"The Lions' Den is a fascinating study of a man's warring emotions as he struggles to rediscover himself while seeking purpose and direction. Stunning!"

-Foreword Magazine

"Powerful and perfectly paced."

-USA News

Opening the front cover of The Lions' Den is like opening the cage of a ferocious animal. It grabs you by the throat and chews you up then spits you out emotionally drained and dazed.

-Denver Post

"Scott Noto masters the literary art of two person point of view with characterization so skillfully layered and a flawless ability to weave in and out of the narrative. A PERFECT 10!!!

-Midcoast Book Review

"After reading the The Lions' Den, it was no wonder it was a hit at the Book Expo."

-The Literary Review

"Beautifully written and absorbing."

-The Sunday Telegraph (UK)

"Scott Noto is a fine, serious writer; he tells a fascinating, moving, and complex story with great skill. This novel marks the debut of a wonderful literary talent."

-International Festival of Authors

THE LIONS' DEN

SCOTT NOTO

A Novel

PELHAM PRESS

NEW YORK•BOSTON•LONDON

Published by Pelham Press, New York, New York.

Member of the Pelham Publishing Group,
a division of Pelham Press, Inc.

✂ Pelham Press is a registered trademark of Seagram, Inc.

Printed in the U.S.A.

Cover photo by Stacey B. Smith

Library of Congress Cataloging-in-Publication Data
is available upon request

ISBN: 0615523528
ISBN-13: 9780615523521

First Edition

This novel is a work of fiction. Names, characters, business establishments, events, organizations, places as well as incidents and dialogues are products of the author's imagination or are used ficticiously. Any resemblance to actual locales or persons, living or dead is entirely coincidental.

For Karen

I can neither imagine nor will I ever accept a world without you in it.

ACKNOWLEDGMENTS

No novelist can—or should—undertake a book this complex and wide-ranging without help. And I am extremely grateful for the people who have helped me make The Lions' Den what it is.

These fall roughly into three groups:

First, the people who helped me nail down the inside information on which the book is based. These include many of my friends and colleagues on Wall Street, as well as the academic and Wall Street economists I've discussed this scenario with, over the years. My gratitude and appreciation to them all.

I wish to express personal thanks to my good friend Robert Angilletta, Director at Citigroup, and former Managing Director, James Donofrio now at Deutsche Bank, who once told me, "A guy like you should be writing novels instead of wasting his time on Wall Street." Although I am still, 'wasting my time on on Wall Street,' I hope they consider this work convincing evidence that they were right. Finally, I wish to thank Congressman Charles Rangel and former Mayor Rudolph Giuliani, simply for being great guys.

In this first group, I also need to thank some people whose names I cannot mention for obvious reasons. These include some high profile people at Blackstone who gave me access to the investment banking Gods in New York and at the Federal Reserve as well as entrée to their lobbyist friends in Washington. Special thanks to my buddies over at CBS, who took me into their confidence and shared information with me. I'd also like to thank a very good friend at the Security and Exchange Commission, who schooled me in government practices and procedures and revealed what he could about some previous high profile SEC operations.

Second, I'd like to thank the people who helped me editorially, who helped me get this story down on paper:

These include my editor and friend, Harvey Ardman, for his guiding hand and determination to tame the monster manuscript I brought to him, as well as for his remarkable editorial skills and his belief in what I was doing. His talent and passion made The Lions' Den a deeper and broader work. I'd also like to thank him for sticking by me and putting up with my stubbornness, and not appeasing me. The moment I met Harvey in Boston, I knew I had struck gold.

I would also like to thank my creative consultant, Dan Zamow, now Senior Vice President at Brean Murray, Carret & Co.. I want to thank him for all the ideas he came up with and sparked in me during our rise together at Lehman Brothers when we were at the World Financial Center, hammering out the details for the Lions' Den and waiting for CEO Dick Fuld to go home so we could sneak in his office, smoke his cigars, drink his scotch and make those endless telephone calls to our contact in Saudi Arabia. If Fuld only knew what went on behind his back. Thanks for the smokes, Dick. And thanks, Danny, for helping me fill in the blanks.

Third, I'd like to thank those folks who helped me after the manuscript was completed: My attorney, Alan Wasserman, Kelly Wallace, my web publicist, and the well respected Dr. RJ Garis, my literary publicist. I'd also like to thank my agent, Sidney Kramer, for believing in the project and in my talent, Stacey B. Smith for the cover art, and the entire graphic design team. Thanks also to the sharp-eyed Cynthia Beatty, who crossed all my Ts and dotted all my Is, literally.

And finally, who can forget Deborah Pendergast and the entire staff at Pelham Press for their professionalism. She and her people have been unfailingly encouraging.

So, thanks for everything, guys. See you again at the awards ceremonies!

"The true soldier fights not because he hates what is in front of him, but because he loves what is behind him."

-G. K. Chesterton

PROLOGUE

Half of them had been late—no surprise—but all were here now, at least everyone whose loyalty he trusted, about fifty in all. They'd come to the colonnaded building at the center of the King's enormous palace compound and gathered in the lavish lounge designed for Royal Family meetings wondering "what now?"

Last to arrive had been the Crown Prince's full brothers—Interior Minister Sha'if and the Governor of Riyadh. Their mother, who was from the Sudairi clan, had taught them from childhood that if they didn't band together, they risked being elbowed out of the hierarchy by the other forty-odd sons of King Ibn Sa'ud. And although they weren't exactly friends, they knew better than to break ranks when times were bad.

Arrayed in a pecking order as rigid as the College of Cardinals, they and other members of the Royal Family lounged on burnished leather chaises and ancient Persian rugs, smugly showing each other their diamond-studded watches, or gazing through the palace's bullet-proof picture windows, uneasily observing the artificially lush gardens and exotic vegetation. A few were just pacing, nervous and worried.

All of the men, the Crown Prince noted cynically, had abstained from their customary Armani, Dolce & Gabbana, Versace, or Prada finery and garbed themselves in *thobes,* the traditional male attire in the Saudi Kingdom. The women were dressed in flowing *abayas* and *hijabs* that completely concealed their makeup, as well as their figures. All had foresworn their Italian footwear, at least for today, for camel-hide sandals.

They were now anxiously waiting for the last of them to arrive: the sovereign King, the holiest of the holy, the richest of the rich, the most powerful of the powerful, the silent, shrunken old stroke victim whose whims dictated their lives, their fortunes, their country, and most of the civilized world.

The Crown Prince let his eyes flit over the bunch of them, his brothers and half-brothers, his uncles and aunts, nieces and nephews, his cousins first, second, and third. They were a disgusting lot for the most part: distrustful, rapacious, dissolute, perverse, a Whitman's sampler of every moral failing known to human kind. He was almost ashamed to share a bloodline with them.

The only non-Royal in the room, and the only person with a weapon, was the huge, swarthy, grim-faced, Lt. Hafez Aziz, the Crown Prince's personal bodyguard. He sat on a hard chair in a far corner, his Uzi gently cradled in his arms.

Even though he was the Crown Prince, the de facto regent, and, at age fifty-two, the Heir Apparent to the throne, if he hadn't summoned his relatives in the name of the King, some would have ignored his call. He had his supporters among the Royal relatives, but many wished him dead, and only a handful would have mourned him. They'd come because they were afraid.

Of course, he, too, was afraid—not of losing his life or his opulent lifestyle. He was afraid of losing the only thing that really mattered to him: power, power over the rabble, power over the fate of nations, the power he ostensibly shared with the decrepit King, power more addictive than opium. He was grateful for the intensity of his fear, for it had driven him to conceive a plan worthy of Alexander the Great. All he had to do now was sell it to his frightened relatives.

He heard footsteps in the outside courtyard, and a stirring of attendants and servants, and he knew the cause immediately. The King was arriving— the eighty-four year-old grandson of the country's founder, a horseman of legendary prowess, a negotiator who'd made even Henry Kissinger sweat, and a man with whom no one wanted to play poker. Once upon a time.

The enormous, deeply carved oak doors smoothly swung open to reveal the King in his space-age wheelchair, his Medusa-like wife and a retinue of about twenty, which ranged from ancient retainers who'd seen more in their time than human beings were meant to see, to trembling and impatient virgins, waiting for a call that would never come.

Several retainers guided the King's wheelchair into a central spot in the room, while Royal relatives scurried out of the way. Everyone stood and gazed at the old man most of them hadn't seen in years, their faces struggling to express respect and admiration while disguising their shock, pity, and contempt.

There he was, big as life—the Head of the House of Sa'ud, Ruler of Saudi Arabia and custodian of the Grand Mosque at Mecca and Mohammed's Grave at Medina. Well, not as big as life. He was withered down to the bare essentials, strapped in a contraption, attached to multiple machines and tubes, his lips permanently frozen into the snarl that had terrified so many of his servants.

Standing over him was that harpy wife of his, the Queen, owner of the Kingdom's most vicious smile, the King's veritable owner and warden, who claimed to understand his grunts and mumbles, and to be able to translate them into coherent statements—hers, not his, as everyone knew, but wasn't foolish enough to say.

The Crown Prince touched his heart then his head in greeting, and the other Royal relatives followed suit, like bobbing toy woodpeckers perched on drinking glasses. The King seemed not to notice until the Queen bent down and whispered in his ear. He lifted a hand and made some kind of feeble gesture, like a dying Pope blessing his flock. The Royal relatives sat, except for the Crown Prince.

"My illustrious family," the Crown Prince began, "I have convened this gathering at the urgent request of our beloved leader, the glory of our land, the King of Kings. Recent events have forced him to conclude that our country has entered a new political phase, one which has put our entire family in grave danger, and put its very survival at stake."

He inclined his head toward the King, who uttered a short series of incomprehensible grunts. The Queen nodded briskly, as though the guttural sounds made perfect sense to her. "The King says that the Crown Prince is speaking the truth."

The Crown Prince nodded. This much had been agreed upon. But now, if he wanted the Queen's support, if he wanted to retain his power and perhaps even his life, he had to persuade the Royal Family to agree to his plan.

"You are all aware of the recent terrorist bombings. And you also know—although we have managed to keep this news from the public—that an attempt was made recently to assassinate His Majesty," the Crown Prince continued. "But here is something you do not know. At that very moment, and at a location 300 miles away, an attempt was also made on *my* life."

An audible gasp came from the rest of the relatives. Several of the women began wailing. The Crown Prince noted the shock and fear on the faces in front of him. After all, he and the King were among the most carefully guarded men in the world.

"Obviously, both attempts failed, praise be to Allah," he continued. "I wish I could tell you that they were thwarted by our rigorous security precautions, but I survived only because the bathroom door in my villa was thicker than our enemies had assumed. And the King—he is with us today because two of his nurses sacrificed their own lives to save him."

In the rear of the room, a heavy-set figure rose to interrupt, the Great Uncle, a man in his declining years well-known for over-estimating his IQ. "What about the assassins? Have we tortured them to reveal the names of other conspirators?"

"Thank you for reminding me, Uncle," said the Crown Prince. "Unfortunately, both assassins sacrificed themselves as well in their attempts on us. We learned nothing from them…"

"Nothing!?" the Great Uncle said, outraged. "We train our security people to…"

"We learned nothing from them, initially, except their identities," the Crown Prince told him. He paused a moment, then spoke again. "The young man who attempted to kill His Majesty was the son-in-law of our Security Chief."

The Great Uncle sat down suddenly, eyes wide in disbelief.

"And the man who tried to assassinate *me* was the half-brother of our Defense Minister."

The room fell silent for a moment.

"These people, they were known religious fanatics?" asked the King's Second Cousin, a man who spent most of his time at his mountain villa near Hitler's Berchtesgaden. "They were Wahhabi?"

"Known fanatics?" the Crown Prince chuckled bitterly. "Hardly. They were both members of the elite, with beautiful families and good lives ahead of them. No, they were not *known* fanatics. But fanatics they were, nonetheless. We found irrefutable evidence in their quarters—religious tracts and letters."

An arrogant young prince sitting on the brocaded silk lounge chair near the center of the room loudly objected. "I was with the Security Chief's son-in-law at Yale. He was a boozer and a womanizer. He scorned our religion."

"Yes," said the Crown Prince, "so it seemed. And so it seemed with the other assassin as well. Western-educated. A collector of Ming vases. Known weakness for cocaine. Nonetheless, a Wahhabi extremist. His wife admitted it…after some persuasion."

One of the *abaya*-clad matriarchs offered a different explanation. "These assassins—they are a strange and horrible exception. Our people adore us. I am always treated with the greatest deference…"

She was interrupted by one of the ranking cousins, a shrewd-eyed man who would have been a rising executive at any major corporation. "I must assume then, honored Aunt, that you have not heard of the attacks and the suicide bombings, that you know nothing of *Al Qaeda*'s attempts to destabilize the Kingdom," he said.

"Terrorists," she replied dismissively. "Murderers. Every country has its share."

"You are correct in many ways, honored Aunt," said the Crown Prince. "But there are more than a few of them here. We have the visible ones pretty much under control—the *Al Qaeda*—It is the invisible ones who worry me—the radical Wahhabi and their Fundamentalist Koranic beliefs. I have personally supervised a sweeping investigation of our institutions—all of them."

"And…"

"…In addition to our schools, I have found that they have spread throughout the civil service, the provincial governments, our health-care institutions, civil engineering, the military, the judicial system, our National Guard, the police—and I include the secret police…"

A woman sitting near him gasped in surprise.

"That's right," the Crown Prince continued, thinking that we must start telling our women more about what is happening in the world. "I said the secret police. Our entire society is honeycombed with these fanatics."

A gravelly voice from the left side of the room boomed out, "We must kill them, every last one of them!" All eyes turned toward the King's First

Cousin, a man who had just become a grandfather and had found something that interested him more than the string of thoroughbred Arabian horses he raced mainly in England and America.

"Kill them all?" the Crown Prince inquired politely.

"Yes," said the First Cousin. "We can wait no longer. We must kill them, like Assad did—he massacred every religious fanatic who had settled in Syria."

"We are breaking up terrorist cells and imprisoning—or killing—all we can find, my cousin. But most of these people have no known connection to terrorists. They are the reserves, you might say," said the Crown Prince. "They are gathering strength and numbers and plotting to undermine our stability from within."

"You mean what happened in Tunisia and Cairo can happen in Riyadh?"

"Why not? Is our monarchy immune to revolution?"

"That is why we must arrest them all anyway," the First Cousin insisted.

"A few years ago, we might have been able to do that," the Crown Prince said. "But today…I am not sure such an order would be obeyed. And even if it were, it could inspire widespread violence, which we might not be able to control."

Now the Crown Prince's younger Brother, a man with a face like Valentino and the ambition of the Borgias, spoke up. "So, my Brother, what are we to do? Politely line up at the chopping block?"

The Crown Prince allowed himself a smile. "Of course not, my Brother, although it would be interesting to see exactly how we'd line up."

Moments later, there was an enormous crash behind the closed double doors at the back of the luxurious meeting room, a huge thunderclap. Panicked Royal relatives screamed in terror, hit the floor or dived behind chairs and couches, or under tables, the Queen taking refuge behind the King's wheelchair, flinging her arms over her face to protect herself from the blast and the debris. The King seemed completely untroubled. The Crown Prince simply watched everyone's reactions.

Almost immediately, a phalanx of palace guards burst into the room through every door, leaping into defensive positions, AK-47s drawn, determined to neutralize any threat. But there was no threat, no blast, no blood. Except for the noise, nothing was amiss.

At the back of the room, the double-doors swung open and Lt. Aziz emerged, propelling an elderly, red-faced servant in front of him. "Your highnesses," the old man began, then burst into tears.

"What has happened, Hassan?" the Crown Prince said, recovering his aplomb. "Are you all right?"

"The rack of pots and pans, hundreds of them…" He couldn't finish the sentence.

The Crown Prince gestured to Lt. Aziz, who grabbed a partner and headed back into the kitchen to investigate. They reappeared a few moments later.

"The bolts pulled out of the ceiling," Lt. Aziz reported.

"An unusual accident, but no sign of tampering," the other guard added.

"Thank you, Aziz," said the Crown Prince.

The bodyguard nodded to his squad, and everyone left to resume their stations. Aziz resumed his position at the far side of the room.

The Royal relatives dusted themselves off with as much grace as they could manage. They'd been thoroughly shaken by the incident.

The Crown Prince absorbed this with considerable satisfaction, then noticed that one fellow, a distant Cousin, a recent college drop-out, steely-eyed, lean, almost gaunt, heavily bearded, had not moved from his chair and was now observing the scene with almost scientific detachment.

Another Royal Nephew broke the silence, a bored-looking Westernized young man who looked as uncomfortable in his *bisht* as a *mullah* in a Speedo. "Well," he said, "that was just so much fun. Let's do it again."

The Crown Prince silenced him with a look that could have bored a hole through armor plating. "We're all on edge," he said. "I know you all must be concerned after what's happened and what I've told you."

The King's First Cousin rose again. "Concerned? That's a mild word for it. You have presented us with a seemingly insurmountable threat, a danger against which we cannot defend ourselves. Have you no solution?"

"Of course he does, Uncle," the bored Nephew said while casually picking dirt from under his fingernails. "We've already lived through it once, and once was quite enough, thank you."

The Nephew's meaning was obvious to all, including the Crown Prince. After 9/11, no one knew what might happen next, especially after it became clear that most of the terrorists were Saudi nationals.

And so, on the day after the World Trade Center towers went down, the Crown Prince had commandeered a dozen Royal Saudi Airline Boeing 747s, as well as the HZ-HMED, the 757 that had been fitted out as the world's most luxurious and most complete mobile hospital, and staffed with world-class specialists.

Late that night, while the world was still in shock, the Crown Prince, with a handpicked security team, had overseen the swift and stealthy transfer of the feeble King and his immediate entourage to the waiting hospital plane. It had taken off immediately on a secret flight to Paris, where a cordon of armed guards were waiting on the tarmac of Orly airport, ready to take him to a safe house in the suburbs.

Meanwhile, thousands of members of the Royal Family—government officials, business tycoons, playboys and their wives, children, hangers-on and servants, had gathered at Riyadh International Airport, where they were unceremoniously packed into the waiting 747s and evacuated from their native land.

At the same time, three other 747s had been making the rounds in Asia, America, and Europe, picking up Royal ambassadors and businessmen and their families—no easy task, especially in the United States, where all air traffic had been halted. It took a personal phone call to the president to make it happen.

Of course, the airlift had turned out to be unnecessary, and some had accused the Crown Prince of overreacting, but if the fanatics had chosen that moment to strike at the Royal Family, they would have enshrined him as a prophet.

The King mumbled something and the Queen translated. "Tell us how long we have, in your best judgment."

"Five years—if we're very fortunate," said the Crown Prince.

"What will happen in five years?" asked an attractive young woman with a California accent, the wife of one of the King's grandsons.

"In five years, they will take control of everything," the Crown Prince said. "Every institution, every government function, every level of power."

The young woman seemed stunned. "Couldn't the National Guard protect…"

"They will control the National Guard as well," the Crown Prince said.

The Great Uncle, who was old enough to remember King Sa'ud and, as a child, had actually met Lawrence of Arabia, lifted his substantial bulk out of his chair and raised a fist toward the ceiling, his *bisht* sliding toward his shoulder. "They will not conquer the Kingdom of Ibn Sa'ud," he proclaimed. "The Royal Family is like the fingers of a hand. Threaten it and it becomes a fist!"

The assembled family members, having first heard this Royal cliché when they were children, reacted with embarrassed silence.

Among those ignoring the remark was the Royal Ambassador to Great Britain, a tall, elegant man. Instead, he chose to dispute the Crown Prince's scenario. "In your fantasy," he began, "the Fundamentalists will control our oil fields within five years. But the Americans will not let that happen, just as they could not let stand Saddam's seizure of Kuwait."

"You are the diplomat, my brother, and I have great respect for your understanding of world affairs," the Crown Prince replied. "But I am not at all sure that what you predict would come to pass."

"You think the Americans would give up their SUVs and learn to live through winter in unheated homes?" the Ambassador asked, provoking audible murmurs of agreement among some of the Royals.

The Crown Prince answered the Ambassador's question with one of his own. "Do you think the Americans could mount another Middle East invasion after what happened in Iraq and Afghanistan? Would their Senate let them? Would their people stand for another round of war, more casualties, more billions down the drain?"

The Ambassador was still not convinced. "Even so, they would have no choice but to protect their interests," he said. "Nixon was ready to send in paratroopers to seize the oil fields during the 1973 OPEC crisis. This president could put a similar plan into operation."

"That is a possibility, of course," the Crown Prince granted. "But let me suggest a different scenario, which I think is a far more likely one: the U.S. will send their aircraft carriers, load troop carriers, and stealth bombers. Right?"

He glanced around the room. Every eye was riveted to him.

"At this point," the Crown Prince continued, "the Fundamentalists make two announcements: First, they'll say they have mined the oil fields and now have the ability to halt oil production for years—and will do so if even one American sets foot on Saudi sand, uninvited, and second, they'll say they have no intention of cutting off oil to the West or raising the price. Their only demand is that all American and U.N. security forces peacefully and quickly leave the Middle East."

The Crown Prince glanced at the Ambassador, who was listening intently.

"So what does the president do?" the Crown Prince went on. "He listens to the demands of the American people, who are tired of war and who don't care where they buy their oil, so long as the supply is not interrupted."

"He'll cut a deal with our enemies?" an uncle asked.

"He'll cut a deal with anyone except al-Zawahiri," said the Crown Prince. "After all," he smiled, "other presidents negotiated with Yasser Arafat."

"That is a very persuasive scenario," the Ambassador said thoughtfully. "I can find no fault with it—except the Americans are unlikely to abandon Israel."

"Let our enemies deal with that problem," said the Crown Prince. "Let's be honest here—none of us give a damn about Israel *or* a Palestinian state, only where it leaves the House of Sa'ud."

"And where *does* this leave the House of Sa'ud?" asked another cousin.

"It leaves us entirely at the mercy of the Fundamentalists," the Queen said flatly, surprising and pleasing the Crown Prince.

"And seeking political asylum wherever we can find it," said the Foreign Minister.

"Or hiding like Nazis in some South American shithole like we were the Boys in Brazil," added a Nephew.

"Not if I can help it," the Crown Prince said.

Now everyone, even the bored Nephew, was looking at him expectantly. "Please tell us your plan, Highness," the King's Uncle implored.

"It is chiefly financial," the Crown Prince began. "It involves raising funds to…"

The Great Uncle interrupted him angrily. "Money? More money? That is your answer? How many hundreds of millions have we already paid these *Wahhabi* devils?"

One of the Matriarchs, an older woman with the eyebrows of a hawk, stood to defend the Great Uncle's challenge. "How much more protection money are we to give to the Mullahs and their poisonous schools?"

The Crown Prince's younger brother strode forward now, and the Crown Prince let him take the floor. "My brother is a highly intelligent man, and we all respect and love him," he said. "But he is acting as though the last twenty years never happened. He has forgotten that our resources, great as they are, are not infinite. He has forgotten how much our brothers in neighboring countries have come to depend on our largesse," the Crown Prince's brother roared on. "He does not realize that our attempts to buy off our enemies have failed. And it is time to admit that." He smiled grimly.

"I have forgotten nothing," the Crown Prince said calmly. "And I agree. Though we have spent a fortune, we have failed to buy off our enemies. But that is not what I intend."

A movement drew the Crown Prince's attention to the back of the room, near the kitchen doors, to the gaunt young Cousin who had reacted with almost suspicious calm to the kitchen disaster. The young man seemed inexplicably restless and agitated. The Crown Prince glanced over at Lt. Aziz, who had also noticed the Cousin's sudden jumpiness and had unobtrusively glided to within an arm's reach of him.

"My honored Cousin," the Crown Prince said, looking at the young man, "have I said something that disturbs you?"

All eyes turned toward the Cousin. "There is one thing my esteemed Cousin *has* forgotten," the young man said bitterly. "He has forgotten that we brought all this on ourselves…"

Lt. Aziz caught the Crown Prince's eye and the Crown Prince, with the slightest shake of his head, signaled his bodyguard to let the man speak.

"We have brought all this on ourselves," the gaunt Cousin said, "because we have all ignored the traditions of our forefathers. We live lives based on corruption and drinking and whoring. We have defiled the Kingdom by inviting the Americans to build bases here, becoming the lapdogs of the Western infidels, giving them a hold on us even the Crusaders could not have imagined.

"Our society is so corrupt," the Cousin went on, "that young men are no longer willing to work. Instead, it is five million Filipina and Indonesian workers who perform the honest labor that was once part of our tradition, while our sons—and yes, even our daughters—debase themselves in multi-million dollar orgies and drunken binges on the Cote d'Azur, or palaces in Marbella or Tangier while our society rots away."

By now, he was wild-eyed and panting. "There is only one way to save the House of Sa'ud," he told his Royal relatives, "and that is to cleanse ourselves of the corruption that pollutes our very souls."

The gaunt Cousin paused for breath, and the Crown Prince took the opportunity to interrupt him. "Since you have been so very helpful telling us all what we have forgotten—what *I* have forgotten," he said without irony, "let me now tell you what *you* have forgotten, honored Cousin.

"We are all living in the closest place on Earth to Paradise, and not just those of us in this room and our relatives, but every Saudi, young or old, male or female." The young man opened his mouth as if to speak, but was overrun by his Cousin's momentum.

"Everyone here gets free health care," the Crown Prince continued, "as well as free college educations. We live in one of the world's driest countries, and yet water is almost free. Our people pay less than almost anyone on earth for utilities and domestic air travel. Our welfare system is the envy of the world. And *that*, my dear Cousin, is what corruption has given us."

The Crown Prince smiled thinly at the gaunt young man and waited for him to back off and remain silent.

"How like you, *honored* Cousin," the young man challenged, "to imply that material rewards can substitute for spiritual rewards, and that successful profiteering is the equivalent of virtue. How like you to talk about a Paradise on earth, when there is only *one* Paradise, the Paradise Allah gives those who deserve it," his eyes were filled with rage. "Riches are not the solution to the problem that worries you, the problem you have created for yourselves, but I have the real solution right here."

The young man swiftly reached under his *bisht* and pulled out a small, shiny, cylindrical object. It was the latest model British armor-piercing fragmentation grenade that, when it exploded, ejected more than 2000 razor-sharp splinters that could kill or maim everyone within thirty feet.

"This," the Cousin shouted, "will purify the Kingdom forever." The Royals stared at him, unable to move, even to scream.

The Cousin yanked the pin of the grenade and reared back to hurl the device into the middle of the room. But his arm lurched forward empty-handed, the grenade having been neatly snatched from his grasp by Lt. Aziz, who had also snaked his other arm around the Cousin's neck.

Aziz said a few words into his lapel mike, and a few moments later, two more bodyguards had come to his aid. They cuffed the Royal Cousin, who was now shouting incoherently, and carried him out of the palace.

Once more, the Royal relatives, grim and shaken, crept out from behind their hiding places. The Crown Prince noticed that the King seemed untroubled, almost oblivious to the commotion. But he'd spotted a brief flash of fear on the Queen's face, a momentary interruption in an expressionless mask.

"My family," the Crown Prince began, speaking over the excited recountings of what had just taken place, "my family, please listen to me.

Listen…" The conversational buzz faded until he had their attention. "I know how much of a shock this has been to you. There is no pain so sharp as betrayal by someone of your own blood.

"At the same time," he continued, "our Cousin has illustrated—better than any words I might utter—the insidious power of the Wahhabi disease. We must treat him gently and hope that he recovers…"

The Crown Prince broke off his steely gaze and continued. "What's important here, what our Cousin has demonstrated, is that we must protect ourselves against the multitudes who suffer from the same infection *he* does."

"Yes," said the Great Uncle, acting as though he was speaking for everyone present, "that much is clear. But you have yet to tell us *how* we can protect ourselves."

"Ah, yes," the Crown Prince said, smiling. "I was just getting to that when I was interrupted. We are going to save ourselves by transferring every bit of our wealth and power to a place where it will be safe from our enemies."

"So, tell us, Great Prince, where abroad will we transfer this *power*?" the Great Uncle asked, looking at the other Royals and grinning broadly.

"In America," replied the Crown Prince.

"America? The United States?"

"That is correct."

"And may I ask how we will accomplish this?"

"Of course you may, my Uncle. We will accomplish this by assuming ownership of *theirs*."

The room fell silent for a moment, then there was laughter. The Crown Prince joined in on it, happily.

"You are speaking about our lives," his Half Brother said. "You are talking about the survival of the Royal Family. You are joking about our future."

"You are right again, my Brother. I am speaking of our lives and about the survival of our family. But I am not joking. I am quite serious…"

"About taking America's power?"

"I was speaking metaphorically. Perhaps it would be more accurate to say *buying* America's power."

This time there was no laughter—skepticism, curiosity, murmurs of doubt, but no laughter.

"We already *have* plenty of interests in America—prime real estate, politicians, and plenty of corporate CEOs and lobbyists," the Half Brother said dismissively.

"That's not what I mean when I say 'buying America,'" the Crown Prince replied. "I'm talking about taking control of America through their economy."

"How?" someone asked.

"Bit by bit," said the Crown Prince. "By acquiring controlling interest in the Fortune 500—starting with GE, Wal-Mart, Intel, McDonald's, CBS, IBM, Microsoft, Mobil-Exxon, Time Warner, AT&T, and *The New York Times*, and other multinationals."

The Half Brother interrupted. "That's preposterous. We are wealthy, but we are not *that* wealthy."

The Crown Prince grinned. "I said *controlling interest*, honored Brother. In many cases, that will amount to only a few percentage points of stock."

The Half Brother was unrelenting. "And what will we do with these *stocks*, honored Brother? Collect dividends? What good will this do us?"

"It will give us an iron-fisted grip on their infrastructure," said the Crown Prince. "It will give us control of the unions. It will give us control of the shareholders. It will give us governors and senators and cabinet members, yes, presidents. We will gain control of the media, and through that, control of the American people. It will allow us to write the laws and to run American foreign policy and commerce. To all intents and purposes, we will *become* America."

The Crown Prince knew this was a critical moment. Either his plan won approval from the most influential members of the Royal Family—right now—or the House of Sa'ud was probably doomed, and so was *he*. He waited for someone to speak out—a powerful Uncle.

After a moment, that Uncle, the country's Oil Minister and one of the most powerful people in the Kingdom, rose to address the others. "I think this is a good plan. Ambitious, but within our abilities. But one question remains, Great Prince: Will the Americans let us do it?"

"That is an excellent question, honored Uncle," said the Crown Prince, preferring a more ringing endorsement. "The answer to your question is crucial to the plan," he said. "What we are doing must remain secret—at least the extent of it. If our actions become public knowledge in the United States, if we are exposed, the public outcry will compel their leaders to stop us."

The Half Brother was on his feet immediately. "Surely, *someone* will discover what we're doing and inform the president. That will finish us."

The Crown Prince was ready for this. "The president may indeed catch wind of some of our activities, but we will reassure him with vague explanations about foreign investment, and he will not look too closely because, after all, he is our friend. We have many friends in Washington."

"And we have the skill to pull this off all by ourselves? This is not like dropping in at Harry Winston's and buying a few million dollars worth of cut gemstones."

"No, honored Brother," said the Crown Prince smoothly. "We cannot do this by ourselves. We will need Wall Street to assist us in our deception, by setting up shell companies within shell companies, so that no one—not even Wall Street—suspects who the real owners are."

The Half Brother was still not convinced. "Why will they do this for us—betray their own country? Tell me that, if you can."

"For the simplest of reasons, my Brother—because it will be in their short-term financial interest. And Wall Street has never failed to act to protect or further its own financial interests."

"Even in the face of threat?"

"*Especially* in the face of threat," said the Crown Prince. "American capitalists sold their technology to the Soviets during the Cold War, even though it was unethical, just as they secretly do today with Iran and China. Give them their money, their lavish homes, their women, and their cars, and they'll do whatever we want."

It was the Crown Prince's own Second Son, nineteen now, who tested him next. "What of the Wahhabi extremists, honored Father? How will they react when this plan comes to fruition?"

"Ah, yes," said the Crown Prince. "Our over zealous religious friends. Well, my Son, they will feel fulfilled and vindicated because they will be left with something they seem to want more than we do. The country."

One of the Matriarchs, a huge woman, wearing a *burnoose* the size of a tent, growled, in a voice that made stomachs vibrate. "What do you mean, the country? Do you truly expect us to abandon the land of our ancestors, our oil?"

The Crown Prince nodded sagely. "Have you looked at that land lately? Are you brimming over with love for this endless sand and this searing heat? And when you're here, how eager are you to return to your palaces and estates in Morocco or France or wherever you've made your *real* home."

He paused a moment to let someone speak, but, as he had guessed, no Royal relatives rose to proclaim their undying love for the Saudi desert.

"Yes," he continued, "I am asking you to give up the land of your ancestors, but I'm asking you to make this sacrifice on behalf of your descendants and yourselves, for that is the only way to assure the safety of the Royal Family and preserve our wealth and power."

"You make it sound so easy," the Half Brother said. "But it will not be easy at all. We all have homes and businesses here. Are you asking us to abandon all this and take the loss?"

"No," the Crown Prince said. "I am asking you to liquidate your holdings here and invest in something of at least equal value, with a more secure future. We will help you find buyers here or abroad."

A hand went up on the right side of the room. It was the Crown Prince's weak-chinned First Son, the disappointment of his life, thirty-one years old, but only chronologically. "Yes, my Son. You have a question?"

"Yes, my Father. If we abandon our land…well, all my friends are here. I have a social position to maintain and a reputation to uphold. What will happen to that if I abandon my country?"

The Crown Prince paused. He didn't want to humiliate his son, but he didn't want to encourage this line of questioning from others who had better reasons to pursue it. He had to say something that would satisfy those concerned with this issue but unwilling to raise it.

"My Son," he finally said, "You will always have the respect you deserve within the Kingdom. And your wealth and influence will impress people you meet wherever you go."

His first Son took it all as a profound compliment and sat down.

The Uncle who usually supported him spoke next. "I am sure you have worked this out in detail, my Prince. Could you share your thinking with us?"

Now the Crown Prince laid it all out: the mutual fund that would, through shell companies, buy controlling interest in America's Blue Chip companies, the contributions Royal families would make to this fund from their various revenue streams plus the liquidation proceeds of their fixed assets in Saudi Arabia and the timing of the operation—the sell-off would be done carefully, to avoid rousing suspicion. The buying would begin immediately.

One by one, the objections and the questions were disposed of and the suggestions accepted or declined.

After about an hour, no one seemed to have anything more to say. "Any more questions?" the Crown Prince asked. He glanced at the Queen, who gifted him with an approving nod.

"I have a question," said the Half Brother. "What about those of us who simply do not wish to participate in this insane conspiracy?"

The Queen bent down to the King, whispered in his ear, and received a mumbled response. Then she rose and addressed the Half Brother. "The King says we are not taking a vote. He reminds you that the Royal Family is not a democracy. Your full participation is mandatory."

There it was, the Crown Prince thought. The deal was done. But the Half Brother was still not ready to surrender. "And if we *still* refuse?"

This time, the Queen did not even go through the motions of consulting her paralyzed husband. "His Highness promises those who do not wish to participate that no harm will come to your children." She smiled.

CHAPTER ONE

Julie Chambers decided to walk uptown. After all, New York was the greatest walking city in the world, and it was still fairly cool, at least for the middle of August. Besides, it would give her time to think.

She knew she couldn't mourn forever. She also knew Jack's death had left a hole in her life that could never be filled. There'd been no time to prepare for it, no lingering illness, no long trail together into old age. Just a plane crash in the desert and he was gone. Just…gone.

Julie stopped to study some shoes in a Fifth Avenue shop window. It had been almost a year since she had any goal other than to forget—not the man she'd known since their college days at Georgetown, not the man she'd married, but the pain. All she'd been able to achieve was a certain numbness.

Then there was that telephone call from Hank and everything was up for grabs again. They had a project that might be up her alley, he said—was she ready to come back to work? She'd been asking herself the same question for months.

But here she was, heading for the tall building on Sixth, the one covered in pink marble. Pink. That was UBS all right, pink—cheap-looking, obvious, vulgar. The building was a perfect match for the programming—a classless conglomeration of reality TV, court shows, soap operas, and tawdry talk programming. As for the news department, well, Jack's death had sucked the life out it. The other executive producer, Fred Fielding, was good, but he wasn't exactly a model of youth, energy, and new ideas.

Even if I am ready to go back to work, she thought, I'm not sure UBS is the place for me. It's a dead-end, emotionally, intellectually, and especially career-wise. I need something new, something challenging, something that will engage me.

Julie walked past the Public Library at the corner of Forty-Second and Fifth. A few dozen people were lounging on the massive stone steps, dozing, reading, licking ice cream cones, sunning themselves. It brought a smile to her face. She loved New York. And she was feeling pretty good.

She crossed Forty-Second Street and walked toward Sixth, past a cigar shop, some jewelry stores, and a women's boutique. "We might have a project for you," Hank had said. That was curious. He needed her. But why? She'd been a good segment producer, but she didn't think they missed her all that much.

She'd skipped breakfast this morning, intending to get a bite at her favorite coffee shop at Sixth and Forty-Second, but it was gone, replaced by a tall, but very ordinary office building.

A year is a long time in New York. Things change. But not everything. On the next block, the sleazy book store was still there—the same one Fred Fielding had chided her about. "See that?" he'd asked one day. "Giuliani missed one. One little victory for you and Jack and the rest of the free speech lefties." Ah, Fred. Such a love.

A block further uptown, Julie found, to her surprise, a sparkling new Starbucks. She slipped onto a thinly padded seat at the counter, and ordered a toffee nut latte and a cinnamon bun. The first section of *The New York Times* was sitting on the stool beside her.

Julie scanned the headlines while she sipped. More attacks in Iraq. Another clean air regulation. Yanks beat Red Sox. Intercoastal Courier bought by Kansas City firm. Wounded UBS Television Producer Leaves Ramstein for U.S.

Wait—what was that? Wounded UBS television producer? Julie read the article quickly.

Ramstein AF Base, Germany, Aug. 13—Fred Fielding, well-known United Broadcasting System news and documentary producer, was released from the base hospital today, a week after being wounded in an ambush near Belfast. His wounds, while not life-threatening, were fairly extensive, but hospital authorities said they anticipated a full recovery.

Suddenly it all made sense. UBS wasn't the least bit concerned about her health and welfare. They needed her to fill in for Fred. That meant there might be a really good opportunity here. Furthermore, she should be able to strike a pretty good bargain.

Julie laughed. How easily I've slipped back into network politicking and salary negotiating—two skills she'd had to master in order to survive at UBS. She had the network where she wanted them all right, but she wasn't at all sure if she could stand to work for UBS, even if she didn't have to report to Fred Fielding.

She glanced at her watch. Hank had said eleven o'clock. Wouldn't hurt to keep him waiting a few minutes, let him sweat a little. But not too much. Hank Kozloff was a nervous, squeaky-voiced, uptight little fellow, in his middle-sixties, though he looked younger. He was also a dear man, a great boss, and probably the best damn news director in television.

Julie drained her coffee cup and continued strolling uptown, stopping at an amazing display of rings, bracelets, and diamond pins in a jewelry store window on Sixth Avenue. She looked down at the plain band of gold she was wearing on the ring finger of her left hand. Now that won't do, she thought. They'll think I'm not facing up to reality. She slipped it into her purse, and a wave of loneliness swept over her.

That won't do either, she told herself. Especially not when she was bound to see lots of old friends and colleagues—Miles Corbin, the president of UBS News, handsome, accomplished, powerful, and cold as dry ice, and Cal Flannery, Marty Cohen, Lisa Green, and the rest of the news crew—and most of all, Paige Hanson, Julie's young and eager assistant, researcher, confidant, and friend.

The tall pink building loomed ahead, stirring memories. Julie checked her reflection in a window. Conservative grey blazer and tweedy skirt. Trim figure. Small, regular features. The barest hint of makeup. Dark blonde hair tightly braided and up. She wished she felt as together as she looked.

Then she joined the stream of people entering the building and slipped into the last elevator on the right side, along with a whip-thin black messenger and his bicycle, two twenty-two year-old secretaries energetically gossiping in purest Brooklyn brogue, a balding salesman with a sample case of some sort who couldn't keep his eyes off the girls' rear ends, and a short, cartoon-faced young man with Downs' Syndrome guarding a battered mail cart as though it were filled with gold bars. She pushed the button for the thirty-fifth floor.

A blonde girl with hair too yellow and a virtual mask of make-up was sitting behind the reception desk. "Can I help you?" she asked mechanically.

"I'm Julie Chambers and I'm here to see Hank Kozloff."

The receptionist made a phone call and in a moment, Hank bounded through the door, smiling and solicitous. "Julie, Julie—glad you could make it. You're looking great, well maybe a little thinner, but great."

"Good to see you, too, Hank."

They awkwardly decided against a hug and settled for a warm handshake.

Hank took Julie into his office directly, bypassing the newsroom. "I wish you'd come to visit us from time to time, but I'm glad you're here now. Tell me, do you feel as good as you look?"

"It's a work in progress."

"It's still hard to believe..." He didn't finish the sentence.

"So, what's up, Hank?" Julie said a trifle too brightly.

"Well, we might have a little project coming up, and the first time I heard about it, I thought—this would be perfect for Julie, if she's ready to come back. Are you? I mean, I don't want to push..."

"Tell me about the project," she said. "Need someone to produce another Bachelor rip-off?"

Hank groaned. "I guess we deserved that."

"I've been watching UBS a little. I may be the only one. Jesus, Hank, *four* reality television shows? How low can you go?"

"I know," Hank said with a sigh. "We didn't even bid on the Summer Games this year, and losing the Oscars was, well, pretty depressing. But I think we may be on the way up."

Julie raised an eyebrow. "With John Blaylock as the president of UBS? That would surprise me."

"You haven't been keeping up, Julie. Blaylock is gone as of two months ago."

"Gone? He died?"

"No, but our stock certainly did…and the Board fired him. And replaced him with Carleton Fisher."

"Fisher? Walter Cronkite's Fisher? The Pulitzer-Prize winning Fisher? *That* Carleton Fisher?"

"The very same." Hank allowed himself a smile.

"I didn't know he was still around."

"He came out of retirement to take the job," Hank explained.

"Well, he's got a big one."

"He's changing everything, Julie—but most of all the news division. He's already doubled the news budget and has approved a new multi-million dollar digital newsroom. He's vowed to win back viewer respect—and ratings."

"What happens if he fails?"

"If he fails, UBS is going to disappear like haze on a summer morning. We can't keep losing millions in revenue each year."

They were both silent for a moment.

"Anyhow," Hank continued, "that's why I called you."

"And not because Fred is out of action?"

Hank laughed. "So you *do* read the newspapers occasionally. No, not just because of that."

"I see," Julie said unconvinced. "So how *is* the gentleman from Georgia? Was he badly hurt?"

Hank snorted. "I understand he's in a lot of pain, but he'll be ok. He got shot in the ass."

"In the *ass*?"

"Yeah. He was in Ireland with Tom, producing a segment in the prospects for peace, when the IRA sprang an ambush and, well, his ass…"

"Is a big target," Julie said, grinning.

"Exactly."

They were both laughing when a man appeared at Hank's door—Miles Corbin, tight-faced and all business. "Something funny, Hank? Oh, hi, Julie."

"Hi, Miles."

Hank looked guilty. "I was just telling her about Fred."

"Yeah, that's hilarious," Miles said dryly. He looked at Julie, appraising her. "How are you feeling, Julie?"

Julie smiled up at him. "Pretty good, actually."

"You look good. But you should do something with your hair," Corbin said. "Ready to go back to work, take on some responsibility?"

"Depends what you have in mind."

"You didn't tell her anything, Hank, did you?"

"No, no, Miles. I know Mr. Fisher said he wanted to describe the project."

"Right," Miles said. He turned toward Julie. "So. You ready to meet Carleton Fisher?"

That caught Julie by surprise. "Meet Fisher? Well, ok, yes, I guess I'm ready as I'll ever be."

They took the elevator to the forty-fifth floor—deep brown carpets, low lighting, teak paneling with a photographic history of the network dating back to its days in radio garnishing the corridor walls. A receptionist who looked and dressed like a fashion model greeted them. "You can go right on back to Mr. Fisher, Mr. Corbin."

Carleton Fisher was a tall, slim, distinguished man, grey-haired with a slight touch of red still visible.

"You must be Julie Chambers," Fisher said. His eyes crinkled when he smiled.

He reached out a hand and she shook it. "Glad to meet you, Mr. Fisher."

"Damn—there it is again, *Mr.* Fisher. You know, the pretty girls used to call me Carl."

Everyone laughed politely. Fisher invited her to sit, offered everyone coffee or a tonic water, but there were no takers. Julie took the seat across from Fisher's desk, while Miles and Hank melted into the background.

"I've admired your work for a long time," Julie said. "Not just your television work. I know you were the assistant managing editor at *The Washington Post* who convinced Ben Bradlee to run the Bernstein and Woodward Watergate stories, despite his doubts."

Fisher laughed. "You weren't even alive then."

"We discussed it in my journalism ethics class at Georgetown," Julie admitted.

Fisher sighed and nodded. "Hank showed me some of the segments you produced for *In the Know*," he said. "We admired that show over at CBS and you contributed solid stuff. Fresh. Lively. Excellent segments. You've got real talent."

Julie did something she hadn't done in a long time. She blushed.

"I also had the pleasure of meeting your husband once," Fisher continued. "Terrific producer. Brave man. A real loss."

"Thank you."

The telephone on Fisher's desk rang softly and he looked at it with disapproval. "I told her not to interrupt us," he said. The phone kept ringing and he picked it up.

"Yes?" he said. "Oh. Okay, I'll talk to him." He put his hand over the receiver and spoke to Julie. "Sorry, gotta take this one. Won't be long."

"No problem," Julie said. She let her eyes skip over Fisher's messy desk, over the stacks of paper, the awards and medals, then at the man himself, half-turned away from her. He was no longer young, but still a striking figure, and he radiated both power and integrity.

"The Hartford?" Fisher said concerned. "And the UAW pension fund?" The color drained from his face and he leaned back into his chair, seeking support.

Julie turned her attention to the wall behind Fisher's desk. More awards, framed. Photos of Fisher with Presidents Carter, Clinton, Bush one, and Ronald Reagan. Family pictures. Engraved plaques from organizations like "The Freedom Foundation," and "Citizens for a Democratic America," with lettering too small to read at this distance.

"Can we fight it?" Fisher said. He exchanged a grim glance with Miles. "Well, then, do it, Charley. Buy us all the time you can. And let me know the minute you have any news."

He hung up, thought for a moment, then turned back to Julie and shook his head and smiled wearily. "So, where were we?" he said, composing himself. "Oh, that's right—talking to this charming young lady..."

"Could you tell me a little about the project?" Julie asked, trying not to sound too eager.

"What do you know about foreign governments investing in U.S. companies?" Fisher asked.

Julie's heart sank. She couldn't think of a more boring subject. She'd been hoping they'd called her in to do some kind of human interest piece. "Not much," she said. "What I read in the newspapers. It's supposed to be a good thing, I imagine."

If this is how Fisher planned to reinvigorate UBS, things were even bleaker than she'd imagined.

Fisher's eyes met hers. "That's the cover story," he said with just the faintest trace of a smile.

"Cover story?"

"Yes. And it has to be believable. If the other networks hear about this, they have to believe we're just doing a piece on foreign investment. That's a curiosity-killer, don't you think?"

Julie had no idea where Fisher was going with this. "Well, yes," she said cautiously, hoping she wasn't sinking her own ship. "What's the *real* story?"

Fisher walked over to the window and looked out toward the Freedom Tower, going up at Ground Zero. "It's a story that may be bigger than Watergate," Fisher said, his back to her. "And far more dangerous to America." Hank and Miles exchanged meaningful glances.

"You're going to have to tell me more," Julie told Fisher. "I mean, right now I don't know enough to be able to say whether or not I want to be involved."

Fisher glanced at Miles.

"We've prepared something for you to sign," Miles said. He slipped a document out of his inside jacket pocket and handed it to her. "A confidentiality agreement. I think you'll find it is ironclad."

This was something new—and odd, Julie thought. She scribbled her name on the signature line, then handed the document back to Miles without reading it. Then she looked back up at Fisher.

For a few moments, he just studied her, saying nothing. When he spoke, it was with overwhelming gravity and conviction. "America is under attack," he said.

Julie was puzzled. "You mean the terrorists..."

"No. I mean in addition to the terrorists. I'm talking about an economic *coup d'état* and maybe a political one as well. I'm talking about a war we just might lose."

Julie stared at him, thinking wild thoughts—He's crazy!...It's the biggest story ever...How could he be right?...He's Carleton Fisher...What have I gotten myself into? She struggled to frame a question. "But who...?"

"The Saudis," Fisher said. "The Saudi Royal Family."

Julie wanted to laugh. "The Saudis? The Royal family? But they..."

"Are our allies," Fisher said. "Yes, so we've thought for all these years, and maybe it was true...then. Allies of convenience, anyhow. Not anymore."

"What kind of proof do you have?"

"Mostly circumstantial," Fisher told her. "But plenty of it. More than enough."

Suddenly, Julie realized how closely Miles and Hank were watching her, trying to gauge her reaction. "Mr. Fisher...," she began.

"Carl," he corrected.

"Carl, does Washington know about this?"

"Yes and no," he said. "The SEC knows. And the president has been told. But he apparently believes Saudi reassurances and he has no plans to act. He just can't get himself to believe they mean us any harm."

"I don't really understand how they could be a threat to us," Julie admitted. "What are they doing? And, for God's sake, why?"

Fisher looked at Miles. "You want to answer the lady's questions, Miles?"

"Ok," Miles said. "This is what they're doing: they're buying us. They're buying controlling interest in the top American corporations: IBM, GE, Pfizer—they're some of the ones we know about. And they're doing all this in secret, laundering money through a cascade of nominees and middlemen intertwined inside whole strings of shell companies."

"Don't forget the media," Hank put in.

"Oh, yes. They've already bought controlling interest in *The Los Angeles Times*, Adelphia, Viacom, and ABC," Miles added.

Julie was shocked. "They have control of *ABC*? How do you know?"

"Well, we weren't the first to hear about this story," Fisher said. "Our source offered it to ABC four months ago. ABC was going to run with it, until the Disney board of directors heard about it. Some were in favor, but some new board members opposed them and got Disney family backing."

"Are you saying that ABC—*and* Disney—is now controlled by the Saudi Royal Family?"

Miles nodded. "That's *exactly* what we're saying."

"You read about the Intercoastal take-over?" Fisher asked.

"Yes, front page of *The Times* this morning."

"We have reason to believe the Saudis are behind it."

"I read the story," Julie said. "It said that Intercoastal is being bought by a firm called Kansas City Investment Partners. Rich Midwesterners, no?"

"On the surface, yes," Fisher said. "Actually, Kansas City Investment Partners is owned by International Travel, which is based here in New York, and the majority interest in International Travel is held by a bank in Buenos Aires. Controlling interest in the bank is held by North American Investments, which is fifty-one percent owned by a cousin of the wife of the Saudi minister of public safety."

Julie thought a moment. "Wait a minute. Couldn't that just be innocent—although convoluted—international finance? There's lots of foreign investment in American industries. Didn't Bridgestone buy Firestone? South Korea, too. I seem to recall that they bought Zenith."

"Yes, but we think the Saudis have something much, much bigger in mind," Fisher said.

"What do you mean?" Julie asked.

"That call I just took," Fisher said. "It was from Charles Schumacher, our CFO. He's noticed some unusual block purchases of UBS stock in the last few days."

"They're after us?" Miles asked in alarm.

"Looks that way."

"My God," Julie said quietly.

"We believe they're aiming at total control of the national media," Fisher said. "So we may not have much time."

For a moment, no one spoke. Julie tried to compose her thoughts. Something about this didn't sound right. It was just too, well, outrageous. Unbelievable. "Look," she said, "I know the Saudis are rich, but even they aren't wealthy enough to buy the Fortune 100."

"You're right, "Fisher said. "But they're being very clever. First, they're buying control of our richest companies, the ones with a lot of cash or huge credit lines or assets they can easily liquidate. Then they're leveraging off these assets to acquire other companies. They're using our own goddamn money to buy us."

"But why?" Julie asked. "What's their motive?"

"We've given that a lot of thought," Fisher said. "Our guess is that it's either the money or power."

"The truth is we just don't know," Miles interjected.

This sounds preposterous, Julie thought. It's the mother of all conspiracy theories. "Mr. Fisher—Carl—how do you know this? Who is your source?"

Fisher looked at Miles, then Hank. "You're a skeptic, aren't you?" he said.

"I'm a journalist," Julie replied without hesitation. "I don't tell stories I can't substantiate and I don't shy away from reporting those that I can, even unlikely ones."

Fisher smiled for the first time since the phone call.

"I'm afraid the source is going to have to remain confidential," Miles said. "That is, unless and if we bring you aboard."

"Well, she *has* signed the agreement, Miles," Fisher said. "She needs to know what *we* know if she's going to make an informed decision."

"I trust her completely," Hank said.

"Do I need to remind you gentlemen that I'm sitting right here, listening to every word you're saying?" Julie said playfully.

"Of course," Fisher said. "Two weeks ago, Randy Dandy Hollingsworth paid me a personal visit."

Julie lifted an eyebrow. "Randy Dandy?"

"Randolph McDaniel Hollinsworth. Chairman of the Securities and Exchange Commission. We called him Randy Dandy at Yale. Name stuck."

"His friends called him that?" Julie asked.

"He didn't have many friends, as I recall," Fisher said. "He was a pompous windbag even in college. Hollinsworth is a typical conservative Republican and runs a pro-business SEC, but he thinks unregulated foreign acquisition of American companies is a threat to national security. He even made a strong speech in Congress denouncing against it. The administration was quite displeased to say the least."

"You're going to tell me that Chairman of the SEC is your Deep Throat?" Julie suggested.

Fisher laughed. "Strange, but true."

"Has he often been a source?"

"Just the opposite," Fisher said. "He's called me frequently since he's been in government, but usually because he wanted to put his spin on a story, or delay it—or kill it, if he could. But this time was different."

"How so?"

"There was none of the usual bluster. He was scared. And he was pleading with me to cover the story. Said no one in the Administration would listen."

"And you believed him?" Julie asked.

"Actually no, not at first," Fisher said. "After all, I'm something of a journalist myself." He smiled wryly. "So I asked questions—plenty of them. He had very persuasive answers. He also had *this*…"

Fisher took a thin blue folder from his top desk drawer and handed it to Julie. "Go ahead, take a look."

Julie flipped through the pages. "Looks like lists."

"Yes, lists," Fisher said. "The names of the top-tier companies being targeted. The offshore shell companies that are doing the buying—there are dozens of them, as well as the Wall Street firms that are brokering the deals."

"Wall Street firms! They're party to it?"

"Powerful forces are at work, Julie. Global Equity Merchant Banks like the Blackwell Group are the gatekeepers for the investment community in Saudi Arabia, manipulating the market, causing a sell-off in a company's stock price."

"This allows the monarchy to move in and acquire majority ownership for a fraction of what the company is worth." Miles added.

"How do they get away with it?"

"They get away with it by buying stock directly from the company rather than through the public market. It's called a Buy Out practice."

"And this is legal?"

"Because the companies are privately owned, they're not subject to SEC laws. But now they seem to be going after our public companies."

"And the SEC is powerless to stop it?"

"Julie, a lot of D.C. politicians, once they leave Capitol Hill, are hired as advisors for Blackwell. And that buys a lot of influence within the SEC."

"And the SEC is a federal agency," Julie said, as if speaking to herself. "Mr. Fisher...I mean, Carlton, besides Blackwell, do we know which other Wall Street firms are involved?"

"Can't be sure," Fisher admitted. "There are so many deals, so many accessories. No one has the whole picture—except maybe Randy Dandy Hollinsworth." He slipped the folder back into his desk drawer.

Julie watched him. "I hate to ask this question, but are you sure..."

"That the information is reliable?" Fisher interrupted. "Quite. I made some calls. Everything checks out."

"Then it's downright diabolical," Julie said. "The Saudis are using our own people to buy us out. And it's all clandestine."

Fisher pounced on the word. "Clandestine. Yes. That's the key to the whole shebang. If the American public finds out what's going on, game over. There will be an outcry the likes of which we haven't heard since the Clinton impeachment. And I hope Congress will lock the goddamn barn door while we still have a few horses in the stalls."

Julie shook her head in wonder. "Did you promise, um, Randy Dandy that you were going to run the story?"

"After he told me about ABC, yes. It's my patriotic duty. Besides, if we don't run this story, one of the other networks will while they still have a chance."

"Besides," Miles added, "it fit with our plans."

Hank explained, "We've been looking for a subject for a major documentary special. Something big and dynamic, something sure to get attention and viewership."

"We're going to re-launch UBS in January," Fisher said. "I want this network to make serious journalistic contributions again, the way it did in its glory days. Right now, all we are is bottom-feeders."

"January," Julie repeated. That wasn't going to be easy.

"I know that's cutting it close," Fisher said, "but I don't know how much longer we can protect the network."

"This can't be just another news special." Miles said. "It has to *make* news. This thing will never explode unless someone lights the fuse."

Fisher nodded. "If we can't get every major network and cable news show to put it at the top of the hour and every major newspaper to give it front page headlines…we've failed. We've failed the American people and we've failed UBS."

"We're going to have to go all out to promote it, then," Julie thought out loud.

"But we can't even say what it's about," said Hank. "We have to tease it, promote it as explosive without saying what the explosion is. Make it a kind of mystery."

"You're right," Miles said. "We don't tell 'em what it is, but we say it's the most important television event we've ever broadcast. We aim for at least a thirty share."

"Oddly enough, ratings don't matter much this time," Fisher said, surprising them all. "It's the nuclear fallout *after* the broadcast that matters. We need to warn the country—and change UBS's reputation—overnight."

"I understand," Miles said. "But the question is, can one show do it? What can we put on the air that will be sensational enough to accomplish all that?"

"May I?" Julie asked.

"By all means," Fisher said.

"We can assume that this battle will be won or lost on Wall Street, am I right?" They all looked at each other and nodded. "Then why not do it like a *60 Minutes* or *In the Know* segment?" she suggested. "Have Tom Gallagher grill one of the investment bankers who's been helping the Saudis."

"That's a great idea," Hank said.

"Gallagher, good as he is, is no Mike Wallace," said Miles.

"I know," said Julie. "But we can feed him the questions."

Fisher tried his best not to smile. "I'll talk to him. Besides, Tom's not the problem."

"No," Miles agreed. "The problem is finding someone on the Saudi side who's willing to go on record. The last thing any of these guys want to do is go public."

"Exactly. Not only do we have to find someone willing to go on record, but we need someone genuinely credible," Fisher said.

"I know the perfect person," Miles said. "Only it won't be easy to cage him, especially if he knows what we're planning."

"Who?" Julie and Hank asked simultaneously.

Miles took *The New York Times* from Fisher's desk and pointed to the Intercoastal headline. "*This* guy. The one who pulled off the Intercoastal deal. Barton Mulvaney. They call him *The Rainmaker.*"

"Mulvaney?" Fisher inquired. "That's a familiar name. Blackwell Group?"

"That's the guy," Miles affirmed.

"So tell me about him," Julie said. "Describe him for me."

"Good-looking, early forties, right out of the pages of GQ, could coax a songbird out of a tree. And wealthy—but he'll never be wealthy enough to satisfy himself."

"Married?"

"A couple divorces, I think," Miles said. "Prefers Victoria's Secret models, one at a time, or in groups."

"I know the type," Julie said.

"Do you?" said Miles. "You remember that Oliver Stone movie? Well, this guy is the *real* Gordon Gekko. He's a slimy son-of-a-bitch who lives by his own rules. And he's ruthless, the kind who follows you into a revolving door and comes out ahead of you."

"Sounds ripe for puncturing," Fisher said.

"If we can get him," Miles said. He eyed Julie—up and down—and smiled. "You might have a chance at it."

"For God's sake, Miles," Fisher said disgusted.

"No," Julie said, "he has a point. It might not hurt if the request comes from a woman."

Miles decided not to press his luck. "Anyhow, he'll never agree if he suspects an ambush."

"So what kind of lie should we tell him?" Julie asked, smiling.

"We'll tell him what I told *you*—we're doing a show on foreign investment," Fisher said. "And we are."

"That might work," Miles allowed, "if he believes you."

"He will," Julie said.

Julie regarded Miles Corbin's Wall Street metaphor a bit cliche. Even a bit naive. Or was it? Gordon Gekko was a cultural touchstone. His provocative catchphrase, "Greed is Good" might have been shocking during its time, but it became a mantra for a new breed of 'me' on Wall Street.

"*Okaay*," Miles said, not convinced. "Let's get back to the show. How does it play?"

"Hmmm...well, we open with John Ayers," Fisher said, biting into it. "He talks about who owns America. European investment. Chinese and Japanese purchases of government securities—and then the Saudis.

He highlights some of their investments—then raises the question: What could they be planning?"

"We should probably do more with the Saudis," Hank suggested.

"I agree," Julie said. "We should do a portrait of the Royal Family—ten minutes or so to show exactly who these people are and how they've been supporting radical fundamentalists throughout the Middle East."

"She *does* have an unerring ear for human interest," Hank said.

"It's what she does best," Fisher agreed. "We should also focus on the cozy relationships the Royal family has with U.S. political leaders."

"Good," Julie said. "We have to help people understand why Washington would ignore what's happening—the buyout, I mean."

"And after that?"

"After that, we go to the Gallagher/Mulvaney segment." Julie said.

"That's fine," Miles said. "But we can't end there. How do we wrap it up?"

"We show what's in danger," Julie said. "We show families going to church. We show the Supreme Court in session."

"I get it," Hank said with excitement. "We show the Secretary of State meeting with Arab and Israeli peace negotiators. We show a prayer in Congress. We show our athletes competing at the Olympics. We show U.S. troops guarding foreign children somewhere as they go to school."

"Yes, children," Julie said. "We pluck every damn heartstring we can think of for maybe five minutes or so."

"Then what?"

"Then we cut back to Ayers," Julie said. "And he says something like this: It took us more than 200 years to build America, blood, sweat, and tears. We created an oasis of liberty and justice and we fought a dozen bloody wars to defend it. And now people from another country and another culture, people who don't share our history, our traditions, or our values and human rights are buying it out from underneath us. Are we going to let that happen?" She nestled in her chair, pleased with herself.

"Damn," Hank said, "that would do it for *me*."

"I think that would do it for the entire country," Fisher said quietly. He leaned back and swiveled in his cushy brown leather chair and looked at Julie with new respect.

"What do you say, Miles?" Fisher asked. "You buy off on the concept?"

"Well, it certainly would end any pretense at objective journalism."

"We'll make it an Ayers editorial," Fisher said. "It will be sensational—like Ed Murrow condemning McCarthy."

"Hmm…when you put it that way, it might work," Corbin said, trying to sound like a paragon of good judgment.

Fisher looked into Julie's eyes again. "Are you up to it?" he asked earnestly. "Are you finished mourning?"

Julie had been expecting the question and she'd already contemplated her answer. She returned Fisher's gaze directly. "Well, that all depends," she said. hoping she sounded sure of herself.

"On what?" Miles asked, appearing annoyed.

"On whether or not you'll meet my conditions."

Miles was brought up short. "Conditions? You have conditions?"

"Let her speak," Fisher said.

"Two, to be exact," she told them. "Number one: I want to select my own crew, especially my own directors and segment producers."

"You mean you want to be boss," Miles observed.

"That's right," Julie said.

"And the second condition?" Fisher asked.

"I want the show to air *live*," she said. "And not live on tape."

Hank was taken aback, "Live?" he said with a squeak.

"Yes. No tape, no seven-second delay. Live from all over the country."

Fisher was surprised. "Young lady, I've done more than my share of live television. You have no idea how many things can go wrong—especially in a telecast of this magnitude. It's like doing a trapeze act without a net."

"That's the point," Julie said. "If we do it live, no one can edit the tape. Also, running it live will make the show much more compelling and newsworthy." She didn't mention her second reason for asking that the show air live: it would give her complete control, which was a bold and scary idea.

"It's still much too danger..." Miles began.

"She's right, Miles," Fisher interrupted. "It would stymie any 'new stockholders,' if they tried to control content. It's a bold idea. Risky, but bold."

Miles nodded skeptically.

"When we launch 'The New UBS'," Fisher went on, "we'll be dropping some of the silly reality and game shows, and re-emphasizing news, drama, and quality programming. I want to use this special as the cornerstone of the effort."

"So that gives us four months to get the facts together, get the players on board, structure the interview, write the Ayers material, and find the picture of America locations," Julie said, contemplating the task ahead.

"You want to do the 'picture of America' sequence live as well?" Hank asked.

"Absolutely," Julie replied. "We need the immediacy and the reality."

"Can you do it in four months?" Fisher asked.

Julie realized the operative word in that question was "you." Could she, Julie Chambers, a former segment producer, good as she might have been, pull off a ninety-minute breakout documentary as complex as this one? Could they trust her with a special so important for the network, so important for the nation—a woman who hadn't worked in a year, who may or may not be finished mourning? "Four months is plenty of time to do the job right," she said, hoping it was enough.

Fisher came around from behind his desk, folded his arms, and looked down at her. "I want to be frank with you, Miss Chambers. If Fred Fielding was up to it, this would be his assignment."

"I know."

"And if we decide to hand you the project and meet your conditions—we'll be taking one hell of a gamble."

"I know that, too."

Fisher gazed at her, trying, it seemed, to measure her talent, her commitment, her strength, her poise. It was the toughest moment she'd ever experienced in any job interview and she wasn't even being asked a question.

"Could you give us some time to talk it over?" Fisher asked. "You'll be notified tomorrow, one way or another."

"Certainly," Julie said. "It was a pleasure meeting you, Mr. Fisher. Carleton."

They shook hands warmly. Then she turned to Miles and Hank and smiled. "See you around, guys."

She walked out of the room, took a very deep breath, then found her way back to the elevators. The interview had lasted just under an hour and it had been a very heady experience—meeting Carleton Fisher, discussing this incredible project with him. She thought she did all right, but she didn't think it would come to anything in the end. They're never going to give this much responsibility to a thirty-three-year-old woman with only four years of network television experience, seven if you count PBS, even if she *was* Jack Chamber's widow. And conditions. She demanded conditions…from Carleton Fisher! Where had *that* come from?

Julie got into the elevator and, instead of hitting "L" for lobby, impulsively pressed thirty-five. As long as she was here, she might as well say hello to old friends. She exited the elevator, waved at the startled receptionist and walked quickly through the door to the newsroom: Twenty or thirty people hunched over their desks at computers or editing machines or watching CNN, and Tom Gallagher holding court in the middle of the room.

"…So we're in this ratty horse barn, middle of nowhere, two a.m., no moon, waiting for these two IRA guys." Gallagher said.

"Who arranged the meeting?" someone asked.

"What the hell's the difference?" said another person impatiently. "Let the man talk."

"Right, well anyhow, we saw the headlights of two cars coming along the valley road and we thought, hey, these are our guys. Then the door bursts open and it's three buckos with machine guns."

"Machine guns?"

"Big ones—and they started firing at us the instant they saw us. Wood's splintering, horses are screaming, we're running like crazy for the back door. Simon's out in front…"

"Carrying the *camera*?" someone asked.

"Shit no," Gallagher replied. "He *dumped* the camera. Anyhow, Simon's out the door and I'm close behind and Fielding is coming behind me, I could hear him panting. Then—bang!—he's yelling 'I'm hit! I'm hit!' at the top of his lungs."

"What did you do?" someone asked.

"Kept running," Gallagher admitted. "But then the other car pulled up—cops—and they shot the guys with the machine guns and Simon and I ran back into the barn. And there was Fred, face down in the straw and horse shit, half his trench coat shot off, bleeding all over the place and screaming, 'They shot me in the ass, they shot me in the ass!'"

The news room burst out in laughter.

"What did you do?" a voice asked.

"Covered his ass as quick as I could," Gallagher said. "As usual," he noted, his body now convulsing with laughter.

In the midst of the hilarity, Paige noticed Julie standing at the door. "Oh my God," she said. Everyone followed her gaze and in a moment, Julie was surrounded by friends and well-wishers, Paige Hanson leading the pack.

"It is so great to see you here," Paige said, hugging her, talking like the excited teenage intern she'd been not so long ago. "We've really missed you."

"Same here," Julie admitted.

Cal Flannery, UBS's technician-of-all-trades, a huge man barely wedged into a wheeled swivel chair scooted over to her. "Hey, beautiful," he said, "long time no see. You coming back?"

Julie smiled enigmatically. "We'll see."

"Your old office is still empty," Marty Cohen said. Marty had been head writer for UBS Evening News for thirty years. He was bald and grey and paunchy and his fingers could fly over a keyboard like frightened field mice.

"They didn't even try to replace me?" Julie asked, surprised.

"Budget," said Lisa Green. Lisa was UBS News's line producer, the lumpy, middle-aged woman who controlled the division purse strings.

"I thought they were increasing the news budget," Julie said.

"They are," Cal agreed. "But the change doesn't kick in until September."

Tom Gallagher finally managed to push through the huddle and he gave Julie a long hug. "I'm really glad to see you here again, Julie. The place hasn't been the same without you. And Jack, of course."

The name took Julie's breath for a moment, but she held on. "Thanks, Tom. Kind of you to say."

As the others drifted back to work, Julie saw Hank come through the door. He spotted her and motioned her back into a nearby office.

"Tom," she said, "what does it mean when the jury reaches a verdict after a few minutes?"

She followed Hank into the office and he shut the door behind them. He picked up his phone and punched out some numbers. "I caught her before she left," he said. "We're in Bill's office."

"Who were you talking to?" she asked.

"Miles," he said. "You know, I'm going to retire next year. I'd love to leave this network proud at what it has accomplished and proud of what it has become."

"I understand," Julie said, although she wasn't sure what he meant.

Hank nodded and Miles Corbin walked in the door. "You told her yet?"

"Not quite."

"Okay, I will. You have the job, Julie. Executive producer. You made quite an impression on Mr. Fisher. He thinks you have fresh ideas."

"Do you agree?"

"Well, I know you and your capabilities," Miles said. This was something short of a glowing endorsement.

"What about my conditions?"

"Yes, we agreed to your *damn* conditions."

"One more thing…" Julie began.

"Yes, the contract," said Miles. "Here's what we're offering: $200,000 for the special, with a two-year option for your services as a producer at $250,000 a year."

"You're not putting me on staff? I'm going to be an outside contractor?"

"Yes, that's the deal." Miles said. "Of course, if the special succeeds, I'm sure we'll be able to find a place for you."

Julie and Hank exchanged glances. "I understand," she said. What she understood was that she was being hired over Miles' doubts.

"It all depends on the special," Miles said. "It has to be sensational. The future of the network depends on it."

"Tell her about the budget, Miles," Hank said.

"You have carte blanche—within reason. Fisher has given his word. We've got to do this one right."

"I'm glad to hear that," Julie said. "Okay, where do I sign?"

Miles extended a hand and Julie shook it. "No more signing necessary," he said. "You can start on Monday."

Julie felt exactly like a bride who'd just said "I do," despite her doubts. "Monday it is," she said.

She was already in the elevator, going down, when the events of the day hit her hard. She was back at UBS. She was going to produce the most important television special in the last ten years. God, Jack should have had it. He's dead. Damn. Could she do it? My God, my God.

The elevator door opened and Julie walked out, trying to sort through her feelings.

The Irish elevator captain gave her a wink and a smile. "Have a good weekend, Missy. Hope to see you again soon."

"Yes," she said, suddenly confident. "Yes, you will."

CHAPTER TWO

On the morning of his forty-fifth birthday, Mario Monelli woke up slightly hung-over from last night's party, and slightly confused. He was still aroused, still thinking about the warm, young, and beautiful temptress he met in the emerald waters of Cancun. It was all so vivid—the wild and passionate night they'd shared at the edge of the ocean, the love that had flowered so quickly, the soul mate he'd finally found, the wonderful woman was now lying beside him.

Then he opened his eyes and she was gone. In her place was his wife, Phyllis, her face caked with some kind of greenish anti-wrinkle cream. She was snoring, drooling on the pillow, and wearing the elastic contraption meant to keep her chin firm.

Underneath the gunk, Phyllis was still a good-looking woman—small, regular features, a damn good body, and cascades of dark brown hair—but he'd long ago given up telling her so. There was nothing she couldn't twist, including a compliment. He slowly and carefully slid out of bed, trying not to wake her, when she stirred.

"Mario," she said, stretching, her nasal voice slicing into his brain, "Gimme my robe."

He grabbed Phyllis's robe from the vanity chair and tossed it onto the bed just out of her reach. She glared at him, but said nothing. The real combat probably wouldn't start until they faced each other over breakfast.

He walked into the bathroom for a quick shower, wrapped a towel around his waist, lathered up his face, and started shaving, mourning the dream, miserable with the reality. It hadn't always been this way with Phyllis, he told himself. But he had to go way back to remember when there was anything like love between them—well before Kyle was born, maybe even before Boomer.

Phyllis padded into the bathroom, without glancing in his direction, sitting down and taking possession of the toilet. "I'm fed up with you staying out all night like Dracula, boozing and whoring with your slimeball buddies," she said, flushing and getting up. As she walked out of the bathroom, she poked him in the ribs, hard.

"Ouch!" Mario said, putting a hand to his face. "Look what you made me do."

"If I'm lucky, you nicked an artery," Phyllis said with a nasty grin.

"Don't get your hopes up, Phyllis," Mario said. "There's no way you're going to outlive me." He wiped his face, stuck a piece of Kleenex on the cut, and brushed his hair, peering at it closely.

"The thinning getting worse, Mario? Don't worry. It's natural when you start getting old."

"Getting old isn't the problem, Phyllis," he said mildly, even though he knew he should keep his mouth shut, "the problem is who I'm getting old with."

Mario walked out of the bathroom, into a walk-in closet bigger than most garages, and started pawing through a row of suits. "Where's my charcoal pinstripe Armani?" he asked. "It should be back from the cleaners."

Phyllis lit a cigarette. "I didn't have time to pick it up," she said.

"Dammit, Phyllis, what do you mean you didn't have time? What the hell do you do all day?"

"Whatever the fuck I want."

Mario knew she wanted to fight. And normally he would accommodate her. But he wasn't up for it today. His head was still pounding from the party last night and he was running late.

He picked out a dove-gray cashmere Italian suit, a black calfskin belt, and a pair of silk argyle hose. Then he hit the revolving tie rack and selected a raw silk Hermes necktie embroidered with tiny turquoise dolphins. He found a monogrammed Brooks Brothers shirt in the middle drawer of his floor-to-ceiling wardrobe and scooped up a pair of gold bull and bear cufflinks from the vanity.

Phyllis watched him dress as though she were observing some particularly repulsive zoo animal. "You know, Mario," she said acidly, "I've always wondered what it meant when people called someone an 'empty suit.' Now I understand."

"Fuck you, Phyllis. You're no prize either."

She nodded thoughtfully. "And speaking of fucking, who have *you* been fucking lately?"

Mario shot her a dangerous look.

"Not me, thank God," she went on brightly. "Anyhow, I'll bet you're still having trouble getting it up."

He wanted to smash her in the face. But as much as he hated her, that was something he couldn't do, not after what he'd seen as a kid. He threaded his belt through his pant loops and reached for his O.J. shoes, a pair of tasseled Bruno Magli loafers, which were on the floor near the bed.

"Oh, can I help?" Phyllis asked. She picked up one of his shoes and scraped her nails over the mirror-shined tip, leaving a trail of gouges.

"You bitch." He snatched the shoe out of her hand and took a menacing step toward her. Phyllis backed off warily, bumping into the dresser and almost knocking over a half-empty brandy decanter.

"What are you going to do, Mario," she taunted. "Hit me?" She poured herself a tumbler-full and drank it, glaring at him defiantly.

Mario looked at her with undisguised disgust. "Jesus, Phyllis, it's six in the morning."

"So you can drink all night long with your asshole friends, but I'm supposed control myself?"

Mario ignored her. He slipped on his suit jacket and headed downstairs, fumbling with his tie as he went.

"You fuck like a kid anyway," she yelled, hurling one of her yellow terrycloth slippers and missing him.

Mario heard noises in the kitchen and realized the boys were already downstairs. He managed a smile. They were good kids, both of them. And, after a long, boring summer, they were excited about going back to school. Hard to believe Boomer would be graduating high school next June. Even harder to accept that Kyle was about to start fourth grade.

Kyle, a dead-ringer for Tom Sawyer, was feeding Benson, the family's golden retriever. Boomer—my son, the swimming star, Mario thought—was slipping slices of bread in the toaster. He was tall, dark-haired, and better looking than his father, and at least as smart, Mario told himself.

"Mom sounds pissed this morning," his younger son said.

"Does she?" Mario replied. "I haven't noticed."

"By the way, Dad," Boomer said, "happy birthday."

Mario waved him off. "Never mind that, Boomer. Tell me, where did the Dow close last night?"

"Up thirty points for the day."

"Yield on the long bond?"

"4.94 on the benchmark. You want toast or a bran muffin, Dad?"

"Okay, what's a White Knight?"

"Dad, come on, enough already."

"Just answer the question," Mario said. Wait until Boomer has his first interview on the Street, he thought. He'll blow 'em away.

Boomer rolled his eyes and sighed. "A White Knight is a friendly company that merges with a firm that's under attack to save it from a hostile takeover."

"Excellent," Mario said and thought a moment. He hated bran muffins, but…"Make it a bran muffin," he said.

"I'll get the juice, Dad," Kyle said.

Mario grinned at his youngest. The kid is really starting to grow up. He watched the boy take the orange juice pitcher out of the refrigerator, carefully fill four glasses, and set them out on the table before going back to eating his cereal while skimming pages of a tabloid magazine.

Phyllis came clumping down the stairs, her robe wrapped around her and a crop of pink plastic hair curlers sprouting from her head. She stuck a foot in the missing slipper, which had ended up at the bottom of the stairs. "Did you start the coffee yet, Mario?"

"Just starting," he said. He opened a cabinet, hoping to find the jar of instant.

Phyllis watched him with contempt, arms folded across her chest. "Damn, you're helpless," she said. She pushed past him and got the coffee-making process started.

"You're right, Phyllis," Mario said angrily. "I *am* helpless. That's why you live in a gorgeous home on the Gold Coast overlooking the Sound in Sands Point. That's why you have a closet full of Dior and Givenchy dresses and why your jewelry box looks like a Tiffany's display case. That's why you have every kind of credit card there is, and why we can send our kids to private school and to a fancy summer camp in Maine, and why we always have two new cars in the driveway."

"That's all just money," Phyllis said.

"Money?"

"Daddy, I didn't know Michael Jackson was black."

"What do you give him that shit to read for?" He snatched the magazine out from Kyle's hand and handed him a copy of the Wall Street Journal. "Since when have you turned up your nose at money, Phyllis? Besides, it isn't money. It's twenty years of me busting my ass sixty to seventy hours a week, while you get manicures, pedicures, dermabrasion, and shop."

Boomer took the bran muffin out of the toaster and put it on a plate in front of his father. "You want butter, Dad?" he said, desperately trying to short-circuit the argument.

"What makes you do it, Phyllis? Someone putting a gun to your head and forcing you?"

"You want to know why, Mario? You want to hear what makes me do it?" There was still Brooklynese in her voice, despite years of speech lessons. "Because I'm dead last on your list, Mario. You know it and I know it..."

Mario's eyes narrowed dangerously.

"You're at the bottom of *my* list? That's rich, Phyllis. You shoulda been a comedian.*" He stood up suddenly, stuffed the muffin into his mouth, and washed it down with a long swig of juice. "Have a great day back at school, boys."

Mario grabbed his briefcase, banged open the kitchen door that led to the garage, strode through it, and whip-slammed it shut hard enough to rattle the row of garden tools hanging from the wall. He took a deep breath, slid under the gull-wing-door of his custom black Maserati biturbo 420 convertible, and hit the button that lowered the top, squelching further thoughts of Phyllis like he was stomping out a trash fire. Then he punched the garage door opener, shoved a Nirvana disc in the CD player, and roared out into the street.

A few minutes later, he merged smoothly onto the Long Island Expressway traffic, and forty-five minutes after that, he was through the Midtown Tunnel, bouncing over potholes and fighting his way downtown through clots of taxis, vans, and delivery trucks toward Lower Manhattan and into the nexus of global finance.

During the trip, Mario thought about the day ahead. This was D-day for Intercoastal Courier. If his plan had worked—and he had every reason to believe it would—Intercoastal will have beaten back a particularly vicious takeover attempt. The Clark family will still maintain control of the company they'd worked fifty years to build. There would still be competition on the southern route across the United States and 60,000 jobs would be saved.

That was what he did, day in and day out, with the help of the Zoo Crew, the sharpest team on Wall Street, as well as the most foul-mouthed, sex-obsessed, ethnic grab-bag gang of money movers Wall Street had seen since Animal House played at the Astor Plaza. They were like the movie version of a World War II platoon, fighting bloody battles in the trenches of Wall Street, not for a beachhead, but for companies like Allied Bendix in 1985, Lockheed in '96, their losing battle with the Barbarians over RJR Nabisco in '88, and now the biggest of all, over Intercoastal Courier. My boys, Mario thought, and I'm damn proud of them.

He slithered through the gnarly bottleneck off the West Side Highway and turned the corner onto Vesey Street, toward the World Financial Center building, where he worked. As he drove into the garage, he honked once, gently and stopped his onyx beauty at the guard booth. Widell, the black uniformed attendant, came out to greet him.

"Morning, Widell," Mario said, exiting the car. "Gonna be another scorcher today."

"Sure is, Mr. Monelli."

"Did you have any money on the Mets last night?"

"Well, you know me, boss. Won myself a hundred bucks."

"Damn, Widell, do you *ever* lose?"

"Not often," the attendant said, grinning and showing a gold tooth.

"Maybe we ought to get you upstairs and have you pick some stocks." He laughed and headed toward the elevators. He heard Widell fire up the Maserati and ease it into its home away from home—an oversized, well-lit parking place six spaces from the guard booth, marked with a small, neatly painted sign: "Reserved for Mario Monelli."

Mario took the elevator to the Winter Garden lobby and approached the security desk that guarded the upper elevator bank. It was manned by two uniformed guards scanning personal items on a conveyer belt. "Check his bag," one said to the other, "he's a terrorist."

"Eat me," Mario said playfully. He placed his attaché on the conveyer and walked between the metal detectors and headed for the elevator.

Two expensively dressed men signed in without glancing at the guards and got on the elevator with Mario. "Hey, Bradley," said one, pressing the button for forty-four, "haven't seen you for awhile. Where you been hiding?"

"Hey, Marshall. I'm over in equity with Blair Reynolds."

"Reynolds? I just ran into him out on the Cape."

"Yeah? Well, he and I are buying some acreage in Vermont. You know, for development."

The elevator stopped on the twenty-seventh floor—Loeb Brothers Institutional Trading. "Any chance I could get in on that?" asked the first man.

"Sure, I'll send you a prospectus," said the second, exiting the elevator.

The doors closed and inside the elevator, silence reigned. Mario idly wondered how many times he'd heard this kind of bullshit from WASPS like this, all of them looking like they'd been stamped out at the same factory, trying to figure out what the hell to do with all their "*fuck you*" money.

Finally, the doors opened onto the thirty-fifth, which was one of three floors entirely occupied by Harrison Hart, a small, very successful and privately owned investment boutique. Mario knew its history very well.

Harrison—its original name—had begun as an investment banking house in 1874, founded by a son of the ninth President of the United States, William Henry Harrison. For the next fifty years, it had remained relatively small, but very prestigious, serving the private interests of presidents, kings, and assorted tycoons. When the Depression hit, it was purchased by a consortium headed up by Douglas Gentry, who'd made his fortune in copper mining. In 1986, Gentry turned his majority ownership over to his son, Tyler. But it wasn't until Tyler acquired the Hart Alliance—and Mario's Mergers and Acquisitions team—that Harrison was able to run with the big boys, like Kolberg, Kravis; Goldman-Sachs; and Blackstone.

The lights were already on in the Harrison Hart lobby, and when Mario walked in he found the Beanpole standing at the front desk going through some papers. The Beanpole was everyone's nickname for Tyler's executive assistant, Rose Pheeney. She looked up and smiled, which didn't improve her horsy face all that much. "Happy forty-fifth," she said.

"Damn," said Mario. "Bad news travels fast."

"Forty-five isn't so bad," said Rose Pheeney. "Not if you're a man. If you're a woman, it's the end of life as we know it."

"I didn't know you were forty-five, Rose," Mario said.

"I'm fifty, and you know it very well. Or was that an imposter who ate half the frosting off the cake last May?"

"Anyone else in yet?"

"Tyler's on the phone with somebody. Outside of that, the place is a morgue."

Mario walked back through the trading floor the length of a football field, with its long rows of computers and monitors that charted the markets, and the swivel chairs in front of them, empty for the moment. The floor's loudspeakers, noisy during the day, were quiet now, and the surrounding offices were still dark. Running down the long wall, frozen on yesterday's closing quotes, were the stock and news tickers. In a little less than two hours from now, the opening bell would kick-start all this into an engine room of capitalism.

Mario headed down a short hallway toward two heavy glass double doors, one etched with a large "M," the other with a large "A." The doors had bronze ampersands for handles—his idea. He unlocked them, went inside, and flipped on the lights. The place was a wreck—torn birthday decoration, open filing cabinets, random stacks of half-empty pizza boxes, empty beer cans—everywhere, a half-eaten piece of birthday cake smeared on a Bloomberg terminal. And occupying Mario's chair was an inflatable naked female with a telephone receiver jammed in each orifice. If HR would've seen the place, they *all* would've been filing for unemployment.

A woman's red patent-leather shoe, half-filled with champagne, was sitting on Glen Novak's desk beside a lacy black brassiere that Mario figured must have come from one of the departing summer interns. Glen must have bagged them all—a genuine woodsman who could talk the panties off a nun—thirty-five, tall, dark wavy-blond highlights combed forward, good-looking with an Esquire wardrobe. Sure he was married, but weren't they all?

Well, no. Barry Nussbaum wasn't married. A real-life *Marty* who lived in an old Riverdale mansion with his harpy mother. According to the stories Barry told, the woman was even worse than Phyllis. Outside of numbers, on synergy reports, on SEC filings, and balance sheets, all of which he manipulated more easily than most people breathed, food was Barry's only pleasure. No wonder Barry was Lou Costello on the way to being Orson Wells.

Dennis McCurdy's desk was the cleanest one in the suite, at least if you ignored the seventy-plus cigarette butts piled up in his ashtray, pyramid style. A two-fisted drinker, Dennis was as tough as a dollar steak and getting a little ragged around the edges, which wasn't surprising. He was pushing sixty, and because of his degenerate gambling, was still working on his nest egg, instead of spending his golden years sailing the Caribbean or golfing at Hilton Head.

Still, Dennis was a critical part of the Zoo Crew. He and Glen were the firm's bankrolling gurus. So far, they'd never failed to raise the financing needed to secure a deal, including Time Warner's $130 billion dollar buyout of Western Fed.

But that's not the only reason why Mario loved the guy. Dennis pulled no punches. And he knew what real pain was. He bore scars. One of them was visible—an eight-inch slash across his chest that he'd picked up when he was a wild kid, running with a whole pack of wild kids in the Pigtown section of East Flatbush, Brooklyn. Other scars were beneath the surface. They were the result of what had happened to his son Michael, his only child.

Mario debated calling in the janitorial service, but decided it would be a waste of time. By the end of the day, he thought, after 500 more telephone calls, 200 screamed obscenities, 100 temper tantrums—fueled by coffee and soothed with Maalox, and the final triumph that will save Intercoastal Courier, the place will look exactly the way it did now. And so fuckin' what? The victory was all that mattered.

They all knew that. That's what made them so damn good. They swore and they catted around, but they never took their eyes off the ball. That's why they were globally ranked and were the third-largest firm by capital, dominating the field in Mergers, Acquisitions, and Divestitures. Not a Harvard degree between them. Not a moment at an Ivy League school. No polish, no manners, no pedigrees, not much style either. Just brains, and that was all they needed. They were the last of Wall Street's old guard.

Mario checked his watch. They'll all be rolling in, in another ten minutes or so, and the air would start vibrating and the place come to life. God, he loved this job. He loved the energy, he loved the feeling that he was doing something that mattered. He pitied the people who walked the streets half-dead, which was almost everyone.

On Neil's desk, a stack of papers a foot high was piled on the right side. By the end of the day, the entire stack would be on the left side, every synergy report absorbed and intelligently acted upon. Neil Granger was the Zoo Crew's research analyst with a brain like a buzz saw and a tall sinewy physique that looked as if it had been chiseled from a slab of testosterone. He was a close human approximation of a Chevy pick-up. Rangy, solid, dependable, and All American in a dirt, sweat, and beer sort of way.

"Hey, paisan!" Mario looked up to see Vinny Maldonado coming through the door, a rough-and-tumble streetwise kid he had found elbowing his way through the loud commodity pits. He was wearing what looked like a Hugo Boss pin-striped suit and carrying a motorcycle helmet. On paper, Vinny was the Zoo Crew's bellhop. But in reality, he was Mario's apprentice.

"Hey, what's with the designer suit?" Mario asked. "Your girlfriend buying your clothes now?"

"Well, you don't want your junior associate dressing like a slob, do you?"

Mario was startled. "Junior associate? You mean…"

"I passed my CFA," Vinny said, beaming. He glanced at Barry's desk, spotted a wayward file, and put it in his own stack.

"No shit—you did it! Damn, Vinny, I knew you could."

Vinny looked Mario straight in the eye. "You went to bat for me, Mario. I'll never forget that. Never."

"So what did Inez say?"

"She said no more excuses. It's time to get married."

They both laughed as Glen Novak burst through the door, followed closely by Neil Granger, and as great a combination since Saturday and Sunday. "She was about five foot-five, blonde—a *real* blonde, I can tell— and she was wearing this flimsy white blouse," Glen was saying. "She had huge tits and really dark nipples."

"How do you know that?" Neil challenged him, "you rip off her clothes right there on the PATH train?"

Glen just laughed.

Barry Nussbaum shortly followed, barreling through the glass doors huffing and puffing, catching the tail end of the conversation. "Another day at work, more stories about women on the subway, girls on the commuter buses, girls on the ferry. Don't married guys ever think about anything else?"

"Sure we do," Neil said. "We think about money."

"What I don't understand is what all these women see in you guys," Barry said.

Dennis McCurdy strolled in, wearing a ragged trench coat he might have swiped from Columbo, and carrying a huge, beat-up brown leather dog-eared briefcase, which he plopped down on his desk. "G'morning, gentlemen. You too, Glen," he said. He walked to the far wall of the office suite and pulled down a huge roll-up map of the world, which was now completely covered with pictures of *Sports Illustrated* swimsuit models. "There. I always feel better when the Wall of Shame is up and running."

"Why so late this morning, Denny?"

"There's a taxi strike you asshole in case you haven't heard," Dennis grumbled, slithering out of his trenchcoat. "I had to flag down a gook pulling one of those rickshaws. I thought I was back in fuckin' Saigon."

Everyone laughed.

All the ingredients were in the glass now, like the 5 whites of a highball: Gin, Rum, Vodka, Triple Sec and Tequila. Potent straight, but smooth when together. And Mario was the straw that stirred the drink. The banter continued for a while longer when Mario picked up a book and dropped it on Neil's desk. "Hey, assholes," he said to his startled team. "Can you fuckin' degenerates stop thinking about tits for a few minutes and turn your attention to the airline we're trying to save? You all know the Carlyle team will be hitting us hard."

The laughing ceased instantly and the Zoo Crew took to their desks like they were sailors manning their battle stations on a warship. At exactly that moment, Mario's phone rang.

"Yeah?"

"Tyler wants to see you," Rose Pheeney said.

"Now?"

"Now."

Mario stopped at Dennis's desk. "You've got the con," he said. "I'll be back in a minute." He paused at the door and looked at his team. "Don't any of you do anything stupid." They all laughed, relishing the joke at their expense. The Zoo Crew were his equals outside the office, but professionally he was their god.

Harrison Hart's décor was, for the most part, a study in glass and bronze, modern and anonymous. There was nothing anonymous about Tyler Gentry's office, however, and nothing modern either. The room looked as though it had been cut out of a nineteenth-century British hunting lodge and brought over whole on the Queen Mary.

There was an arched brick fireplace—the only working fireplace in the World Financial Center—wood-paneled walls decorated with photographs from Tyler's life...the young Tyler in a Harvard lacrosse uniform, Tyler in the Congo jungle, holding a shotgun, Tyler—swaddled in furs and down—holding up an ice axe at a Mount Everest base camp, Tyler—drained and exhausted—crossing the finish line at the Boston Marathon, Tyler on the set of "Band of Brothers," posing with friend, Steven Spielberg.

In addition, glass cases scattered around the room displayed actual souvenirs—the ice axe, the shotgun, a stuffed bison, a battered WWII helmet and the like. The furniture was massive—all brown leather and oak-framed.

Mario had not been able to stifle a laugh the first time he'd seen the office, and that laugh had earned him a dirty look from Tyler, and lingering resentment.

Tyler was in his natural-athlete-tanned-and-very-fit mid-forties, a perfect touch of silver in his sideburns, with the bearing of a full bird Colonel. As Tyler saw it, he represented an entire culture, a privileged culture, a superior culture, the culture whose natural habitat was Greenwich, Connecticut and Pound Ridge, New York. And Tyler had built Harrison and his House of Lords in his own image: Sagittarius, half-man, half-horse with a license to shit in the street. The Hart people—especially Monelli's group—were a distasteful necessity. Harrison's House of Commons, Tyler would often joke. But it was hard to argue with their bottom line.

Forcing a smile, Mario opened the door to Tyler's office and sailed in like a warm breeze. Tyler looked up. "Sit," he said brusquely.

"Good morning to you, too, Tyler," said Mario, lowering himself into the guest chair.

"We lost Intercoastal," said Tyler, who always had a penchant for blunt talk. "It's gone."

Mario sat up and furrowed his brow in apparent confusion. "What? What do you mean? Gone?"

"I mean we failed. *You* failed. The raiders won. The biggest deal in the last twenty years, and we have no part in it."

Mario's mouth went dry.

"Old man Clark called me early this morning. He lost the Prudential proxies."

"No one even knew they were in play, Tyler. We stopped Carlyle at twenty-two percent. We had them beat."

"It wasn't Carlyle, Mario, it was the Blackwell Group—Barton Mulvaney, working for Kansas City Investments."

"Fuck! Mulvaney!? Again! How the fuck did that asshole find out the Prudential proxies were in play?" Mario was having trouble getting his arms around all this. "It was a done deal."

"It's a done deal, all right. Mulvaney has fifty-two percent right now, and Clark is resigning from the Intercoastal Board before the bell. I'll bet the story makes the late edition of *The Times* this morning."

Mario could feel the sweat collecting under his shirt. This just can't be happening. "Son-of-a-bitch," he snarled through clenched teeth. "Son-of-a-*bitch!*"

Tyler leaned back in his chair and aimed a cold, level gaze at Mario. "I figure it's going to cost us about a half billion dollars in fees and commissions."

Mario nodded. He'd never lost anything this big or even close to it. And this wasn't the first time he'd lost to that smug son-of-a-bitch Barton Mulvaney.

Then Mario remembered Monty Clark, who'd founded Intercoastal in 1957 with two DC-6s he mortgaged his house to buy, hired his wife as the bookkeeper, persuaded three Army Air Corps pilot buddies to fly for practically nothing and built the company into the third-largest courier service in the United States.

He remembered Monty Clark's pride. He remembered the love and admiration his employees had for the man and he remembered, most of all, the promises he'd made to the Clark family and to the unions representing almost 125,000 employees. This was a leveraged buy-out. Before the buyers were finished, half the fleet would be pieced off or liquidated. What kind of a future would the employees have now? What about pensions?"

"Did you hear what I said?"

"About what?"

"Mario, we got shut out of a $160 billion dollar deal. We were supposed to garner over a half billion dollars in fees and commissions. What do you think that's going to do to our expansion plans?"

"Won't help," Mario admitted.

"We may be making a serious mistake," Tyler said, shaking his head.

"What do you mean?"

"We've been fighting to save these companies, and we've been doing it well. But our competitors are beginning to pull ahead of us now."

"What are you saying, Tyler?"

"I'm saying that the world's changing, Mario. There's a lot of foreign money out there, buying who knows what. There's a lot more profit in takeovers than there is in defenses."

"You know how I feel about that, Tyler."

"That's what really puzzles me, Mario. Apparently, you care more about saving the jobs of some clock punchers than you do about your own success—and your own company."

"I'm gonna tell you a story," Mario began. "About my old man."

"I've heard it," Tyler said. "It's in everything that's ever been written about you. He was a steam fitter at the Brooklyn Navy Yard."

"Yeah, that's right," Mario said. "Every night he came home…"

Tyler sighed.

The phone rang and a moment later, Rose Pheeney came on the intercom. "The Chairman wishes to speak to you," she said. "He's calling from his airplane." Her voice carried a hint of warning.

Tyler's face fell and he anxiously reached for the phone. "Great story, Mario. Send it in to *Reader's Digest*." Mario pressed down on Tyler's hand, preventing him from picking up the phone.

"Leave him on hold," he said. "I'm going to tell you the part of the story you've never heard."

"On hold? Are you crazy?"

"Five-hundred says you don't have the balls."

Tyler withdrew his hand. "Tell Patterson I'll be with him in a moment," he said into the intercom. He flashed Mario a daring look. "Be quick, Monelli."

"You know why my father worked so hard, why he worked so hard he killed himself doing it?"

"No idea."

"He did it so his sons wouldn't have to. See Tyler, every man in the yard had a dream: to send his kids to college. My old man wasn't any different."

Tyler nervously eyed the flashing button on his phone and shifted in his chair.

"But some Wall Street shark shattered his dream along with the dreams of 10,000 other men at the Navy Yard—all of them first-generation Americans. Do you know who that shark was?"

"What difference does it make?" Tyler said. He was growing impatient now.

"It was your father, Tyler. It was Douglas Gentry."

Tyler's mouth fell open. Mario finally had his full attention.

"So Douglas Gentry's boy goes on to Harvard with Barton Mulvaney and the rest of the lucky sperm club, wearing their cashmere cardigans and sipping sherry by the fireplace with their pinkies up, bragging about their polo shots. Meanwhile, Vito Monelli's boy goes to work lugging clothes racks up and down the garment district working on his GED."

Tyler was staring at Mario. He'd forgotten the phone.

"Now ask yourself this, Tyler: How many kids whose folks worked for Intercoastal will end up working menial jobs? How many dreams will be crushed."

Tyler just listened, silently.

"That's why I take it personally," Mario said. He dipped into his pocket and removed a gold money clip from a wad, then peeled off five, crisp, hundred-dollar bills and flipped them on Tyler's desk, beside the blinking phone. "You have bigger balls than I thought, Tyler. I guess you *do* piss standing up. Here," he said, tossing Tyler the phone receiver. "Now lick Patterson's ass."

Heading back toward the M&A department, Mario could hear the raucous hilarity even before he got to the glass doors.

"Hey, Mario," Dennis called out, as Mario entered the office suite, "we're taking Vinny out to *The Silicone Valley* tonight to celebrate his passing the test…"

"Yeah, we're chipping in to buy him a lap dance with Monica and her mammoth mammaries," Neil said, laughing. "A hundred bucks. Cough up."

"Hey, Mario," said Vinny, "what's the matter?"

Mario told them.

He told them about Barton Mulvaney and the Prudential proxies.

He told them about the half billion dollars in fees, gone.

He told them about Monty Clark.

He told them they could forget about the bonuses they expected to make on the deal.

Their faces turned to stone and silence blanketed the room.

"We lost one, guys," Mario said. "We just plain got beat."

"But how?" asked Neil. "How did Mulvaney know about the Prudential proxies?"

"What difference does that make?" Glen asked bitterly.

"God, I'd rather lose to anyone except Mulvaney," Dennis said. "That Irish prick is going to be insufferable."

Neil Granger angrily snatched the red shoe off the Bloomberg terminal and flung it against the wall with all of his might, shattering it at the heel. At that moment, Dick Hamilton walked in, briefcase tucked under his arm. "What's *that* crap?" he said, pointing to the soiled pizza boxes piled on his desk.

No one in the Zoo Crew spoke up. They'd forgotten about Hamilton. They'd *wanted* to forget about Hamilton, bald, pencil-thin, the lone Harrison carry-over retained in the Harrison Hart M&A Division. They'd wanted to forget he was a former vice president of Yale's Scroll and Key secret society, a rector in the Anglican church and probably a spy for Tyler.

"What's going on here?" he asked. "No one's shouting. No one's cursing. You're not doing your Animal House routines. Did you boys strike out in the bedroom last night?" he teased.

"We fucked every intern in the place," Glen barked at him. "Not that it's any of your business, asswipe."

"We have to dump every last share of Intercoastal before the news gets out," Mario told his team, ignoring Hamilton. "If we're aggressive, we ought to be able to recoup what we pumped into due diligence."

"Well, what are we standing around for? Stop farting around and tell our guys on the floor to start dumping," Dennis said, giving Mario a mock salute.

CHAPTER THREE

Mario eased the Maserati into his garage, turned off the engine, and sat there. The day had started badly, gotten worse, and, he expected, was about to fall apart completely. Finally, he took a deep breath, slid out of the car, and walked into the kitchen.

Phyllis was waiting for him, eyes ablaze. She was wearing red lycra stretch pants and a gold lamé top.

"Where have *you* been?" she demanded.

"Sorry I'm late," Mario said. "There was a little celebration for Vinny. He passed his test and…"

"You missed dinner," Phyllis informed him coldly. "And the Bernards' party started about"—she checked her watch—"a half-hour ago. Why do you think I'm dressed up?"

"Damn, I forgot all about that," Mario said. He wasn't in the mood for a party, but Rick Bernard had been Mario's closest friend at Hart. They were still pretty close, despite the bad ending to the merger five years ago.

Phyllis and Brenda Bernard had grown up together, first in Brooklyn, then in Levittown, when both families had moved to the "suboibs," and they'd remained good friends. And their boys, Boomer and Danny Bernard, best friends since grade school, were still inseparable and always at each other's houses, which was easy, since the families lived across the street from each other on the same cul-de-sac.

"It's only their twenty-fifth anniversary, Mario," Phyllis said. "Why would you remember anything like that?" Her smile would have made a cobra cringe.

Mario headed upstairs to change clothes and to get away from Phyllis. "Oh, by the way," she said, following him, "we got a reply from the Winged Foot Country Club today. Don't you want to know what they said?"

"I could care less."

"Well, they turned us down. Again."

Mario shrugged, grabbed a plaid sport jacket and a pair of tan pants from his closet and began changing.

"You don't care about our social standing?" Phyllis asked bitterly. "They look at us, see 'Toidy-Thoid' Street, and sneer behind our backs and you don't care?"

"I look at them and see WASP snobs," Mario said. "I look at them, with their perfect little pointy noses in the air, and wonder why they don't drown when it rains."

"They don't respect you," Phyllis said. "You haven't made the right friends. Just those assholes at work. And Tyler—why didn't you ask him to help, like I told you?"

"Because I don't give a shit about our *social standing,* Phyllis."

"What *do* you care about, Mario? And you better not say *me.*"

"I care about Boomer and Kyle," Mario replied. "I care about my friends. I care about the people I work with. I care about the companies I defend and the working people I try to protect."

"You're so full of bullshit, Mario, it's amazing it isn't shooting out of your ears. By the way, some clown from the Wall Street Journal called asking for you...*The Times,* too."

Mario knew they weren't calling to wish him a happy birthday. I'm going to be paying for the Intercoastal catastrophe in more ways than one, he thought. I'll have to talk to those smear merchants in the press eventually, which is like eating ground glass. Then I'll have to hear what those snipers masquerading as journalists on cable news say about me, which isn't going to be good either.

"What did they want?"

"They wanted to talk to you about some Intercontinental thing, whatever."

Here it comes, Mario thought. "Yeah. That was ours."

"Big Man Mario and his infamous Zoo Crew blew it big time," she said, relishing his failure.

Mario zipped up his pants, fastened his belt, and slipped on the sport jacket. "Let's go," he said and started downstairs.

"By the way," Phyllis said brightly, "Boomer got a college acceptance today."

Mario's face lit up and he spun around, "From Harvard? He's finally off the waiting list?"

"From Brooklyn College," Phyllis said, laughing, twisting the knife.

Mario whirled toward her, fists clenched, ready to hit her. Then the anger gave way to simple hatred. "You've really taught me something, Phyllis."

"Yeah, what's that?"

"The true meaning of the word *cunt.*"

He turned and headed across the street, Phyllis following close behind, clutching an anniversary present for the Bernards. Muffled party sounds wafted toward the street from behind the Bernard house directly ahead of them, and cars already filled the long, curving driveway and spilled into the tree-lined street.

Mario and Phyllis took the flagstone path to the back porch and found themselves in a crowd of partygoers—the Bernards' friends and neighbors—dancing, drinking, and sitting in groups at umbrella-covered tables, while a small band played on the other side of the huge tiled pool.

Mario maneuvered through the throng, saying his hellos, trying to spot Rick, while Phyllis headed in the opposite direction, looking for Brenda.

Mario finally found Rick inside the house, alone in the upstairs study, sitting in a big burgundy leather recliner, drinking. "Hey, paisan," Rick said loudly. "What's your medicine?"

"The usual."

"You know where the pharmacy is."

Mario opened the doors of the wet bar, poured himself a double dose of Jack Daniels, and studied his friend for a moment. It was the same old Rick, of course, tall, movie-star handsome, with that famous 1000-watt smile. But underneath the grin, Mario could sense tension and uncertainty. "What's up, Buddy?" Mario asked, concerned.

"Twenty-fifth anniversary, that's what's up," Rick said, rattling the cubes in his glass.

Rick raised his glass and Mario clinked his against it. "Well, congratulations, old friend."

"Yeah, happy birthday to you, Mario, and happy congratu-fucking-lations to me." Rick got up and refilled his glass. "Hey, I heard about Intercoastal. What happened?"

"If it's alright, I'd rather not talk about it."

"C'mon, what happened? How did Mulvaney get the proxies?"

"I'm still not sure."

"I know what you mean. There's plenty *I'm* not sure of either."

"What are you talking about?"

"I might as well tell you. I'm leaving New York, Mario."

"Business trip?"

"In a way. I'm moving."

Mario laughed. "Moving? What do you mean you're moving?"

"It's true. I got an offer I couldn't refuse. Twice the power and three times the green."

Mario was dumbfounded. "You're going to accept that offer from the Carlyle Group? You're going to Washington? I don't believe it."

"The Carlyle Group? Do you honestly think I'd work for a bunch of ex-presidents and greasy politicians? You know what I think of politicians. Christ no, I'm not moving to D.C.."

"But you said you're moving..."

"A lot farther than Washington, Mario."

"Stop yanking my chain, Rick. What the fuck are you talking about?"

Rick put his drink down and pulled up the corners of his eyes with his forefingers. "Hong Kong," he exaggerated in a Chinese accent.

"You're moving to *Hong Kong*? To China?" This was almost beyond belief.

"Ah, Number One Friend is finally catching on," Rick said with a maniacal grin. "You are looking at the managing partner of the biggest fucking private investment bank in the People's fucking Republic of China, China Minsheng Banking Corp."

"The Chinese are moving into big-time investment banking?" asked Mario. "They're not satisfied with making everything you can buy at Wal-Mart?"

"It's a new frontier, Mario. The chinks are very fucking ambitious. Internationally inquisitive. They're looking to expand. And they want *me* to help them look for Western marquee names."

Mario just stared. He'd never seen Rick this way before, almost raw with—what was it? Rage? Recklessness?

"But I thought things were going well for you over at Montgomery Clark."

"At the beginning." Rick admitted. "But ever since they took the company private last year, being at a board meeting is like being at a fucking synagogue."

Rick poured himself another drink and gulped it. "So this is my idea," he said, wiping his mouth with his sleeve. "I want you to go with me. I want you to head up my M&A division."

"*Me*? You want *me* to come with you? To Hong Kong?"

"Hey, I know it's sudden," Rick admitted. "But what the fuck—you and I were once the hottest team on the Street. Who better than you?"

"After the way it ended?" Mario reminded him.

"Sure, why not?" Rick said expansively. "I still think you should have resigned. But what's past is past. We'll start fresh. It's a whole different *hemisphere* for God's sake!"

Mario just shook his head, over and over again. "Can you see me eating chop suey, Rick? I can't live in Hong Kong. I'd feel like a Martian."

"I'll buy your contract from Tyler. And we'll hit your bid. You'll be eating filet mignon every night."

"It's not the money."

"We work on Wall Street, remember," said Rick, "it's *always* the money."

"Not anymore."

"You're serious," Rick said, lowering his drink.

"Well, I've really found my niche at Harrison Hart," Mario said.

"You mean you're waiting to be made partner," said Rick.

Mario ignored him. "I can't pull the boys out of school, not now. Just not the right time."

Rick withdrew his arm, sighed, and refreshed his drink.

"I forgot. You're forty-five now. Too settled in your ways. A couple of years' adventure in the Orient is just a little too exciting for you."

Rick gave him a devilish grin. "Think of the Chinese women, man. I know you like those little feet."

"I can get all the Asian broads I want right here in Manhattan. I'm just not the right guy for you, Rick."

Rick fingered the rim of his glass and sighed. "Yeah, I thought you'd say that. Because of the way the merger with Harrison ended, right?"

"No. I'd love to work with you again, Rick. You know that. But not in The People's Republic of China."

"You're still worried about communism?" Rick joshed.

"I'm a New Yorker. And I'm an American. A patriotic one. I remember the last time a major Asian country got interested in banking."

"You're paranoid, Mario. China is just interested in being our trading partner. Selling us stuff, that's all."

"Just like Japan. All *they* wanted to do was sell us Toyotas and Sonys and Seikos. Remember? Next thing you know, they're buying up trophy real estate and financing our deficit along with India and Malaysia, and dicking around with their currency."

"Oh, I see," Rick said. "Loyal to your country, but your wife is another story. Tell me how that works."

"Maybe we should stay away from that," Mario warned.

Rick sobered up for a moment. "Sorry," he said. "I was outta line. Let's change the subject."

"Yeah, let's," agreed Mario.

"So tell me, Mario, how is the Zoo Crew? I miss those degenerates."

"They haven't changed a bit," Mario said, grinning now.

"Tell me, old buddy, ever think about Keyes?"

Mario looked hard at Rick, who was back on forbidden territory. "From time to time," he said.

"Course it didn't matter anyhow," Rick sailed on drunkenly. "You were there when it happened, weren't you?"

"What? You don't remember?" Mario asked indignantly. "We were *all* there, standing right beside you, watching our friends from Cantor swan-dive above the impact zone."

"Oh, yeah, I remember now. You're the one who reminded me Keyes was up in Windows, right above them, having breakfast."

"That was a long time ago," Mario said. "No sense rehashing it."

Rick turned away from Mario and took another long drink from his glass. "Yeah, you're right," he sighed. "That was ages ago. Life goes on."

"That's right.," Mario said. "And now you're going to China."

That snapped Rick out of it. "Yeah, China. A whole new world. Still wish you were going with me."

"Isn't in the cards, Rick."

Rick walked behind the bar and drained his glass. "Think any of the Zoo Crew might be interested?"

"I seriously doubt that. Glen's ole lady just ain't well enough. And Barry...poor guy would shrivel up if you took him away from his mother."

They both laughed.

"Well, don't worry. I'll find someone, I'm sure."

Mario paused a moment, thoughtful. Then, he decided to say what he was thinking. "You know, there is one guy...he's green though."

"That's okay. I like them that color. What school?"

"Hard knocks."

"You and him share the same alma mater."

"He's young...but he *gets* it. He has incredible instincts. Only you'd have to wait for him. He's a raw talent and I haven't finished polishing him up."

"That's okay, Mario—I'm not leaving for a while. What's this guy's name?"

"Vincent Maldonado. Puerto Rican kid from up in the Bronx."

Rick looked at Mario sharply, then chuckled. "I like the idea of a Latino in China. I'll bet he'd fit in there better than he does at Harrison Hart."

"You may be right," Mario chuckled, then had a sudden thought. "What about Brenda and Danny? How do they feel about moving to Hong Kong?"

"Oh, yeah," said Rick, stumbling over his words a little. "My very beautiful wife. And my *very* beautiful son. Well, Mario, old friend, that's a whole fuckin' 'nother story."

"What do you mean?"

Rick looked at his watch, but could barely focus on it. "Come on, it's time, let's go downstairs."

"It's time for what?"

"You'll see."

On the way downstairs, they passed Danny's bedroom. The boys were playing video games and pigging out on potato chips and root beer.

They were a well-matched pair—Boomer, with his engaging Mediterranean looks, flashing dark eyes and dark hair, Danny, blue-eyed and blond, his Scandinavian ancestry in full view, looking like a young Bjorn Borg.

"Who's winning?" Rick asked.

"Me," the boys said simultaneously.

Their fathers laughed. "Come on," Rick said, leading Mario downstairs and out onto the terrace, into the noisy, drunken crowd, to a spot in front of the band.

"There you are, Rick!" shouted Andy Stoval. Stoval, a small man with a very big nose, was an internist with a thriving North Shore practice. "Where ya been? Let's get the anniversary couple together and take some pictures."

"Good a time as any," Rick said, grinning, "and your very last chance, too. Hey, Brenda?"

Mario spotted Brenda nearby, looking up at the sound of her name. Phyllis was standing next to her, looking stunned and angry.

"I'm coming, Rick." Brenda was a tiny woman. Once upon a time—maybe as recently as ten years ago—she'd been quite pretty, a porcelain-doll with striking blonde hair and tanned and glowing skin. But the hair was graying now and the skin around her eyes was beginning to wrinkle.

Brenda threaded her way through the crowd. Rick took her hand and slipped the other arm around her waist. The cameras flashed again and again.

"Speech," someone yelled. A few people applauded, half-heartedly.

Rick climbed up on a chair, a bit unsteady, and held up a hand. "As a matter of fact, we have a fuckin' announcement to make." He was slurring his speech like Foster Brooks at a Dean Martin roast. The crowd ignored him.

"Hey!" someone shouted. "Listen up. The man has an announcement."

Someone else hushed the band and the bandleader handed Rick the mike.

"Ladies and germs," Rick began, the mike booming. "I mean ladies and gentlemen. I have an announcement to make. Oh, I already said that." The partygoers finally stopped talking and started paying attention.

"What's the announcement?" Dr. Stoval asked, heckling. "You two having another kid?"

"No, it's nothing like that," Brenda said tightlipped.

"Ladies and gentlemen," Rick began again.

"Come on, out with it," said his heckler.

"First let us say, we thank you for being here," said Brenda, rescuing Rick from his near stupor. "And we'll cherish fond memories of good and devoted friends." She took a deep breath and looked at Phyllis, hoping for support. "Rick and I have filed for divorce."

The crowd fell into a stunned silence, then broke out into nervous laughter.

"It's true," Brenda said quietly, and the stunned silence returned.

Mario, beyond surprise now, poured himself a drink at the bar and leisurely sprawled out on a lounge chair near the pool.

"We're not mad at each other," Rick offered.

"No," Brenda agreed. "It's an amicable divorce."

Suddenly, every one of the thirty or forty guests on the terrace and around the pool was as sober as a bomb disposal expert.

"You hear her?" Rick asked, pointing to the crowd. "An am-amica-bibbble-fuckin'-divorce."

"With no more fuckin'," Dr. Stoval said, laughing coarsely. No one joined him.

"We're still friends," Brenda was telling everyone, "and we always will be. But Rick is taking a job in Hong Kong and Danny and I are staying here until Danny graduates high school." There were tears in her eyes now. "We just couldn't have held up if we'd had to tell everyone separately," she continued. "I know this must be a shock, but it's really for the best."

"That's abso-fuckin'-lutely right," Rick said. "It's for the abso-fuckin'-lutely best."

"Also, by making a joint announcement," said Brenda, "we're telling all of you that we want to remain friends with you. We're not taking sides and neither should you."

The crowd watched them, quietly expectant, as if there were more to come. But there wasn't. Rick handed the mike back to the band leader, and in a moment, the band resumed, sounding a little louder than before against the silence of the crowd.

"Listen, everyone," Brenda said loudly, smiling a little too brightly, "this is a party. We want you all to have fun and enjoy yourselves."

"That's right," Rick said. "Eat, drink, and *fuck* Mary." He was definitely drunk now.

For the next ten or fifteen minutes, the party went on hold and the excited buzz of gossip took over. But eventually people began eating and drinking and even dancing again. Mario guessed that Brenda had gone off somewhere with Phyllis, probably to an upstairs bedroom. It wouldn't be an amicable divorce by the time Phyllis finished poisoning Brenda's mind.

People were still drinking and gabbing when midnight came, but Mario decided he'd had enough. He walked through the house and found Rick sitting on the front lawn, his back against a tree, looking up at the night. He didn't seem drunk anymore.

"Here, you need this more than me," he said, handing Rick his drink.

"Sorry, paisan," Rick said, taking it. Mario sat down next to his friend.

"Sorry for what?"

"For doing it that way."

"Oh that. Well I must admit it certainly put a damper on the party," Mario said wryly. "And all along I thought you guys were happy."

"We were. For a long time."

"Is there someone else?"

"Are you kidding? I'm too scared to cheat on my taxes," Rick said.

"That's too bad," said Mario. "It might've saved your marriage. So what happened?"

"That's just it. We don't know. We just woke up one morning and saw a stranger lying next to each other."

"Why didn't you come to me?"

"You? Go to you?" Rick chuckled. "There's more screaming going on at your house then at an Islander game in the coliseum." They both laughed.

"Why didn't you bail out sooner?"

"I was worried about Danny."

"And now?"

"Danny is almost eighteen. Now it's time to worry about myself."

Mario smiled. "I suppose that you guys have already talked settlement?"

"Actually, we have. Brenda insisted I take half."

"Half? You're kidding, right?"

"She's still a good person, Mario."

Mario nodded thoughtfully. He was thinking more of Phyllis than Brenda.

"So I'm starting a new life," Rick said. "It's gonna be exciting. Sorry you won't be with me…"

Mario looked at his friend with envy. He envied Rick's courage to leave behind a son he adored and to live his own life.

"I can't leave the boys," Mario said. "Especially Kyle. It would destroy him."

"If it doesn't destroy you first." Rick stood and brushed off his pants. "Well, I better be getting back. I got a party to host."

"I don't know how much of a party you got left in there," Mario said.

Rick turned back, as if he forgot something. "I don't know why," he said, "but the one thing that struck me that morning… more than anything else, more than the bodies splattering into the courtyard, was the millions of pages of paperwork floating down from the towers just after the second hit. It had this sort of eerie calm to it, very peaceful, like the tail on a kite I once had long ago. And I thought—I thought to myself, how many hours and needless deadline pressures where placed on preparing those reports… and in the end… who really cared?" Then he paused for a moment. "I have one life. And only I get to choose how its lived." Then he looked at his friend. "Mario, can you do me a favor?"

"Sure, buddy, name it."

"Will you keep an eye on Danny…just till I get settled out there?"

"Sure, Rick. You can count on it."

"Friends for life?" asked Rick.

"Friends for forever," said Mario.

CHAPTER FOUR

After a quick, invigorating walk uptown from Turtle Bay, Julie Chambers pushed through the revolving door at UBS at 8:25 a.m.. She was feeling just about every known emotion, from eagerness and fear, to sadness and joy. It had been just about a year ago that she and Jack had last come to work together, but that seemed like another lifetime.

She picked up a *Times* at the lobby newsstand, then headed up to the UBS newsroom, back into the eye of the hurricane—camera operators wheeling equipment into place, writers working frantically at their computers, set decorators sprucing up the news desk, editors cutting tape. In other words, home.

Julie headed toward the producer's office, flipped on the light and found herself looking directly into the rough and rugged face of Fred Fielding, who was sitting behind what she thought was going to be her desk. His rumpled trench coat was draped over his arm and a pair of crutches were leaning against the guest chair.

"Fred! I…" she stammered.

"Mornin', Julie," Fielding said expansively. "Welcome back."

"I thought you…"

"Were out of action? Never underestimate the old man, Julie. You should know that."

Then, to Julie's relief, Fielding hobbled over to the guest chair and sat down heavily. "Go ahead," he said, waving at the chair behind the desk. "It's yours. I was just resting my aching bones."

Julie laid her briefcase on the desk and straightened some papers. "Good to see you, Fred," she said, hoping she sounded unfazed and wondering if she were still in charge of the special.

"I convinced the docs to let me out from time to time," he said. "I was visiting the refrigerator much too often." He patted his bulging paunch.

"So how are you feeling, Fred? How badly were you wounded?"

"Hell, I got my ass half shot off by machine gun fire. How do you *think* I feel?"

Julie stifled a smile. "You got shot in the rear end, Fred?"

"You find that funny?"

"It's just surprising. I've never known you to run from a story."

Fred didn't laugh. "You know," he finally said, "if I were okay, *I'd* be sitting behind that desk, in charge of the project. Carl Fisher and I have been friends for years."

"I know that."

"So the only reason you're there is that the grand master is sidelined for awhile."

The phrase annoyed her, but when you'd produced as many award-winning hours of television as he had over his thirty-five years in the business, you probably had a right to refer to yourself as "the grand master."

"Now *you've* got the hot potato, Julie," Fred went on. He grinned his big Irish grin at her. "Think you can handle it?"

Julie smiled. She'd worked for Fielding on several shows and she'd never been entirely comfortable with him. Even though he had lived in New York for better than half his life, he was still a Georgian at heart—condescending to women and over-familiar in that gruff, loveable, sexist "Southern Gentleman" way. Still, it wouldn't do to provoke him. "I think I can do the job, Fred—with a little help and advice from you. You're the best."

Fred beamed and practically patted her on her head. "I'll do what I can, young lady," he said paternally. "Of course, I won't be able to come in every day and when I do, I won't be able to stay long."

"Well, any time you can share with us…"

Fielding nodded. He was hurting. "Gotta go now. We'll talk later." He rose unsteadily and somehow got his crutches under his arms. Julie rushed to his aid, draping his trench coat over his shoulders, cape-like. She walked him to the elevators. When the door opened, Paige Hanson emerged and Fred limped in.

"He's back?" Paige asked, wide-eyed, after the door had closed.

"Hi, Paige," Julie said. "No, Fred's not back, not really. He'll stop in from time to time, stick his nose where it doesn't belong, but I think I've got him under control. You know, he can't sit down for more than five minutes."

Paige giggled her cute little girl giggle. "So I heard." She handed Julie a file folder. "I got what you wanted on Barton Mulvaney," she said.

"Great," Julie said, opening the file. "Now, could you set up a production meeting in the conference room for 9:30?"

"Right, boss."

At about 9:25, the production team including several key newsroom managers gathered in UBS's cramped and somewhat shabby conference room. Julie took the chair at the head of the table.

"You all know what this is about," she began, feeling a bit nervous. "But I thought I'd tell you anyhow. We're going to make a ninety-minute documentary, a prime-time *news* special."

"Foreign or domestic?" asked Marty Cohen, the thin, fast-talking, and usually sarcastic writer, trying to figure out how big a slice of pie he was getting.

"Well, both," Julie said. "It's about foreign ownership in America's biggest businesses."

"Hmm," Marty said dubious. "I assume we've picked a date when everyone else will be into reruns."

Everyone chuckled.

"I know it doesn't sound all that exciting," Julie admitted. "But there's an angle to the show that's pretty damn sensational, even scary."

Now she had everyone's attention.

"What I'm going to tell you now must be between us and only us. No sharing with spouses, significant others—even other UBS people. Right now, the only people who know are Mr. Fisher, Miles, Hank, Fred, and myself."

She glanced around the table, making eye contact with everyone in the room. One by one, they offered their promise. Then, for the next few minutes, she briefed the staff about what the Saudis seemed to be planning. When she finished, the room was silent. "Well?" she asked.

"I'm having a little trouble getting my mind around this," said Todd Simcox, a former media professor at UT-Austin now writing feature pieces for the UBS magazine shows. At UT, they'd called him "the hippie," but here he was "Tex" and he played the part a little too well, never appearing without his Stetson and cowboy boots.

"Okay, well, let me tell you a little more," Julie said. She described how Randy Dandy had practically begged Fisher to do the special. She also told them about the blue folder and what had happened at ABC.

Carol Twitzel, a school-teacherish woman in her mid-fifties, was the first to speak. "My God," she said, "I thought you were being pretty melodramatic about the secrecy. Now I understand."

"I'm sorry," Marty said, sounding genuinely contrite. "I just wasn't entirely sure you were serious."

"The whole thing is serious," Julie said. "It's also the most important story we will ever put on the air. Carleton Fisher is going to use this documentary to kick off what he's calling 'the new UBS.' He wants to make us a serious network again."

"That was even before *my* time," Cal said.

Julie laughed. "Before my time, too, but that doesn't matter. What matters is that we're doing something that is genuinely important to both America and to the network."

"So how are we going to do this?" Cal asked. "Stock footage, interviews, man-on-the-street stuff?"

"Yes, some of that," Julie said, opening her pad. " Now let's get down to some specific assignments."

She turned to Bill Huffman, UBS's affiliate manager, who had yet to say a word. "Bill, I'm going to need at least ten live remotes—fifteen would be better. Can you work up a list of affiliates who have competent interview/camera teams?"

"It won't be a very long list," Bill said glumly. But then, Bill was a glum sort of man. He hadn't smiled since his wife left him, and no one ever heard him laugh. But he'd never failed to deliver what he promised.

"Wait a minute," said Cal Flannery, pulling himself erect in his chair. "Did I hear you say ten to fifteen *live* satellite feeds? What are we using them for?"

"Focus groups and man-on-the street interviews."

"But fifteen feeds, Julie, we haven't run that many since the last presidential election. Do you know how much money it's going to take just to get the control room back up to speed?"

Lisa Green shook her head. "I can't approve that," she said with a nasty smile. "That's not in the news budget."

"Would $100,000 be enough to upgrade the control room and the rooftop microwave antenna array?"

That stopped Cal cold. "You can get Miles to sign off on that?"

"I can and I will," said Julie.

Lisa Green sat up sharply, opened her mouth, desperate to object, then sagged back into her chair, mute.

Julie turned to Carol Twitzel. "Now, Carol. We're going need the best montage you've ever done—five minutes, with music."

"About?"

"Well, let's call it 'America the Beautiful.' I want a collage of images, historical and contemporary, overlaid with music of Americans living their idea of the American dream."

Carol nodded, making notes. "I'll get on it."

"Now, Tex," Julie said, "I need a two-part feature from you. Stock footage, voice over, maybe twenty minutes total."

"Portrait of the Royal Family?" Tex guessed.

"That's the first part. Second part is a quick history of U.S.-Saudi relations since World War II. Emphasize the U.S. oil connections, the financial ties to Halliburton and Bechtel, and the close friendships with U.S. political figures."

"What about me?" Marty asked. "Got any work for me?"

"Of course," Julie said, consulting her notes. "I need three pieces from you: an intro—a couple of minutes, maybe—and a five to seven minute piece that traces Saudi investments in U.S. firms, uncovering the shell companies they're using to disguise their purchases."

"Hold on a minute," Marty said. "How do I find out about these Saudi investments if they're secret?"

"See me after the meeting, Marty," Julie said. "I have a folder full of the information you'll need. I also need you to write five minutes of closing commentary for Ayers to read."

Marty nodded. "I suppose you want something 'fair and balanced,' right?"

"Not this time," Julie told him. "This time we're going to tell the simple truth. Think of George Washington warning the colonies about 'foreign entanglements'."

"You can count on me, Julie," Marty said.

Cal Flannery looked up from his notes. "Here's something I don't understand, Julie. You've only assigned about fifty-odd minutes and you're running out of writers and producers. What are we going to put on the air during the other forty or so minutes?"

"Ah, yes," Julie said. "What I'm planning in the final segment is an interview with a Wall Street banker who thinks what the Saudis are doing is good for America, and Tom Gallagher asking the toughest questions imaginable, exposing the truth."

"You're going to find a Wall Street guy willing to submit to that?" Carol asked.

"Well, I have someone in mind, but I'm not sure we can get him. So I'm going to need some quality backups."

"So, I assume we'll tape Tom and this guy in the studio for a few hours," Cal said, "then edit it."

"No," Julie said. "We're going to go live."

There was a moment of silence. They all looked at one another.

"Did you just say 'live'?" Tex asked mildly.

"Live," Julie repeated. "That's the only way I can be sure no one will be able to interfere."

"Talk about reality TV," Carol added.

Julie turned to Paige. "Paige, start making me appointments to meet some of the other investment bankers and financiers who've worked on the Saudi deals. Tell 'em we're doing a major special on foreign investment—nothing more. Tell 'em we expect to get as many viewers as the Super Bowl."

Paige was wide-eyed. "We do?"

What a sweet, innocent kid, Julie thought. "No, Paige. I was exaggerating. There will be wild celebrations upstairs—and big pay raises down here—if we get *half* that many."

"Did I hear you say pay raises?"

During the next few days, production research went into high gear. Marty surrounded himself with reams of material on the Saudi Royal Family, checking out the deals described in the blue folder.

Meanwhile, Julie tried to get an appointment with Barton Mulvaney. She phoned. He was in a meeting. He was golfing at Shinnecock country club, he was "in Paris for a few days," he was conferring with an important client, he was car racing in Germany, he was "trekking through the Andes," he was anywhere but in his office. She managed to get his e-mail address, but he or whoever answered his e-mail didn't respond to her.

So, in between her attempts to make contact with Mulvaney, Julie and Paige talked to dozens of Wall Street raiders and bankers whose names were on the blue folder lists, found some who were willing to talk—but not very articulate, and some who were very articulate, but not willing to talk.

"We're running out of candidates," Paige said.

"Why don't you run down who's left on Marty's list for me?"

Paige opened her notepad. "Okay. Henry Metcalfe won't be available in January. He'll be vacationing in Bali."

"Bali."

"And Tony Roche, over at Morgan Stanley, has fifteen minutes free a week from next Tuesday. In the morning. He's willing to see you then in his Beverly Hills office. We could shop afterward," she added brightly.

"I don't think so," Julie said dryly. "Okay, what about this Alex the terrible?"

"Alex Volkov? He's scheduled for some kind of elective surgery the week of the special. His assistant wouldn't be specific."

"Alright, then how about Stanley Frank?"

"Barely speaks English."

"Tomkins?"

"He has a great face…for radio," she joked.

"Okay, who else is on the list?"

"Let's see. Steinmetz, Collingwood, Perelstein, Conway, Meklis, Swartzman, Edgerton, van Krule, Saaritan, Forstman, De Boef, Hoffman, and Wolfinger have all refused. That leaves Smythe, Trager, Bromberg, Mockler, and Mulvaney…."

At that moment, Fred Fielding appeared at Julie's office door, leaning heavily on his crutches and panting. "Did you say 'Mulvaney'?" he asked Paige, who seemed flustered by his presence.

"Oh, hi, Fred," Julie said smoothly. "Yes, Barton Mulvaney. We were talking about interview subjects for the show. He's a candidate, but I can't get past his gatekeepers."

"He'll talk to *me*," Fred assured her. "Known him for years. His VIP box at the Meadowlands is right next to mine. He's the guy who just won the Intercoastal battle, you know."

"Could you set up an appointment for me, Fred?"

"Consider it done."

Two days later, Julie paid a visit to the Blackwell Group, a Wall Street private equity firm at 120 Broadway. She told the disinterested receptionist her name and that she had an appointment with Barton Mulvaney. The receptionist told her someone would be with her shortly.

Julie sat down and thought about the Mulvaney interview. She had two goals, she told herself. The first was to see if the man had a compelling personality, a presence. After a few minutes sparring with him, that would be pretty obvious, she thought.

The second goal was much trickier. Would he competently defend the Saudis' acquisitions? What made this thorny, she knew, was that she couldn't mention the Saudi Royal Family. If she did, it probably wouldn't be more than a few minutes before he knew the surprise UBS was planning. Damn, she thought. What have I gotten myself into?

A few moments later, a tall, impossibly good-looking, brush-cut blond man in his mid-twenties came out to greet her.

"Good morning, Miss Chambers," he said, the odd curl of his lips spoiling his otherwise perfect face. "I'm Vaughn Stewart, Mr. Mulvaney's associate. Please come with me."

The young man led her to a large, walnut-paneled corner office that had a spectacular view of the West Village. An expensive Celestron telescope was perched on one window sill. The other displayed a meticulously detailed model of an Airbus A380 painted in Intercoastal colors.

A man who could have been Vaughn Stewart's older brother—a John Ayers TV anchorman type—came out from behind a glass-top desk the size of a ping pong table. He had a strong chin, a straight nose, and his skin glowed with health.

"Hello," he said, smiling warmly, shaking her hand, "I'm Barton Mulvaney. You must be the woman who's been trying so hard to get hold of me."

"Julie Chambers," said Julie, extending a hand and glancing into eyes that were coldest android blue. "Glad to meet you, Mr. Mulvaney."

He shook her hand. "Bart, please. And may I call you Julie?" He nodded to his associate, who discreetly left the room.

"Of course, Bart," Julie said, catching a glimpse of the glistening wristband of an absurdly expensive watch, peeking out from the monogrammed cuff of his Brioni shirt.

"Sorry I had to keep you waiting."

"Quite all right," Julie said. "It gave me a chance to look at some of the artwork in the lobby. That's quite a collection."

"Thank you. I'm especially proud of the Dali. I acquired that one for the firm myself, at auction. Had to outbid the Guggenheim in Bilbao to get it."

"It's very striking," Julie said.

"Well, even investment bankers have good taste," Bart said with a sly grin, "at least some of them." His eyes swept over her slowly.

"They do like to acquire nice things," Julie observed, ignoring the inspection. "Like Fortune 500 companies."

"Ah, yes," said Bart, gesturing at a chair across from him. "And that brings us to the reason for your visit, doesn't it. I understand UBS is doing a special on foreign investment."

"That's right. And we want to put people on-camera who can help us understand what it means."

Bart's eyebrows rose slightly. "But you're doing an exposé, right? You're going to make it look like foreign investment is destroying the country."

Julie was taken aback. "What gave you that idea?"

"Well," Bart said, smiling, "the media isn't exactly known for its even-handed treatment of Wall Street and big business. Besides, you're from UBS...right? You have that hatchet man—what's his name—Tom Gallagher."

For a moment, Julie wondered who was interviewing whom. "You're right, of course," she said, "television tends to sensationalize and over-simplify. And UBS is guiltier than most."

"I suppose you're going to tell me that Carleton Fisher is on the scene now and he's going to make all the difference," Bart said.

"Well, his reputation for integrity is well-earned," Julie said, "but, no, that's not what I'm going to tell you. What I'm going to tell you is that *I* am producing this television special. I want to present all sides of the issue. I'm committed to it. I'm staking my career on it."

Mulvaney nodded thoughtfully. "Ok," he said at last, "I believe you."

Julie was enjoying the fencing. "Now it's my turn, Bart. I'm trying to find someone who can convince me foreign investment in America is a good thing."

"And you think I might be your man?" Bart asked. "Why is that?"

"Well, I know that you managed your first European transaction in 1992 when you advised the Spanish government on its hostile takeover of Telefonica, the national phone company. You were only twenty-three."

Bart grinned.

"You also worked on Net Global's spinoff of its wireless unit the same year, as well as its $110 billion dollar purchase of Royocal, the world's second-largest transaction ...next to Intercoastal of course."

"Intercoastal?" Bart asked innocently. "What does that have to do with foreign investment? The buyers are from Kansas City."

"And the Kansas City consortium is owned..." Julie paused, meeting Bart's eyes directly, "... by a bank in Buenos Aires."

Bart was a little taken aback. "What makes you think *that*?"

"I have my sources," Julie said.

"Hmmm," Bart said, "beauty, brains, and guts. Well, well, well."

Here comes the blush again, damn it, Julie thought. "Also, highly professional," she reminded him briskly. "Now tell me what's good about Intercoastal being bought by a South American bank."

Bart grinned, and there was a certain charm in his grin. "If you'll have dinner with me..."

Julie returned the grin. "Do you always hit on women five minutes after you've met them?"

"Usually I don't wait that long. But in your case, I made an exception."

"How about making another exception and answering my question?"

Mulvaney sighed deeply and leaned back in his chair. "Okay, if you insist. Here's the essence of it: Foreign investment frees American capital. It allows the U.S. to make its own foreign investments. The result is that countries have a vested interest in each other's success and stability. Nothing could be healthier for a global economy."

Julie decided to risk one more baby step along the razor's edge. "So why do some critics think foreign investment, especially foreign acquisitions of American companies, is bad for the U.S.?"

"They're not looking at the big picture." Mulvaney leaned forward and made deliberate eye contact.

"You know when Fred said I'd be talking to a television producer from UBS, I never imagined..."

"What did you imagine?" Julie asked.

"Someone who looks like Fred," laughed Bart.

He talks well, has an impressive narrative Julie thought to herself. He's convincing. He's certainly presentable, almost *too*-good-looking. And he's a lot too slick and sure of himself. But not without appeal. "And you can give our viewers the big picture?" she asked, getting back on subject.

"Sweetie, looking at the big picture is what I do for a living."

"Are you willing to say all this on-camera?"

Bart grinned. "And let Tom Gallagher carve me up like Chris Matthews? I'm not *that* crazy."

"You think you can't handle Gallagher?" Julie asked, returning the smile, challenging him.

"Gallagher's not the problem," Bart said. "The problem is you guys in the control room, feeding him questions intended to torpedo me.

"We're not going to..."

Bart laughed. "Listen, I play mind games with billionaires, Julie. I'm not going to do something stupid just because a pretty girl calls me a chicken."

"You're pretty tough, aren't you? There's no way you'll do it?"

Bart leaned back in his chair and thought a moment, acting like the man in the driver's seat, which is just what he was. "I might," he said at last.

"Don't keep me in suspense."

"Here it is: forget about putting me up against Gallagher. He's just a face man. But I *might* be willing to discuss the subject with another investment banker."

"Whose views parallel yours?"

"On the contrary. Find someone who disagrees with me, if you can. I'll appear with anyone who knows what he's talking about, as long as it's someone in the business."

"Any suggestions?"

"Are you asking me to do your job for you?"

"Ok, just promise me this: if I find another investment banker willing to take you on, you'll agree to be on the show."

Bart grinned. "I could probably be persuaded."

"Good," she said. "That's what I was hoping to hear."

Mulvaney stood and moved toward her. Julie glanced at her watch. "Oops," she said, "I have an appointment uptown."

"You never said if you'll have dinner with me." He'd put his hand on hers and she found it was surprisingly warm.

"Maybe another time," she said, smiling and withdrawing her hand. "I'll be in touch."

"In touch," Bart said, a suggestive note in his voice. "Now I like the sound of that."

CHAPTER FIVE

Mario sat at the table, waiting, toying with the silverware, readjusting the heavy linen napkin on his lap and getting annoyed. Frank was late, which was like saying the sun rises at dawn. Damn. Well, they'd made an agreement and he was going to follow through. Mario caught the eye of the elegantly dressed waiter, who hurried over to him.

"Maurice, I'll have a crabmeat cocktail and a Delmonico, medium rare. And Frank will have Chicken á la King."

"The chicken," Maurice said, his left eyebrow lifting almost imperceptibly.

"Well, he's late, Maurice. And it will be good for him."

"Yes, sir." Maurice said, suppressing a smile. He turned and briskly headed for the kitchen.

Mario leaned back in his seat and gazed at the room. He liked Delmonico's and its wood-paneled walls and etched-glass windows. He and Frank had made a wise choice for their weekly lunch.

Of course, he couldn't be angry at Frank. Not really. Hell, not ever. There'd never been a better, more protective older brother. Whenever Mario headed for trouble, he reminded himself, Frank had always popped up, nudged him just far enough in the right direction, then backed off and made Mario think he'd saved himself. It was masterful.

Maurice reappeared with a bottle of merlot and poured Mario a taste.

At that moment, Frank showed up, chubby, breathless, and sweating. Frank was almost a comic figure—a stout man in his late forties, with small, perky ears, like a Jack Russell terrier and thick, horn-rimmed glasses. But he had enough wit and charm to make him a union mouthpiece and one of the Democratic party's chief political fundraisers.

He sat down heavily across from his brother. "Did I make it?" he said, panting.

"Nope."

"Shit. What did you order for me?"

"Chicken á la King."

"Fucking chicken! Not a sirloin or a filet? Not even a porterhouse? Chicken?"

"I ordered it because it'll be good for you." Mario patted his flat stomach. "And maybe it will convince you to be on time next week."

Frank sighed. "Bring it on, I deserve it." He looked around. "Nice place."

Maurice uncorked the wine again and Frank took a taste. "Lovely," he said.

"So, Frank," Mario said, not letting up, "what's your excuse this time? Traffic on the Manhattan Bridge?"

"The Teamster meeting ran long."

Mario nodded understandingly.

"By the way, Mario, I read about Intercoastal. That's a bummer."

"Yeah. I still don't know how it happened. Somehow, Barton Mulvaney got hold of a big block of proxies we were sure we controlled."

"There'll be other deals, Mario. And you'll win 'em."

"I know. But this one really hurt. I let a lot of people down. But enough about me. How's it going with you? How's Millie and the girls?"

"Millie is still a pain, but she's *my* pain. The girls are doing good. How are the boys? Any word from Harvard?"

"Still waitlisted."

"Tell Boomer give it some time. It's still early," said Frank. "So, what about you? How's things with Phyllis?"

"Couldn't be better, Frank. We're living miles apart in a parallel universe inside a 10,000 square foot home."

"So nothing has changed, I see. How's that golf game? Still killing worms?"

"I'm not an old hacker yet," Mario answered.

"Well you just turned forty-five," Frank reminded him.

"I'm five years younger than you, Frank. Always *will* be."

"But you're no kid anymore." Frank was serious now. "Look at you. Hair thinning, touch of grey..."

"It's premature, like your ejaculations."

Frank sighed and took another sip of wine. "So what's it like on the home front? Any chance of a truce between you and Phyllis?"

Mario snorted. "When the Arabs and the Israelis kiss and make up, we'll be right behind them."

"I wish there was some way I could help."

"You can help by getting me a divorce."

"You're thinking about your neighbor's divorce. Gave you ideas."

"If Rick and Brenda can do it without killing each other, why not Phyllis and me?"

"Because it's not a level playing field, Mario. Especially in New York. Child support is now a percentage of income. Attorneys used to be able to negotiate that. You'll also be responsible for the entire mortgage. And that's not all."

Mario almost gagged on his wine. "There's more?"

"New York State has done away with mandatory joint custody."

"God...!" He lowered his voice. "Goddammit Frank, I gotta be able to see my kids."

"Well, you'll still get standard visitation."

Mario groaned.

"You mean I get to see Kyle every other weekend, while Phyllis spends every other *day* telling him what a lame bastard I am. Fuck. What else?"

"Well, you'll also have to pay enough alimony to keep her living in the style to which she's become accustomed."

"But she never worked a day in her life."

"Doesn't matter," said Frank. "Did you provide for her?"

"Whoever came up with that law should be hung by his nuts."

"It's New York State, Mario. I told you to marry that crazy Albanian bitch in Jersey or Connecticut. But nooooo...you had to have the big Corleone wedding out in fuckin' Long Beach with that Luca Brasi bridal party, and her crazy brothers holding the fake tommy guns...*real* class."

"That was *her* idea."

"What's with the berry juice? I need a *real* drink. Waiter, scotch."

"So I'm more or less screwed is what you're telling me, Frank."

"Listen, what do you care about money? You carry your talents and abilities with you. You'll never be scratching for dough so long as your brain still works."

Maurice brought the food and they both concentrated on eating for awhile.

"Well, things may be bad with Phyllis," Frank said, "but you still got something on the side, right?"

"Frank, you know I've never had any problem getting laid. The problem is finding a place to do it."

"I've never understood what you and the Zoo Crew have against hotel rooms."

Mario shook his head. "Because I don't want every concierge and bellhop in Manhattan greeting me by name. That kind of reputation I don't need. I'm *already* being sodomized in the papers."

"Okay...so, how about an apartment...you know, like that movie with Jack Lemmon and Shirley...Shirley... What was it called?" Frank asked.

"The Apartment."

"Yeah, that's it. You could do that."

"Maybe," Mario said with lukewarm enthusiasm. "It's an idea."

"Just no divorce, okay? Find a way to live your life despite Phyllis. Once Boomer graduates college, we'll talk again."

Mario considered his brother's advice. "Yeah, I'll try. Besides, I have a more immediate challenge."

"What's that?"

"The Zoo Crew is playing Mulvaney's bunch at Chelsea Pier tonight."

Frank laughed. "Another nasty shootout between the Hatfields and McCoys?"

"Fuckin' A," Mario assured him.

Maurice removed the dishes. "Dessert, gentlemen?"

"Give me a small dish of chocolate ice cream," Mario said. "Nothing for him."

"Now wait just a damn minute…" Frank protested.

The game was set for 7:30 p.m., but the Zoo Crew steamed onto the Chelsea Pier's hardwood court just before seven and found Mulvaney's team already on the floor, running plays. There were six of them: Mulvaney, Vaughn Stewart, plus three others who looked like they'd won the genetic lottery, barely six months out of the Ivy League and still wearing their Delta Kappa Epsilon T-shirts, plus a towering black kid.

"Look, boys," said Mulvaney, holding the ball. "Our opponents have arrived: the uncouth, the unfit, and the unwashed, direct from their most recent catastrophe, the loss of Intercoastal."

"Your mother takes it in the ass," Dennis announced loudly across the gym.

"Notice the wit, Vaughn," Mulvaney observed. "That's the kind of polish you get from two years at Buffalo State College."

"You think you're hot shit, Mulvaney," Neil said. "But you're not even warm."

Bart just smiled and tossed the ball to the tallest of the three Royals who zipped down the floor before passing to the lanky black teenager, who slam dunked it like LeBron James.

"Who's the ringer?" Glen asked, pointing.

"He's not a ringer," Vaughn explained condescendingly. "He's a bona fide Blackwell employee. Hey, Antwan," he smugged, "guy here wants to see your company ID card." Antwan loped over to the group.

"This I gotta see," Mario said. The black kid went to the bench and dug out his wallet from his gym bag. He pulled out a card and handed it to Mario, who studied it carefully. "This says you've been an employee since August fourteenth—that's three fucking days ago."

"New job," said Antwan, grinning.

Vinny challenged him. "Just what do you *do* at Blackwell?"

"He's a communications assistant," Vaughn cut in.

"You mean he's a fuckin' mail boy," Vinny said. He grabbed the card from Mario and flung it toward Vaughn.

"You never play fair, *do* you, Mulvaney?" Neil asked with disgust.

"I don't make the rules," said Bart. "I just obey them."

"Enough of the bullshit," said Mario. "How much?"

"Start the bidding," shrugged Bart.

"I've got a grand says we're going to win this game," Mario said.

"A grand?" Mulvaney said derisively. "Well, I understand…after losing Intercoastal, that's all you bums can afford."

Behind him, Vaughn Stewart tossed the ball to a blond-haired frat boy, who shot it from about half court. It clanked off the rim and rolled to the bleachers.

"Make it *five* grand," Mario countered.

"Me too," Neil said.

"Count me in," said Dennis.

"Same here," Glen put in.

They looked at Barry, who hadn't said a word since he'd walked into the gym. "You want me to bet $5,000 that we'll win?" he asked dubiously. Neil gave Barry a withering glance. "Okay, okay," Barry said. "Five grand. I'm in."

"What about Omega House?" Mario asked, pointing to the frat boys.

"They're in," Mulvaney answered for them. "What about your, um, Hispanic associate?" Mulvaney said. "If he's playing, he should be betting."

Vinny went pale. "Five grand? I..."

"I'll cover you," Mario told him. "And what about the African-American gentleman on *your* side?"

"I'll cover him," Mulvaney said. "Not that it will matter."

"One more thing, Bart," Mario said. "If we win, I want to know how you found out about the Prudential proxies."

Mulvaney hesitated, then grinned broadly. "Sure, Mario. If you win, I'll tell you *exactly* how we did it. But I'm sure the secret is as safe as your daughter's virginity."

"I don't have a daughter."

"I know."

A basketball bounced away from one of the Royals frat boys. Mario scooped it up and in one smooth and violent motion, heaved it at Bart. Mulvaney caught the ball just before it slammed into his nose, turned and fired it toward the basket, almost from mid-court. The ball rainbowed through the air, clanked off the rim, and rolled in.

Mulvaney turned back to the Zoo Crew, grinning. "Why don't you dumbos throw your jocks on, if you got anything to stick in there, and get out here on the court so we can give you the beating you deserve."

"You're going to get yours, fuckstick," Barry threatened, shaking a fist at Mulvaney.

Bart glanced at Barry's belly. "I'm really going to enjoy watching your friend waddle down the floor."

"Let's change and get back out here," Mario said. "We have money to win."

"Oh and Monelli, we'll have an ambulance parked...just in case that forty-five-year- old body goes into shock."

"You're an asshole, Mulvaney," Mario said.

"Fuck you, too," Bart laughingly replied.

The Zoo Crew found its way to the locker room and began changing.

"God," Neil said, "I want to kick their asses into the Hudson."

"So do I," Barry said morosely. "But they've beaten us two years in a row and they're younger and faster this year."

"And blacker," Dennis noted wryly.

"How long do you think the game will last?" Glen asked casually.

Dennis looked at him suspiciously. "Why? You in a hurry to go someplace?"

"Well, I got a date."

Barry made a wicked guess. "You got more dates than a calendar."

"On the night of the playoffs?" Mario said incredulous. "You can't bench your cock for just one night?"

Glen shrugged. "What can I tell you?" he said. "It wants to get in the game."

"*Rudy* at Notre Dame saw more playing time than that wet noodle," Dennis laughed.

"So who is it *this* time?" Asked Barry.

"Laura Oh."

"The egg roll over in Hedge Funds?" Neil said. "You're doing an inside job?"

"She's married," Barry reminded Glen. "She wears a ring or haven't you noticed."

"After a few drinks, *no* one's married," Glen said with a sly grin. "Speaking about marriage…sure hope you know what you're doing, kid?"

Vinny laughed while slipping on his gym shorts.

"Serious, kid, how well you know this conchita?"

"It's Inez," Vinny playfully reminded him. "And we've known each other since grade school."

"Take it from us, kid, you only know them *after* you marry them," Neil said. "Before that, they're one big fucking mystery. Remember that flick, a *Bronx Story?*"

"*Bronx Story?*"

"Yeah, you remember, the one where Bobby D drove a bus.

"A Bronx *Tale.*"

"That's what I said. Remember when that half a wise guy told the young kid to watch out if his date opens the car door for him."

"Yeah, I remember," laughed Barry. "I also remember how many girls began opening car doors for guys after that."

"And how many guys began watching to see if they did it," Glen added.

"Inez does that," Vinny said innocently.

"Listen to this guy, Inez does it."

The Zoo Crew laughed.

"Forget what they do in the movies, kid," Dennis said. "Just date 'em, don't marry 'em. That way, things don't pan out, you grab your hat and coat then take the L out of Lover and tell her its Over. That simple. But *you* sign that paper... next thing you know you're in court and your wife is sitting next to that Allred bitch."

Neil put his arm around Vinny. "There's only one way to know if a woman will change after marriage."

"Yeah, and what's that, Dr. Phil?" Vinny asked.

"When your hiding the salami with her the first time, just as she's getting into it... finish quick, then act like your all embarrassed. But don't apologize. *Then* watch how she reacts."

"And what does *that* tell you?"

"It's a crystal ball into the future."

"I hate to break it to you morons, but we have a tournament tonight. Remember?" Mario asked, obviously annoyed.

The married advice stopped, and, for the next few minutes, Mario laid out the game strategy.

Barry was sitting on a bench, bending over his belly, panting, struggling to lace his shoes. When he finished, he looked up to find everyone watching him. "What?" he asked.

"Do you know your role on the team?" Mario asked.

"My role?"

"Yeah, Barry," said Glen, "and we're not talking about the rolls of flab."

"Barry, you got seventy-five pounds on that black kid," Mario said. "Crash those boards. Knock him on his ass two or three times. He'll get the idea."

Barry nodded and swallowed hard.

"And, Neil," Mario continued, "when you set a pick on Mulvaney, I want him to feel like he's been hit by a tsunami. That way, Vinny can penetrate."

"Vinny, penetrate?" said Dennis. "You're sure he knows how to do that?"

The Zoo Crew laughed and headed upstairs, their adrenalin pumping. Mario fell back and caught Vinny at the bottom of the steps.

"Don't pay any attention to them. Marriage is what two people make of it. You and Inez all set for Sunday?"

"Yeah, we just picked up the rings. I really appreciate you standing up for me, Mario, being my best man and all."

"Glad to do it. Do you know everything that's expected of you?"

"Yeah, we covered it all during Pre-Cana."

"I'm talking about the game tonight..."

The basketball game against Mulvaney's team was almost as much a disaster as the Intercoastal deal. Mulvaney, along with his black ringer and fresh crop of Ivy League glory boys, left the Zoo Crew gasping for breath, feeling like fat old men, and $5,000 lighter in the wallet, each. It was a more than a twenty point blow out.

Afterward, the Zoo Crew retreated to the locker room, angry and miserable. They listlessly changed into their street clothes without bothering to shower—except for Glen—then, bitterly cursing under their breaths, wrote checks to Mulvaney. As always, Mario covered Vinny's losses, although he would have given Vinny his rightful share if they'd won.

"Who wants to be the mailman?" Mario asked. Everyone silently turned toward their lockers. No one wanted to humble himself before Bart and fork over the winnings—just one week after forking over Intercoastal.

To spare them the indignity, Vinny snatched the purse from Mario and headed back into the gym to deliver it to Mulvaney and his gang. When he returned, grim and crestfallen they piled into a cab and headed to an old Wall Street haunt where traders cheered their profits and drowned their losses. The mood was glum.

Harry's at Hanover Square was a circa 1875 Wall Street hangout only a short walk from the New York Stock Exchange set on the ground floor of a pre-Civil War brownstone. Here, bulls and bears congregated in gold ties and suspenders, drank German beer, and stoked up on reliable, but not exciting, Continental fare, and a good looking woman could have caused a stampede.

The Zoo Crew were sitting at a booth sucking on imported beer and still bitching about the loss when Mulvaney's team entered. "Bart just walked in with those flying monkeys," Neil said quietly, without expression.

Mulvaney and his frat boy bandits swaggered up to the bar like they were the Earp brothers and ordered a round. Then Vaughn spotted the Zoo Crew and nudged Bart. Both of them walked over.

"Well, well," said Bart, "if it isn't Jerry's kids. You guys didn't look so good tonight."

"We'll give you a better game next time out," said Neil.

"Next time you should try the Special Olympics."

"Very funny, Bart," Dennis said. "Come to gloat?"

"Not my style," Mulvaney replied. "Besides, it was just what I expected."

Mario slowly turned in Bart's direction and Mulvaney grinned. "No hard feelings about the game, right? And no hard feelings about Intercoastal either, okay?" He extended a hand.

"Wrap it around your dick," said Mario, gulping his beer.

Mulvaney shrugged, still smiling. "You know, Mario, it's not that I'm better than you are. All my guys are better than your guys—look at Talbott here. Princeton, first in his class. And Troy, same thing. Or Hunnicutt. Dartmouth. Valedictorian. And of course my protégé Vaughn here. Haavaad, you know. Handpicked him myself out of Wharton."

"Academic knowledge is no match for the knowledge acquired," Mario said.

"Since when?" laughingly replied Bart.

"The great stock market bubble blew up lots of companies, Bart, and polluted the Street with toxic assets, dreamed up by goober heads like these with their $650/hr. globetrotting tutors from the *Princeton Review*." Mario looked at Bart challengingly.

"So higher education is useless, is what you're saying," said Bart.

"No, that's *not* what I'm saying," Mario replied. "I'm saying that an MBA from one of your gladiator schools will be a useful cog in *any* corporate machine. But there's no point in pretending this kid of yours can actually *run* anything. it's just another way privileged assholes like yourself use pricey, overrated credentials as leverage against less affluent kids. PhDs, BAs, MBAs...it's all BS."

"Mario's right," Vinny agreed. "All them degrees are just fancy wallpaper."

"It's *those* degrees," Vaughn corrected smugly.

"Now me?" Mario continued, "I'll take a street savvy kid with nothing more than drive and a basic education—like Vinny here for example, and throw 'em against any one of these show horses in your gene pool."

"Let me get this straight," Bart said. "You want to put this mutt of yours against a magna cum laude?"

"Vinny will magna cum on his face."

"That's right," Neil said and gave Vinny the high five.

Bart looked at Vaughn and snickered. "He must be interested in losing more money."

"Look, Bart," said Neil, trying to cool things down, "you already *got* our money, so how 'bout you find your own booth and take these Ken dolls with you."

"Bidding starts at fifty grand," said Mario.

"That's chump change," Bart replied.

"Okay," Mario said, "what do you have in mind?"

"Show me your balls, paisan. A hundred grand split anyway you like." Mulvaney looked around at the Zoo Crew. "How about it boys, wanna piece?"

Neil looked at Dennis and Dennis looked at Barry and they all looked at panic-struck Vinny. No one could manage anything but a weak nod.

"Just what I thought," Bart said with a smirk. He started back toward the bar, his posse following.

"Make it a million dollars," Mario announced loudly.

The tavern suddenly went mute, like a vintage E.F. Hutton commercial.

Bart glanced nervously at Vaughn. The Zoo Crew stared at Mario, bug-eyed. Mario calmly took another sip of his beer. "Whose got balls now, Bart?"

Bart looked at the Zoo Crew. "You boys in?"

"This is strictly between you and me, Bart."

"Okay, Mario," said Bart, "if that's the way you want it." Bart turned to his posse. "Gimme something to write on?"

Mario handed Bart a paper napkin. "Here," he said, "use *this*."

Neil leaned across the table to Mario. "Are you fucking outta your mind?" he said. "That Ken doll of his has more degrees than a thermometer."

"He can shove each one up his ass," Mario said. "Vinny has instincts. And that's something you can't get at *Whore*-ton."

"Neil's right, you fucking lost it, man," Barry said.

"Maybe," Mario answered and turned to Dennis. "Denny, you write it down."

By now, a small group of traders from JP Morgan and Credit Suisse had abandoned the bar area to come over and watch.

Dennis slipped on a pair of bifocals, uncapped a black, felt-tipped pen, and nervously spread the napkin out in front of him. "Okay, what's the bet?"

Mario leaned forward with his beer. "How 'bout this? Vinny tops your guy in a major deal."

Mulvaney considered the suggestion. "What size deal?"

"Anything over fifty million in assets," answered Mario.

"No, make it a hundred," Neil cut in, exchanging an affirming nod with Mario.

"Okay, but he's gotta be lead banker, and it has to be listed on the New York," Bart insisted.

Mario thought a moment. "It's a bet," he said.

Dennis carefully recorded the agreement on the cocktail napkin while Mario and Bart watched, as well as both teams and the score of patrons now crowded around them. "Okay," he said. "Just needs your marks."

Both men signed their names and Dennis witnessed them.

"Wait a minute," said Neil, reaching for the ketchup bottle. He squeezed two small dollops on the napkin, while everyone looked at him as though he'd lost his mind. "Fingerprints," he said. "So no dishonest asshole can weasel out of it." He looked at Mulvaney.

Mario dipped his thumb into the ketchup and pressed it onto the napkin. He licked his finger and looked up expectantly at Bart.

"Typical low class Zoo Crew horseshit," Mulvaney said with a scowl. But he added his fingerprint in the appropriate place.

Dennis separated the plies and handed one to each man. Mulvaney daintily extended a thumb and forefinger, taking the napkin by a corner as though it might contaminate him, and dropped it into his Cognac-colored Pratesi briefcase. Mario tucked his in his wallet.

"Come on, boys," Bart said. "Enough slumming." He nodded once to Mario and headed back to the bar, splitting through the crowd that had gathered.

"Okay guys," Mario said. "I've had it. I'm heading home." He rose.

"Some night," Barry said, shaking his head in awe.

Mario grabbed his cigarettes, slid out of the booth, and walked out of Harry's. He was heading for the World Financial Center garage when Vinny caught up with him.

"Mario, you gotta call it off," he said, trying to keep pace.

"Call it off? Why? I can't. Besides, I don't want to."

"But why?" Vinny asked. "Why are you doing this?"

Mario stopped. "I'll tell you why. I've been listening to people like Bart all of my life, telling me I didn't have the education or the class or the pedigree, that guys like me have no place in their world. I'm sick of it and I don't want it to happen to you. Because the way I lost Intercoastal to Mulvaney yesterday, you'll be losing to Vaughn, tomorrow. And you got plenty of tomorrows, kid."

"But I don't know if I can beat 'em," Vinny said. His voice was full of doubt and fear.

"I know that, Vinny. But I also know that you *can*—and you will. You see, I know a lot about you that you don't know about yourself. All I have to do is look in the mirror to see it." He grinned, then turned and walked away, leaving Vinny standing in the middle of Wall Street.

The Lexington Avenue express squealed to an ear-piercing stop on the downtown side of the Bowling Green subway station, a few blocks from Wall Street, and disgorged streams of professionals, hurrying toward the exits, faces expressionless. It was 8 a.m. and the August heat hadn't yet risen to nearly suffocating heights.

One of the men in suits, a tall fellow with dark hair and deep-set eyes, pushed his way against the foot traffic, heading toward the uptown end of the platform, which was a dead end, except for a small rusty door. Unlike the rest of the subway riders, this man's face was anything but blank. It was serious, almost grim, as if he were on a mission of great importance.

And in his mind, he was. He was Elliot Case, chief enforcement officer of the Securities and Exchange Commission, and he was a man with very specific orders from his boss: to get proof that prominent people on Wall Street were conspiring with the Saudi Royal Family to transfer ownership of the main components of America's economic strength to a group of Arabian sheiks.

For Elliot Case, this was a mission based on disbelief, disbelief that the Saudis would attempt something so daring and treacherous, disbelief that any good American, banker, broker, or financier would actually betray his country, and finally the greatest disbelief of all, that the President of the United States would do nothing about it.

Elliot felt that only two people stood between the United States and catastrophe: himself and Randall McDaniel Hollinsworth. And the country wouldn't be safe until they exposed the plot and unmasked the plotters, foreign and American.

And so he'd flown from Washington himself to make sure the wiretap operation was going smoothly. He reached the rusty door, took a quick look around—no one was paying any mind—and knocked in a pre-arranged pattern.

The door opened and Case's beefy deputy, Chester Hinkley, ushered him in. This was one of the SEC's best-kept secrets, a wire tapping center that accessed the land lines and cell phones of every major player on Wall Street. A dozen men were working on the electronics, setting up a computerized audio capture operation.

"When do we go online, Chester?"

"Noon, maybe a little earlier."

"That's good," Case said. "Make sure we do backups of everything— and keep those hard drives under lock and key."

Hinkley pointed to what looked like a bank safe from 1935. "I'm the only one with the combination," he said.

CHAPTER SIX

The limo carrying Mario and the Zoo Crew pulled up to the front entrance of the biggest, gaudiest, most over-the-top hotel in Atlantic City or maybe anywhere except Las Vegas, that outrageous gold and white fantasy known as Trump Taj Mahal.

Mario generally regarded Donald Trump as an overrated, egomaniacal asshole, who spent most of his time trying to convince the world he was a brilliant, self-made money manipulator. But even if the man was all hype, his casino *wasn't*, and the Zoo Crew knew it. And it was the perfect place for a party in Vinny's honor or any other excuse to throw one.

The huge white carved stone elephant at the entrance, one of seven, bedecked in red and gold, the seventy minarets sprouting from the gambling hall, the towering white slab of the hotel itself—all of this was home court for the Zoo Crew, just a quick flight down to Atlantic City on Harrison Hart's private plane for a sinful night of booze, blasphemy, and debauchery.

"Pretty fantastic building," Vinny said, as the Zoo Crew poured out of the limo, the doors held open by turbaned mahouts.

"Nothing compared to what's inside," Mario said, leading the way to a lobby festooned with German crystal chandeliers, and a marble registration counter more than one hundred feet long, served by a bevy of gorgeous young women dressed like belly dancers.

At the VIP check-in, they were met by "Princess" Sarita, a strikingly beautiful Hindu girl whose job it was to pamper the hotel's heavy hitters. She greeted each member of the Zoo Crew by name and genuflected prettily when Mario introduced her to Vinny.

"Have any of my friends arrived?" Mario asked.

"About a dozen," Princess Sarita said. "They're already up in the suite with their women." The suite she referred to was Mario's favorite, the 4,500-square-foot Alexander the Great suite, the grandest accommodation in the hotel.

"With their women?" Vinny asked. "You mean their wives?"

"No, Vincent," Mario said in a fatherly way. "Not their wives. Their wives are at home, like ours."

"*Wives?* You mean they're married?"

"No Vinny, the guys are single, their *wives* are married."

"Speaking of women," Glen said, "where are *ours*?"

The Princess escorted the Zoo Crew to the private Alexander suite elevator, and a tunic-clad elevator man whisked them skyward. In a moment, the door opened on a large marble vestibule. The bronze double doors to the palatial suite were wide open, and the rock music was so loud it was impossible to hear yourself talk.

Inside, the party had already started and when the Zoo Crew entered they were greeted by loud raucus cheers like it was an event at the old Palladium. Zoo Crew friends from Goldman Sachs were there, as were colleagues from Brown Brothers, Spear Leads, and Toronto Dominion, the outfit that had financed many Zoo Crew deals. Every one of the men had a drink in one hand and an arm around one of those stunning, half-dressed blondes or redheads, who went by names like Crystal, Dawn, or Bambi.

Behind them, in one corner, were tables laden with shrimp, caviar, and pastries, two chefs carving roast beef and cooking *filet mignon* to order and a wet bar staffed by three toga-clad bartenders.

The suite itself was decorated for royalty: Billowing white-silk panels on the ceilings, snow-white carpeting throughout, burgundy-colored leather couches and chairs, sheet glass tables with wrought-iron bases painted in gold leaf, famous paintings—possibly reproductions—and flat-screen television sets covering the walls, playing porn, pro sports, or first-run movies, and a huge hot tub in one corner. Just off the main room was a lavish gambling den overflowing with slot machines and gaming tables, everything in play.

"My God," Dick Hamilton said with both awe and disgust. "*This* is the Alexander the Great Suite? It looks more like Caligula's Palace." It was also Hamilton's first time on a Zoo Crew junket, added at Vinny's suggestion.

Bill Bronson, Fallon Financial's golden-haired, wonder boy, famous for his perfect features and aristocratic bearing, rose from the hot tub, dripping and nearly naked, a cuban tucked in his kisser, and greeted the newcomers. "Well, if it isn't the Lions' pride—how the fuck are you, Mario? Why so late?"

"Don't worry about us," Barry said, heading for the food, "we'll catch up in no time."

"Yeah," Glen said, "if our dates ever get here."

"Heard what happened with Intercoastal," Bronson told Mario. "I'm sorry it worked out that way, although it's good for my morale to see that the great Zoo Crew fucks up occasionally."

All eyes were on Mario, waiting for the explosion. But it didn't come. "Glad we could make you feel better about yourself," Mario said. "But hell, that was yesterday. Today we eat, drink, and screw, in honor of Vinny here."

Bronson lifted a glass. "To Vinny," he said. "Enjoy your final hours of freedom, my friend." He walked back to the hot tub, where a small harem was waiting for him, and slipped in as gracefully as a porpoise.

"Well," said Barry, "I don't know about the rest of you, but my date has arrived. Her name is *filet mignon* and I hear her in the other room calling to me."

Dennis, as was his habit, had found his way to the gambling room, where a crowd had gathered around the roulette table, screaming encouragement to a good-looking blonde in a red silk dress that was doing a very poor job of keeping her warm. Dennis managed to squeeze in beside her.

At the bar, the line was three deep and the bartenders were going nuts trying to serve everyone. The food tables had been decimated and were in the midst of what must have been an emergency re-supply. Meanwhile, the bathroom pharmacy, stocked with Ecstasy, Quaaludes, Speed—as well as shrooms and pure Colombian cocaine had become a compulsory visit for every pleasure-worshipper in the suite and which was fuel to their many excesses.

Mario watched for awhile, then turned to Neil. "You know," he said, "if our dates don't show up soon, this is going to get ugly."

Finally, just before midnight, the elevator door opened again and out walked Madame Maiko and her Orient Express, clad in silk gowns of red, green, and yellow, and made up to perfection. They might have come directly from Tokyo, but they'd actually just choppered in from the mainland of sin, Manhattan.

Neil was the first to spot them. "Good, you're here Madame Maiko, and looking even lovelier than usual."

"Ah, Mr. Neil," said Madame Maiko. "I mean, Mr. Godzilla. How nice to see you once more."

"Godzilla," Neil said, "that's me. And I'm about to wreck Tokyo again."

Madame Maiko and her girls giggled naughtily and disappeared into the back bedroom, closing the door behind them.

"Well, well," Dennis said, pointing to the bedroom door. "Look at this." The door was decorated by a framed object—a plasma television set. He turned it on and the interior of the room appeared.

"I'll be damned," Mario said, and he glanced around the hallway.

The Zoo Crew watched the television set with unconcealed lust as the girls daintily went about their business—turning the place into an oriental tea room. "I never get to go first," Glen said, slurring his words. "So I think it's my turn this time."

"Remember why we're here," Mario said. "This is Vinny's bachelor party."

"You're right," Neil said. "The kid should go first."

Mario sent Barry to fetch Vinny, and he returned a few minutes later, practically dragging his charge. "The Yankee game was just getting good," Vinny said. "What do you want me for?"

"Tonight you are a man," Glen said, switching on the TV.

Vinny stared at the geishas gliding around the room, adjusting the lights and the cushions. "Oh no," he said. "Not me. I promised Inez."

"Goddam it, kid, it's not like you're married yet," Mario said, shaking his head.

"What can I tell you guys. I love the woman. Besides it wouldn't be Christian."

"Are you kidding?" said Glen. "It's *very* Christian. That's why God made it one of the commandments."

"Oh yeah, which one?" Vinny asked.

"Number eight. Thou shall not commit adultery…unless in the mood."

"What Glen is trying to say," Mario interrupted, "is you better take it while you still can."

"Besides," added Neil, "its not really cheating if you're wearing a condom." He winked.

"A Condom." Vinny repeated. "With a whore."

"Kid, every woman's a whore in the hands of the right man."

"What do you guys get out of this? You all got beautiful wives?"

"It doesn't matter how beautiful a woman is," Neil said. "Men get bored boning the same woman. It's encoded in our DNA. Screwing around actually *helps* our marriages."

Vinny sighed and shook his head. "I'll be inside watching the Yankees."

Neil turned to Mario. "We gotta toughen up this kid," he said.

"I have another idea," Mario said, grinning. He looked up at the screen, then switched it off. "Let's give Dick the privilege of going first."

"He'll never go for it," Neil said. "Not with the joker in the deck."

A sinister smile stretched on Mario's face. "Just you leave him to me," he said, and headed toward the party room. A few minutes later, he was back with a very reluctant Dick Hamilton.

"This isn't fair, Mario," Glen protested, on cue. "Why should little Dick go first?"

"I told you *not* to call me that," Hamilton said coldly.

"Aw, give him a chance, Glen," Neil said. "I'll bet he's never had a real Japanese massage before—have you, Dick?"

"Well, not Japanese, no."

"Good," said Mario. "It's settled. You go first, Dick."

"I don't know. I'm not sure I trust…"

"Look, you overblown gasbag," Neil said, "Mario is doing something nice for you. If you insult him by refusing his gift, it'll be the last time we invite you anywhere."

"Well, um, okay I guess. I mean if it's just a massage. Thanks."

Dick walked into the bedroom and closed the door behind him. Neil switched on the television set, to reveal the geishas approaching what was obviously a very nervous Dick Hamilton. The Zoo Crew crowded around the screen to get the best possible view, except Glen, who went to get an audience.

Inside the bedroom, and fully visible to anyone watching the television screen, Madame Maiko bowed low to Dick and handed him a large, steaming towel. "You wash now?" she asked, with a strong Japanese accent.

"Wash?"

"Yes, wash you, Papa-san. Wash you arr over."

The other geishas, all but one of them tiny, beautiful, and dainty, gracefully approached their visitor, their kimonos swishing as they moved.

"What are you going to do?" Hamilton asked nervously, looking for a way to retreat.

"Properly prepare you for your massage, Sir," said Madame Maiko.

At that moment, Glen returned with more than a dozen people in tow. Dennis shushed them and pointed. While the Zoo Crew and friends watched the television, transfixed, the geishas supple fingers began untying, unbuttoning, unfastening, and unzipping. Dick Hamilton's clothing came off with astonishing swiftness, exposing an almost hairless chest, a belly that bulged far more than his clothing had let on, and chalk-white legs that seemed inadequate for their task.

Hamilton protested weakly, but two lithe geishas quickly disposed of his clunky cordovan wingtips and argyle socks, which had been held up by black elastic garters. Last to go: his white boxers. And when the geishas slipped them off, they uncovered an ass that looked like twin cratered moon mounds. They also revealed Big Dick's little penis.

Madame Maiko took him by the hand and led him to the bed. He laid down awkwardly, on his back, trying futilely to cover himself. Madame Maiko then snapped her fingers at the troupe of geishas, who immediately began oiling his extremities and moving toward the center of his body.

In the hallway, everyone strained to see. Dick Hamilton was getting an erection.

Then the tallest of the geishas straddled Dick and began massaging his inner thighs, leading steadily upward. "Wait," Dick said fearfully, "don't you touch me there!"

But the geisha was not to be denied, moving toward Hamilton with mouth open wide. Before he could protest, the cherry red lips had engulfed his little erection and had started sucking voraciously. After a few minutes, he was panting and helpless.

The geisha sucked faster and faster, until Dick's body was rigid with need. Then, the geisha pulled away and Dick spurted again and again. When it was all over, he sat up, his face a mixture of shame and fear. "My God, my God," he said.

"Oh, it's ok, papa-san," the tall geisha said, winking. "We've got the same equipment, you know." The geisha's kimono slipped open, revealing that this dainty flower of the orient was actually a wiry Japanese guy, hung like a stallion.

"Oh my God!" Dick said. "Oh my God, oh my God!"

"I guess he's found the joker," Glen said, and started snorting with laughter. Neil put a hand over Glen's mouth, but it was too late. Glen was quickly joined by chuckling from Dennis, then outright chortling from Mario and finally Neil till there was no stopping it, no matter how much the others tried to shush them. The hilarity that erupted outside the back bedroom was a delightful combination of hooting, howling, and horse laughs.

Dick Hamilton bolted upright on the bed and searched furiously for the source of the merriment. Then he noticed the tiny camera pointing toward the bed and turned a distinct shade of pink.

He leaped out of bed with a roar, snatched up his clothes, trying desperately to cover himself, and threw open the door, coming face-to-face with scores of laughing eavesdroppers.

"You're all...you're all... you're all degenerates!!!" he sputtered. Then he ran out of the suite, carrying his clothing in his arms.

"Wait, Dick," somebody called out. "You forgot your fortune cookie."

Ten minutes later, four hotel security men, each built like an NFL offensive lineman and wearing a turban, arrived, escorting an almost hysterical and half-naked Dick Hamilton. "Ok, gentlemen," one of them said, "party's over. Get your personal belongings and say good night..."

The room cleared out faster than it had filled up, leaving Dick standing pathetically in the middle of the room, wearing one shoe and carrying the rest of his clothing.

Downstairs, two of the guys in turbans hustled the Zoo Crew directly into their waiting limo. Just as they were about to pull away, Dick bolted through the front doors, still half-naked, arms flailing, his face a mixture of terror, humiliation, and desperation. "Wait!" he yelled plaintively. "Wait for me!"

Neil looked at Mario and shrugged. Mario sighed deeply, then, with the greatest reluctance, opened the limo door. Dick practically fell into the vehicle and the limo headed back to the airport, practically rocking with laughter.

The plane ride back to New York was mercifully brief, considering how drunk the guys were. Even so, Barry threw up half the buffet the moment he stepped onto the tarmac at LaGuardia. Dick was in shock.

The Zoo Crew staggered into the Marine Air Terminal, which services private planes, and out onto the sidewalk. A limo driver of obviously middle-eastern descent called to them. "Are you the Monelli party?"

"That's right," Neil said. The Zoo Crew piled into the limousine waiting to take them back to lower Manhattan.

The long black car crossed the Fifty-Ninth Street bridge and cut over to the FDR drive for the trip downtown.

"I gotta go," Barry said. "I gotta go bad." He pounded on the taxi's inside partition. "Let me out! I gotta pee!"

"And I gotta take a shit!" Glen said, farting loudly and stinking up the car.

The driver pulled up abruptly, in front of Trinity Church and the NYSE. "Out," he said.

"What?" Mario said.

"Out! I don't drive pigs," the driver shot back. "And that's what you are, pigs!"

They tumbled out of the limo, helter skelter, Neil slamming the door behind them so hard that the moon roof popped open.

"Fuck you, Osama."

"Damn," Barry said. "I gotta go *now!* I mean *now!'*

"Follow me," Glen said, stumbling up the stone steps of Federal Hall, toward the statue of General Washington. "I see the perfect spot." Barry huffed and puffed his way up the steps and toward the pedestal where George Washington took the oath as president. He was followed by Neil and Dennis.

Neil unzipped his trousers and began peeing upward, with a strong, steamy stream that fell just short of Washington's boots.

Mario was disgusted. "Jesus, Neil. What kind of fuckin' idiot are you?"

But the rest of the Zoo Crew, even Mario, followed his example, seeing who can piss highest, Barry and Neil, managing to wet George's knickers, then his cape, till the Zoo Crew had the Commander-in-Chief of the Continental Army in the full throes of a golden shower. They were laughing and joining streams with great abandon when the squad car pulled up.

A few minutes later, the Zoo Crew was handcuffed and hauled into a paddy wagon, still carefree and jovial, except for Dick, who was protesting, "I hardly know these men and I wasn't even peeing," and Barry blubbering with that loveable exuberance, "Can't we all just get along?"

The paddy wagon pulled to a stop in front of Manhattan South's First precinct and the Zoo Crew tumbled out, still drunk and laughing, except for Barry, who was now crying.

"Maybe they'll ask us to provide urine samples," Glen said.

"Ok, gentlemen," said one of the uniformed cops who'd brought them in. "Move it!"

The Zoo Crew did as it was told. Inside the big, ugly brownstone building, they were taken to a back room and booked.

"Any of you patriots want to make his phone call now?" asked the desk cop.

"I would," said Mario.

"Okay, piss 'n boots, it's all yours." The cop pointed to a phone on a desk and Mario picked it up and called Frank, who was annoyed at being awakened, but, as usual, ready to help his brother in any way he could.

After saying goodbye, Mario handed the receiver to the desk cop. "You'll be getting a call soon from the DA," he said. "God, I always wanted to say that."

The cop snorted. "Okey dokey, Mr. Wall Street, but while we're waiting, we have a nice room where you and your little piss party can hang out. Not too crowded tonight." He exchanged a meaningful look with one of the other desk cops, who laughed.

"This way to your suite, gentlemen," said one of the uniformed cops. He led the way down a dank corridor with a concrete floor and cinderblock walls.

Mario was trying to remember the drunk tanks of his younger disco days in Red Hook—tempered steel bars, a floor smeared with vomit and feces, a room full of professional drunks and homeless derelicts—when he thought he heard something. "Is that music?"

"Damn," Glen said, "I hear it, too."

"Same here," Neil said. "What the hell?"

It was unmistakable now, soft, pleasant music, coming from the other end of the hallway, someone singing melodiously.

Barry, who knew his Broadway music was the first to identify it. "That's Judy Garland," he said. "I recognize the song—it's *The Man Who Got Away*."

The Zoo Crew and its uniformed escorts turned a final corner and came face to face with a green-painted chain-linked fence, closing off an area about twenty feet square.

Aside from a couple of drunks sleeping in one corner, the only occupants of the holding cell were half a dozen oddly-dressed people sitting in plastic deck chairs, in a semi-circle around Judy Garland, who was standing on a table, belting out the song and dancing suggestively. The Zoo Crew stared in disbelief. "Man," Glen said, "I didn't realize I was *this* drunk!"

"Judy Garland" was six foot two, with a bad case of five o'clock shadow. The music was coming from a boom box on the floor. Marilyn Monroe, despite the glorious blonde hair, was horse-faced and had weightlifter legs. The others were even blurrier caricatures of the real people they were impersonating, except for Liberace, who, in his pink spangled tux and wavy hairpiece, was a reasonable facsimile of the late pianist/entertainer.

"They've locked us in here with a bunch of weirdos," Neil said to Mario.

"Let's see now," Mario said. "We've been peeing on a statue of George Washington in public, and *they're* the weirdos?"

"What's that?" Barbara Streisand said delighted. "You peed on George Washington? I have absolutely longed to do that. Now I'll have to find some other statue. Is there a George Bush anywhere nearby?"

Neil shot Babs a wicked look, "You pee standing up?"

"I pee standing up *or* sitting down," Barbara said sweetly. "I'm bi-urinal."

"You mean these are all guys?" Vinny asked, confused.

Dennis sighed. "Ah, Vinny, Vinny, you have so much to learn."

"Yes," Mario said. "They're drag queens, except for Liberace here, and Richard Simmons."

"I'm a drag *king*," Liberace offered. "Or a duke or a count. Something royal, I'm sure of that."

"What are you, um, guys doing in the drunk tank?" Glen asked. "You don't look drunk. You look like freaks, but you don't look drunk."

"We were having a little *soiree* at my place," Liberace explained. "A little Broadway, a little Hollywood, a little singing, a little dancing, a little fooling around. We just got a little bit rowdy."

Mario was puzzled. "Rowdy?"

"We have some very straight neighbors, if you get my meaning."

"You queers had just better watch yourself," Dennis chimed in, still slurring his words a little.

"Well, here we both are, stuck for a few hours in a very unpleasant place. Perhaps we can do our part by providing entertainment and helping us both forget our surroundings."

Neil and Mario looked at each other as though maybe this guy wasn't a total lunatic.

"Hmm," Mario said. "I think we'd appreciate anything that would make the time pass more quickly. What do you say, boys?"

Ethel Merman looked at Marilyn Monroe and grinned. "Let's put on...a *show*!" And so they did, a boisterous, rollicking, madcap show, all singing, all dancing and lots of comedy, a fairly professional show, since most of the drag queens were longtime entertainers.

Liberace began by introducing the "Divine Miss M, Bette Midler," who sang and danced a bawdy, rip-roaring, burlesque version of *Copacabana* that brought the Zoo Crew to its feet, applauding and whistling.

Bette Midler took her bows, curtseying girlishly, exposing the full length of her red fish-net stockings and momentarily flashing frilly red silk panties. At this, Marilyn Monroe minced over to the Divine Miss M, batting her eyelashes, and slowly ran her hands over Miss M's bulging breasts. "Ooooh," she said in her little girl voice, "you're just so cute I might have to become a lesbian."

By this time, Neil was laughing so loud he'd fallen off his chair and was rolling on the floor. Dennis was practically in tears and Barry and Glen were guffawing so hard they were having trouble breathing. Dick had that "deer in the headlights" look, and Mario was applauding and whistling loudly. "More," he said, getting into the spirit of the show. "More! More!"

"Thank you, thank you, thank you," Liberace said graciously, emceeing again. "And now I want to introduce the famous blonde bombshell who saw more naked Kennedy rear ends than anyone else except Rose Kennedy herself, the one and only Marilyn Monroe."

Marilyn jumped up on the table like a gymnast, a male gymnast. She looked directly at Mario and smiled seductively. "Are you the president?" she asked, practically cooing.

Neil looked at Dennis and Dennis looked at Barry and Barry looked at Glen, who turned to Mario, who caught Vinny's eye. "Well, what do you think, Vinny? Am I the president."

"Sure are."

"Good," Marilyn said in a throaty stage whisper, "then this is for you." She turned on the boom box and very convincingly lip-synced the words to "Happy Birthday, Mr. President," while dancing suggestively and flirting with Mario outrageously. When the music came to an end, Marilyn hopped down off the table, pranced over to Mario and gave him a big, sloppy wet one, right on the lips before he had a chance to object.

Mario came up sputtering. "Hey, hey, you watch yourself—you're pushing it."

Marilyn looked back over her shoulder. "Remember, sweetheart, a kiss is just a kiss."

"If I was you Mario, I'd get tested," Glen said.

A brace of nearly identical, red-faced Irish cops, both with bellies that must have put them at or over the NYPD limit, came strolling around the corner and up to the drunk tank gate. "Ok, you miscreants," one said in a brogue he must have picked up from his grandfather, "the show's over. Bail's been posted."

The Zoo Crew were up and headed out before the gate stopped swinging open—except for Mario.

"Hey, man," Mario told Liberace, "that was a helluva show. Are you ladies gonna have any trouble getting out of here?"

"Naw, my lawyer should have us out within the hour."

Liberace pulled a business card out of a pocket and handed it to Mario through the bars.

"Roger Duvall," Mario read out loud, "architect and interior decorator."

Liberace bowed. "I am a master of many arts," he said with a wink.

Mario slipped the card into his wallet and hurried to catch up with the rest of the Zoo Crew.

At the front desk, they signed a few papers and exited the police station, feeling grubby and groggy. They mumbled exhausted goodbyes to Mario, then headed up to Penn Station via taxi.

"Don't forget the wedding, Best Man," Vinny reminded Mario.

"*I'll* be there. Just make sure *you* show up."

Mario considered walking back to the Financial Center to retrieve his car, but thought better of it. He was bone-weary and his head was pounding. He looked up Broadway, hoping to spot the "on-duty" light of an empty cab. No such luck. Well, okay, he thought, the jailbird is being forced to take the subway. He headed into Chinatown, to the Canal Street subway entrance, planning to take the RR train one stop to Chambers Street.

Mario walked down the subway stairs, only to find that the entrance was closed for the night. He shook the accordion steel gate a few times, hopelessly, then headed back up the steps.

Three young Asian men were blocking his exit to the street. Their eyes were cold and threatening. "You need a ride somewhere?" asked the tallest of the three, a stocky man in a yellow bandana and diamond nose stud.

Mario suddenly felt clear-headed. He knew he was in trouble. "Naw, my car is just a few blocks away. I can walk."

"Then why you in the subway, man?" asked another of the men, who wore a scraggly goatee.

"Well, I just…"

"Hey, man," said the third, grinning mischievously, "you got the time?"

Mario knew they he didn't give a damn about the time, but keeping up a pretense of civility was his only chance out of this. He checked his watch. "2:35," he said.

"Nice watch," said the thug, reaching out a hand. "What kind is it?"

Mario lunged for the top of the steps and managed to get to street level before the smallest of the trio tackled him and sent him heavily crashing into the pavement.

Then they were on him, all three of them, a furry of sharp jabs to his face and chest, aiming vicious kicks at his ribs, one thief ripping the Rolex from his wrist, another grabbing his wallet.

Still on the pavement, Mario swung back awkwardly, fist slamming into the chest of his smallest attacker, who reeled backward, momentarily off-balance, then surged forward, grinding a booted foot into Mario's jaw.

The attackers dragged him into nearby Cortlandt Alley, away from the mercury vapor lamps on Canal Street, melting into the shadows of a construction scaffold. Mario heard a click, then felt the tip of a switchblade against his throat.

Time seemed to slow down now. "Please," he begged, in a voice he didn't recognize, "please don't kill me."

Then another figure entered his field of view, an old man, a black man, wrapped in rags. Suddenly, the knife pressure eased. The man crouched into a defensive position, took two steps forward and knocked the knife-wielding thug off his feet with a single blow.

The biggest of the three Asians swung wildly at the man, who gracefully slipped the punch and struck his opponent with a short, fast, powerful uppercut that left the young man sprawled on the sidewalk, dazed.

The other two thugs rushed the black man almost simultaneously, but he clothes-lined one of them and took out the other one with a picture-perfect left hook. By this time, the big one was up again and wielding a knife. The man knocked the thug down with a shot to the jaw. As the thug fell, the man kicked the knife toward the far end of the alley.

Now Mario was up on his feet, unsteady and hurting. But his attackers were fleeing—he could still see them running down Canal Street toward Broadway. Mario brushed himself off as best he could and took inventory.

"Are you okay?" the man said, slightly out of breath, handing Mario his wallet. "Did they get anything else?"

"My watch," Mario said, staring at the old man. "But I'm all right. What about you?"

"Never laid a glove on me," the old man said.

"I've never seen anything like it. You took on all three of them. For a moment there, you reminded me of Sugar Ray."

The old man laughed. "Leonard or Robinson?"

"Never saw Robinson."

"I wasn't that good. No one was that good."

"So you're a fighter then?" Mario asked.

"Was. About a million years ago."

"What's your name?"

"They called me Chocolate, Kid Chocolate, back then."

Mario's head was mostly clear now. "And now..."

"And now I'm the champ of Cortlandt Alley," the old man said. He grinned, showing several missing teeth. "Name is Shaw, Gus Shaw. My friends call me Gus."

For the first time, Mario looked at him closely under the street lamp. He was an average-sized man, skin quite dark, almost handsome features blurred, evidently, by years of ring warfare, matted hair, covered in rags that were once decent clothing, feet bound and looking swollen, eyes surprisingly clear and intelligent, none of the stench that usually wafted up from an indigent.

"So why did you help me?"

"It was three to one against you. Just didn't seem like fair odds to me."

"It felt like there were six of them. I was watching my life unfold in my mind's eye when you suddenly appeared."

"Wasn't really so sudden, friend. Lotta times, people don't even see me and Sam."

"Sam?"

Gus nodded toward a battered shopping cart where sat an orange alley cat purring atop the debris. "They don't notice us nosing through the garbage, looking for cans. Don't want to."

Mario opened his wallet. "Look, man, I don't know what would have happened to me if you weren't here. The least I can do is..."

"Close your wallet, friend. I'd just drink it away."

Mario shrugged and slipped his wallet back into his pocket. "Hey, ya hungry? I could take you..."

"Where? Nothin's open now, not even Mickey D's. Anyhow, I doubt they'd let me in."

"Where do you go to eat then?"

"Soup kitchen. The Armory. I never go hungry for long."

Mario found himself looking into the man's eyes. He felt like he was being questioned, judged, assessed somehow. "Could I ask a personal question?"

"How did I get here?" Gus said with a smile. "You people always ask. Well, I had a good long run. Did a lot of things, good things. Did some bad things too. I'm just where I should be..."

Gus looked at Mario's suit. "But a man like you...you don't belong here, friend—"

"Call me, Mario, please."

"You don't belong here, Mario. You belong at home with your family, safe and warm."

"You're probably right about that," Mario admitted.

"No 'probably' about it," Gus said. He pointed at a lone cab, coming down Broadway. "I think that's for *you*."

They both watched as the cab crept up to the curb.

Mario thought a moment, then took a business card out of his wallet and gave it to the man. "If you ever need something—anything—that's my phone number."

The old man held the card out in the glare of the street lamp and examined the card as if it were the first one he'd ever seen. "Mario Monelli," he read.

Mario shook Gus's weather-beaten hand, surprised by the rough, cracked skin and the calluses. "Thanks again, Gus. I won't forget it."

Chapter Seven

Gus.

Mario couldn't get the man out of his mind.

At work, Monday was a disaster. Everyone was still wrecked after the wedding reception. And then there was still the cold, hard reality of what had happened with Intercoastal. The energy and vigor Vinny usually supplied was also missing. He and Inez were off on a week-long honeymoon to the Grand Caymans, Mario's wedding gift.

So Mario's thoughts often turned to the old boxer who'd saved his bacon on Canal Street. Who was he? Had he told Mario the truth about himself?

That Thursday night, when Harrison Hart was practically deserted, Mario sat down, fired up his computer and went to Google to find out what he could about Gus Shaw.

Within ten minutes, he'd come came across a mention from 1950s *Ring Magazine* and was able to call up an article about a Golden Gloves tournament a black teenager from Detroit named Gus Shaw aka "Kid Chocolate" had won. It even had a picture of Joe Louis shaking his hand.

Mario printed out the picture and studied it. Shaw was shorter than Louis, but well-muscled and glistening with sweat. He gazed at the face with a magnifying glass. He recognized the smile, a friendly, expansive grin. But the eyes in the picture were innocent and untroubled, the skin unwrinkled, the hair black and luxuriant. Still, it was Gus.

Mario stuffed the picture in his desk drawer and went back to the computer. He could find only one other Gus Shaw reference, an article from *The New York Times* dated June 12, 1967. The article described a fight, a main event at the Astoria's Sunnyside Garden, in which Gus Shaw—"Kid Chocolate"—a leading contender for the middleweight crown, knocked out Tommy Harper, another highly rated fighter, who died immediately after the fight.

Was *that* it? Was *that* responsible for what had happened to Gus, for the fact that this once proud and accomplished man now owned nothing more than a rusty shopping cart and lived at the edge of survival?

There was one clue in *The Times* article and Mario decided to follow up on it: Shaw, *The Times* said, had trained at the famous Stillman's Gym, the Mecca of the boxing world from the nineteen thirties to the sixties, now replaced by an apartment building.

After a couple of minutes on EastsideBoxing.com, Mario found a man who'd spent the better part of his life at Stillman's, a man who remembered the boxers, the trainers, the promoters, the fight reporters, the wise guys, a man who knew all the great stories, an ancient fighter and corner man named Eddie Garford.

It took almost no time to ferret out Garford's number and get him on the phone. Mario gave the man his name. "I'm trying to get some information about Stillman's gym, in the old days."

"Stillman's, you say," Garford said, voice crackling with age. "You say you have some questions about Stillman's. Well, I'm your man. Did ya ever go there? Ever see it?"

"No, I just…"

"Well, you shoulda seen it. Big old union hall, walls plastered with fight posters. Ceiling high enough for a trapeze act, always a smoky haze in the air."

"I didn't know," Mario said, trying to think how to advance the conversation.

"Yeah," Garford rambled on, "Lou Stillman never spent a nickel on it. But no one ever saw a fight there without paying for it—Jack Curley sitting at the door at the bottom of the steps, collecting a quarter from everyone, didn't matter who you were, Joe Louis, Marlon Brando, you paid or you didn't go up them stairs. Did ya know Lou Stillman?"

"No, I just…"

"He'd sit up there on that raised chair, up against the wall, and bark out insults over his loud speaker. And no one argued with him. They could all see the gat poking out of the tweed jacket he wore all the time."

"Sounds like a nasty guy, Eddie…"

"Old beat cop. Took over the gym after World War I, didn't know anything about the business, not when he started."

"Did you know any of the famous fighters?"

"My friend, I knew *all* of the fighters—Harry Greb, Benny Leonard, Sandy Saddler, Graziano, Willie Pep, now *there* was a fighter—not like *today's* cream puffs."

"They all trained at Stillman's?"

"Oh, yeah. You should have been there when Ray Robinson skipped rope or hit the speed bag. It was like watching Fred Astaire. And I knew the Hollywood types who hung around, Sinatra, Tony Bennett, Dean Martin. I was there when Paul Newman trained for *Somebody Up There Likes Me*. But I have a feeling you're not looking for a trip down memory lane, friend. You tracking somebody down?"

"In a way," Mario said, figuring the guy was sharper than he thought. "But I already know where the guy is. I'm just interested in his story."

"Who's the guy?" Garford asked.

"Shaw, Gus Shaw."

"Gus Shaw? Goddamn, I haven't heard that name in over forty years. Fought under the name of Kid Chocolate. Helluva fighter. Won the National Amateur Welterweight title when he was nineteen. Big right, fast left jab. Heart like LaMotta. After he bulked up a little, lot of people thought he was going to be Middleweight Champ. You say you know where he is?"

"Yeah. I guess you could say he's down and out now." Mario decided not to be too specific.

"Hey, that's too bad. But not surprising."

"What do you mean, Eddie? Why isn't it surprising?"

"You know about his last fight?"

"The one at Sunnyside Garden? Yeah, it was in the newspapers. His opponent died."

"It was worse than that. The fighter he killed? He was one of Gus's friends."

"What do you mean, friend?" Mario asked. "How close *were* they?"

"Gus and Tommy Harper were like blood brothers, well not really blood, but, you know. My memory ain't so good no more, but I seem to remember something about a gang. Yeah, that's it. They were both in gangs in Detroit in the fifties, during the race riots, and Harper saved Gus from getting his head opened up by a bunch of white punks with tire irons, and he got him into the fight game. Or maybe it was the other way around."

"You mean Gus saved his friend."

"Yes. No, wait, I'm wrong. *Gus* was the one who got saved. Tommy was older. He was *already* a fighter."

Mario was puzzled. "But then, why did the two of them fight each other?"

The old man laughed. "Why? Because they didn't have any choice, that's why. It was the only way either of them could earn a title shot. Harper was being groomed as a contender and they put Gus, the black guy, against him to take the fall. That was the way things worked back then. Goddamn dirty business."

"But Gus wouldn't do it?"

"I don't know the whole story. I wasn't in on it. But I saw the punch that ended Tommy's life—Tommy got tangled up in the ropes. Then Gus hit him with a flurry of punches, like he was in some kinda rage, gave him a fearful beating. It was awful to watch. They tried to revive Tommy, but it was no good."

"What happened to Gus?"

"Life kinda went out of him after that—started hittin' the bottle. He never came back to Stillman's. Never fought again. Gave up a title shot with Emile Griffith at the old Felt Forum."

"I read Gus had a wife," Mario said.

"*And* a son. He loved that kid. His ole lady brought 'em into Stillman's once, when the kid was a baby. Quite a looker she was. A white girl."

Mario sighed. "Well, that's quite a story, Eddie. Thank you for telling me."

"Yeah, it's not one of my favorite memories."

"But it sounds like you have a lot of great memories about Stillman's."

"Yeah, well, it was my life. I could tell you stories…"

Monday, Vinny was back from his honeymoon in the Grand Caymans and not as tan as he should have been.

"What's with the prison pallor, Vinny?" Glen asked. "The old lady wouldn't let you out of the bedroom?"

"Aw, leave the guy alone," Barry said, "he's a newly-wed. He's probably having trouble walking."

Vinny threw up his hands and laughed. "Okay, you guys—enough already." He opened his briefcase, took out a small framed honeymoon photo of himself and his new bride and placed it on his desk with great care.

M&A's double glass doors opened and in walked Tyler Gentry, accompanying a tall, fetching red-head with the body of a movie star and the cool self-confidence of a NASCAR driver. She was wearing a black Yves St. Laurent business suit, and when they caught sight of her it blew their eyeballs through the back of their skull.

"Well, hello there," Glen said with a big grin, "how're doing?"

The woman looked at him as though he were an animal of some lower order.

"Gentleman," Tyler said, "I'd like you to meet Kathleen Sweeney, formerly of Bear Stearns and Wingate Capital."

Mario extended a hand and the woman shook it briefly, but firmly. Neil and Dennis did the same and Barry offered a wave. Vinny just sat back and watched.

"Kathleen is coming aboard," Tyler went on. "She's just been approved by the partners."

"You can call me Kat," the woman said. She looked around the suite, immediately spotting the Wall of Shame, with its display of the latest *Sports Illustrated* swim suit models. "Hmm," she said, lifting her eyeglasses and peering at a picture of a slender blonde woman wearing a pale purple thong. "I didn't know it was available in that shade of lavender."

"I like it in black, myself," Glen said.

Kat ignored him.

"Miss Sweeney—Kat—comes to us with impressive credentials in the field of education," Tyler said. "But her banking experience is minimal. So I've decided to start her off as your assistant, Mario."

"What?" Mario said startled.

"Your assistant," Tyler repeated.

Mario still didn't get it. "I don't understand."

"We'll put you at, umm, let's see, *that* desk," Tyler said to Kat, pointing to the desk next to Mario's, now solely occupied by Vinny.

Vinny regarded Tyler without expression, then looked at Mario.

"You're kidding," Neil said.

Dennis didn't understand yet. "She's taking Vinny's job?"

It was Tyler's turn to be confused—or act confused. "Vinny's job? Of course not. He's still your man Friday. This is totally different."

"Tyler, Vinny just got his CFA," Mario said. "He's ready to step up. Remember our discussion last year?"

"Passed your CFA, did you?" Tyler asked Vinny. "That's admirable. Mario's always had a lot of confidence in you."

"But Mario said he was going to make *me* his assistant," Vinny objected.

Tyler smiled paternally. "Well, someday, maybe. Perhaps when Kat moves up. Mustn't rush things, you know. In due time."

"You're gonna let this happen?" Vinny asked Mario. Before Mario could answer, Tyler cut in.

"It's not his call," Tyler said. "Anyhow, it's a done deal."

"Listen," Kat said, "I don't want to make any trouble here."

Tyler turned toward her. "You're not the problem, Kat," he said graciously. "We just need to get a couple of things straightened out. Young man needs to understand his situation, that's all."

Vinny looked hard at Tyler. "Fuck you, Tyler." He grabbed his briefcase and bolted.

"Kid, wait!" Mario said, but Vinny was already through the glass doors.

For a moment, everyone in the suite was stunned. Then Mario shot Tyler a furious look and chased after his protégé, getting to the elevator just after the doors closed. He made for the stairwell, leaping stairs three or four at a time.

He shot through the Winter Garden lobby and ran into the garage just in time to see Vinny swing his leg over his motorcycle and reach for the starter button.

"Vinny, for God's sake, wait!"

Vinny switched off the engine and sat back and Mario straddled the motorcycle's front wheel, hoping to stop him from moving. "I don't want to hear it, Mario," Vinny said. "You made me a promise."

"I'll find something for you, Vinny, something better. I've been exploring an idea."

"No more promises, Mario. I'm sick of 'em." He strapped on his helmet, hit the starter button, and his motorcycle roared into life once again.

"Vinny, listen to me!"

"Get out of the way, Mario." He swung the bike around, but Mario grabbed the handle bars.

"I've got a million bucks riding on you, ya fuck!"

"Since when did you ever give a shit about money?" He shoved Mario out of the way, screeched through the gate, and was gone.

A few minutes later, Mario barged into Tyler's office, enraged. "Tyler, you are one of the biggest assholes I've ever met. You've lost me—us!—one of the smartest, most ambitious, hardest-working young men on Wall Street, a fuckin' star in the making."

"Come on now, Mario. Don't get your panties in a knot. Vincent is a nice kid, but he's the wrong image for Harrison Hart. You didn't really expect him to follow in your footsteps, did you? That Horatio Alger shit is dead. A fairy tale, like unicorns and dragons. Yeah, I know all about your little bet with Bart—not so little. You should have told me before you made it."

"Tyler, you gave me your word—once he got his CFA, I could bring him aboard as my associate."

"Kat's got an MBA from Boston University."

"Who gives a fuck! Vinny has a genuine feel for the Street."

"But no degree."

"Dammit, Tyler, he's got *ambition!*" Mario shouted, slamming his fist into Tyler's desk.

They gave each other a long, hard look, and Tyler took a deep breath.

"I didn't have any choice, Mario. Your team is the only one in the firm without a woman. We're beginning to look non-compliant. I've been getting a lot of heat about that from HR and the diversity committee. We have one now, you know. Perhaps you didn't get the memo."

"Yeah, it's pinned next to the Wall of Shame. Look, we can fix this, Tyler. Just give the woman some other job."

"This one suits her perfectly. Adds a little class to your outfit, too, which isn't a bad thing."

"She's a fucking school teacher, Tyler. And you didn't even have the courtesy to ask me before you hired her," Mario said.

"Look, you know the deal, Mario. You and your crew have a lot of independence around here, but I do the hiring and I do the firing."

Back in Mergers and Acquisitions, Mario found Kat setting up Vinny's desk *her* way. She handed him the framed picture of Vinny and Inez. "I hope I didn't upset any apple carts," she said.

Mario took the picture without commenting and stuck it in a desk drawer.

"So, Kat," Glen said, "after work...you and me...what do you say?"

"Okay," Kat replied, stopping what she was doing. "I'm going to say this once: what I do after work is my business and it's not going to involve you, any of you." She glanced around the group to make sure everyone was listening. "I don't shit in my own bed. You got that?"

"Yes, ma'am," Dick piped up. "I'll make sure the boys behave themselves."

Kat studied Dick for a moment. "You're the one they call 'Big Dick,' aren't you?"

Neil and Dennis tried to restrain their laughter.

The next morning, Kat came in carrying a roll of paper under her arm and wearing something blue and slinky and unbuttoned enough at the top to force Glen to avert his eyes. She walked directly to the Wall of Shame and started examining it critically.

"Jesus Christ," she said in disgust, "which one of you guys is responsible for keeping this up?"

"Well, I..." Glen said.

Kat ripped one of the pages off the Wall of Shame, crumpled it up and tossed it into a wastebasket. "I wouldn't be caught dead wearing panties like those."

"I think that was *my* contribution," Dennis admitted.

Kat tore down another page. "What's the matter, boys, have they stopped sending you the current catalog?"

Mario just sat back and watched the show, thinking it didn't matter how many pages she tore up, so long as she kept coming into work dressed the way she was now. He was having trouble remembering why he was so pissed off at Tyler.

And in a far corner, Dick suppressed a nasty little grin and kept silent.

"Hand me some tape, somebody," Kat said.

"Yes, ma'am," said Dennis, "happy to oblige." He put his tape dispenser in her outstretched hand.

Now Kat unrolled the paper she'd been carrying and taped it over the vacant spot she'd created. It was a Chippendale poster—a group of impossibly good-looking men with muscles oiled and packages bulging from their Banana Hammocks.

The Zoo Crew watched attentively as Kat, standing with her back toward them, stretched to put a piece of tape at the top of the poster. The movement caused her dress to rise, revealing a long length of well-shaped thigh.

Barry, who been chomping on a pencil, opened his mouth and the pencil fell to the floor. Dennis bit into his knuckles. Mario tried to get everyone's mind back on business. "Hey, Glen," he said, "hand me that opposition report on Martin Air Conditioning, will ya?"

Glen was transfixed by Kat.

"Glen? Glen? The synergy report."

"Oh, yeah. Sure, boss, right here," Glen said, handing Mario the stapler instead, his eyes staying with Kat.

"There," Kat said, turning around. "That's better." She looked around the room. "Don't you all think so?"

"Much fairer," Dennis said.

"And more balanced," Glen said, earning a warning look from Kat.

"What do *you* think, Mario?" asked Kat.

"I think things will never quite be the same here," Mario said without further explanation.

Later that week, Mario and Kat were summoned to Tyler's office, where Tyler, Dick Hamilton, and the director of human resources, Judith Clarke, were awaiting them.

"Go ahead, Ms. Clarke," Tyler said, looking distinctly uncomfortable.

"I'll get right down to business," Ms. Clarke said. She was a young, tightlipped woman with wire-rim glasses. "There've been some complaints about the two of you."

Tyler shuffled some paper on his desk and tried to ignore the conversation.

"*What* complaints?" Mario said, glancing at Hamilton.

"For one thing, Mr. Monelli, we've heard grievances about the wall paper in Mergers and Acquisitions. You've got a sexual harassment suit just waiting to happen."

"They're just some swimsuit catalog pictures," Mario said. "A little adolescent maybe, but harmless."

"That's not the point," Ms. Clarke said. "It promotes a sexually charged atmosphere."

"Look," Kat interrupted, "I'm the only woman in the section and I'm not in the least offended. So that should take care of that."

Ms. Clarke went on. "We've also had a complaint about you as well, Ms. Sweeney."

"Already? I've only been here a week."

"It's because of the, well, provocative way that you dress."

Kat stood, boldly displaying herself. "Just what's wrong with the way I dress?"

Judith Clarke cued Dick Hamilton with a nod.

"Well, for one thing," Dick said, "the buttons. Even if you stand straight, your bra is visible, and if you bend forward..."

Kat smiled. "You poor frustrated little boy. Upset by a little cleavage. Well, I wouldn't want you to suffer." She took two steps toward Hamilton. "Here, Dick. Could you button me a little? I mean, just so I don't offend you anymore."

Kat took Hamilton's hand and drew it to her neckline, but he pulled it away, horrified and embarrassed. "Well," Kat told Hamilton, "if you're not willing to button me up to suit your notion of what's proper and what isn't, then I have a simple solution for you."

"What's that?"

Kat smiled prettily. "Just turn your back whenever I walk by."

Dick glared at her for a moment, then turned on his heel and marched out of the office, as though he'd won his point.

"Look, you officious little piss-ant," Mario boldly said to the HR director. "There's nothing wrong with the way Kat dresses *or* with our little posters. You're wasting our time on nonsense."

"Well, it's my job to make sure no one is offended..." Ms. Clarke said, backing away from him.

"Right. Well, no one *is* offended except me—by this political correctness gone wild. May I?" Mario reached for the document on Tyler's desk—glanced at it—then gingerly folded it in half before tossing it into the waste basket. "That's what I think of his bullshit complaint."

Judith Clarke looked at Tyler, then without a word lifted herself up and walked out of the office, visibly angry.

"Gee, *that* went well," Tyler said.

Tyler politely dismissed Kat and lined Mario up in his sights.

"Have you lost your mind, talking that way to the director of HR?"

"It's not enough we got compliance snooping through our e-mails and monitoring our private phone calls now," said Mario. "Now Big Dick and Ms. Kunta Kunte are questioning office morality and we..."

"I think you made your point, Mario."

"No, you called me in here, now let me finish. Some women *like* to come to work and have men stare at their tits. It increases productivity."

"How so?" asked Tyler.

"It keeps men sitting at their desks."

"That boorish behavior went out in the eighties, Mario. These people in HR have a lot of clout now. They may pursue this legally. You think you'll make partner *then*?"

"I'll deal with that when the time comes," said Mario. "In the meanwhile, Kat wears what the fuck she wants."

Mario left Tyler's office and found Kat waiting for him outside the office.

"Hey," she said, "thanks for going to bat for me."

Mario looked at her coldly. "I didn't do it for *you*, Kitty Kat," he said, then walked away from her.

It was a busy week and Mario wasn't able to spring himself until late Friday afternoon. Then he headed straight for Cortlandt Alley, hoping Gus would be there. Mario made his way past the garbage, the broken boards, and bent pipes, down to a bundle of rags lying beside the rusty grocery cart—Gus's rusty grocery cart, he was sure.

"Gus?" He put a hand on the rags. Suddenly, a callused, cracked-skin ashy-looking black hand shot out and grabbed him like a vice. "Gus, it's me, Mario."

The bundle of rags turned over. "Ah, my Wall Street friend." He released Mario's hand. "Not a good idea to sneak up on someone that way."

"For a moment I thought you were…"

"Dead? I was in the middle of my afternoon nap." Gus shook himself and sat up. "What's up? You get yourself in trouble again?"

"Naw, I brought you something to eat." Mario handed Gus a Big Mac in a bag and sat down next to him. "You know, I looked you up on the Internet."

"Oh really? Nothin' more to know."

"Not according to Eddie Garford."

Gus's eyebrows knit for a moment, then cleared. "You talked to Eddie Garford? Where the hell did you find *him*?"

"Through a boxing magazine."

Gus just shook his head in wonderment and stopped eating the sandwich. "What did he say about me?"

"Told me how promising you were. He also told me about your last fight."

Gus stopped eating. "That was a long time ago," the old man finally said. "Another lifetime."

"We all carry demons, Gus."

"Yes, Mr. Monelli, I 'spect we do." He gave Mario a long look.

Mario was taken aback for a moment. It was as if the old man knew something about him. But of course that wasn't possible. "Sometimes guilt can be hard to bear," Mario said thoughtfully.

"It can be the fight of a lifetime," Gus said.

"Gus, Eddie Garford also told me that you had a wife and son."

"That old fool didn't miss nothin'. Yeah, had 'em and lost 'em. Wife took off on me a long time ago. Took my boy with her. She died a while back, I heard. But I don't have no idea where my son is."

"I could find him for you, Gus."

Gus looked at Mario for a long time. "You wouldn't be doin' me, or him any favor."

Mario looked at the weathered old face and the wise old eyes. "If that's the way you want it, Gus." He reached into his pocket, pulled out a gold money clip stuffed with bills, and peeled off a handful. "Gus…here, get yourself some decent shoes."

Gus inspected his bare swollen feet, which were bulging out of a pair of ravaged, laceless sneakers. "Don't need any."

"Look here," Mario said, trying to salvage the old fighter's self respect. "Someday some other idiot is going to get himself in a jam and need a helping hand from you. I want to be sure you're there. Here, take it."

Gus nodded and took the money, and the two of them clasped hands.

"Where are you going *this* time?" Phyllis asked suspiciously.

"LA," Mario said, packing like the experienced traveler he was.

Phyllis opened a nightstand drawer and pulled out a box of condoms. "Here," she said, tossing it to him, "don't forget *these*."

Mario caught the box one-handed and threw it in his suitcase just to spite her.

At that moment, Kyle walked into the bedroom, carrying a Spiderman doll, saw the suitcase and stopped dead. He looked at his mother, then at his father. Then he began to tear.

"Hey, champ," Mario said, surprised and concerned. "Why the water works?"

"You're going away."

"Yeah, but just for a few days. I'll be back soon."

"Not like Danny's daddy?"

"Nah, what kind of soldier leaves his best buddy behind?"

"A bad soldier, daddy."

Although it was Boomer who pumped life through Mario's heart, it was Kyle who commanded his soul. Maybe because the boy was fighting a learning disability and could never aspire to his older brother's potential.

He scooped Kyle up in his arms and brought him to his room, tucking him inside a Marvel Super hero bed frame. "I'll be back before the weekend. We'll go see that new action film, the one with Vin Diesel."

"Dark Fire, daddy? Promise?"

"Scouts honor."

"Can we see it on IMAX in 3-D, daddy?"

"You betcha."

The boy dried his eyes and Mario gave him a hug.

It was after midnight, but the streets of coffeehouse row, in one of Cairo's seediest sections, were still filled with pedestrians, mostly angry-looking young men, most of them in traditional Arab dress.

They sat at the sidewalk cafes, sipping from tiny cups of dark-brown liquid, and arguing noisily, about Israel, about America, about Iraq, about Osama, about Mubarak, about women, about the price of just about everything. It was a ritual way to bring the Sabbath day to an end.

In the rear of one of the least reputable coffee houses, two men shared a table about the size of a manhole cover. Although both were in Arab dress, one was pale-skinned and had blue eyes. He was drinking coffee. His tablemate, a swarthy, heavy-browed man in his early twenties, was smoking a handmade cigarette and looking around the café nervously.

"There was no need for us to meet face to face," the young man said, "especially not in public."

"I want to see if you're justifying what we're paying you."

"Get on with it," the younger man repeated.

"Okay. According to your note, Al Qaeda is gearing up for another big attack on American soil."

The young man nodded. "They have recruited fifty men."

"Saudi nationals?"

"Saudis, yes. But also from Pakistan, Syria, and Yemen. The training will take place in Hamburg, Germany."

"But you do not know where this attack is supposed to take place."

"No one has yet been told. All I can tell you is it is planned to take place on a day of great celebration."

"You're sure?" the light-skinned man asked.

"I'm one of them."

"Achmed, that is very dangerous."

The young man smiled cynically. "Dangerous? And what is my life worth now? Nothing. I expect your customs will prevent me from entering America...some passport problem."

"I'll take care of it. Can you tell me anything about the nature of the attack?"

"Only that it promises to be much bigger than 9/11. That is all we have been told. We have also been told it will happen very, very quickly."

"Are we talking about a bomb? A biological weapon."

The young man shrugged.

"What about a time frame?"

"It's only a feeling...they haven't said anything...but I'd say no later than a year and maybe earlier. No sooner than nine months is my guess."

"Anything else?"

"Just a code name for the operation: El Hesab."

The fair-skinned man had never heard the word before. "What?"

"It means 'the price' or 'the bill.'"

"Hmmmph. Can you tell me anything else?"

"No. I will contact you from Hamburg the moment I have heard anything more. Now, do you mind if I get out of here. I feel like everyone is looking at us."

"Go," said the light-skinned man. "And be careful!"

The young man departed quickly, not looking back. Ten minutes later, the westerner rose, paid the bill, and strolled off. Soon, he was back at his hotel and on a secure landline, talking to his superiors.

Within a half hour, the NSA was searching radio and telephone calls worldwide for any mention of "El Hesab." CIA databases were also being searched and the alert also went out to the FBI, Customs, and the ATF. The word even reached the secret SEC Wall Street wiretap operation.

CHAPTER EIGHT

Mario leaned back in the comfortable business-class seat and studied the Martin Air Conditioning documents. The long commercial flight to LAX out of Newark provided him the perfect opportunity to review everything before meeting the client.

Across the aisle, Neil was sound asleep, which was just as well, Mario thought. He'd probably been up half the night, putting the wood to some gorgeous female while his wife, Elaine, was still sneaking Twinkies at an exclusive fat farm in Durham, N.C.. And even Neil needed some R&R now and then.

Neil was as WASP-looking as Prince Harry—tall, perfect features, chiseled nose, a fine crop of medium-brown hair. He looked as though his Anglo-Saxon roots stretched back to the days of the Magna Carta, the perfect image of a Princeton lad, or maybe Yale. Except for one thing. Neil Granger didn't have a drop of WASP blood in him. In fact, he wasn't even Neil Granger, at least not originally.

The man sound asleep across the aisle was—originally—Makarios Kanfantaris, born to first-generation Greek parents who settled into the Greenpoint section of Brooklyn in the early fifties. His father, a shoemaker by trade, was killed in a botched hold-up when his son was only six.

Neil was a magna cum laude graduate of Purdue University, who had financed his own education by gambling, first in Las Vegas, then, when it came time to earn his MBA at Duke, at the blackjack tables of Monte Carlo.

It wasn't until a few years after college that Makarios Kanfantaris bade farewell to himself—two years of frustration on Wall Street, presenting stellar grades and a flawless appearance, and getting no offers at all. Then one day, Makarios Kanfantaris walked into Manhattan Civil Court and walked out as Neil Granger, and the world of banking and finance opened its doors to him.

Mario didn't fault Neil for the name change—might have done it himself, if it hadn't been for his mentor—Austin Keyes, who didn't give a damn what his heritage was, or where he went to school…or didn't.

Mario had arranged for John Martin, the founder and CEO, to meet them at the hotel, along with his two sons, Brian, the company president, and Chris, the vice president of manufacturing. Their chief legal advisor and the director of public relations would also be there.

He'd also told Martin to schedule a board of directors meeting for the next day, so that certain protective measures could be put into place before the annual stockholders' meeting.

In their phone conversations, old man Martin had seemed a canny sort. He was a visionary, maybe even a leader of men, but way out of his depth when dealing with a serious attempt to buy his company out from under him.

This was always the hard part—getting the CEO to understand how best to defend his company, getting him on board with the strategy without making him feel like an outsider. But over the phone, John Martin had sounded like a good man, in desperate need of help and asking for it with a certain amount of humility.

Mario and Neil met the Martin team in their Beverly Hills hotel suite. John Martin, a broad-shouldered, barrel-chested man in his middle sixties, looked like the sort of man you'd want leading your wagon train through Indian territory. His eldest son Brian was a charmer with a shock of blond hair and a surfer-boy tan. His other son Chris looked like the old man must have looked at age thirty-two.

They were accompanied by their attorney, Howard Silberman, and the director of public relations, Marsha Makey. They'd brought two company accountants and the controller.

After the usual awkward small talk, Mario got down to business. "Let's start with this: why are we here?"

"We're looking for a legal way…" Silberman began.

John Martin interrupted. "We're trying to save my company from those goddamn Texas buzzards circling over us."

"Exactly," Silberman said.

Mario exchanged glances with Neil. "So, let me get this straight," he said. "You don't want do *any* kind of deal with Nevco Industries? No matter how sweet a deal they're offering."

"My father meant exactly what he said," Brian stated. "No sale, no merger, no you-sit-on-my-board-and-I'll sit on yours, or any of that joint CEO bullshit Weill and Reed did over at Citigroup."

"They're looking for a total victory," Neil said to Mario, who nodded.

Mario pulled Glen's opposition research report from his briefcase. "My team tells me that this is a genuine, *bona fide* hostile takeover attempt. Your company's in play John, and it's going to be decided by a proxy fight at the stockholders' meeting two days from now."

"Can we win that fight?" the older Martin asked. There was real fear in his eyes, and this obviously wasn't a man who scared easily.

"I can't guarantee anything," Mario said. "Nevco is getting good advice from their investment people in Dallas, and they appear to have a pile of cash."

"But let's concentrate on you for now," said Neil. "What's your capital position? How are your lines of credit?"

"We're overextended," Brian admitted. "We've been putting most of our capital into the new plant in Georgia. It's going to make us a fortune, but it doesn't start operation until late next year."

"This sounds absolutely horrible," Marsha Makey said. "How in the world am I going to put a good spin on this? How can I reassure the stockholders? And what about the key employees?"

Mario smiled patiently. "You're going to tell them the Martins have no intention of selling and have every confidence that they can beat off the threat."

"Can we?" John Martin said. "Can we win this one?"

"Maybe," Mario said.

"Yes, we can," said Neil, simultaneously.

Martin glanced from face to face. "Which is it?"

"Yes, we can," Mario said.

"Maybe," Neil said at the same moment.

Mario and Neil looked at each other. Martin barked out a laugh and everyone else joined in.

"Okay, this is what they're trying to do," Mario said. "They're attempting to buy a majority of the voting stock, then, at the stockholders' meeting, vote the board of directors out of office and appoint their own. Then, their hand-picked board will approve a blanket tender offer from Nevco, and it's goodbye to Martin Air Conditioning."

"Then they'll leverage your assets to pay the debt level financing— equipment, machinery…everything," Neil added.

"Do you know what they plan to do?" Martin senior said. "They plan to move production to Southeast Asia. That would eliminate 11,000 jobs."

"So, okay, Mario," Brian said, "looks to me as though we have to find some way to buy back as much of our stock as possible, before the proxy fight."

"That's the Frank Capra version of a proxy fight," Mario said. "Little old lady plops down a big brown paper bag full of stock certificates in front of the loveable old founder—that's you, John—and says, 'You have *my* vote, Mr. Martin,' and it's just enough to give the founder the victory over his evil opponents, and then the closing titles flash on the screen."

"That's not the way it really works?" Chris asked.

"Usually not. Anyhow, it's not the way it's going to work *this* time," Mario said.

"Okay," Brian Martin said, "no little old lady. So how do we get the money to buy back enough stock to retain control."

"We don't," Mario said. "We let *them* win."

"But once they own the majority of our stock, we're finished," Marsha Makey said glumly. "It's just one big surrender, and if that's what you came here to tell us, could have stayed in New York."

"I said we were going to let them win the proxy fight," Mario responded. "I didn't say we were going to let them take over the company. And we're not."

"But how, without enough money?"

"You have the board ready to meet tomorrow, right?" asked Mario.

"Yes, and they're all on our side," said Brian.

"Good," Mario said. "Now let's go over the play book. Here's what they need to do…"

The Martins had rented out a small, elegant, movie theater in Santa Monica with about 500 well-cushioned seats. By nine a.m. on Wednesday, most of them were occupied, by the odd assortment of housewives, pension fund managers, retired folks, and brokers—the well-dressed, ill-dressed, and inappropriately dressed.

John and Brian Martin, Howard Silberman, and Marsha Makey sat at a table on the stage, along with Vern Chernak, Martin's CFO. Mario and Neil sat in the theater's front row, where they could easily communicate with the cast onstage.

First, John Martin talked about the company's previous year ("very profitable"), his hopes for the coming year ("should be even better"), and his plans for the years to come ("our expansion will give us a clear path to industry leadership").

Then, it was Vern Chernak's turn to present the company's financial data, which gave the accurate impression that the company was, heavily invested in expansion, but sound.

Brian Martin followed with a Power Point presentation about market penetration, manufacturing efficiency, and new product development on the way.

"Isn't it time for the fireworks to start?" Neil whispered to Mario.

"Yep, right about now."

On stage, John Martin was at the microphone again. "Ladies and gentlemen, it's time to re-elect the board of directors for another term. Since it is unopposed, I ask for your unanimous approval in a voice vote. Do I hear any objections?"

"Here it comes," Neil whispered to Mario.

A handsome, dark-haired, well-dressed man, one of several sitting in the middle of the theater now, rose quickly. "Mr. Chairman, I have an opposing slate of board members to offer."

John Martin looked at him hard. "And you are?"

"David Kohl, of Kohl, Cromwell and Sebastian. I represent Nevco Industries and a group of stockholders that now holds a majority ownership of stock in Martin Air Conditioning. We hereby cast all of our votes for the opposing board."

There was a collective—and very audible—gasp from the other stockholders in the audience.

"I think this is a legal issue," Martin said calmly, turning to Howard Silberman. "Could we have your opinion, Mr. Silberman?"

Silberman nervously pulled the table mike closer to him. "I'm afraid your vote is out of order, Mr. Kohl."

"How so?" Kohl returned fire.

"Well, we have a staggered board at Martin Air Conditioning. Only one quarter of the board members are up for re-election each year. That is the maximum number you can replace."

"Since when does Martin have a staggered board?" Kohl asked. He fumbled in his briefcase for a moment. "I have the company charter right here, and it calls for an annual re- election of the entire board."

"Not anymore," said John Martin. "The board amended the charter."

He glanced down at Mario, who gave him a thumbs up.

"When?" Kohl demanded, furious.

"Yesterday, as a matter of fact," Martin said.

The suit sitting next to Kohl whispered something to him, then Kohl spoke again to Martin. "I see," he said. "But if we replace three board members a year, we'll obtain a majority in three years."

"Well, that's true," Silberman explained. "But when the board is considering a tender offer or any other kind of merger or purchase of the company, it can only be approved by a supermajority—a vote of eighty percent of the board or more."

"And this is in the charter, too, as of yesterday?"

"That's correct, Mr. Kohl." Martin glanced at Silberman, who nodded vigorously.

Kohl sat down and conferred hurriedly with several advisors sitting in his row and was soon back on his feet. "Wait! On behalf of the stockholders I represent, I hereby summon a special stockholders' meeting for tomorrow morning to consider our tender offer from Nevco Industries."

Martin gestured at Silberman, who took the mike again. "Sorry, Mr. Kohl. The charter specifically gives the board the exclusive right to call a shareholders' meeting."

Kohl's face was turning red now. "But we have the voting majority. I can prove it."

"Not as of this morning," Brian Martin said. "Yesterday, the board voted to allow those who have owned Martin stock for five continuous years to purchase an equal number of shares at fifty percent of current market value."

"What? You've created a poison pill?" Kohl said incredulous. "There was no such thing in your charter yesterday."

Brian Martin looked down at Mario and Neil and smiled. "I think you're right, Mr. Kohl. But, of course, that's history."

Kohl stared at the ensemble on stage. Then he stuffed his papers back into his briefcase, pushed his way down the row of theater chairs, stepping on a few feet in the process, strode down the aisle, feigning bravado, and left the building. His advisors and other allies followed suit. A few of those who remained started clapping and soon the entire audience was applauding and whistling.

Martin now ran through a few remaining housekeeping measures to make the board's re-election official. Then he closed the notebook in front of him.

"Ladies and gentlemen," he said, "the last forty years have seen our company rise from an unknown air condition contractor in Los Angeles to the third-largest manufacturer of air conditioners and home heating units in America. I think that our progress will continue, to our benefit and yours. I thank you for your support."

Once again, applause broke out in the theater.

"I now declare this stockholders' meeting closed," Silberman said with great satisfaction and relief. "Thank you all very much for attending. See you next year."

A cheer rose from the audience and John Martin waved in response. Then the crowd began to filter out of the theater.

Martin hopped off the stage, looking ten years younger than he was, and hurried over to Mario and Neil. He made as if to shake hands with them, but ended up embracing them both. "I just don't know what to say," he said.

"We were just doing our jobs," Neil grinned.

They were soon joined by both Brian and Chris Martin. "That was amazing," Chris said. "You predicted everything he'd say and do—and he was tough."

"Yeah, but not a street fighter," Neil said, pointing at Mario.

"Gentlemen," said John Martin, "I know some other people who'd like to thank you."

Fifteen minutes later, the company limo drove up to a vast, beautifully landscaped steel and glass two-story structure a few hundred yards off the Santa Monica freeway interchange: Martin Air Conditioning and Heating World Headquarters.

John Martin led the parade through the lobby and out onto the catwalk overlooking the busy, noisy plant, a sea of people, assembly lines and machines of all kinds. The factory line manager, a burly man named Sam Cebrowski, came out of his office to greet him.

"Hi, Sam," Martin said. "Could we do a one-minute total shutdown? I have some news for the troops."

"Sure, boss," Cebrowski said. "Give me about a minute to get the signal out."

The factory noises—clanging, hissing, honking of electric vehicles, steel cutting and drilling, chains rattling—slowly dropped off and the movement of people and machines gradually ground to a complete halt. Cebrowski came out of his office again and plugged a microphone into a wall station, handing it to old man Martin.

"Good afternoon, ladies and gentlemen, friends, and colleagues. His voice reverberated loudly. "This is John Martin. I've just come from our annual stockholders' meeting and I have some good news for all of you: Martin Air Conditioning has defeated the take-over attempt."

The cheers that came from all over the factory floor were long and genuine.

"This means that your jobs are secure, and probably for quite some time to come. We're all going to keep doing what we do so well: making the best damn air conditioners and heating systems in the world."

More cheers.

"It was a tough battle," Martin continued, "and we very nearly lost it."

He began to choke with emotion and handed the microphone to his son Chris, who continued where his father left off.

"We *would* have lost it," Chris said, "if it hadn't been for the brilliant work of two men who work for our New York investment partners Harrison Hart. Mario Monelli and Neil Granger."

He paused for a moment, and the applause started in one corner of the building, quickly spreading across the entire factory floor until it was louder than the cacophony of full production.

John Martin regained his composure and tapped the mike with his finger. "Okay, okay," he said. "They deserve that and more. I'm going to take them around the floor now and give you all a chance to say hello. Now, hmm, I guess there isn't any nice way to say this—time to go back to work."

There was laughter from the floor, the kind of laughter that comes from happy, satisfied employees who like and admire the person they work for. Then the noises and the machines started up again.

John Martin and his sons, Brian and Chris, escorted Mario and Neil down to the lower pavilion, where a couple of electric vehicles awaited them. They spent the better part of an hour on a victory lap, tooling around the plant, stopping to talk to supervisors, foremen and line workers, and giving the boys from Brooklyn a good idea what Martin Air Conditioning and its people were like, bringing them face to face with the people whose jobs and families they saved.

They met back at the catwalk. "Hope you enjoyed it," Martin said.

"It helps, John," Mario told him. "It lends some humanity to what we're doing for a living."

"You've made a big difference in the lives of a lot of people," Martin told Mario and Neil. "I'd like to find some way to show my appreciation."

Mario laughed. "Well, there's the advisory fee…"

"No, not money," old man Martin said. "Something more personal."

"I could take them to the party tonight," Brian told his father. "They might enjoy it."

"Thanks for the invite," Mario said." But we're flying back to…"

"Party? Any chance there might be some women there?" Neil asked with a glint of mischief in his eyes. "Single or otherwise."

Brian looked at his younger brother, then smiled. "Wouldn't surprise us. How about I pick you both up at the hotel at, oh, let's say four o'clock."

Neil looked at Mario. "We can fly back in the morning," he said.

"Okay," Mario finally relented.

Mario and Neil came through the hotel doors at four o'clock sharp and found the Martin sons waiting for them in a white Bentley convertible. The top was down and Brian was at the wheel, wearing black bathing trunks, a vividly colored Tommy Bahama silk shirt, a pair of futuristic looking Oakleys, and the smile of a man who knew he really looked good. Chris was in the front passenger seat, outfitted in the latest Prada leisurewear.

"So tell us, fellas, where are we going?" asked Mario, sliding in the rear seat beside Neil.

"Our friend lives out in Holmby Hills, about twenty minutes away," Brian said.

"Holmby Hills?" Neil asked.

"Yeah. It's just above Sunset Boulevard, not far from Beverly Hills and Bel Air," said Chris.

"Well, if your friend's crib is anything like this car— it must be *some* place."

Brian exchanged a sidelong glance with his brother. "You could say that."

Twenty minutes later, the Bentley pulled up to a pair of huge wrought iron gates, leading to a driveway that snaked up the hill to a large structure, barely visible through the dense foliage and trees.

Brian rolled down a window and spoke briefly to the man in the guardhouse, who smiled, nodded, and pushed a button. The massive gates swung open and Brian eased the Bentley up the driveway and over a short stone bridge. A green lawn spread out on one side, complete with shade trees, swaths of azaleas, ferns, and rhododendrons—and a group of pink flamingoes loping up the hill.

Mario looked back toward the gate to see a Rolls pulling up to the guard house. "Ok, fellas, I give up. What the fuck *is* this place?"

"Gentlemen," Brian said, "welcome to the Playboy Mansion."

Neil looked at Mario, stunned.

"The Playboy Mansion?" Mario asked. "Are you telling us that your 'friend' is Hugh Hefner?"

"Amazing as it may seem, yes," Brian said, guiding the car past a pair of white marble lions that guarded a set of imposing hillside stairs. A topless young woman was sitting astride on one of the lions, chatting with a handsome man in a short, white, terrycloth bathrobe.

"How the fuck do you know Hugh Hefner?" Neil said, his head swiveling as the car moved forward, so he could keep his eyes on the bare-breasted goddess.

Now the main building loomed larger. It was a huge, crenellated, mullioned slab of olde Engishry, a lushly-landscaped gray gleam of granite walls and slate-shingled roofs and gables, intersecting at various angles.

The white Bentley drove over a short stone bridge. On the other side: what looked like a natural lake, complete with island and waterfalls, edged in irregularly shaped rock and populated by bevies of half or totally naked people, most of them—the women, at least—young and beautiful, swimming, sunning, and making out.

"When Hef bought the property in the early seventies, Dad was the air conditioner contractor. He and Hef got pretty tight. And we've inherited the friendship."

They pulled up to the front of the mansion and turned the car over to a uniformed valet. Chris took off toward the swimming pool and Neil and Mario headed for the main entrance.

"Hey, hey, not so fast you two," Brian said. "Let me show you around the grounds first."

"The grounds," Mario said. "You want us to see the *grounds*, when we all know that there are *women* inside the building?"

"There are women on the grounds, too," Brian assured him. "I just think you should get an idea of where you might spend your time here, outside of the main house."

So Brian gave them the tour, taking them first to the outbuilding on the left. It contained a green house, an aviary, and aquarium and a reptile collection, beautiful people wandering through the exhibits. None of the girls were wearing tops, quite a few were absolutely naked and the men were in bathrobes or pajamas. A couple was making love on the zebra-striped couch and, aside from a couple of voyeurs, no one was paying any attention.

"Are these girls for boning?" Neil asked.

"Patience," Brian said, and led them back out onto the lawn, past a beautifully-landscaped tennis court, where two ranked male professionals were engaged in a serious match and several beautiful women were doing their best to disrupt it. Beyond the tennis court, a nude volleyball game was in full swing.

"Man, I wish I had the silicone concession in L.A.," Neil said.

"This way to the main house," Brian said, laughing.

He led them up the stone sidewalk, though the enormous oak doors. A Playmate was holding forth at the cloakroom, her breasts barely contained by a stingy crop top, which revealed a dizzying cleavage.

"May I take your jacket?" she asked Neil, who didn't need to be asked twice.

"May I take your tie?" she asked Mario, who ripped it off and handed it to her.

"May I take your shirt?" she asked Neil. "And your pants?"

Mario got the idea and stripped down to his underwear, and the Martin Brothers weren't far behind. When they were almost naked, the girl presented them with a choice of bathrobes and pajamas, silk or terry. Mario chose red pajamas, Neil a blue paisley bathrobe.

Neil reached for his left hand and started to slip off his wedding ring. The movement caught Brian's eye. "You don't have to bother with that," he said. "No one cares."

Mario and Neil exchanged glances. "My friend," Mario said, "we have died and gone to *fuck* heaven."

"So, Brian," Neil said, "what are the, uh, rules here?"

Brian laughed. "Anything goes," he said.

Neil and Mario walked into the parquet-floored Great Hall, which was filled with lounging couples and an impressive selection of beautiful women, and strolled through the crowd.

A small redhead jiggled her way across the room and caught Neil's eye. "Excuse me," he said, blocking her way, "I don't want to be rude or anything, but I just have to tell you how lovely your hair is. I've never been able to resist a redhead."

She smiled, then took Neil's hand.

"Where are we going?" Neil asked.

"To the Red Room," the girl answered. "I'm meeting a girlfriend there. She's a blonde. Can you resist blondes?"

"Actually, no," Neil said, grinning. He winked at Mario, then disappeared with the girl into the crowd.

"What's goes on in the Red Room?" Mario asked Brian.

"Oh, it's a large, comfortable suite with fat leather couches and enough sexual energy to power San Francisco. Gets pretty dirty."

"Only if it's done right," Mario said, then started off after Neil when he bumped into a man with a familiar face. "Say, aren't you…"

"Yep," the familiar face said in a horse voice. "Gotta go…don't want to keep the lady waiting."

"Nice meeting you," Mario said, a little surprised at how aged the Aerosmith god looked.

"Wasn't that Joe Perry…?"

"Sure was," Brian said. "Look around…you'll see a lot of faces you recognize…I think that's Bill Maher over there…and look there…Kanye

West with Terence Howard? And over there, isn't that Dorothy Dickinson, the porn star?"

"My God, this place is everything they say it is," Mario said.

"This is just a moderate-sized party. When there's a big event like the mid-summer nights 'August bash,' all thirty rooms can fill up."

"So where should I go, Brian?" Mario asked.

Brian shrugged. "Introduce yourself. I'm heading out to the grotto." He left Mario standing in the middle of the Great Hall, where almost all the women were topless with a narrow, perfectly manicured landing strip of hair between their legs and perfectly symmetrical rear ends jacked higher than a prom dress in June.

Mario took the stairs to the second floor to do a little exploring. He heard laughter coming from a room down the hall and headed in that direction, through a gallery of framed photographs of Hefner and his famous friends.

He looked inside the room the laughter had been coming from. It was dimly lit, but he could see the bodies and silhouettes draped over the couches and on the giant oval bed, more women than men, there legs in different time zones, screwing their brains out as if the world were ending in an hour.

It was wilder than anything he'd ever seen at the old Plato's Retreat or other hedonistic night spots in Manhattan, but there didn't seem to be a spot for him, and he wasn't all that fond of watching. Still, just as he turned to leave, a woman's arm arose from the pile and waved him into the heap of writhing bodies.

Mario spent about an hour in the room, caught in the ether, at one time lying back and allowing himself to be serviced by three gorgeous women. They kissed, licked, and sucked while he fondled—mainly breasts, some of the fullest, creamiest he'd ever had the privilege of touching.

Afterward, he threw his robe back on and made his way to the grotto, a large, stone-lined cave that looked as if it had emerged from the sea millions of years ago, with a ceiling of fused glass panels and the distinct hum of dozens of water jets. The place was full of friends and lovers, among them Brian Martin, who was sprawled on a rock, next to another Playmate. He was sucking down a daiquiri while she was jerking him off. Brian gave him a wave. Mario figured Neil was probably still inside the Red Room of the main house, proving what a great stickman he was and impressing Hef's entire harem with his marathon stamina.

Mario made his way back to the main house to try out the caviar and perhaps find Neil. After a bit, he sidled over to the bar and got himself something to drink. Maybe I'll never get to heaven, Mario thought, in fact, it's very unlikely. But it could hardly be better than this. The bartender gave Mario his drink. Then Mario realized it was time for a pit stop.

He caught the bartender's eye and gestured anxiously. The bartender pointed a thumb toward the rear of the lounge.

Mario slipped though the heavy walnut door, past two Laker players, and found himself in a small, but elegant bathroom, chrome, glass, and black marble everywhere. Besides the attendant, there was one other occupant in the room, a small man in a silk paisley robe and gunfighter black pajamas, standing at a starkly modern urinal with gold-plated fixtures.

It was Hugh Hefner, older than the pictures of him Mario had seen, very grey now, but still slender and erect.

He turned slightly, toward Mario. "Enjoying yourself?" he asked.

"Oh, yeah," Mario laughed. "By the way, Mr. Hefner, I'm Mario, Mario Monelli. I'm a guest of the Martin family."

Hef nodded. "Good people, the Martins."

"Yes…they've shown me what Paradise really looks like."

Hef closed his robe and smiled. "You mean *this* place?"

"Of course."

"I guess a lot of people see it that way. For me, it's a wonderful adult playground, but it's a long way from Paradise."

"Well if this isn't Paradise, I don't know what is."

Hefner smiled ruefully. "*I* do. I've been there a few times. And with any luck I'm going there again…to find her."

"Find who?"

"Paradise is where my true love is," Hefner said.

"She here tonight?

"No," Hef said sadly. "Sometimes I wonder if she exists," he sighed. "This place is just a substitute. I know how far short it falls of the real thing."

"You mean you'd give up all this for one woman?"

"If it's the right woman…in a heartbeat."

"But you've been married…more than once."

Hefner nodded reflectively. "That's right. I've been lucky enough to find that one woman, and more than once—but foolish enough to louse it up. Thrice. It's not going to happen again."

"Well, I wish you the best of luck," Mario said.

"Thank you," Hefner replied, "and the same to you."

"Yeah," Mario said, washing his hands. "But I think it's a little too late for me."

"Ah, stuck in a bad marriage, are you?"

"Yeah. It's the cross I have to bear," Mario said.

Hefner lit his pipe and gave Mario a searching look. "You have children then."

"How did you know?"

"Why else would you stay?" he said sadly.

"Yeah. I can't leave my kids," Mario said.

Hefner took a deep breath. "Hard to hurt those you love. But if there's one thing I learned, its that no parent ever did their children any favor staying in a bad marriage. Perhaps they may benefit more if you had the courage to live for yourself."

"Sounds a bit selfish, don't you think?" Mario replied.

"A selfish man doesn't stay in an unhappy marriage, Mario. Only a weak one does."

The attendant handed them each a monogrammed towel and they dried their hands.

"Just one piece of advice, if you don't mind an old dog like me giving advice."

"No, Mr. Hefner, not at all," said Mario.

"Don't live your life as though you'll do better next time. Life is a celebration. Shouldn't *you* be celebrating?"

Hefner shoved his pipe in his mouth and winked, then walked out of the bathroom, into a covey of Bunnies, who squealed at the sight of him.

CHAPTER NINE

Paige appeared at Julie's open office door, clutching a stack of file folders.

"Oh, come on in," Julie said, "and shut the door behind you."

Paige did as requested, taking a seat in front of Julie's desk.

"I've been thinking about Mulvaney," Julie said. "We have to find the right opponent for him, or he's going to end up convincing our audience that the Saudis are our very best friends."

Paige nodded solemnly. "We could pit him against Gallagher or Ayers, providing they have enough prep time."

"I'm afraid our guys can't learn what Mulvaney already knows about the subject matter. Besides, he's contemptuous of them—and not just them. Just about everyone in the media."

"So..."

"So...we have to find the right adversary for him," Julie said. "And it isn't going to be easy."

"That's what I thought you'd say," Paige said. She dropped the stack of file folders on Julie's desk.

"What's this?"

"Every Wall Street maverick who opposes foreign investment I could dig up."

"Girl, I forgot how good you are."

There was a knock on Julie's door, then it opened before she had a chance to ask who it was. Fred Fielding hobbled in, swinging a single crutch.

"Well, well, if it isn't the two prettiest women at UBS television," he said cheerfully. "Hello, ladies?" He shrugged off his trench coat, stuck it over a coat hook, leaned his crutch against the other guest chair in the office and sat down heavily, as if he owned the place.

Paige smiled broadly, too broadly at Fred, then at Julie. "Happy to see you, Fred," she said, in a tone of voice that Julie knew meant *Who the fuck does he think he is and what the fuck is he doing here?*

Fred accepted the remark at face value. "Always glad to see you, too, Paige."

"How are you feeling?" Julie asked.

"Good enough today to come in and help you out for an hour or so."

"That's great," Julie said, glancing at Paige. "We can always use help."

"So how is it coming?" Fred asked. "The show I mean."

"We're making progress," Julie said cautiously.

"Good. We're all counting on you, Julie. But you don't have to go it alone. I'm here to help and we have some terrific people."

"Yes, I know," Julie said. This was getting tiresome.

"I recommend that you bring in Cal Flannery. And Marty Cohen…"

"Yes, and Lisa Green."

"Excellent. And the first thing you gotta do is have a production meeting."

"Already had it."

Fielding thought a moment. "Splendid. I didn't need to be in on it. They can handle the technical stuff. With your direction, of course. You're a *fine* producer."

"Thank you," Julie said. He was condescending and she was getting annoyed.

"Of course, it can be tricky. Especially the sound."

"The sound?"

Fielding nodded sagely. "That's right. I've seen it screwed up—more than once. I remember when I was working with Cronkite, we had a big, breaking story—airplane crash in Chicago with hundreds dead. Cronkite decided to go on the air with what we used to call a 'Bulletin' until someone decided that term was too frightening. Anyhow, I wrote the piece in about ten minutes and got it on the teleprompter and we cut into Guiding Light, infuriating twenty million housewives."

"What happened?" Paige asked.

"So Cronkite smoothes down his hair, and gives the control room the high sign. Off goes the soap opera and on goes the 'Bulletin' title card. Camera lights up and Cronkite starts speaking in that wonderfully gravelly voice of his, grave, but reassuring, and he's perfect as usual. We cut back to the serial and start congratulating ourselves, and then the phone rings and it's Bill Paley."

"*The* Bill Paley?" Paige asked.

Fielding looked at her fondly, as though she were a small child inquiring about the Easter bunny. "William to you, Paige. Yes, *the* William Paley, the president and founder of the CBS network, a man almost as powerful as the president of the United States, at least back then. Anyhow, he had some rather unpleasant news for us: Not a word of Walter's bulletin went out on the air. Someone screwed up—messed up—the sound. Twenty million people didn't have a clue about what he said."

"That's terrible," Julie said, wondering where Fred was going with this.

"Oh yeah, that's a good word for it," he said. "And you gotta remember, Cronkite's crew was the best in the business. These were all experienced pros, absolute crackerjacks. They didn't make mistakes."

"Were they fired?" Paige asked.

Fielding smiled. "That might have been easier to take. What happened was that Paley showed up in the studio, which was kind of like the king of England showing up in the locker room of the New York Giants, and while we were all busy snapping to attention and looking busy, he talked to the young producer."

Julie was surprised. "You could hear what he was saying?"

"Oh, yes," Fielding said. "He wasn't speaking softly. What he said was that he expected to get thousands of letters of complaint from viewers, complaints about interrupting the soap opera and complaints from those who wanted to know what Cronkite said. And he expected the producer to answer every last one of them, in his own handwriting—this was before word processing. And you know what that producer did? He answered them."

"That's a lot of letters," Paige said awed.

"It was either that or his job," Fielding replied.

"I see," Julie said. She was getting tired of this.

"Don't you care to know who that young producer was?" He waited for a response, looking at Julie, then at Paige.

Julie sighed. "Okay, Fred," she said, humoring him, "who was he?"

"That young producer," Fielding said, making a punch line out of it, "was Carleton Fisher."

Paige looked at Julie in astonishment, but Julie's eyes were on Fred.

Julie was silent for a long moment. "I'll check the sound personally," she said, forcing a smile.

"Oh, I'm sure you will, darlin'. Of course, the concept stuff, that's where I can really help."

"What do you mean, 'the concept stuff'?" Julie asked cautiously.

"Well, you know, the show format, putting the elements together so that there's a coherent theme. How you're going to tell your story, know what I mean?"

"We've really worked out the concept pretty precisely, Fred."

"Damn, darlin', I'm sure you have, but why don't you tell the old master? If you did it good, I can make it great."

Julie hesitated a moment, then handed Fred a single sheet of paper. "This is general, but you'll get the idea."

"I've got some work to do," Paige said. "Good seeing you, Fred."

Fred put on his glasses, then flipped back the first page and started reading, mumbling to himself. "Let's see...open with Ayers talking about foreign investment in the U.S....portrait of the Saudi Royal Family...and U.S. dealings with the Saudis...Gallagher interview with Mulvaney... segment on American history and values at risk...um hmmm..." He looked up at Julie. "So you liked Mulvaney?"

"I don't know if 'like' is the right word," Julie said. "But he's one of the investment bankers who's helping the Saudis, and he's got an interesting narrative, good appearance—perfect for our purposes."

"So Gallagher is going to expose him?" Fielding asked.

"We may put another banker against him—someone with an opposing viewpoint, if we can find the right guy."

Fielding smiled indulgently. "Tell you what, darlin', I'm going to check my little black book and see if I can find the guy you need. I've been around the block a few times, you know."

"I know, Fred. You didn't get that row of Emmys by reading teleprompter copy," Julie said.

"Hard work, darling'…that's the real secret. I'll get on the blower and see what I can scare up." Fielding shifted in his chair, obviously uncomfortable. "Meanwhile, I'm going to take a look at the outline and see how we can improve it." He rose laboriously and tucked his crutch under his arm. He waved one hand at his trench coat, ineffectually. "Could you give me a hand?"

Julie smiled. I'd like to give you a hand right out the window, she thought. But she took his coat, draped it over his shoulders, and opened the door for him. "Thanks for stopping by, Fred. Take care of yourself now. Don't overdo it."

She picked up the phone and punched in a number. "Marty, could you come in here for a minute?"

A few seconds later, Marty Cohen plopped himself down in the visitor's seat. "What's up, boss?"

"How's the writing coming?"

"I've got a draft of the opening and I'm working Ayer's closing commentary.'

"What about the Saudi investment piece—that's absolutely critical," Julie said. "The material in the blue folder—is it enough?"

"Oh, yeah," Marty said. "And it's terrifying. I don't need any more facts, I just have to figure out how to present them clearly and without talking down to the viewer."

"Marty, this isn't yesterday's UBS. It's tomorrow's UBS—thoughtful, intelligent, responsible. It's okay to be smart."

"You got it, boss," Marty said, genuinely pleased. "And if this keeps up, I might actually start liking my job again."

After he left, Julie summoned Carol Twitzel. "When do you think I'll be able to see a rough cut of the 'America the Beautiful' montage, Carol?"

"We've got the stock footage and the stills in house now and we'll be shooting them tomorrow. Rough cut Friday morning?"

"That's fine. Let me know if you have any problems. I'd like to get this in the can as soon as possible because I may have another assignment for you."

"I think you'll be happy with what I'm doing," Carol told her.

Julie spent the rest of the afternoon schmoozing the outlying UBS affiliate station managers that would provide remotes, and compiling lists of academics, ex-government officials, and Wall Street wise men critical of foreign investment in the United States.

After a few hours of this, Paige appeared at her door with her coat on. "Julie, it's almost seven o'clock," she said.

"I know. I'm going to stay awhile and read," Julie said, patting the stack of file folders on her desk.

Paige frowned. "How late do you plan to stay?"

"All depends. I could take the stuff home, but it'll be quiet here." Julie looked back up to find that Paige hadn't moved.

"I just don't like to see you working so late."

Julie smiled. "It's the best thing for me, Paige, really. It's exactly what I need."

Paige opened her mouth to speak, then thought better of it. "See you tomorrow," she finally said.

Julie watched her go for a few moments, then opened one of the file folders. It was filled with newspaper clippings about a investment banker named Barnett Russell. She went through the papers, listlessly. Boring. Looks like a chipmunk. She picked up her felt tip pen and marked the folder with a big red five.

She flipped open another folder. Same kind of stuff, different guy. Looks presentable, gives a lot of speeches so he might be a decent talker, regarded as a contrarian, which could be either good or bad. After browsing the biographical data, she marked the folder with a six and picked up another.

Oops, a woman, with a face like a clenched fist. That wasn't the kind of debate she wanted. She marked this folder with a big "R" for rejected and put it aside.

She went through another folder, then another, and another, and time passed. The "R" stack grew taller, and the fours and fives accumulated as well. But the eight was rare, there were only a few sevens, and not a single nine or ten. It was discouraging, but this was only the preliminary round.

Julie glanced up at the clock on the bookshelf across from her desk. It was almost 9:30 and the night seemed to be slipping away. Time to go home. But why? To what? To whom? To no one. She let her eyes drift away from the clock toward the picture of Jack on the shelf above.

He was wearing the smile of a man who'd found his way in life, who was doing what he'd been born to do, a man who'd found his life's companion.

Then all the memories came flooding over her, a thousand moments at once—riding bikes together in Martha's Vineyard, stuffing each other's mouths with sushi, working late together on a story, picking out a watermelon at D'Agastino's, kissing, watching him drool in his sleep, sharing a bathtub, dining out fancy, eating in on Chinese takeout, lying in bed and watching Casablanca on television, arguing about something silly and making up...

No.

You can drown in those memories, she reminded herself. You *have* been drowning in them. It's time to stop. You *have* to stop. You have something truly important to accomplish, something Jack would be proud of. She turned to the file folders and started in again.

Half an hour later, Hank knocked on her door.

"You still here?" he asked, scolding.

Julie glanced at her watch and laughed. "Time flies when you're having fun."

"Right," said Hank, who wasn't buying it. "Anyhow, it's time to go home."

"But..."

"And I'm leaving *now*, with *you*," Hank said. He waited until she got up and slipped on her coat.

In the garage, they walked to Hank's brown Honda, got in, and headed out.

"How does it feel, being back at work full time."

"It's like I never left. Everyone was watching me for a couple of days, but that's stopped, thank God."

Hank cut over to Park Avenue and started downtown. "I thought I caught a glimpse of Fred today in the hallway, but maybe I was seeing things."

"Nope. Fred was here all right. Came in to offer his help."

"I hope he didn't help you *too* much," Hank said.

"If it were up to him, he'd be producing my show and I'd be fetching coffee for him, but I think I can handle him. I know how to appeal to the gentleman in him."

"I thought that part was shot off."

They both laughed.

The next day, Julie was back at her desk bright and early. After she dealt with her mail, she was off to NYU to talk to a renowned economics professor—a former Clinton appointee—an expert in international investment, a scholar, and potentially, a Mulvaney opponent. He knew his stuff, alright, but talking to him was like watching the yule log.

Then it was lunch with a Morgan Stanley banker at the Harvard Club. Surprisingly, the banker turned out to be quite charming, but given to long pauses while he considered his answers to simple questions. That evening, Julie dined with a WTO economist, who was much too involved with global politics.

The next day was more of the same—except that the economics professor was at Columbia, the investment banker was at Brown Brothers Harriman, and the politician was at the UN. None of them, she concluded, was any match for Bart.

After that, it was a day in Washington, talking to a highly recommended official at the Fed, a young woman at the Treasury, a Congressman on the House Ways and Means Committee, and an economics attaché in the State Department.

A few of them were pretty good, but no one had Mulvaney's unique combination of expertise, good looks, speaking ability, and intellectual firepower. If she put any of them up against him, the special would end up proving the wrong point.

So, Julie thought, she'd just have to dig deeper—and hope the right person was out there somewhere.

The SEC's surveillance headquarters at Bowling Green station was in full operation. Half a dozen steel tables had been brought in, and each one of them was covered with electronic equipment, all connected by enough wires to serve as a root system for a giant oak tree.

Field agents wearing headphones were manning the tables, watching as the hard drives filled up with recorded telephone calls. Every so often, one of the computer operators would burn a DVD and hand it back to the work station, where other field agents fed them into DVD drives, examining them with a program that contained algorithms that could spot specific words and phrases.

Chester Hinkley, who was supervising the operation, prowled the tables like a fourth- grade teacher watching her students struggle with the multiplication tables. At each stop, he uttered his mantra: "Anything from any Wall Street source?"

Most of the operators answered in the negative, although some said their equipment had flagged some "chatter"—attack, Osama, bomb, Qaeda, nuclear, North Korea biological, kill, assassinate, and others. Context checks, however, had revealed nothing suspicious.

"How about it, people? We're looking for the Holy Grail and our Holy Grail is Saudi Royal Family. Do we have any hits that even remotely resemble that phrase?"

"Nothing yet, boss," said someone at the central work station.

"Okay," Hinkley said. "One more thing. We're also supposed to be looking for that Homeland Security keyword: **El Hesab.** Anything yet?"

Hinkley sighed deeply. "Okay people. But keep at it. Keep sharp."

CHAPTER TEN

On Labor Day, in backyards all across America, the grill gets cleaned, the hotdogs and hamburgers, or the ribs and steaks come out, the badminton net gets put up, the friends, relatives or neighbors come over, and a barbeque commences.

So it was in the backyard of Mario and Phyllis Monelli, except theirs was not a tiny patch of grass surrounded by a chain link fence, behind a row house in Astoria, Queens.

The Monelli summer compound was an architectural gem, a huge, multi-level, modernistic structure, cedar-sided, with immense windows that would have fitted nicely on the observation deck of the Chrysler Building, the whole thing shrouded by trees and thick plantings.

But the house's most outstanding feature was its location, smack in the middle of millionaires' row in East Hampton, Long Island about 150 yards from the blue Atlantic Ocean, perched on a steep cliff, overlooking a white sand beach, set back in a cove, so that the waters were as calm as a bay.

A spiral staircase made of teak curled down from the edge of the cliff to a dock, where Mario had moored the handsome, forty-foot Sea Ray he'd bought two years ago. On weekends, his guests—including neighbors Jerry Seinfeld and Billy Joel—could be seen snorkeling or roasting marshmallows at midnight campfires on the beach.

Mario had purchased the house five years ago from actor Paul Sorvino, and, on the advice of one of the Monelli's many marriage counselors they'd consulted over the years, had told Phyllis it was hers. Only somehow he'd never managed to remember to sign the papers.

The Zoo Crew, their wives, and a thin complement of friends and neighbors started showing up, and by noon, the gang was all there, with background music adding to the festivities.

Mario had hired a barbeque specialist out of San Antonio, Texas, and he and his assistant were cooking bucketsful of ribs, filets, and chicken wings, on a stainless steel grill that Mario knew for a fact was identical to the one at Camp David.

A wet bar had been set up back and a pair of female bartenders, formerly of the Coyote Ugly saloon, were dispensing alcohol, including beer on tap. Phyllis, who always had a drink in her hand, had put her foot down absolutely when it came to recreational chemicals—"there are going to be *kids* here,

Mario, including our own sons," so it was bring-your-own-smoke (or sniff) for the Zoo Crew, and beware of Phyllis and the kids.

But if there were ever a day for good behavior on the part of the Zoo Crew, this was it. The reason for their restraint was simple: wives. Glen's wife, Amanda, a cute blonde, a real sweetheart in her late twenties, was confined to a wheel chair, hoping for a remission from the multiple sclerosis that had struck her down three years ago.

Neil's wife, Elaine, a dark-haired beauty-pageant winner, now massively supersized, despite her stay at a Durham N.C. weight facility, seemed permanently stationed near the grill, where she was vacuuming down a little bit, in fact *quite* a bit, of everything. Mario couldn't even look at her without remembering a party *last* summer where Glen had made a fool out of himself and humiliated Elaine by asking her when the baby was due.

And then there was Barry. No wife. No date. Instead, he brought his mother, a small, sixty-five-year-old, cantankerous Sephardic woman with hard eyes, a perpetual frown, full of demands. "Barry, get me my suntan lotion," "Barry, find me a chair in the shade," "Barry, don't go swimming, you've just eaten." He took it all, without complaining. After all, she *was* his mother.

Dennis had brought his wife, Marie, as well, which was unusual. She'd rarely appeared in public since their son Michael was killed on 9/11, along with the rest of Ladder Co. 21. The little brunette had been full of laughter before that, and full of life. But all that was gone now, maybe forever. Dennis treated her with touching kindness.

Among the last to arrive at the barbeque was Vinny and his new wife, Inez. Vinny went out of his way to thank Mario for paving the way with Rick, who was anxiously awaiting him to arrive in Asia.

"You deserve it," Mario told him. "Beautiful new wife, great new job, wonderful new opportunities—you know, I envy you, Vinny."

"And a baby on the way," Vinny reminded him.

Also at the barbeque, a bunch of kids: Boomer and Danny, playing in the surf or riding on jet skies with two golden-haired teenage girls, little Kyle and Neil's munchkins, a seven year-old boy and a five year-old girl, building sand castles while Benson, the family dog, barked and romped among them.

The men spent the first part of the day swimming, raucously playing volleyball or Frisbee, eating, drinking, and snorting to excess, as usual. Gradually, the neighbors, began to drift away, probably to other barbeques, and the relatives bade their farewells.

Sometime around dusk, after Vinny and Inez left, the Zoo Crew, stuffed, exhausted, sunburned to a crisp, but feeling no pain, found themselves chugging beers and smoking grass, aboard the deck of Mario's boat, which was docked at the water's edge.

"Did you catch those girls running down the beach an hour ago or so?" Neil asked.

"Yeah, I saw 'em," Mario said, tossing Neil another beer. "I might have followed them except for…you know who."

"Yeah, my you-know-who was watching me like a hawk," Glen said.

"Same here," Barry said.

"Barry, Barry, Barry, " Dennis said, "our you-know-whos are our *wives*, not our *mothers*. You're the only one of us who could have gone after those babes without getting the evil eye."

"The evil eye?" Barry asked. "Have you noticed the look my mother gives me when she needs something and I can't produce it immediately?"

"Someday you're going to tell her to go fuck herself," Glen said.

They all laughed. A few hundred yards out to sea, a big sailboat cut across the water, following the shoreline. A shapely girl in a practically nonexistent bikini waved at them and every one of them waved back.

"You know," Neil said, still waving, "we're all prisoners. Doesn't matter *how* much dough we make."

Dennis asked what he meant.

"Well, the world is filled with broads," Neil replied. "But we can't get to them, or at least not very often. It's like we're all wearing one of those electronic ankle bracelets, only it's around our testicles."

"That's not exactly it," Dennis said. "We have the opportunities. There are women anywhere, and if one of us can't find any, all he has to do is ask *you*. The problem is, and always has been, where do we take them?"

"A hotel?" Barry ventured.

"Whenever I take a girl to a hotel, she tells me it makes her feel like a prostitute," Neil said.

"Once I tried to take a woman to an unused office—guy was on vacation," Dennis said.

"What happened?" Mario asked.

"His secretary *wasn't* on vacation."

"I took a girl to a friend's apartment once," Glen said.

"That's an idea," Mario said. "Was it always available?"

"No, and that was the problem. He used it for the same thing, so I could never count on it."

"Why don't we just get our own place," Barry said.

"You intending to bring your mother there?" Neil joked.

"Sure, we could get an apartment, but what happens if two or three of us need to use it at the same time," Dennis said.

"So we get a big apartment," Barry suggested.

"And do what? Wave to each other in the hallway and take turns in the bathroom?" Neil asked.

"Even if we had a place," said Glen, "what good would *that* do, what with Big Brother Judith Clarke and her PC cops watching our every move?"

"I know," said Neil. "You can't even look at a woman's tits or tell a dirty joke anymore without risking your career."

"That's for sure," Glen said. "I remember it used to be pretty routine for big producers to order strippers up to the trading floor, while some hot shot salesman was being serviced in a conference room. No one was shocked. We laughed."

"That's true," Dennis said. "And guys bragged more about their sexual adventures than the money they brought in."

"Yeah," Glen agreed. "We've all been neutered by political correctness."

"How much money we make for the firm last year?" Mario asked. "Four hundred million…a half bil?"

"That sounds right, but what's *that* got to do with anything?"

"We're putting up those kind of numbers and we gotta sit back while these piss ants in HR dictate what we can and can't do? Especially in our personal lives *outside* of the office."

"I agree, Mario, but there's nothing we can do about it," said Glen.

"There's plenty we can do about it," Mario said casually, gazing out at the blue Atlantic. "It would be expensive, but it would be worth it—*if* we could keep it a secret."

The Zoo Crew looked at each other.

"You gonna torture us with that Playboy Mansion story again?" Glen asked.

"No, no…it just gave me an idea, when we went there, I mean," Mario said.

"Stop fucking with our heads, Mario," Dennis said.

"Okay. What I'm thinking about is a private club, just for us and maybe a few of our good friends on the Street in our situation. A comfortable and luxurious place, you know, with plenty of food and booze always on hand, a place you wouldn't be ashamed to take a movie star."

"I see," Glen said skeptically. "So what happens when I arrive at the door with Charlize Thereon and…"

"I assume you're talking about the day Hell freezes over," Neil interrupted.

"It could happen," Glen said. "You never know. Anyhow, what happens if I knock on the door and one of you guys is already there with some slut he picked up on the PATH?" Neil shot him a dirty look.

"I'm not talking about a studio apartment, Glen," Mario said. "I'm talking about a venue where all our desires are realized."

"You're fucking serious?" Glen asked.

"Damn right I'm serious. Come on, Denny said it himself, we've been talking about this for years. We were just playing around until our marriages straightened out. Remember? What about it Glen? Think Amanda's ever gonna get out of that chair?"

Glen shot Mario an unforgiving look and forgot about the white powder he was sucking up his nose. "That's not fair, Mario. You know I'll never leave her."

"I know, Glen. But I also know she's never again going to be the woman you married. Same with you, Dennis. Forgive me, but the best part of Marie died right alongside Mikey that day. And you're in the same position, Neil. We all know you love Elaine, but we also know she doesn't turn you on any more."

"It's easy for *you* to say, Mario," Glen said. "You don't love your wife."

"I did, once, Glen. Very much. But that woman is long gone and she ain't coming back. I'm like all the rest of you—I need a place where I can be myself, where I can enjoy life and have what I deserve. Difference is, you guys don't *want* to leave, with me...I *can't* leave."

This time, no one argued with him. It took Barry to break the long silence that followed. "How much you figure this will cost?" he asked.

Mario laughed. "It would be you to bring up money. But whatever it costs, we can afford it. Except for Intercoastal, we've had a hell of a year."

Glen took a deep breath and shook off the dose of reality Mario had laid on him. "It'll have to be convenient," he said. "Nothing too far. I can't leave her alone very long."

"It'll be convenient," Mario assured him. "And we'll fly below HR's radar and all those other bastards in Internal Affairs."

"You're talking like this is a done deal," Barry said. "It's just an idea. A *wild* idea, if you ask me."

"So where do you take *your* women, Barry?" Mario asked.

"Yeah," Neil said, "you take them up to Riverdale for a threesome with your mother?"

"Fuck you, Neil. I take them to their place when I can."

"How's that working for you, Bar?" Mario asked.

Barry shrugged weakly.

"You see, that's our problem," Mario said. "We spend so much time scheming, and covering our tracks, that by the time we got it figured out, we're too stressed to get it up."

"Speak for yourself," Glen said.

Everyone was nodding in agreement.

"We'll need to set up a dummy corporation to own it, and house rules or by-laws that govern the way it operates, so none of us can be tied to it," Dennis said.

"If we all anteed up, somewhere in the neighborhood of fifty grand, that would give us enough working capital," Mario said. "Not a bad start...but *just* a start."

"That's a lot of hotel rooms," Glen said.

"Not if you're talking a lifetime," Neil told him.

At that moment, Boomer, Danny and the two WASPY girls they'd hooked up with came running across the sand, past the pier. On the boat, all discussion suddenly ceased.

After the teenagers disappeared inside the house, Neil spoke. "Gentlemen," he said, "we just had a demonstration of the most important aspect of this project, if we agree to undertake it. It has to be absolutely confidential."

"You're right," Glen said. "If my wife ever got wind of it, she'd climb out of that wheel chair and kill me. And I know it sounds corny, but I don't want to lose her."

"Same here," Neil said. "Elaine—well, look at her. You all remember how beautiful she was. I keep hoping that she will be again."

Dennis sighed deeply. "The only way I'd get involved with this idea is if I were absolutely certain Marie never found out. She's *already* on the edge."

"If my mother found out, she'd would circumcise me...*again*," said Barry.

"And if Phyllis ever caught on to what we were doing," Mario said, "she'd clean me out and take the boys. So I need to keep this under wraps, too. Let's start by agreeing on that—and the fifty grand."

"I think we're all out of our minds," Barry said.

A week later, Mario called the Zoo Crew to an after-work meeting on the thirty-ninth floor, to be held in the small Harrison Hart conference room adjoining the company library. When they got there, they found a huge map of New York City sprawled on the conference table. Little red circles marked about a dozen locations.

"Gentlemen," Mario said, when they'd all arrived, "I've been doing some preliminary work on our project, as promised."

"Me too," Glen said. "And I've come up with a name."

"Do tell," Neil said, mocking him.

"Okay. Well, we're the Zoo Crew, right?" He looked around the room. "And we protect companies like lions protect their den."

"A den?" Dennis asked.

"That's right," Glen allowed, "and like all lions we need a den to call our own."

"Any objections?" Mario asked, looking around the room. "Good. The Lions' Den. It's settled. So we have a name."

"What we don't have—yet—is a location. Now I've met with half the real estate agents in the city. I haven't been able to find the right place."

"What?" Dennis said, "Nothing in SoHo or Gramercy? What about Chelsea?"

"Nothing on the west side, Mario?" Neil asked. "No available co-ops, or brownstones, or even loft buildings in the village that could be remodeled? None, in all of Manhattan or even across the river in Jersey City or Hoboken?"

"Oh, there's plenty of those," Mario said, "but they're either too public, or too small, or not centralized enough, or the co-op boards would never allow it, or there are zoning problems or something."

"Maybe a quarter mil between us isn't enough between us," Dennis suggested. "Maybe we should up the ante."

"Jesus," Glen said, "this is ridiculous. This is New *fuckin'* York City. All we're looking for is a nice place to get laid, for cryin' out loud."

"Yes," came a sultry voice from behind a set of bookshelves, "it can be difficult to find a place to fuck." The Zoo Crew turned and beheld Kat strolling out of the library stacks into the conference room. She was eating an apple and holding a book. "Especially if it's a *sperm* of the moment thing... *ba dum bum*." The Zoo Crew stared at her, gape-jawed.

Mario asked the question that was on all of their minds. "How long were you, uh, standing there, Kat?"

"Oh, I was in the library before you boys came in," she said brightly. "I was rummaging around in the stacks, doing some research. I heard everything."

"Shit," Glen muttered. "Shit, shit, shit!"

"I guess that ends *that*," Neil said, shaking his head.

"Stop jumping to conclusions, Neil," Kat instructed. "Something good has just happened here and none of you are sharp enough to see it."

"Meaning what?" Mario asked.

"Meaning I'm not the type to run down to Judith Clarke and tell her my colleagues are in the executive conference room planning..."

"You blackmailing us, Kat?"

"Don't get your zipper stuck, Neil." Her eyes strayed to one of the red circles on the map. "Is this one of your potential locations?"

"It's one we're considering," said Mario, not looking down at the map.

"Well, you may also want to consider that the theatre traffic will add forty-five minutes to your commute home." She removed her reading glasses and guided them along the map. "You can detour through Hell's Kitchen in order to hit the West Side Highway, but if you live in Jersey it'll take an hour just to get to either the Holland or Lincoln tunnel."

Neil glanced at Mario, then back at Kat. "What about the West Village? We would have easy access to both the East and West Side Highways, as well as all the tunnels and bridges."

"That's true, Kat said, "but the Twenty-Third Street district zoning law prohibits any dwelling in the garment district over four stories, unless it's also a commercial building with a loading zone."

"How is it you know so much about city ordinances, Kat?" Barry asked.

"I have four brothers and a dozen uncles and they're all in city government—cops, firefighters, building inspectors, assistant district attorneys, facility managers, some of them pretty high up on the food chain. In fact, my godfather is an appellate judge."

Barry was the first to understand. "So, if there's any zoning problem…"

"I can make it go poof," she said. "Likewise building inspection problems. I'm privy to city building de-acquisitions before any real estate agent gets wind of them. I can also tell you about city development projects before they hit the newspapers. And if you should run into any legal problems…"

"You can make those go away, too?" Barry asked hopefully.

"What makes you think we would accept help from you, Kat?" Mario asked.

"Because without me this will always be a dream."

Neil decided this was the time to take Kat down a peg or two. "If your family is so damn influential," he said, "how come they couldn't get you reinstated at your teaching job?"

"What do you mean reinstated?" Mario asked.

"Kat woman over here told her third-grade class there was no Santa Claus and got canned for it. Ain't that right, Kat."

"So, you checked me out. Kudos. I'm impressed. You're right. My brothers don't have all that much influence with the Archdiocese. If you're talking about the city government and municipalities, though, they practically run the place."

"You really have that much influence?" Barry asked.

"I'm the baby sister, the only girl in the entire extended family."

Mario caught Dennis's eye and Dennis shrugged. He got the same reaction from Neil, then Barry. Glen was resting his head on the table, face down.

"What do you want from us, Kat?" Mario asked.

"Who says I want something?"

"You're ready to keep quiet about what we're doing and even help us," Mario pointed out. "You *must* want something."

Kat thought a moment. "Okay, first, I want you to stop treating me like I took the lollipop from your little apprentice. I deserve to be judged on my own merits."

Mario didn't bat an eye. "You said 'first.' There's more?"

"Yeah. I want in."

The Zoo Crew looked at each other and laughed.

"Why?" Mario asked.

"Couple of things you guys don't know about me," Kat replied. "I'm as much a player as any of you…"

"We got that," Glen said. "We also got that you're not playing with any of *us*."

"Nothing personal, Glen, honey," Kat said with a little purr. "But play is play and business is business. No mixing. And I need this place as much as any of you. I live in a very classy eastside townhouse and I don't want the doorman telling my high-society neighbors I'm bringing a different person home every night. Wouldn't fit my image." She looked at Mario. "Capice?"

Glen caught the odd word. "Person."

"Yeah," Kat said. "I swing both ways. Doesn't matter."

Glen's eyebrows shot up to mid-forehead, and Barry's jaw dropped. But it was Dennis who had the perfect comeback, "No," he said matter-of-factly, "of course not. Doesn't matter at all."

"We'll let you know, Kat," Mario said as sincerely as he could manage.

Mario spent weeks talking to more real estate agents, visiting property after property and finding something wrong with each one of them. Either they were too visible, or zoning regulations prohibited what the Zoo Crew had in mind. There was only one solution and Mario knew it. The rest of the Zoo Crew knew it as well. That afternoon, Mario set up a meeting in the conference room and asked Kat to come.

"We've discussed this at length, Kat. We've decided to accept your offer, on one condition."

Kat laughed. "And what might that be?"

"Here it is," Mario said. "No special treatment or privileges because you're a woman. You're going to get treated like everyone else in the Zoo Crew."

"That's all I've ever asked for," Kat said and smiled. "Now let's see if we can find ourselves a little piece of heaven."

A week later, Mario asked the Zoo Crew to meet him and Kat at the East Side Heliport.

"We're flying someplace?" Glen asked.

"Just to keep the trip short," Mario said.

They all squeezed inside a small chartered helicopter, which flew up the East River, over the bridges connecting Manhattan with Brooklyn and Queens, past the luxury apartments of the Upper East Side and Gracie Mansion.

"Where the hell are we going?" Barry shouted over the whopping sound of the blades.

"Trust me on this," Mario yelled back.

"Trust me?" Neil said, turning to Glen. "Doesn't that mean 'fuck you' in Italian."

The chopper set down on Ward's Island, at the tip of Manhattan, on a grassy field just north of the footbridge to the city, and west of the Triborough

Bridge and the parallel Hell's Gate Bridge, which ran between the Bronx and Queens.

"Where the fuck are we?" Glen asked, looking around, trying to orient himself.

"Gentleman—and lady," Mario said proudly, "this is Ward's Island and the future site of the Lions' Den."

The Zoo Crew scanned the site, everyone confused.

"It's mostly park now," Kat added. "But it used to be a potter's field, and there was a hospital for immigrants here."

"You're thinking of building something here?" Dennis asked.

"No, no…we already got the building. Needs some work, but when we're finished with it, it'll be perfect."

"How did you find out about this place?"

"The fire department once had a training facility here," answered Kat. "My uncle is the ex-deputy commissioner."

Neil looked around. There were half a dozen old stone buildings on the island. "One of *those* buildings?" he asked, dubious.

"Yeah," Mario said. "It's just a short walk. We'll put in a flagstone path later." All he had to do, he thought, was get their imaginations working.

"I feel like I'm a million miles from the office," Dennis said.

"Exactly," Mario told him. "It's really isolated, but it's only about twenty minutes from Lower Manhattan. And every highway and tunnel out of the city is easily accessible.

"Okay," Neil said. "Let's see it."

Mario led the party through ankle-high grass toward a smallish, three-story stone building at the south end of the island. They stopped about thirty yards away from it and Mario made a grand, sweeping gesture of introduction.

Barry stood looking at the building, eyebrows knit, biting his lip. "That's it?"

"Magnificent, isn't it?" Mario said.

"It's really something," Neil said, trying hard not to disagree. "Just what is it?"

"It used to be part of the Manhattan Psychiatric Hospital."

"A nut house?" Glen asked. "What are we going to do, start it up again?"

Kat ignored him. "Except for my uncle, no one even knows the city is selling it. Municipal buildings are usually auctioned, but he's arranged for us to buy it below the opening bid."

"Which is?" Barry inquired.

"Just $234,000."

"Of course it needs to be cleaned up," Mario admitted. "But it's going to be stunning, I guarantee you."

"I just wish it were a little closer," Dennis observed.

"But that's good," Mario told him. "Nobody's going to be bothering us up here, no crowds, no traffic, *no* Judith Clarke—under the radar, like we wanted."

"And we won't have any zoning problems," Kat assured them. "No one will even know we're here."

"How much is this going to cost us when it's finished?" Barry asked.

"I haven't figured that out yet," Mario said. "It's gonna cost us, that's for sure. But we'll have an asset that matches any other property in Manhattan.

"Shall we go in?" Mario suggested. He led the way, excited.

They opened the door, and entered the building, suddenly finding themselves in the dark. Mario had brought a flashlight, but it barely made a dent in the blackness, and the tiny windows were mostly blocked by foliage. The building was old and full of debris and cobwebs. The place reeked of mold.

"I haven't been able to get the electricity turned on yet. Another couple of days and you'll be able to see it better," Kat explained.

"C'mon, guys," Mario said, leading the way. "I'm going to take you for a tour." He headed down a dark hallway, stopping at each room and turning his flashlight into the gloom within.

"We must be in the asshole of the world," Dennis said.

"This was the conference room," Kat said, her voice echoing off the stone walls. "And the room across the hall was used for collaborative diagnosis."

"Now back here," Mario said, turning a corner, "is the kitchen. It's huge—more than big enough for our needs."

"Holy shit!" shouted Glen.

"What's wrong?" Mario asked.

"Over there, I saw a creature with evil red eyes and an ass bigger than Barry's. Quick. Kill it!"

Mario swung the flashlight around toward the darkest corner of the room. A large rat was casually observing them, as if he were the master of the domain and they were the intruders.

"I'm out of here," Glen said, panicked, and he headed for the door.

"Right behind you," said Barry.

"What a bunch of candy asses," Kat said. She snatched the flashlight out of Mario's hand, took three steps, and swung the light toward the rodent, which scurried off, barely avoiding the blow. "I think it's safe now," she said sarcastically.

Glen and Barry rejoined the group and Mario led on, back to the grand staircase, shining the flashlight around so the Zoo Crew could see the elaborate carvings and fixtures.

"So, when did the Adams Family leave?" Dennis asked. "Or is Lurch still hanging around?"

Mario walked to the center of the grand lobby. "Don't you guys have any imagination?" Mario asked, using his arms to create imaginary pictures. "Can't you see it after the decorators are finished…"

"Don't forget the exterminators," Glen said.

"Maybe we should give the Ghostbusters a crack at it, too," Dennis chided.

"It's going to take plenty of work, that's for sure." That was Neil's way of saying it was going to cost a fortune.

"I'd say six or seven million, depending on how upscale we go," Barry said.

"Jesus Christ," Dennis said softly.

"Seven million?" Glen said, in awe. "Ain't no pussy worth seven million."

"I wouldn't even masturbate in this shithole," Neil said.

"Where are we going to come up with that bread, Mario?" Dennis asked.

Barry pulled out his Blackberry and started crunching numbers. "Let's say we mortgage the place for seven million. At five percent and fifteen years…"

"Yes, it'll be expensive," admitted Mario."But we're going to have the best private club in the world."

"Mario, I hate to say it," Glen said, "but I think this is beyond my reach. I mean it's great and all that, and I'm sure it would be wonderful once we clean it up, but I'm going to have to opt out of this one. You know, Amanda's medical expenses are stretching me pretty thin."

"Sure, Glen, I understand. I'm disappointed, but I understand." But he didn't.

"You better count me out, too," Dennis said. "It's a bold idea, but there's a reason no one's ever done it before. We'd have to be nuts to take this place. No pun intended."

"Use your imagination, Dennis," Mario urged. "Picture it the way it will be when it's finished. Trust me."

"I do trust you, Mario," Dennis said. "But I have to part company with you this time—this is just…well…too much, even for us."

Mario turned to Neil. "You know me, boss," Neil said. "Where you go, I go. But if it's just you, me, and Kat woman, I have no idea how we can swing it."

"We already own the building, Neil," Mario said.

"Then we'll just flip it and get our money back," Neil countered. "We'll still have a chance to find the right place."

"You're all idiots," Mario said, steaming. "No imagination, no balls. We have an incredible opportunity here and we're going to blow it because you're all pussies."

"The way I see it, Mario," Dennis said, "this is *your* big daydream. For the rest of us, it would be a good thing—but frankly, we could live without it."

"We *have* been living without it," Glen pointed out.

"Well, fuck you," Mario said. "Fuck all of you. Go take your women to Howard Johnson's for all I care."

He stormed outside, toward the helicopter, furious, the Zoo Crew following, silently.

The ride back to Wall Street was awkward and uncomfortable.

CHAPTER ELEVEN

The next few days at Harrison Hart's M&A Department were not happy ones—none of the usual horseplay and hilarity, in fact, no talking at all, about women, about money, about fantasy football, nothing except about business. And for the first time since destiny had brought them together at Hart, what the Zoo Crew had seemed to be slipping away from them.

While the others communicated in flat, quiet monotones, Barry worked away at his desk. He finally caught Mario just after work, when everyone else had gone home, and asked to talk to him.

"What's on your mind, Barry?" Mario asked.

"I think I may have a way to do this Lions' Den thing."

Mario hesitated, then shrugged. "Say what you have to say."

"Okay. You've got a great idea for a private club, but just too few members to make it financially."

"So we add ten more guys," Mario said. "Won't be hard. Will that do it?"

"Nope. But ninety more would."

"What? That's your solution—add ninety more guys?" This was going nowhere, Mario thought.

"Do the math, Mario. With a membership of 100, we could easily support a fifteen-year, eight-million-dollar mortgage, including renovation and upkeep. If we went for a thirty-year, we could do it with about sixty-five members."

"This was just supposed to be for us, not every horn dog on The Street," Mario objected.

"Except for me, it would only be for married ones...with *our* problem."

"What married guy is gonna pay..."

"If you build it, they will come," Barry winked. "Only we'll be playing on a *different* 'Field of Dreams.'"

Mario considered what Barry was saying. "You used the word 'members.'"

"Like at a health club. We sell gold key memberships for $1,000 a month, all inclusive."

Mario shook his head. "Won't work. Everybody in Lower Manhattan will find out about it in about fifteen minutes and our wives will be next. Next thing you know, I'm living in a basement apartment, driving my kids to the movies every other weekend in my Chevy Geo."

"Thought about that," Barry said. "The membership contracts will have a non-disclosure clause. Sort of like a disclaimer."

"Keep talking," Mario said. This is starting to make sense, he thought.

"Anyhow, Mario, look at it this way: it's like meeting your boss in a dirty bookstore. Neither of you wants to talk about it afterward, much less tell anyone else. Mutual assured destruction," Barry said, grinning.

"Okay," said Mario, "but let me ask you a question: with all of those members, how would we keep control of the place?"

"We incorporate. We're the fucking officers and the only stockholders."

"Barry, you're a fuckin' genius. But will everyone else get on board?"

"Not only is everyone on board, but they're already in the cockpit waiting for our captain to take us up."

They both smiled.

"This is the first time you've been to my office in what, five years?" Frank said. He was in the middle of eating a hot pastrami on rye.

"I've been meaning to visit," Mario said, looking around the messy office appreciatively, although there wasn't much to appreciate—wooden desks, a carpet that had seen better days, fixtures that were brand new—twenty years ago—and windows that looked out over the Kings County district courthouses of downtown Brooklyn.

"Hey, you want coffee?"

"Yeah, two lumps. Cream."

Frank relayed the request to Margaret, his gal Friday, who appeared soon afterward with a little tray carrying not only two steaming cups of coffee, but a selection of Pepperidge Farm cookies.

"So, what do I owe the pleasure? Is someone suing you, Mario? No paternity suits, I hope." He laughed.

"No one is suing me, Frank. But this needs to be confidential. It's about a project I'm working on—and it's a good thing."

"You want to consult me on a confidential legal matter and it's a good thing? Okay, tell me about this project of yours. Building a separate bedroom away from Phyllis?" He laughed again.

"Are you finished, Frank?"

"Sorry."

Mario quickly laid out the Lions' Den's basic details and the Zoo Crew's plan for financing it.

Frank nodded slightly, contemplating what he had just heard. Then he punched the button on his office intercom. "Margaret," he said, "could you call the psych ward over at Bellevue. There's a lunatic in my office."

Margaret's voice came over the intercom. "Yes, Mr. Monelli," she said, giggling. "Shall I ask them to bring a straight jacket?"

"Good idea. And a Hannibal mask."

"Having a good time, Frank?" Mario asked. "You don't like our little project?"

"Oh, I like it all right. It's a very entertaining idea. But I can see a dozen different ways it could get you arrested, or lose your career or your family."

"Arrested? You're exaggerating, Frank. Anyhow, if there *are* any pitfalls, I'm sure you'll figure out how to avoid them."

"You think I'm gonna risk being disbarred over this?"

"You're acting as a legal adviser, Frank. No one's breaking the law."

"Remember the last time you went into business with the Zoo Crew. You bought that race horse. The one you swore was going to be the next Secretariat. What was its name?"

"Rear Guard," Mario said.

Frank tried not to laugh. "That's it," he said. "*Rear Guard.* Didn't the name give you a clue?"

"Will you forget the fuckin' horse, Frank?"

"Okay, Mario, but I'm really not the man to do this. You really should be talking to some of your slimy corporate lawyer friends on Wall Street."

"I'm just asking you to be our legal adviser Frank."

"Right," Frank said, finally resigned to it. "Okay, let's start at the beginning. This place is going to need a liquor license?"

"Well, sure. But we got that covered."

"I hope so. What about zoning regulations?"

"All been fixed."

"Have I ever told you how much I disliked that word, Mario?"

"Relax, Frank, we have a contact in the city administration. Someone influential who will take care of all of the details."

"And they'll do it legally?"

"It will be legal because *they'll* be doing it."

"I assume you've got the building permit covered as well?"

"All fixed. Sorry, all taken care of."

Frank leaned forward in his chair. "Mario, are you absolutely sure you want to go through with this, um, thing? It's going to take up a lot of time, not all of it fun, it's going to cost a lot of money—more than you think, I'm sure, it could end up making you some enemies on The Street, and if Phyllis ever finds out…"

"I've weighed the dangers, Frank. But Hef said something to me that night that really got me thinking. He said, 'You're living your life as though you'll do better next time.' Well, there isn't any next time, Frank. My time is here, right now. In five years I'll be as old as pop was when he died."

Frank looked at his brother thoughtfully. "I understand all that, Mario, but…"

"I'm just living my life despite Phyllis…like you said."

"Stop looking at me that way, Mario. You're making me feel like I'm stealing your candy bar. I'll help. Okay?"

Mario smiled. "Thanks, Frank."

"We'll need to set up a shell company where we can wash the money so it leaves no paper trail to the stockholders."

"Good thinking, Frank."

"Then we'll need to set up another off-shore bank account and draft some confidentiality agreements between the Zoo Crew."

"No problem."

Frank turned a page on his legal pad. "Good. Now let's get to the incorporation stuff. Where do you want it incorporated?"

Mario shrugged. "New York, of course."

"I'd ask your attorneys, or whomever you choose, to set it up in Delaware, or better yet, the Cayman Islands," Frank said, answering his own question.

"You know what's best."

"What's best is to forget about this whole crazy idea. But you're not going to do that, are you?"

"Keep going," Mario said, pointing at Frank's legal pad. He knew his brother would make sure it was done right.

"You're definitely going to need a manager, a kind of combination *maitre d', concierge* and purser."

Frank threw his pen down and put his face in his hands and sighed. When he came up for air, he was smiling. "I know the perfect guy," he said. "He couldn't be more perfect if he were made for the job."

"Who's that?" Mario asked. "What job—the manager job?"

"Duncan Spencer. He's a client of mine. Managed the Plaza Hotel for three years. British servant type, used to arrange vice for high-ranking politicians while in New York."

"Trustworthy?"

"You kidding? He *has* to keep quiet. If he's caught doing anything illegal, he'll be deported."

"Perfect. Let's set up a meeting," Mario said.

Frank scribbled a note on his pad. "Okay. Now, what's the name of your contractor? And your architect?"

Something occurred to Mario. He slipped his wallet out of his pocket and began rifling through it, finally coming up with a dog-eared business card. "What about *this* guy," he said, handing the card to Frank.

Frank studied the card skeptically. "Roger Duvall," he read. "What do you know about this guy?"

"Not a lot. I just met him."

"Margaret," Frank said into the intercom, "could you come in here a moment."

The door opened and Margaret entered. She was a formidable looking woman in her mid-fifties with a glint of mischief in her eye. "What now, Matlock?"

He handed her the business card. "See if you can get Burt to give me a quick fix on this guy."

Margaret took the card and left.

"Burt?" asked Mario.

"My PI—private investigator to you. He knows where the rocks are and what's under them. Or who."

A few moments after she left, Margaret buzzed in. "I have Burt on the line."

Frank pressed a button on his phone. "Burt, I'm putting you on speaker. I have my brother here. He's the one who's making the inquiry."

"Hey, Burt, this is Mario."

"Nice to meet you, Mario," came the voice over the speakerphone.

"What do you got for us?" asked Frank.

"Turns out I had a file on Duvall."

"Does he have a record?" Mario asked.

"No, no—just the opposite," Burt said. "Everything I have on him is positive. He's very respected in his field, done some impressive work for some important people, designed the Exxon exhibit at Epcot, lead architect on the Absolut Vodka corporate headquarters, played a major role in creating the layout for the Museum of Modern Art, even worked on the new tower at Ground Zero."

"Pretty impressive stuff," Mario said.

"Thanks, Burt," Frank said. "Let me know if you find anything we should be concerned about."

He punched the button ending the conversation and turned to Mario.

"See," said Mario. "We're going to do our due diligence on this, Frank. It's not some stupid, wild-eyed adventure."

Frank gazed at his brother ruefully. "As I recall, Mario, that's what Napoleon said just before he invaded Russia."

The next morning, Mario called Roger Duvall, who, to put it mildly, was quite surprised to hear from him. "I don't get much work from my drunk tank contacts," he admitted.

"Let's call it a happy coincidence," Mario suggested. "Anyhow, I've got a project on my hands, and from what I hear, you might be the perfect man for it."

"Oh, my dear, I'm not perfect. But I *am* very, very good."

Mario laughed.

"Now, dear, tell me about your project," Roger continued.

"Well, I can't tell you the details, not over the phone. Are you free this afternoon?"

"As a bird, my love."

By the time Mario got to the East Side Heliport, it was drizzling and threatening a downpour. Roger showed up dressed like Howard Hughes— dashing studded calfskin jacket, vintage smoked flying goggles with round lenses, immaculate jodhpurs, pressed to a knife's edge. He was carrying an enormous umbrella, decorated with a fairly good reproduction of Monet's "Water Lilies."

"Better circumstances than last time," Roger observed. He held his hand out and Mario shook it firmly, but briefly.

"So, where are we headed, love?"

"North—to Ward's Island, at the uptown top of Manhattan."

The pilot waved them aboard the helicopter and minutes later, they landed on Ward's Island. They walked toward the grey stone building Mario had picked out.

"Oh, my," Roger said in admiration, "that's part of the old Manhattan Psychiatric Center, isn't it? I have friends who…oh, never mind.. What do you want to do with it?"

"I want to make it into a private—extremely private—club for some of my high profile Wall Street, umm, associates, a luxurious and comfortable place where they can bring their women friends and relax, without interruption."

A sly smile crossed Roger's lips. "Of course," he said. "What a perfectly delicious idea."

They stood in front of the building, gazing at it, Mario hoping, Roger evaluating, measuring it with his eyes from one angle, then another. Mario handed Roger the key and the decorator marched up to the massive front door and disappeared inside, Mario following.

They were in some kind of grand lobby now, with a ceiling three stories high. Roger walked around, poking a head into one room, then another, then climbing the stairs and repeating himself.

"So exactly what do you boys have in mind?" Roger said, taking a deep drag on his cigarette holder.

"I wanna create the ultimate fantasy," Mario replied.

"You know," Roger said, still taking stock of the place. "I once did something similar for Steve Wynn—on a much smaller scale of course."

"The Steve Wynn who owns the Bellagio?"

"The very same."

Now Roger set off on a tour of the building, Mario watching as patiently as possible. Finally, after about fifteen minutes, he could contain himself no longer. "What do you think, Roger? Will it work? Can you do it?"

"Oh, yes," Roger said expansively, "yes indeedy. Absolutely yes. I can make it into what you've been imagining, Mario, a very citadel of hedonism. Hefner will shrivel up with jealousy."

"Is seven million enough?"

"For starters. I may have to cut a corner or two. Are the blueprints in that tube?"

Roger fished the blueprints out of the tube Mario was holding, unfurled them and began studying them, uttering an occasional "hmmm," "oh my!" and "good lord."

"And how long do you think will it take, Roger?"

"Well, let's see," Roger said, looking up. "The building is rock solid, no pun intended. We can make the room layout work just fine. The electricity and the plumbing are a mess, but that's to be expected. With a decent-sized crew—and I know exactly the right girls—maybe three months."

"This is highly confidential, Roger. You can't put it on your resume."

"Of course, dearie, my lips are sealed."

As they stepped out of the main door into the dusk, Roger raised his umbrella and Mario put on his trench coat.

"You know something, Roger," said Mario, as they strolled arm in arm through the fog, toward the chopper, "this might be the beginning of a beautiful friendship."

SEC Chairman, Randy Hollinsworth, stood in the middle of his office, trying to concentrate on putting golf balls into a little metal cup. "Not even a whisper?" he said. "No connections at all?"

"I'm afraid not," said his chief investigator, Elliot Case. "We've run the tapes through the NSA's best computer algorithms, and we have yet to come up with anything warranting closer investigation."

Hollinsworth putted again, and missed. He laid the club on a windowsill, looked past the Washington Monument and out toward the Potomac for a few moments, then sat down heavily behind his desk, frustration clearly etched on his face.

"What search terms are you using?" asked Ben Hersh, the SEC's deputy director. Hersh hadn't come to the SEC the usual way, as a famous Wall Street high roller. He'd gone to Fordham Law School, been part of the New York State Attorney General's organized crime task force under Rudolph Giuliani, and had grown up in a tough section of south Boston, and was known as much for his tenacity as his brains.

"Everything we can think of," Case responded. "Saudi, Royal Family, buyout, takeover, abdication, refuge, majority interest, Swiss accounts—about fifty terms, altogether, individually, and in many different combinations."

Hollinsworth shook his head, grimly, "And we haven't caught a thing?"

"We've intercepted over 11,000 possibles, but they've all been false alarms," Case said. "And you wouldn't believe how many conversations are about sex. If you can believe them, half the married guys on Wall Street are getting more ass than a public toilet."

"You heard anything from your friend, Fisher?" Ben asked.

"He told me he has his best people working on it," Hollinsworth said. "And if we don't get anything from the intercepts, they may be our last chance."

CHAPTER TWELVE

It took almost two weeks of late-night meetings at Craveth, Swaine, and Moore, New York's acknowledged experts in corporate law, to put The Lions' Den, Ltd. together—two weeks of sometimes angry arguing and debating, two weeks of compromises, loophole closing and covering-everyone's-ass amendments to the corporate charter and the by-laws, two weeks of subsisting on cold pizza and warm diet soda.

What finally emerged, at least apparently, was a completely legal entity, all irregularities, questionable provisions, and grey areas invisible except to expert and highly suspicious eyes, vague and innocuous Delaware incorporation papers, a numbered bank account in the Cayman Islands, and plans for overseas structured financing, to assure security.

Guiding this fledgling enterprise was a full board of directors, which by some astounding coincidence, comprised the entire membership of the Zoo Crew: Mario, ordained as president and CEO; Neil, vice president; Barry, CFO; Glen, secretary; Kat, director of government relations; and Dennis, director of security. Frank Monelli was appointed chief counsel.

All of this was wrapped in non-disclosure agreements designed to preserve the confidential status and operations not only of the officers, but of everyone who might ever become a member, security provisions so tight they would have impressed the sentries guarding Area 51.

Mario and the Zoo Crew came up with a list of more than thirty-two high profile Wall Street friends that they knew, without doubt, were a) wealthy, b) trustworthy and c) married and incurably horny and d) whose behavior made them vulnerable to scandal. That left sixty-eight spaces to fill, a good portion of which they hoped would come from the recommendations of the first thirty-two.

At the same time, Kat spoke with a few of her relatives in government and obtained a liquor license and all relevant zoning and building clearances.

Finally, they got the money. That was settled at a meeting at a run-of-the-mill chophouse in the west forties, Mario bringing Barry for his mortgage expertise. Bill Bronson, Fallon Financial's IPO golden boy, just back from Belize and sporting a glowing tan, was already waiting for them at a rear table, a large black briefcase sitting by his knee. It contained mortgage documents that would yield eight million dollars in cold hard cash in exchange for lifetime privileges at the Lions' Den. Mario nodded. "Anything I have to worry about in these documents?"

"Not a thing. You've got the boilerplate the partners reserve for their own children. But...there is one caveat: this is a one-time offer, paisan. You can't dip into the well again. Eight million—untraceable—is major coin," Bill reminded him. "I had to go overseas for part of it. No other bank is going to rescue you if you get in over your head."

"Where overseas did you go for it?"

"You mean who banked us?" Bill replied. "Let's just say *In-fidelity Trust*." That was his way of saying, it's best you don't know.

"Thanks for the warning, Bill, but don't worry. I know what I'm doing."

Mario slipped the papers into a jacket pocket. "I'll have my brother take a look at these and get them back to you before the day is over."

"And you'll have the check tomorrow morning," said Bill Bronson. "Who do you want it made out to?"

"The Lions' Den Co., Ltd.," Mario told him.

"Lions, eh?" Bill smiled and said. "They have big schlongs."

That afternoon, Mario phoned Roger on the cab ride to Brooklyn. "Okay, my friend. The financing is in place. You can start drawing up the plans."

"Halfway finished, m'dear," Roger said. "I'll call you when they're ready for your inspection."

Mario and Neil arrived at Frank's Brooklyn office just before noon. They'd gathered to meet with the most likely candidate to manage the Lions' Den, Duncan Spencer.

At twelve o'clock sharp, Margaret escorted a tall man into the conference room, conservatively dressed, complete with a grey fedora, with the bearing of Field Marshal Montgomery. "Gentlemen," Frank said, "this is Duncan Spencer. Duncan, this is my brother Mario and his associate, Neil Granger."

"Good afternoon, gentlemen. Please beg pardon for my tardiness." His words curved richly around his muted British accent. He tugged the gloves from his hand one at a time and handed them to Frank, along with his hat and overcoat, neatly folded.

Mario was puzzled. "You were on time to the minute."

"In my profession, perfect service demands being five minutes earlier than expected."

"Have a seat, Spencer," Frank said.

"Care for a soft drink?" Mario asked.

"Tea would be splendid?" Spencer said hopefully.

"Margaret, get him some tea." Frank said.

"We've read your résumé," Mario said. "Your credentials are quite impressive. You were the manager of the Royal Garden Hotel in Kensington for three years?"

"Yes, sir. I moved on after we were given our fifth star. I was asked to supervise the staff at the Hotel Amarante on the Champs-Elysées in Paris."

"A five-star hotel?" Neil asked.

"Well, yes, naturally," Spencer replied. "At any rate, I was there for about six years until some American chaps, who turned out to be the owners of the Plaza Hotel, convinced me to cross the pond and supervise their operation here in New York."

"Impressive," Mario said. "Has my brother told you what's on our minds?"

"Only that you're looking for someone to oversee a very exclusive gentlemen's club."

"Yes, a club for high-profile wealthy men and whatever, shall we say, *guests* they might happen to bring with them," Mario replied.

"If I have the good fortune to look after the establishment," Spencer said, "I would expect that my duties would be to supply the members their every desire, hopefully before they knew they had it."

Mario looked at Frank, obviously impressed.

"But we're not talking about a brothel," Neil added.

Spencer feigned shock. "A house of ill repute? Nothing so tasteless, gentlemen. I would never associate myself with anything less than top class, unless, of course, a guest required it."

That kind of flexibility could be very useful, Mario thought. "Now, Spencer, if we hire you, you'll be responsible for the entire facility—that includes day-to-day operations-devoted to insuring everyone's pleasure."

"You might get some pretty off-the-wall requests," Neil cautioned. "Some may be in a grey area, you know, when it comes to legality."

"Grey is one of my favorite colors," Spencer said.

"Then there's the matter of sex," Mario said. "What's your attitude toward sex? At the club, I mean."

"Of course, I only indulge on special occasions, since I have such a delicate constitution," Spencer replied. "But I encourage others whenever I can."

"What did he say?" Neil asked Mario.

"He said he approves of fucking."

"I have to raise one more subject," Mario went on. "Everything that happens in our little club must be, well...confidential. Who goes there and what they do while they're there can never be revealed to anyone."

"You down with that?" Neil asked.

A strange look passed over Spencer's face. Then, quite unexpectedly, he started tittering.

Mario looked at Frank.

Spencer took one deep breath and instantly regained control. "Pardon me, gentlemen," he said, "but it's the irony. You see, gentlemen, my previous employer terminated me, with prejudice, I might add, precisely because I was unwilling to reveal information to him or to the authorities about certain, shall I say, occurrences in the hotel."

"You were fired because you wouldn't rat? Neil asked.

"Precisely," Spencer said. "I am the soul of discretion. It is a quality that has been ingrained in me since birth. I learned it from my father, who learned it from *his* father, who learned it…well, my family have been members of the serving class since the days of Queen Elizabeth. The first, of course."

Mario looked at Frank. "Did you know that's why he'd been fired, Frank?"

"I knew that there'd been some kind of scandal at the Plaza regarding some U.N. officials and that Spencer was the chief casualty, but I didn't know the details. He wouldn't tell me, which is why I can't help him fight deportation."

"You mean you would rather be deported than give up names?" Mario asked.

"Just doing my duty, as I saw fit," Spencer said with convincing modesty.

They talked for another half hour about the services that the Lions' Den would offer, about the employees it would need, about the likely character of the members, and the grand opening schedule. The meeting was about to break up when Spencer raised another subject.

"Oh, one more thing, gentlemen. About that deportation order hanging over my head."

"Ah, yes," Mario said. "When are you scheduled to leave for the U.K.?"

"They're kicking him out early next month," said Frank.

"Kat could probably take care of that," Neil suggested to Mario.

"You chaps would earn my undying loyalty."

"Exactly what we had in mind," Mario said, exchanging grins with Neil.

Mario and Tyler Gentry strolled toward the clubhouse, entrusting their clubs to their caddies. It was the third time in a year they'd flown down to Augusta to golf at Bobby Jones' famous course, the site of the annual Master's Tournament.

Tyler always invited someone on his golfing excursions and picked up the tab. But it never really cost him anything because there was always a bet involved and he was an accomplished golfer, and his guests knew better than to beat him. More often than not, in fact, Tyler ended up making a profit on the weekend, and his guests had to grin and bear it, even Mario.

"What happened to you at the Amen Corner?" Tyler asked, twisting the knife a little.

"I don't know," Mario said. "Somehow, I always end up in a stand of pine trees hacking worms. Maybe I need new clubs."

"Remember, Mario, clubs don't make the golfer," Tyler said. "The golfer makes the clubs."

"So you keep telling me," Mario said evenly. He wished he hadn't given his clubs to the caddy. He wanted to bounce one of his titanium drivers off Tyler's skull, just to see how it would sound—a thunk? A thwang? A kind of loud pop? Who could say.

They were approaching Augusta's beautiful but unpretentious clubhouse now, a two-story, white colonnaded wooden structure, surmounted by a wide cupola, guarded by a giant live oak and ringed by sidewalks lined with rose bushes.

"Where to?" Mario asked.

"The upper veranda?" Tyler suggested.

"Anyplace, as long as we can get out of the sun. I'm melting."

They climbed the outside stairway, past a stand of azaleas and settled into two dark green wicker chairs when a smiling, white-coated elderly black-skinned waiter approached them. "Afternoon, Mr. Gentry," he said. "Good day on the course?"

Tyler tried to put it gently. "For me, yes. For Mr. Monelli, well, not so much."

"Maybe next time, Mr. Monelli," the waiter said diplomatically.

"Bring us a couple of mint juleps, Tucker," Tyler said.

Mario had prepared for this moment, which he knew was inevitable. He fished his check book out of his golf jacket. "How much?" he asked.

"We can take care of that later, Mario," Tyler said. "Let's just relax and enjoy the beautiful landscaping."

"How much?" Mario repeated.

"$11,500. I took twelve holes and beat you by a total of nine strokes."

Mario didn't bother to check Tyler's calculations. He scribbled in the numbers, ripped out the check and handed it to his boss. "Good game," he said.

"Well, you're getting better, Mario. Someday you're going to surprise us both."

"It'll be *quite* a surprise," Mario said, reminding himself that this was never going to happen.

"Speaking of surprises, Mario, I was surprised to hear about this little club of yours."

God damn it! Mario thought. How could he know? "Club? You mean the Callaways you've been touting?"

"Mario, Mario, I'm talking about the secret men's club you and your guys are building out on Ward's."

"I don't know what you're talking about, Tyler." But he did.

"C'mon, Mario, think I don't know what goes on in my own office? Tyler sees all and knows all—everything that happens at Harrison Hart."

Either he's been bugging my office, Mario thought, or Hamilton somehow got wind and blabbed. Anyhow he thought it best not to deny it. "I wasn't trying to keep anything from you, Tyler. The whole thing is just in the talking stage."

"That so?" Tyler asked. "Then what about the building?"

"Oh, that's still in the option stage, too."

"You know, Mario, before we merged with your company we kept a number of swank Fifth Avenue apartments...for executives and their girlfriends. Oh, not for me, of course," he chuckled. "I'm a happily married man, as you know."

Mario finally realized how he should handle this. "We could use some seed money, though. Got a spare two hundred grand lying around?"

That got the desired response. "Oh, well, no, no, I'm not looking for an investment. Besides, I have fiduciary responsibilities to the firm, and there's the partners to consider. You understand, I'm sure."

"Relax, Tyler, I was joking," Mario said, affecting a disappointed expression. At that moment, to Mario's relief, Tucker arrived with their drinks.

CHAPTER THIRTEEN

"Today is green light day," Roger had told Mario over the phone, meaning that the sketches and blueprints were ready and construction could begin as soon as Mario gave the okay.

Mario and Neil grabbed their coats and hailed a cab.

"Where does our friend live again?" Neil asked.

"Somewhere in the meat packing district," Mario said, getting in.

Neil laughed. "Take us to the corner of Gay and Gay," he jokingly told the driver.

The cab dropped them off in front of Duvall's SoHo loft, a non-descript, four-story structure bedecked with iron fire escapes. A small art gallery with big windows occupied the street level, and beside it was an odd, even creepy, brown steel door.

Mario pressed the buzzer beside the door and was rewarded with an almost-immediate buzz. The door swung open, revealing Roger smiling down from them on a television screen. "All hail, gentlemen from Wall Street," he said. "The elevator awaits. Press the top button."

Directly in front of them, Mario and Neil found a tiny elevator that looked as though it had been made in a jewelry shop. At the top floor, the elevator door slid open and the two men stepped out into a huge room, two stories high, with millions of dollars of original art hanging from the rafters—Warhols, Lichtensteins, Hockneys, Rauschenbergs, and Harings.

Roger was awaiting them, majestically dressed in a flowing, muted rainbow-colored caftan and a purple beret, a living parody of a sixteenth-century Flemish painter. He was barefoot and holding a snow-white Persian cat.

"Jesus." Neil said in a voice only Mario could hear. "This dudes taken more balls to the face than Johnny Bench."

"Be nice," Mario whispered, "he's an artist."

"Welcome to my humble abode," Roger said with a little bow, beckoning them inside.

The floor was dotted with outrageous sculpture and furniture, a collection of multicolored mushrooms the size of small children—actually chairs. On the sound system, Michael Feinstein was playing something by Gershwin. The room's finishing touch: an excess of cat statues of every imaginable size, color, and shape.

"Have a seat," Roger purred, pointing to a cluster of mushrooms.

"Do you actually live here?" Neil asked.

"The living quarters are one floor down," Roger said, opening a gold cigarette case. "This is my studio, where I work."

Mario looked around the room. "How come no architect's drawing boards?"

"Got your image of an architect's studio from The Fountainhead, have you?" Roger said. "Well times have changed."

He pointed to a back corner, toward a group of Mac G5 computers, each with its own LCD monitor, resting on a bevy of modernistic work stations.

Mario and Neil awkwardly sat on the mushrooms, which turned out to be quite comfortable. "So," Mario said, "you have some sketches to show us?"

"Of course," Roger said. A remote control appeared in his hand and he pushed a few buttons. Venetian blinds slowly descended to cover the large plate glass, and the studio lights simultaneously dimmed. An LCD screen the size of a garage door rose from a panel inside the parquet floor.

"We're gonna see Baywatch?" Neil asked hopefully.

Roger hit the remote again and the screen lit up instantly. It showed a huge jungle clearing, bordered by a dense combination of undergrowth, vines and towering trees. Here and there, monkeys hung perilously from high branches while two giraffes overlooked the scene from behind the trees, and a tiger's face was visible in the bushes. A sweeping stairway with ivory elephant tusk railings twelve feet long ascended toward the top of the jungle canopy.

"What the hell is this?" Mario asked. "A page out of *National Geographic*?"

"*Au contraire, messieurs*," Roger replied. "This is the grand entry hallway of the Lions' Den."

"You're shitting me," Mario said.

"Please. You're speaking of the one perversion in which I do not partake."

"My God," Neil said, "it makes the grand ballroom of the Titanic look second-rate."

Roger bowed, neatly catching his beret as it fell off his head and restoring it in a single motion. "Let's take a look at another room."

The vision on the screen dissolved into another, a room based largely on Pride Rock, King Musafa's rocky perch, topped off by a pleasing arrangement of rhinoceroses and hippopotamuses that, at a second look, turned out to be luxurious leather-covered couches and lounge chairs. The walls were frozen dioramas of the African veldt, lighted from behind—to the left, a herd of wildebeests loping through the elephant grass, and in the distance—to the right, a troop of rhinos romping at the edge of the jungle.

Dominating the front view was Africa's highest peak, the snow-capped mount Kilimanjaro, perhaps twenty or thirty miles away. As Mario watched, a pack of hyenas crossed the screen, the motion so startling that he almost fell off his mushroom. "What the…"

"The front wall is a giant LCD television screen," Roger explained.

"Yankee Stadium has one similar. What you're looking at is a screensaver."

Once more, the image faded away, blending into yet another. This one depicted an irregularly-shaped watering hole, surrounded by vine-covered trees and protected from the elements by the leafy green canopy above. Lolling nearby were a collection of animals—zebras, impalas, warthogs, and a group of baboons, and, in the pool itself, the water bubbled invitingly. Mario and Neil watched, awestruck.

Finally, Roger showed outside elevations. "In the interests of being inconspicuous, all I've done here is clean up the exterior, make any repairs needed and put in some decent landscaping," Roger said. "It doesn't look shabby anymore, but it's not going to attract any attention either. And that, gentlemen, is the whole show." The screen went dark.

Mario realized that Roger was angling for compliments, but it wasn't any strain to deliver them. "Roger, you've outdone yourself," he said. "This is a true masterpiece."

"I agree," said Neil. "It's only a damn shame so few will see it."

"There's one thing you haven't mentioned, Roger, and it worries me," Mario said.

Roger grinned. "Money."

"Yes, exactly," Mario said. "Can we really build this fantasy land within our budget?"

"Yes, of course. Well, almost," Roger said. "When you figure in everything, it comes in at or around nine million."

"I said our budget was eight million," Mario said relieved, but not about to let Roger know it.

"I know," Roger replied. "But, we also know there was a cushion there."

"Well, Roger, how about this? If we give you the green light today, would you give us your word to do your very best to trim that budget by half a million?"

Roger didn't know what to say. "I can give you my word I'll try," he finally said.

"What do you think, Neil?"

"I don't like it, but if he sincerely tries…" Neil said.

"Oh, then I will," Roger said.

"Then do it," said Mario, rising from the mushroom chair. "Make it look exactly like the pictures." He offered Roger his hand and they shook.

A few weeks later, Mario took a chopper out to Ward's Island, bringing Dennis along for the ride.

It was a gorgeous fall day—crisp, sunny, the leaves just beginning to turn. The weeds had been cleared out from in front of the Lions' Den and the building's dark-grey stones had been sandblasted to a silvery white. It's starting to come along, Mario thought. In fact, it's starting to look—there was only one word for it: classy.

Three panel trucks, two pickups, and a new Porsche 911 Cabriolet were parked unobtrusively to one side of the building.

They walked inside as power drills droned and sanders swirled and white dust rained from drywall. They drifted from room to room across bare plywood floors. Finally, Mario stopped and cocked his head to one side. "What the hell?"

Someone inside the building was singing. Loudly.

"*I am the King of the sea, the ruler of the Queen's Navee, whose praise Great Britain loudly chants*," sang one strong male voice.

"*And we are his sisters, and his cousins, and his aunts!*" sang a chorus of other male voices, melodiously.

Mario and Dennis looked at each other, totally confounded, then headed resolutely for the back rooms where they found Roger, dressed in a red, comic-book version of an admiral's uniform, swinging his arms like an orchestra conductor, directing a trio of muscular young carpenters dressed in outlandish bright blue eighteenth-century British seaman's uniforms, all of them busily drilling conduit holes and singing, "*When at anchor here I ride, my bosom swells with pride, and I snap my fingers at a foeman's taunts...*"

Off to the right, a studly young quartet of electricians, busily installing new wiring, added their voices to the chorus: "*And so do his sisters, and his cousins, and his aunts!*"

"What the hell is this?" Mario said loudly.

"Aha!" said Roger expansively. "Our honorable employer and one of his stalwarts have come to gauge our progress. Welcome aboard, gentlemen."

"What the fuck is going on here?" Mario repeated, putting a little edge in his voice. "It looks like a 4th of July party at Elton John's house."

"My good man, you have walked into a combination HMS Pinafore rehearsal and building reconstruction operation," Roger explained. "We're doing it off-off-Broadway next month. I can get you tix." He winked broadly at Dennis, who took two steps backward in confusion.

"Well, thank you for sharing," Mario said, "but I'm interested in what's happening with our building, the one we're paying millions to remodel."

Roger beamed. "We are making absolutely splendid progress, my dear man, and I'm sure my ensigns would love to boast of their accomplishments." He slipped his arm around Mario's and led the way to the trio of sailor-suit-clad workers framing the interior walls. "We've just finished ripping out the old drywall and we're about to put up new partitions."

"Looks good," Dennis said.

"Shall we check out electrical?" Roger asked, and led the way to an adjacent room where hunky electricians were stringing BX cable and metal conduits through the ceiling beams and walls.

Dennis examined the work approvingly. "They're doing it right, paisan."

"Anyone for plumbing?" Roger asked, smiling. "Maybe you fellas would like to see how my boys lay some pipe."

Dennis shot Mario a sidelong glance.

"Leave it alone," Mario told him.

Roger marched toward the rear of the building. In a room behind the main hallway, a detachment of sailor-suited plumbers was manhandling a mammoth jungle green hot tub into position.

"The trees will be coming in at the end of the week," Roger said.

"Hey Roger! I mean Admiral Duvall!" someone called. "Delivery!"

At the front door, they found a quartet of black men, one of them holding a clipboard.

"You Duvall?" asked the man with the clipboard.

"The very same, good sir," Roger admitted. "You have a delivery for us?"

"A couple of crates," said the mover a little suspiciously, evidently trying to get his mind around Roger's costume. "Sign here."

Roger signed the bill of lading with a flourish and the moving men returned to their beat-up truck, hand-painted with the legend "Brothers Movin' Brothers," and pulled out two heavy and elaborately built wooden crates. It took all four men to carry each crate to the entrance at the main hallway, where Roger wanted them placed.

"What's in the box?" Dennis asked.

Roger paused, uncertain for the first time. "Statues. Very old. Very beautiful."

"Let's have a look," Mario suggested.

Roger waved the carpenters over and they went at one of the crates with hammers and crowbars. It took them a few minutes to pop the lid, and only a little longer to remove the thick excelsior packing and to cut through what seemed like endless layers of bubble wrap.

Mario and Dennis peered into the crate. What they saw was an extraordinary, life-sized lion carved in granite, with rubies for eyes, a mane made of filigreed gold, and claws of sapphires. "My God," Mario breathed. "That's amazing!"

"Is it real?" Dennis asked, stunned.

"Very real," Roger said, kneeling down and petting the golden mane. "It was excavated from a Sumerian archeological site in Jordan. It's about 2,700 years old, dating from the period when Gilgamesh ruled Uruk. And its twin is in the other crate."

"Twins? Where did you get it?" Dennis asked, genuinely curious.

"From an old friend," Roger said. "Let's call him an art dealer—in the Middle East."

Mario and Dennis turned to leave.

"Oh, one more thing," Roger said. "I'm going to need another half million in cash, preferably hundreds."

"Excuse me?" Mario said. He knew he must have missed something, or misunderstood.

"For the family," Roger explained.

"What family?" Dennis asked.

Roger rolled his eyes. "You're being terribly dense, m'dear. And here I thought you were both men of the world."

Mario raised an eyebrow. "You mean…"

"Yes, the Lacugna family and their friends, silly," Roger went on, almost whispering. His cat gracefully leaped into his arms and he petted it reflexively.

Dennis missed Roger's remark. "What was that?"

"He's talking about the mob," Mario told his friend.

Roger corrected him. "The representatives of the various unions and building departments is a more discreet way to put it."

"I thought Giuliani locked up all those guinea bastards," Dennis said.

"Not all of them. But it's the Russians we really have to worry about."

"The Russkies? What could they do to *us*?" Mario asked.

"Hmmm," Roger said thoughtfully. "Well, they could shut down construction. Forever. Or set the place on fire. Or machine gun the guests on opening night… if they're in a bad mood and running low on vodka."

"I thought no one would know about our building," Mario said.

"They keep tabs on construction material," Roger explained. "All over the five boroughs, Long Island, Westchester, and New Jersey. Donald Trump couldn't build an outhouse without greasing the right palms."

"You believe this shit," Mario said to Neil. "Roger, any more surprises and I'm gonna be in your shorts using your balls as speed bag. Got that?" Mario said and walked away.

Roger looked at Neil. "What the matter with *her* today?"

Back outside, Mario flipped open his cell phone and called Frank. "Bad news," he said. "We're going to have to donate a half million to the Lacugna family."

"Yeah. So?"

"Well, I certainly didn't plan on that."

Frank was surprised. "You didn't?"

"I know, I'm stupid. Don't rub it in. Listen, Frank, I know you know the Lacugnas. You're the fuckin' mouthpiece for the Teamsters. Can't you…"

"Sorry, Mario. The butchers from Brighton are in charge now. They make the Italians look like altar boys. My advice is that you just pay them and forget it."

"Yeah, well forget it." Mario said.

"Forget it? Let me explain something to you, Mario, because I don't think your brain works too good—the one in your head. The one in your pants works fine. Remember when the Yankees won the World Series a few years back…"

"Whats that gotta do—"

"Shut up and listen. Well that night a few of their star pinstripes were out celebrating with their wives and girlfriends at the Venezian room on the upper West Side. I know this because the Gambino's own a piece of the joint. That same night, Johnny Lacugna walks in with Frankie "nails" Russo and he sees these guys at his usual table. And sitting with them is the mayor of New York, a fellow Napolitan, a scumbag I helped get elected. The *maitre'd* explains to Big John that the players reserved the table and offers Big John another table. But Big John doesn't want another table, he wants *his* table. The one he always sits at. And he wants it fucking *now*.

"The *maitre'd* walks over to the Yankees, the New York *fucking* Yankees, Mario, and the Mayor of New York, and tells them they have to give up the table. Big John picked up their tab the rest of the evening, only it wasn't at that table. That'll give you an idea who runs this bitch, Mario. It's not Wall Street, its not City Hall, the jews, the liberals, the fags or Al *fuckface* Sharpton. And its certainly not the Teamsters. Capice? Am I getting through to you, Mario?"

"Yeah," Mario said dejected and flipped shut his cell phone when Dennis came out.

"Everything alright?"

"We gotta kick up to Big John." Mario said, angrily walking past him.

"What the fuck…"

Frankfort, Germany

She could hardly believe her eyes. After two fruitless weeks of prowling around behind the bear cages at the Frankfort Zoo, there it was: a ragged slip of yellow paper no bigger than her palm. She bent down, pretending it was litter and needed to be tossed into one of the zoo's brown garbage cans, and swooped it up.

Then, as she'd been taught, she headed for the women's room. Once inside, with the stall door bolted, she took a look at the paper. A single character was written on it, in what looked like childish script. She checked her watch. Fifteen minutes. Perfect timing. She walked casually toward the snack bar, bought a chocolate ice cream cone, and found a seat on an empty bench.

Three minutes later, she had company: an old lady with thick legs and a babushka. When she sat down, she was so short that her feet no longer touched the ground. She slide away from the old woman, but the old woman followed. "Stay in one place," she grunted. "These old bones don't move so well."

So this was her contact? This was someone's grandmother. Great-grandmother. Well, it was a damn good disguise, if that's what it was. "What's new with your family?" she asked, using the code phrase.

"You know my son, Simon? He and his boys are moving to New York."

"All of his boys?"

"All four, and some of their friends."

"When will they arrive?"

"Hard to say. They have some other stops. But they should be there in time to get the package."

"Package?"

"Oh yes. A very valuable package. A fruitcake, I hear, very big, just bursting with flavor."

"When is it supposed to arrive?"

"Well, you know how the mail is these days. Best I can tell, sometime in the next six weeks."

The next day, the CIA notified Homeland Security, and Homeland Security contacted all of the other agencies overseeing American borders: a dirty bomb or a bioweapon is being shipped into the United States and will be picked up by an Al Qaeda cell in Manhattan. Police along both coasts were put on high alert.

CHAPTER FOURTEEN

"I look stupid in this yellow tunic with the fuzzy rocks on it, or whatever they're supposed to be."

"You look like Fred Flintstone, or at least you will when you put on the turquoise tie."

"Like I said, stupid."

"Stop complaining," Phyllis said. She put on the orange headpiece—cartoon hair—and the clamshell necklace, and admired herself in the mirror, as Wilma. "It's a lot better than your George and Martha Washington idea."

This was exactly what he needed, Mario thought, another argument with Phyllis, this one over a fucking Halloween party. He had other things to worry about. Important things. Roger was spending money like a Japanese businessman at a Manhattan Geisha house. He had to find some way to cauterize the money bleed. The Zoo Crew had managed to cover the mob money, but now they needed to raise still more cash, and they needed to raise it quick. "First you break my balls into accepting Tyler's party invitation, and now you're complaining about the costume." Mario said. "Do you *ever* do anything, Phyllis, but bust balls?"

"Only when I have a reason," she said, hiking up her tunic.

"Then tell me what the hell was wrong with my second idea, the Tarzan and Jane costumes?"

"You as Tarzan, that's what. Tarzan with love handles and a fat ass. You would have looked ridiculous."

"And I don't look ridiculous now? I don't know why I let you talk me into this, Phyllis."

"This is the first time Tyler has ever invited you to one of his private parties," she reminded him, "and a lot of important people will be there."

"You mean country club people? Daughters of the American fuckin' Revolution? That's why you want to go, Phyllis, to promote yourself onto the society pages."

Phyllis opened her mouth to reply, but was interrupted by the door bell.

She hurried downstairs to get the door, and found Danny Bernard standing there, his blond good looks hidden by a Dracula costume that included a comically-evil Lugosi mask. "I vant to suck your blood," he said, trying for a Transylvanian accent. "Oh, hello, Mrs. Monelli. I mean Wilma. Very cute."

"Thank you, Danny. Your costume is very convincing."

Mario came down the stairs. "Good God!" he said.

Danny laughed. "My mother wanted me to dress like an angel, but I told her I wanted to look *bad*." He checked his watch. "Where's Boomer? We got to get going."

A reasonable imitation of Elvis Presley, complete with pompadour and sideburns, appeared at the top of the stairs and danced his way down, wielding a guitar and singing, off-key, "You Ain't Nothing But a Hound Dog."

Mario applauded. Danny booed and laughed. "You look more like Elvis Parsley than Elvis Presley," he said.

"Very funny," Boomer said and grinned. "So, did you tell them yet?"

"Tell us what," Mario and Phyllis asked at the same moment.

"I got accepted into Stanford," Danny announced proudly. "Mom got the letter today."

"Way to go, Dan boy!" Mario said. "This is cause for celebration." He went into the kitchen and returned with a fist full of cold beers.

"Have you told your father?" Phyllis said. "Rick must be thrilled."

"I tried, but he'd already left for Shanghai. But I sure can't wait to tell him."

They clinked bottles and Danny made a toast. "To Boomer and me. Wall Street here we come."

"Hey, Danny, show my folks your ring," Boomer urged.

Mario was puzzled. "What ring?"

"Our class rings came in today," Boomer said. He held up his right hand and Mario studied the jewelry appreciatively.

"Looks like a ruby," he said.

Phyllis peered at the ring. "Quartz, dyed red."

"Mines Onyx," Danny said, holding up his ring.

"Quartz, dyed black," Phyllis said with the certainty of a woman who knew her jewelry.

"What made you choose a black stone, Danny?" Mario asked.

"Because I vanted to show my *dhark zide*," he said, sounding more like Lugosi than Lugosi.

"I remember when me and your father, as a token of our friendship, traded rings back when we were seniors at New Utrecht High," Mario said, "then returned them on graduation day."

The boys looked at each other.

"Sure, why not?" they said.

Boomer put on the ring with the black stone and Danny slipped on the ring with the red stone. "Friends for life?" he asked Boomer.

"Friends forever," Boomer affirmed, and they clinked rings.

"Let's get going," Danny said. "Kayla and Jenny are probably already there."

"Wait a minute," Mario said. "Boomer's costume isn't quite complete." Mario opened the door to the hall closet, rummaged around the back, pulled out a garment bag, and handed it to Boomer. This was Mario's most valued possession, a weathered brown leather jacket he paid a fortune for at a Graceland auction.

"Why don't you wear *this*?"

"The *jacket*?" Boomer said, awed.

"I think The King deserves it," Mario told him, grinning.

Boomer carefully slipped the jacket out of the plastic bag.

"What's so special about some crummy jacket?" Danny asked, leaning forward to examine it.

Boomer gently unzipped the inside pocket. "Here," he said. "Read this."

Danny peered at the lining. "Made *expressly* for Elvis Pressley," he read, "for use in 'King Creole.' What's 'King Creole'?"

"It was Elvis's best movie, and the last one filmed in black and white before he got drafted," Boomer said.

"Impressive," Danny granted. "That must make it very valuable."

"You bet it does," Boomer said. "And it's all mine when I'm eighteen. Right, Dad?"

"We'll see," Mario said.

"But you promised," Boomer whined.

"I said, we'll see. Now put it on and let's see how it looks." With his father's help, Boomer did just that, inspecting himself in the mirror.

"You're sure to win first prize tonight for best costume," Danny said.

"Gee, it looks great," Boomer gave his father a lengthy hug. "Thanks, Dad."

"Just see that it comes home in perfect condition…without eggs on it."

"I will, Dad, I swear."

Phyllis handed Boomer the keys to the Hummer. "Make sure the car comes home in perfect condition, too."

Mario and Phyllis—Fred and Wilma Flintstone—pulled up to the dock about nine p.m. and joined Superman and Lois Lane and Dorothy and the Tin Woodsman, who were walking toward the WFC marina. The sounds of partying and music drifted toward them.

"*That's* Tyler's boat?" Phyllis asked, awed. "It looks like a small cruise ship."

"Yeah, that's *The Depository*. And he never shuts up about it," Mario said. "It's a Bennetti Classic. Forty-three meters."

They were welcomed at the gangway by a striking blonde, dressed like a Radio City Rockette. "And you are?"

"Mario and Phyllis Monelli. Yabadabadoo."

The girl consulted her list. "Welcome aboard."

Phyllis reached for the list. "Who else is coming?" she asked.

"Cut out that shit," Mario said, yanking her away from the girl, onto the boat's main deck and into the skewed reality of a Halloween party. They were surrounded by cartoon personalities, historical figures, politicians, mythical characters, and celebrities of every description.

There was so much old money on the yacht, it was a miracle it didn't list and sink. Costumes or not, Mario thought, I recognize half the people here—the men anyhow. That's Laird Johnson in the Mickey Mouse suit, and Edgerton Lowry as Rambo. The guy in the Henry VIII outfit was McDonald Charles. He glanced forward—David Painter as Darth Vader.

And what the hell am *I* doing here? Mario asked himself. Where do I fit in to this gathering of billionaires, these products of the right schools, inherited wealth, secret societies, and private clubs? Why did Tyler invite me—just to prove that I will never belong, no matter how much money I make?

He watched the Rockettes serving drinks to the old men, and saw the old men examining them, their hunger transparent, their actions restrained only by their fear of scandal, lack of opportunity or watching wives, most who were trophies of years past looking a little shop worn and nervous.

As the yacht pulled away from the dock for its cruise up the Hudson, one of the Rockettes approached them. "What would you like to drink?"

"Brandy for me," Phyllis said.

The girl went off to fetch the drinks. "Make that one your first and your last, Phyllis."

"I'll do what I want, Mario. You don't own me."

Mario shrugged and went off to make contact with Tyler and left Phyllis to fend for herself. Tyler was nowhere to be seen on the main deck, so he found the stern ladder, just aft of the bar, and descended to the lower deck. Thinner crowd, but still no Tyler.

He climbed back up the ladder, two flights to the upper deck, and more celebrity look-alikes—Richard Nixon, Frankenstein's monster, Charlie Brown, Tyler's wife, Helena, a gaunt, patrician, dark-haired woman, evidently pretending to be Helen of Troy and falling far short. But no Tyler.

Up three more steps to the sun deck, and there was Elvira the vampiress— And around her, a pair of hairy arms belonging to Tyler, who was half-dressed in a Roman toga, an anachronistic pair of Birkenstock's on his feet, and a ring of laurel leaves circling his distinguished temples.

"Jesus Christ!" Tyler said, "Oh, it's you, Monelli. You scared the shit out of me."

"Who are you supposed to be, Nero?"

"You see me playing a fiddle? No, I'm Julius Caesar, thank you very much."

"And you're going to tell me this is Caesar's wife?"

"Come on, Mario. It's a party."

Mario's eyebrow's went up. "Are you sure you want to do this here, Tyler?"

He waited for Tyler to make the obvious conclusion, and before long, he did.

"Gotta get out of here." He dragged the more-than-willing Elvira toward one of the sun deck windows, opened it and stepped onto the boat's upper deck, pulling the girl after him. And this, Mario thought smiling, was the same Tyler who'd told him how happily married he was. "Find Helena," he asked Mario. "Tell her...tell her... tell her something came up." He was acting like a man who swallowed a bottle of Viagra.

Mario glanced at the wood protruding from inside Tyler's sheet and knew what it was that came up. He enjoyed watching Tyler's moral compass change direction, his circumcised needle now pointing north.

"But, Tyler," Mario said, pretending innocence, "I thought you're happily married?"

Tyler shot Mario a sidelong glance, then he and Elvira hopped down onto the deck and awkwardly stepped into the Zodiac rubber dingy at the stern. They clumsily untied it and sped off.

Mario turned to go downstairs. Phyllis was standing there on the ladder, shaking her head in disgust.

"What are you going to say to his wife?" she asked.

"Exactly what Tyler asked me to." He pushed past her without waiting for a response, stopped to talk briefly to Helena, then got lost among the party-goers.

After a few hours of this, they were back on the road, heading home. Mario drove through the Midtown Tunnel and east on the Long Island Expressway, through light traffic.

"Until tonight, I thought Tyler Gentry had some class," Phyllis finally said, picking up where she'd left off. "I can't believe he left his own party to fuck some bimbette young enough to be his daughter."

"What Tyler does is Tyler's business," Mario said.

"Just don't let me ever catch *you* cheating on me like that. You'll walk out of court with nothing but your limp dick in your hand."

Mario laughed, but he knew Phyllis wasn't joking. That was the one thing that stopped him from dumping her—that and the boys. They were like hostages to his good behavior.

Soon, they were off the expressway, driving through suburbia, heading toward their house, not talking anymore. Approaching their street, Mario caught a glimpse of flashing blue and red lights filtering through the trees and backed off the accelerator.

Now they came into the cul-de-sac and there were more flashing blue and red lights, half a dozen ambulances, and police cars parked helter-skelter in front of the Bernard house, and a throng of pajama-clad people, adding to the commotion. "What the fuck?" Mario said, curious and a little worried.

"Oh my god, that's Brenda's house," Phyllis said.

Mario pulled into his driveway, and ran toward Rick's house, Phyllis close behind him. A cop at the door stopped them from going inside. "What's going on?" Phyllis asked fearfully.

Suddenly a neighbor's voice called out from behind him.

"Mario, Phyllis."

"Nathan," Mario said. "What the hell is going on? What's with all the fucking cops?"

"It's Danny."

"Danny? What about 'im?"

"He's dead."

"He's what! How?" Phyllis was disbelieving.

"What happened?" said Mario.

Nathan paused for a moment, then shook his head. "No one knows. The police won't tell us anything. It's gotta be a suicide. He wasn't the same ever since Rick left."

"Where's *my* son?" Phyllis asked, beginning to sound hysterical. "Boomer! ...Boomer!..."

Now Mario and Phyllis raced back toward their own house, through the crowd of curious neighbors. "Jesus Christ, what's this all about?" asked one man, dressed only in a plaid silk robe and slippers.

Mario and Phyllis ignored him and kept running, passing Danny's car hooked up to a police tow truck, flinging open the front door of their house, and yelling, "Boomer! Boomer, are you here?"

No answer.

Mario vaulted up the steps, heading toward Boomer's room, Phyllis behind him, screaming out her son's name.

Boomer's door was closed, locked. Mario kicked it open. Boomer was lying on the bed, face down, still in his Elvis costume, his head buried in his pillow, sobbing.

"Boomer, thank God you're okay." Mario said.

The boy turned over, stretched out his arms for his parents and, as they both hugged him, started sobbing again.

"It's Danny," he said, trying to catch his breath. "He's dead. Danny's dead, Dad."

"We know," Phyllis said, cradling him "But are *you* okay?"

"The cops were everywhere when I got home," Boomer said, between heaving sobs. "They told me about Danny."

Downstairs, someone called into the house, through the open door. "Hello? Anyone there?"

"Yeah," Mario said. "I'm coming."

A hollow-faced, man in a food-stained topcoat was waiting at the front door. He extended a hand as Mario hurried downstairs. "Detective Draven, Manhattan homicide," he said. "You must be Mario Monelli."

They shook hands. "That's right."

Mario caught Draven eyeing his costume.

"Halloween party," Mario explained.

Draven nodded. "Mind if I come in and talk?"

"Not at all," Mario said, a little puzzled at the detective's interest.

Phyllis came down the stairs.

"Your son is here? Boomer, they call him?"

Phyllis looked at Mario and Mario gave the detective a long, hard, suspicious look.

"I just need some information," the detective told Mario. "I don't want to make a big deal out of this. You can stop me anytime if you think it's getting too much for him."

Mario didn't have any real choice. But he was also sure Boomer had nothing to hide. The whole thing was a tragedy for everyone. Suddenly, he thought of Brenda Bernard—and Rick. My God, Rick. And Danny. Jesus Christ, how could this have happened?"

"Phyllis, go over and see to Brenda," he said. "She's gonna need you."

"But Boomer…"

"He'll be all right. But Brenda must be falling apart."

"I'll be back soon," she said. "Call if you need me."

She grabbed her coat and left. Mario turned back to Detective Draven.

"I'm going to let you talk to my son," he said. "But remember, Danny was his best friend. He's totally devastated by this."

"I'll be on my best behavior," the detective assured him.

Mario went upstairs and Boomer came down with him, still distraught.

"Mike Draven," the detective said, offering Boomer his hand. "I'm very sorry about your friend, son. Would it be all right to ask you just a few questions?"

Boomer looked at his father, then managed a nod.

"Thanks. Now you and the Bernard boy went to a high school party tonight, right?"

"Yeah, Halstead. I drove my mom's truck."

"What about your dates?"

"Their parents were chaperoning. They drove them there and back." Boomer's eyes filled with tears and he looked away from the detective.

Draven gave him a few seconds, then went on. "Did you and Danny Bernard leave at the same time?"

"No, he took off earlier."

"When did this happen?"

"I'm not really sure. Must have been around ten o'clock maybe. Anyhow, that's when I noticed he wasn't around."

Draven jotted down a couple of words. "You two have an argument?"

"What? No, no argument. We never argued. He's my best friend. Was."

"Then you'd know if he was using drugs," Draven asked casually.

"He wasn't into drugs," Boomer said. "He *hated* the whole idea of drugs. We both do. Did."

"Didn't his parents recently split up?"

"What are you suggesting?" Mario asked, interrupting. "That Danny killed himself? That's ridiculous. I saw him earlier this evening and he was fine, thrilled about getting into Stanford."

"No, Danny Bernard didn't commit suicide tonight," Draven replied. "He wasn't murdered either. He died of a crystal meth overdose. His body was found in Harlem, in Sugar Hill on the roof of the old King Movie theater."

"In Harlem? That's impossible!" said Mario. "He wasn't a user. Was he into drugs, Boomer?"

"No, Dad, I swear."

"How would you know?" Draven asked.

"We were best friends."

"Best friends don't always tell each other everything."

"We did!"

"When you drove home from Halstead, did you happen to come home by way of Harlem?" Detective Draven asked.

"No, I took the tunnel."

"Okay. So when did you get back?"

"Back home? I don't know, 'round eleven."

"Can anyone back that up?"

"Yeah, yeah, the babysitter was here. I told her she could go home."

"Babysitter? What's her name?"

Mario interrupted again. "Our babysitter's name is Mandy Lipkin. She lives a couple of blocks down the street."

"She'll say you got here by eleven?"

"I'm sure she will," Mario said. "And so will my younger son, Kyle."

"No, Dad, Kyle was sleeping when I got home."

"And once back home, you never left the house again?" Draven asked.

"I already told you that. Dad, why is he asking me all these questions?"

"Okay, detective, that's enough." Mario interrupted, shielding Boomer.

Draven closed his notebook and stuffed it into a jacket pocket. "I guess I got everything I need. I'm really sorry, son. It's painful losing a friend. I've lost a few myself over the years." He smiled tightly, then walked out.

Mario turned and looked at Boomer. "I'm going next door to see what I can do. Stay here and watch your brother."

On the way next door, Mario saw Andy Stovall, clad in his pajamas, rushing into the Bernard house, carrying his doctor's bag. Once more, the cops stopped him at the door. "I'm the best friend," Mario said. "I think I'm needed in there."

"You're Monelli?"

"Yes."

"They're upstairs, your wife and the mother. Doctor's with them. And some other neighbors."

Mario could hear Brenda screaming upstairs, calling out for Danny, then Rick. He hurried upstairs, pushing his way through the neighbors lining the hallway and squeezed his way into the master bedroom. Five policemen and a pair of paramedics were trying their best to restrain Brenda so Andy could give her a sedative. Phyllis was standing nearby, phone to her ear, shouting at someone. "I said *Rick Bernard!* Hold on? Operator, I've been holding this fucking line for twenty minutes!"

Suddenly, Mario didn't want to be here at all. He turned away and threaded his way through the neighbors in the hallway and stopped in front of Danny's room. Then he impulsively pushed the door and slipped in. Moonlight was flooding in through the window, streaking across the swimming trophies on the window sill, and the Eli Manning poster watching him from the wall. The only thing that was missing was Danny. Mario felt as though the entire room were empty. He felt as though *he* were empty.

He sat down on the bed, embracing Danny's pillow, and gazed at a framed photograph on Danny's desk. It was taken three or four years ago. Danny was wearing his swimming goggles and holding a trophy. Rick was standing beside him, his arm around his son. Mario remembered the moment. He'd taken the picture.

How had this happened? Mario asked himself. How had he *let* this happen? He remembered his promise to Rick—to look after his son. And now this. When he couldn't bear to be alone with his thoughts anymore, he returned to the master bedroom to find Brenda now lying on her back, practically comatose. Stovall was taking her pulse.

"You get a hold of Rick yet?" Mario quietly asked Phyllis.

"They're getting him to come to the phone," she said.

"He doesn't know yet?"

"No, he knows. The American Embassy relayed the news a little while ago. But I thought we should talk to him."

"You're right," Mario said. "Give me the phone."

Phyllis handed it over.

"Hello," he said, "this is Mario Monelli. I'm Rick Bernard's best friend. I need to talk to him." He listened for a moment. "Did you tell him who I was?" He listened again. Then he hung up, slowly.

"He isn't there?" Phyllis asked.

"He's there. He doesn't want to talk to me."

The funeral was held at St. Catherine of Siena Roman Catholic Church in Farmingdale, Long Island under a threatening grey sky. Even though school was in session, high school kids and teachers from the prestigious Halstead filled two-thirds of the pews, the rest occupied by an assortment of the Bernard's friends and neighbors spilling onto the sidewalk outside. Mario and Phyllis took seats on the left side of the altar, near the front.

Finally, after everyone else was seated and the priest was ready to deliver the eulogy, Rick and Brenda entered the church, his arm around her, her eyes red-rimmed, he wearing dark sunglasses, both of them wearing plaintive expressions and walking in a daze. They took their places in the front row. Try as he might, Mario was unable to catch Rick's attention.

The eulogy was mercifully short and received with tears and stunned silence. Life doesn't work like this, Mario thought. Children don't die before their parents. Yet this was the scene, playing itself out before his eyes. Then there was Rick. What could he say to him? And what if it had been Boomer? He couldn't even allow that thought to take root in his mind.

Then the service was over. The priest motioned to Boomer and some of his friends and they came up to the altar, hoisted the charcoal grey coffin by its brass rails, and slowly carried it down the aisle, followed by Father Mackey and a bevy of altar boys. All precisely choreographed to the Ava Maria.

Once outside, they descended the stairs to the waiting hearse, Rick and Brenda close behind, barely holding on, the rest of the congregants following solemnly. The limousines were lined up behind the hearse, and behind them came a long train of cars, many belonging to classmates from Halstead attending the funeral.

They got into their car and, after a few minutes, the more-than-forty-car procession began moving through the streets slowly and turned onto the Southern State Parkway, the headlights glistening on the wet road. The rain had slowed to a light drizzle, but the skies were still threatening.

"Why didn't you say something to Rick?" Phyllis asked.

"He'll come to me when he's ready. I didn't want to force it."

"He's your best friend, Mario. He needs you, even if he can't admit it."

"I'm not going to push him, Phyllis. He's really hurting."

"That's exactly why you should go to him."

"Phyllis?"

"Yeah?"

"Shut the fuck up."

The ride to Calvary Cemetery was agonizing, but brief. Mario followed the line of cars down the winding cemetery road to the little gathering of people, parked, and walked across the grass toward Danny's gravesite, Phyllis taking her own route.

The coffin was already sitting on the lowering mechanism, above the empty grave. Mourners surrounded the site, under umbrellas, and the Monellis joined them on the outer fringes, barely close enough to see what was going on and too far away to hear Father Mackey, despite the crowd's silence.

Brenda shrieked and Mario realized that the coffin lowering must have started. The shriek turned into wailing, and several of the Halstead school girls joined in. On the other side of the gathering, Mario could see Boomer standing there, whimpering, beside a girl he'd never seen before. The girl's face was streaked with tears. The Zoo Crew stood nearby, among a throng of people from Wall Street who had come to pay their respects to Rick.

After the grave was shoveled closed, Mario went looking for Rick. He spotted his best friend across the lawn, holding up an umbrella with his other arm around Brenda's waist, slowly heading for the limo. Mario walked quickly to catch up with him.

"Rick," Mario said. Rick turned. Mario opened his mouth to speak, but the words wouldn't come.

Rick Bernard took off his sunglasses and regarded Mario without expression. "Thanks for looking after my boy, Mario," he said. Then he and Brenda got into the limo.

CHAPTER FIFTEEN

Paige handed Julie four folders and a couple of videotapes. "That's everything," she said.

"Good," Julie replied. "Now how do I look?"

Paige stood back and assessed her boss. Charcoal-gray suit with a short skirt, but not too short. Not a hair out of place. Brimming with energy and confidence. "You look great," she said.

Julie checked her watch. "I'd better get going."

On the way to the elevator, she ran into Hank. "Ready for the command performance?" he asked.

"As ready as I can be."

When they got to Carleton Fisher's office, Miles was already there.

"Those for us?" Miles said, pointing to the folders Julie was carrying.

"Yep," she said. "One for each." She passed them out.

At that moment, Fred Fielding hobbled in, puffing. "Sorry, folks," he said. "The wound has been acting up."

"Nothing serious, I hope," Fisher said.

"I'll be fine. Got a folder for me?"

Julie groaned silently, but smiled anyhow. "I didn't know you'd be here, Fred, but you can take mine."

Fielding awkwardly plopped down on the couch and started reading.

Fisher opened his folder and paged through it quickly. "What's the bottom line, Julie?" he asked. "Where do we stand?"

"I think we're in pretty good shape," Julie said. "We've got agreements from fifteen affiliates for remotes. Carol has found us some heart-wrenching interview subjects. Ayers' opening and closing segments have been written, and they're terrific."

"They're in the folder?" Fielding asked.

"Yes. And I've got a rough cut of the America montage right here, on tape."

Fisher put the tape on his desk. "I'll look at it later. Now, what about our centerpiece—the debate you've been telling me about. Have we agreed on our antagonists?"

"Yes," Julie said. "Well, one of them—Barton Mulvaney. He's our target.

"What's his likeability factor?"

"He's likeable enough initially. But after awhile, it's obvious that he's an arrogant son-of-a-bitch," Julie said. "I have some tape of a CNBC interview of him."

"Later," Fisher said. "What about our assassin?"

Julie felt her muscles tense, even though shed been expecting the question. "That's what I'm working on right now."

Fred pursed his lips. "You mean you haven't found the guy who's capable of drawing Mulvaney out in the open and expose what the Saudis are up to?"

"That's quite discouraging m'dear," said Fisher.

"I had a few candidates, but they declined once I told them who'd they be facing."

"You gotta find us someone who can bait Mulvaney," Corbin said.

"I'm open to suggestions," Julie said helplessly. It really annoyed her not to have a candidate to present. And she knew it weakened her position, especially with Miles and Fred.

"I know someone," Fred said thoughtfully. "He has terrific credentials. Trusted by almost everyone. I recall a piece he wrote in *The Wall Street Journal* some years back about the dangers of Japanese investment in America. Scared the shit out of everyone. I'm sure he'd feel the same way about the Saudis."

"You're thinking about George Van Wert?" Fisher asked.

"I thought he hung up his spurs," Hank said. "He must be pushing, what now, seventy?"

"He's alive and still active. A very wise man," Fielding said. "A patriot."

"But he's not strong enough," Hank protested. "Mulvaney's a wolf. He'll eat him alive."

"I agree," Julie said. "We need someone strong enough who can win this fight."

"That's what we *all* want," Miles said. "Maybe we should talk to Van Wert. And, Fred, I think it's time for you to get a little more involved, if you're up to it."

Julie glanced at Hank, silently begging for help.

"Now wait a minute," Hank said, "I've been watching Julie. She's been doing a superb job with her team. I trust her implicitly, and I'm *very* confident she's going to come up with exactly the right person for us."

"I'm sure my doctor will allow me to put a little more time into the project," Fielding offered.

Fisher gave Julie a long, hard look. "Let's give it a few more days. If you haven't found a better candidate, say by Thanksgiving, then we'll approach Van Wert."

"Understood," she said, trying to sound professional and confident, but feeling embarrassed, even humiliated. On the other hand, Fisher hadn't taken the decision away from her—yet. She glanced at Miles, who was shaking his head as if she just gotten away with murder.

Three days.

She'd already been going at it for three months now, without success. She hadn't found the right man at Jones Day nor did she find him at Warbus Pincus and Davies Ward, or any of the other giant brokerage houses or big buyout firms she'd visited.

At least half of the prospects simply weren't right for the task—they were unappealing, or too boring, or they were on the wrong side of the issue, or worse, they would never connect to a wide cross section of the American public.

Most of the rest disqualified themselves. She'd heard more excuses than a grade-school teacher collecting homework assignments. "I don't want any publicity," "I'll be abroad," "I'm not good on television," "It's against company policy."

So now what, with three days left? She didn't like what she'd heard about George Van Wert, that he was a Wall Street dinosaur, whose "fire in the belly" had burned out long ago. But if she couldn't come up with a better opponent for Mulvaney, the network would be stuck with him. And she would lose most of the influence she had with Carleton Fisher.

The next morning, Julie was at her desk by 7:30, going over the B lists and hoping to reconsider someone she'd judged too harshly. It was a waste of time. She needed new candidates. She needed a miracle.

Then a thought occurred to her. There was one person she hadn't talked to, an old and dear friend, a fatherly figure for her and Jack—when Jack was still alive: Milton Jaffe, the senior senator from Ohio and, the ranking Democrat on the Senate Commerce Committee. She and Jack had met him during their days at Georgetown, studying journalism. Jack had served on his staff, even helped with his re-election campaign. Jaffe had been a good friend ever since.

She flipped through her address book, and impulsively dialed the old crusader's home number. The phone was picked up on the second ring. "Jaffe here."

"Senator? It's Julie, Julie Chambers."

There was a pause, then, "Julie! I'm *so* glad to hear from you. How are you?"

"I'm back at work at UBS, believe it or not. Working again for a living."

"That's great to hear, Julie. But I knew you'd get there."

"Wait a second—how are *you*?"

"Just a touch of flu," Jaffe said. "I'm already on the mend. I'm really delighted to hear that you're back at work."

"It's like riding a bicycle, I guess. Carleton Fisher has me producing a special."

"I've known Fisher for thirty years," Jaffe said. "A genuinely good man. I'm glad UBS brought him in. So, tell me about this special of yours."

"Well, that's why I'm calling you—that and the fact that I've been very tardy returning your calls after—well after..."

"Dear, I understand. But I'm really glad to hear from you. You're sounding, well, like yourself. Now tell me about this special and how I can help you."

Julie laid it out, hinting at the Saudi aspect of the show without specifics, describing the kind of person she was looking for and what she needed him to accomplish.

Jaffe waited a long time to respond, and when he did, he was serious. "Julie, I think we shouldn't discuss this on the phone."

"Really? Why?"

"Well, you never know about phones these days," Jaffe said, trying to joke.

"I see," Julie said. She was being warned to watch out for herself, that she might be getting into dangerous territory. She'd known that, of course, but hearing it from Jaffe made it much more real. "Okay, let's talk about my problem—finding a perfect adversary for Barton Mulvaney."

"Yes. I understand the difficulty. You're looking for a Wall Street insider who's not afraid to ruffle a few feathers."

"But someone patriotic," Julie added.

Jaffe laughed. "That's like looking for an honest politician."

"Seriously, do you know someone or anyone who might lead me to someone?"

"Have you talked to Fitzgerald Galvin?"

"The head of the New York Stock Exchange? He's either been traveling, or too busy to see me. And now I don't have any time left. I have to find someone by tomorrow, or I'm going to have to take a man named George Van Wert."

"That old gasbag? He'd be a disaster. Listen, I'll call Galvin and get back to you."

"Thanks, senator. It would mean a great deal to me."

Jaffe's secretary called Julie back a half hour later. "The senator has arranged for you to meet with Mr. Galvin in his office at eleven tomorrow morning."

After a half-hour in the waiting room, Julie was ushered in to see the Chairman of the New York Stock Exchange, Fitzgerald Galvin. Galvin was an elegant man in his middle fifties, who spoke without detectable emotion and, for that matter, said very little. He gave Julie exactly thirty minutes, during which time he had tea served in Wedgwood cups.

For Julie, the conversation was highly disappointing. Galvin said he wasn't sure Americans would tune into a television program about foreign investing, he didn't think there was any reason to worry about it, and he wasn't acquainted with anyone on The Street who had any serious objection to it.

"And that's really all I can tell you. I wish I could be of greater help. Now if you'll excuse me, today is an early close and I'm leaving for Nantucket to spend Thanksgiving with my daughter."

Two minutes later, Julie found herself back outside, gazing at the six massive Corinthian columns of the New York Stock Exchange building, wondering what to do next.

She walked until she found herself in front of a bar and grill. Lunch. Maybe that would help. The place was crowded with men in suits, very few women. She walked in anyway, sat down at the bar and ordered a veggie burger and a beer.

When her order came, she drank the beer, but couldn't force herself to eat. The bartender noticed. "Not hungry, after all?"

"I'm stymied," she said glumly.

"Beg pardon?"

"I've just run into a wall."

The bartender, a round-faced, grey-haired man with a twinkle in his eyes, looked around playfully. "No wall here," he said with a smile.

"At work," she said, her chin resting on her palm. "I've run into a wall at work."

The bartender made a walking motion with his fingers. "So? Go around it."

Julie looked up at the man. He has a very kind face, she thought. "The wall doesn't seem to end."

"Get a ladder and climb over it," the bartender said.

"No ladder."

"There's always a way," the bartender said. "*You'll* find it."

Encouragement was always good, even from a stranger. Julie forced herself to take a bite of her burger and looked around the room, glancing at the theatrical neon stock ticker and two Munifacts machines mounted over the rectangular bar. "Why is this place so crowded?" she asked the bartender. "Everyone else on Wall Street seems to be rushing home to their families to start the Thanksgiving weekend early."

"Well, for a lot of Wall Street people, this *is* their family, or their second family."

"So they're friends?"

"Or rivals, even enemies—but still brethren, if you know what I mean. They live out half their lives here, it seems, gloating or trying to forget their mistakes, or making excuses. But they always come here afterward."

"After what?"

"Their triumphs—or their losses."

"And you watch."

"I think of myself as an observer of life. The name's Mike, by the way," he said, extending a hand.

"Julie," she said, smiling and giving it a shake. "So tell me, Mike, anything really interesting ever happen in this joint?"

"Well, you remember *Bonfire of the Vanities*, the Tom Hanks' movie?"

"Sure."

"They filmed a couple of scenes right here."

"That's the most exciting thing that's ever happened here?"

Mike refilled her glass. "Interesting, probably. But not the most exciting. The most exciting was a wager."

"Wager? Just an ordinary bet?"

The bartender considered the question, then lowered his voice. "This was no ordinary bet m' dear," he said confidentially. "It was for a million dollars."

"Come on," she scoffed playfully, "A *million* dollars? Just one bet?"

"You've haven't heard about it? Everyone on Wall Street has been talking about it for weeks."

"I'm not in the industry."

"Ah, that explains it. Well, it was after work one night not too long ago...." The bartender related the whole story, telling her about Mulvaney and Monelli.

"Did you say Mulvaney?" Julie asked. "*Barton* Mulvaney?"

"Yeah, that's the guy. Hey, didn't you say you're not in the business?"

"I've heard of him," Julie said. "But the name Monelli is new to me."

"He's pretty well known in the neighborhood. He's a mergers and acquisitions guy over at Harrison Hart. He's a player, one of the best, they say."

"So this wasn't a friendly bet, I imagine." Julie said, interrupting.

Mike chuckled. "Friendly? Those two *hate* each other. Goes way back. And just a few weeks ago, Bart burned Mario on the Intercoastal deal."

"Hmmm....the Intercoastal deal. That's interesting," Julie said. This was getting better and better, she thought. "Do you know where Harrison Hart is?"

"Yeah. World Financial Center, over on Vesey Street. That's just..."

"Yeah, I know where it is. Listen, thanks, Mike—you've been quite helpful."

"Me? What did *I* do?"

Julie dropped a twenty dollar bill on the counter, smiled at the bartender, and hurried out.

No time for phone interviews, she thought as she headed toward the World Financial Center. He was either going to be there or he wasn't, he would either see her or he wouldn't, he was either the right guy or he wasn't, there was no more time, there were no more chances. She was throwing a Hail Mary.

Julie had expected the usual beautiful blonde barely-out-of-her-teens receptionist in the Harrison Hart lobby, but it was late in the day, and the desk was being manned by the horsey-faced woman. She was stacking some papers and evidently about to leave.

"Can I help you?"

"I'd like to see Mario Monelli."

"And you are?"

"Julie Chambers. I'm a producer at UBS television. I'd like to talk with him."

"Do you have an appointment?"

"No," Julie said. "But please, it's urgent."

Rose Pheeney picked up the phone and relayed the information while eying Julie. "No," she said into the phone, "she doesn't have a camera." Then she hung up. "You're in luck, honey. He'll be with you in a minute."

Julie breathed a sigh of relief. She looked around the luxurious glass-and-steel lobby, whose walls were lined with original oil paintings by Picasso, Miro, Monet, Renoir, and a melting orange-and-green landscape that must be the work of Salvador Dali. She chose a seat under the Dali, so she didn't have to look at it. Then she heard a man's voice behind her. "I guess I won't have to write UBS that letter after all."

Julie turned and found a man approaching her, a fairly tall, well-built man with rolled-up shirt sleeves and a loosened tie knotted at a rakish angle, evidently Mario Monelli.

"I beg your pardon?" she said.

"Last week, my eight-year-old boy was home from school, sick, when his mother caught him watching one of your soaps on the tube—a half-naked couple in bed insinuating intercourse. Now I'm no prude, lady, but I don't think an eight-year-old should be exposed to that kind of thing."

"Maybe his mother should keep a closer eye on the boy," Julie replied.

"Yeah, maybe I should be writing the letter to *her*." He chuckled and extended a hand. "I'm Mario Monelli," he said. "What can I do for you?"

"And I'm Julie, Julie Chambers," she said.

"Hello, Julie Chambers. Did I forget an appointment or something?"

"No appointment. I just took a chance you'd be here." She let the first impression wash over her—not a matinee idol, but more than presentable. Strong-looking, very self-confident and straight forward.

"I see. Who sent you?"

"Hmm...no one, exactly. I just heard about you. I only need a few minutes of your time."

"Do you have anything identifying you as a UBS employee?"

Julie showed him her company ID card. "You could call Hank Kozloff, the news director.

Mario regarded Julie with a combination of interest and suspicion, weighing his first impressions of her.

"Come, follow me, we'll talk in my office." Mario escorted Julie through the expansive, but practically empty trading floor. Mario beat her to the M&A suite by a few steps and managed to get the Wall of Shame rolled up before she saw it.

"Pardon the mess. The cleaning staff hasn't had a chance to...Can I get you anything, water, a Coke?"

"No, thank you" Julie said, looking around the suite. It looked like a frat house, the desks littered with coffee cups and cigarette butts competing for space with framed snapshots of children and dog-eared manila folders. She took a seat—Neil's chair—and crossed her legs, noticing Mario's effort not to be obvious about looking.

"So Julie—if I can I call you Julie—what brings you here?"

Julie, busy regarding Mario, trying to evaluate him, forgot to answer. She hated the office, but enjoyed the timbre of his voice and his quick way of speaking.

Mario reminded her that he was asking a question. " I said what did you hear about me?"

"I heard that you're one of the best."

Mario flashed her a mischievous look. "At what?"

"The mergers and acquisitions business," Julie said with just the faintest trace of a smile.

"Ah. Yes. Well, I hope you're not looking for an argument."

They both laughed.

"Seriously, why are you here—what do you want from me? Stock tips?"

"Well, no, it's just that I heard about you and..."

"I know, you said that already."

"Yes I did, didn't I. I guess you can say I'm looking for an opinion."

"Opinion, about what?"

"Foreign investment in the U.S." She waited for his reaction.

"That's it? No warm up? Nothing about my history or anything—just foreign investment?"

"For a start."

"Okey dokey," Mario said, and launched into it. "On a small scale, foreign investment in U.S. equity or treasury debt is just fine, or investing in a little real estate. It gives other countries a stake in our growth. But on a large scale, it's suicide."

"Suicide," Julie repeated, "How so?"

Mario flashed her the kind of look teachers sometimes direct toward slow learners. "Look," he said, reaching for a rubber band and entangling it in his fingers, "America was built on industry, on manufacturing. But we've already sent most of that overseas. And we're spending our money to buy the products, not adding to our own prosperity, but contributing to the trade deficit."

"But buying foreign products isn't the same as having foreign countries invest in American companies, is it?" Julie asked.

"You're right. It's not. But imagine this. Today, Nike is making a profit from those Asian-made sneakers it sells here. What happens when a substantial amount of that profit goes to foreign investors? It's just another way to drain money out of America, and even more insidious than the outsourcing."

Julie was impressed—this guy was strong, clear, and direct. He talked like it really mattered to him. She pushed harder. "But it does help the global economy, doesn't it?"

"Maybe, in the short run—ten or fifteen years. But in the long run, it's a disaster for the entire world. We're the world's marketplace, the globe's great consumers. What happens when we can't afford foreign products?"

"I hear what you're saying," Julie said, continuing to push him, "but the American economy is so much stronger than any other…"

"Let me give you a little taste—Julie, your name is? In 1962, eighty-eight percent of the cars sold in North America were made right here in the good old USA. By the big three: GM, Ford, and Chrysler. Now, only a *third* of the cars sold in North America are made by U.S. car manufacturers."

"But I hear American cars are much better than they used to be—can't the trend be reversed?"

"Yeah, if you believe in miracles. The labor costs are so much lower abroad, and so are the health care and pension costs. We can't make the investments necessary to match Koreans on price, the Japanese on quality, and the Europeans on performance. We've already lost the electronics and apparel industry for similar reasons, and we're going to lose the steel industry unless we're very lucky. So instead of them sharing in our growth, we're getting their leftovers. So much for your *fucking* global economy." Well, that was a little rough, Mario told himself, but she's the one who came to *me*.

He'll have to do a lot better than that if he wants to shock me, Julie thought. She served him another question. "Okay, but what about this: don't foreign companies create manufacturing jobs right here in America? We do have Toyota and Nissan plants here, you know."

"Sure we do," Mario volleyed. "And we get one new job here for every five we give *them*. And we wouldn't get *that* if we didn't play kiss ass with Toyota, Nissan, *and* Honda, giving them tax breaks and special regulations. Hey, why aren't you taking notes?" He tossed her a pencil, not hiding his annoyance.

Damn, Julie thought. He's right. He had her mesmerized. "Okay," she said, picking up a pencil and opening her notebook. "But, as an investment banker, if you refuse to participate and help foreigners invest in or buy

American companies, aren't you leaving a lot of money on the table?" Julie knew how Barton Mulvaney would have answered this question. Money was what drove these guys. Monelli, too, she expected.

"Some," Mario admitted, trying to sound reasonable. "But I've never had a problem making money, and by protecting U.S. companies from venture capitalists advising on foreign buyouts, I'm helping keep America whole. I think that's worth something. Don't you agree?"

Julie didn't know why, but somehow she trusted this man—at least a little.

He spoke with passion—and conviction…in language simple people could understand. That was all too rare. "Mr. Monelli, I haven't been completely honest with you. The program I'm working on isn't really about foreign investment, at least not in the usual sense."

Mario gave her a long, hard look. "Look, tell me the truth or let me go back to work."

"Okay, here's the truth: UBS has come into possession of some very troubling facts about a clandestine and massive foreign effort to buy out the whole top tier of America's flagship companies—DuPont, GE, the television networks, the entertainment industry. Everything. It's a full-scale economic ambush, and the special I'm putting together is intended to expose it, and, we hope, garner public support to stop it."

She waited for a reaction, and it was a long time coming. "Who's the conspiracy theorist behind all this?" Mario asked, obviously unconvinced. "Do you seriously expect me to believe what you just said?"

"I didn't believe it either, not at first. Although we've yet to learn their intentions, I've seen the details of their actions. I've seen the facts. I know the sources, who are absolutely unimpeachable. But I can't reveal them to you. At least not yet."

"Okay," Mario said, "let's say I believe this story of yours. Where do I fit in?"

"We need someone to make our case on television credibly and convincingly. And it can't be a journalist. It has to be someone on the inside—like the scientist who exposed the tobacco industry."

"I see. So Wall Street is involved—you think."

"Wall Street is *definitely* involved. In some ways, it's being victimized and manipulated. But most of it is pure, unabated greed. And we all know that Greed is man's proverbial yoke."

"So I hear," Mario said. "Well, how about this: let me see what you've got. I'll evaluate it, and then I'll let you know."

"I can't do that," Julie said. "I've already told you more than I should have. If you agree to get involved, then I'll share everything I have."

"I'm supposed to take this on faith?" Mario asked. He didn't know what to make of what this woman was telling him. She seemed honest, even earnest, but…

"Okay, I'll give you one example," she said. "You know who bought Intercoastal?"

"Of course. It was a Kansas City consortium."

"I can prove it was no such thing. It was actually financed by a bank in Buenos Aires, and they were working for, well, a Middle Eastern power."

Mario stared at Julie, dumbfounded. "You're out of your mind."

"The money trail has been traced all the way back. In great detail. By an agency of the U.S. government. We have all the documents. The experts tell us they are genuine, without question."

"Why come to me? Why not go to the authorities?"

"That's been tried. But either they refuse to believe it, or they refuse to act, or they're in collusion."

"So you believe it's up to you, your network."

"Who else? We're going to set out the facts, then stage a debate over what they mean to the American people and the future of the country."

"Have you lined up an opponent?"

"In fact we have. Barton Mulvaney. Know him?"

Mario leaped out of his chair. "Mulvaney? What is this, some kind of set-up?"

"No. Nothing of the sort, Mr. Monelli. Everything I've said to you is true. And when Mulvaney agreed to participate, I'd never even heard your name."

Mario regarded Julie skeptically, but continued. "Does he know what you're planning?"

"Only in general. He thinks the show is about foreign investment."

Mario put a finger to his lips, sat back down in his chair, and considered what he'd just been told. He was amazed. He was also infuriated, especially when he thought about Intercoastal. "This is all pretty sudden," he said. "What am I, Miss Chambers, second choice? Third choice?"

"It's Julie, and no. You're the first person I've asked, Mr. Monelli."

"It's Mario, and when is this all due to air?"

"Mid-January."

Mario visibly relaxed. "That means I have plenty time to think about it."

"Not really," Julie said reluctantly.

"Something else you haven't told me?"

He might as well know it all, Julie thought. "Yeah, if I can't sign up a better candidate by tonight, I'm going to be stuck with someone I think can't do the job."

"And what makes you think *I* can?"

Julie looked at Mario directly. "I don't know. Intuition, I suppose."

The idea of going head-to-head with Barton Mulvaney on national television was almost irresistible, except that there was always a chance he'd make a fool out of himself. "Look, you came in here a few minutes ago and dumped a load of bricks on my face. You expect an instant decision?"

"No. But I'd like you to seriously consider what I've said and tell me as soon as possible because time is running out."

There was something about this woman Mario found intriguing, he decided, something that made him want to say yes to her. "Let me sleep on it," he said.

The moment Julie walked out of the World Financial Center, she flipped open her cell phone and excitedly called Paige. "Paige, I think we found our shooter. See what you can dig up on Mario Monelli. I'll be there in half an hour."

By the time Julie got back to the office, Paige had printed out more than 100 Internet references that chronicled Mario Monelli's career.

"He sounds absolutely terrific," Paige said, sounding like a teenager asking about her best friend's date at a pajama party. "So tell me about him!"

Julie decided against teasing her. "Well…he's in his mid-to-late forties, decent looking I suppose."

"How do you think he'll do on television?"

"Well, he can talk, that's for sure. He has a lot of poise and self-confidence. He doesn't have Mulvaney's polish, but then he doesn't have Mulvaney's annoying slickness either."

"But is he willing to go up against Bart?"

"He's pretending to be reluctant, but frankly I think he relishes the idea. Still needs some convincing, though. What do you have on him?"

Paige spread her printouts over Julie's desk. Mostly they were brief mentions in the financial press, featuring Mario and the Zoo Crew's footprints in various mergers and takeovers, some dating back as far as twenty years. There was also a three-year-old piece from Crain's Business news, a one-page profile with a picture of Mario on the cover during his negotiations with Time Warner.

In the profile, the journalist called Mario "one of Wall Street's smartest operators, the engine that made Hart so successful, and the reason Harrison president, Tyler Gentry, wanted the merger."

They kept turning pages. A *Business Week* article called him "one of Wall Street's white hats, and one of the few people feared by Carl Icahn and the takeover sharks."

"Damn," Julie said. "He's in *Forbes*. He's in *Barron's*. He's not a mirage. He actually does exist. Look at this, Krugman of *The New York Times* called him 'a working class hero.' The man who single handed saved twenty-one thousand manufacturing jobs from being outsourced to India."

"What's his academic background?" Paige asked.

Julie poured through the clippings. "Two years at City College, night school." Then a thought occurred to her: How could he even get his foot in the door of a major Wall Street outfit with an associates' degree from CUNY when every investment banker I've talked with is an Ivy Leaguer?

"Hey, Julie, listen to this," Paige said, and began to read. "… A Horatio Alger story, Mario was a native of Brooklyn's Red Hook section, who went to work bussing tables and lugging clothes racks through the garment district while helping put his brother through Fordham law school. It was at the Hart Alliance's company cafeteria where he was discovered by Hart CEO and mentor, Austin Keyes…"

Julie grabbed the paper and read the article for herself. Then she looked up in disbelief. "He was a busboy."

"Unbelievable. How did you find him?" Paige asked.

"By accident, really," Julie said. "Just dumb luck."

"So, no George Van Wert?"

"Not if I can convince the boys Monelli is our man."

"How do you think they'll react?"

"I'm not worried about Hank, of course. But I'm pretty sure Miles and Fred will try to undercut me. Listen, Paige, run downstairs to the library and see if we have footage on Monelli. Anything you can get your hands on. Doesn't have to be current."

"You mean *this*," Paige said, holding up a tape. "It's him on MSNBC."

"Girl you're the best,' she said, taking the tape, scooping up all the Internet printouts and heading for the door.

"Where you going?" asked Paige.

"To climb over a wall," she said.

Julie ran upstairs thinking about how she would sell Mario whose storybook odyssey from street urchin to Wall Street gave her chills—piting him against Mulvaney, a gun-toting, blue blood diva born into a Wall Street dynasty but whose intuitive understanding of the complexities of the LBO elevated him into the uplands of Wall Street immortality.

Miles Corbin looked up as Julie entered Fisher's office. "Never mind, she's here," he said into the receiver and hung up the phone. Fred and Hank were already there, all of them looking pretty glum. Even Fisher seemed downcast.

"You left instructions we're to pass on Van Wert?" Miles said sternly. "Why?"

"Because I think I've found someone better," Julie said brightly. All of her instincts told her that Mario Monelli was the perfect dragon slayer. All she had to do now was to persuade the jury with her closing argument. And she knew there were two jurors in the room—Miles and Fred—who would relish her failure.

"Tell us about him," Hank said.

"Okay," Julie said. "I'm going to start by telling you what he *isn't*. He isn't a scion of the moneyed classes who run Wall Street. He's not movie star material. And he's not from the Ivy League."

"Then what is he?" Fred asked.

"He's just a working class guy who's fought his way up the ladder solely on brains and guts."

"Question *is* does he have the brains and guts to accomplish what we need?" Miles said, directing the question to Fisher.

"I'm over *here*, Miles." Julie reminded him.

"Does he have a name?" Hank asked.

"Mario Monelli." She swallowed hard.

"Mario Monelli?" Fred repeated, scrunching his face. "Where did you find *him,* in San Janeiros' feast, grabbin' his crotch, sayin' fugheddaboudit?"

"Fred…shut up," said Hank.

"Okay, Julie," said Miles. "Now that you've told us what this guy *doesn't* have, how about giving us some idea of what he *does* have. What's his background? What has he achieved? What's he done that would make him a credible opponent for Mulvaney. Remember, Barton Mulvaney has quite a résumé."

"So does Monelli," replied Julie. "He's one of the top five mergers and acquisitions men in America, and a staunch opponent of foreign investment. He led a movement that helped boot the Japanese out of Wall Street in the late eighties when they were buying everything in sight. He heads his own team at Harrison Hart—in fact, Tyler Gentry, who heads the firm, acquired Hart some years ago just to get Monelli's team on board."

Miles wasn't satisfied. "But Mulvaney's a mergers and acquisitions guy as well, isn't he? Do we want two of them?" He looked at everyone.

"Of course we do," Julie said. "That's what this whole Saudi effort is all about. And these two are no strangers to confrontation—especially with each other."

"Can you be more specific?" Fisher asked her.

"Certainly," she said. "Mulvaney is the shark many raiders use to help them bite off companies they want. He hunts their weaknesses and advises the raiders how to take advantage of them."

"And Monelli?" Fisher prompted.

"Monelli works for the other side—a dark angel for the companies under attack. He shows them how to strengthen their stock price so that they're less vulnerable."

"Isn't Monelli the guy who lost the Intercoastal proxy fight?" Miles inquired.

Julie was surprised. "So you *do* know who he is?"

"I remembered," Miles said without expression.

"Well, yes, he *did* lose Intercoastal, and it discredited him."

Hank had a thought. "He must be furious at Mulvaney."

"Furious is a poor word for it," Julie replied. "The bad blood between them is almost legendary on Wall Street."

"Wall Street has *always* been a river of bad blood, Julie."

"But theirs is visceral, culturally and socially driven. And the candle *still* burns hot. Right now, they've got a million dollar bet going."

That caught Fisher by surprise. "What's that?"

"The way I hear it, each of them is grooming a protégé, and they've bet a million dollars that their guy will be first to close a major deal—the *same* deal."

"Did you say one million?"

"Sounds like real drama," Hank observed. "Might be just what we need to smoke Mulvaney out."

"Yes, but do we really want hostility and overheated passion?" Miles asked.

"I'd give my right arm for a bare-knuckled brawl on live television," Hank said. "In fact, I can't think of anything better."

"Wait a minute, Julie," Fisher said. "You've told us that Mulvaney is very picky about who he'll appear with. He was adamant. What happens if he vetoes Monelli?"

Julie laughed. "I don't think there's any chance of that. He'll relish the idea of taking on Monelli—and even if he doesn't, he wouldn't risk losing face at the Harvard Club by backing away from the fight."

"That's all good," Fred said, "but this guy Moretti—he has to have *some* charisma. Otherwise, Mulvaney might make him look like a fool."

"Mario Monelli isn't going to lose this fight," Julie said with conviction.

"How can you be so sure, Julie? Fisher asked. "Didn't you just meet him yourself?"

"You're right, but sometimes it's obvious. Monelli—and that's his *right* name, Fred—is down-to-earth, gritty, savvy. Mulvaney is pretentious."

Fisher fired another question. "But would you call Monelli persuasive?"

"Well, he sold *me* and he wasn't even trying to. He doesn't hide his emotions, and he speaks with great conviction, which will resonate with John Q. So does Bart, but he always seems to have some kind of secret agenda. I wouldn't trust him to hold my sandwich at a picnic."

"And what makes Monelli so tough?"

"Let me put it like this," replied Julie. "He put his older brother through Fordham law school lugging clothes racks up and down the garment district. Do that twelve hours a day and you can wrestle bears."

Everyone in the room looked at each other.

"We have Monelli on tape?" Fisher wanted to know.

"Right here," Julie said, handing Fred the tape. Fred slid the video tape into Fisher's player, and they all settled back to watch. Julie crossed her fingers not having viewed the tape prior to handing it over. But she hadn't any choice.

It was a clip from a business program. The interviewer, an overly-attractive girl who seemed scarcely out of college, was interviewing a well-dressed, well-built, dark-haired man with deep-set eyes.

"It's a few years old," Julie said. "But you'll get the idea."

"Mr. Monelli, I understand that you've tangled with Mike Milken—and won. Could you tell me about that?" It was Hanna Nettler of MSNBC, blonde, clear-eyed, and too young to grasp the financial complexities she'd been hired to discuss.

"I think you're talking about Indiana Railroad," said the man across from her, looking a little uncomfortable to be in front of the camera. "There was a group that wanted to buy the company and sell off most of its assets to raise cash for another buyout."

"And Milken was behind it?"

"He was a source for the financing, yes. It was a hostile takeover attempt, financed with junk bonds."

"Which were Milken's specialty…"

"That's correct, Hannah." There was a little twinkle in Mario's eye. Any trace of discomfort was gone.

"So what happened?"

"My people and I did an in-depth strategic analysis and found a white knight—Chicago and Northwestern. It turned out to be a perfect fit."

"So Indiana Railroad survived?"

"Yes, but that's not the main thing. The merger saved 15,000 jobs—the raiders were set on restructuring them out of existence. It also saved the pensions of everyone who worked for both companies, as well as several small Midwestern cities that would have lost their rail service and died." There was a new note in Mario's voice, a hint of pride.

"How did you get it to work? Indiana Railroad was about to go into Chapter 11 Bankruptcy, wasn't it? Both rating agencies had them at C minus." She sounded like she was reading from notes.

"Yes, but the infusion of capital from Chicago and Northwestern let them restructure their debt. My team and I streamlined assets and helped negotiate a different capital structure by accelerating share buybacks. Then we got the union to restructure the labor agreements. It was all a matter of mutual trust and respect."

"Do you and Michael Milken still talk?"

Mario smiled slightly. "No, not really. He was out of circulation for a long time, as you know, and our paths don't cross that often these days."

"Well, thank you for talking to us, Mr. Monelli. And—what can I say—good luck with your next deal."

"Thanks," Mario said, "but it's hard work that matters, not luck."

The screen in Fisher's office went blank and everyone turned toward him for his verdict. "I can see why you're proposing this guy," Fisher said. "His political views are just right for the show. I can imagine his reaction to the Saudi threat."

"I think he'll do a good job defending his point of view," Hank said. "But it's more than that. Julie's right, he's got *conviction*. You don't see that very often, at least not on Wall Street."

Fisher reached for his pipe, then decided not to light it.

"He was okay in that little clip," Fred Fielding said, "but we don't have any guarantee he can kill the dragon."

"That's what worries me," Miles Corbin said. "Your man is a bit rough around the edges. Unpolished. It's not *his* fault, but he simply doesn't have Mulvaney's breeding or pedigree. You have to admit he's a little bit, well, ethnic."

Julie tried to contain her anger. "Most of *America* is ethnic, Miles."

"Listen, we're not PBS," Carleton Fisher reminded everyone. "We're not targeting an audience of intellectuals who spend their off hours reading Tolstoy. Our audience is the average man and woman, the average family. They're almost certain to relate better to Monelli than Mulvaney."

"Do you have a commitment from him, Julie?" Hank asked.

"I haven't made the offer yet, but I'm confident he'll agree to appear."

"Happy Thanksgiving, kids," said Fisher, "looks like we got ourselves a fight."

Neither Miles nor Fred had anything else to say. They knew the decision had been made and that further discussion was futile.

So did Julie, but she was careful to hide her elation. Hank on the other hand *wasn't*. He reached for the phone. "We'll get Brian Cates to direct?"

"Not so fast," Julie interrupted pressing down hard on the receiver.

"But, Julie, Cates is our best," Hank said.

Julie looked at Fisher. "I pick my own crew, including directors, remember?"

"Who do you have in mind?"

All eyes followed Julie's and they landed firmly on Fred.

"Any objections, Miles?" Fisher said, smiling broadly now.

Harold Bloom, one of the four transcribers in the SEC's Wall Street secret listening post, lifted his fingers from his computer keyboard and carefully adjusted his headset. Then he stepped on the transcribing machine foot pedal again, listening intently.

Bloom's unusual motion caught the attention of his superior, Chester Hinkley, who was continually surveying his entire squad of listeners and transcribers. He watched the man to see if more was coming, or if the fellow was simply trying to get comfortable, or fidgeting.

Oddly enough, Bloom repeated his actions precisely. He ceased typing, fiddled with his headphones and tapped his foot pedal again. Then, he did it once more. Hinkley sat up straight in his hard wooden chair and waited for Bloom to say something.

After two more repetitions of this little performance without a word or signal from Bloom, Hinkley couldn't stand it anymore. He walked over to Bloom and tapped him on the shoulder, which caused the man to nearly jump out of his seat.

"Something interesting?"

"Just a phrase. Probably doesn't mean anything."

Hinkley sighed. Getting this man to speak up was just about impossible. "What phrase?" he asked.

"I don't have any idea what it means, if anything," Bloom replied.

"Tell me the words, Harold."

"Lions' Den."

"Lions' Den? That's it? Sounds like a metaphor."

"Yes, I thought so, too, the first time I heard it."

Now Hinkley was interested. "You've heard it before? When?"

"Oh, all week long—six or seven times."

"From what sources?"

"A variety. I'd have to look up their names."

Hinkley contemplated this for a few moments. "Put the phrase on the report to Washington," he said. "And look up the names. See if you can have them before two o'clock."

"Two o'clock? But that would cut into my lunch hour."

"I'll tell you what. When you give me the names, then you can take lunch."

CHAPTER SIXTEEN

By the time Mario got to the deli, the streets were deserted and Sol was blocking the door. Mario tapped on the glass. "One more customer before you close for Thanksgiving?"

Sol unlocked the door and held it open. "You said the magic word."

"What's that?"

"Customer."

Sol walked behind the glass counter, with its amazing display of meats, salads, and other deli dishes, retied his apron and looked at Mario.

"Gimme a corned beef on rye, an order of potato pancakes, a Coke, and a piece of cheesecake, to go."

"Ya wanna double it up, like last time?"

Mario hesitated. He knew he should, but he was having trouble finding the heart for it. He was having trouble finding the heart for anything much these days. He hadn't been able to take his mind off Danny for more than a few minutes, or the look in Rick's eyes.

A few moments later, Sol was handing Mario an overstuffed brown paper bag. Soon, Mario was walking through the empty streets, approaching Cortlandt alley. Then he heard something confusing: a roaring sound and a torrent of water pouring into a nearby sewer drain, coming from inside the alley. He snaked around a pair of fifty-five-gallon drums, and there was Gus, totally naked, in front of an open standpipe, washing himself. He was still a fairly imposing figure, slender, but well-muscled, despite the ravages of time, wear, and decades of self-imposed deprivation.

"Damn, Gus," Mario said, "you're gonna catch your death of cold."

"I'm used to it, Gus said. "Hey, hand me that towel." He pointed to an ancient, threadbare Statler Hotel bathmat on his cart's bottom shelf.

"This thing?"

"Yeah. Maid didn't bring any fresh linen today."

Gus dried himself off, shivering, then looked at Mario expectantly. "Just happened to be in the neighborhood?"

"Brought us lunch," Mario said, showing him the bag.

"What, again? I told you, no telling what all that decent food is gonna do to my system." He wrapped himself in the bathmat, picked up a rusty wrench and shut off the standpipe.

"Eat it anyhow," Mario said, tossing Gus a sandwich.

Without any concern for modesty, Gus rewrapped himself in his customary castoffs and scavenged clothing, sat down on a box, and began wolfing down his sandwich.

Mario sat down across from him, spreading out his meal on his knees. He lackadaisically picked at a potato pancake with a white plastic fork.

"You're still troubling yourself about the boy," Gus said.

"Danny. Yeah."

Gus looked up at him, sharply. "Sleeping okay?"

Mario nodded.

"And work, still hard to keep your mind on it?"

Mario nodded again. Then he perked up. "But I have this opportunity to be on television."

"On the tube, you serious?"

"Yeah, some producer came to see me today. A real looker. Seems they're looking to do some sort of…to be honest I don't know what they're looking to do. All I know is they want me to do it."

"Sounds interesting," Gus said, trying to be encouraging. "Will you still bring me sandwiches when you're a big celebrity?"

Mario laughed half-heartedly.

Gus looked at him thoughtfully. "It won't always hurt this much," he said, after awhile.

Mario looked up at him.

"Don't underestimate the power of time, Mario."

"How has time helped *you*?" Mario asked, genuinely curious.

"Are you kidding?" Gus said. "Every time I walked into that ring, I knew everything what was gonna happen. He had a move, I had a counter. He thought the bell would save him, I knew I still had ten seconds. I was in control. Only I wasn't really in control. Fate was standing right beside me, ready to count me out."

"What does this have to do with me?"

"Well, same thing with you. You think you're in control, ain't nothin' gonna happen unless you say so. But fate is standing right next to you, lickin' its chops, ready to sucka punch you."

"You mean like with what happened to Danny? It wasn't my fault, it was fate? If that's true, why do I feel so goddamn guilty?"

Gus tore off a chunk of potato pancake, dipped it in applesauce and popped it into his mouth. "Because you think *everything* is your fault."

"You mean I shouldn't feel guilty?" Mario said.

"Okay. I got a question for you: What could you have done differently?"

"I could have forbidden them to go to the party, or I could have taken them myself."

"You'd have done that forever?"

Mario took a deep breath and shook his head.

"Of course not. You had every reason to believe the boy would be responsible. You couldn't have known that boy would end up dying." Gus made a fist and held it up. "Look at this," he demanded. "Look!"

Mario looked. Gus's hand was scarred across the knuckles and swollen, and the skin, ash-colored and cracked in several places.

"I killed a man—with this. I ended the life of my best friend—with this. I *earned* my guilt. You...you didn't do nothin'. But that friend of yours—he abandoned his son, climbed out of the ring and told you to take his place, letting you take the beating that was meant for him. And your *still* taking it. Don't you think it's time you get out?"

Mario thought about the old fighter's words. Gus seemed to have a deeper view of the world than he did, maybe a clearer view.

Then something occurred to Mario. "I have an idea," he said. "Come to my house tomorrow for Thanksgiving dinner."

"Naw, Mario, don't worry 'bout me. I'll go to the armory and get some grub like I always do Thanksgiving."

Mario stood up. "No, Gus, not tomorrow. Tomorrow you're coming home with me." He was adamant. "Besides, you would be doing me a favor. My oldest son, Boomer, the kid...well the kid is in worse shape than I am. Maybe a few words from you..."

Gus looked himself up and down, at the oversized pants, the clothesline belt and the ludicrously mismatched laceless sneakers. "What's your missus goin' to say when I walk in like this?"

"I'll handle her. You just be here and ready by two."

Mario headed back to Harrison Hart to retrieve his briefcase. Back in M&A, he found his briefcase, stuffed it with a few documents he wanted to review during the long weekend, and headed out. When he got to the lobby again, he found Tyler waiting at the elevator banks in his overcoat.

"Anyone else back there?" Tyler asked casually.

"Not anymore," Mario said.

"So Mario, what are your plans with the family tomorrow, staying home?"

"My brother is coming over. You?"

"The usual."

He had a feeling Tyler had something on his mind.

"Say, how's that thing coming by the way, that project of yours?"

Ah, here it was. "Which one?" Mario asked, baiting Tyler to say it.

"You know, that club you're building. Where is it, Randall's Island?"

"Wards," Mario said offhandedly. "Moving along."

Ever since the Halloween party, Mario had expected Tyler to approach him. But it had taken weeks. He admired the man's self-control.

"So, how's the membership drive coming along?"

"Well, we have a few spots open, but what we're really looking for is one last associate. Right now it's a bidding war between some guys at Goldy and Dresdner."

"Hmm," said Tyler, "an associate? What's that?"

"That's someone with special privileges, Tyler—guaranteed accommodations, prime rooms, first-class service."

"I see. And what does it cost to become an associate?"

"A hundred grand upfront, plus common charges," Mario said casually. "But the associate is also responsible for bringing in ten standard members, at the usual $50,000 entrance fee."

"You and your guys—the Zoo Crew..."

"We're all associates," Mario said. Mario knew Tyler didn't relish getting in bed with him and the Zoo Crew, nor any of Hart's House of Commons. Poor bastard must have had a horrendous time finding a place to get laid Halloween night.

"And how long would a new associate have to sign up these members?"

Mario pretended to contemplate the question, but he knew that Tyler was hooked and that the Lions' Den money troubles were over—*if* he could reel him in. After all, when it came to women, men were primal no matter what their breeding.

"Well, I'd say two weeks."

"I see," Tyler said, hand to his chin, thinking.

The down signal on the elevator bank chimed and the doors opened on the car directly in front of them. The half dozen people inside moved back to let Mario and Tyler in. But Tyler waved them on and the door closed.

"Let's get something straight, Mario, it's not that I don't love my wife. She's been everything a good wife should be, except..."

"Say no more," Mario said. "Everyone will understand."

"Ten members you say?"

"Minimum," Mario replied. "I would think that among your circle of friends..." He let the sentence dangle.

Tyler fell silent for a few moments, thinking, perhaps calculating, considering acquaintances. "This has to be absolutely confidential, Mario," he said, finally. "If Helena or the partners ever found out..."

"Let me be frank with you, Tyler. You're going to see people you know, and they're going to see you. But it's a matter of mutually assured destruction. No one can say anything without revealing his own sins."

Tyler straightened himself to maximum height. "Come with me," he said, and he walked back to his office, flipped the lights on, and got his checkbook out of his desk.

"Make it out to the Lions' Den Ltd," Mario said.

CHAPTER SEVENTEEN

They pulled into the driveway, parked, and walked to the front door, Gus checking to make sure his buttons were buttoned and his zipper was zipped.

Mario opened the door and stood aside to let Gus enter. "We're here, Phyllis," he called. This better go well, he thought. If that bitch says or does anything…They were in the kitchen before he could finish the thought. Phyllis stood at the counter, working on the turkey, her back to the entrance way.

"Phyllis," Mario said politely, "this is my friend, Gus. Remember, I told you about him."

"Nice to meet you, Mrs. Monelli. You have a beautiful home."

Phyllis looked over her shoulder. "Yeah, the boxer. Mario told me about you."

She turned back to the counter and continued working on the turkey.

"Where are the boys?"

Phyllis didn't bother to turn around. "In the yard with the football."

"C'mon, Gus, I'll introduce you."

"Mind if I like wash up first?" Gus said.

"Sure—wait, I have a better idea. How would you like a hot shower?" Phyllis turned, shooting daggers at Mario. "And come to think of it," Mario said, studiously avoiding Phyllis's glare, "I think I have some clean clothes that would fit you reasonably well."

They left Phyllis stewing, along with everything else she had going on the stove. Mario led the way upstairs, Gus following hesitantly. "Holy mother of jesus, I never seen a bedroom like this," he said.

Mario opened his wall closet filled with fall casual wear, more than he'd ever wear.

"Whatever you see here, Gus."

Gus gave Mario a long look. "Naw, I couldn't…"

"Sure you could," Mario said. "I got closets full, just going to waste. That door leads to the bathroom. Help yourself to one of my bathrobes."

Gus put a hand on his dirt-encrusted shirt. "What should I…."

"Give it to me and wash them for you," Mario said.

Gus took a step toward the bathroom, then stopped. "Thanks, Mario," he said, then disappeared into the bathroom. "Jesus Christ," Mario heard Gus say through the door.

Mario rummaged around in his closet and picked out some of what he'd outgrown—the pants with the thirty-four inch waist that hadn't fit since the Harrison merger, selected the accessories. He stacked everything at the foot of the bed, and left Gus to what he knew must have been his first hot shower in years.

The doorbell rang as Mario was coming downstairs, and he got it. It was his brother, Frank and his sister-in-law, Millie, who were seldom part of Monelli Thanksgivings. They entered in a flurry of friendly greetings and laughter, and Frank presented a bottle of wine to Phyllis.

"Very nice, Frank, thanks," Phyllis said. "Did you know we have a guest."

"So I heard," said Frank. "Is he here yet?"

"Upstairs, freshening up," Mario said, taking their coats.

"What's happening in the game?" Frank asked, heading into the living room.

"Mario!" Phyllis's nasal summons beckoned Mario as he was about to plop down on the couch beside Frank and watch the Detroit Lion-Dallas game. "What?" he shouted back.

"Come in the kitchen for a minute. I wanna talk to you."

"Jeez, Phyllis, now?"

"Yeah, now."

Mario looked at Frank, then pushed the door open and trudged into the kitchen.

"Now what?" he asked as Phyllis was glazing the yams.

"Get the card table and one of the folding chairs. They're in the basement."

"Why?"

"Well, you don't think for one minute I'm going to have that bum eating at my dining room table on Thanksgiving," Phyllis said. "Set it up in the living room, where we can't see him. He can eat with Benson." She looked at her sister-in-law, Millie. "He brings niggers to my house."

"Please, Phyllis...it's Thanksgiving," Millie said.

"Okay, he can eat with us," Phyllis said. "But not off my Lenox. He'll use a paper plate and plastic flatware, and like it."

"If he does, you'll be eating on a paper plate, too, Phyllis."

Mario returned to the living room and glanced at the television set. "What happened to the game?"

"Its halftime. The Lions are getting crushed."

"Always a blowout on muthafuckin' Thanksgiving."

"Never mind the game," Frank said. "So tell me about this woman producer came to see ya. You really considering doing this?"

"The only reason I said I'll think about it was the fact that I'd be going on opposite that arrogant snake Mulvaney."

"You're like one of those dogs at the Florida racetrack, Mario. Wave a Mulvaney bunny at you and you're off and running."

"I just want to sink that fucker's ship and this may be my chance to do it."

"By pissing each other off on television."

"There's more to it that I can't tell you, Frank. At least not yet."

Frank looked at Mario skeptically, but something on television had caught Mario's eye.

"...and not only has Bank of America bought an interest in a Chinese bank," UBS news anchorman John Ayers was saying, "but a Chinese Bank, Minsheng, is rumored to be looking for Wall Street properties. In other news..."

Mario hit the mute. "Minsheng, that's Rick's new outfit."

"Ever hear anything from him since...?"

Mario just shook his head, glumly.

"So, Mario," Frank said, his tone of voice signaling a subject change, "this guy upstairs...You never was one to pick up strays. I mean, I'm all in favor of charity—and you told me how this guy saved your ass. Still—Thanksgiving dinner? With your family...with Phyllis?"

"I told you he was a boxer, didn't I?"

"Yeah, when Jesus was a baby."

"I'm serious, Frank. He was a terrific middleweight. I did some research on him."

"And now he's a bum."

"To the eye," Mario said, a little annoyed with his brother. "But there's something about him, I don't know—deep. He's done a lot of thinking about life."

"So what's he think about living in the gutter?" Frank asked. "Doesn't he have family?"

"As a matter of fact, he did. A wife and kid. I don't think he knows what happened to them." Then Mario had an idea. "Hey wait a minute, Frank, what about that Magnum PI guy of yours..."

"You mean Burt?"

"Yeah. Think *he* could find the boy?"

"Are you kidding? Burt could find what bleacher seat Jimmy Hoffa is buried under at the Meadowlands. I'll give him a hoot."

Then Gus appeared on the staircase, and they both stopped talking.

This wasn't the same man Mario had taken upstairs earlier. It was a slender black gentleman, clean-shaven, clear-eyed and smiling broadly, nattily dressed in clothing slightly too big for him—crisp khaki pants, a tartan-plaid flannel shirt with a Ralph Lauren logo, Nikes that looked like they'd just come out of the box.

Frank was confused. "*That's* Gus?"

"The very same," Gus said with a wide smile.

Frank and Gus shook hands and introduced themselves.

Phyllis barreled out of the kitchen with Millie to announce that dinner was served. They both stopped dead in their tracks when they saw Gus, Millie puzzled, Phyllis eyeing Gus as though he was a felon. "I recognize that clothing," she said after a moment. "That's Mario's stuff—were you prowling in our closets?"

"I put it out for him," Mario growled. "It's a Thanksgiving gift."

Phyllis looked over Gus again. "Well," she said with just the slightest edge, "clothes *do* make the man. I wonder what *you'd* be without them, Mario." She flounced back into the kitchen.

Mario would have followed her, but for Frank's restraining hand. "Sorry about that, Gus," Mario said.

"Ain't no big deal."

Boomer burst through the French doors twirling a football, Kyle close behind. "Is dinner ready yet?" he asked. Then they saw Gus and their mouths dropped open.

Gus stepped forward and extended that big, scarred hand of his. "Gus Shaw," he said. "And you must be Boomer....and *you're* Kyle. Nice to meet you both."

Kyle stared up at him in awe. "Are you the boxer who saved my Daddy?" he asked, in his little boy voice.

A smile came to Gus.

"That was a while ago, but I think I'm the guy you mean." He took Kyle's tiny hand and shook it.

Millie stuck her head out of the dining room. "Everything is on the table."

"We'll be right there, honey," said Frank.

Everyone trooped into the dining room, where Mario made the seating arrangements, situating Gus away from Phyllis. They took their places and Boomer reached out a fork to spear a slice of turkey.

Gus held up a hand. "Just a moment, son. I'd like to say a few words."

Phyllis opened her mouth to speak, but thought better of it.

Gus interlocked his fingers and closed his eyes. Everyone awkwardly joined hands. "I wish to thank this wonderful family for having me to this fine supper, at their beautiful home. I'm proud to be here..."

"Among friends," Mario said.

"Yes, among friends," Gus said, before going into the lord's prayer. When the blessing was over, everyone let go of each other's hand.

Now came the filling of the plates, with Boomer and Kyle leading the charge, piling on the turkey, scooping up mounds of mashed potatoes and peas, taking more slices of cranberry sauce than they were entitled to, then drowning everything in thick brown gravy.

Gus waited until the whole family had loaded up, except for Mario, who gestured for him to go first. He took a thigh, as well as modest helpings of the side dishes and trimmings.

"So, Gus, my brother tells me you were a middleweight?" Frank asked.

"Yes, sir, started out as a welter," Gus said, slicing off the drum stick. "But I couldn't stay away from the turkey." He ate a piece, eyes twinkling.

"What name did you fight under, Gus?" Boomer asked him.

"They called me Kid Chocolate."

"Just like the candy bar." Kyle said.

"Ummm, Kid Chocolate? Now where did I hear that name?" Frank said.

"My brother is a big fight fan, Gus," said Mario.

"That's strange, I knew all the middleweights from your time," Frank went on. "Kid Chocolate, you say?"

Gus gave Mario a nervous look from across the table as Frank struggled with his memory.

"Let's see, there was Dick Tiger, Griffith, Gene Fulmer, the Argentina kid, Monzon…and the guy who got put away for murder out in Newark, the one Denzel played—what was his name?"

"Ruben Carter," Gus replied. "They called him Hurricane, because of how fast he could throw punches."

"Did you fight him?" Kyle asked.

"No. He was in prison by the time I started getting good fights."

"Dad said you once knocked down Sonny Liston," Boomer said, chomping on his corn.

"It was only a sparring match, just before the Clay, I mean Ali fight. The first one. Liston was a heavy, you know. An ex-con, a real badass. And he didn't stay down long, believe me, at least not when I hit him."

"Quick, best fighter pound for pound you ever saw, Gus?" asked Frank.

"Oh, that's an easy one. The Sugarman. Ray Robinson."

"Could Ali have beaten Marciano?" Boomer asked.

"Hard to say, good as Ali was, he never came across a fighter like Marciano who could hit with both hands."

"Hey, Gus, tell us…"

"Alright, boys, enough about boxing. Let Gus eat," Mario said.

Boomer outmaneuvered Kyle for another slice of cranberry sauce, and left his little brother frustrated and pouting.

Gus turned to Kyle. "So, young man," he said, trying to distract him, "must be good to have an older brother to watch out for you."

"He doesn't *always* watch out for me," Kyle said. "Sometimes, when the older kids pick on me and laugh, on account I got left back, he doesn't help."

"Hmmm," Gus said, casting a disapproving glance at Boomer. "Show me what they do."

Kyle made a fierce face and threw a left toward Gus, who easily deflected it and mocked a counter-punch. "Did you see what I did when you threw the punch? I blocked with my right and surprised you, and while you were still surprised, I made a move with my left. You get that?"

"I think so."

"Good. Now *you* try." Gus launched a half-speed left at Kyle, who blocked it easily and punched Gus in the stomach hard enough to get a grunt. "Take it easy, boy," he said, smiling, "lotta turkey in there, and we want it to stay put." Phyllis watched the scene with distaste.

Millie brought out a dish of marshmallow candied yams, and the boxing banter ceased, while everyone reloaded their plate. When the conversation resumed, it was small talk about recipes, Wall Street, Caribbean cruises, and other trivia. And so it went for nearly an hour.

Once the table was clear, Phyllis and Millie brought out the desserts—an array of Italian pastries, Spumoni and, of course, espresso. Mario got a bottle of anisette from the liquor cabinet and filled the adults' glasses.

The boys, after peppering Gus with more boxing questions, asked him to join them in the backyard. "I'll come soon," he said. "Let me talk with the adults for awhile."

"Well okay," Boomer said. "But hurry."

Phyllis took a long sip of Sambuca, then lit up a cigarette, and turned toward Gus.

"Didn't you once kill a man in the ring," she said pleasantly. "Tell us about that."

Gus looked at her without expression.

"Kid Chocolate, that's it!" Frank erupted and said, "I remember now! It was Tommy…Tommy…" he said, snapping his fingers, "Tommy Harper up in Queens. It was the same night of the Quarry-Burns card."

Gus nodded, tried to pass it off. But he couldn't hide the profound sadness in his eyes.

Kyle bounced back into the room, took Gus's hand, and started tugging. "C'mon, uncle Gus, show us more about boxing? Please? Please?"

"Sure," he said with a sigh, and followed Kyle through the French doors, out into the brisk November night air.

Phyllis locked eyes with Mario from across the dinner table, then reaching for her cigarettes, got up. "Time to take care of the dishes," she said with a smug grin, then disappeared into the kitchen, leaving everyone else at the table gaping, except for Frank who was utterly bewildered.

"What did I say? Millie, Mario…"

"You're such a stupid ass," Millie said, picking up a tray, bringing it into the kitchen.

"Will somebody tell me what the hell just happened."

"Give me your legal opinion, Frank," Mario said grimly. "Is it still against the law to murder your wife?"

Mario got up and went to the window overlooking the back yard. Kyle was playing with the football. Gus and Boomer were off to the side, deep in conversation.

After a while, Gus came back into the living room, with Kyle propped on his shoulders, and Boomer, both feigning punches at imaginary opponents, and at each other, careful not to connect. It had been a long time since Mario had seen both his sons enjoying each other's company, or Boomer so happy.

"Thanks for talking to him, Gus," he said.

"He's a good kid," Gus replied. "They *both* are." Then he turned to Mario and sighed. "Maybe it's time for me to call it a night, Mario. Get out while the getting's good. Besides, Sam'll start wondering if I've abandoned him."

"Sam? Who's Sam?" Kyle asked.

"Sam is my cat. Picked him out of a trash can a while back. He was tied up in a garbage bag."

Kyle had a thought. "Does Sam like turkey?"

"Sam will eat just about anything," Gus said.

Kyle ran into the kitchen and came out a few moments later with a Zip-Loc bag full of turkey scraps.

"Your mother see you do that?" Mario asked.

The boy grinned and shook his head. He handed the bag to Gus, who thanked him.

"Are sure you gotta leave, Gus? It's still early," Frank said.

"I'm a bit worn out."

Kyle ran over to Gus and hugged him. "Don't go."

"Another time, young man. Remember to keep your right up."

Boomer stood there, not knowing what to do, and Gus shook his hand, quite formally. "Watch out for your little brother. He's all you got. And remember what I told you."

Gus turned toward Phyllis, who was sitting on the other side of the room, smoking a cigarette. "Thanks for the hospitality, ma'am. Great meal."

She waved at him half-heartedly.

Five minutes later, Mario and Gus were back in the Maserati and heading toward Manhattan, Gus now the proud possessor of another item from the depths of Mario's closet, a green nylon golf jacket from L.L. Bean.

Mario glanced over at Gus, who was gazing out of the window, deep in thought. "The boys sure took to you, Gus," he said.

Gus looked over at him and smiled, but Mario could see his thoughts were elsewhere.

"Sorry about Phyllis. She can be pretty tough to take."

"Why haven't you thrown in the towel?"

Mario reached for his wallet and flipped it open to the photo jacket of the boys, "Two reasons," he said simply.

"I know what ya mean," Gus said. "When ya young nothing matters but everyone else's happiness. But after the years beat 'cha up, you look back at your wasted youth and realize nothing ever really mattered but 'cha own."

That was odd Mario thought. Hefner had told him the same damn thing.

"And what about you, Gus. Is this *your* life, forever?"

"It's the life I've chosen," Gus said.

Gus lapsed into silence, but Mario couldn't tell if he was lost in thought or just tired. Soon, they came to the toll booths at the Queens-Midtown Tunnel. Ten minutes later, they were driving across Canal Street and bouncing over potholes toward Cortlandt alley. When they got there, Mario stopped the car and shut off the engine. "Chilly night, Gus, would you rather I take you to the shelter?" Gus just sat there not moving...and not talking. "Gus...Gus, you okay?"

"We came up the ranks together, as fighters," Gus finally said. "Amateur stuff to begin with. We sparred a lot, learned together. We were a perfect match, but somehow, we never fought each other. We refused to."

Mario looked at Gus, but Gus was staring straight ahead. He couldn't tell whether the old man was talking to him, or to himself.

"We were the finest prospects in Detroit, maybe the whole Midwest," Gus went on. "We turned pro at the same time. Went through the bums and the palookas, cutting 'em down one by one."

Gus paused, lost in his nostalgia for a moment. Then he continued.

"Few years later, there's nobody left but me and Tommy—and the champ, of course. We *had* to fight each other. Couldn't get out of it—and whichever one of us survived, he was gonna have a shot at the title."

Gus stopped, then forced himself to go on.

"We were pretty evenly matched physically, but Tommy was a better man than me. Bigger heart. And I loved him. He saved my life during the riots. I owed him that title shot. Maybe I'd get mine later. I was going to take a dive."

Mario knew, instinctively, that Gus hadn't told this story to anyone before, at least not since it happened, and maybe not even then.

There was a long silence, then Gus finally turned to Mario. "That night, before the fight, he comes into my dressing room and asked me to lay down."

"What?"

"He said they were starting to call him 'the great white hope,' and he stood to make thousands, as heir to the current champion, Emile Griffith... said, I owed him. And that a *nigger* should always pay his debts."

Gus looked away and Mario could feel him drifting again.

"We get in the ring and we touched gloves, and he's grinning at me like we have a secret. I *hated* him at that moment. Then the bell rings, and I went after him with all the fury there was inside of me. I'd never fought that way before in my life. I had him down twice in the third round.

"But the bell rings for the fourth, and then the fifth, and I'm on him again, my brain exploding with adrenalin. And I put him down again, hard. Only this time, he didn't get up."

This was the millstone on Gus's shoulders. This was the cross he bore, the weight that had crushed him.

"So they get me back to my corner and I'm looking at him lying there, the doctors working on him, and he slowly turns his head in my direction. Then it hits me. This is what Tommy wanted. For me to give it everything I had. He had a feeling I was gonna throw the fight. But he also knew the only way to get me to forget that I owed him, was for me to hate him."

"My God, Gus."

"Our eyes met and I watched the life go out of him." Tears were dripping down Gus's face.

They were both silent now.

Now, finally, Mario had a window into the tormented soul of this man, and he realized what Gus had been living with.

A patrol car came down West Broadway and slowed up, giving them a long hard look. They watched the car disappear in the distance and then, when Gus looked at Mario again, he was his old self—wise, ironic, knowing.

"Mario—that boy. The one you feel responsible for..."

"Yeah, Gus?"

"It ends tonight."

Gus bundled himself against the wind, got out of the car, and headed into Cortlandt alley.

A small, weathered fishing vessel was silently bobbing in the water, coast in view. A single man—old, wizened—was at the helm, half-asleep.

Then something on the horizon caught his attention: a speedboat, heading in his direction. He sat up straight, sipped his coffee and watched, without much curiosity, as the vessel approached.

The speedboat cut its engines just a few yards from the fishing boat and a well-built young man addressed the old skipper and handed him a small envelope.

Then the speedboat's engines roared back into life. It made one slow circle around the fishing boat and headed back the way it came. On board, the young man turned to an older man in a business suit, and handed him the envelope.

The older man carefully ripped open one end of the envelop and shook its contents—a single piece of notepaper—into his free hand. Using a pocket calculator, he deciphered the messages and read it: "Valuable package shipped last week from Syria, after final payment received."

The head of the anti-terrorism unit looked at the coded message from the company's man in Cyprus.

He alerted the Treasury to look for substantial U.S. bank transfers to Syria, sent the text of the message to U.S. Customs, with a request to look for the package, then forwarded it to Homeland Security, knowing that it would be too vague for them to act on, but determined to cover his ass.

CHAPTER EIGHTEEN

"I'm freezing my nuts off!" Glen said, walking quickly down Water Street.

"I don't know why we just didn't cab it to the heliport," Mario said glumly.

"Because Barry, our fat CFO here, is looking for any way to save us a few pennies," replied Dennis. "As if a few *more* bucks will make any difference."

"Speaking of money," Neil said, turning toward Mario, "has Tyler delivered his ten members yet?"

"The last two came in an hour ago," Mario said, gloating a little. "He also asked me if we had room for a few more."

"How few?" asked Neil.

"Like another fifteen."

"Who did he sign up?" Kat asked.

"Let's see," Mario said, "there's Romney from Credit Suisse, Steinberg from Dreyfus, O'Sullivan from Wells Fargo, even a couple of hitters from Blackrock—"

"Christ, this thing is growing more legs than a fucking caterpillar," Glen said.

"Lot of guys out there in our same situation."

"So, where does this leave us, Barry, financially I mean?" Neil asked.

"I think we're going to have a fairly comfortable surplus," Barry said, panting like he was back in the gymnasium at Chelsea Piers. "Even after we make our last payment to Big John and the Russkies."

The conversation was interrupted by the whapping blades of a big, black Bell 430 gliding down the East River, fast approaching the heliport. "Gentlemen," Neil announced, as the noise grew louder, "I think our ride is here."

The Zoo Crew scurried under the downdraft of the whirling blades and boarded as the blades slowly turned above them. At that moment, Frank poked his head into the cabin. "Room for one more?" he asked.

"Right on time," Mario said, helping him up. "Let's get this show on the road."

Mario tapped the pilot on the shoulder, the whirling blades picked up speed, and the chopper lifted off the pad and headed across the FDR and up the East River.

"Glen," Kat said frostily, "do you think you could stop pressing your thigh against mine?"

Glen sighed and moved slightly.

"Roger says we'll be ready for the inaugural ball Friday night," Mario said.

"It better be," Barry said. "We can't afford any more overtime."

"So, Kat is it?" Frank shouted over the deafening sound. "I heard you told your third-grade class there wasn't any Santa Claus." He was being funny.

Kat regarded him without expression.

"Whats your name, honey?"

"Frank."

"Well Francis, there can only one hero on Christmas and that guy died on the cross. Capice?" Kat replied, *not* being funny.

Frank raised an eyebrow and looked over at Mario who was grinning.

The chopper circled Ward's Island, then gently sat down on a new asphalt landing pad, which was outlined with a circle of colored lights. "Well," said Frank, "I hadn't seen *this* before."

They all clambered out of the chopper and were starting down the log-bordered flagstone path—also new—toward the building, when suddenly, Glen stopped. "What's that?" he asked, listening intently.

The others stopped behind him and went silent. "Sounds like...drums," Mario finally said. "Jungle drums."

They walked on a few more paces, tripping motion sensors that were half-hidden in the bark of the logs lining the walkway. The jungle drums got louder, and they were interrupted by the trumpeting of a distant elephant.

"What is this, a theme park?" Dennis asked." I'm at fucking Six Flags."

They continued down the path, and the jungle noises increased in number and volume. The elephants and lions were joined by a chorus of chattering monkeys and the chirping of exotic birds.

Ahead stood an archway of dense, intertwined vines and, when they passed through it, the Zoo Crew—and Frank—found themselves on a flat, perfectly manicured lawn, decorated by small stands of African wattle trees and bush willows.

Surmounting this lawn was a living replica of an African plantation home, a large, squarish clapboard structure densely covered in vines and surrounded on three sides by a weathered veranda, which was protected by faded khaki tenting.

"Fuck me," Barry breathed. "Is this the right building?"

"Are we on the right continent?" Neil asked, awed.

Mario walked up to the building, wondering what had happened to the stone, and how the vines had grown so fast. What he found was a veneer of weathered wood, covered by a fine netting of the sort used to make toupees. Artificial vines were threaded through it, and augmented by amazingly realistic *trompe l'oeil* painting. The illusion was perfect.

At the rough-hewn log doorway to the building, under a pair of infrared heating units, stood a pair of towering, deep ebony, perfectly matched Maasai warriors. Each was carrying an iron-tipped wooden spear, and wearing a loincloth, to which was clipped a cell phone. The warriors expressionlessly and simultaneously crossed their spears in front of the door, blocking their entry.

"Tell him Monelli and his friends are here," Mario instructed. One of the warriors spoke briefly into his cell phone. A moment later, Roger Duvall appeared, arms wide in welcome, smiling broadly. He was attired in a pith helmet, and a safari suit of khaki-colored English canvas similar to the one worn by Stewart Granger in *King Solomon's Mines*. A battered pair of Zeiss binoculars circa 1935 hung from his neck, and a Hemmingway-esque beard adorned his cheeks and chin.

"Gentlemen, gentlemen, gentlemen," he said expansively, "welcome to the Lions' Den, Africa's best kept secret, a hedonistic outpost of civilization in the heart of the dark continent. Please come inside. I assure you the natives are friendly."

Frank looked at Mario, barely managing to stifle a laugh. "After you, Stanley," he said with mock graciousness.

"Why thank you, Livingston."

As they entered the building, the hostess, an exotically beautiful woman, in a nearly translucent sarong, handed each of them a small, braided rawhide whip, coiled, but ready for action. "What's *this* for?" Barry asked the woman, stretching it around his waist like a belt.

"That is for your protection, gentlemen," the hostess told them. "Use it in the unlikely event that one of the wild animals threatens you…or any other way that would give you pleasure." She winked.

Neither Neil nor Mario was surprised by the transformation of the grand hallway—they'd seen pictures of the African dioramas in Roger's studio, the huge jungle clearing, bordered by a dense combination of undergrowth, vines and towering trees, a montage of primates hanging from the high branches, the giraffes just over the trees, the spotted leopard in the bushes, the stairway with the enormous elephant tusk railings ascending toward the top of the jungle canopy.

Arching over this fantastical construction was a weathered bronze sign: *Welcome to the Ivory Coast.* The staircase was flanked, on both sides, by the matched pair of enormous antique stone lions that Mario and Neil had seen delivered from Jordan. They had a kind of mystic majesty that transcended even their size and antiquity. They seemed to be alive, ready to roar, ready to leap, but unable to move.

They expected something like this, and they'd warned the rest of the Zoo Crew to be prepared. But the reality was as different as a photograph of Angelina Jolie was from the real thing.

There were not only sights, but sounds—lots of them, elephants, birds, monkeys, drums, buzzing insects, and there were also smells, the perfume of jungle flowers, the dank odors of tropical rivers, the occasional whiff of dry grass in the sun; an asthetic and olafactory exercise in Disney engineering.

Frank gazed at his surroundings, transfixed.

"You okay, Frank?" Mario asked.

"I'm...I'm in shock. I just never dreamed...."

"Well, you helped make it possible."

"Much as I like the place, I'd just as soon not be reminded of that," Frank said.

"Gentlemen," Roger said, addressing the group, "there is much more to see. Follow me please. And watch out for crocodiles—just kidding."

The next stop on the tour was the cocktail lounge. But it was a cocktail lounge unlike any other—a plank-for-plank replica of *The African Queen,* the boat from the movie of the same name. On one side of the boat was a rough slab of mahogany, twenty-five feet long, and serviced by barkeeps dressed like Bogart and Hepburn, except younger, bronzed, and built.

One thing was missing from this setup, however—a cash register. In fact, the Lions' Den lacked any reminder of money whatsoever. It was as if they had entered a world where everything was for the taking, as it was in the wild. *And* on Wall Street—or at least *used* to be. Members could leave their wallets at home—so long as they were up to date with their common charges, deducted automatically from numbered, untraceable accounts Frank had set up in the Cayman Islands to protect member identities.

Roger made sure the bartenders took care of the Zoo Crew's needs, then waved them on into the room next door, the lounge, with its tables made of elephant hooves, and its sling-like chairs of ropes and vines. A pair of scantily clad native women stood by to take orders.

The room's ceiling was a dome of bright blue sky, with puffy cream-colored clouds lazily floating by. Africa's highest peak, the snow-capped Mount Kilimanjaro, was visible in the distance. A pack of hyenas crossed the veldt from left to right, barking as they ran, disappearing into a grove of short, squashed-looking wisteria trees.

Frank jumped. "They moved! I saw them run!"

Mario grinned, and just then, a pair of gazelles loped out of a stand of chestnuts, gamboled over the veldt, and stopped for a drink at a small watering hole.

"It's video," Roger explained. "A projection screen combined with digital scenic and sound effects, thanks to George Lucas's special effects outfit, Industrial Light and Magic."

"Jesus Christ, Roger," Dennis said, "you're a goddam genius."

"I thought you knew that when you hired me."

"What's on the menu," Barry asked.

"That's Spencer's territory," Roger said, "but I can tell you that there is no menu. There are a few specials, different every night, but you can ask for anything you want and the kitchen will prepare it for you."

"I have died and gone to heaven," said Barry.

Neil was surveying the room. "Isn't it awfully bright in here?"

Roger checked his watch. "Yes, it's mid-afternoon on the first floor. Dusk will be falling in about two hours. It's all adjustable."

Duvall led them across the grand hall, toward a pair of huge doors made of logs, bound together with rawhide. The bronze sign over them read *Tim-Buck-$2*.

As they approached, the doors swung open automatically, revealing a fully-equipped gambling parlor—slots, roulette wheels, baccarat tables, and pit stands for those who preferred playing 21, all this in a jungle clearing surrounded by dense undergrowth and a babbling stream that had attracted a group of birds of Paradise.

"Not in operation now, of course," Roger said. "But Friday night, I predict, the place will be packed."

"What else is on the first floor?" Mario asked.

"The only other public rooms are the theater and the watering hole—it's a huge, hot tub, complete with animatronic wild animals, our steam room, the Sahara, with a half million cubic yards of sand imported from the desert itself, and also includes a desert diorama, of course. Other than that, there's the kitchen, the offices, some storerooms, and utility rooms."

"And upstairs?" asked Frank.

"Upstairs," said Roger with a gleeful leer, "are the, um, man caves."

"Let's go upstairs," Glen said with a mischievous glint of his own.

As they ascended the stairs, the quality of the light slowly changed. The sun grew dimmer, the stars began twinkling, then the moon appeared overhead, in perfect imitation of the scenes that once appeared on the inner ceiling of the Hayden Planetarium.

Now, they made their way along the Serengeti Trail, the rough path through the dense jungle that served as the upstairs hallway and the gateway to the bedrooms. The fires of isolated tribal villages popped up in the dark landscape. The occasional lions' roar gave way to distant snoring and an occasional snort, mostly drowned out by a cacophony of croaking frogs, all captured in Dolby sound.

At the end of the Serengeti trail, seemingly miles away, they could see the world-famous Victoria Falls, fed by the Zambezi River. Suddenly, a cool breeze started up, carrying with it a mélange of jungle scents, smells and odors pumped by dual hydraulic engines Roger had flown in from McDonnell Douglas. It seemed as if they were outdoors.

Mario just shook his head in surprise and delight. "I knew it was going to be spectacular, Roger, but I had no idea how real it was going to look."

"Thank you," Roger said, beaming.

Now he escorted the Zoo Crew through a series of what he called full-sized dioramas—rooms to everyone else, specifically bedrooms for the members. Some of these, Mario and Neil had seen in Roger's studio. But here they were in 3-D, as real as they would have been if such places actually existed on the dark continent—a clearing in the rainforest, carpeted with grass—but under the grass, invisible, a vast expanse of Tempur-Pedic mattress; a cozy cave behind a waterfall, perfect for an orgy, with large, strategically placed foam rubber rocks—perfect pillows; a compound of Xhosa tribe thatched huts in various sizes, with soft African music floating through the ether.

Roger paused outside of a door that bore a bronze plate that read *The Lions' Lair.* "Gentlemen, please pay close attention. I'm about to show you my masterpiece."

He swung open the door and bade them enter. Suddenly, they found themselves in an enormous grotto, lit by flickering wall torches, carpeted in deeply cushioned artificial grass that would have brought tears to an NFL groundskeeper, a wet bar that provided ice cubes shaped like enormous diamonds, a kidney-shaped hot tub, couches that looked like boulders, but were actually made of leather-covered foam rubber, and every other luxurious accoutrement known to man.

Within this cave were seven commodious tents, reminiscent of those used by desert nomads, but made of high-denier (and opaque) nylon. These were, in effect, the Zoo Crew's separate bed chambers, their little erotic cocoons, complete with silk bedding, as well as a fine selection of erotic oils and toys. They were lush, luxurious fuck nooks.

One of these tents, a dome made from tightly woven red silk, was larger than the others. Roger took Mario by the elbow and led him to the entrance. "This," he said, "is Mustapha's Refuge. It's reserved for the CEO—whomever *he* might be," he winked.

Mario peered inside. The dome was a moving diorama, with birds, animals, elephant grass silhouetting in the wind, clouds moving across the sky. An extraordinarily realistic lion and his mate apparently slept nearby, within the dome.

"Takes my breath away," Mario said. "The whole place does."

Roger smiled broadly, turned to the rest of the Zoo Crew, and waved his hand theatrically around the Lions' Lair. "This, gentlemen, is *your* room and yours alone, yours and your guests, that is. You can eat, drink, and make merry at any time of the day or night—the room will always be available to you."

"I gotta hand it to you, Mario," Dennis said. "Never in my wildest dreams did I imagine anything like this. It's like Xanadu."

The final stop was at the first-floor office of the facility manager, Duncan Spencer. Duncan took the men on a tour of the service facilities, including the superbly equipped kitchen. He introduced them to the supervising chef. "Gentlemen, I would like you to meet Chef André Poincaré, formerly chef of the Deauville Arms, in Nice. Andre, these are your employers."

Barry wandered over to the pantry, opened the double doors—and gaped. The shelves in front of him were filled to overflowing with an incredible selection of gourmet groceries: common and exotic spices, rare vinegars and oils, coffees and teas imported from all over the world, European and Asian cookies and biscuits, imported grains, legumes, pasta and nuts.

"Where's the *real* food?" Barry asked.

Chef André lifted an eyebrow, but restrained himself from saying something sarcastic. "In here, sir," he said, opening a refrigerated locker. It was a cornucopia of caviar, cured sausages, escargot, fresh tenderloin, hams, pate, smoked fish, different varieties of salami, tuna, and whole birds.

The next stop involved a trip to the wine cellar, which contained what looked like an infinity of wine racks. A man in a crisp white uniform approached them.

"Gentlemen," Duncan said, "this is our Chief Sommelier, Gunther von Austenberg. Gunther, these are our employers."

The sommelier led them through the maze of wine racks, stopping occasionally to display a bottle. "This," he said, "is Chateau Latour Pauillac Premier Cru Classe-1945, a splendid year. And over here we have a Chateau Mouton Rothschild Bordeaux 1947..."

"My God," Barry said, slapping a hand to his forehead. "I've heard of that wine. It's over $8,000 a bottle." He pulled out his Blackberry and began crunching numbers.

"Hey, Barry, why don't you set that thing to vibrate, then shove it down your shorts and call yourself." Neil said.

After touring through wine country, they headed back upstairs, Mario and the rest of the Zoo Crew accompanying Duncan back to his office, where they met the servant staff, composed entirely of illegals of various nationalities, for whom Kat had secured green cards through her family connections at the INS in return for their silence about the Lions' Den.

They left Duncan's office and wandered back into the main lobby. Roger spotted them and walked over. "Well, does it meet your expectations?"

"It surpasses them," Mario said.

"In every way," Dennis added.

Roger doffed his pith helmet and bowed deeply. "Thank you very much." He shook hands with each of them, one by one, and kissed Kat on the cheek.

"The final payment will be in your office tomorrow morning," Mario said.

"Oh, pooh," said Roger. "Who cares about money? Oh, that's right. *I* do."

"Will you grace us with your appearance Friday night?" Neil asked.

"No love, I don't want to take the spotlight away from you kiddies. But best of luck with opening night—I know it's going to be boffo."

They showed up, all seven of them, dressed to the nines, Frank included, just before seven p.m., having made their excuses to their wives—late meeting, major client coming in from out of town, big deal cooking, whatever—and having been believed or disbelieved, or adding to growing suspicions.

Following Mario's strong suggestion, they came without women on this night and no other. Even Kat came stag. Too much was riding on the opening to indulge in their own fun. They had to make sure everything was going well, that everything was working the way they'd promised. It was a magnificent place, the Lions' Den, but it had cost them every last nickel they were able to raise, and they knew a few unhappy members could close it faster than a Broadway bomb.

At this point, Mario and the rest of the Zoo Crew took up their stations, Mario and Neil flanking the stone lions and greeting the members as they arrived, Kat in Tim-Buck-$2, Glen patrolling the second-floor bedrooms, Barry, who rarely skipped Shabbos, overseeing food and drink service, Frank shadowing Duncan Spencer, Dennis keeping an eye on the video theater and the watering hole—all of them communicating via walkie-talkies.

At around eight p.m., the helicopters, small charter boats, limousines, and taxicabs began dropping off the members—mostly men in their forties and fifties, a few older, a few younger, with their expensive clothing, expensive haircuts, and expensive women, invariably blonde, younger and more attractive than their escorts.

The warriors uncrossed their spears precisely at 8:30, and began allowing people to enter, after checking member IDs. Stationed in the grand lobby, Mario and Neil were the first to encounter them, and the encounters all played out more or less on the same theme:

"It's amazing, Mario—better than I imagined."

"Congratulations, I'm proud to be a member."

But what Mario and Neil enjoyed most of all was not the unending stream of compliments, satisfying as they were, but the expressions on the faces of the members and their women friends—they were elated, astonished, thrilled, and overwhelmed.

At about nine p.m., Tyler showed up with several of the members he'd recruited—the biggest of the big, CEOs and CFOs and board chairmen, not one of them worth less than 100 million dollars, all of them escorting women directly from the pages of Vogue.

"I'd like to welcome you and your friends to the Lions' Den, Tyler," Mario said. "I'm sure you'll all have a good time here, and I hope you'll come back regularly."

Tyler briefly acknowledged Mario, clearly not wanting to emphasize their relationship. The others were distracted—amazed, really—by the architectural fuck sanctuary in which they found themselves. Some nosed around the big public rooms on the main floor, others drifted upstairs, couple by couple, to find places where they could slake their appetites, or, as one of them put it to Mario, "screw our brains out."

The Zoo Crew watched—and guided—this parade of horny middle-aged married executives and their buxom honeys with mixed emotions. Of course, they were delighted with the way their baby was being received.

At about ten p.m., Glen came down the staircase to report to Mario. "You won't believe what's going on upstairs. We have some real animals up there, and I don't mean the hyenas in the dioramas. And here I am walking around with wood in my pants and no place to put it."

"Patience, my man, patience. We had to make sure opening night was perfect—and it is. Tomorrow, and from then on, and on, and on."

Then Kat was at Mario's elbow. "How goes it?"

Dennis came out of the theater and walked over to join the group. "You'd think the place had been open for five years. Not a glitch."

"Everyone's happy?" Kat asked.

"Delirious," Dennis said, "and I'm not even exaggerating much."

Duncan Spencer, who'd been practically invisible all night, suddenly showed up at the Zoo Crew's impromptu meeting. "Gentlemen, the entertainment has arrived. Shall I alert the members?"

"Start moving everyone downstairs," said Mario.

Spencer vanished and a few minutes later, loud elephant trumpeting rang out from the club's speaker system, followed by Duncan's cultured voice. "Ladies and gentlemen," he said, "for all of those who may be interested, the evening's entertainment will begin shortly in the grand lobby."

Most of the members and their guests had gathered in the main lobby, at the foot of the grand lions. The lights went dim. Spotlights strobed the staircase and the jungle drums grew suddenly louder, and, a dozen nubile, bare-breasted women in native attire and headdress, a racially mixed collection of Alvin Ailey ebony beauties, who exuded sex from every pore, came gliding down the Ivory Coast staircase in a kaleidoscope of glitz and color. A quintet of African drummers followed them.

On the floor, the dancers moved in sinuous rhythm, at first slowly, then faster and faster, the earthy beat of the jungle drums keeping up with them, leading them, swinging their fevered bodies in shameless abandon, spraying sweat onto the crowd.

Mario was watching the crowd when Tyler approached him with a luscious brunette glued to his arm. But Tyler said nothing. All he did was to extend his hand and shake Mario's once, briskly, before retreating upstairs with her.

CHAPTER NINETEEN

The contrast between the two men could not have been more perfectly scripted. Mario, the humble Wall Street long shot with the blue-collar work ethic, contrasted perfectly with the stylish, gregarious blue-blood, Mulvaney. And Julie, along with the network brass, was salivating at the thought of it. When Julie arrived at Harrison Hart, she found Mario waiting for her in the lobby, looking more handsome than she remembered.

"Can we go into your office," Julie said. This had to be done privately, she thought.

"Sure," Mario said, wondering why is she being so mysterious.

Mario led the way to his office through the M&A suite, past the Zoo Crew—every one of whom was busy on the phone, but none of whom was too preoccupied not to notice Julie and the way her skirt hugged her backside.

Julie sat down across from Mario. He couldn't help thinking there was something very appealing about her, a certain liveliness and grace.

"Mind if we close the door?" she asked.

"Not at all," Mario said, more puzzled than ever. He drew the blinds and took a seat behind his desk.

She unzipped her handbag, took out a manila envelope, and handed it to Mario, without comment. "Read," she said.

Mario leaned back in his chair, opened the envelope and started on the first page. It was a full-blown forensic of every move he'd made in defense of Intercoastal Courier, including a few he thought were known only to himself. He glanced up at her.

"Read the next page," Julie urged quietly.

Mario turned the page. There it was—every move and countermove Barton Mulvaney had made to defeat him. Mario realized he hadn't had a chance. Mulvaney and the Blackwell Group not only had enough proxy votes to sway the Intercoastal board, but secured votes in reserve as insurance.

"Where did you get this?"

"There's one more page," Julie pointed out.

Mario flipped to the last page, wondering what more could be said about the Intercoastal deal. Then he found out. The financing to make the purchase was entangled in a string of transactions, laundered from Blackwell to three mid-western banks, to five banks in South America, to a series of shell corporations in Europe, to three government agencies and a holding company in Turkey, to the Ministry of Finance in Saudi Arabia, to a single personal account that belonged to the Crown Prince."

By the time Mario looked back up at Julie, the color had drained from his face and the small hairs on the back of his neck stiffened. "Is this all you have? Is this the whole thing?"

"No, there's more."

"And they all lead back to Saudi Arabia, to the Royal Family?"

"That's right."

Jesus Christ, Mario thought. Our big ally in the Middle East, ambushing us financially, the monetary equivalent of 9/11. He felt sick at heart, and frightened for his country. "Where did you get this stuff? Which agency?" His tone was insistent.

Julie didn't know how to answer him. "Mario, I...."

He studied the documents. Expensive paper, but there was nothing on it except the financial details. Probably second sheets, he decided. Then he noticed something—the paper was watermarked. He held it up to the bright light on his desk, and there it was: The Great Seal of the United States of America and the words "Securities and Exchange Commission."

Mario looked up at Julie. "They're from the goddamn SEC."

She offered him the tiniest of smiles and changed the subject. "Do you think that Mulvaney knew what he was doing?"

"You mean, did he *know* the Saudis were the source of the financing— and they were taking control of Intercoastal?"

"The question is: would he have known their motives?" she asked.

Mario just shook his head. Bart might've heard whispers, he thought, but as bad and unscrupulous as Bart was, Mario couldn't see Blackwell or other private equity firms actively betraying their own country. Maybe this was a one-off. "I can't believe Bart is privy to their intentions," he finally said. "But then neither are you."

Mario's office door opened without warning and Tyler Gentry walked in, then stopped when he saw Julie. "Oh, pardon me," he said, smiling, "I didn't know you had, um, company."

"Julie Chambers, I'd like you to meet Tyler Gentry. He's my boss," Mario said. "Tyler, Julie Chambers is a television producer at UBS."

"Glad to meet you," Tyler said, taking Julie's hand but not letting go of it. "What brings you to Harrison Hart?"

"Actually, I'm here on business."

"Business," replied Tyler looking at Mario and lifting an eyebrow. "May I ask what business?"

"UBS plans to interview him."

"Really? About what may I ask?" He finally released Julie's hand, but only after patting it, and he plopped down in the chair beside hers.

"It's an exposé about foreign investment," Julie explained while looking nervously at Mario.

"So tell me, Miss Chambers, how did you happen to come across Mario? May I call you Julie?"

Jesus Christ, Mario thought, the horn dog is actually flirting with her.

"Certainly. Mr. Monelli has a unique viewpoint." She wanted to end this encounter as quickly as possible."

Tyler looked at Mario. "So are you giving Miss Chambers the red-carpet treatment, Mario...showing her what goes on *behind* the scenes?"

"Behind *which* scenes?"

"Well, what about the trading floor over at the New York Stock Exchange. Have you had a chance to see it, Miss Chambers?"

"No, not the trading floor," Julie admitted.

"Well, you really should make it a point to visit."

Mario was getting perturbed listening to Tyler treat Julie Chambers like some fucking tourist, not a journalist. "What is it you wanted with me anyhow, Tyler?" he asked.

"Oh, I was just checking on something technical. Not important. But seriously, Julie, I'd be happy to give you a look at where the real action is on Wall Street." He smiled in what he must have considered his most endearing manner.

Mario rolled his eyes. Tyler was going to show Julie where the "real action" was? Not if *he* had anything to do with it. "She came to see *me*, Tyler. Want to see the Exchange?" He asked Julie, thinking this might be the quickest solution.

Julie caught on instantly. "Let's go," she said.

Mario stuck the envelope with the SEC papers into his suit jacket pocket. Then he and Julie said their goodbyes to Tyler and walked out of Mario's office, leaving Tyler sitting there, wondering what the fuck just happened.

Without a word, they boarded a crowded elevator, Mario grinning broadly and Julie struggling to suppress a giggle.

"That was amazing," Julie said, laughing.

"I thought he was never going to shut up," Mario agreed. "Do you really want to see the Exchange?"

"Sure," Julie said.

They crossed the busy traffic on the West Side highway and walked down Liberty Street.

"Difficult boss?" Julie asked.

"We had some difficult times blending the two outfits when we merged, but we did it."

"And now?"

"Now, I head the most profitable unit in the firm."

Julie nodded knowingly. "Ah, so it's all about money."

"Of course. This *is* Wall Street, remember? Power, money, and women—they're the bacon, lettuce, and tomato of The Street."

"I guess I'm the tomato," Julie said thoughtfully. "That makes you the lettuce and Tyler the bacon, right?"

"I've always wanted to be a figure of speech," Mario laughed. He hadn't had this much fun talking to a woman in—well, he couldn't remember.

They were deep in the Broad Street canyon now, stone and concrete cliffs on both sides, standing on a sidewalk that only saw the sun at high noon, directly across Federal Hall and the grey stone classical-revival building where fortunes had been made and lost for more than a century.

"You know, you don't have to take me to the Exchange," Julie said.

"You're not interested?"

"I'm interested, but it has nothing to do with the story and I should be getting back to the office."

"I understand," Mario said, wishing he could find a way to prolong the conversation. "As much as I'm enjoying myself, I got to be heading back to work myself, Julie."

"Listen, I'm going to have more things to show you and lots of questions to ask. But maybe it's not a good idea for me to come to your office," she said. "How about after work, you available?"

"Possible." He flashed on an image: the two of them sitting across from each other at some intimate SoHo restaurant, he looking into those sparkling green eyes.

"Oh, wait," Julie said. "You have something of mine."

Mario thought a moment, then patted his jacket pocket. "Oh, you mean *this*." He pulled out the envelope with the SEC documents and handed it to her.

The moment Mario got back to his desk, Tyler called him. "Have a good time?"

"Tyler, what's with you? Why were you acting that way in my office?"

"Never mind that and tell me more about this television show, Mario." There was nothing playful in his voice now.

"It's an expose on foreign investment in the U.S. Just an interview. I'm not the only investment banker being profiled."

"Okay, but why *you*? This isn't exactly your field."

"I've defended against foreign takeovers, Tyler, remember? That's why you acquired Hart—and wrecked a few thousand lives." He didn't bother keeping the resentment out of his voice. "Besides, she said something about a fresh face."

"Yeah, you're fresh all right. Just don't get yourself into anything you'll regret, or anything that could be damaging to the boys upstairs *and* the company. Not if you want that partner..."

"Yeah, yeah, don't worry about it."

"And, Mario, about that girl..."

"Goodbye, Tyler," he said, then hung up without waiting for a reply.

Julie called Mario the following day. "I'm sending you a package by special courier," she said. "It's more of what I showed you in your office. Please read it as soon as you can, and maybe we can discuss it after work tonight."

"Okay," Mario said. "I have Ranger tickets for tonight, but if you want to meet for a quick dinner, we could do that."

Less than an hour later, Mario was in his office studying the documents Julie had sent. They were, essentially, a series of case histories—material devoted to take-overs brokered by some of Wall Street's premier sharks and buyout firms, dating back anywhere from two months to two years.

The earlier reports were relatively sketchy, perhaps because Randy Dandy and the SEC didn't realize the extent of the activity at first. The later reports, like those documenting Intercoastal's acquisition, were highly detailed forensics.

None of these reports, Mario thought, was particularly surprising—by itself. Except for the complex string of dummy corporations and multiple banks, they were quite ordinary. But added together, they were staggering. They amounted to a very well-orchestrated attempt to acquire the economic heart of America.

On a hunch, Mario began separating the reports into piles, one for each industry sector. The result was strange. Three piles were much higher than the others: media, transportation, and communication. High tech was a distant fourth, and there were nothing in manufacturing, consumer goods, or agriculture.

Mario considered the disparity. Why would Saudi Arabia concentrate on transportation, the media, and communication? These were hardly the wealthiest sectors. Nor the most profitable. If he were advising someone on what stocks to buy, this wouldn't be the group he would recommend.

Who would want to buy or control these companies? Mario tried to put himself inside the head of the Saudi Royals who were organizing this massive offensive. Suddenly, he understood their whole strategy. It was incredibly bold. And before long, it would be impossible to stop.

They met at a no-name steak house not far from Madison Square Garden. Julie wore a cream-colored pants suit with a purple turtleneck sweater. "Absolutely *mahvelous*," Mario thought, remembering how Billy Crystal said it on Saturday Night Live when he was imitating Fernando Lamas.

"Well, what did you think?" she said, as they sat down at a table in the back.

"Absolutely incredible," Mario said, unable to take his eyes off of her.

"I mean about the papers. Did you have a chance to read them?"

Mario tried to stop thinking inappropriate things about her. "Yes, yes I read the documents. It's worse than I thought. Worse than you told me."

Julie was startled. "How can that be?"

"It's not just the takeovers, it's the *pattern* of the takeovers. It's not just that they're targeting important American companies, it's *which* companies they're buying."

At that moment, a slender, pockmarked Hispanic waiter steamed up to their table. "Drinks?" he asked, without much interest.

"Bring us a bottle of your finest Chianti. And we're ready to order."

The waiter pulled out his pad. "What'll you have?"

"Tenderloin, medium. Baked stuffed potatoes. Asparagus," Mario said. "He looked over at Julie and grinned. "How do you want your steak, Julie?"

"Medium rare," she said. The waiter left with their order. "Now tell me about this pattern."

"They're starting with the media," Mario said. They're trying to control the news flow and the movement of people."

"Yes, we know that, but why?"

"Because it's crucial that their plan remain secret. If it leaks out, their plan is dead on arrival. The market will shut down foreign purchases. Endgame."

"Yes," Julie said, "you're right, but…"

"See, they're planning a staged takeover. Media and communications being first: control news and ideas to make sure no one knows what they're doing. This allows them time to initiate the second step: acquire the manufacturing and technological base of the country. Then—consumer goods, agriculture, and retailing. That's how the Nazis did it."

"The Nazis? I'm lost…"

"Think about how cable news distorts what happens around the world *and* in America. Think of the lies they spread about politicians they don't like or how they portray religion. Now imagine if the neo-cons or left wing extremists who own these media outlets fall under the control of the Saudis."

Julie nodded, fascinated.

"Now apply the same model to all the major news networks, *The New York Times* and *The Washington Post*, *The Boston Globe*, and all the radio talk shows."

"They'd control what we saw and heard," she said. "They'd control what we *think*."

"And what we did. We wouldn't be getting information about the world from the news media, we'd be getting propaganda—propaganda that could easily alter foreign policy and even our laws."

"In time," Julie said, trying to soften what Mario was saying.

"Yes. It would take some time. Five years, maybe ten. By that time, they'd control everything important or at least everything that matters."

"I understand now," she said. "If the Saudis seize control of the right components of our economy, they have the economic power. They get all the profits, pollute without restraint, even sell our technology to the highest bidder..."

"That's right."

"I should tell you that there've been some serious offers for UBS."

"Jesus Christ," Mario said. "Then there's less time than I thought."

"You think UBS is in danger?" Julie asked, knowing the answer before she asked the question.

"I think that if we let the Saudis do this, America as we know it will be toast. The same thing is already happening with Muslim influence in western europe. And there's another thing you need to know, Julie. You're in personal danger—everyone associated with the program is in danger. I would be, too."

Julie was shocked. "You mean..."

"I mean if the Saudis are willing to attack America with such venom, they're not going to let anyone or anything get in their way."

"You're scaring me, Mario."

"I'm scaring *myself.*"

"You said before that you'd be in danger, too," Julie began. "Does that mean you've made up your mind to do it?"

Mario sighed deeply. "I'm leaning that way." He checked his watch. "Better chow down now if you expect to see the face-off."

"The face-off?" Julie asked.

"We'll talk more during the game," Mario said.

After dinner, Mario took a chance and held out an arm. She took it. They walked down Seventh Avenue and into the slow-moving crowd gathered at the front entrance of Madison Square Garden.

An usher took Mario's tickets and escorted them behind the Ranger's glass at center ice. Someone in the box waved to Mario.

"Who was that?" Julie whispered.

"The coach."

The National Anthem began and the crowd stood, quietly. Then the referee dropped the puck and the game was on.

For the next half hour, Mario and Julie didn't exchange a word that wasn't about hockey, she asking questions, he patiently teaching.

"Who's that one, number sixteen?" Julie asked, pointing to a man dashing across the ice.

"Bobby Holik," Mario said. "Rangers' best scorer."

Someone from the Rangers' opponents caught up with Holik and smashed him into the boards right in front of the Rangers' bench and the crowd roared angrily. Julie bent toward Mario. "That's legal?" she asked.

"Oh, yeah. But not good for *us.*"

Overall, it was a boring game between two bad teams. Mario was watching twelve semi-toothless millionaires on the ice, trying to crunch each other, but he was also thinking about the Saudis. He was thinking about what he'd gotten involved with. He was thinking about Julie.

Then the horn sounded and the period ended, half the spectators heading toward restrooms or snack bars.

"I thought we were going to talk business," Julie said wryly.

"We are," Mario replied. "Right now. I've been thinking about this whole thing, Julie, and I'm sorry but I can't do it."

"What do you mean?"

"Just what I said. I'm not the man for the job."

Julie was dumbfounded. "Bad joke," she said.

"No joke," Mario replied. He knew how disheartened she must feel, but somehow he had to make her understand. "Julie, this is too important for a nobody like me. I don't have the credibility, not as far as the public is concerned."

"But you have the knowledge. And the passion."

"But not the pedigree or the credentials."

Julie suddenly felt a wave of anger sweep over her. "You're *afraid*! You're afraid of the Saudis. Or is it Bart you're afraid of?"

"You're right, Julie," Mario said. "I *am* afraid. But not of Bart. I'm afraid that no one will take me seriously—that Mulvaney and that silver tongue of his will talk his way out of whatever I say. You need someone notable, someone highly educated, who can formulate arguments on the fly and articulate them well. And that's not me."

"But you're all we've got," Julie said, almost pleading. "I've been searching for the right person for months and you're head and shoulders above everyone else."

"Look, I'll help you find someone—the *right* person. I know plenty of people."

"*You're* my choice." Julie was feeling dispirited. Without Mario, the whole thing wouldn't work. It was back to square one and production was already lagging.

Mario hated the reaction he'd triggered, the expression on Julie's face, the obvious disappointment—in him. "I'll do everything I can behind the scenes, Julie. I'll tell you what you need to know about Mulvaney and how to fight him."

Julie looked into Mario's eyes. "Look, Mario, I'm going to prepare you. I'm going to teach you the tricks of the trade. You're going to look and sound great."

"I know myself better than you do, Julie. I'm not willing to risk the future of the country on my television performance, and you shouldn't either."

"Mario..."

"My decision is final."

Back on the ice, the time for the next face-off approached. Most of the spectators were back in their seats.

"I think I've had enough hockey for awhile," Julie told Mario.

"But there's a lot of time left in the game," Mario said.

"I'm sorry." She rose from her seat. "I'm going to catch a cab."

Mario rose beside her and led Julie out of the arena, all the while trying to come up with a way to smooth things out, but he couldn't think of anything.

Out on Seventh Avenue, Mario hailed her a cab. "Where to?" he asked, opening the passenger door for her. She climbed inside and told the driver "Turtle Bay."

"Keep me informed," Mario said, meaning it.

"Of course," said Julie, *not* meaning it.

Mario hopped a cab downtown, got his car, then drove toward the midtown tunnel, mind churning. He had long hankered, after an acknowledgement from the Wall Street establishment, that he rates among the first rank of pound-for-pound players, but thus far there had been a reluctance to bestow that accolade given his perceived tendency to duck foreign buyouts of American multinational companies. Regardless of the validity of this viewpoint, there can be little doubt that he now had a priceless, if perilous, opportunity to demonstrate to his critics his authenticity. But still could he do it, he wondered?

One moment, he knew—without any doubt at all—that he had been absolutely correct, that he simply wasn't the right man to take on Bart, and that the stakes were simply too high, and if he fucked it up—he didn't even want to think about the repercussions.

But the next moment, he pictured himself face-to-face with Bart, exposing the man's greed and lack of anything remotely resembling ethics or morality.

He stopped thinking about the decision at hand and started thinking about Julie. He wanted her approval, and that certainly wasn't the way to get it. But he knew he wasn't going to have another chance. She wasn't going to consult him. She wasn't going to call him. He'd seen the last of Julie Chambers.

Julie was half asleep when the phone rang. She fumbled for the receiver and picked it up just after the third ring, answering with a drowsy hello.

"It's me," a voice said. She might be half asleep, but she recognized that voice all right.

"Oh yeah, hi." Her tone of voice was polite, non-committal.

"I'll do it," Mario said, "I'll go on television—on one condition."

"What's that?" She was sitting up in bed now, fully awake.

"Promise you won't let me make a fool of myself."

She could hear the crushing self doubt in his voice.

"You know I will, Mario. But tell me, what made you change your mind?"

There was a long pause.

"I don't know," he said. But he did.

Three uniformed U.S. customs inspectors approached what looked like an abandoned warehouse on the loading bay of Pier 16 in Long Beach, California. Manny Terenada, the senior inspector, jiggled the door handle. No luck.

"A locked door of an abandoned building?" Iris asked rhetorically. "That doesn't make any sense."

Out in the river, a small tug waddled by and gave a toot.

"Do we have a search warrant?" asked Al Barnes, the new man on the job.

Inspector Terenada gave his partner a dirty look. "If we find something, we'll get a search warrant."

Al lifted his leg and gave the door a ferocious kick and it caved in, tearing off its hinges. Manny tried the light switch and a row of fluorescents buzzed on. "Well, well, someone's paid the electric bill," he said.

The interior of the structure was practically empty, except for a few dozen cardboard boxes and a couple of battered steel filing cabinets. The inspectors each pulled out a drawer and started pawing through the folders.

"Nothing here," Al said. "Just old bills of lading."

"Same here," Iris said, bored.

"Wait, here's something," said Manny. He held up a half-crumpled yellow Post-It note.

"What does it say?" Al asked.

"It says, 'Release the 'package' only to Roger Duvall.' The word 'package' is in quotes."

Back at the office, Manny fed the name "Roger Duvall" into the national government database. What came back was the man's age, address, marital status (not married), occupation: architect and interior designer. Outside of a misdemeanor charge, later dropped, for public indecency, he had no priors.

Manny shrugged. Well, he thought, what's the harm. He entered the information into the database.

CHAPTER TWENTY

By the time Julie got to the office the next day, Paige was already there and waiting for her. "Well—how did it go? What happened?"

"He went back and forth on it for awhile, but we've got a firm commitment from him now." Julie liked the sound of those words.

"Tell me about it."

"We ended up at the Garden watching the hockey game...."

"You're kidding," Paige said. "It's about time you started having fun."

"Listen, I'm going up to tell Hank. Would you get Barton Mulvaney on the phone for me? We have to firm up that commitment."

A few minutes later, Julie had Barton Mulvaney on the line.

"Ah...Julie Chambers, always nice to hear your voice," Bart said.

"Well, I've got some good news for you."

"News," said Bart. "You mean you've decided to accept my dinner invitation."

"I thought I'd drop by and talk to you about it in person."

"I'm tied up all day," Bart replied casually, not even pretending to be truthful. "But I'm free for dinner."

There was no refusing this guy, Julie thought. "All right, dinner. But early. I have another engagement tonight."

"Well, we'll see about that," Bart said. "How about meeting me at Bouley's—that's on Broadway, between..."

"I know where it is," Julie said. She'd been there once, and she'd had to reserve a table a month in advance.

Julie walked into Bouley's just after six o'clock, and made her way through the groupings of fresh-picked apples in the entryway to the *maitre'd*'s station. She mentioned Barton Mulvaney to him and asked if he'd arrived. "Ah," said the elegantly dressed *maitre'd*, "his table is in the Red Room."

The Red Room was low, with ceiling arches, muted rose-colored lighting, and an ambience that was unremittingly romantic, exactly as she expected.

Bart rose to meet her, kissing her hand while the *maitre'd* gracefully pulled out a chair for her and slid it under her as she sat down. As he retreated, the sommelier arrived.

"Wine, Charles. You know what I like," Mulvaney said. Then he glanced at Julie. "My you're looking ever so lovely."

"Thank you," Julie said, trying to be gracious but not encouraging.

The *maitre 'd* reappeared, with a single menu, which he handed to Julie. "You don't want a menu?" she asked.

"They know what I like."

What an arrogant, supercilious bastard, Julie thought. She looked at the menu. "So, what do you recommend?"

"I'd try the tasting menu. Nice variety there."

"Sounds good."

A waiter materialized at the table, and took Julie's order, then disappeared. After that, the two engaged in some trivial small talk while waiting for their drinks to arrive.

They were starting to run out of conversation when the food arrived on a little silver cart. The waiter placed a dish in front of Julie that looked more like an artist's pallet than a meal, twelve bite-sized portions.

"A little bit of everything," Bart explained unnecessarily.

Then the waiter started unloading dishes in front of Mulvaney—seared *foie gras,* buttermilk and black truffle chicken breast, lobster with baby bok choy, baby pig, rack of lamb, black bass roasted in a scallop crust, In other words, everything on the menu.

"You intend to *eat* all that?" she asked in disbelief.

"Oh, heavens no. I'll just eat what I want."

My God, Julie thought, this man may just be the biggest pig I've ever met. "I see."

"So," Mulvaney finally said, between bites, "what's the big news?"

"We've found a suitable challenger for you."

"At last?" Mulvaney asked with a sly smile. "Grapevine tells me you've been searching all over town. Okay, who's this opponent you lined up? I'm sure I know him."

Julie decided to do a little teasing. "His ideas about foreign investment are really quite different from yours, which should make for a lively exchange."

"Are you gonna tell me his name or do I have to start guessing?"

"His name is Mario Monelli." She waited for the reaction, and it came almost immediately.

"Mario Monelli?" he laughed. "I thought UBS was trying to improve its image."

Julie was taken aback. "What do you mean?"

"Jesus, have you *talked* with him? I don't think he ever finished high school."

"Well, that would make a nice contrast, wouldn't it?" Julie said brightly. "So how about it, Bart? Are you on board?"

"Jesus, I don't know. He's not very credible in my circle. I think I'm going to pass."

"I see, Bart. He's not worthy enough to debate, but he's worthy enough to write you check for a million dollars…*if* you win."

Bart was flabbergasted. "What? You know about that? Did *he* tell you?"

"Everyone on The Street knows, Bart." She leaned in toward him, her anger just barely concealed. "Just like everyone is going to know you ran from this fight. That ought to do wonders for your reputation...in your circle."

The sommelier arrived then, a bottle of wine in each hand. He showed them to Bart, who approved with a cursory glance. Then came the uncorking and the pouring, followed by a period of serious eating.

After a few minutes, Mulvaney came up for air. "I was wondering, Julie—how much do you really know about Monelli?"

"I've read everything that's been written about him, of course, and I've seen his television interviews." Julie wondered if Bart was about to tell her something that would knock Mario off the horse.

"Then I assume you know about this club he and those clowns at work are involved with?" Mulvaney asked.

Her brow furrowed. "Club? No. What club?"

"I don't know much about it. It's shrouded in mystery. It must be something very exclusive...and very enticing. I hope it's legit. I wouldn't want to see you, or the network, involved in anything shady or unethical."

"Thank you for your concern," Julie said. What a hypocrite, she thought. Still, she'd have to ask Mario about this.

The *maitre'd* appeared at the table. "All is well?" he inquired, smiling, looking at Julie.

"All is delicious, George," Bart assured him.

The *maitre'd* smiled and departed, and Bart turned his attention back to Julie, taking her hand and gazing into her eyes, seductively. "Now this is what I had in mind for the rest of the evening..."

Julie interrupted, taking her hand from his. "I'm afraid I can't stay."

"So soon? Where are you going? What could be more important—or more fun—than spending the rest of the evening with me?"

Oh, brother, she thought. "And here I thought you were a gentleman, Bart."

"A gentleman is nothing but a patient wolf, Julie." He grinned.

Well this is one Red Riding Hood you won't eat, Julie said to herself.

"Bart, you're charming and you're hard to resist, but like I told you this afternoon, I do have another obligation."

"Obligation? Don't tell me you're one of those 'Sex and the City' types who's gotta run home to her cat?"

"I know exactly what you were thinking Bart, and it's not going to happen." Bart just smiled and leaned closer, as though he thought she were offering nothing more than token opposition. "There's a jazz club I know in the West Village—one of the Marsalis boys is playing. We could go there. Then go back to my crib on Sutton Place. Have you ever seen the UN building from a warm Jacuzzi on a penthouse roof, Julie?"

From the way Bart was leering at her, Julie decided, he was already picturing her naked. "Sorry, it's all very tempting, of course, but like I said before, I have another engagement. But thanks for the invite. And for dinner. Do I have your commitment to do the show?"

"Sure, Julie," he leaned back and said, smugly, "I'll debate Monelli. And I'll beat him like a red-headed stepchild."

"Good," she said, "I'll have my assistant send you a release. Now if you'll excuse me, I have to get home to my cat."

She took two steps, then turned back toward Mulvaney. "Oh, and by the way, Bart, in case I neglected to mention…we're going live."

"Big mistake, Julie," Bart admonished her, as she turned to walk out. "Like the prosecution letting O.J. try on that glove."

Julie hurried along the cobblestone gutter that was Franklin Street, past windows decorated with Christmas lights, heading toward TriBeCa, producing little clouds of cold fog with every breath. Now she had the final piece in place for the main event—the commitments. But Bart had planted a little seed of doubt in her mind about Mario. It was something she had to clear up fast.

But there was one piece of information she couldn't share with Mario— not yet. She had to pick the right moment to tell him that the show would air live, otherwise, she could lose him. She wouldn't tell him tonight. Tonight was a celebration.

Now, up ahead, she could see the dark green awning of the TriBeCa Grill now garnished with garlands and Christmas lights. She stepped inside the restaurant and pushed through a slew of suits lurking at the bar, anxiously poking away at their Blackberries and chatting up the lovelys. She spotted Mario waiting for her, having a drink, and talking with a man, short in physical stature, who had his back to her.

Mario looked past the man's shoulder and waved her over. "Hi Julie," he said, helping her off with her coat. "I'd like you to meet someone. Julie Chambers…Marty Scorsese." Julie looked at the famous director standing next to Mario, startled.

"Nice to meet you, Julie," Martin Scorsese said, shaking hands with her. Then he turned to Mario. "Gotta run, Mario, I'm meeting Bobby to talk about this year's film festival." He shook hands with Mario and turned to Julie.

"A pleasure meeting you, Julie. And watch out for this *paisan*, he's dangerous."

"So I've heard," Julie said, sliding on a barstool next to Mario. Then he winked at Mario and wandered off.

"What can I get you?" said Mario.

"Chardonnay is fine," she said. Mario ordered her one. "You didn't tell me you knew Martin Scorsese."

"And DeNiro and Pesci," he said with a laugh. "That's what makes me dangerous?"

"Well, I *have* been told you might be involved in something that's not kosher."

Now it was Mario's turn to be startled. "Who said *that*?"

"As a matter of fact, it was your good friend, Barton Mulvaney."

"What? What did that slime ball tell you?"

"He said something about a secret club of some kind."

Oh, fuck, Mario thought. "What kind of a secret club?"

"He didn't know. Something you're not telling me," she said.

"Oh, I know," Mario said, snapping his fingers, hoping his brain would provide him with the right cover—and that she'd believe it. "There's this small social club for Wall Street execs some of my colleagues started. Bart was blackballed because he's an asshole. He blames it on me and he's toxically bitter about it."

"I see," Julie said, smiling. "Anyway, Bart has agreed to be on the show. That's my news for the night."

"I guess we're off to the races, then," Mario said, toasting her.

Mario finished his drink and signaled the bartender for the check. The bartender came back with two doggie bags. "The glazed brisket sandwich is in this one," he said, holding it up, "and the buttermilk onion rings and the sparkling water are in this one."

"What's this?" Julie asked, fearing a repeat of Mulvaney's one-man smorgasbord. "You haven't eaten?"

"No, this is for a friend of mine," Mario said. "C'mon, I've got my car here. We'll drop off the food, then I'll take you home. Okay?"

Soon afterward, Mario pulled up in front of Cortlandt alley and opened the door for Julie. "Your friend lives near here?"

"No," Mario said. "He lives *right* here." Mario held out his hand and, after a moment, she took it and allowed herself to be led into the alley, if a bit reluctantly.

Gus was sitting in a broken-down recliner, his orange cat on his lap, reading a book by the light of a bare bulb overhead, which was hanging from a string of extension cords leading who knows where. He rose as Mario and Julie approached, carefully placing the cat on the pavement.

"Delivery," said Mario, handing Gus the bags.

"Hope you ain't expecting a tip," Gus joked.

"Julie," said Mario, "I'd like you to meet a very good friend of mine, Gus Shaw. Gus, this is Julie Chambers. She's producing the television show I told you about."

Gus stood and touched the brim of his longshoreman's cap. "Very happy to meet you, Miss Chambers."

"It's Julie," she said, completely charmed, "and I'm very happy to meet you too…Gus is it?" She couldn't believe it. One moment Mario is drinking with Martin Scorsese, the next he's feeding the homeless.

By this time, Sam had strolled over to Julie and nestled against her leg, purring. "That's Sam," Gus said. "A very good judge of people."

Julie was unable to contain her curiosity. "Have you and Mario been friends long?"

Gus and Mario exchanged looks. "Not long," Mario said.

"But time is not the only measure of friendship," Gus added.

"No," Julie said slowly, surprised and impressed. "It certainly isn't." She took a long hard look at Gus. He didn't look like much—an old black man with a wizened face and bulldog demeanor.

And yet…the man had been sitting here, reading. What kind of street person had a pet? And what kind of street person had a friend like Mario, bringing him food from fancy restaurants?

Julie scratched Sam's head, which caused him to purr even louder.

"Gus, how come you're not wearing the clothing I gave you?" Mario asked.

"That's my Sunday best, Mario. I'm saving it for special occasions."

"It's getting chilly—wouldn't hurt to wear the jacket. I'm going to see about picking you up a coat."

Gus looked at Julie, smiling. "The man thinks he's my mother. So, hey, how are the boys doing?"

"Oh I tell ya, I got 'em gloves" replied Mario. "They're boxing now."

They both laughed, and Julie wondered what this was all about. She also wondered, finally, what Gus had been reading. She picked it up from his chair. It was a worn Library Edition of "For Whom the Bell Tolls," by Ernest Hemingway. "You like Hemingway, Gus?" Julie asked.

"Someone tossed out a bunch of these old books and I grabbed some," Gus said. "This is one of the better ones, but I also like that Steinbeck fella."

"He's one of my favorites, too," Julie said thoughtfully.

"Ready to go home?" Mario asked Julie. He wanted to cut the conversation short, before Gus started talking about things Mario would rather tell her himself—or, who was he kidding?—things he hoped she would never discover.

"Ready when you are," she told Mario, then turned toward Gus. "Glad to meet you, Gus," she said with genuine pleasure.

"My privilege, ma'am," Gus said, touching the brim of his cap.

They got into the car, and in the glow of the street lights, she found herself looking at Mario with new eyes.

"So, Mario," Julie said, "how did you and Gus meet?"

"I was walking back to my place one night, pretty shit-faced, and some muggers attacked me. Gus jumped out of the alley and, well, I'm alive. Anyhow, we've gotten to be pretty good friends."

They turned onto Julie's street and pulled up beside the luxurious Turtle Bay apartments and parked.

"You know," Julie said, "your friend Gus had a point."

"Yeah, what's that?"

"I really don't know much about you, except what I've read. I mean, just as matter of due diligence, I'd like to find out a little more about you. Especially since we'll be working together." She was trying to sound businesslike, but wasn't sure she'd succeeded.

He shut off the car engine. "Umm, let's see" he said. "Where do I begin? I was born eight pounds, three ounces..."

Julie laughed.

"Look, sounds like this might take a little while, and it's getting cold in here. You drink coffee?" Julie asked.

"Only if it's a lot of trouble," he jested.

She smiled. "Why don't you find a spot and I'll make us some."

"A parking spot—around here? He laughed. "That could take all night."

Upstairs, she unlocked the door, turned on the lights, and took Mario's coat from him and hung it on the coat rack. Then she headed for the kitchen.

Mario took the opportunity to look around. Classic contemporary furnishings, not ostentatious, but high quality and well-chosen. Silver-framed pictures of an older couple—parents, no doubt—and of a younger woman wearing a Swarthmore sweatshirt and who looked a lot like Julie, a sister, perhaps.

And, finally, there was a small picture, framed in wood, and sitting on Julie's desk, of a handsome, hazel-eyed man with wavy, sandy brown hair, and a Nikon strung from his neck. A brother? Maybe, maybe not.

"I have espresso," Julie called from the kitchen.

"Great, make it a double," Mario called back.

He ducked in the foyer and quickly called Phyllis, telling her he was meeting with the television producer, and not to wait up. He neglected to mention the producer was a woman.

Julie returned with the coffee tray, putting one cup in front of Mario and sitting down across from him. "So," Mario said, taking a sip. "You have questions?" He caught an interesting scent—perfume. Had she been wearing it earlier?

"Yes," she said, taking out a little notebook and curling up on the couch. "I'd like to start with Harrison Hart. You told me that because the M&A division is the most profitable in the firm, you manage to stay out of the bear trap."

"That's true, relatively. As long as we keep winning our battles, we enjoy full autonomy from Tyler Gentry and Harrison's House of Lords."

"Has it always been that way?" Julie picked up a pencil, but didn't do anything with it.

"Actually, it's a pretty complicated situation. You see, Tyler and the other partners at Harrison engineered a merger with Hart some years ago precisely to acquire our M&A team."

"I'm surprised Hart let you go."

Mario laughed without pleasure. "That's hardly what happened. There was a turf war after we came aboard. Tyler and the partners forced the resignation of some senior Hart executives, including our company president, Austin Keyes. Is that *L'air du temp*?"

Julie looked up from her notepad.

"Your perfume," he said.

"Yes," said Julie. "Yes, it is. So how do you feel about it?"

"I like it on you."

"I meant the merger," she said, bringing Mario back into the fold.

Mario paused, looking for the right words. "It was a terrible situation, not only for me, but for everyone at Hart. But the severance deal made Keyes one of the richest men on Wall Street, not that he lived to enjoy it."

"He's dead?"

"He was having breakfast up in the Windows of the World restaurant when..."

Julie nodded silently, understanding.

"He was my mentor," Mario continued. "Raised me from a pup."

"So you and your team ended up in what is now called Harrison Hart?"

"That's right. All except one. He didn't have the stomach for it and quit. My best friend. Or we used to be. Now he's in China to make a name for himself."

"You don't speak because of the merger?" she asked.

"Cuts deeper. I'd rather not get into it," Mario sighed. "Anyway, Tyler fired the head of M&A, a position Bart was being considered for." Julie furrowed her brow in apparent confusion.

"I know what you're thinking," said Mario. "Then what am *I* doing at the helm? Well let's just say it was part of the arrangement."

"What kind of arrangement?"

"The merger was billed as 'a merger of equals,'" Mario explained. "But later that fall, Keyes found out Harrison's partners lied. They never intended the combined companies to be equals and forced Keyes out. It destroyed any trust the Hart people might have had with Harrison. And without trust, you can't lead."

"So then what happened?"

"The firm started to hemorrhage talent. And that really spooked the partners. They needed Hart—under my stewardship—to help recreate the

Harrison brand. So me and Tyler called a cease fire and negotiated a peace treaty."

"What kind of peace treaty?" She was genuinely intrigued.

"We agreed to lay our guns down with the assurance I'd be made partner, giving Hart representation on the board. Exactly what they promised Keyes."

"Where did that leave Bart?" Julie asked.

Mario took a sip of his coffee, looking at her with a devilish grin.

The light dawned. "I see," said Julie. "Tyler gave *you* what he promised to Bart."

"Yeah. It was a blow to Bart's ego...*and* his reputation. He swore revenge. And he got it with Intercoastal."

"Now I'm beginning to understand what's going on between you two," Julie said. "What about your team—?"

"The Zoo Crew? What about them?"

She smiled. "That's what you call them, the Zoo Crew?" She took another sip of coffee, and jotted down a note.

"Yeah. Fits us pretty well. We like it."

"You're animals?" she teased.

"That's the way the Harrison people see us," Mario answered, deadly serious. "They're Rhodes scholars from Yale, and all the other *'fuck you'* schools, married to blonde, cookie-cutter wives, power lunching on escargot and Haut Brion wine. We're red-faced ethnic kids from City college, feeding on cold pizza and warm Pepsi, married to some girl in the neighborhood we knocked up back in the day. And we're out there kicking Ivy League ass every day."

"If you guys were all so loyal to Keyes, then why did you remain at Harrison Hart?" she asked.

"Because Keyes was dead. And it would have been a futile gesture to leave. Not only that, it would have meant cutting ourselves out of the company's future growth—and exerting our power."

"You're planning a revolution?"

"No. But we were tempted. The day after the Keyes' disaster, Tyler and the partners marched into the building like the Nazis marching into Paris. I'll never forget the feeling of being conquered."

"So if I understand correctly," Julie said, "Tyler is like the camp commandant and you're the Allied commanding officer. He needs you to control the prisoners and keep the talent from escaping. Otherwise..."

"The firm would plunge into chaos." Mario nodded. "Separate P&Ls, separate trading floors, even separate bathrooms, and cafeterias. They want no part of us and we want no part of them."

"All this over one man?" Julie asked.

"When I become partner the war will end and we'll unite the firm," said Mario. "I owe that to Keyes." Mario got up, stretched, and walked over to the wall unit that held Julie's stereo and CD rack. "Mind?"

"No, go right ahead." Julie watched Mario sift through her CD collection, wondering if he'd find something he liked. She hoped so, but it didn't seem likely. But he took a CD out of its plastic case and slipped it into the player. In a moment, the soft, melodic piano jazz of Errol Garner was floating out of the speakers in surround sound.

"One my favorites," Julie said. Her eyes met Mario's for a moment and held.

"You got anything stronger besides coffee?" Mario asked, hoping she'd catch his meaning.

"Red or white?" she asked.

"White—if it's cold."

She came back from the kitchen juggling a bottle and two glasses. Mario did the pouring, while Julie put her feet up on the couch and curled herself around a pillow.

Julie guessed that Mario was done talking about his rise on Wall Street when another question occurred to her. "Gus mentioned 'the boys,' you know, the ones with the boxing gloves. Was he talking about the Zoo Crew?"

Mario filled his glass and grinned. "No, he was talking about my sons."

"That's right, you have a little boy!" Julie reminded herself. "Kyle, right?"

"Just turned eight. And my oldest is seventeen.

"You also have a teenage son." She said with flattering surprise. "What's his name?"

"Boomer."

"That's an unusual name."

"Named him after an old buddy of mine from East Islip who went on to play pro football. He's looking at universities now."

'Which ones?"

"We've checked out Dartmouth and Cornell. After the holidays, we're driving up to New Haven to see Yale..."

"Seems like the entire Ivy league is laying roses at Boomer's feet."

"All except for one school," said Mario.

"Harvard," she guessed.

"He's waitlisted. We still haven't heard."

"You and your wife must be very proud."

"You mean my ex-wife," Mario heard himself saying, feeling as detached from his own words as he was from Phyllis. He took a long sip from his wine.

"What happened?"

"Nothing good. That's why we're divorced."

They laughed.

"And what about Kyle? Is he a future scholar, too?"

"My little guy? I'm afraid he's not the student his older brother is."

"Oh, and why is that?"

"Actually he's developmentally delayed…three years."

"Oh, I see," Julie said. She tried to think of a way to change the subject.

"What about you?" Mario gestured to the picture on her coffee table. "Your husband?"

Julie followed his glance. "He was." There was a pained catch in her voice. "He was killed in the Middle East covering a story." She caught her breath and looked away.

"When?" Mario asked.

"Been over a year now." She took a drink of wine.

"I'm sorry," Mario said gently. "That couldn't be easy."

"It's one day at a time," Julie said, smiling a little too brightly.

"How long were you married?" Mario asked, hoping to comfort her somehow.

"Almost nine years," she said. "But we knew each other since college."

"You must miss him."

"Terribly," she heard herself say.

"So you've thrown yourself into your work."

"I enjoy my work."

"But you can't put your arms around a job, Julie. Life goes on."

She nodded, then excused herself and took both empty glasses into the kitchen and refilled them. Then the tears came. She thought she'd finished with them. But they were flooding down her cheeks now, and even worse, she'd started sobbing.

Mario's arms were around Julie before he was even conscious of the urge. She sobbed into his shoulder and he held her, surprised by her softness. It lasted for what seemed to be a long time.

Julie pulled back, her face tear-streaked, mascara running, embarrassed. "I don't know what happened to me. I haven't cried like that in…"

Mario liftd her chin and gently kissed her. That lasted a long time, too. It was a soft kiss, but it had a lifetime of passion behind it. When they broke, Mario took his clean, white carefully-folded handkerchief out of his pocket and started wiping Julie's tears, looking into her eyes, and she into his.

After a moment, Julie grinned, took the handkerchief from him and wiped her own tears off the shoulder of his suit jacket. Then he took her hand, brought her back into the living room, and sat down on the couch with her where they talked and talked.

"…the day after Christmas, they told me Jack's plane had crashed over Fallujah. I felt like part of me had died as well." Her eyes engaged Mario's.

"Why do people you love always seem to die around the holidays? Everyone I loved in my life died this time of year. Jack, my father, my grandparents. Even the dog I had as a child."

"Now I understand why you don't have a Christmas tree," Mario said.

"I didn't feel like putting one up this year. What for? What I want I'll never find under a Christmas tree."

She reached behind her head and Mario heard something snap. Suddenly her thick blonde mane fell to her shoulders, framing the warmth of her face. Unlike the airbrushed, surgically enhanced creatures that hung on the Wall of Shame, this woman was slender, healthy, naturally beautiful, and genuine, and instead of the artificial sexiness so many women attempted, she radiated a quiet self-confidence.

He gazed into her eyes, which were green, and warm, and deep. He liked looking into them.

Mario and Julie talked for hours, getting to know each other, feeling comfortable with each other. Then, just before midnight, Mario finally took his leave.

In the following weeks, they saw a great deal of each other. It was dinner at Le Cirque or the Four Seasons, lunch at Patty's Pizza Shop under the Brooklyn Bridge, long, deep conversations at the MoMA, popcorn, wine and Casablanca on television at her place, ice skating at Rockefeller Center in front of the huge Christmas tree despite snow flurries, making out behind some bookshelves at a mid-town Barnes & Noble, exchanging naughty texts and emails via Twitter and Facebook, snuggling up under the blanket during a horse-and-buggy ride through Central Park, even decorating a small tree Mario brought home to her.

Their time together changed them both. Julie was living again, laughing again, feeling again, dressing to be attractive. Everybody at work could see it, and some commented—"you're just so full of energy," or "I don't know what it is, but you've definitely got your mojo back, girl," as Paige put it.

The same was true of Mario. He was just as dedicated as before, but the grimness was gone. He was more easy-going, not obsessing over the Lions' Den...or caring for that matter. He was, as Neil said more than once, "a man who looked like he was actually enjoying his life."

Somehow, they never made it to Mario's fictitious apartment in Battery Park—he always found an excuse: "Got a buddy crashing there for a few days," "Your place is a lot closer." "It's all torn up—they're renovating."

But he knew this couldn't go on forever. He couldn't expect Julie to believe the apartment excuses, forever, nor could he count on Phyllis always believing he was working late with the television producer.

Some of the time they spent together actually was related to the upcoming special. Julie devoted a fair amount of time working with Mario, coaching him for his television appearance. "The best advice I can give you," she said, "is to be yourself."

"My uneducated working-class slob self?"

"I mean your confident, passionate, clear-headed, eloquent self."

Mario laughed. "That's the way you see me?"

"That's the way you *are.* "

"What else? I'm sure you have a whole set of tips and warnings."

Julie took a deep breath. "Okay, here's one: When Bart is talking, *listen* to him. Don't take that time rehearsing your answer to the previous question. Otherwise you'll lose focus."

"That makes sense," Mario admitted.

"Here's another one: You don't have to answer a question instantly. Take a few moments. The words will flow better, and it will give Marty and me a chance to check out the supporting data and feed you through your earpiece."

"Roger that."

"And whatever you do, don't bloviate."

"Huh?"

"Don't expand your answers. Keep them short and precise."

"Yeah," Mario said thoughtfully, "and if I ramble, you can always edit the tape."

Uh-oh, Julie thought—he doesn't realize we're going to be live. Well, maybe it's best not to tell him, at least not until he feels a little more confident.

On another night, Julie brought in both John Ayers and Tom Gallagher to get Mario comfortable with both men, and to help sharpen his oratorical skills. "When I ask a question," Gallagher told him, "just forget about the camera and talk to me as though we're having an ordinary conversation."

Julie and Mario also spent a lot of time puzzling over how the U.S. government could ignore what the Saudis were doing, despite the evidence that the SEC had accumulated. Julie finally had Mario sit with UBS news head writer and research director, Marty Cohen.

"Here's the terrorism part of the story," Marty said. "The Royal Family is using oil money to pay off its Islamic radicals. They're paying protection, so the oil fields won't be attacked, and so they can retain power."

"Yeah," Mario said. "I guess that makes sense."

"You think so? Well, you know what the Islamic radicals do with the money?"

Now Mario understood. "So you're saying that we're financing our own destruction."

"Exactly."

"So why don't we shift our oil purchases elsewhere?"

"No can do," Marty told him. "Only a little bit of the oil money goes to the terrorists. The rest comes back to the U.S., in return for military hardware—planes, tanks, etc. An arrangement set up by Henry Kissinger in the early seventies. American defense companies live off these contracts.

"The bottom line," he said, "is that practically everyone in America with political power is on the Saudi payroll, directly or indirectly. That includes Washington lawyers, PR firms, lobbyists, defense contractors, senators, America's Middle-East ambassadors, and CIA station chiefs—and the president and his cabinet."

Mario just shook his head. "You're telling me that the Saudis can call in a favor any time they like?"

"That's right. So long as the Crown Prince keeps buying our weapons and banking our oil and buying our debt, no one cares what happens in the Saudi kingdom."

"I had no idea the political hold the Saudi Royal Family has on us."

"And it goes all the way back to FDR. Every president…every goddamn one of them. Even Kennedy. All the way back to that bag of money Khashoggi left for Nixon in San Clemente. It was never returned."

But most of the time Mario and Julie were together, there was no talk at all about the special. There was, at long last, when Julie was ready, when her trust for Mario was complete, love-making—tentative at first, new to both of them…gentle, affectionate, and intimate, but eventually fast, hot, and urgent.

Each of them was completely into the other and into the moment, no fantasies, no selfishness, no detachment. They luxuriated in each other's touch, in exploring each other's bodies, skin to skin, finding surprises and delights.

Two days before Christmas, while having an intimate dinner at Acapella's, an Italian restaurant in Lower Manhattan, they exchanged gifts. Mario gave Julie a set of beautiful diamond earrings, which she put in on the spot. Then she handed him a small, gift-wrapped box. Inside was a silver-colored iPod. It was pre-loaded with all the music they'd heard in the last few weeks—the Erroll Garner, the Nutcracker Suite, the music they'd danced to at Butter's, the ice skating music from Rockefeller Center, the Christmas music that had drifted out of the Fifth Avenue shops.

She watched him unwrap it, watched his expression as he realized what it was, and their eyes met, as they had so many times before, and they embraced each other with exquisite tenderness, a tenderness that led to an almost endless kiss, a kiss that transported both of them.

The day before Christmas, following the company's annual holiday party at Ciprianis—the only time Harrison's House of Lords and Hart's House of Commons socialized—Mario decided he'd rather be someplace else. He made one stop—back at the office, picked up a gift-wrapped box, and once again donned his overcoat and left.

Mario found Gus at the remote end of Cortlandt alley, where the winter winds couldn't reach, but the temperature was still low. Gus was huddled up under some newspapers, eyes closed, wearing the golf jacket Mario had given him. A scraggly plastic Christmas tree about three feet tall stood beside his chair, its battery-operated colored lights—all five of them—blinking irregularly. Sam was sleeping underneath it.

"Hey, champ," Mario said, hoping his friend wasn't really asleep.

Gus opened a single eye, returned the greeting, shook himself free of the newspapers, and stood.

"Merry Christmas, Gus," Mario said, handing the box to the old fighter.

"What's this?" Gus asked, taking the box and looking at it curiously.

"It's a Christmas present, me to you."

"You want me to put this under my tree?" Gus asked, joking.

"No. Open it now. I want to see the expression on your face."

Gus carefully removed and folded the wrapping paper, as if he'd find a good use for it sometime, and slid the top off the box, pushing aside the tissue wrapping. He pulled out a puffy dark green jacket.

"It's from L.L. Bean—their warmest down jacket. It's waterproof, too. Some gloves are in the pockets."

"I can't get you to stop taking care of me," Gus said, slipping it on.

"Doesn't look that way. Hey, Gus, it's cold out here, how 'bout spending Christmas Eve with me and the boys tonight. You can sit by the fire."

"Thanks, Mario, but a man should be alone with his family tonight. Sam and me are going to the Houston Street shelter with a bunch of my street buddies."

"Well, another time then?" Mario didn't want to push him.

"Sure," Gus said half-heartedly, then changed the subject. "So you almost ready for that television show?"

"Yeah," Mario said. "I've been working a lot with Julie. She's been telling me how to behave during the debate."

Gus smiled. "All work?"

"Well…" Mario started, and then stopped when he couldn't figure out what to say next. He didn't have to. Gus already knew.

"So what did Julie say when you told her you were married."

Their eyes met and Mario looked away.

Gus shook his head. "Yeah, I didn't think so. And your missus, she doesn't have a clue either, does she?"

Mario didn't say anything.

Gus sighed. "Ain't no difference between a wise man and a fool when he falls in love."

Driving home through the torrent of traffic fleeing the city for the Christmas weekend, Mario could think of nothing but Julie. One moment, in his mind, they were together in bed, laughing with each other. The next, he was trying out excuses and explanations, and imagining Julie's reactions to them. Nothing was working.

Mario pulled into his driveway, taking some pleasure in the twinkling Douglas fir he could see through the living room window, and the kids nearby. Moments later, he walked in through the kitchen entrance and heard Nat King Cole's "Come All Ye Faithful" wafting from the living room.

Phyllis was standing there, hands on her hips, hell in her eyes. "Well, if it isn't Santa's missing elf. And where the *fuck* have you been?"

Her anger caught Mario by surprise. "At work. We had our Christmas party, then I stopped by to see Gus and give him his present."

"Did you simply *forget* that we were having Christmas Eve dinner here at three. You know, with Maria and Charlene *and* their husbands *and* their kids?" She was enraged.

"I just…damn, I guess I *did* forget," Mario said apologetically. "I don't know what I was thinking. Are they still in the dining room?"

"No, fuckhead. We waited around and ate an hour late—the ham was like a brick—and they waited and waited and finally went home. While you were making nice with your good friend, the punch-drunk nigger. Or some woman."

"You've got it wrong, Phyllis. You know where I've been. I've been working with the television producer, getting ready for the special. It's only a month away."

"You're a liar! You're a cocksucking liar and I've had enough of you!"

"Another Christmas out the window," Mario muttered, slipping off his coat.

"Out the window? I'll give ya out the window."

Phyllis marched into the living room, where Kyle was checking out the boxes under the tree, trying to find the ones with his name on them so he could guess what might be inside.

"Watch out!" Phyllis snarled. In an explosion of rage, she ripped the electrical cord out from the wall, reached through the branches of the Christmas tree, grabbed the slender trunk with both hands, tore it out of its moorings—while Kyle watched, disbelieving—and hurled it through the living room bay window, shattered glass flying everywhere, cold air flooding the room.

"And this…" Phyllis said, rummaging around in the pile of gift-wrapped packages. "This is my Christmas present to you, you undeserving fuck!" She found a small box, put it on the floor and stomped it again and again and again, leaving the package flattened and its broken contents—a Cartier gold watch, crystal shattered—scattered over the antique Persian carpet. Mario glared at Phyllis as though he were finally ready to kill her. And Kyle just sat on the floor, staring at his parents, tears running down his face.

CHAPTER TWENTY-ONE

Paige walked down the hall and around the newsroom, spreading the message. "Full staff meeting at ten o'clock," she told each of the members of Julie's teams, getting grumbles, cheery okays, and shrugs in return. Julie's office was her last stop.

"Everyone's on board," Paige told Julie.

"Is Fred here yet?" Julie asked.

"Nope. I e-mailed him, but I don't know if he got the message."

Julie checked her watch. "Well, he still has another five minutes. He'll make it."

Paige nodded, opened her mouth to speak, then closed it.

"What?" Julie asked. "Say it. I won't bite. It's about Fred, isn't it?"

"Well…yes. It's really nothing. I just don't get it."

"Get what?"

Paige took a deep breath. "Julie, I know you don't like the guy. Sometimes, he makes my skin crawl with his patronizing Southern gentleman routine."

"I know what you mean," Julie said with a little laugh.

"So why did you make him director of the most important segment of the show? I just don't understand."

Julie leaned back in her chair. "Sit down, young lady. You've asked a good question and I think you'll learn a lot from the answer." Paige sat.

"Fred feels like he's in competition with me. He thinks *he* should be executive producer of the show. Also, he's not so young any more. He's beginning to worry that he's losing his edge. He's scared."

"I hadn't thought of it that way," Paige admitted. "But I still don't understand why you'd make him director."

"Two reasons—I don't want him taking pot-shots at me. I want him to have a greater stake in this. That way if I go down…"

"He goes down with you," Paige said. "I see now."

"Besides, Fred really knows what he's doing. Having him aboard will help us."

At that moment, the phone rang and Paige picked it up. "Hello…yes, she's right here. Okay, I'll tell her," she said, then hung up and turned to Julie. "That was Miles. He wants you in his office."

"Now?"

"Yes. He sounded quite urgent. Want I delay the meeting?"

"No," Julie said, grabbing her coffee. "Best you start without me. I shouldn't be long."

"Me? But I don't know..."

"Of course you do, Paige."

Julie hurried upstairs, wondering what Miles thought was so pressing. When she got to his office, she found Miles sitting behind his desk, looking more than normally pale. Hank was sitting in a corner guest chair, eyes averted.

"Thanks for coming right up, Julie. I'm not going to beat around the bush. I just got a call from Carleton. He's with Chuck Shumacker, our CFO. There's been a run on UBS stock."

For a moment, Julie couldn't breathe. "How bad?" she finally said.

"Not critical...yet, but unmistakable. The bankers give us three or four weeks, Fisher says."

"Three or four weeks before..."

"Before our 'suitors' own a majority of our stock and control the UBS board."

To Julie's surprise, Miles took a bottle of tequila out of a desk drawer and poured himself a drink. "You want one?" he asked.

Julie shook her head.

"*I* can sure use one," said Hank. Miles set out another glass and poured Hank a double shot. She'd never seen Miles Corbin acting this way. It was as though the skin had been stripped off the arrogant son-of-a-bitch he usually was, revealing someone small, weak and—there was no other word for it—frightened.

"Can we fight back?"

The question finally roused Hank. "We might be able to delay them a couple of weeks," he said, dejected, "but they seem to have an in with all the major shareholders."

"'They' is a holding company in Missouri with a post office box address Randy Dandy says is represented by the Blackwell Group," Corbin said.

"I imagine its owners speak Arabic," Julie replied sardonically.

"Very likely," Hank agreed.

Until this moment, the Saudi economic onslaught on America had seemed theoretical, distant. But this was different. This hit them all where they lived.

"So does this mean we're canceling the special, Miles?" Hank asked.

"God no!" Corbin said. "We're not canceling *anything*. But we have to move up the air date. Ready or not, Fisher wants the special to air next week at eight p.m. Eastern."

Julie was flabbergasted. "Next week?"

"That's right," Corbin said. "One week from tomorrow night."

"But we're hardly ready. We're scheduled to air in forty-five days, right before the February sweeps," Julie protested. "That would be well before..."

"Actually, Carleton wanted to air the show *tomorrow night*…"

Julie couldn't help interrupting. "Tomorrow night!"

"…but I told him if we did that, no one would watch it. I convinced him we had to have time to promote it. I asked for a month. He gave me one week." Miles concluded, then gulped another shot.

Julie just sat there overwhelmed, unable to speak. She couldn't argue with Corbin's logic. It would be difficult, but, she hoped, not impossible. "Okay," she said. "One week from tomorrow night. It will be ready to go, no matter what it takes."

"Good. Now you two get downstairs and rally the troops."

Julie headed to the conference room, Hank beside her, and found her staff locked in debate. Fred had already gone, she discovered, but she'd get to him later. She gathered all her segment producers, and associates who quickly joined everyone in the conference room, bodies spilling out of the doorway.

"Okay, everybody, take a deep breath. I have news." She looked around at their faces: Cal Flannery, stoic, ready for anything…Marty Cohen, nervous, impatient… "Tex" Simcox, smiling as though he knew what was coming… John Ayers, asking why he was called into another meeting.

Julie glanced at Hank, who shrugged and held up his hands. It was her show. "Okay, people. We've had a deadline change," Julie said. "We're going on the air next week." There was a collective gasp from the group, then an outbreak of whispering. "Can we do it?"

She looked around the room and found most people were nodding, although no one seemed thrilled.

"Well, it's not any strain on me, so long as I get the script a few hours before airtime," said John Ayers, in that famous baritone of his. "But I do have a question: what's the hurry?"

Julie opened her mouth to speak, but it was Hank who came to her rescue. "The boss has heard rumblings that one of our competitors—the one with the Eye—is planning a similar project. He's worried that we could be scooped."

There were nods of understanding all around the table.

Back in their offices, Julie's team worked frantically to finish up the montage and the scripts, and to get everything else ready to air. Meanwhile, Julie, Hank, and even Miles, spent the remainder of the morning making urgent phone calls to affiliate stations, sponsors, and technical teams, changing schedules, getting new commitments.

It wasn't until noon before Julie realized she had to notify two more people: her cast for the main event: Barton Mulvaney and, oh my god, she thought, Mario. She called Mulvaney, who wasn't fazed by the news.

"Sure, darling, I'll just switch a couple of appointments, not a problem," he said.

Julie decided that in Mario's case, however, a phone call wouldn't do. She had to break the news to him very gently. They'd both been counting on the weeks prior to the special to hone his debate skills and prep him on how to unmask Mulvaney and the Saudis. Now the extra time was gone, and whether or not it was true, Mario might conclude he wasn't yet ready for the man Wall Street called "The Rainmaker."

She picked up the phone and called him at work, skipping the pleasantries and trying to keep the urgency out of her voice. "Can we meet for lunch somewhere downtown?" she asked as sweetly as she could manage. "Maybe a good seafood place."

"I'll meet you in front of the Seaport in an hour," Mario said.

Julie was standing outside Pier 17 early, and feeling nervous—the first time she'd felt nervous about Mario in weeks.

Mario steamed up to the entrance of the South Street Seaport just before one o'clock, cheeks red from the cold, puffing. He gave her a quick kiss and bundled her into the mall-like building.

They took a window table at the Sequoia Restaurant, looking out at the ships docked in the harbor.

"So," Mario said, after the waitress took their orders, "what's up? I didn't expect to see you until tomorrow night."

"Well, I have some news," she said, sounding serious.

Mario frowned. "Bad news?"

"There seems to be a run on UBS stock."

"Who?"

"No one's sure. But the SEC thinks the Blackwell Group is advising."

"You know what this means?" Mario asked. "It means that the hostile bid is already underway. UBS has one, maybe two months of independence."

Julie swallowed hard. "Yes. That's the way Fisher and Corbin see it, too. They've moved up the air date of the special. It's going to air next Thursday night, January third. The promos begin tonight."

"Whew!" Mario said, a little overwhelmed. "So when do you want me to begin taping?" He was trying to sound enthusiastic, but he couldn't conceal his fear.

Julie had rehearsed half a dozen ways of saying it, but now it just came out, plain as can be. "We're not taping it." She looked at him almost imploringly, hoping he'd understand and she wouldn't have to explain.

That makes no sense, Mario thought. "Not taping? What do you mean?"

She closed her eyes and prepared herself, as though she was getting ready to leap in the chill waters of the East River. "We're going live," she said, then opened her eyes to watch Mario's reaction. Mario didn't react.

"Live?" he gulped.

She nodded affirmatively, afraid of his reaction.

"You mean no one's going to edit out my bad grammar or my fumbling if my thoughts get tangled up in my words."

She nodded again, and tried smiling this time, hoping he'd be reassured.

"Why live?" he said, looking panicked.

"Lots of reasons: makes it look fair, unrehearsed, untampered within the editing room. Also, it's real and the audience knows it. Anything could happen. Besides, it will prevent any meddling if the Saudis move faster than we expect."

"You knew this, didn't you." Mario said quietly. "You knew all along."

Julie sighed deeply. "I was going to tell you..."

"When? As I was walking into the studio."

She leaned across the table and held his face steady, trying to reassure him. "Sweetheart, darling, listen to me...listen...you can do this," she said softly, but insistently. "And I'll be right in the control booth...in your earpiece. I won't leave you. We'll take him down together."

Mario looked out the window at the two bridges that tied Manhattan to Brooklyn.

"Mario, I know you're worried—but I also know you can do it."

Mario recognized the words. He had told Vinny the same thing that night at Harry's which only added to his crushing self-doubt.

Mario turned to face her. "You don't understand, Julie, it's not just me I'm afraid for. It's you, too. I don't want you to risk everything, including your career, on a live show."

"I've *already* risked everything when I fell in love with you," she said.

Mario felt an onrush of love, but the fear remained. "But there's so much riding on this, Julie. If I blow it, the country's going to lose everything." He tossed his napkin down and slid his chair back.

"Where are you going?" Julie asked, really getting concerned now.

"Out for some fresh air," Mario said.

He strode out of the restaurant, onto the promenade deck without looking back, Julie following. Once they were outside, Mario walked to the railing and gazed at the choppy water of the East River, taking quick breaths of the crisp cool air.

Julie came up to him from behind, put her arms around him and rested her head on his back, whispering to his ear. "It's going to be fine, darling, I promise. I'm going to be right there in the control room, making sure you're not humiliated—like I promised."

Very slowly, Mario began to catch his breath. He turned, and his arms enveloped Julie. "I'm okay now," he finally said.

Julie looked at him closely, trying to gauge his frame of mind. "Good. Now let's go back inside and finish our lunch."

And that's what they did. By the time dessert came, Mario was pretty much back to his usual self. But Julie knew he could use a little more reassurance, and they could both use a little more of each other.

"Things are crazy right now," Julie said. "How about we get away for the weekend. Someplace quiet. Just the two of us. I know a great little bed-and-breakfast up in the Berkshires. Or maybe we could go skiing up at Lake Placid."

Julie's suggestion came as a very welcome surprise. It was just what he needed, Mario thought, just what *they* needed. He could send Phyllis and the boys off somewhere on a family trip, then bug out at the last minute. Then he could take Julie to the Monelli cabin in the Catskills. "I have a cabin in the Catskills up past Woodland Valley," he said. "It's on a lake with a great view of the mountains, huge pine trees. Big fireplace."

"Sounds perfect," Julie said approvingly. "You want to pick me up Friday after work?"

Mario's brain was in over-drive. "No," he said thoughtfully, "let's drive up separately. I've got a late Friday afternoon meeting up in Mount Kisco, and I probably won't be able to get there until nine o'clock or so."

"The key is under the mat?"

"I keep it on top of the door frame. I'll e-mail you a little map."

Mario waited until very late Friday afternoon to drop the bomb on Phyllis. "I can't go with you. Tyler's sending me to Chicago this weekend," he said. "I won't be back until Monday."

"Goddamn it, Mario! This was *your* idea! 'It's been a long time since we visited your mother,' you said. 'let's go see her this weekend.' I've been *begging* you for months, and finally, just before we go, you pull this shit. You're a fuckin' prick, you know that."

This was no more or less than he'd expected. "I'm really sorry, Phyllis. But you can still go with the boys."

"You're damn right I'm going. I'm not going to disappoint my mother. Not after that shit you pulled on my sisters."

"I'll send her some flowers," Mario said, tossing a little gasoline on the fire.

"Flowers! You think that'll make up for it? Whadda schmuck."

Mario made the trip to the cabin in two hours flat, giving him plenty of time before Julie would be there. Then, he went through the cabin like a CSI detective, searching for evidence, careful to erase any trace of having a wife. There wasn't much—Phyllis was meticulous about matters of personal hygiene. All he could come up with was a pair of her boots, a woman's razor on the edge of the tub, a glass with a lipstick print on the kitchen counter, and a pair of earrings on the bedroom nightstand. He was trying to cover his tracks like he was Tiger Woods.

He stuffed everything into a garbage bag and stashed the garbage bag in the tool shed. He draped one of Boomer's football jerseys over a living room chair and tucked one of Kyle's model cars under the couch. They made the room look lived in. Then he selected some choice logs from the firewood rack and lit a match. In a few minutes, the cabin was warming up nicely and it looked cozy enough for a honeymoon.

Julie's blue Prius pulled into the snow-covered driveway and parked behind the Maserati. It was a little after eight, which pleased Mario because he knew she must be as eager to see him as he was to see *her*.

He hurried down the porch steps as she buzzed down the window.

"Excuse me, sir, is this Mario Monelli's cabin?" she said, pretending innocence.

"It ain't Abe Lincoln's," Mario said. "Come on, let's get inside. It's cold out here." He grabbed her small suitcase, put an arm around her, and brought her into the warmth of the cabin, closing the door behind them. Then, as she started slipping out of her ski jacket, his arms were around her again and the two of them were kissing hungrily, as though they hadn't seen each other for years.

Somehow, they made their way into the bedroom, still kissing, and they flopped onto the bed. "Wait," Julie said, reaching for a blouse button.

"*I'll* do it," Mario said, and while he did, she did the same favor for him.

They were naked to the waist now, lit only by the glow of the fire in the other room, but it was a moment to absorb the sight of each other, the kind of moment that always ends with a kiss or a smile or in this case, both.

After that, it was hands, caressing, fondling, experiencing the texture of their lover's skin, the curves of their lover's bodies, the intimacy of each other's most private places before slavishly burying themselves in each other. It was as if there was no world outside of the cabin.

Afterwards, Mario brought back two glasses of wine and they lay beside each other. "You know," Julie said, "it's pure luck that we met."

"How so?"

"Well, your name wasn't on any research list I was given. I'd never heard of you until I talked with the bartender at a bar and grill not far from your office. I was telling him my woes—I hadn't been able to find anyone qualified or willing to go up against Bart—and he mentioned you."

"Yes, I am well-liked among the bartending set."

Julie laughed and hugged him and the hugs turned into kisses, and then they started to make love again. And when they came up for air, it was more because the room was getting chilly than because they'd had enough of each other.

"I'll put on more logs," Mario said, wrapping a sheet around himself.

Julie followed him into the living room, wearing nothing at all.

After he restocked the fireplace, Mario turned to say something to her and saw her standing there, her silhouette outlined by the flickering flames, lithe, but also womanly.

"My God," Mario said softly, "you are so beautiful."

"It's the poor lighting," she suggested.

"Come here," he said. She came to him and he enveloped her in his sheet, so they were naked together. Then it was back to the bedroom, and eventually spooning as they slept, Mario's arm wrapped around her.

For just an instant, in the middle of the night, she stirred, became aware of the arm and thought she was with Jack. But no, this was a very different man. A good man, a loving man, but someone new, a second chance. For Mario, it was a second chance as well, maybe his last. He had discovered in Julie the embodiment of all the women he had loved or lusted after. His surrender to her was total.

Early the next morning, the brilliant sunlight poured through the uncurtained cabin windows. Mario woke to find Julie looking out at the snow, falling onto the lake.

"It's a beautiful day," she said. "We should go out and enjoy it."

"You're absolutely right," Mario said, nuzzling her neck. He could easily have spent the day in bed with her. "There's ice-skating at Brown's Hotel, and we could get a great breakfast there."

"I'm sure there's no food in the Monelli cupboard," Julie said.

"Well, I didn't have time to…"

"*I* did," she said. "There's a bag of groceries in the car. Why don't you bring it in? I'll take a shower, then fix you the greatest omelet you ever had."

"Okay, but I have to chop some wood first. We're almost out."

"Bundle up," Julie said. She watched adoringly as Mario threw on his clothes.

"Give me a half hour," he said. He kissed her and got the groceries out of her trunk and brought them in, then left again.

Julie stretched and headed for the shower. The cabin had an electric hot water tank, Mario had told her, so she could luxuriate for awhile, which is just what she did, soaping herself down, shampooing her hair, and letting the hot water invigorate her like rainwater.

Finally, she stepped out of the shower and wrapped herself in one of the white Turkish towels she found on a bathroom shelf. She wiped the steam off the bathroom window and looked out. Mario was chopping wood out in back of the cabin. Quite a man, she thought. And mine.

Julie took a towel to the bathroom mirror and took a look at herself. A happy woman looked back at her, a woman who was pleased with life. It had been a long time since she'd seen that kind of reflection, and it made her smile.

When she opened her toiletry kit, she found a toothbrush, but no toothpaste. It seemed unlikely, but maybe Mario had some. She reached for the mirror, but it was flush against the wall, no medicine cabinet behind it. Hmm…maybe the little cabinet beside the sink.

She opened the top drawer. An old razor, an empty blade pack, and a plastic deodorant dispenser. No toothpaste. She tried the next drawer, which was empty. She almost closed it, then realized it was binding. Something was stuck between the drawer and the side of the cabinet tracks. She lifted the drawer out of its slot and something fell on the floor—an ivory-color plastic compact—no it was a birth control pill pack.

Julie smiled. Well, this probably wasn't the first time Mario had invited a woman to his little getaway in the woods. She picked up the plastic container and noticed a label pasted to the top of the package, which she read. "Phyllis Monelli. Take as directed." How old was this thing? She wondered. Could it have been sitting in that drawer since his divorce almost five years ago? Julie checked the label again and saw it was dated six months ago.

She wandered out of the bathroom, the ivory plastic disk in her hand, walking into the living room, her mind cycling through the information again and again, like a cell phone looking for connectivity. Nothing made sense.

Julie sat down on the couch, looking at the round, plastic container in her hand, trying to find a logical explanation, one that exonerated Mario. But she couldn't. Then it dawned on her. She had been lied to. Mario was married. As in still. That was the simple, ugly truth.

And it explained a lot. It explained why Mario never took her back to his apartment. It explained why he never spent the whole night at her place. It explained the late-night phone calls, or why he'd given her his cell number, but not his home number. The man was a liar. She felt her heart sink as she said the words to herself. He was a liar and a cheat, and she had to get away from him—now.

As Julie rose from the couch, the phone rang. Who was calling? His wife? She fought the impulse to pick it up and answer it, and while she was hesitating, the answering machine clicked on.

"Mario, pick up. It's Neil. We've got big trouble at the Lions' Den. Some of Tyler's friends are insisting we have whores here, so they don't have to furnish their own dates. They say they sometimes only have an hour or two to get away from the wives, and they don't have time trying to find…shall we say companionship. Call me quick, paisan. They're about to lynch Duncan."

Then there was a beep and the machine clicked off.

Julie was stunned. Mario was the head of some kind of sex sanctuary for married men? Bart was right. Who *was* this man? How could he have fooled her so easily? Was she *that* vulnerable, *that* needy? *That* gullible? At another time, perhaps, she would have cried. But now anger prevailed, cold hard fury. She felt used. She felt dirty, despite the shower.

Julie slammed the pill container down on the table, then walked to the bedroom, dressed and stuffed the rest of her clothing into her sports bag. Then she stomped out of the cabin, slamming the door behind her.

At almost the same moment, Mario came through the cabin's back door carrying an armload of wood. He stamped his boots free of snow. "Julie?" he called. "How are those eggs coming? I'm starved."

When there was no answer, he walked into the kitchen, looking for her. "I figure after we eat, we can build a snowman. Julie…Julie…" He checked the bathroom. What the fuck? I wonder if that li'l vixen is outside, he thought, waiting to hit me with a snowball I bet. He headed for the front door, then stopped when he noticed something on the living room table.

Mario picked up the pill container, puzzled, and he read the label. "Oh shit!" He heard a car start up and whisk out of the driveway, and ran to the front door. "Julie, wait…!" He yelled to the Prius as it sped off, fishtailing and spraying snow behind it.

"Oh, fuck me!" He ran back inside and dialed her cell number. No answer, not even the voice mail. He tried again and again and again. Still nothing. She'd cut him off.

Monday morning, Mario was on the phone to UBS. There'd been no answer at Julie's apartment all weekend, but he knew she had to show up at work.

The network operator put the call through to Julie's office, but Paige intercepted.

"This is Mario," he said. "Is Julie in yet?"

"Ah, Mr. Monelli," Paige said coolly, "this is her production assistant, Paige Hanson. Yes, she's in, but she isn't accepting calls right now. However, she did ask me to relay a question. She wants to know if you intend to keep your commitment in regards to January third."

Mario felt his heart sink. Julie was communicating through a surrogate. She must have lost all trust and respect for him.

"Of course I will," he said, almost angrily. "My word is my bond. But I need to see her. There are things I have to explain."

"I'm sorry, Mr. Monelli, I'm afraid that won't be possible. I'll be your contact here at the network. You can call me if you have questions, and I'll keep in touch with the details and so on."

In the middle of the afternoon, Mario took a cab up to midtown, to the big pink building that was UBS headquarters. Determined to have his say, he talked his way past a guard and two receptionists, and slipped into the news department, unnoticed by any of the staff, and came across a man wearing a cowhide Stetson.

"Excuse me," Mario said. "You know where I can find Julie Chambers?"

"That's her office right there, partner," Tex said. "But missy ain't in."

"No. Where is she?"

"Down in editing. Been there all morning."

"Where's editing?"

"Fifth floor, west side of the building, next to studio C."

Mario made his way downstairs past the various studios and came across a young woman as she came out of a room.

"Is that the editing room?"

"Yes, it is," Paige replied, befuddled.

"Julie's in there?"

"Yes, she is." He gathered steam and pushed past her. "Sir…you can't go in there." Mario barged into the room, where Julie and Carol Twitzel were sitting at an editing console, running some footage.

"I'm sorry, Julie, I couldn't stop him…" Paige explained, hurrying in after him.

"It's ok," Julie said, then looked at Carol. "We'll finish this up later. Great job."

The two women looked at each other, shrugged and left—reluctantly. When they were gone, Julie turned to Mario, her hands folded across her chest. "Maybe it will be easier if you just say what you came to say, then leave," she said.

"Look, I admit I let things go too far. But I didn't mean to lie to you. You gotta believe me. I was going to tell you."

"When, Mario? When she was refilling her prescription. You're married, say it."

"The marriage is bullshit. We don't even fuck."

"Apparently, considering how many pills were still left."

"It's over, Julie. It's *been* over."

"If it's over, then what the hell are you still doing with her? Why don't you get out?"

"Because I'd be leaving my kids and all that I've worked for. And that terrifies me, Julie, even more than this fucking show."

"But not as terrified of losing that sex club of yours. Am I right?"

Mario gulped. "How do you know about the Lions' Den?"

"You really should check your phone messages."

"That was all before I met you, Julie. Before I fell in—"

"Don't" she said. "Don't even say the word. And all this time I imagined you as this icon of integrity, and what was good in this world. But you're really no better than all the rest of them."

"Julie, that night at the cabin…"

"Oh, yes, I do want to thank you for that—for considerately *fucking* me in the family cabin instead of parading me in front of your Zoo Crew pals at your private club." She was trembling with pain and anger. "I only have one question, Mario," she said through her tears. "Of all the women in this city, why me? Did I look that vulnerable?"

"I never meant to hurt you, Julie."

"What do you think you've done?" she sobbed.

There was nothing Mario could say and he knew it. Her eyes were so filled with disillusionment, he could barely look at her.

The intercom buzzed, and Paige's voice came through, loud and clear. "Julie, is everything all right down there?"

"It's fine," she sniveled. "Everything is just fine." She clicked off the intercom. And burst into tears.

Mario desperately wanted to go to her, but he couldn't even move.

"Please, just leave," Julie said, still crying.

Mario opened his mouth, but couldn't think of anything to say. Then he did as she asked and left.

Back in her office, Julie was going through the latest draft of the John Ayers' opening, trying, but unable to concentrate, when Hank poked his head inside.

"How's it going?" he asked.

"We're in pretty good shape, I think. No serious problems."

"Good. Glad to hear it," Hank said, inviting himself in. "I hear you had a visitor this morning."

By the way Hank was looking at her, Julie knew this wasn't a social call.

"I won't ask how it started," he said, "because it's *your* life and none of my business."

"You're not going to tell Miles are you?" She was relying on their friendship and mutual respect.

"Give me a good reason not to," he said.

"Because it's over…and because he's married." She looked directly into Hank's eyes. "Things have been very rough for me after Jack, Hank. But things will be fine…really."

Hank put his arms behind his back and looked at her. He was making a final judgment. "I hope so, Julie…for *their* sakes," he gestured at the busy newsroom visible through her office window. "For *all* of our sakes."

Late the following afternoon, Tyler stopped by the M&A suite and found Mario alone at his desk, working. He was unkempt and unshaven. "Good god, what happened to *you*?" Tyler said. "You look like a Bangkok whore at dawn."

Tyler didn't normally wander through the Zoo Crew's hood, which made Mario suspicious.

"What's on your mind, Tyler?"

"I got a call this morning from an old Harvard buddy of mine, Miles Corbin," Tyler said. "You know, one of the senior executives over at UBS. He asked if we would do him a favor and let him stage the debate right here on the trading floor. Kind of give it that *on-location* feel."

"What did you tell him?"

"I said, 'What do *we* get out of it?'"

Mario smirked. "You looking to make money off this, Tyler?"

"Well, I thought we deserved *something* for our trouble. Anyhow, Corbin says, 'tell you what, why don't you come to the network's New Year's Eve

Party at my house tomorrow night. It's legendary. And bring some of your top lieutenants if you want.'"

"That's what this is all about? You want me to go with you?" Mario asked. "Sorry, I've got other plans."

Tyler lifted a leg and sat on the corner of Mario's desk.

"You know it's funny," he said, reaching for one of Mario's crystal paper weights.

"What's funny?" Mario said, looking up at him.

"How a man can be happy with any woman so long as he doesn't love her."

Tyler grinned devilishly. "You fell for her, didn't you?" he said. Mario was startled. "Tyler knows all, Tyler sees all, remember?"

Mario didn't have the energy to deny it. Instead, he nodded, feebly.

"Don't tell me," Tyler said, reveling in it. "Let me guess. You didn't tell her you were married...and now she wants nothing to do with you. Am I right?"

Was it that easy to figure out? "So how do I get her to trust me again?" Mario said, as much to himself as to Tyler. He wasn't used to talking to Tyler this way, this openly.

"You don't," Tyler said. "Trust is highly overrated anyway. It's just another way of taking each other for granted and not paying attention to your relationship. You've tried talking to her?"

"I can't get within ten feet of her."

"That's why it's too bad you won't be ringing in the new year with us," Tyler said, lifting himself up and heading toward the door. "Oh, did I forget? Miles mentioned that everyone from the news division will be there..." He paused, letting his words sink in, and when Mario didn't react, he repeated himself. "*Everybody*, Mario."

Mario finally understood.

Geneva, Switzerland, Banque Privée Edmond de Rothschild
The Office of Dr. Hans Von Wharton, director

"I've told you again and again that we cannot reveal any information about our depositors or their transactions," said Dr. Hans von Wharton. "This is common knowledge. And yet you come asking to see confidential records. I do not understand."

U.S. Treasury Agent Walter Dellinger, a large and intimidating man, fixed von Wharton with his well-known icy gaze, a look that had withered the resolve of treasury ministers and bankers throughout the world. "Then you won't mind the headlines that say you're refusing to cooperate in a terrorist investigation and putting civilians at risk."

Von Wharton tried to stare back, but stronger men than he had given in to Dellinger's stony glare and he was no exception. "I will give you and your colleague brief access to the documents you are requesting, but only on one condition: that this be entirely unofficial, that it set no precedent, and that no one other than your immediate superiors have any knowledge of my, uh, generosity."

Von Wharton lead them to a private room and directed his assistant to provide them with any documents they requested.

It was not until five a.m. the next morning that they found something interesting. Field agent Tifton pointed it out to Dellinger. "It's a $200,000 wire deposit from the Grand Caymans that arrived here seven weeks ago and was immediately transferred to Beirut."

"Do we have a name on the account?"

"We do," Tifton said. "It's Roger Duval."

CHAPTER TWENTY-TWO

"Explain it to me again," Phyllis said, almost patiently. "Yesterday, you were dead set on staying home for New Year's Eve. Now, you're worried that we're going to be late to a party that's being thrown by someone I never even heard of. Why is that, Mario? Inquiring minds want to know."

Mario was in the closet, trying to decide which tie to wear, and Phyllis was in the bathroom, still working on her hair and makeup, two complex and time-consuming tasks. But the door between them was open, and the conversation went on as if they were face-to-face.

Mario took a deep breath. "Like I said, Phyllis, I'm going because the host is a top executive at UBS network, and he wants me there."

She came out of the bathroom and began struggling to get into a scarlet chiffon evening gown that, she insisted, had shrunk since she bought it.

"Besides, I think you can really get something out of this party."

"Tell me how, again."

"Well, to begin with, it's in East Greenwich, Connecticut," he reminded her. "There's going to be a lot of high society there, a lot of community leaders."

"From the community of East Greenwich?" Phyllis asked sarcastically. "Well la-di-da." She presented her back to Mario and he dutifully zipped her up and clasped the little hook at her neck.

"Not East Greenwich high society, Phyllis, *New York* high society. Tyler tells me it's quite an exclusive event."

"That's interesting," Phyllis allowed.

He slipped on his suit jacket and looked at the time on his new gold Cartier. "You almost ready?"

"You go on down," said Phyllis, putting on the finishing touches. "I'll be there in a minute."

Downstairs, Mario found Boomer getting ready to go out. "Where are you headed tonight?" he asked.

"One of my buddies is throwing a party."

"You going with that Reardon girl?"

"Yes, Dad. With Jenny."

"Go easy on the booze tonight. Where's your brother?" Mario asked.

"He's at Brandon's house. They're having a sleepover, remember?"

"Oh, yeah."

Boomer took a little jewelry box out of a plastic bag and stuck it in his pocket, which caught Mario by surprise. "You're really going all out for this girl, aren't you?"

"Yeah," Boomer said, a little embarrassed.

"Well, good for you. Good for her, too. It's nice to see you taking showers again regularly, wearing clean clothes, doing your homework. She's a good influence."

Boomer walked toward the door, then stopped. Something was on his mind, but he was reluctant to share it. "Can I ask you a question, Dad?"

Mario laughed. "You need money?"

"No, that's not it. I've just been thinking, you know, about Jenny."

"I'll bet you have," Mario replied with a mischievous grin. "What's the question?"

Boomer steeled himself and spit it out. "Dad, how can you tell if you're really in love?"

"Jesus," Mario said, surprised. "I didn't know it had gone that far."

"It hasn't...I'm just asking," Boomer said.

Mario considered the question for a moment and found himself thinking about Julie. "Umm, let's see. I guess there are many answers," Mario said, putting a hand on Boomer's shoulder. "But only one that makes any sense to me is, you know you're in love when she's the most important thing in your life. When nothing else matters."

Boomer considered his father's words. "When nothing else matters," he repeated, nodding. "I'll remember that."

"Listen, be careful tonight. Lotta crazy drunks out there. Stick to the main roads. And if the weather gets really bad, I'll come get you in the Hummer." He opened his wallet, took out a fifty dollar bill, and looked into his son's eyes before handing it to him.

"What's a blanket tender?"

"It's when an issuer redeems its shares in order to gain more of a controlling interest. Happy?"

Mario forked over the fifty.

"Thanks, Dad," Boomer kissed him, wished him a Happy New Year and left the house.

Mario and Phyllis arrived at Corbin's place in just under an hour, the anonymous female voice of the GPS unit verbally guiding them right to Corbin's mailbox.

"Can you see the house?" Phyllis asked.

Mario peered up the long driveway. "I can't make it out yet, but I see a little sign directing us to the parking area."

They turned off into a lot already occupied by several dozen luxury cars, including three other Maseratis and two Ferraris. They surrendered the keys to the valets and followed the other arriving guests down a long, snow-covered walkway toward the huge, Georgian-style mansion. It was set in what seemed like the middle of an oak forest, in practically perfect privacy, and surrounded with arboretum-quality plantings. The sound of music could be heard faintly through the closed windows.

A uniformed servant opened the door for them and, as soon as they entered, another servant took their coats. They found themselves in what Corbin called his living room, but what most other people would have described as a grand ballroom, with a fifteen-foot Douglas fir in the center of the room, underneath a cathedral ceiling.

A covey of pretty girls, dressed like elves, were circulating through the crowd, balancing silver platters overflowing with all the common and most of the uncommon delicacies. An eight-piece band and small choir was stationed in the far corner of the room on a split-level stage, playing holiday music.

Halfway across the room, Mario saw Glen, standing next to his wife Amanda's wheelchair. Neil's wife, Elaine, was standing nearby, sipping on what looked like sparkling water, looking much thinner after her two-month stay at the Rice University eating disorder clinic.

This surely was a different crowd than Mario was used to, although he recognized a few faces—the mayor of East Greenwich, several local television personalities, a woman who looked exactly like Martha Stewart, and probably was, several CEOs and, dammit, some of Blackwell's head honchos, which meant that Bart was in the water. What he didn't see anywhere in the room, however, was his reason for being there and the reason why he lied to Phyllis—Julie.

"I'm going to go get a drink," Phyllis told Mario.

Mario put a hand on her shoulder. "Phyllis, take it easy on the sauce tonight. Lotta opportunities for you to make important and useful friends. Don't fuck it up."

"Mario, this is a *New Year's Party. Everybody* drinks on New Year's."

"Well, that just means you'll have more opportunities if you just, you know, stay cool. See anyone out there worth talking to?" He was doing his damndest to make it sound like advice, not manipulation.

Phyllis scanned the room like she was a heat-seeking missile. It was swarming with wealthy couples she'd never met, but heard of. "I think," she said, "that's Katerina Wellborn over there."

"Yeah?"

"She's the board chair of the Metropolitan Institute of Art," Phyllis explained. "Also, I think, the organizer of the annual New York Society Ball."

"Sounds like she'd be worth meeting," Mario said. "Why don't you go over and tell her how much you enjoy her museum."

Phyllis nodded, and Mario was relieved to watch her walk toward the museum lady, mustering the courage to approach her. Maybe, he thought, just maybe my shithead of a wife will not humiliate herself tonight.

Mario looked back into the crowd, trying to spot more friends or acquaintances. Dennis was standing at a bar, his wife, Marie, nowhere in sight. Probably not up for a party, Mario thought. And no Kat—"I have better things to do on New Year's Eve," she'd said, and Mario was certain that was true. But Barry was there with his mother, straining on his leash. What a picture. He soon felt a tap on his shoulder.

"Hey, Mario." It was Tyler.

Mario turned and nodded. "Tyler. Happy New Year."

"Thanks. Come with me," Tyler said, "some people I want you to meet."

Tyler took Mario by the arm and dragged him toward a small knot of people, a few of whom he recognized. "Hey, everybody," Tyler said, "this is Mario Monelli. Mario, I don't know how many of these folks you know— but this is Miles Corbin, an old Harvard classmate and president of UBS News…"

Mario and Miles shook hands. "Beautiful house," Mario said.

"….And you recognize Tom Gallagher and John Ayers, I'm sure…"

"We've already met," Mario said, nodding to the two men.

"…and this is Fred Fielding," Tyler went on. "He's one of the great journalists of our time."

"Glad to meetcha," said Mario.

"And of course you know Bart…"

"Yeah, we've met," Mario said, putting on a smile. He'd half expected Julie would be part of the group, but she was still among the missing.

"I understand this is your first major television appearance," Corbin said genially.

"That's true," Mario said. "My first, his last."

"Nice watch," Bart said noticing the elegant wristband of Phyllis's Christmas gift. "Do they make them for men?"

"Now, now, boys," said Fred Fielding. "Save some of that energy for the show."

The small talk lasted until Mario realized he was the only one without a drink. "Excuse me, gentlemen," he said. "I think I have a little catching up to do. Where's the closest bar?"

Miles pointed across the room.

At the open bar, Mario found Dennis and Barry among those getting drinks.

"You believe this fat putz brought his mother?" Dennis said.

"What was I gonna do," Barry explained. "We *always* spend New Year's together."

Neil came over to refresh his drink. "So, Barry, you gonna tongue kiss your mother at midnight?" he teased.

Mario looked around, trying to spot Julie.

"You know there's gonna be quite a crowd watching you on TV," Neil said.

"Fuckin' A," agreed Dennis. "Every gin joint and sports bar from Battery Park to Gramercy is booked solid Thursday night. Even the Lions' Den is booked solid. You and Bart, toe to toe—

"Word is spreading faster than a cold through kindergarten class," said Barry.

Mario shook his head. "It's that damn bet. Everybody's dying to see us kill each other on television."

Glen joined them at the bar. "Some late money just came in on you boss, knocking the odds down twenty to one."

"You mean The Street is betting twenty to one I lose?" Mario asked.

"Lose?" Glen said slyly. "They're betting twenty to one you won't even show."

Glen and Dennis began laughing, and Neil and Barry joined in. They were *still* laughing when the big oak front door swung open bringing in a gust of snowflakes, as well as Paige Hanson and Julie Chambers, her cheeks glowing with the cold, looking wind-swept and beautiful. Mario waited till their coats were taken and they had a chance to mingle. Then he had another drink, to help him work up his nerve. Then while he was picking his way through the crowd, he noticed Miles unobtrusively take Phyllis by the arm and pull her toward Julie.

"Phyllis," he said, "I'd like you to meet Julie Chambers of UBS. Julie, this is Phyllis Monelli, Mario's wife."

"Please to meetcha," Phyllis said, holding out a hand.

Julie briefly took hold of Phyllis's hand. "Same here," she said politely, feeling sick to her stomach, almost unable to believe she was standing face to face with Mario's wife, and taken totally by surprise.

Although rattled, Julie still had enough presence of mind to introduce Paige, but Paige came very close to freezing. She took Phyllis's hand and opened her mouth to say something, but barely managed a weak hello.

"So you work at the network that's putting on the show with my husband?" Phyllis asked, examining Julie so closely she might as well have been using a jeweler's loupe.

"Actually, Julie's the show's executive produce*r*," Miles interjected with a smile.

"*You're* the show's producer?" Phyllis asked, incredulous. "The producer Mario has been working with for all those long hours?"

"Well, I…."

Phyllis didn't wait for an answer. "Excuse me," she said coldly, looking around the room wildly.

Even from across the room, Mario knew what had happened and what must have been said.

Phyllis was plowing through the crowd like a bulldozer, heading straight for him. "I want to talk to you *now*," she said loudly.

Neil cut her off. "Phyllis, why don't I get you a drink."

Phyllis glared at him. "A drink?" she said loudly. "Yes, that's not a bad idea. A drink would do just fine right about now." The last remark was aimed at Mario.

Neil escorted Phyllis to the bar, leaving Mario gazing across the room at Julie, who was looking spectacular in her silver satin shift. For just an instant, their eyes met, then she turned away and walked through a set of French doors in the middle of the living room.

Mario slipped through the milling crowd, toward the doors through which she had just passed. It led into a large, glass-enclosed sun room, filled with exotic foliage.

Julie was standing at the far end of the room, looking out at the snow glinting in the outdoor spotlights, her back to the door. Mario closed the door behind him, and the party sounds faded away.

"Julie?" Mario said softly, almost timidly.

She turned, with eyes so sad he could hardly bear to look at them. "Hello, Mario."

"It's a nice party," Mario said.

She sighed. "Is it?"

"Miles really knows how to put on the dog."

"I met your wife," Julie said, ignoring Mario's remark. There was no emotion in her voice whatever.

"I know," Mario said.

"Do you think you should be out here?"

"I wasn't planning on coming at all tonight," he replied.

"Why did you?"

"Because I couldn't let it end with us that way. I needed to come tell you just how sorry I am, Julie. And that you don't have to worry. I won't bother you anymore, if that will make you happy. I only hope that one day, you'll find it in your heart and forgive me."

They locked eyes, then Julie turned back toward the window again.

"I know I've let you down," he continued. "But Thursday night I'm gonna do my best, Julie. I want you to know that. And afterward, I'll be out of your life."

At that moment, the live music in the living room resumed playing, and the band, by purest chance, played a melody they'd danced to for hours at Butters.

She turned away from him, eyes filled with tears, as the bandleader sang the words as best he could…

"I can only give you love that lasts forever,
And a promise to be near each time you call.
And the only heart I own
For you and you alone
That's all,
That's all…

I can only give you country walks in springtime
And a hand to hold when leaves begin to fall;
And a love whose burning light
Will warm the winter's night
That's all,
That's all..."

The music ended, to muted applause, and Mario and Julie stood in the middle of the sun room floor, then Julie put a hand to her mouth, sobbing, and hurried back into the house, and disappeared into the crowd.

Inside, everyone counted down to one, and there was a burst of hooting and hollering from the living room, and the band struck up *Auld Lang Syne.*

Mario stood at the sunroom door and watched the cascading balloons and the confetti raining down on the roomful of smooching couples—Glen and his wife, Neil and *his,* Barry and his mother embracing and all the others. "Happy New Year, Julie," he whispered to himself. He sighed deeply, then headed back into the party feeling more alone than he had ever felt.

Neil stopped him the moment he set foot through the doors. "Is everything ok? I just saw Julie running to the bathroom."

Suddenly, Barry appeared. "Mario, watch out for Phyllis," he warned. "She made a fool out of herself with that Wellborn dame. Now she's totally sloshed and saying some really stupid shit."

"So? What else is new?" Mario said, disgusted.

Someone clinked a knife against a glass, and Miles Corbin climbed up on the temporary stage beside the band and reached for the mike to address the crowd, and the band stopped playing.

"Good evening, everyone," Corbin said. "I'd like to thank you all for coming tonight and, on behalf of Christine and myself, wish you a happy and healthy new year."

A few people started applauding, but Corbin held up a hand.

"As you all know, UBS is just days away from airing its highly anticipated and ground-breaking special entitled '*America for Sale.*' I'm not just speaking for myself when I say it is an event not to be missed."

He nodded at Carleton Fisher, who was standing nearby, and everyone laughed.

"And I want to take this occasion to thank—in advance—those principally responsible: Hank Kozloff, Fred Fielding and, most of all, our wonderful young executive producer, Julie Chambers." He gestured in the crowd to Julie, who just returned from the bathroom. She bravely managed a smile.

More applause. Again, Corbin held up a hand.

"The event boasts two of the greatest practitioners Wall Street has seen. And it is each others destiny that they were brought together for what UBS anticipates to be the most seismic collision of this or any other era, since the *Thrilla in Manila*. Everyone chuckled.

"I want to express my personal gratitude to two men, Barton Mulvaney… and Mario Monelli, for their courage in taking on this critical subject… and each other. Gentlemen, you have honored UBS and your profession by agreeing to participate."

Barton Mulvaney confidently waved an arm, like a champion prizefighter about to enter the ring, and Mario, flanked by the Zoo Crew, acknowledged the applause with a slight nod. But his mind was still on Julie.

Miles raised his glass. "Everyone, a toast. To the two princes of Wall Street. In just a few days, one of them will be crowned king." The crowd toasted the two men and the band briefly played *Jolly Good Fellows*.

"You fools!" came a female shout from the back of the room. The music died and everyone turned, puzzled. But Mario recognized the voice and the attitude. It was Phyllis, drunk and enraged. She was holding a champagne glass in one hand and a bottle of champagne in the other. "You think this man is a Jolly Good Fella? Well, he's a fake. He's got 'cha *all* fooled." The booze had erased her years of speech lessons.

Phyllis stumbled toward the center of the room, parting the crowd like it was the Red Sea. Mario had begun pushing his way toward her the moment she'd interrupted Corbin, and now they met, Phyllis still yelling in derision.

"A toast," she said, pouring champagne into her glass and raising it high. "To Mario Monelli, the king of Wall Street, the one whose wife can't set foot in Shinnecock and Winged Foot because his highness's bloodline ain't right."

Every eye in the room shifted to Mario, more with interest than disbelief.

"The one who dropped out of high school with an eighth-grade reading level. Let's wish him a happy fucking new year because he'll be fucking every woman in sight. Everyone—except the one who sleeps next to him every night."

"Phyllis, for *God's* sake!" implored Glen's wife, Amanda.

Phyllis was too far gone to hear her. "Let's toast his career because he started as a busboy, and a busboy is all he'll ever be."

She lurched forward like a crazed dog, thrusting her face into Mario's, her mouth contorted in a fiery rage, saliva spewing, pulling the pin and hurling another verbal grenade. It took Dennis and Neil to muscle in and pull her away from him.

Then, for a moment, the room was silent, as everyone tried to digest the surreal scene they'd just witnessed, their eyes inevitably turning toward Mario, who felt like the emperor with no clothes.

In the back of the room, Julie was standing beside Paige, stunned by what she'd just witnessed, amazed at the venom in Phyllis's voice, understanding for the first time what Mario's life must be like at home, and why he needed the Lions' Den to make his misery more bearable and less continuous. She wanted desperately to go to him, to soothe his humiliation, and would have done just that, except for the tug on her sleeve. It was Paige, guessing her thoughts, holding her back while looking at her, and gently shaking her head.

With Neil and Dennis keeping Phyllis in their grip, Mario approached her again. "You promised you would behave yourself," he said, seething. Then, seeing the bottle she was holding, he ripped it out of her hand.

"And what about you, *darling*?" she asked. "Are you behaving *your* self?" She shot a look in Julie's direction for all to wonder.

"I'm taking you home," Mario said.

"But it's New Year's, dear. I've just started having a good time." She looked over at Katarina Wellborn, who was the picture of disapproval. "What are you looking at you WASPY, purebred bitch?" she snarled.

"Phyllis, shut up or I'm going to *shut* you up," Mario threatened.

"Try it," Phyllis said, tossing her drink in Mario's face. "There, now both of you are nice and wet."

The crowd, even the Zoo Crew, gasped, except for Barry and his mother, who, while they never stopped watching, also never stopped eating. Near the bar, Miles Corbin and his wife were arguing. Mario took out his handkerchief and wiped the champagne from his face.

"Get her coat," Mario asked Neil urgently.

While Mario was dragging Phyllis out of the room, she stumbled over the split level stairs leading to the hallway, and fell in front of Julie. Mario kneeled down to help her, along with Julie, their eyes locking as he hoisted Phyllis up.

"Always the dutiful husband," Phyllis said, before being whisked out of the house.

In the parking lot, Mario opened the Maserati's passenger door and practically threw Phyllis inside the car.

"Hey," Phyllis said, "That hurt!"

"Shut up," Mario said. He slammed the door closed and started the car, wound around the circular driveway and headed back out to the main road, straining to see through the blowing snow.

"That's it," Mario said. "I want out. I'm finished with you."

"You're finished with *me?*" Phyllis said savagely, slurring her words. "Who the fuck do you think *you* are?"

"I said what I meant, Phyllis. I want a divorce." His voice was colder than the wind howling outside of the car.

"And what Mario wants, Mario gets, right?" she replied. "What's wrong with the heater in this $200,000 pile of shit?"

Mario glanced at his wife with undisguised hatred and switched on the heater. A chilly gust blew out of the vents.

"You *would* like a divorce, wouldn't you? You and that television whore. Don't look so surprised. You make a handsome couple. May you forever be happy. Only you can forget about a divorce. She's not gonna be around my children, she's not gonna live in *my* house."

Mario did his best to contain his fury. "Okay. But I'm not gonna live with you either. I'm packing and getting out."

"I've heard *that* song before." She laughed.

"I mean it this time."

"You leave now and you leave with nothing but your dick in your hands. You're dumb, but you're not stupid."

"I could kill you, Phyllis."

"Go ahead. Just make sure when you do, you bury me with my money and my jewels. That bitch will have to dig for it."

He was on the Thruway now and the snow was getting worse. Up ahead, all he could see on his side of the road were a few tail lights. "You can keep everything. Just give me the boys," he said.

"Give you the kids? Not a fucking chance."

"Then I'll fight you for custody."

"Yeah, I bet you and that slick shyster brother of yours got it all worked out. Well, go ahead, do it," she dared. "Not a court in the world will take 'em away from me. Just remember, a mother is a mother, forever," she said, poking his face. "A father could be anyone in the street, so I guess we'll let the courts decide."

A new wave of anger washed over Mario. "You're going to force Kyle to take the stand and choose between his mother and his father? Are you really that heartless?"

Phyllis snickered. "You can have Kyle," she said. "It's Boomer I want. He's money in the bank and I want what a mother deserves."

Mario slammed the brakes, sending the car into a fast, terrifying spin and crunched into a soft snow bank.

The car had barely stopped moving before Mario launched himself at Phyllis, pinning her to the seat with one hand and raising the other, fist clenched, intent on crushing her face.

The very real fear in her eyes stopped him. "Don't hurt me," she begged.

He pulled back, sat down heavily in his seat again, and stared at the snowflakes, trying to regain control.

At Corbin's house, some of UBS's top brass had privately gathered in the sun room for a war counsel to talk about what had just happened.

"That was the most disgusting public exhibition I have ever seen," Fred said, "We can't put this guy on the air. It would be irresponsible."

"Did you know he doesn't have any higher education?" Miles asked Julie.

"He attended City college for a while."

Fred stifled a laugh.

"Knock it off, Julie," Miles said, "I'm talking about *real* higher education."

"Yes," Julie admitted, and her admission visibly irritated Miles, "but that's one of the remarkable things about him—he's become one of the most prominent men on Wall Street based on savvy and charisma."

"He does have *that,*" Fred agreed. "I think he'd be quite a compelling figure on any show. Only not *this* one."

"I don't care if the guy grew up in an inner-city orphanage. He's just an aberration on Wall Street that's unlikely to be repeated. That's one more reason he's not the right guy for us," Miles argued.

"But everything is set, Miles. How could we do the show without him?" Hank inquired.

"*I* could do it," Tom Gallagher said.

"Yeah, you could do it," Julie said. "You're a man of unlimited talent, or so you tell us. But it means that *we* take over the role of expert."

"Julie makes a valid point," Hank said in her defense. "This Bart guy is a gunslinger. No offense, Tom, but this guy is too dangerous. We could make total fools out of ourselves…"

"And end up with Mulvaney winning this damn thing," said Julie.

"We're lucky if we're not reading about that little scene in the tabloids tomorrow," said Fred, moving in for the kill.

"Whatever we do," Miles said, "we can't use Monelli."

"I don't agree," Julie said. "I've thought—from the very beginning—that our argument should be made by someone who isn't part of Wall Street's elite. And nothing I saw tonight has changed my mind."

"What about that psychotic wife of his?" Miles said, looking directly at Julie, and she knew there was an ambiguity to his question.

Julie didn't flinch. "I thought he handled the situation as best he could. Besides, we're putting *him* on television, not his wife."

"It still may not be too late to get Van Wert," Fred said. "It would be the same set up."

Julie couldn't believe her ears. She was on the verge of losing control of the production. "I believe this is *my* decision, gentlemen."

"Why should *you* be the one to make the decision?" asked Miles.

"Because that's what you guaranteed me when you hired me," she replied.

"*That* may have been a mistake," Miles said loudly.

That was as far as Fisher was willing to let it go. "Let's turn down the volume, folks. You too, Miles," he said, and the arguing ceased. "The way I see it," he continued, "I have a decision to make."

"But you promised me…" Julie objected.

Fisher interrupted. "You're absolutely right. But things have changed, and whether or not you wish to hear this, he presents for this network a gauntlet of concerns that make him a shaky commodity. The country—and UBS itself—are at risk. And as president and chairman of this network, I have a responsibility. Do you understand?"

"Yes," Julie said. It was the only possible response.

"Now, before I make my decision, there's something I need to know from you, young lady." He was focusing on Julie as though no one else were in the room. "I need a genuinely honest answer, Julie—no ego, no cover-your-ass stuff. I need you to be truthful, not only to me, but also to yourself."

She felt like a little girl, being judged by her father.

"Do you believe in him? Do you believe in this man with your very heart and your soul? But more importantly, do you trust him with the fate of our country and the future of this network. Because that's what we're talking about here."

Everyone in the sun room looked at Julie with baited breath. And she answered with the gravity of someone in the confession booth. "I believe in him with all my heart and my very soul."

"And *you*, Hank?" Fisher asked, keeping his eyes locked on Julie's.

"I back my producer," Hank replied steadfast. There was a long silence.

Fisher weighed the factors a moment, then nodded. "All right, we stay the course."

Miles looked at Fred and lowered his head. The verdict was in and there was no challenging it.

Fisher reached for his overcoat. "Now if someone will kindly call for my car while I get Mrs. Fisher..." Before leaving, he glanced back at Julie one last time. "I hope your intuition is right, young lady."

"Some New Year's," Tom said, following everyone out of the sun room. Only Julie and Hank remained.

"Thanks for going to bat for me, Hank."

Hank nodded ruefully. "Do you believe in him, Julie? Or do you love him?"

He walked back into the house, leaving her to think about his words.

Phyllis got out of the Maserati as soon as Mario pulled into the garage and strode angrily—and a bit unsteadily—into the house. Mario slammed the garage door and followed her inside, seething. He took off his tux jacket and hung it on a chair when the phone began ringing. He picked it up, gripping it hard enough to bend the plastic. "Yeah," he said murderously, "what is it?"

It was Boomer. "Dad, Jenny and I are in the Denny's parking lot and..."

"Outta gas again?" Mario asked, his voice filled with irritation.

"No, I..."

"What is it, money? You don't have enough money? I didn't give you enough money?"

"Jenny and I were listening to the radio, and the city called a cold winter emergency. The weatherman said the temperature is going to be five below tonight, and that everyone should stay inside or seek shelter, and I started thinking about Gus. You know how he hates the shelter."

Mario forgot his anger. "Which Denny's?"

"Garden City, by the mall."

"Wait for me. I'll be there in ten minutes."

Mario pulled an old down comforter out of the linen closet, grabbed his red sub-zero Patagonia jacket and headed for the garage.

"Where the fuck are you going?" Phyllis demanded.

"Out," Mario said. He slammed the door behind him, hopped into the Hummer and drove off to pick up Boomer and his girlfriend.

The trip into the city was fast, despite the blizzard, thanks to the Hummer's four-wheel drive and Mario's heavy foot. They pulled up in front of Cortlandt alley and found the old man lying near his chair, covered with snow, barely conscious.

"Jesus, Dad, they beat 'em up and took his coat."

Mario was on his hands and knees in an instant, brushing off the snow with an ungloved hand. "Help me get the jacket on him," Mario told Boomer and his girlfriend, and they propped him up.

Boomer zipped up the jacket and Mario bundled the comforter around his friend. "Is he all right, Dad?" Boomer's voice was filled with fear.

"He's alive, but in bad shape," Mario said. "Gus? Gus? Stay with me."

Gus's eyes flickered open for a moment, then closed again.

"We gotta get him someplace warm," Mario said grimly. "And we gotta do it fast."

"Is there a shelter around here?" Boomer asked.

"I'll find out," Mario said. He ran back to the Hummer and hit the OnStar button.

"There's one just a few blocks from here."

Boomer and Mario grabbed Gus and half-carried him toward the Hummer.

At that moment, Gus opened his eyes again. "Sam," he said.

"His cat," Mario told Jenny. "See if you can spot him."

Jenny hurried back and found Sam cowering under Gus's chair and picked him up. Mario took the wheel while Boomer and Jenny hopped in the back with Gus.

"Dad, hurry, I can't stop him from shaking."

They pulled up outside the shelter, a two-story, grey stone building with a warmly illuminated sign that read, "We welcome all who are poor, hungry, or without shelter."

"I'll make the arrangements," Mario said. He hopped out of the truck and darted into the building. What greeted him was nothing less than the ante room of Hell—hundreds of homeless people, mostly minorities, some drunk, some sick, some crazy, as well as dozens of families with dirty, ill-clothed, insect and rat-bitten children, most of them crying, some accompanied by the weary cops and out-reach teams who'd brought them here.

The place was dimly lit and cold, and some enterprising young thugs were hawking blankets and hot coffee allocated to helpless indigents, hoping to squeeze their last dollar from them. On top of this, there was the almost unbearable human stench—sweat, shit, vomit, body odor, rot, and decay, an obvious breeding ground for tuberculosis, and only two nurses treating dozens of hyperthermia cases.

Mario was horrified. He couldn't bear the idea of leaving Gus in the hands of these people, in a place that reeked of violence and misery. Were they all like these, the city shelters for the poor and homeless? No wonder Gus hated going there.

"Maybe we should take him to the hospital, Dad?"

"Hey, you," said a man handing out blankets, who didn't look much better than the people he was serving. "You want something?"

"I have someone in the car who's freezing. Is there room here for one more?" As he asked the question, Mario found himself praying that the answer was no.

The man laughed. "Room? We're stacking them like cordwood. There's barely room for you to be standing there. I can't help you."

Suddenly, Mario was infuriated. "What? You can't help? Isn't it your *job* to help people? You're supposed to help people, aren't you?"

The shelter manager decided to make an effort. "There's a third-story walk-up shelter on Front Street, near the Brooklyn Bridge. They might have an empty bed."

Mario had some trouble finding the building, which was on a street without street lights, in an industrial area. "Come on," he told Boomer and Jenny, "help me take Gus upstairs. One way or another Gus is going to get a bed here, even if I have to buy the fucking place."

Slowly and carefully, the three of them carried Gus up the dingy stairway, the old fighter flickering in and out of consciousness. Jenny stuck Sam into her pocketbook, then slipped past the men to open the door at the top of the stairs.

The lady at the reception desk, an older woman with cavernous cheeks came around the counter to help with Gus, who was half-conscious again.

"Do you have room for him?" Mario asked.

The woman just shook her head. "We just gave away our last bed. We don't even have any more mats. Have you tried the Bowery Mission?"

"We been everywhere," Mario said. "Look, you gotta help me. He's real bad. At least let me throw some blankets on the floor for him." He reached into his pocket for his wallet, then realized he'd left it at home. "Shit! Boomer, give the lady some money. A donation."

Boomer found a ten in his pocket and handed it over to the woman. "That's all I have."

"Well, I do have a cot in my office that I use occasionally. Bring him in there."

They helped Gus to the cot, and laid him down, at which point he opened his eyes. "Where's Sam?" he managed to ask.

"I've got him," Jenny said. She pointed at her purse. The cat's head had popped out of it and he was looking around with mild curiosity.

Then Gus started coughing. It quickly escalated into a very worrisome hacking that left him salivating phlegm and gasping for breath.

"Is he ill?" asked the shelter lady.

Mario shrugged uncomfortably, hoping that the cough wouldn't disqualify Gus for the bed. "I don't think so. I don't know. Do you have a doctor here?"

"A nurse practitioner. I'll call him."

The nurse practitioner was a very large, white-suited man with a shaved head and an attitude, probably from being overworked. He bent over Gus for a closer look at him and Gus rewarded him by coughing in his face. "He's got a cold," the nurse informed them.

"Could you keep an eye on him?" Mario asked.

The nurse cocked an eyebrow. "Somethin' special about him?"

"He's my friend," Mario said.

"Oh, I see. Well, I'll have the maid get the silk sheets and have room service deliver a *filet*. How would he like it done?"

Mario reached for his wallet. "Listen," he said confidentially. "I'm going to give you…" He stopped in mid-sentence. "Fuck. I left my wallet. Boomer, do you have any more cash?"

"About three bucks, Dad. I had to borrow ten dollars from Jenny."

"It was my last ten," Jenny said.

Mario quickly unfastened the watch on his arm and handed it to the nurse practitioner. "Take it. It's a Cartier."

"Yeah, right. I could go up to Canal Street and buy one of those off a dink for twelve bucks."

"Dad, are you crazy? Mom spent five grand on that."

The nurse raised an eyebrow, then took the watch.

"I'll be back tomorrow morning," Mario said. "Just make sure he's warm and comfortable. Call me if he gets worse."

The nurse turned toward Gus. "Now let's see if we can get you cleaned up and settled in," he said.

CHAPTER TWENTY-THREE

Even though it was New Year's Day, Mario was up early and at the New York City Rescue Mission before nine o'clock. A different woman, older, sterner, and less welcoming, was at the front desk.

She looked him up and down, noting the expensive down jacket and letting him see that she noticed. "And how can we help you today, sir?"

"I'm here to see my friend."

She was skeptical. "*You* have a *friend* here?"

"That's right. Older man. Black. He was in bad shape when I brought him in."

"Ah. Come with me."

She led the way into the office and to Gus's cot. Gus was asleep, which Mario thought was good. Very gently, Mario put a hand on Gus's forehead. "My God," he said to the woman, "he's burning up! Get me the nurse."

"I think he's on a break," the woman said dryly. "You want me to give him a message."

"Yeah," Mario said. "Here's the message: Get your ass over here before I start breaking things."

"You don't have to threaten, sir," the woman said, trying to placate him. She left, and Mario bent over Gus. "You awake, Gus? Can you hear me?" He took the old fighter's hand, which felt clammy and warmer than normal.

The nurse strode up to Gus's cot. "Oh," he said, recognizing Mario, "it's you."

Mario turned on him. "I thought we agreed that you would keep an eye on my friend."

The nurse, though he was a big man, was alarmed by Mario's intensity. "I checked your friend like you asked," he said defensively. "He was fine."

"Oh really? He's burning up. Touch his forehead."

The nurse put a hand on Gus's forehead, his white coat riding up and exposing Mario's Cartier buckled to his wrist. "He does seem a little warm," the nurse admitted.

Mario was furious. "A *little* warm? A *little*? Call an ambulance, you asshole. And give me my watch back."

The nurse hesitated a moment, but saw the fury in Mario's eyes. He ripped the watch off his arm and carelessly tossed it to Mario, who caught it deftly. "Yessir, *boss*," he said sarcastically, trying to salvage a little self-respect. "Right away, *sir*."

The ambulance came from New York Downtown Hospital, the one closest to the rescue mission. Orderlies loaded Gus into the ambulance, Mario supervising, and then he rode with his friend to the hospital.

At the admitting desk, Mario wrote out a check for $10,000. "This is for a private room and a private nurse around the clock. And if it costs more than this, just let me know. In the meantime, get on the blower and get me the chief resident…now!" He flipped her the phone receiver.

Mario stayed with Gus until a doctor examined him.

"It's not good," the head resident told Mario. "Double pneumonia."

Mario felt utterly helpless. "But he'll be all right though…?"

The head resident was a young, friendly sort with a ready smile, but he wasn't smiling now. "Maybe if he were younger, or in better shape…"

"What are you kidding," Mario interrupted, "the guy is a bull."

They moved Gus to ICU where Mario watched while they started an intravenous drip and set up a plastic oxygen tent over his head and torso. When Mario couldn't stand to watch any more, he left.

The days before the television special were among the worst of Mario's life. He didn't sleep well, he didn't eat well, he didn't review the material the network sent to him to help him prepare for the debate. All he could think about was Julie—and now, Gus.

And it was starting to take a toll on him at work. In the midst of an important merger negotiation, he neglected to instruct the client's anti-trust attorneys to institute crucial protective by-laws, and had to be rescued by Neil.

Mario excused himself and went to the men's room to splash some water on his face, to wake himself up and regain his concentration. Neil barged in after him.

"You realize we almost blew three months of hard work."

"Thanks for bailing me out in there. It won't happen again."

Mario meant every word of that, but it wasn't enough for his wingman.

"Nurse your broken heart elsewhere," Neil admonished him and strode out, not letting his boss off the hook so easily.

Soon afterward, Mario was standing beside Gus's bed again, next to the private nurse he'd hired, when the old fighter finally awoke. He looked around, through half-closed eyes, puzzled, trying to find his bearings.

"You're in the hospital, Gus," Mario explained, clutching his hand. "You've been sick."

Gus managed to focus his eyes. "Mario?" he asked, his voice barely audible.

Mario told Gus about New Year's Eve, how he and Boomer brought him to the rescue mission after finding him badly beaten and left for dead in the snow inside Cortlandt alley.

Gus motioned Mario closer. "Your boys okay?"

"They're fine. Worried about you."

Gus opened one eye wider than the other. "Where's Sam?"

Mario smiled. "*He's* doing just fine."

Gus briefly raised himself up on one elbow, as if trying to get out of bed, then he fell back, and was silent.

"Gus?" Mario said, "Gus? He shot a panicked look at the nurse.

She bent over Gus for a moment. "He's just passed out," she said. "I don't think he'll be conscious again for awhile."

On the way back to the World Financial Center, Mario searched his mind for ways he might revive Gus's spirit. He thought of bringing the boys to see him, but rejected the idea, thinking it might be too much for the old man, might even be too much for the boys.

Then he remembered Gus's son. He hadn't heard a word from Burt, Frank's PI—had the man come up with anything? When he got back to Harrison Hart, Mario gave Burt a call.

"I just left you a message at the house," Burt told him. "Not only did I find the son, Augustus Shaw Jr., but I found a grandson as well, Andrew Shaw."

"A grandson? Jesus Christ. What can you tell me about them?"

"The son retired from the marines five years ago. Now he's a manager of a small suburban bank outside Miami, married, and the grandson is a sophomore at Drexel. An engineering student. I'll fax you the phone numbers and addresses."

Wait until Gus hears about this, Mario thought. It's going to give him a reason to get better.

But Gus heard neither about his son, nor grandson that day, or the next, not because Mario didn't tell him, but because he was either unconscious or not lucid enough to understand. His lungs were filling up with fluid and doctors were unable to get his fever down, or say whether or not the old man would ever be fully conscious again—or how long he'd even live.

On the afternoon of the television special, Mario went back to the hospital. He had to get through to Gus, tell him about his son. He couldn't do anything else until he did that, at least.

He opened the door to Gus's room and found him lying quietly in his bed, eyes closed. Mario looked at the nurse, who held a finger up to her lips. "He's sleeping," she whispered.

"Has the doctor seen him yet?"

The nurse sighed. "Yes. He doesn't think the antibiotics are working. It may not be long now."

Mario glanced at Gus. He seemed quite peaceful, except that his breathing was too fast. He walked out of the room in turmoil, he had to go back to Harrison Hart and ready himself for the show—it was only a couple of hours away now, but he couldn't leave Gus's bedside. For one of the few times in his life, he didn't know what to do.

With show time fast approaching, the UBS control room was a picture of controlled panic. In addition to Julie's crew, each of which was overseeing their part of the project, there was a platoon of technicians at the control boards, making sure every aspect of the telecast was ready to launch.

Julie had a chair in the midst of the chaos, overseeing the crowd of technicians, watching the monitor wall, which showed each remote location, each labeled by city name. Her headset and the switching panel in front of her gave her the ability to establish instant voice contact with anyone on the team from any city.

She was studying the middle wall monitor, the one that showed the scene at the Harrison Hart trading floor, watching the two camera operators focus and zoom, first on the speaker setup, then on the audience that had already gathered on the floor.

"The setup is looking good, Fred," Julie said into her mouthpiece. "But could you check the light levels on the two chairs? I think the one on the right is just a little too hot."

On the middle monitor, Julie watched the lighting technician at Harrison Hart making the corrections. "That's perfect," she told Fred. "Oh, Fred, listen, I know you know this, but I'm nervous enough to remind you: I want reaction shots of both men, especially when things start to heat up."

"You got it," Fred assured her.

Then Paige was at Julie's side. "The video clips are all cued up," she said.

"Keep an eye on the technicians," Julie instructed. "I don't want a single second of dead air."

Julie surveyed the wall of monitors in front of her. At the remote locations, crews were in various stages of preparation: in Minneapolis, the chairs for the focus group room were all set up and someone was putting up a wallpaper-covered back wall. In Tucson, tech crews were positioning lighting equipment. In Atlanta, the focus group, a perfect demographic sample—was already in position and getting restless. In St. Louis, they were still laying carpet. In New York, a panel of economists, politicians, and journalists was coming together in a downstairs studio.

"Cal," Julie said into her mouthpiece, "would you inform the slow-pokes that we're less than two hours from air time and they'd better get moving?"

Cal, who was standing at the other end of the control room, holding a clipboard and taking his own inventory of the remote feeds, gave Julie a wave.

"Everyone should be up to speed in the next fifteen minutes or so."

"And they know their local anchors have to be ready to go on air with focus-group results the moment after the post-debate commercial break, right?"

"Right," he affirmed. "And I've made sure Tex is going to be getting the voting results in real time and ready to broadcast right after the 10:23 commercial break."

Julie ran her eyes across the monitors to the one in the lower right corner, which was linked to a camera outside of Federal Hall. John Ayers was standing on the steps, his face ruddy with the cold air, and a wardrobe woman was adjusting his scarf.

Julie hit the mike switch. "John, this is Julie."

"Ayers here."

"John, I need you to go inside until just before air time. Your nose is so red you look like you should be pulling Santa's sleigh. Gotta protect the talent, you know."

Julie asked the camera operator to give her a wide shot, then a 180-degree pan while she watched on a monitor in the lower corner of the UBS control room video wall. Two or three hundred curious bystanders were already gathered at the camera location, ready to watch Ayers launch the show, all of them standing placidly behind the wooden barricades the NYPD had set up.

And behind them were the UBS satellite truck, with its enormous white dish, and three UBS equipment vans, one for each of the two camera crews that were inside Harrison Hart and Ayers' crew outside the New York Stock Exchange.

Julie leaned back in her chair and looked around the control room—sound men checking the levels on their sound boards, transmission techs metering the broadcast signals, electricians taping down critical connections.

Up until that moment, she'd been too busy to think about the deeper meaning of what she was doing, what was happening here and all across the country on this night. But now it swept over her, an outburst of nerves that left her pulse pounding and her teeth chattering, So much at stake...for the country, for the network, for herself, for Mario.

Fielding's voice was in Julie's headphones again. "Mulvaney's here," he said. "Gallagher's in make-up. No sign of Monelli yet."

Julie looked at the studio clock and frowned. "He should be there soon. Let me know when he arrives."

Fifteen minutes later, she still hadn't heard from Fred Fielding, so she contacted him again. "No Monelli?"

"No Monelli. What's he trying to do, give me a heart attack?"

Julie took a deep breath and waved Paige over to her chair. "Mario hasn't showed yet," she said.

"I'll make some calls," Paige said, trying to reassure her.

"Try his house." Julie said. "And the Downtown Athletic Club...and Harry's Pub. I'll call that crew of his. Maybe *they* know."

Mario must be delayed by something, Julie thought. I just *know* it's something beyond his control. It doesn't matter what's happened between us, he'll honor his agreement.

Julie dialed Harrison Hart and got Neil on the phone. "Neil, this is Julie Chambers at UBS."

"Julie Chambers?"

"Yes. We're looking for Mario. He hasn't shown up yet and we're starting to get nervous. I called his cell, but he's not picking up. Any ideas?"

"I'll put the boys on it and we'll get back to you as soon as we know anything."

"Thanks."

"Don't worry he'll be there. He wouldn't disappoint you for the world."

The sentence just hung in the air, while a million thoughts raced through Julie's mind.

Back at New York Downtown Hospital, Mario was in tremendous conflict. He had to leave for the show. And yet he couldn't tear himself away from Gus whose breathing and fever was getting worse. And yet he could not be in two places simultaneously. Which love would he honor?

He looked at Gus, inside the plastic oxygen tent, frail, still breathing too quickly, his face contorted with pain. There was just no way he could appear on a goddamn television show while his friend lay dying.

Mario walked into the hallway, pulled his cell phone out of his pocket, and hit a button. "Tyler? It's Mario."

"Where the hell *are* you man? They're going crazy here looking for you."

"I'm at New York Hospital with a friend. He's real bad. I can't leave him."

Tyler was flabbergasted. "Say that again. What friend? Never mind—when are you getting here?"

"That's why I called. I don't know if I *can*."

"Wait a second. You mean you're going to blow off tonight?"

"I don't think he's gonna make it," Mario repeated. "I don't want him to be alone when...I mean if ..." His voice was fragile, on the edge of breaking.

"Did you tell Julie yet? She needs to know immediately."

"I can't face her, Tyler. That's why I'm calling *you*." There was a long pause.

"This is gonna do you a *lot* of damage, Mario. And not just to UBS. After Intercoastal, this is going to be the nail that seals your coffin on The Street."

"It's not about me anymore, Tyler." There was no life in Mario's voice now.

"Go ahead, Mario, sit with your sick friend," Tyler said. "Say a prayer for him, too. And say one for Julie. I got news for you, pal, that girl laid it all on the line for you the other night after the UBS brass threatened to kick you to the curb after that little scene your wife graced us with. Corbin told me she put all her chips on your number, buddy boy. It'll be sad watching her go down in flames tonight."

Mario heard the phone beep and Tyler was gone.

It was 7:30 pm and the control room was percolating like mission control before a shuttle launch. Julie heard Paige's voice in her earpiece. "Julie, phone for you, line four." Julie felt a wave of relief sweep over her. This must be Neil, calling to tell her that Mario was on the way. "Yes?"

"Julie, it's Tyler."

"Tyler?"

"I'm afraid I have some bad news for you," he said.

Her stomach fell to the floor.

"Mario's not going to make it."

"What do you mean not make it?" she said. "Is he okay? Has something happened?"

"He's fine, but a friend of his *isn't*. He's keeping vigil with him at New York Hospital. He's not expected to last the night and Mario won't leave him."

Julie knew immediately who this friend must be. Only Gus—and what Mario felt for the man—would stop him from keeping his word. For a moment, Julie simply couldn't speak.

"I'm afraid you're going to have to do the broadcast without him."

The impact began to hit her.

She had a live program airing in less than an hour and she'd lost her Top Gun. Her mind flooded in a wild search for answers—abort the show? No, the whole country would be watching? And what would she tell UBS sister stations—all 200 of them. And the sponsors. What about *them*? What about the lawsuits? Delay it until next week? No. By next week, the opportunity might be gone, and the United Broadcasting System might be as well.

She hung up and looked around the control room. Everything was moving right along. According to the monitors, the remote locations were all set with their focus groups, and of course there was John Ayers, still freezing his nuts off outside Federal Hall, while a throng of spectators numbering close to a thousand now and growing, reached deep into Broad Street canyon, amid the giant Christmas tree, glistening in the night, and illuminating the American flag that masked the face of the NYSE building, everyone waiting for the broadcast to begin.

Julie finally took her heart in her hand and called Miles Corbin. "Bad news," she said. "Mario's a no show."

There was a pause, then, with remarkable calm, Miles said, "I see. Meet me in Fisher's office as soon as you can get up here. I'll call Hank."

They all arrived at about the same moment, and Julie could see from the expressions on their faces, that they all knew the situation was at DEFCON 5.

"First of all, Julie," Fisher said, "I want to know if there's *any* chance at all that Monelli will get to the set in time."

"I think we have to assume there isn't," Julie said. She could hear her pulse beating in her ears.

"Probably drunk somewhere," Miles said. "Maybe he got spooked."

Fisher fixed him with a blank stare. "There'll be plenty of time for recriminations and post-mortems, Miles. What we have to decide— immediately—is what to do *now*."

"If we're going to run the show tonight—and I don't think we have any choice—we have two options," Hank said. "First, we get George Van Wert down here, pronto. He knows his way around the general subject and we'll brief him by cell phone on his way to Harrison Hart."

"What's the second option?" Miles asked.

Julie spoke up. "We do away with the panel and put it all on Gallagher. We tell him it's going to be a hostile interview and me and Marty will feed him questions remotely."

"But will Mulvaney go for that?" Corbin asked. "He's expecting Monelli. He *approved* Monelli."

"He's ego is bigger than Trump's," Julie said. "He'd never pass up the opportunity to go on television solo."

"And who could object to good old George Van Wert?" Miles added.

"I could," Julie said. "Mulvaney will trample him. He's old, he's tired, and he's slow."

"And he's all we have," Fisher observed. "Miles, you take care of it. Get him down to the Financial Center and brief him. The segment doesn't begin until forty-five minutes into the telecast, that's the third station break. Still some time."

Miles glanced at Julie, smiling slightly—it was his little moment of triumph.

"What do we tell the affiliates?" Hank asked.

"Tell them *nothing*," Fisher demanded.

"Now, Julie," Fisher began—and she was sure he was going to take it all away from her, certain she failed—"I want you to talk to Tom. Get him ready for a long, hostile interview. Get your questions in order."

"But I thought Van Wert…"

"We don't have him yet, and we don't know if he can do it. If he says yes, I want to prepare both options and make an airtime decision after I see him."

"Okay," Julie said, turning to leave, "I'll get Gallagher prepped."

"Good," Fisher said. "And by the way, Julie, I want to remind you of one thing."

She turned around to face him. "What's that?"

"It was *your* idea that we do this live."

He couldn't get his mind to think about the Wall Street bars and haunts across lower Manhattan, packed in eager anticipation from Little Italy to Houston Street. Nor about family, friends, and neighbors, gathered at his home in Long Island, like it was a Pay Per View event, or the victory celebration that awaited him across the river at the Lions' Den. Neither did he ponder the repercussions to Harrison Hart, legally, as well as to himself, professionally. None of it no longer mattered.

Mario, alone in the hospital chapel, offered his prayers for his friend's recovery. It was all he could do now and he was very fearful that it would not be enough. He didn't have much hope left, but he knew where his place was, and after a few moments of solace, he walked back to Gus's room.

The nurse met him at the door. "He's awake!" she said. "He asked me if you were here."

Mario hurried into the room flashing a big smile and knelt beside the bed. "Well, well," he said, "so how was your beauty sleep?"

Gus managed a smile of his own. "I'm still tired," he said.

"Are you comfortable?" he asked, taking Gus's hand.

Gus lifted an eyebrow and looked at Mario slyly. "Do you know how long it's been since I had clean sheets? And a pretty nurse to take care of me?"

Mario laughed and Gus joined in, but Gus's laugh almost immediately turned into long, hard, hacking coughing, interrupted only by brief gasps for breath. Mario and the nurse exchanged anxious glances, but after a few moments, Gus got his coughing under control. The effort took all the humor out of his face.

"Listen, I have some good news for you, Gus," Mario said, as soon as his friend was able to focus again. "I located your son. He's living in Florida. Clearwater."

Gus shook his head, as though he were hearing something impossible.

"That's the truth," Mario said. "Got his address and his phone number. And that's not all I found out."

"What do you mean?"

"You have a grandson, Gus. Boy named Andrew." Mario waited for the reaction, but it was a long time coming. He wasn't sure whether the old fighter was drifting off or lost in thought.

Finally, Gus spoke. "I have a *grandson*?" He was grinning broadly.

"That's right. Sophomore in college, studying engineering up in Philly."

Gus broke out in a coughing fit again, worse than before. It was several minutes before he was breathing regularly, and even then, the phlegm in his lungs rattled audibly. The nurse nervously adjusted Gus's oxygen tent, then checked his saliva tank, which Mario noticed was filling up what looked like white clam chowder, being sucked from Gus's lungs. "Do you want to see him, Gus?"

"I'm not sure....if he can get here...fast enough," Gus said. He was crying now. "Mario," Gus said, "there's a chain around my neck." He tried to touch his neck, but couldn't lift his hand enough. "Take it off," Gus said.

Mario reached under the oxygen tent, unclipped the chain and pulled it from Gus's neck. It came away with two small, burnished gold ornaments—tiny boxing gloves. He stared at them, almost in awe. They were relics of another life, reminders of a time when there was nothing but tomorrows.

"This is your Golden Gloves prize, Gus. The one Joe Louis gave you."

"I want you promise me you'll give it to my grandson. Tell him to never let it go."

Mario thought for a moment, then placed it back in Gus's palm and curled the old man's fingers around it. "You can give it to him yourself."

"I can't fight the man upstairs, Mario. I'm old. And I'm tired. Can't come out for the last one."

Gus's eyes drifted to the TV hanging from the wall. A reporter was describing the scene outside the NYSE. "What day is it?" Gus asked.

"It's Thursday, January third," Mario said.

Gus was quiet, thinking. "Ain't you supposed to be somewhere tonight?"

Mario glanced over at the TV. "Yeah. Right here."

"You'll disappoint her."

Mario felt a stab of pain. "I already *have.*"

"I thought you loved this woman."

"I do."

"Then how can you let her down?"

"Because I love you, too."

"Don't give up your title shot for me, Mario. This is *your* night to be champ. Me, I had my shot. I didn't take it. But this...this is *your* time."

"I'll fight him another day, Gus."

"You can't win this on the street. Take it from an old street fighter who knows—you gotta fight this beast in the ring. Otherwise, you'll be fighting it forever in here." He feebly gestured to Mario's head. "You may not win her love. But you just might win her respect." Gus's voice was soft, but urgent. "You'll thank me one day."

"I'm afraid."

"Don't be. I'll be in your corner the whole time, stitchin' ya up." He put the necklace back into Mario's hand. "Take it," he said. "Keep it with you. And don't let go. Not for a moment...," Gus said, drifting now.

Julie ran her eyes across the wall of monitors, settling on the center one. She watched John Ayers take his place at the top of the stone stairs leading up to Federal Hall. A make-up person patted him down one last time and someone else adjusted his coat. His breath was coming out in little puffs of condensation, a nice effect that would make the broadcast that much more immediate.

Then Ayers rubbed his hands together in what could only be described as eager anticipation. "Magic time."

In the control room, the digital clock hit 7:59:30. Julie ignored the butterflies in her stomach and checked the Harrison Hart monitor, hoping against hope to find Mario sitting in his designated chair. No sign of him. "Twenty seconds, John," she said into her headset. "Go to station break," she instructed a technician. "Roll intro." The UBS logo popped up on every control room monitor.

Julie cued the control room director to begin the voice over intro. The control room crew exchanged nervous glances—the show was starting, but one of the stars was missing.

"Live from Wall Street, John Ayers." The announcer's voice came over the network feed.

"Okay, John," Julie said quietly into her mike, "you're on."

On the center monitor, the control room crew watched Ayers appear from behind the enormous black, cast iron statue of George Washington, and confidently stride down the majestic stone steps of Federal Hall, the television lights turning the Broad Street canyon into something approaching daylight.

"Wall Street," he began, in that wonderfully rich and reassuring voice of his, "is the financial capital of America. And the world. This is where fortunes are made and lost. And where new companies are recognized for their strength and potential. This is where companies are bought and sold—and lives hang in the balance."

He paused and looked into the camera with grave sincerity. "And *this*," he said, "is where America is facing its greatest economic challenge in the history of the Republic, where America is locked in an intense struggle with incredibly wealthy foreign interests over the fruits of U.S. capitalism. This is where an event unprecedented in our nation's history is now unfolding. Good evening, everyone. I'm John Ayers. Tonight, we're going to explore..."

"Run main title," Julie told the Program Manager. And up came the words, in a large and disturbing type face, "AMERICA FOR SALE," accompanied by ominous music. When the title was over, Ayers resumed his spiel, while Julie once again checked out the Harrison Hart set. Still no Mario, but Mulvaney was already in his chair, looking like the cat who was about to eat the canary.

She picked up a phone and called upstairs to Hank. "What's the story with Van Wert?"

"Miles is on the phone with the old boy as we speak" Hank said, "What about Tom? Can you brief him in time if Van Wert doesn't pan out?"

"I'm on it."

"Keep me informed," Hank said and hung up.

On the middle monitor, Julie saw that Ayers was almost finished with his lead-in… "So this is the question we're going to examine tonight: Are these foreign investments actually good for us, or are we giving away the heart of American power—and influence—in exchange for short-term profits? In short, are we selling our country?"

"Roll the first montage," Julie instructed Stan, her control room director. Ayers' image dissolved into Carol Twizel's brilliant theme of America, beginning with archive footage from the bicentennial. Then the phone rang again. Julie scooped it up quickly.

"Yes?"

"Good news, we got Van Wert," Hank said. "Miles is personally picking him up and taking him to the Financial Center. Get word to Fred."

"Will do."

Instead of watching the montage, Julie kept a close eye on the monitor displaying the scene at Harrison Hart—spectators jamming the live set on the trading floor.

"Fred," she said, "what in hell is going on?"

"It's a freaking madhouse, Julie," Fred said into his headset. "Everyone in the building has crowded in here. We've had to lock all the exits. We're getting a lot of shit from the fire warden."

"Miles should be there with Van Wert any minute."

"Van Wert!"

"Monelli's officially MIA," she sighed.

"My God," Fred said softly. "So we're going on, but with Van Wert?"

"You got it," Julie confirmed.

"I just love doing live television," Fred said. "Okay, have them come up through the freight elevator. I'll alert security."

Julie asked one of the cameramen to give her a wide view of the door by the freight elevator, and he zoomed back obligingly.

A few minutes later, the door opened and Miles Corbin emerged, with an arm around the shoulder of George Van Wert, who was slightly disheveled, eyes blinking like a befuddled owl. Miles cut through the crowd, guiding him toward the television setup on the other side of the trading floor.

Julie spoke into her microphone. "Someone give Miles a headset."

A hand intruded into the frame with a headset and Miles put it on. "How is he?" she asked.

Miles quietly turned away from Van Wert. "We got him up from a nap and he's not as sharp as I'd like, but he'll come around."

"Gloria?" Fred said. "Get Mr. Van Wert ready for the camera."

"Come with me, Mr. Van Wert," Gloria interrupted.

They headed for a perimeter office, which was being used as a make-up room.

"Have you briefed him, Miles?" Julie asked.

"As much as anyone can in fifteen minutes.

"Can he do this?"

Miles paused. "I think he'll muddle through. Let me get some coffee in him and be back to you. Is Tom ready to give it a go in case?"

"Marty's given me a list of about ten tough questions, and he's working on the follow-ups. We can feed them to Tom, but he won't know what we're driving at."

"It's your call, Julie. Fisher made that clear."

Thanks a *lot*, she thought bitterly. "Yes, and I intend to make it," she said. "But not quite yet. Let's see if Van Wert wakes up. I'll have Tom ready to step in on a moment's notice."

A few minutes later, while Julie watched in the control room, Van Wert appeared at the door of the make-up room, his cheeks now as rosy as a teenage girl's, and Gloria led him to the chair opposite Mulvaney's. Bart regarded the old man at first with mild surprise, then with amusement.

He has just realized Mario won't be there, Julie concluded, and the disgusting expression on his face was just a harbinger of the price they were all going to pay. As Van Wert sat down in the debate chair, the spectators grew quiet, and a buzz went through the crowd, evidently confused by the fact that both chairs were now occupied, and Mario wasn't sitting in either one of them.

Suddenly, a raucous outburst of cheers, whistles and hollering broke out in the northeast corner of the trading floor where a legion of Hart's rank and file had gathered.

"Fred, what's happening?" Julie said. "What's all the noise about?"

"I don't know!" Fred shouted into his headset.

"Miles?"

"Oh, fuck me," was all she heard Miles say.

The tsunami of cheers whipped around the floor and hit its peak as Mario emerged from the throng of spectators, patting his back as he made his way toward the setup on one side of the trading floor, Neil and Kat riding shotgun—a bevy of television lights looming over Tom Gallagher, standing at a podium, facing two swivel chairs set in front of the Futures Desk, one occupied by Barton Mulvaney, the other—at the moment—by George Harold Van Wert.

"Julie, it's Monelli!" Fred shouted through his headset.

"What!"

"He's here!"

At UBS, everyone in the control room yelled in excitement when Mario appeared on the screen. "Talk about a fuckin' entrance," one video technician said to another.

Back on the trading floor, Bart stood up, his game face firmly in place, craning his neck to see what was going on, just as Mario passed a relieved Tom Gallagher and his panel of moderators and stepped over the equipment cables into Bart's domain. The two men nodded minimally, conspicuously avoided a handshake, unintentionally furthering the theatrics.

"You're in the jungle *now,* baby," Bart warned Mario.

Mario noticed Van Wert, sitting in the chair opposite Mulvaney, like a man with a concussion, but he didn't break eye contact with his rival.

"George," Mario said calmly, "Get the *fuck* out of my chair."

Fred intruded himself between Mario and Van Wert. "Goddamn it, Monelli, where the hell have you been? Never mind. Get over to makeup. We've got seven minutes. Gloria?"

"Tell Julie I'm sorry," Mario said. "I can explain."

"Later," Fielding said. "After the show."

Gloria took his arm. "This way to make-up, Mr. Monelli."

Julie was amazed and relieved to see Mario—but there was no time to figure out her emotions. "Fred," she said into her headset, "thank George very much and give him a nice seat, away from the action. We're going back to plan A."

Watching the scene on her monitor, Julie saw Fielding talking to Corbin, who was giving him an argument.

"Miles," Julie said into her mike.

Corbin looked up at the camera. "This isn't right, Julie," he said into his headset, "Van Wert is doing a lot better. He's going to be fine."

"It's my call, as you so politely reminded me, Miles, and my call is that we go on with this exchange, *as planned.*"

She looked up to see Hank watching her from the other side of the control room, and waved him over. "Would you tell Fisher we're going ahead as planned?"

"You know he said to go with Van Wert."

"I know. Tell him we're going with Monelli."

"I hope you know what you're doing."

She glanced up at the control room monitors. The second segment was almost over. At Harrison Hart, Van Wert was clinging to his chair, protesting. "You can't drag me down here, then pull me at the last minute."

"I'll make it up to you, George," Miles explained. "Tomorrow, we'll interview you about what was said tonight, and put the segment on the evening news."

Van Wert reluctantly surrendered the chair. "But I can put it all in perspective," he promised, as he was escorted out of camera range. Bart and Mario settled themselves in there chairs ready to square off like heroes in Greek tragedy.

Julie checked the broadcast monitor. Ayers was now on the bottom step on Federal Hall, ready for the hand-over to Tom Gallagher after his review of U.S. Saudi relations.

"Ladies and gentlemen, you are about to witness something unprecedented, a live, real-time television exchange between experts with two diametrically-opposed views, a debate with the highest possible stakes for the future of our country. And let *you*, the American public decide…"

"And moderating this important debate will be Tom Gallagher."

In the control room, Julie cast her eyes down the rows of remote-location monitors. All of the focus groups were in their seats, and toll free numbers appeared at the bottom of the screens. Then she turned toward the middle monitor, and she got a brief glimpse of Mario sitting before the camera, armed only with his passion and her belief in him. He seemed completely determined and ready—only someone who really knew him could see the fear and uncertainty under his veneer. Her heart went out to him.

CHAPTER TWENTY-FOUR

"Thank you, John, and good evening everyone. I'm Tom Gallagher, and we are live inside the World Financial Center, ready to get underway for this much-anticipated debate. Or should I say discussion. By any event, this segment of *America for Sale* should prove very interesting, so let us begin. Before we introduce our two guests, let's meet our distinguished panel, the people who get to ask the questions..."

"Jesus Christ, Julie," Fred said into his headset, looking at Mario. "He's sweating like Mike Tyson on Jeopardy."

"He'll be alright, Fred."

"...now, it's time to introduce our two guests," Gallagher went on, "two remarkable men, both of them experts in foreign and domestic investment and cross border acquisitions..."

Mario watched Fielding direct camera one to zoom in on Mulvaney, who was sitting back in his chair, preening for the camera, legs crossed casually, attitude and attire reminiscent of a Ralph Lauren model.

"To your left is Barton Mulvaney, of the world-famous Blackwell Group, an equity buyout firm which he co-founded.

"Mr. Mulvaney, who is the son and grandson of investment bankers, is a Wall Street icon and Rhodes scholar, having earned his first million dollar bonus just six months after receiving his MBA from the Wharton School of Business. We are very proud to have him."

Mulvaney's smile broadened and he nodded, more in agreement than appreciation.

Fielding touched the shoulder of the second cameraman, who came in tight on Mario, who was leaning forward in his chair, twisting a fist in his palm, wearing an expensive suit, but looking as though he was dressed above his class. He was very nervous, and trying desperately to hide it.

"Seated to my left—your right—is Mario Monelli, managing director of mergers and acquisitions at the Harrison Hart Alliance, which happens to be the scene of this live exchange. Mr. Monelli's path to Wall Street prominence was very different from Mr. Mulvaney's. No blue-chip background, no prep school, no Ivy League degree..."

Mario sat in his chair a picture of nervous energy, adrenalin pumping through his veins, hating the way he was being described, clutching Gus's necklace so tight in his palm that his knuckles were white. This is the real thing, he kept reminding himself, it's happening *right now*.

"Mr. Monelli started at the low end of Wall Street, breaking through Wall Street traditions and the Old Boy Network to join the elite in the investment banking stratosphere. Today, he is a rising star in the world of high finance, and we are very pleased to have him with us tonight."

Mario was breathing so rapidly it appeared he might lose consciousness. Suddenly, there was a voice in his earpiece—Julie's voice. "I'm here, Mario, watching and listening to everything."

Mario involuntarily glanced at the camera lens, as if he might find Julie there. Then, when he realized what he'd done, he smiled at his folly.

"If you forget something, or get rattled, I'll help you out. Just remember our practice sessions. Take a deep breath, take your time, and you'll be fine."

The phone rang again and Julie picked it up.

"Julie, we agreed on Van Wert. What in god's name are you doing?" Fisher shouted.

"Risking everything I have," she replied and hung up, before ordering a technician to lock the control room door.

"Like all debates," Gallagher was saying, "we have some rules—very simple ones, since, so far as I know, no one here is running for president." He smiled at his own witticism and a few easily amused spectators on the trading floor affected a laugh. Then he went over the simple rules.

"If there aren't any question, let's begin," Gallagher said. "Our first question will be asked by Peter Meyers of *The Wall Street Journal*, and it will be directed to Barton Mulvaney."

"Mr. Mulvaney, *is* it good for America when foreign companies or foreign governments invest or take controlling interest in U.S. companies?"

Mario watched Bart lean forward in his chair, smiling and exuding his usual overweening self-confidence. "I'd be happy to answer that, Pete. There is no question that foreign investment benefits America, and in many ways. Most experts agree.

"I'll give you just a few reasons. First, foreign and cross-border acquisitions of American companies bring an infusion of capital and give foreign governments a bigger incentive to seek better trade relations with the United States, creating a broader market. Second, they create thousands of new jobs for American workers—jobs that generally pay more than U.S. employers are willing, and these workers gain valuable "know how." Thirdly, they generate tax revenue, and lastly, it spreads money throughout the local economy, stimulates small business, and encourages research and development. It also makes us more competitive in the global marketplace..." Bart sailed on in his reptilian languor, flexing his imposing vocabulary, ever so slowly, accenting each point with an arched brow and savoring Mario's discomfort with glee.

When he finished, Bart leaned back in his chair, poised, pugnacious and quite satisfied with himself. Julie spoke into her mike, talking directly to

Mario, through his earpiece. "Ok, take a deep breath." She watched Mario do as instructed. "Now answer—and don't rush it."

"Mr. Monelli," Gallagher was saying, "is Mr. Mulvaney accurate in his assessment?"

Mario just sat there looking at the lights and the crowd around him, and it put the zap on him. Tom looked over at Fred, almost panicked.

"Julie, do something," Fred whispered into his headset.

"You can do this, Mario," Julie said into Mario's earpiece.

"Well, if he *is* accurate," Mario finally said, "it would be the first time." The spectators were momentarily silent, then broke into laughter. In the control room, Julie just smiled, knowing Mario was a master at disarming people with his sense of humor.

"But let's look at his arguments anyhow," Mario continued. "He says foreign investment stimulates research and development. That's true—but you know who benefits from that R&D? The company's foreign owners. It's called 'technological transfer' and eighty percent of it goes abroad."

Mario looked at Bart and smiled. "He says that foreign investment in the U.S. produces jobs here. But most of those jobs simply replace pre-existing ones in U.S.-owned companies. At best, the country gains no more than 15,000 jobs annually, while workers' wages and pensions stagnate, and employers refuse to pay for health insurance."

Mulvaney was deliberately avoiding Mario's eyes, instead rubbing his chin as if nothing his rival said was worth acknowledging.

"Now, about that added tax revenue," Mario went on. "Very little of it gets to the federal government. Foreign companies are experts at hiding revenue *and* profits."

"How?" asked Tom.

"A lot of creative Wall Street accountants out there," Mario replied. "The kind who went to American gladiator schools like my opponent here. The amount of tax fraud and money laundering is astonishing, washed through offshore shell companies.

"The other points he made are also incorrect," Mario continued, still coolly looking at Mulvaney. "Our workers get 'know-how'? No. It works the *other* way—our workers *teach* foreign competition how to do it. And this business about stimulating the local economy? American companies already do that. They don't need foreign help."

Looking at the focus group monitors, Julie saw a spike in Mario's approval. She spoke quietly, on her line into Mario's earpiece. "Exactly. Round one for Monelli." Mario took stock of himself and was pleased. He was now calmer and in control although still breathing heavily.

Gallagher intervened. "Would you care to rebut, Mr. Mulvaney?"

"Yes," Bart laughed. "I'd like to say that most of Mr. Monelli's points are based on faulty or outdated statistics. Furthermore, he's ignored the most important thing about foreign investment: We do it, too. We're investing in—or buying—companies throughout Europe, Asia, and Latin America. It's one way we're showing confidence in foreign economies, just as they invest here because they have confidence in *our* economy."

"Tom," Mario interrupted, "I wanna rebut his rebuttal…"

"You have fifteen seconds to respond, Mr. Monelli," Gallagher said.

"Well, my friend Bart here is absolutely right—we *are* buying and investing in foreign companies, but the foreigners are doing it at twice the rate we are, and the disparity is growing. Just look at our staggering trade deficit as we borrow from China to buy oil from the Middle East in order to finance our domestic agenda."

"Mario, we can't stop doing business with the rest of the world," Bart interjected. "If we become isolationists…"

"I'm not saying we're to isolate ourselves economically, *Bart*."

"Then why are you spewing protectionist rhetoric?"

"Because soon there will be nothing left to *protect*," Mario countered and turned back to the panel of moderators.

"Tom, foreigners own more than thirty percent of the United States debt market with most of that in treasuries."

"Yes," Mulvaney interrupted smoothly, "that's true, but he's drawing the wrong conclusion from it. The right one is that it's foreign capital that is fueling our economy, keeping inflation low, which improves our standard of living, forcing our industries to become better and more efficient, and helping millions become homeowners."

"And *that*," Mario interrupted, "is why in the last twenty years, the U.S. has shifted from being a net creditor nation, to which the world owed a third of a trillion dollars, to owing the rest of the world nearly *twelve* trillion dollars, leaving the world awash in dollars that are easily used to buy off big chunks of America."

"Give us an example," Tom said.

"You want an example," Mario replied. "I'll give an example. The U.K.'s BP bought Amoco for forty-eight billion dollars—now Amoco's profits go to England. Deutsche Telekom bought VoiceStream Wireless, so their profits go to Germany, which is where most of the profits from Random House, Allied Signal, Chrysler, Doubleday, Cyprus Amax's US Coal Mining Operations, GTE/Sylvania, and Westinghouse's Power Generation profits go, as well. Ralston Purina's profits go to Switzerland, along with Gerber's; TransAmerica's profits go to the Netherlands, while John Hancock Insurance's profits go to Canada. Even American Banker's Insurance Group is owned by Fortis AG in Belgium…"

"Good work, Marty," Julie said to her head writer.

"Listen to this:.." Mario unfolded a crumpled piece of paper. "This came from the National Security Review, the June issue. It says, 'Foreign governments have spent nearly $375 *billion* last year in foreign and cross border acquisitions, and that number is projected to increase to nearly $700 billion over the next two years.' Are you happy with that, Bart? Do you think that's a good thing?"

"Gentlemen, gentlemen," Gallagher said, holding up his hands, "*We're* the ones who get to ask the questions. But Mr. Monelli raises a valid point, Mr. Mulvaney. Is it good for America to be heavily in debt to the rest of the world?"

"I know that ten or even fifteen trillion dollars sounds like a huge amount of money," Mulvaney said, "but it's less than twenty percent of our GDP. As a nation, we make that much every ten weeks."

"True, but our debt is increasing very quickly," Mario countered, "because we've abandoned the principles of tariff-based trade that built American industry, and kept us strong for over 200 years.

"Tom, the cold hard truth is that the unholy alliance between Washington and Wall Street has sold out the American worker. Driven by the insatiable greed of Wall Street profiteers, and accelerated by the false promise of free trade, our manufacturing base has been chased out of this country, entire industry sectors have been wiped out, and along with it, the livelihood of millions of hard-working Americans..."

Then for the next few minutes he took Bart to task, railing against unfair trade agreements with Mexico and China, before being distracted by the tap-tap-tap signaling ten seconds of rebuttal time remaining.

"Consider this, Tom, China, right now, is using our trade dollars to build their military."

"But so is England and Israel, Mario," Bart laughed.

"But China owns three trillion of foreign currency reserves, Bart. One day they'll stop buying our debt and start selling dollars to buy oil or Euros. And that will position them to swallow us, without firing a single shot. Tom, did you know the parts for our nuclear missiles are now made in China, a country who last year threatened us with nuclear weapons...

"And it's not just China. Foreign companies are right now buying up our water systems, our power generating systems, our mines, and our few remaining factories...

"Our oil comes from a country that birthed a Wahhabist movement that ultimately led to fourteen Saudi citizens flying jetliners into the World Trade buildings and the Pentagon. Germans now own the Chrysler auto assembly lines that turned out tanks to use against the Nazis in WWII. And the price of labor in America is being held down by over fifteen million illegal workers, a situation that was impossible twenty-five years ago when the unions were the bulwark against dilution of the American labor force..."

He opened his mouth to continue, then heard Julie's voice in his earpiece—"You're bloviating," she said. "Let Tom get on to the next question—we're almost there."

"Okay, the next question—and it will be asked by Regina Brand of the *National Review.*"

"Gentleman, everyone has heard a lot about foreign investment in U.S. companies, ever since Japan bought Rockefeller Center back in the 1980s, and still more after China tried to buy UNOCAL, and Dubai's failed bid to acquire our ports: If we continue to let foreign companies and governments gain a major foothold in American enterprise, aren't we surrendering control of our economic future?"

"Mr. Mulvaney, do you wish to comment on that?" Tom said.

"I would be happy to because it's one of the gross misconceptions about foreign investment. And I'm going to kill it here and now. It is true—but only in theory—that foreign governments could exert political pressure on the U.S., if they owned or controlled enough big American companies..."

Mario raised an eyebrow, and leaned forward, angry and impatient, ready to edge into Bart's answer, but Julie, watching the focus group monitors, intervened. "No, no. Don't interrupt. Let him reach for the cheese."

"It's possible," Mulvaney continued, "that some foreign government could blackmail the U.S., perhaps into a U.N. vote against Israel, or to change immigration policies, or convert their dollars into Euro, or threaten to dump U.S. Treasury debt, maybe closing some of the major U.S. factories they own. Toyota was rumored to have threatened plant closings if the federal government bailed out GM. But it will never happen."

Mulvaney glanced over at Mario, and then at Tom. He was about to deliver the *coup de grace*, the blow that would deliver an early knockout and bragging rights at the Harvard Club, afterward. "No foreign government would do this," he said, "because it would undermine *its own* economy worse than it would hurt ours. It would cause the dollar to fall, making American workers unable to afford foreign goods. If the damage were great enough, America would slip into a deep recession, which would knock the value out of the companies the foreigners had invested in."

Mulvaney leaned back and grinned triumphantly at Vaughn, his protégé. Then he thought of something else. "Besides all that," he said, "the foreign-influence scenario assumes that individual investors would do what their governments told them to, in concert. And we all know there's no telling investors, foreign or domestic, what to do with their money. Right, Mario?"

Gallagher intercepted the question. "Gentlemen, this is a very spirited exchange, but remember, we're the ones who get to ask the questions here. Do you have anything more to add, Mr. Mulvaney?"

Bart steepled his fingers. "Here's the bottom line," he said, like a business school professor addressing a class of freshmen. "When an economy is as robust and as important to the world economy as the United States, its chief creditors have a strong incentive to keep it healthy. So our debt actually gives us *more* power, not less.

"Anyhow," Mulvaney continued, "all this paranoia about foreign investors dictating U.S. policy is ludicrous. It originated in the 1980s, when it looked like Japan was buying everything American, before my colleague here launched a personal crusade and rallied support on Wall Street and cut Japan off from financing—even though it wasn't true, but it appeared that way. Today, we know that many foreign countries invest here—Britain, Canada, the Netherlands, Japan, China, the Arab Emirates. And they have only one thing in common: they've invested in the U.S. because it's safe and profitable."

"Thank you, Mr. Mulvaney," Tom said.

In the control room, everyone's attention was now on Mario. Julie looked at him, trying to gauge his state of mind. He seemed very calm, and there was the slightest trace of a smile on his lips.

Mario caught Barton Mulvaney's eye and nodded approvingly. "I have to admit it, Bart, you've stated your argument quite well. In fact, except for one thing, I don't think I've ever heard it put more convincingly. The problem is you're completely and tragically wrong."

Mulvaney opened his mouth, but no words came out.

"The truth is," Mario said, "we *are* being threatened *right now, at this very moment* by a fabulously wealthy country. For at least two years, maybe longer, this country has been secretly and systematically gaining control of some of America's flagship companies..."

"You don't know what you're talking about," Mulvaney interrupted.

Mario smiled. "Not only is a foreign country buying control of our core assets," he said, "but there exists on Wall Street a rogue circle of private equity firms that are knowingly brokering these deals."

A surprised murmur swept the trading floor and, in the control room, Julie and Paige gripped hands and exchanged tense glances.

"Now you're making accusations?" Bart asked, combatively.

"It's not just an accusation, Bart. I have written proof of what I'm saying."

"Impossible," Mulvaney replied, but he seemed less sure of himself than before.

"Gentlemen," Tom Gallagher said, trying to regain control, "this is a debate, not a private discussion. Mr. Monelli, you've made a pretty sensational claim. Can you substantiate it? What nation are you talking about?"

"The kingdom of Saudi Arabia—the Saudi Royal Family..."

There were gasps on the trading floor. Julie cast an eye over the control room monitors that displayed the national focus groups. Mario's words had them riveted.

"That's preposterous," Bart scoffed. "They need us as much as we need them. They wouldn't do anything to harm us."

"Bart, a few months ago, you and I were locked in a desperate battle for the control of Intercoastal Courier. And your side won that battle. Do you know who your side was?"

Bart's face flashed with anger. "It was a Midwestern holding company," he said.

"Yes. And who owned them?"

"What do you mean? It was a consortium of Midwestern banks."

"Nope, sorry. The funding came from a South American holding company."

"What? But what does that have to do with…"

"With the Saudi Royal Family? They were the secret funders of the holding company." By now, the momentum had shifted, and Bart's self-confidence had evaporated and settled comfortably on Mario.

Mario pulled an envelope from his jacket pocket, got up and handed it to a surprised Barton Mulvaney.

"What's this?" Mulvaney asked, as Mario returned to his chair.

"See for yourself."

The dialogue had come to a standstill while Bart was reading Mario's papers. But Tom was never at a loss for words for very long. "Ladies and gentlemen," he said into the camera, "Mario Monelli has made some explosive charges about the Saudi Royal Family's involvement in taking control of a major U.S. company, and Barton Mulvaney is looking at what his opponent says is the proof. How about it, Mr. Mulvaney? Is Mr. Monelli correct?"

All eyes shifted to Bart, who had gone pale. "We would have had no way of knowing," he said directly to Mario.

Mario nodded, not truly convinced. "And what would you have done if you *had* known, Bart? Would the Blackwell Group have refused to shepherd that acquisition?"

The question caught Bart flatfooted but he managed to fight himself off the ropes and pull himself together. "These papers," he said evenly, "may show that the Saudis was involved with Intercoastal. But that's *all* they show. Your wild charges about a Royal family plot to control America's core assets…that's only your crazy fantasy."

The crowd of spectators on the trading floor were completely silent, even George Van Wert, their eyes fixed on Mario, waiting for his reply. It was the same in the UBS control room. Julie resisted the urge to coach Mario—he was doing just fine, according to the focus group monitors, and she didn't want to break his momentum.

"Intercoastal is just one recent example of what the Saudis have been doing, Tom. It's hardly the most important. The Saudis have also bought a controlling interest in IBM, Merck, and General Electric, which leaves them well positioned to control CBS, AOL, and Time-Warner. And if you don't believe me, here are the documents to prove it." Mario handed Mulvaney another sheaf of papers.

For a moment, Mulvaney had no reply. Then he brought the fight to the center of the ring and started slugging back. "Where are you getting these documents? This isn't public information."

"Where I've gotten these documents is beside the point," Mario countered. "It's what they *say* that matters. They *prove* I'm telling the truth."

"Wait a minute," Mulvaney said, waving the papers Mario had given him. "Anyone could have manufactured them. Prove they're authentic."

Mario shrugged. "Why don't you check the watermark like *I* did?"

Mulvaney's eyebrows furrowed. He took one sheet from the batch and held it up to the lights. Then his face fell.

"What does it say?" Tom Gallagher asked.

Mulvaney mumbled something.

"Excuse me?"

"It says 'United States Security and Exchange Commission,'" Mario said, almost defiantly. "Is that genuine enough for you, Bart?" Mario asked innocently.

"It's that producer," Mulvaney snarled. "She's telling you what to say in your earpiece."

Mario ripped the earpiece out of his ear. "This thing? Here, *you* take it!" He tossed the earpiece toward Mulvaney, who made an awkward and unsuccessful effort to catch it.

Back in the control room, Julie reassured an alarmed tech crew not to panic at Mario's insistence on going without a net. By God, she'd been right about this man. He was everything she'd hoped for. Well, almost everything.

Mulvaney was desperately paging through the documents, trying to get a handle on them. Meanwhile, Julie nixed the commercial break, risking a lawsuit with the sponsors.

"Okay," Bart finally said, "even if these documents *are* genuine, there's *no* evidence that the Saudi Royal Family is anything other than a normal investor—not evil conspirators, intent on doing us damage."

"What they proved," Mario retorted, "is that the Saudi Royal Family is buying controlling interest in America's most important companies. And they're doing it through off-shore money laundering set up by like kind Wall Street brainiacs who engineered the destruction of Enron and Worldcom."

"Excuse me, gentlemen, if I could get a word in here," Tom Gallagher said a little sheepishly. "I have a question for Mr. Mulvaney: did you know the Saudis were investing in the U.S. on *this* scale?"

"No," Mulvaney said. He was visibly sweating now, on the run, falling back on boiler plate ripostes like "And that's another thing. How could this have escaped the notice of the entire U.S. government?"

"It didn't," Mario said calmly. "The proper agencies discovered what the Saudis were up to. But the administration scoffed at them and pressured them to drop their investigations."

"Why would they do that?" asked Tom Gallagher.

"I don't know," Mario said with a wry smile, "but I can guess. We all know that Washington is filled with Saudi friends—senators, judges, ambassadors, Wall Street power brokers, and leaders from both parties. They go hunting and fishing and golfing together. Even frequent the same call girls. They go to each other's weddings and birthday parties."

Bart tried to fight himself off the ropes. "I just don't buy that, Monelli. You've taken a relatively few investment deals and built them into some kind of conspiracy. They're nothing of the kind."

"How would you know, Bart, if you're not involved?"

Gallagher turned to Mario, as though he still had control of the debate. "Mr. Monelli, would you care to elaborate?"

"As a matter of fact," Mario said, "I would. I believe the Saudi buyout is part of a top secret plan—top secret until this very moment—to gain control of America's economic core, and to use that power to bend the policies of the American government, foreign, and domestic, to serve Saudi purposes."

"What?" Mulvaney was almost yelling. "What the hell are you talking about?"

"Fred, have Tom go to commercial" Julie instructed, in a tactical move.

"Gentlemen, excuse me," Tom Gallagher said, looking at Fred, "but I'm afraid the answer to that question will have to wait till after we break." He smiled into the camera. "We'll be right back." Fred cut away to commercial.

"Monelli," Bart said, "you have thoroughly fucked yourself. That is the most outrageous thing I've ever heard."

"You have it backwards, Bart," Mario said. "As usual."

Vaughn rushed over to Mulvaney, panic in his eyes, and tried to get his mentor to look at some papers he was clutching. Bart ignored them.

"We'll be back on air in three minutes," Fred told them. "Just time for a pee break, if you hurry."

Neil bolted out of the audience and grabbed Mario by the arm. "You got this muthafucker on the ropes," he said. "Come on, let's use Tyler's private john." Mario followed his friend into Tyler's office—and found Tyler standing at his desk watching the wall monitor and grimacing.

"Well, well," he said, "if it isn't Jesus Christ, superstar himself. I'm sure the partners are going to drill me a new one. I hope you know where you're going with all this, Mario. You're in *very* dangerous waters."

Mario flashed a grin, then disappeared into Tyler's private bathroom.

Back in the UBS control room, Paige came over to Julie. "I have to admit, he's doing pretty well. The focus groups love him."

Julie just shook her head. "He was so nervous—now it turns out that he's a natural.

"Very true," Paige said.

"Okay, everyone," Julie clapped and called to the control room crew, "coming out of commercial..." Neil walked Mario back to his chair as everyone scurried back into position.

"Now put this Irish prick away in the next round so we can go to the Lions' Den and throw down."

On the set, Tom Gallagher cleared his throat and looked directly into the camera lens. "Good evening, ladies and gentlemen. Tom Gallagher back with *America for Sale*. Just before break, Mr. Monelli accused Saudi Arabia of seeking to control the American economy. And Mr. Mulvaney challenged that allegation as I recall. Would you care to respond to his challenge, Mr. Monelli?"

"I'm going to stand by every word I said," Mario told him, "And I'll tell you why. I have carefully analyzed the Saudi investments and purchases—I got the details from an unimpeachable government source. And I've found there's nothing random about what the Saudis are doing. There is a distinct and very ominous pattern to what they're doing."

"A pattern," Gallagher said, "what type of pattern?"

"They started with the media and communications industries. And they're moving on to the transportation industry. Intercoastal was their first purchase, but they have already started accumulating other airline stock as well."

"So they have an investment plan," Mulvaney interrupted. "Every smart investor needs an investment plan."

"I think what Mr. Monelli is saying, is that the Saudis have a hidden agenda."

"That's *exactly* what I am saying," Mario said. "And the first item on that agenda is to control the flow of news. If the American public gets wind of what they're doing, the outcry will force the government to respond, no matter how many politicians have feathered their nests."

"Oh really," Mulvaney said sarcastically. "So why are they letting *you* spill the beans, Mario. You escaped their all-seeing eye?"

"Only accidentally," Mario said. "They didn't know what UBS had discovered. Even so, they're already buying UBS stock and, at the rate they're going, they'll control the network in a month or less."

A nervous mumbling swept through the trading floor audience.

"Tom, you better get in there," Fred warned, fearing a backlash. But Gallagher stood down. He was only taking orders from the control room.

"That doesn't mean they'd interfere with editorial decisions," Mulvaney said. "They're just interested in a profitable…"

"Profitable network?" Mario said, laughing. "Have you looked at UBS's earnings lately, Bart?"

"So maybe they think they're buying it on the cheap."

"They're buying it because they want to control content. That's exactly how a takeover of a foreign government begins," Mario said. "Ask your old poly sci professor buddies at Harvard, Bart. ABC and the *Chicago Sun Times* were just the beginning."

"What happened at ABC?" Tom Gallagher said.

"It's pretty simple," Mario replied. "ABC got hold of this information before I did, and they were planning to break it eight months ago. Then one of the Saudi shell companies got control of the network and killed the story. Fired the reporters, too."

The entire trading floor fell silent, in shock. Even Barton Mulvaney was speechless.

"You can prove this?" Tom Gallagher managed to ask.

"Your producer has sworn and notarized depositions, both from ABC's management and its editorial staff."

Watching this unfold on the monitor wall, Julie put her hand over her mike. "Marty, would you get on that right now? *The Times* is going to be demanding to see them tomorrow morning."

"I'll get on it right after the show," Marty told her.

"What I don't understand," Gallagher was saying, "is what their motive could be."

"I've spent a lot of time thinking about that, but I'm not sure," Mario admitted. "If they were simply investing, they'd want America to continue to be safe and stable. But this is a culture dedicated not to the global economy, but the globalization of Islam."

"The Royal family are *not* fundamentalists, Mario," injected Bart. "Most are western educated."

"Which makes their growing influence in America even more frightening," Mario exclaimed. "Tom, they're buying us with the blind...," Mario looked over at Bart, "or *not* so blind help of some of Wall Street's best and brightest—whose only loyalty is to money.

"If Washington doesn't do something about this, we're going to have another 9/11, this one aimed straight for the Fortune 100. It's an attack on the America *built* by people like my father, a common immigrant laborer, and Bart's father, a Wall Street zillionaire.

"You're right, Tom," Mario sailed on. "My opponent and I *are* from two different Americas. But we're *all* pawns on this chessboard now. And the Saudis are only a few moves away from a checkmate. We must stop them *now!*"

The entire trading floor audience burst into spontaneous applause, surprising both Gallagher and the UBS crew. Neil jumped onto a desk, vigorously twirling a towel and egging on the crowd. Julie, meanwhile, looked down at her monitor and saw Ayers and the camera crew in the frigid wind, watching the special from a small screen set up near the UBS van outside the NYSE. They were all grinning.

After a few moments, Gallagher spoke.

"In all my years in the news business," he said, "I don't think I have ever heard a more compelling plea." Then he remembered Bart. "What about *you*, Mr. Mulvaney, what do you have to say about all this?"

Bart, a spirited pugilist of the old school, was utterly vanquished, his face bloodied, his marbled body sagging, his noble ambitions sapped by the ubiquity of Mario's passionate uppercut. Only a will that exceeded his good sense kept him upright.

"Mr. Mulvaney."

Bart was just staring in the distance. He didn't realize Gallagher was addressing him. "Mr. Mulvaney?" Gallagher repeated himself.

Mulvaney's eyes narrowed. "Yes," he said in a voice devoid of spirit.

"Would you care to add comment?"

"I want everyone to know that I've been ambushed. I had no idea Saudi investment was going to be discussed, and I had no idea what the Saudis have been doing."

Then he stood up, removed his lapel mike, and walked off the set without further word. It was clear that he would not be coming out to fight another round. Off camera, Mulvaney's posse desperately tried to get him back on the set, but he brushed right past them.

"Ladies and gentlemen," Gallagher said, looking into the camera, "we'll be back in a moment."

Applause and cheering broke out on the Harrison Hart trading floor, and well-wishers and colleagues swarmed around Mario like paparazzi lining the Red Carpet on Oscar night, congratulating him, telling him it was a unanimous decision on all scorecards. Even George Van Wert. "You spoke very well," he said.

Mario didn't have time for any of it. Instead, he retrieved his coat, pushed his way past the adoring throng, and hurried toward the elevator banks. He was anxious to get back to the hospital—and Gus.

"Hey, Mario, where are you going?" someone yelled.

Mario stepped inside the elevator, pressed the button for the lobby, then looked up and grinned. "I'm going to Disney World," he said as the doors closed.

The program continued after the commercial break, but the debate was over. Next, viewers were treated to the opinions of a panel of political and financial experts, all of whom demanded that the federal government set up a fact-finding commission—and immediately rescind—all Saudi purchases of stock in any U.S. company.

The panel of experts was followed by focus group reports from cities all over America—dozens of ordinary citizens, outraged at their government's failure to spot and thwart the Saudi threat, some demanding an investigation, praising Mario's courage, and most of them dismissing Barton Mulvaney with contempt.

Just before Ayers began the close, with a stirring Murrow-like warning, Carleton Fisher appeared in the control room, Hank trailing behind him. The entire tech crew turned toward him and fell silent. Julie looked up to find Fisher approaching her, his face a picture of disapproval.

As she rose, ready to take her medicine, Fisher wrapped his arms around her, then, grinned broadly. "He was fantastic," Fisher said. "You knew all along the bad blood between them would draw Bart out. But what you did, young lady, was nothing short of mutiny."

"It took all the courage I could muster," Julie said.

"I want you to know that when I saw what you were doing, I came within an ace of aborting," Fisher admonished.

"What stopped you?"

Fisher held her at arm's length, shaking his head. "If there's one thing I've learned in all my years, it's to never argue with a woman's intuition."

"I can hardly wait to read the reactions in tomorrow's papers," said Hank.

"And on the networks," added Fisher. "The Today Show and Good Morning America have *already* requested footage.

"Hey, Julie, everyone's meeting over at Maxim's for a late-night steak and celebration," Tom said from the monitor. "How about joining us?"

"Sorry, can't," replied Julie, still thinking about Mario.

"Stop in at my office first thing tomorrow morning," said Miles, now back at the studio. "I think we have a contract to write." He winked and joined Fisher and Kozloff.

The moment Fisher and his entourage left the control room, the tech crew burst out into loud, prolonged applause, enough to make Julie applaud back to them. "This was truly a team effort," she reminded her crew.

Then she spoke into her mike. "Fred—Fred, can you hear me?"

The video feed was still visible on the center monitor and she saw Fred turn toward her. "I'm here."

"Is Mario still there? I want to congratulate him."

"Sorry, Julie. Elvis left the building as soon as it was over."

Julie threw her coat on and hurried to New York Downtown Hospital, where she learned that Gus was in ICU. Unwilling to wait for an elevator, she practically ran up the stairs, then down the hallway. She pushed the door to his room open—and found the bed empty, and freshly made. Mario was sitting in the corner on the floor, a lost, empty look on his face.

"Mario?" she said, rushing toward him. She knelt beside him and gently lifted his head. He looked down at his bloodied hand and her eyes followed. She touched his hand and it slowly opened for her. Inside was the necklace, bloodied, but still intact, the charm's tiny impression carved into his palm. Julie took the necklace from his palm, then wrapped her kerchief around his hand. She looked into his eyes, searchingly, and he looked into hers—then broke into sobs. She cradled him against her chest and they wept together, ignoring the unbridgeable gap that remained between them.

It was a grey, overcast, windy day at Resurrection Cemetery on Long Island. Six inches of dirty snow covered the ground, most of it there since New Year's night. In a far corner of the main burial ground, there was a coffin-shaped wound in the snow, exposing a rectangle of moist, dark earth.

The rectangle was surrounded by the chromed railings of the coffin lowering mechanism.

A small knot of people stood nearby: an overcoat-clad priest, tall, thin, delicate-looking; two grave diggers in jean jackets and worn coveralls, one leaning on his shovel, the other adjusting the lowering mechanism, and Mario, with his two sons, bundled against the wind.

Mario checked his watch. "You might as well go ahead, Father. I don't think anyone else is coming."

The grave diggers placed the coffin on the lowering straps and stood, ready to activate the framework that would sink it into the ground. The priest took his place at the head of the grave and opened his Bible.

Then Mario heard a car engine. He looked across the cemetery, through the grim, leafless trees and saw a bright yellow cab approaching quickly, on the curving cemetery road. "Hold on," he told the priest, and everyone watched as the taxi edged near.

The cab stopped along the path, a short distance from the newly dug grave, and two tall, well-dressed, light-skinned black men emerged, the slightly shorter one about Mario's age, the taller and trimmer one perhaps a few years older than Boomer. Mario and his sons watched them trudge through the snow and approach the gravesite.

"I'm glad you could come," Mario said, extending a hand to the older man. "I'm Mario Monelli. These are my boys, Boomer and Kyle."

"Augustus Shaw, Jr," the older man said. "My son, Andrew."

Mario sensed the emotional undertones in Shaw's voice. This wasn't just a son mourning his father, he realized. There was anger here, too, and disappointment, and resignation.

"When did you see your father last?"

Shaw pointed to Kyle. "When I was about his age. He disappeared, walked out on us."

"He was really hurting, Augustus."

"Yeah, my mother told me all about it." His eyes wandered to the coffin. "She never stopped loving him, you know, despite everything."

"He was an easy man to love," Mario said.

"We're you with him when…"

"…when he died? No. But he died with dignity," Mario said, even though he knew there was little dignity in dying alone.

"How long did you know each other?"

"Only a short while." Mario told the man, "but we grew very close in that time." He wanted Augustus to know that his father was a good man, a decent man. "He helped me through a rough period. My boy, too."

"Mind if I ask you a question? How did a man like you even get to know someone like my father?"

And Mario described the night in Cortlandt alley, and gave Gus Jr. a sense of their strong bond and the respect they each shared.

"Makes me wish I'd known him, too," Augustus admitted.

"You know, Dad," Andrew said, "I have grandmother's scrapbook of him." He looked at Mario and the boys. "She said he could've been a champion if it hadn't been for…you know…"

Augustus was looking at his son in surprise. "I guess your grandmother told you the stories, too," he said.

"She said she wanted me to know what kind of man my grandfather was." Then he looked at Mario. "Did he really live all those years on the street, Mr. Monelli?"

"That he did," replied Mario. "Now he'll always live in my heart."

"Sure wish I knew him," Andrew said.

"Maybe this will help." With his bandaged hand, Mario reached into his trench coat and pulled out Julie's blood stained kerchief. "Your grandfather wanted you should have something." He opened the kerchief folds and took out the necklace. "Joe Louis give 'im this the night he won the Golden Gloves. He was sixteen. Before he died, he said…he said to me, 'give this to my grandson. Tell him to always keep it close during his most trying times. And never let go…no matter how hopeless things may seem.'" He regarded for a moment the impression of the tiny boxing glove scarring his palm. "I know *I* never did." He placed the necklace into the young man's hand, then glanced at Augustus, who smiled and nodded his approval.

"Take good care of that, Andrew," Mario told him. "It's all he owned. Now it's yours."

"I will, Mr. Monelli."

"Here, let me." Augustus took the necklace, put it around his son's neck and fastened the clasp. "There. Just where it belongs."

The priest cleared his throat rather loudly. "Gentlemen, are we ready for the service now?"

Mario squeezed Boomer and Kyle's hands, and Augustus put his arm around his son's shoulder. "We're ready now, Father," Mario said.

"God, I love that Monelli bastard," said Randall Hollingsworth. "He took what I gave Carleton Fisher and blew the Saudis out of the water."

"You know anything about this guy, Mulvaney?" asked Deputy Director, Ben Hersh.

"Nothing that wasn't on the program," said Hollingsworth. "But we're going to keep a closer watch on that Blackwell Group he pimps for. I do have one piece of news, though."

"Which is?" asked Elliot Case.

"Milton Jaffe told me he plans to introduce a bill in the Senate to regulate foreign investment in the U.S., by country."

"If anyone can get anti-takeover legislation passed, it's Milton Jaffe," said Ben.

"Senator Jaffe, Randy?" asked Case. "I heard the senator was ill."

"He's dying," said Hollingsworth. "Liver cancer."

"Is there enough fight in the old boy to take on the president's billionaire conservatives?" Case asked.

"I remember a little colored girl, once upon a time, wanted to go to an all-white university. The state of Alabama said she couldn't. Milton Jaffe said she can." That was all Hollingsworth needed to say. "I'm going to give him the notarized originals of the Xeroxed documents I gave Fisher, plus all the electronic surveillance."

"You want me to run them over to his office, Randy?" Ben Hersh offered.

"No. They're all in a safe in my house in Massachusetts," Hollingsworth said. "I'm going to fly up and bring them back with me. I don't want the documents out of my sight until I see the senator."

CHAPTER TWENTY-FIVE

Julie awoke early the next morning, stumbled out of bed, started the coffee maker and went to retrieve the copy of *The New York Times* she knew she'd find waiting outside of her apartment door.

Then she walked back to the studio kitchen, poured herself a cup of coffee, and glanced at *The Times'* front page. One headline—just above the fold—took her breath away: *Wall Street Banker claims Saudis Plotting Economic Coup on United States.*

She speed-read the article. It was a recap of last night's UBS news special, written with plenty of "alleged" and "claimed" qualifications, detailing Mario's charges and theories, that, if true, threatened a scandal equal to Watergate.

Julie took her first sip of coffee. This was just the beginning, she realized. The world was about to change, and for just about everyone.

When she arrived at UBS, the newsroom was already in an uproar. Paige, who was on the phone, was the first to spot her. "Here, it's for you. They've been calling since 7:30."

Julie took the phone. It was Jean Bryson, *Newsday's* senior editor, asking for a telephone interview. Julie asked her to call back in the late afternoon. "That's after my deadline," the woman complained. "Sorry, I can't talk to you until then," Julie said.

Just as she was hanging up, Hank walked into her office. "You saw *The Times* piece?"

She nodded.

"Well, we've also had calls from *Newsweek, Harper's, The Washington Post, The Dallas Morning News,* and *The Wall Street Journal,* as well as the other networks—and the morning hasn't even begun."

"They want interviews?"

"Yes, but, as expected, the networks also want footage clearance. Every one of them intends to do a story on the evening news tonight," Hank said.

"Even ABC?"

"Yep, even ABC. 'The cat's out of the bag,' they said. 'No one's going to stop us from running the story now.'"

Julie leaned back in her chair and shook her head in amazement. "So what were the overnights—did we draw the ratings we hoped?"

"All the right people saw it," Hank said. "And that's all anyone cares about. I've already had half a dozen calls from friends at other networks, congratulating me."

Julie's phone rang once, then, a moment later, Paige buzzed her. "It's Jim Lehrer at PBS," she said.

"Tell him I'll call him back," Julie answered. She and Hank were grinning at each other, then Julie turned thoughtful.

Miles Corbin knocked on the doorframe and Julie waved him in. "Well," he said, "how's our little Joan of Arc today? Ready to take on another army?"

"Not quite," Julie said. "I'm still totaling up the loot from last night's victory."

"I just thought you'd like to know—I drove in from Connecticut this morning—it's on every radio talk show. The callers are livid. Laura Ingraham, believe it or not, said that if it's true, the president should be impeached. I don't even want to tell you what Imus said.

"Amazing!" said Hank.

"And here's some more news," Corbin said. "I've just been on the phone with Fisher. He's having lunch this morning with the Senate majority leader. Seems we ruffled many a feather on the Hill and up at 1600. So guess what we're going to do?"

"What are we going to do?"

"Fisher plans running the show...*again*, taped version, Sunday night, preempting the NFC Conference championship game. Half a dozen sponsors are already bidding. We'll have it out on DVD in a week. YouTube is *already* airing segments."

"You're kidding," said Julie, barely containing her excitement. This was turning out to be a bigger deal than everyone thought.

On the morning after the television special, the phone at Mario's bedside rang just a few hours after the round of parties thrown for him in pubs all around lower Manhattan, culminating with the uproarious celebration at the Lions' Den, all of which he'd forced himself to attend.

Mario picked up the phone on the third ring, hoping that the first two had been the result of a wrong number. "Yeah?"

"Mr. Monelli, Ed Thatcher of *The Wall Street Journal*. I'd like to do a piece on you for tomorrow's edition—hope I didn't wake you, by the way."

"Wake me? At five a.m. You gotta be kidding. Call me at the office."

"Of course. Sorry to have called so early, but my editor called me an hour ago and told me to get right on it, before anyone else got to you?"

"Anyone else?" Mario asked, but the caller was already gone.

Mario hung up the phone and it rang again before he could take his hand off the receiver. "Jesus Christ, what now?" he said.

"George Blevens of *The Washington Post*, Mario. We met about a year ago. Do you remember me?"

An image formed in Mario's mind, a picture of an unkempt little man with thick glasses and a heavy beard. "Yeah, I remember you, Blevens. What can I do for you at five in the morning?"

"Well, I've been assigned to investigate the Saudi story and I was hoping to get an hour of your time, this afternoon. I can fly up there. We can meet, oh say around two?"

"Don't know my schedule yet, Blevens. Call me late this morning and I'll let you know."

"I could do that," Blevens said agreeably.

The second call had awakened Phyllis. "Who's that on the phone?" she asked groggily.

"Newspapers. They want to do stories about last night's show," Mario explained.

The phone rang again and Phyllis turned over and put a pillow over her head.

Four more members of the press checked in before Mario went to work, and he told them all: He'd get back to them. And on the way into the city, he got three more calls, including one from *Business Week* and *US News and World Report*, these to his cell phone, the one with the unlisted number.

Mario sat in the Maserati, just one more car in the morning traffic, trying to make sense of the sudden attention. He'd thought that his fifteen minutes of fame would pretty much end after last night, despite Julie's warning months earlier that the press might pursue him. "They'll go after the Saudis," he'd said, "but *me*, they'll forget all about." Now he realized that wasn't going to happen.

He handed his car keys to Widell in the underground garage, and rode the basement elevator upstairs to the Winter Garden lobby. The security team playfully hounded him like groupies, pretending to be autograph seekers. Mario smiled, taking it all in stride.

Upstairs, as he approached his office, he could hear the phone ringing. He hurried to pick it up.

"Hello, Mario? It's Larry King."

"Larry King? *The* Larry King?"

"The very same—this *is* Mario, isn't it?"

"Yeah, Larry. What can I do for you?"

"For starters, you can come on my show tonight and talk about the Saudis with me."

"I thought you retired."

"Whatever gave you *that* idea? I haven't had a chance to look at that program you did last night, but everyone is telling me you were amazing. I want to give the Lion of Wall Street a chance to reach a, er, different audience. What do you say?"

"I say not tonight, Larry. I don't feel much like a lion. I'm exhausted. I got about three hours of sleep last night."

"Okay, well then what about tomorrow night—I'll bet you're not booked yet..."

Mario and the Zoo Crew spent most of their morning fielding calls from the pundits. By noon, Mario had given in to better than half the people who wanted to either write an article about him, ask him questions about the Saudis, or book him on their radio or television show.

On the very day Mario buried Gus, he participated in not one, but two different prime time, Sunday morning political television talk shows.

The first was ABC's This Week, with George Stephanopoulos.

"The Saudi ministry is quite upset, Mr. Monelli" Stephanopoulos began the discussion. "Not only have they demanded an apology from our state department, but they've recalled their ambassador. The White House has issued this statement in response."

Stephanopoulos rolled a clip of the White House Press Secretary's statement emphatically denying every allegation Mario made on UBS. When it was over, Stephanopoulos turned to Mario. "Pretty strong words. What are your thoughts?"

"George, step back and consider," Mario replied. "The Saudis have acquired wealth without working. They have made enormous profits without producing. They've stockpiled all the latest technological equipment, and yet they haven't any technology. They have trillions of dollars in the bank, but control no real capital. They have never demonstrated the capacity to convert their vast wealth into real power...until now. At the slightest scowl from Uncle Sam they sign any agreement, make any deal to assure Washington that they're our allies."

"If they aren't our allies" Stephanopoulos probed, "then exactly what *is* our relationship?"

"Examine the facts, George," Mario said. "Less than twenty-four hours before the attacks on 9/11, the Saudis pumped an extra nine million barrels of crude, most heading for the U.S. As a result, oil prices in the West remained low and U.S. inflation spiked marginally in spite of the single most devastating attack in history."

"Okay, let's assume you're right—they knew of the attack in advance. But why would they want to help us by pumping more oil prior to such an attack?"

"To keep their U.S. investments here safe, George. To keep the price of Middle East oil stable and protect their profits, while at the same time being careful not to inflame the radicals threatening their power."

An hour later, Mario was at NBC on Meet the Press, sitting across from David Gregory. It was a solo gig, thirty minutes, uninterrupted.

"Mario, why has Washington been so lethargic about regulating foreign investment in the United States?"

"Simple," Mario replied. "Because there are economic incentives for practically everyone—ex-presidents, former ambassadors, incumbent senators, and congressional and cabinet members. You play the game, keep your mouth shut, and the Royal family will take care of you, find you a job, perhaps fund a chair at a university or buy you a Lexus or townhouse in Georgetown. Is this the fulcrum we want the global economy to balance on?"

A few nights later, Mario found himself sitting across the comeback kid, a Larry King special that CNN had promoted shamelessly for a week as "the first real conversation with the Lion of Wall Street."

As soon as the show started, Larry hunched his shoulders, leaned forward and smiled. "You're considered a hero by millions, Mario, and we don't have many of those in America. I can't remember the country this galvanized since fifty American citizens were taken hostage outside the American embassy in Tehran."

Mario tried to shrug it off. "You have a question for me?"

"I have many," King chuckled. "But first let me start with *why*, Mario? Why has it been so easy for the Saudis to gain such a foothold in America?" Mario folded his hands and looked hard at King.

"Larry, most of the Saudis' U.S. investments are made through offshore entities. That lets them get around their own strict laws and conceals from us who the true purchasers are."

"And who *are* they?"

"They're the ones who run the country, who control the oil, and who pay protection money to the Islamicists, the people who take bribes and fly to Morocco whenever they want to get laid by someone other than their eleven wives…"

After the break, Larry took callers' questions for Mario. There were questions from every cross section of America, and Mario answered each of them, including the clueless ones, with patience and intelligence.

"Mario, tell me," Larry said, concluding the show, "what's happened since you exposed the Saudi plan? Has the Royal Family been stopped?"

"I wish I could be sure, Larry. I do know that the Eagle…"

"By Eagle you mean the SEC, correct?"

"Yes," Mario said. "The SEC is thoroughly investigating any entity trying to buy big blocks of stock in any major US company. The Royal Family isn't going to be able to hide behind fictitious buyers much longer."

"So they no longer pose a threat."

"I didn't say that. It'll make it harder to disguise these acquisitions to responsible banks and investment houses, making these deals more transparent. But I believe a few rogue Wall Street firms are actively cooperating with the Saudis. They're aware of the threat, but they're making a fortune in advising fees…"

The next day, it was more of the same, only this time on the radio with Rush Limbaugh, a booking he accepted against his better judgment. It was such a heated and hostile exchange that Mario declined further offers from the radio talk show bigmouths, even Hannity and Bill O'Reilly.

Toward the end of the week, Mario was lying in bed, half asleep, more or less watching the late night news, when he was startled to hear the anchorman announce that the U.S. Attorney General handed down indictments, charging two former U.S. Congressmen with fraudulently allowing the Saudi Royal Family to purchase stock in their names.

Next, it was a phone call from an investigative reporter from the *Huffington Post*, telling Mario the paper was about to break the story that the vice president of the United States had personally directed the Enforcement Division of the SEC—without the knowledge of the chairman—to "deep six" reports detailing Saudi stock purchases involving U.S. companies and their subsidiaries. "My editor told me to get your comment, and run with the story," the reporter said.

"I'm glad some of the high-level corruption has been uncovered," Mario told the reporter, "but this had better not be the last indictment. I'm sure there are plenty more involved."

That afternoon, Mario got a call from the dean of Harvard Business School. Would he be interested in being the guest lecturer in the Practical Business Ethics class this spring? The irony left Mario speechless for a moment—Harvard wants *me*? He thought. I ought to tell them to fuck themselves.

"Of course, there'll be a handsome honorarium," the dean said, sensing reluctance. "Shall we say $50,000?"

Then Mario thought about Boomer. "No need for that, dean. I'd be delighted to lecture. No charge. Just send me the details."

Ever since Keyes fished Mario out of the executive dining room and groomed him for better things, there'd been a tangible benefit just for being Mario Monelli—not only money, but friends and connections, and many other kinds of goodies. But now, thanks to his new-found celebrity, these tangible benefits got a huge upgrade, including increased demand for his advice, and higher fees.

A lot of the upgraded benefits involved pleasure. NFL Commissioner Roger Goodell extended an invitation to Mario to join him, as his guest, in the Commissioner's skybox at the Super Bowl in New Orleans. Not to be outdone, hockey czar Gary Bettman did the same.

Then there was the appearance on Letterman, a brief visit, but more than long enough for the genial talk show host to praise Mario's "lion-like courage" and to introduce the Lion of Wall Street to "one of your distant cousins," a real live lion, trotted out on stage and suitably tranquilized for the occasion. Mario petted the animal nervously, and jokingly asked if the segment was over yet. The next morning, the Today Show ran a clip of the whole thing.

That week, Dreamworks called Mario with an offer: would he take a small speaking role in Spielberg's next movie? Mario declined. Random House called with a book offer. "You don't have to write a word," they told him. "We'll have a first-rate ghost writer interview you. But it will be your name on the cover." Thanks, but no thanks, said Mario, seeing all this for what it was: people trying to ride the wave and capitalize off his name.

But there was nothing he could do to stop Phyllis from cashing in. "I called Katrina Wellborn," she told Mario one night. "We had a nice chat."

"She took the call—after that drunken scene New Year's?"

"I explained that I was having a diabetic reaction."

Mario laughed. "Too much alcohol in your sugar stream?"

She shot him a look. "She was very happy to hear from me, Mario. She invited me to a Monday afternoon museum fundraiser as her guest."

Mario didn't really know what to make of all this—the notoriety, the attention, the privileges, the publicity. It was a new life, new prestige, new prominence. He knew, he didn't really deserve it. He owed everything to Julie—and she was rarely out of his thoughts. He would have given up all the attention for a single evening with her. But he'd made a promise to stay out of her life, and he loved her enough to keep his word.

Most public scandals have a fairly short shelf life. Not "Saudigate," the moniker the media gave the affair. Instead of fading away, Saudigate—to Mario's amazement—gained steam with each passing week, as did the investigation that extended its tentacles in a score of new directions from Wall Street to the White House.

A month after the UBS special aired, the president held a nationally televised press conference. "Your name is going to come up, watch," Neil insisted and Dennis agreed.

"God, I hope not," Mario said, feeling the weight of his sudden celebrity. "Enough is enough."

After the president gracefully fielded a half dozen questions about his friendship with the Saudi Royal Family, the red-haired virago in the front row cleared her throat and, in her famous gravelly voice, put it to the Chief Executive.

"Well, Mr. President, since you tell us that your connections to the Royal Family are really just social acquaintances, I'd like to know your opinion of the man who brought this story to the attention of the American public, Mario Monelli."

A look of distaste flashed across the president's face, quickly, but not so quickly that an alert observer would have missed it. "I don't know Mr. Monelli personally," the president said, his aw-shucks smile finally asserting control over his features, "but I'm sure he's a good man and a fine Wall Street professional. I just don't believe most of his assertions are accurate."

"He oughta be impeached," said Barry.

"Then hung upside down...by his nuts," Dennis added.

"We can only hope so," Mario agreed.

Julie and Marty Cohen were talking about Mario when Hank walked into her office. Marty was first to greet him.

"I thought you'd like to know how the re-broadcast did. We have the Nielsen figures now," Hank said.

"Good news from the front, I hope?" Julie asked.

"Well, you decide. We got a forty-three point overall rating, and a seventy-two share."

"Seventy-two?" Marty was incredulous. "You mean that three-quarters of all the television sets that were on Sunday were tuned to the rebroadcast?"

"Those are Super Bowl ratings, Hank," Julie said, in awe.

"That's exactly what Carleton Fisher said, Julie," Hank told her. "By the way, he'd like to see you in his office this morning—at your convenience. I'm sure it's about your contract."

Julie smiled. "At *my* convenience?"

"That's the way he put it," Hank said. "And here's something else you'll enjoy: within minutes after the re-broadcast was over, we'd sold more than 200,000 copies on DVD—that's almost $4 million. Keep that in mind when you talk to Fisher."

"Maybe I'd better go see him *now*," Julie smiled.

Upstairs, Fisher came around his desk, took Julie's hand and held it warmly. "Come, my dear, sit with me," he said, leading her to the beige leather couch that overlooked the southeast window, the view dominated by the delicately carved spire of the Chrysler Building.

On the wall in front of them was a large plasma television set, carrying the UBS feed, alongside four smaller screens, one each for the other networks, all tuned into typical morning programs. The volume had been muted.

"So how's my star producer this morning?" Fisher asked.

Julie felt the beginnings of a blush. "I don't think..."

"You've seen the new numbers?"

Julie nodded. "Very gratifying."

"More than that, Julie. It's the beginning of a turn-around for us. We're not out of the woods yet, but we're on our way."

"In other words, it's becoming a Carleton Fisher network," Julie said.

Fisher laughed. "Don't lay it all on me, Julie. You've played a vital role. And I need you to continue to *fill* that role.

"So, I want to make the relationship official. I've had legal draw up a contract. It comes with a $100,000 signing bonus. Also, I'm doubling your base pay."

The whole thing blew her away. All the uncertainty, all of the risks she'd taken—and now this. She wished Jack were alive to see it. She wished…she wished she could tell Mario.

"Did you catch the attorney general on *Face The Nation*?"

"What did the old wind bag have to say?" Julie asked.

"Plenty," Fisher replied. "The Justice Department is raising the flame under the kettle. Insiders tell me two congressmen plan on calling a press conference within the week. I expect both to resign, you know, to 'spend more time with their families.'"

"Oh, how touching," Julie replied.

"Anyway, Tom is down there waiting for the story to break."

Just then, something on one of the television screens across from them distracted Fisher. Julie followed his gaze. CBS had interrupted regular programming with a special report. Fisher reached for the remote and turned up the volume.

"…witnesses told police that the plane exploded in a brilliant flash of light moments after takeoff. NTSA agents are expected to arrive within the next few hours, and the FBI won't comment about suggestions that the crash had suspicious causes…"

Fisher flipped to CNN, which was just breaking the story.

"…his wife and teenage daughter were also reported to be aboard the plane…"

"Who's wife?" Fisher directed his question at the bank of television sets, flipping to ABC, which was just interrupting "The View."

"…Randolph McDaniel Hollingsworth, Chairman of the U.S. Securities and Exchange Commission was returning to Washington from his home in Weston, Massachusetts…."

"My God," Fisher said, looking over at Julie with undisguised horror. Then he switched channels again, this time to UBS and John Ayers.

Another channel switch.

"…will not confirm that a SAM missile struck the Hollingsworth plane, causing the deaths of the SEC chairman, his wife, and teenage daughter, in addition to the pilot…"

Fisher cut back to Ayers, who was interviewing someone, split-screen.

"…too early to make any kind of comment about a missile or a bomb," said Frank Rhegetti, NTSA accident investigator according to his title.

"Is there any evidence that this may have been an assassination?" Ayers asked.

"It could have been engine failure. We just don't have any information."

Rhegetti disappeared from the screen, which filled with Ayers' image. He was holding a hand to an ear. "Yes," he said. "Go ahead and run it." He looked up. "Ladies and gentlemen, I'm told we have that tape now."

Ayers' image vanished, replaced by a shaky shot of two seven year olds in red and green snowsuits, laughing, running, and ineffectively throwing snowballs at each other. Then, in the background, a small private plane appeared, angling toward the sky. Whoever had been filming the kids tilted the camera up to follow the aircraft.

Suddenly, a small, bright spot appeared underneath the plane, at ground level, then shot into the sky and rammed the aircraft, which instantly exploded in a spectacular fireball. The camera sank, to follow the debris falling from the sky, and once more, the laughing youngsters appeared in the frame.

"Julie, I want you go home and pack a few things. Then I want you to check into the Waldorf immediately."

She was startled. "Why," she asked, "do you think I might be in danger?"

"I don't know," Fisher said, reaching for the phone. "But I don't want to take any chances. Maybe this will be enough for them, then again, maybe it won't."

"Enough for whom? What do you mean?"

"I think the Royal Family has just sent us a message," Fisher said.

Five minutes later, Julie was racing through the chaotic newsroom. Once in her office, she phoned Mario, telling him what had happened, suggesting he take a vacation.

"It's nice to know you're worried about me," Mario said.

"Of course I'm worried about you, Mario. They've just killed Randy Hollingsworth, and you could be next on their list."

"What about you?"

"Fisher is having me check into the Waldorf for awhile. Now what about that vacation?"

"Impossible. We're up to our ass in paranoia. Every company thinks they're next on the Saudi hit list."

"Would you consider hiring a bodyguard?" she asked, almost imploring.

"Sure. Want the job?"

"Stop joking. Please."

"I think you may be getting a little over yourself. But I'll tell you what I'll do—no more media appearances, no more interviews. I'll lay low."

After a week at the Waldorf, and no threats or attacks on anyone else, Julie decided to take her chances on living normally. But she followed the Hollingsworth investigation closely. The NTSB confirmed that explosives caused the crash, but it was unable to make a conclusive judgment about the apparent missile on the videotape.

Washington, however, reacted as though there were no question that Hollingsworth's death was an assassination. The Democrat-dominated House of Representatives easily passed a measure that prohibited foreign countries from acquiring more than a set number of U.S. firms or investing a certain amount in America, the figures based on U.S. GNP. And Julie was delighted when her old friend Senator Milton Jaffe and his blue dog Democrats announced a similar bill in the Senate, with the added provision that some of the Saudi purchases would be disentangled and reversed.

But Julie knew that the steam was leaking out of the reform movement. The administration had fired a few West Wing officials, the president had denied complicity so often the public was beginning to believe him, and the Republican leadership in the Senate was proposing toothless measures that seemed to have a better chance of passing than Jaffe's stringent ones.

At Harrison Hart, Mario's life was slowly returning to something resembling normal, the crowds that camped outside his home grew sparse, partly because he was now turning down all public appearance. It wasn't just that he had come to dislike celebrity and the invasion of privacy that comes with it. He had two more reasons to cool it.

First, there was Tyler, who observed that the partners thought it would be good if Mario retreated from the limelight and concentrated on business. In addition, Mario was taking serious flak from the Lions' Den members. "Your celebrity is endangering our investment *and* our anonymity," was the consensus.

So Mario stopped saying yes to the media—a decision that detracted from the story's attention—and tried to stay out of the public eye. Nevertheless, he'd finally become a man of stature among his peers. No longer was his face pressed against a plate glass window, a fact of which he was reminded late in March when he got a gilt-edged invitation to the famous "Prosperity Ball," where the kings and princes of Wall Street mingled with captains of business and industry from the world over, and with powerful politicians and world leaders past, present, and future. This year, it was being held at the Encore in Las Vegas, the newest and most luxurious "in your face" hotel in the world.

He showed the invite to Tyler.

"Looks like you've arrived," Tyler said.

"Seems that way," Mario admitted. "I assume you'll be going, too?"

"Invited every year," Tyler said, trying half-heartedly not to sound condescending. "Oh yes, and one more thing: I think it would be best if you left your wife at home. Unless you plan on burying her in the desert."

Tyler smiled and departed, leaving Mario to his thoughts. The Prosperity Ball, where the *Haves* meet the *Have Mores*. He wondered whether Rick would be there—and if he was, would he be ready to forgive him?

Roger Duvall slowly became aware of a noise, a rude, impatient pounding. He struggled to open his eyes, curious about what might be causing it. Beside him, in bed, lay the young Greek God, eighteen years old, he hoped, naked and oblivious. The result of too much wine and way too much weed.

The pounding continued. Roger dragged himself out of bed and slipped into his favorite purple silk bathrobe. What was going on, he wondered. Was the loft on fire? He took the freight elevator down to the front door.

Two nondescript men in dark suits and sunglasses were waiting for him. He huddled behind the door to escape the draft and opened it. "What is it?" he said irritably.

"Roger Duvall?"

Duval sighed. "Yes. And who, may I ask, are you?"

"Special Agent, Rod Brooks, FBI," said the taller one. They flashed their badges.

"Special Agent, Thomas X. Martin," said the shorter one. "Would you please get dressed and come with us, sir?"

"What? Now? Why?" Roger was both frightened and surprised.

"You're wanted for questioning."

"Look, if it's about the boy, he assured me he was over eighteen."

The FBI agents looked at each other expressionlessly. "Please get dressed sir," the taller one repeated.

Roger went back upstairs, the FBI agents accompanying him, and he slipped into something casual, then grabbed his shearling bomber jacket. Whatever this is, Roger thought, I'll be back in an hour. He didn't want to wake the boy.

But he emerged from his bedroom to see Mutt and Jeff tossing his place, spilling out drawers, going through papers, sweeping video tapes into a bag. "I hope you have a warrant," Roger said. Neither agent bothered to answer.

The shorter one headed for the bedroom, and a few minutes later, the boy stumbled into the living room, totally naked. "Any drugs you find aren't mine," he told one of the agents. "They're his."

"Thanks a lot," Roger said sarcastically.

At a nearby FBI field office, a team of agents began by questioning Roger's parentage. His father was middle eastern, he said, but his mother was American, and he was born in the U.S. "Why do you want to know about my parents?" he asked, disturbed by this line of questioning.

"We'll ask the questions," said Agent Martin. "Now tell us about your father. Was he Egyptian or Syrian? What connections did he have to Al Qaeda?"

"Al Qaeda? You've gotta be kidding. I don't have any idea. I've only met him twice, when I was a kid."

"Okay," the agent said, putting that one aside, "Now, could you tell us about these?"

He showed Roger the post-it note found in the dockside warehouse and a fax of his signed wire transfer for $200,000 to the Syrians' Swiss bank account.

Now Roger realized what this was all about—or he thought he did. "Look, I'm just an interior designer. I haven't done anything illegal. I just paid a man for some art works, and if it was illegal to take them out of their country of origin, I don't know anything about it."

"Don't try to snow us," said Agent Brooks. "We know your Syrian contact is an Al Qaeda financier. We also know you didn't pay $200,000 for some smuggled art works. We have a pretty good idea what was in that package, and you're going to save yourself a lot of grief if you just level with us. Where is the package now?"

Duval was mystified, but desperate to clear himself. "There's nothing mysterious about it, er, them. They're just a pair of ancient granite lions I picked up on the black market. I had no idea that the Syrian was involved in anything else—especially Al Qaeda."

"Tell us what you know about the recent Massachusetts Air Charter flight crash."

"My god! You don't think I had anything to do with that."

Agent Martin looked at Duvall coldly. "Do you know about the laws that prevent the FBI from torturing prisoners?"

"Yes, I remember when they were passed."

"Well, we don't," Agent Brooks said, connecting two wires to a rotary transmitter, with a gleam in his eye. "We haven't been informed yet, right, Tom?"

The interrogation lasted for hours with the agents grilling Roger over and over again about "the package" and about the wire transfer, Roger's father, and the airline disaster. By the time they were finished, Roger was so terrified that he had wet his pants and told them everything he knew about the Lions' Den, but the agents didn't believe him. They were sure they'd uncovered the secret terrorist cell CIA intelligence had been months looking for.

After the initial questioning, to Roger's great surprise and dismay, they'd didn't say, "hey, go home, this is all a silly mistake." They arrested. When Roger hysterically protested and cited his civil liberties and voiced tearful demands for a lawyer, the agents laughed him off. Instead, they flew him in shackles to Charleston, South Carolina, without allowing him a phone call, imprisoned him in a brig aboard a Navy warship, where he awaited to be transported to Guantanamo Bay and classified as an enemy combatant.

CHAPTER TWENTY-SIX

On the limo ride to Teterborough Airport in New Jersey, the home base of many New York area corporate jets, Tyler spent most of his time on the phone, as usual. And the phone calls continued on the flight to Vegas on Harrison Hart's private Gulfstream jet.

Mario, on the other hand, was lost in thought. The last few months had truly been eventful—the Lions' Den, Julie, the television special, the departure of Rick Bernard, his guilt over Danny and Gus's death.

Most of it had been resolved, one way or another, as often as not, painfully. But what had happened with Rick—and Danny—was still an open wound. That was one reason he'd accepted the invitation to come to the Prosperity Ball, the hope that Rick would be there. He couldn't let that friendship die.

By the time they landed on the tarmac and taxied up to the VIP section of Las Vegas's McCarran International Airport, a stretch white limousine was already waiting for them. Soon afterward, Mario was ensconced in an executive suite at the Wynn Las Vegas, the most luxurious hotel in the world.

It was one of the grandest hotel rooms Mario had ever seen, with its wall-to-wall and floor-to-ceiling windows, and its panoramic view—the twinkling architecture of Las Vegas on one side, the great mountains rising from the desert floor that surrounds the city, on the other.

By itself, the room was remarkable enough—and of course the Wynn Resort, with its country club, casino, restaurants, night clubs, etc., etc.—was more than a match for the accommodations, although maybe not for the Lions' Den. But what was really amazing to contemplate was that on this weekend, the entire place was filled with a good percentage of the most prominent business people in the world.

Who knows, Mario thought, above him a queen might be primping. Next door, the CEO of one of the world's largest companies might be shaving. On the other side, it might be a Supreme Court justice and his wife, and on the floor below, perhaps, a prime minister.

The Prosperity Ball—at least that's what they were calling it this year. In previous years, it went by a different and more honest name: the Predator's Ball. It had been the ultimate celebration of greed and acquisition, by some of the most rapacious and most acquisitive men alive. It was a celebration of money, and its accumulation by any means, the rest of humanity be damned, a celebration sponsored by Michael Milken.

But, what with the scandals—Boesky, Kozlowski, Madoff, Enron, and AIG just to mention a few, greed had became a naughty word, as non-PC as a racial slur. And the image that came to mind when the word "Predator" was uttered had burdened it under the dead weight of its history.

And so, someone with good PR sense had renamed the thing, and Milken had ceded the event to people free of scandal, and now we had the Prosperity Ball, which had a nice, egalitarian ring to it, and which didn't draw attacks from the socialists, the communists, the poor, or the middle class, none of whom realized it wasn't meant for them.

With an afternoon to kill—the main event would be that evening—Mario slipped into casual clothes and took a stroll along the Wynn Esplanade, outside, window shopping at Cartier, Vuitton, and Chanel, then browsing at Wynn Penske Ferrari-Maserati. It wasn't just the affluent who were buying whatever caught their eye, it was the women they had brought.

This is something for which this annual event was justly famous—and why the power elite rarely brought their wives. Instead, they either brought their mistresses or selected companions from the apparently endless supply of unattached beauties and dinner whores who could be found almost anywhere at the resort, for nowhere, and at no time was it more true that "What happens in Vegas, stays in Vegas."

After a late afternoon massage, Mario returned to his room, changed into a cashmere sport jacket and a pair of woven silk trousers and took the elevator down to the ballroom level. He was getting hungry, but he knew the Lafitte Ballroom would feature tables overflowing with every imaginable delicacy and open bars that could accommodate any taste.

It was relatively early in the evening, but people were already beginning to filter into the grand ballroom. It was an odd crowd—mainly older men, accompanied mostly by much younger women—all acting out the age-old attraction between beauty and money.

There was Bill Gates, choosing an appetizer from a silver plate, sharing a laugh with Carl Icahn and George Soros. Not far away, Warren Buffett was conversing intently with Sumner Redstone. And beyond them, Mario noticed Michael Dell arguing with Marc Cuban, or maybe it was the other way around. For a moment, Mario felt like a little boy catching a glimpse of Joe DiMaggio. But here he was, amazingly enough, one of the guests at the world's most exclusive party.

Mario wandered around the ballroom, sampling the food tables, getting himself a dirty martini, circulating among the guests, and listening to snatches of conversation, usually about money or politics. He finally chose a position at a far wall, where he could watch the entire spectacle, listen to the orchestra, and, hopefully, spot Rick.

After a few minutes, Tyler found him. "Glad you came?"

"I feel as though I'm on some kind of movie set," Mario replied.

"Well, there's no better place in the world to network," Tyler said. "And I mean just that. Come with me. There's some people I want you to meet."

Mario obediently accompanied Tyler on a tour of the room, getting introduced to important people from many fields. Some of the people Mario met discreetly mentioned seeing him on television, but most stuck to commenting on Tyler's introduction—"Mario is one of the most talented merger specialists on Wall Street. He just received the Frost and Sullivan strategy award in Palo Alto and was named best executive at the tenth annual Wall Street business awards."

While he shook hands and made small talk, Mario let his eyes drift over the crowd, searching for Rick. He had a friendship to save, to revive, and renew. But he couldn't find him. He did spot someone else, however.

There she was, in a fetching blue silk dress, looking more beautiful than ever, her hair swept over her ear, just grazing her shoulders. She didn't see him, and he took the opportunity to indulge himself in the sight of her, catching a flash of her green eyes, then a moment of her smile, then the graceful motion of her hair when she turned her head.

Standing there, halfway across the room, Julie was animatedly talking with Carleton Fisher and another man, an older man. Mario thought he looked familiar, but couldn't quite place him.

Then, suddenly and unexpectedly, she turned and saw Mario. He felt himself smile and, after a moment of indecision, she smiled back at him. Then she turned to her companions.

"Tyler, who's the old guy talking with Julie and Carleton Fisher?" Mario asked. "I can't quite place him."

"You don't know who that is?" Tyler asked surprised. "That's Senator Milton Jaffe, heads the Senate Commerce Committee. He's about to introduce legislation that what would limit foreign investment here."

"I see," Mario said, unable to take his eyes off Julie.

"Stay the hell away from him," Tyler warned, "he's a shark hunter. Broke Haldeman in half during Watergate summer."

Mario weighed the warning and found himself walking in her direction.

"Hi, Julie," he said. "You're looking beautiful."

She blushed. "Hi, Mario."

"Good to see you again, Mr. Monelli," said Carleton Fisher, shaking his hand.

"Mario," said Julie, "I'd like you to meet someone. This is Senator Milton Jaffe. I told you about him, remember? Senator, this is Mario Monelli."

They shook hands. "I knew you looked familiar," Mario said.

"Your face is familiar to just about everyone," Jaffe replied. "I missed your original appearance on television, but caught the rebroadcast. You were quite magnificent."

"Thank you," Mario replied.

"Carl, Julie—will you excuse me and Mr. Monelli for a moment?" The senator gently put an arm on Mario's shoulder and guided him away.

"Certainly," Julie said.

"Are we going somewhere?" Mario asked, surprised.

"I thought we would get ourselves a drink. There's something I'd like to discuss with you." He started walking and Mario went along, taking a path around the couples dancing to the orchestra music.

"You know that I'm sponsoring a bill in the Senate intended to put strict limits on foreign investment here."

"I've been reading about that. I hope you succeed."

"Then you also know that it promises to be a tremendous fight."

"You're not optimistic?" Mario was a little surprised. "I thought everyone was clamoring for legislation regulating foreign investment."

"If by 'everyone' you mean the American public, you're right. But if you include Washington, that's an entirely different story."

Mario was genuinely perplexed. "But wouldn't anyone who opposes your bill be committing political suicide?"

Jaffe sighed deeply. "Oh, no one will do it publicly, Mario. They'll amend the bill to death or just find a way to sabotage it without being blamed for its failure. After all, it *is* Washington."

This was making no sense to Mario. "What can they possibly say against it?"

"Well for one thing some feel it will infuriate our European allies, who have heavily invested here—like Holland, Germany, France...even the Brits."

"Why not restrict it to Saudi Arabia?"

"Not so easy, Mario. Is Saudi Arabia the government of the country or is it the Royal Family? If you look at what they've been doing, the majority of purchases are by individual members of the kingdom.

"How can we prohibit individuals from investing?" Jaffee asked. "Look, we both know the country is in danger, Mario," he said grimly. "So does almost half the Senate. Somehow, I have to convince a few more of my colleagues."

Mario shook his head, disgusted. "What could they be thinking?"

"Money, that's what they're thinking," Jaffe said. "Like you said on Larry King, many of them are making a fortune from the Saudi purchases. But even those who aren't, are afraid what will happen to the American economy if Saudi Arabia, even China, stops dumping billions into it. They sincerely believe that poses a much greater threat than letting the Saudis continue. That's why I need you in my corner, Mario," Jaffe said earnestly.

"What can *I* do?" Mario asked, gnawing his teeth at what he anticipated the senator would ask.

"If I'm ever to rally enough congressional support, I'll need you to testify before the Senate Subcommitee on Foreign Investment."

"Me? Why me?" Mario asked.

"Because you have a fetish for ethics. Your testimony would put tremendous pressure on those senators who are open to persuasion."

"Senator, all the hard information I cited came from the SEC. They're the one performing the autopsies on all these takeovers."

"That's not enough. What I need is someone who can expose Wall Street's underbelly, its dirty business and dirty secrets. And you bring something to the table that I can't find anywhere else, passion…conviction…genuine patriotism."

"I hate to say this, senator, but that's just being a mascot. I don't know how that would convince any senator to change his mind and vote for your bill."

Jaffe laughed, more ruefully than with good humor. "You're overestimating our senators, Mario. They're gawkers and gossips, just like everyone else in America. Celebrity impresses them. They'd be in awe of you, and impressed that someone of your stature and integrity would be willing to testify in front of them on a national stage."

Integrity? Me? Mario chuckled to himself, imagining the expression on the old boy's face if he ever learned of the fuckfest he shepherds on Ward's Island. "Even if I have nothing new to say?" Mario said.

"Your appearance would persuade the American people all over again that the Saudis must be stopped—and the senators would feel the heat, believe me. I think it would gain us at least three votes. You're a hero, Mario, and everyone loves a hero."

None of this was what Mario wanted to hear. He had good reasons, very good reasons, to avoid the hearings at all costs. Testifying would just be inviting catastrophe. Some hot-shot playing Woodward and Bernstein could find out about the Lions' Den and set off a tabloid feeding frenzy, putting member identities at risk. He'd be a pariah, not a hero, even in the eyes of the Zoo Crew. Even his own family would hate him. This old geezer would end up hating him, too, the revelations jeopardizing passage of his bill. And there was no way he could explain this to the senator.

"It's your zeal that would excite them, Mario. Your sincerity. Your ability to cut through all the bullshit and break things down so even a child can understand them, just as you did that night. You know you're one of the most trusted figures in America?"

"That's ridiculous."

"Ask the president if it's ridiculous. Your poll numbers are better than *his*."

"So I should risk having my family wind up like Hollingsworth's?" Mario asked.

"They would have killed you already," Jaffe said, behind hardened eyes. "But they won't. You still got a lot of light on you. So their only recourse is to discredit you like big tobacco did to Wigand. Oh, not the Saudis of course. They'll just try and intimidate you. You're the last person they want testifying in front of the Senate. No, I'm talking about the enemies within. In Washington…and on Wall Street."

Tyler was right, Mario thought. He should have kept his distance from this man. He was persuasive and persistent.

"I know what I'm asking, Mario," Jaffe said. "I know how much courage it will take. But if there's one thing I've learned during my tenure in the Senate: advocating a cause isn't enough. You have to be willing to risk everything. That's where true greatness lies."

Mario nodded thoughtfully, trying to find a way out of the bear trap.

"Jack Chambers had that greatness, too, you know," Jaffe said. "He put his life on the line to tell a story, to tell the nation the truth. He *lost* his gamble, but what a noble effort it was." Then he looked toward Julie. "I imagine that's what Julie loved most about the man." Jaffe was playing all his aces, Mario thought.

"How do you know I'm that kind of man?" Mario asked.

"Because you've already demonstrated it on television. And because I know that Julie wouldn't risk her reputation on a coward. Nor would she her heart."

They were approaching Julie now, having circled around the room.

"Would you give it serious thought?"

"I'll think it over and let you know."

"You'll let him know what?" Julie asked, coming to meet them.

"I've been asking Mr. Monelli to appear before my hearing," Jaffe said. "He's a tough nut to crack."

"I see," said Julie, mischief in her eyes. "Well, maybe I can persuade him a bit."

At that moment, the ballroom's orchestra struck up a gorgeous melody, and a number of couples stepped out onto the hardwood dance floor.

"Would you care to dance?" Mario asked Julie

"That's up to the senator. I'm *his* date tonight."

"You two young kids go ahead," Jaffe said and smiled.

Mario presented himself to Julie and, in a moment, his arms were around her and they glided across the floor as though they'd been dancing for a lifetime.

"I was surprised to see you here," Mario said, whispering into her ear.

"When the senator asked me to come, I just couldn't say no, especially now."

"Now?"

"He's been ill."

"I see."

"So what did you two gents talk about?"

"He wants me to get me up in front of a packed circus and repeat my last performance."

"Well, you always told me you wanted to see Washington."

"Not from *that* angle," said Mario.

"What did you tell him?"

"I told him keep dreaming, speaking of which, I had a great one about *you* last night."

"You had a dream…about *me*?" she asked skeptically.

"Wanna hear it?" he said with a glint of mischief in his eye. "Don't worry, it's clean."

"Sure, go ahead," she playfully dared him.

"Well for starters, we were in Bora Bora, lying next to each other in one of those glass-bottom, thatched huts…"

The music swelled and Mario gave Julie a fancy twirl that left them both grinning, and drew appreciative looks from some of the nearby dancers. There was a difference in Julie, and this time Mario knew what it was—her defenses were down and the disappointment was gone.

"You're not still angry with me?"

"Oh, I'm still angry, or at least I should be," she said without sounding angry at all, "but I've never had a good memory for anger."

"When we get back to New York…" Mario started, working up his courage, "can I see you again?"

"Mario, we've already been through…"

"I've asked Phyllis for a divorce, Julie." The playfulness was gone.

"I can't listen to…" she tried to pull away.

"You *will* listen," Mario said, firmly holding her back. "Frank is trying to work out an arrangement that'll let me keep the boys."

"But you'll lose everything you've worked for," she said, gazing into his eyes.

"You'll never have anything, unless you risk *everything,*" he said. "And I'm holding everything that matters, right here."

"What about that Lions' Den club of yours?" she asked.

"I'm through with it," Mario offered immediately.

They continued to dance, but there was no more talking about the past. They were making repairs, the sort of repairs that make whatever was broken more durable.

Mario and Julie remained together on the dance floor for several more dances, holding each other, talking softly into each other's ears. And then she said, "Hey, big boy, would you mind dancing me over to the ladies room?"

"Not at all," Mario said, twisting back to see where she wanted to go.

She slipped out of his arms and disappeared into the ladies' room. Mario took up station outside the door, to wait, still searching for signs of Rick.

Julie was back in a few minutes, but Mario scarcely had time to greet her before he was approached by two swarthy, dark-haired young men in flawless business suits and white and red checkered headdresses.

"Mr. Monelli?" said one.

"Yes? What can I do for you?"

"Would you mind coming with us, sir? Please." It sounded more like a command than an invitation.

"Would I come with you *where*?"

"Our employer wishes to have a word with you."

Julie spoke out now. "Who is your employer?"

"That will become apparent."

"Why all the mystery?" Julie asked, worried.

"I assure you, my employer just desires a brief meeting. There's no danger of any kind."

Mario turned to Julie. "Why don't you get us both a drink while I see what this is all about." He gave her a peck on the cheek and a reassuring smile."

Mario and the two Arab men took the express elevator directly to the Tower Suite. When the door opened, the two young men stepped out and disappeared, and Mario found himself alone in another world. He'd seen luxurious settings before. He'd visited the finest hotels in the world. He'd been a guest in the homes of men who were fabulously rich. But this was something truly incredible to behold. It was the fantasy of a person with unlimited and unimaginable wealth.

This, Mario told himself, is what the Taj Mahal must look like on the inside—pillars of filigreed gold, walls of intricately inlaid tile, covered with billowing red, orange and blue silk panels, a marble floor spread with huge, multicolored Persian rugs, and topped off by a golden dome inset with circular windows that offered a panoramic view of the surrounding landscape and Vegas strip—a feature he'd glimpsed from outside the building.

Except for the hard reality of it all, Mario thought, he might have entered the Disney version of Aladdin. He wouldn't have been surprised if a troupe of half-naked Arabian belly dancers emerged from behind the drapes, clinking tiny finger cymbals and engaging in the kind of sinuous body movements that could hypnotize a cobra.

Then someone *did* emerge from behind the drapes, a tall, black-haired, black-eyed, dark-complexioned man, a bit on the heavy-set side, his expensive suit so well tailored that his heft was hard to spot. He radiated power and self-confidence, but there was also a controlled ferocity to him. Pinned to his suit lapel was a small, jeweled red crescent. He motioned to his personal bodyguard.

"That will be all, Aziz," he said.

He waited till Lt. Aziz left the room, then extended a hand and smiled the way hunters smile when they have their prey in their sights. "Well, well, Mr. Monelli, we meet at last."

Mario returned the smile, unfazed. "And you are?"

The man momentarily inclined his head toward Mario, in a sort of perfunctory bow. "I am Mohammed bin Sa'ud bin Abd al-Aziz Al Sa'ud al-Kabir, the Crown Prince and Heir Apparent of Saudi Arabia."

Mario stared for a moment. Fuck me. He wasn't ready for a face-to-face conversation with the future king of Saudi Arabia—and he hoped that conversation was all the Heir Apparent had in mind. He took a deep breath. "I'm pleased to meet you, Your Highness."

"As I am, Mr. Monelli, " said the Crown Prince. "Won't you please join me for some tea." He gestured toward two big chairs covered in elaborate multi-toned brocade.

"Actually, I'm keeping someone waiting downstairs."

"Miss Chambers will be just fine, I assure you."

The two men sat down across from each other. Then the Crown Prince clapped his hand, and a lithe Arabian serving girl, appeared from behind the drapes, carrying a silver tea service. The men watched her silently as she poured, her eyes locking with Mario's over the silk veil that partially covered what Mario was sure was a lovely face.

"You didn't have to search me out," Mario observed.

"Of course I did. I had to meet the man who has had such a major impact on my life and that of my future kingdom." He offered Mario a cigarette from a sterling silver case. Mario declined, but the Crown Prince indulged.

"That's a two-way street," Mario said.

The Crown Prince smiled his intimidating smile. "Yes. I saw the television appearance that made you so famous. Very impressive performance."

"Thank you," Mario said.

The Crown Prince's smile faded and disappeared. "That doesn't mean I liked what you had to say."

"I understand. I've put a wrench in your plans."

The Crown Prince looked at Mario sharply, then smiled and stirred his tea.

"So tell me, Mr. Monelli, how are your sons? I understand your oldest is about to enter college."

"That's right," Mario said, feeling a momentary cold chill. "They're just fine, thank you."

"I have children, too. Seventeen of them. Two of them are going to Harvard. Maybe they will cross paths with your boy," he said, sipping his tea.

"Maybe so." God, he hoped not.

"Are you enjoying your stay in Las Vegas?" the Prince inquired.

"Yes. I come here often. It's one of my favorite places."

"Really?" said the Crown Prince, feigning surprise. "I'd think you were getting all the entertainment you could handle on that little island off Manhattan that you and your *Zoo Crew* frequent."

Mario almost scalded his lips on his tea. "You know a lot about me," he said.

"Well," said the Crown Prince, "you *are* a very famous man...one with a... rather salacious appetite for life's pleasures, even by Saudi standards."

Mario had no idea where this was going, but he didn't like it. It reminded him of that scene in "The Godfather" where Michael, aware of his brother-in-law's treachery, toyed with him, just before killing him.

The Crown Prince took a long sip of his tea and leaned forward. "If I were you," he said, "I'd stay out of the public eye for awhile. Perhaps forever. I think you've made enough TV appearances. And I see no reason for you to attend any congressional hearings or to speak to any government investigators."

"And if I don't, what do you have in mind for me?" Mario asked mildly. "Another plane crash?"

"Don't be so melodramatic, Mr. Monelli. Some of my cousins are hot-headed and they are occasionally over-zealous, as I am sure you are aware. But I have no intention of causing you or your family any personal grief. I am not a violent man. In fact, I am a very generous man. I hope you will give me the opportunity to prove that."

"That's not likely," Mario said. "Anyhow, your offer of generosity seems wrapped around a threat."

"On the contrary, I am merely informing you. If Senator Jaffe's bill moves through the Congress, your president will have no choice but to sign it. That would be most inconvenient for my people."

"You mean the radicals you lost control of?"

"Sure, its no secret we've lost control of our country," admitted the Crown Prince. "And our citizens are slaughtering yours. But you can depend on us to keep your cars on the road and your houses warm. And, by the way, you'll feel better if you don't think about the unpleasant reality that your oil bank is sitting on dangerously shifting sands."

Mario laughed, which caused the Crown Prince to grin. "You find something I said amusing to you, Mr. Monelli?"

"That's your threat? You'll cut off our oil? We both know oil is fungible. The only way you can cut our oil supplies is to stop *pumping* it and stop selling it to anyone. Once it's on the market, anyone can buy it at market price."

The Crown Prince's eyes narrowed and gleamed with insane obsession. "All speculation, isn't it? There are many ways the senator's bill could fail, especially if a few obstacles are, shall we say, thrown in its way."

"You mean like OPEC moving away from the dollar and accepting Euro."

"Your letting your imagination run wild, Mr. Monelli. It is not my intention to destabilize the dollar. Your leaders are doing a competent job of that on their own."

"But you and your *friends* can float an international currency that could greatly impact the preeminence of the United States in a global economy."

"And risk the value of my family's stake here? Now that would be quite foolish of me. No, Mr. Monelli, I have other ways to persuade Washington."

They were both leaning forward in their chairs, almost nose-to-nose now, neither one of them blinking. "It doesn't matter anymore," Mario said. "The American people will weather anything."

"And whom will the American people look to for leadership," laughed the Crown Prince, "the president? In ten years time, your president will be powerless, a figurehead, more or less like British royalty is today."

"I wouldn't bet on that," Mario said. "But I do wonder why you put this plan into motion."

"The answer to that, Mr. Monelli, should be obvious to a man in your position. It's an investment, shall we say…"

"Well, *this* man sees it as an attack on the country that—more than any other—has helped you stay in power. Now if you want to *remain* in power, I suggest you hop back on your camel and return to the desert."

The Crown Prince laughed soundlessly, then waved his hand at the panoramic window. "Mr. Monelli," he said, his voice hardening, "this *is* the desert." He clapped once, then stood, and Aziz reappeared. "Perhaps we will meet again," he said, flashing a wide smile.

"Don't count on it," Mario replied walking to the elevator."

"Keep an eye on your stock market, Mr. Monelli. You have more surprises ahead."

The elevator door opened and Mario stepped inside, this time unaccompanied. He waited for the doors to close, then gave the inside of the elevator door a furious kick. "Muthafucker!"

Julie was downstairs, standing directly across from the elevator bank, waiting, visibly concerned. The doors opened, and she rushed toward Mario and pulled him close.

"That fucking cocksucker," Mario shouted, "muscling me like Tony Soprano. I don't care how rich that towel-head son-of-a-bitch is."

Julie tried to calm him. "Well, at least it's over now. After I found out who lived in the Tower Suite, I didn't know what to think," Julie said. "What did he want?"

"He tried to intimidate me, that maggot fuck!"

"Did he actually threaten you?"

Mario thought a moment and calmed down. "No, no open threats. He gave me some *advice* though—'avoid the public eye, don't do any testifying,' that sort of bullshit."

"Anything else?" she asked.

"Oh, yeah, he *did* threaten to have OPEC cut off oil supplies to the West if Jaffe's bill passes, but he knew I knew he was full of shit. We need his oil, but not as bad as he needs our country." Mario told her about the kingdom's plans to transfer their wealth, and everything else, except the Crown Prince knowing about the Lions' Den. He would deal with that gem of a problem first thing back in New York with the Zoo Crew.

"They also killed Hollingsworth."

"He *said* that," she asked in disbelief.

"He didn't have to," Mario said. "But I know. I could see it in his eyes."

Julie felt responsible for what had happened. It was she who'd put Mario in harm's way, who'd pushed him into taking this on, and this was one of those times she wished she hadn't.

Julie held him at arm's length. "What are you going to do?"

"I don't know, Julie. What would you like me to do?"

Julie just shook her head. She had no answer.

CHAPTER TWENTY-SEVEN

Mario studied his handwritten list of clients under proxy attack. "Where do we stand with Pierpont, Dennis?" he asked.

Dennis tapped a few keys on his computer and peered at the screen. "Amalgamated Ore now owns forty-five percent of Pierpont's stock, including convertible debt."

"Glen, call Ron Wittington. He's CFO at Pierpont. Tell him that the White Knight defense worked as planned," Mario said.

Glen laid aside his March Madness picks and looked up from his computer screen. "Will do."

"Do you think the Crown Prince was serious, Mario?" Dennis asked. "They probably had a few things in the works when you exposed them, but it's been a few weeks now."

Mario shook his head. "I take him seriously, Denny. Maybe if Washington had taken some bold action, we could all relax. But we know that didn't happen. I think all the media coverage has only driven them further underground."

"How can we spot them, then?" Kat asked.

Mario just sighed and shook his head. "That should be the SEC's job, and maybe it *would* be if Hollingsworth was still around. Now, I don't know. But at least we'll be dug in when they hit the beaches."

The phone rang and Neil grabbed it. "Yeah…oh sure, hold on." He handed the receiver to Mario. "Your wife."

"I'm busy, what is it?"

"Well, I just thought you'd like to know that our son has been accepted at Harvard," she said.

Mario almost dropped the phone. "Accepted?" he repeated, looking at everyone anxiously. "Are you sure?"

"I have the letter right here in my hand," she said.

"He made it!" Mario yelled triumphantly to the Zoo Crew. "Boomer made Harvard." The Zoo Crew quickly came around their desks and crowded around Mario.

"Ask her if he knows yet?" Neil asked.

"Phyllis, does he know?" Mario repeated into the phone.

"Not yet. He's at school."

"Tell him I'll see him tonight. And tell him I love him."

There was silence on the line for a moment. "Yeah. I'll tell him."

The Zoo Crew shook Mario's hand, patting him on the back, happily congratulating him. The jubilation was long and, for Mario, very satisfying. He picked up the phone again.

Everyone knew who he was calling and scurried back to their own desks to give him some privacy.

"Hi, Sweetie," he said when she answered.

"You're a mind reader," Julie said with an edge of excitement in her voice that rivaled his own. "I was just about to call you. The most incredible thing has just happened."

"Over here, too." Mario beamed. "Those Harvard bastards finally accepted Boomer."

"Congratulations. When?"

"Now. We just got the news, *now*. Phyllis called to tell me. Only good news she ever gave me in twenty years. Now what's *your* news?" Mario asked.

"Well, sir, I would like you to know that *America For Sale* has just been nominated for five Emmys, including best news special. I was nominated."

"Terrific. You deserve it, baby. You're going to win, too. I'm sure of it."

"It wouldn't have happened without you."

"Yeah, well, you can forget about being without me. You're never going to be without me again."

Kat was poking a finger down her throat.

"Would you be disappointed if I gave you a rain check for dinner tonight..."

"That's all right, Mario, I understand. You need to celebrate tonight with your son."

A few weeks later, Mario and the boys gathered in front of the big screen television, a big bowl of popcorn between them, to watch the Emmy Awards live from Radio City Music Hall. Phyllis was conspicuously absent, attending one of Katerina Wellborn's charity events.

Normally, Mario hated television award shows. Nothing was more excruciating, he thought, than sitting through a boring night of egos gone wild, watching the pretentious pat each other on the back, acting as if they had saved the world. But tonight was different.

The show opened with the camera panning across the crowd—the usual assembly of celebrities from the television and entertainment industry.

"Why are we watching this crap instead of the Rangers?" Boomer asked.

"Because I told you, the show I was on was nominated," said Mario. "Go watch hockey in your room tonight."

But Boomer hung around anyway.

Then the show started, and the host and hostess for the evening, walked out into the glitz and glamour of the stage, greeted by a roar of applause.

As the evening progressed, the usual "galaxy of stars" presented awards for every category accompanied by clips from the nominated programs.

Then, finally, after what seemed like a dozen commercials, a couple of well-worn sitcom stars appeared on stage hand in hand and, after a lame attempt at some comedic repartee, decided to get on with business. "What's next, honey," the man asked.

The sitcom queen squinted her eyes at what must have been the teleprompter. "Says here our job is to award the Emmy for the best television news special of the year...The nominees are..." she said, running through them as clips flashed on the screen, and ending with "UBS for America For Sale, Julie Chambers, executive producer." The camera featured a silent video clip of Mario and Bart locked in heated exchange on the Harrison Hart trading floor. The Radio City audience burst into applause at the image of Mario.

"Hey, Daddy, that's you," Kyle perked up in excitement.

The clip was frozen and split-screened beside a live shot of Julie sitting at a table among high-ranking UBS executives. She was wearing a simple off-the-shoulder baby-blue satin evening dress. She smiled into the camera and Mario was sure it was for him.

"And the envelope, please..."

The man handed his co-star the envelope. "And the winner is..." She ripped it open and breathlessly announced "UBS for 'America For Sale,'..." The audience erupted and the sitcom star had to speak over the applause. "Julie Chambers, executive producer..."

The music swelled and the theater broke into applause, as the camera panned toward the UBS contingent for the reaction shot.

Everyone in the aisle was crowded around Julie, celebrating the moment, shaking her hand or embracing her, and she was tearing up, occasionally glancing directly into the camera, which made Mario feel she was thinking of him.

She walked gracefully down the aisle, lifting her dress as she walked up the steps and onto center stage, where the sitcom stars congratulated her, and a gorgeous model handed her the Emmy Award. And then she stepped up to the microphone, looking a little nervous, Mario thought.

"Wow, she's pretty, Daddy," Kyle marveled, innocently.

"She sure is," Mario agreed. Boomer said nothing and looked at his father, who was fixated on the television.

Julie unclenched a hand and stretched out a little piece of paper. And then she spoke. "Every television program is like a symphony," she began. "And I had the honor of conducting *this* one. But in the end, it's the orchestra that makes the music." And then followed the names of her production team. "I'd also like to thank Carleton Fisher, Miles Corbin, and Fred Fielding for their courage and for having faith in me. Hank Kozloff for sticking by me." Hank blew her a small appreciative kiss from the audience. "But most of all to a special someone for loving *me,* and who taught me—you can never have *anything*... unless you risk *everything.* Thank you." The music started up again and the model escorted everyone off stage.

In the den at Mario's house, Kyle laughed, "Hey, Daddy, isn't that what *you* always say?"

Mario brushed it off. "It's a common saying." Then his eyes met Boomer's, and he saw something *uncommon,* a look he hadn't seen before.

Frank called Mario at work the following morning and suggested they have lunch. He had news about the negotiations with Phyllis's attorney, and it had to be discussed face to face.

They met at Peter Luger's in Brooklyn, and this time Frank was early.

Even so, Mario was there first, and he ordered the wine and steaks.

"How long are you going to make me suffer, Frank?" Mario asked. "Tell me what's happening."

Frank took a deep breath. "Okay. I think I've gotten you a really sweet money deal."

"Yeah?" Mario said, motioning for the waiter. "Talk to me."

"Well, first you're going to have to give up the bank accounts, the stocks and the bonds, the annuities, the IRAs..."

Mario's eyes widened. "That's a *sweet* deal?"

The waiter arrived with the wine, and the two men held their silence until he was gone.

Frank said, "Here's the good part: you get to keep all future earnings."

"No alimony?"

"Nope, no maintenance. Phyllis wanted a lump sum anyhow, and with the way *your* career is on fire, I figure you can earn it all back in five years or less."

Mario swallowed hard. "That's true, but Jesus, Frank, you know how long it's taken me to salt all that dough away?"

"Just be glad Phyllis doesn't know about the offshore account. The one they didn't find out about during the financial discovery."

"What? What offshore account?"

"What am I a schmuck?" Frank said, a little exasperated. "I'm your goddamn brother. You can be straight with me."

The waiter arrived with their steaks, and there was a momentary pause in the conversation.

"About the Lions' Den..." Mario began...

Frank popped a bite of steak into his mouth. "I don't want to know about that."

"Yeah, well you need to know about *this*," Mario said. "Remember that little pow-wow I had with the Crown Prince?"

"What about it?"

"Well, he referred to the Lions' Den. I'm afraid he could use it against me if I testify for Jaffe."

"So don't testify."

"I have no intention," replied Mario. "I'm just hoping that by severing my connections with the Den, he'll find some other way to come after me."

"Jesus, brother, I don't know if I can get you out of this one."

"Frank, if you can get me through the divorce, that's all anyone could ask."

"Yeah, well…" Frank took a long sip of wine.

"More bad news?" Mario asked.

"I had to give her the house," Frank confessed.

"That's okay, I figured as much," Mario said. "Now the beach house is another story."

"Had to give her the beach house, too," Frank said.

A pained expression crossed Mario's face. "Waiter," he called out, "bring me some Vaseline." Then he turned to Frank. "Both houses, Frank? What, am I going to have move into Gus's old spot?"

"It was the price of saving your future earnings, Mario. From the financial standpoint, you come out ahead this way. Buy yourself another beach house. You and Julie can pick it out together."

Mario brightened a bit, imagining the two of them with the real estate agent. "Yeah," he said, "we'll drive out there together and find something we both love."

"Not in the Maserati," Frank said, eating.

"That cunt wants my car?"

"Phyllis was very specific about it."

"That vindictive bitch. She wouldn't know how to drive my car if A.J. Foyt gave her lessons. She's just trying to stick it to me."

Frank laughed. "That's exactly what she told her lawyer."

"Fuck it, who cares anyway," Mario said. "She can take it all. So long as I walk out with my Elvis jacket and joint custody."

"Well, you'll have the jacket."

The waiter brought espresso for Mario and a dessert menu for Frank.

Mario couldn't even look at the espresso. "You mean she's going to fight shared custody, Frank? The money, the houses, and the car wasn't enough? She wants the kids, too?"

"No, she's willing to give you joint custody of the boys…with one condition."

"What kind of condition?" Mario asked, feeling an emptiness in the pit of his stomach.

"She'll agree to joint custody, providing you don't marry Julie."

"What!?" Mario felt the bile rising. "She's trying to dictate what *I* do with the rest of *my* life? Who the fuck does she think she is? She can't do that! It isn't legal."

Frank shrugged sadly. "I'm afraid it is, Mario. If you and Phyllis agree to it, the judge will make it part of the divorce decree."

Mario just sat there, steaming, unable to say anything, feeling trapped.

"Look," Frank said. "Boomer's going to be of age and off to Harvard soon, and Phyllis won't be able to dictate *how* much time he spends with you…"

"But we're talking at least ten years with Kyle," Mario said.

"Yeah. She can't stop you from seeing Julie, but if you marry her, I'm afraid you won't be spending much time with Kyle."

Mario felt devastated. He was *already* neglecting the boys due to the overwhelming demands at work, so there was no substitute for taking them to a ballgame on a Sunday afternoon, or sitting at home with them watching television.

Then there was Julie. He wanted to spend the rest of his life with her, share everything with her—the boys included. Marrying Phyllis was a tragic mistake—the result of being young and stupid and wanting to do the right thing—but now he had the opportunity to correct the mistake, to live life as it was meant. But he also knew that a scorned woman left on the balance sheet was a treacherous commodity, especially where young children were involved. And Phyllis was already a few olives short of an antipasto.

"Well, I won't let her stop me, Frank. I'll fight her."

"You might want to rethink that, Mario. I've seen these nasty tug of wars. Never do the kids come out in one piece. Don't do this to my godson. Let me negotiate visitation."

"I made Kyle a promise, Frank. A soldier doesn't leave his buddy behind."

"I know you did. But the one thing I learned when I was a divorce attorney is the one who loves the kids most isn't the one left holding the rope. It's the first one who lets go."

The next day, back at his desk, Mario had trouble concentrating. He just stared out the window, thinking about the "Sophie's choice" Phyllis had given him. Whichever choice he made, he lost. Even worse, Phyllis *knew* that's how he'd see it, and that he would never use Kyle as a pawn.

He dreaded telling Julie. He feared she'd do something selfless, such as ending the relationship so he could be with Kyle, or, even worse, compromising herself and accepting the relationship as is, with no hope of marriage, or of a real life together. Whatever path he chose now, he had to take full responsibility for it. It had to be his choice and his alone.

Feeling someone standing over him, Mario glanced up and found Barry looking at him, curiously. "Everything alright?" he asked.

"What's on your mind?" Mario said, annoyed.

"Well, I've been making some calls about Microsoft. Some of the activity is normal stuff: institutional trading—pension funds, insurance company purchases. But I'm getting a lot of I-don't-knows, from people who *should* know. Could be nothing, but…"

"Stay on it, Barry. I want to be absolutely sure."

At that moment, a messenger walked through the M&A glass doors, sheepishly handed an envelope to Mario, then quickly departed.

Mario looked at the envelope. Thin, no return address, just the note that it had to be delivered personally. Slipping a letter opener into the flap, Mario neatly slit the envelope open and withdrew the single sheet of paper that was inside.

It was a photograph, a portrait, of Mario himself—a photo from *Newsweek*. It had been altered. There was a bullet hole in the exact center of his forehead, a little ragged on one edge. A string of letters cut out of newspapers had been pasted across the bottom with a cryptic note that read, "He talked too much."

What the fuck?

Mario stared at it, a picture of himself shot to death, murdered, lifeless—unreal of course, but beautifully and realistically Photoshopped. The thing scared the shit out of him. He looked at the Zoo Crew. They were busily working or on the phone lining up dates, oblivious. Mario didn't have to ask himself who sent him this grim message. He knew.

And then bravado took over. He was supposed to be scared by a picture? The Crown *fucking* Prince had no idea who he was dealing with. Where Mario had grown up, cars had a habit of exploding, and buildings went up in flames. Body parts got broken at someone's whim. The people he'd grown up with put the bleeding heads of dead horses into the beds of their enemies—the idea didn't originate in the movies. And the Heir *fucking* Apparent thought a doctored photo would rattle *him*?

Mario looked at the picture again and the bravado ebbed. It was quite something to see a picture of yourself, dead. He folded the photo in half, then in half again, then slipped it into the paper shredder,

"Something important?" Neil asked, mildly curious.

"It's nothing," Mario said. He didn't want to alarm the Zoo Crew, and God knows he didn't want to alarm Julie either.

When Mario got to Julie's apartment that night, she was already there. They hugged wordlessly, then kissed, hungry for each other. Then, still saying nothing, Mario picked her up and carried her into the bedroom.

"Mario…" Julie began.

"Shhh," said Mario, depositing Julie on the bed, gently.

Then the clothes started coming off, interrupted by kissing, fondling, intimate touches, eyes locked together, and soon everything became more urgent, the love-making slow at first, but intense, then gathering speed as the two bodies joined together to celebrate their passion for each other.

It had been this way ever since Mario and Julie had returned from Vegas. Ever since he had semi moved into the Millennium Hotel across from Ground Zero.

He spent as many evenings with her as he could, and as many overnights as his responsibilities with Boomer and Kyle would allow. But the love-making seemed different each time—sometimes silent, like tonight, sometimes filled with laughter, sometimes accompanied by words of fevered passion, many of them. There was a rightness to the relationship, not just emotionally, but physically, and both of them felt it. But it also had a temporary quality, good enough for the time being, but only in anticipation of something more permanent, something truly settled—which could not happen until Phyllis was truly and permanently out of the picture.

After the love-making, they ordered sushi from Nobu and had it delivered. While waiting, they showered—together—and came within an eyelash of ending up in bed again. But hunger prevailed, and by the time the doorbell rang, they had put on bathrobes, the table had been set, and the wine had been poured. Mario paid the delivery boy while Julie unpacked the sashimi and sushi platters.

"So how are things at work?" Mario asked. "Are they still treating you well?"

"Like a princess," she said. "Especially Fred. As far as he's concerned, I can do no wrong. Miles Corbin, too."

"Thank God the man finally came to his senses."

"How about you?" Julie asked. "Back to normal yet?"

Normal? Mario thought. If it's normal to get pictures of yourself as a corpse. "More or less," he said casually. "Could you pass the wasabi?"

She handed him the green paste. "You're having lunch with Frank tomorrow?" Mario knew this wasn't a question about his social schedule. He had told Julie Frank was negotiating with Phyllis's attorney, so it was her subtle way asking about the progress.

"We had lunch *today,* as a matter of fact," Mario said. "The negotiations are coming along, but it's no picnic."

Julie, sensing that there was more going on here than Mario was saying, got up, came around behind Mario, and leaned in to kiss and hug him. She was trying to make it all right and, for a little while, she succeeded.

Two more envelopes were waiting for Mario when he got to work after the Easter weekend. He didn't bother to open either one. He didn't want to see what the photo-shopper had cooked up, and he'd already gotten the message. So, into the shredder they went.

"You didn't open your mail," Barry observed, curious. "How come?"

"Junk mail," Mario said.

"But…"

Mario interrupted. "Any progress with that Microsoft investigation, Barry?" It had been nearly a week since he'd asked Barry to make sure all the buyers of significant blocks of Microsoft stock were legitimate.

"Nothing tangible yet," said Barry, who knew when to stop asking questions. "But I think I'm getting closer."

Neil looked up from his desk, across the room. "I might have something," he said, "but it's not related to Microsoft."

"What's that?" Mario asked, surprised.

"Well, something strange is going on with Tyler."

"Tyler? What do you mean?"

"It's probably nothing," Neil said, "but I was talking to Rose Pheeney the other day when a call for Tyler came in from China."

"What kind of business does Tyler have in China?" Mario asked, intrigued.

"I asked Rose the very same thing," Neil went on. "Seems that Tyler and the partners recently have been talking to people there quite a bit. Late night conference calls sometimes."

"Maybe I should ask her about it," Mario said.

"I already did. She doesn't know anything. Or so she says."

That caught Mario's interest. Rose doesn't know what Tyler is up to? She checks him in and out of the bathroom every time he moves his bowels.

"I'm playing squash with Tyler tomorrow," Mario told them. "I'll see if I can find out what's going on."

Mario and Tyler played squash at the Downtown Athletic Club that afternoon. They'd tried to make it a weekly event, but they were both so busy that once a month was about as often as it happened.

Originally, squash was intended as a way for Mario and Tyler to get to know each other, but it had evolved with time into a fierce contest, an unstated struggle for dominance between two men—both of whom were accustomed to running the show.

Unfortunately for Mario, Tyler was a much better player, in fact, a better athlete in general, which carried over to their golf outings. It wasn't a matter of Mario playing just hard enough to lose to his boss. He gave it everything he had, and it still wasn't enough. Only this time, for once, Mario didn't mind losing—not if he were able to find out what Tyler was cooking up.

By the time they got out of the showers, the locker room was empty. Mario figured this was as good an opportunity as any. "You're a terrific squash player, Tyler," he said. "But I hear the Chinese are even better."

"The Chinese? I didn't know." Tyler looked confused, but wary.

"You haven't ever played with any of your Chinese friends?"

"If you're talking about Raymond Ko, he's Japanese."

"No, I meant your Chinese friends in China—you know who I'm talking about."

"I…goddammit, Monelli, you've got yourself a helluva grapevine."

Mario shrugged.

"I was going to tell you all about it," Tyler continued.

"So tell me," Mario said, managing a smile.

"It's a financing deal for Harrison Hart," Tyler said. "I'm pursuing ways to shore up our capital. It's all still in the exploratory stages. Not even all the partners are privy to the details yet."

"Not even Peter Patterson, who's in Beijing right now?"

"My, you do get access to information, don't you? Look, I was going to bring your crew aboard in the next few days," Tyler went on, improvising. "I'm going to need you to conduct a top-drawer study."

"Why all the secrecy?"

"Because if word got out that we were looking for additional financing, there will be blood in the water, and it could put us in play."

"Anyone in particular?"

"Well, I always worry about Mulvaney making good on his threat after we merged with you guys," Tyler said, "especially now, after you blew out his candle that night. And let's be frank, Bart could tiptoe through a beach and not leave a footprint. He did with Intercoastal."

That's interesting, Mario thought. He's trying to distract me from what's going on in China. "I understand," he said. He'd let the matter drop for now, but he knew Tyler was definitely trying to throw him off the scent. But why?

That evening, when Mario pulled into his driveway, he was surprised to see the Hummer there. He'd been expecting to take the boys out for dinner, but maybe Phyllis was playing mother and cooking for them. And sure enough, when he walked into the kitchen, there she was, standing at the stove. Boomer and Kyle were sitting at the kitchen table. Kyle excitedly jumped in Mario's arms. Boomer didn't acknowledge him.

"Hello. I'm a little surprised to see you here."

"The boys deserve a good home-cooked meal," Phyllis said brightly. "And there's enough for you, too, if you want to eat with us. Kyle, take that outside. We're going to eat now." Kyle did as he was told, taking his model rocket outside, and returning without it.

"What are you making?" Mario asked, suspicious. He was *always* suspicious when Phyllis was anything less than a total bitch.

"Baked ziti," Phyllis answered. "Sit. Wouldn't hurt us to be civil with each other for once."

A little late for that, Mario thought, but he sat down across from Boomer and rolled his sleeves. "So, Boomer, how's Jenny?"

Boomer took a moment to answer, apparently reluctant to pursue the topic. "We broke up. I thought you knew."

"You never said a word about it. How would I know?"

Boomer shrugged and shoved a forkful of baked ziti into his mouth.

"So what happened? You two argue about something?"

Boomer took another bite, ignoring the question.

"Answer your father," Phyllis ordered, helpfully.

"We broke up. There's nothing to tell," Boomer said defensively.

"That's too bad," Mario said. "I liked Jenny. She's a nice girl."

Boomer didn't look up from his plate.

"Who dumped who?" Phyllis inquired, tactlessly.

"It wasn't that way, *Mother*," Boomer said, his voice taking on a nasty, sarcastic tone. "She doesn't like my friends."

"What's wrong with your friends?" asked Mario. "They're all smart kids…"

"…and come from good families," Phyllis added.

Boomer sat and steamed for a moment. "Look," he said, struggling for control, "I don't want to talk about it. I just want to eat. I'm running late."

"Late for what?" asked Mario.

"Boomer won tickets to see the Stones tonight," said Kyle.

"You got tickets?" Mario asked, turning to Boomer. "Even my guy in the Pit couldn't get 'em. Awesome. Give me a few minutes to eat and wash up."

"What for? Who said anything about *you* going?" said Boomer.

"You're not taking me?"

"No, they're for me and my friends."

"Are you kidding me?" Mario said disbelieving. "Who was it took you to see Bruce at the coliseum? And what about Metallica?"

"That's your problem."

"You can't talk to your parents that way, young man…" Phyllis said.

Boomer looked up at his mother defiantly and slammed his fork on the table. "Then I won't talk to you at all," he said, abruptly standing and storming out of the dining room. Mario and Phyllis stared at one another, dumbfounded.

"Boomer, get back here," she warned, but Boomer didn't even break stride.

"Mario, don't." She said.

Mario ignored her and angrily pursued his son into the living room, almost as surprised by Boomer's attitude as he was about being left out of Boomer's plans.

"What the hell do you and your friends know about the Stones, you little pisshead?" Mario growled. "You don't even know who Brian Jones is? I saw Mick at Wembly in '79."

"Yeah, well ya won't see 'em tonight, at least not with *my* tickets," Boomer said, slamming the front door behind him.

Mario bent forward to look out the new bay window. He watched Boomer stride angrily to his car, and drive off, spraying pebbles. "What's bugging *him*?" Mario asked Phyllis. "The only time he talks to me is when he needs money."

"It's probably the girl," Phyllis explained.

"Gotta be more than that," Mario said. "I've never seen him react that way before."

"He'll cool down. He always does."

"I'm going to wait up for him," Mario said. "If you don't mind, that is." He looked at Phyllis, realizing that he was asking for permission to stay in his own goddamn house, and hating it.

"Be my guest," Phyllis said, feigning magnanimity. "Just make sure you don't come upstairs."

He fell asleep on the couch in the den, with the television set playing. When he woke up, it was morning again, and Phyllis was puttering around in the kitchen.

"You still here?" she asked, when he appeared in the doorway.

"Yeah. I was waiting up for Boomer. Must've fallen asleep."

"So, where you staying these days?"

Mario ignored her and fixed himself some coffee, and after about ten minutes, the Jetta pulled into the driveway. Boomer emerged and walked into the house.

"Well, young man," Phyllis said, firing her words like bullets, "you've gotten yourself into some serious trouble. Where did you spend last night? We were frantic."

"I fell asleep in the car," said Boomer.

"Suddenly your bed's not good enough," Mario said.

"What do *you* care. You don't live here anymore."

"See that, Mario." Phyllis flashed her coldest smile. "He's turning on you, the way you turned on me, when you found out I was pregnant. Hah! Some wedding *that* was."

Mario looked at Phyllis in horror, once again amazed at her incredible timing. He wanted to ram her words back down her throat, but he was too late. He turned toward his son, who was looking at them with contempt.

"I've always wondered why you two got married," Boomer said, much too calmly. "Now I know. Well, the hell with you, both of you."

Once again, Boomer stormed out of the house. This time, neither Phyllis or Mario said a word.

A dozen heavily armed commandos, shrouded in black wetsuits, faces obscured by night vision goggles, leaped effortlessly, one by one, into a fourteen-foot, black-painted inflatable dingy.

At a signal from the leader, the men dipped short muffled oars into the murky water and slowly pulled away from the shore. The boat glided silently, picking up speed, unseen by the few other watercraft that happened to be in the area.

Fifteen minutes later, the little raft came around at the western edge, scraping pebbles. They hopped out of the boat, in synchronized fashion, and pulled the raft ashore, stowing it under some bushes. The leader consulted a small laminated map, lighting it with a tiny red LED flashlight.

He pointed north and waved his men into line and they set off. As they approached, they came to a sudden stop and one of the men held up a small infrared detector. "The place is deserted," he said quietly. "No signs of life."

The leader nodded curtly and motioned his men forward. At the main door, one of the men took out some kind of instrument, fiddled with the lock for a moment, and the door swung open. The commando crew entered swat-style, machine pistols at the ready, covering each other, their ultra-bright flashlights dancing around the room like searchlights in a prison yard.

The commando leader stood in the center of the room and surveyed the scene. "Fuck me," he said, almost in awe. "In the name of God, what kind of a place is this?"

The team spread out inside the building, backing each other up.

After about twenty minutes, they reassembled in the grand hallway. "Report," ordered the leader.

The upstairs team spoke first. "Nothing up there but bedrooms—but my God, you wouldn't believe the décor. It's some kind of fantasy brothel...in Africa I think."

The commando leader nodded and turned to another pair. "We found the same thing, Colonel."

"Anyone find weapons of any kind?" the leader asked.

Everyone shook their head in the negative. "They do have a big kitchen in the back," one commando said. "And a really kick ass bar," added another. "I found the office," said the third. "There's a safe."

"Lieutenant Brasco, make me a complete set of images. Lieutenant March, you're with me in the office. Let's get that safe open."

Lieutenant Brasco dipped into a pocket and pulled out a camera the size of a stick of gum and proceeded to take pictures.

Meanwhile, the commando leader and Lieutenant March opened the office safe and made photocopies of the documents inside.

"Get every damn page of it," said his superior. "And do a disk copy on the computer hard drive."

A hour and a half later, the commando team neatly arranged the contents of the safe, making certain they'd left no evidence of their visit. Then they snuck back to the rubber raft and paddled back to a mother boat waiting for them a few hundred feet off the shore of Manhattan.

CHAPTER TWENTY-EIGHT

For Julie Chambers, UBS News Director Hank Kozloff was ageless. But according to company policy, mandatory retirement age was sixty-five.

And so, as winter began to fade, Kozloff's colleagues, Julie included, set up a retirement party for him—nothing elaborate, just a friendly, informal event.

Then, one afternoon, Hank was led into the commissary on a ruse, and found practically everyone at UBS News, there to surprise him and wish him a happy retirement. After Hank's gratifying astonishment at the celebration and congratulations from everyone, Miles Corbin climbed up on a chair and took over as master of ceremonies.

Miles related some of the highlights of Hank's career at UBS, dating back to when he was a young maverick with a crop of hair and thirty-two-inch waist, and offered the customary words of praise before presenting him with lifetime first-class passes for two on the world's leading airlines and cruise ships. "Happy retirement, Hank," he said. Everyone applauded.

Kozloff stared at the certificates in disbelief. "My God," he said, "I didn't know it was still possible to get something like this."

"You deserve it," Miles said, grinning.

Julie watched it all with pleasure. Hank was one of her favorite people, someone willing to take a bullet for her, risking his own legacy. Of course, it brought up a question—the question everyone, including Julie, had been asking themselves ever since Hank's retirement was formally announced: Who would be his successor at UBS?

Miles Corbin slipped out of the crowd with a piece from Hank's retirement cake, and came over to Julie. "Really got him by surprise, didn't we?" He took a bite of cake. "Julie, do you remember the job Hank had before becoming news director?"

Julie shot Miles a side-long glance. "That was a little before my time, Miles."

"He was the chief of the Washington news bureau. Covered the entire federal government. Fielding has been doing the job more recently, but… well he really doesn't have the physical stamina to do it anymore."

"I wouldn't be too concerned, Miles, Fred's a horse," she pointed out.

"That's true," Corbin said. "But even a horse needs to rest his tired feet."

Julie began wondering why Corbin was telling her all this. "Come on, Miles, drop the other shoe."

"Okay," Miles sighed. "We're moving Fred up into Hank's old spot, but we'd like you to take over the Washington job."

"Washington?"

"It's a very big job, Julie, and who knows, maybe when Fred retires…"

"What are you saying, Miles?" she asked, skeptically.

"I can't make the guarantee—who knows what will happen in the next few years—but if you do down there what you did up *here*—in spite of the skeptics…"

Julie decided to take the chance. "Like you?"

Miles grinned. "You just need a little more seasoning, a little more experience."

"Be honest, Miles," she said. "Did I get this because I'm a woman?"

"You got it because you earned it," came a voice from behind.

She turned, and there was Carleton Fisher, drink in hand. "I see you've given her the good news, Miles."

"A reward for a job well done," Miles replied.

"In that case, I don't know what to say," said Julie.

"Say you'll accept," Fisher said.

Mario unlocked the door and opened it, and the smell of delicious cooking wafted like a tropical breeze. "Honey," he said, "I'm home."

"Did you remember to bring the Chianti?" Julie called from the kitchen.

"Got it right here," he said, coming up to her from behind, wrapping his arms around her and nuzzling her on the neck. "Umm, something smells great. What are we having?"

"That, my dear, is mussels fra diavolo." She pointed to the cookware on the stove.

"Really? You're a brave little WASP, cooking Italian for a boy who grew up with old-country Italian cooking."

"Anyone can cook Italian now, Mario," Julie said with a pointed little grin. "They have recipes. Whole books of them."

"Still pretty courageous," he said, lifting the lid off the saucepan and taking a whiff.

They sat and ate and talked about their lives. Mario talked with Julie about the boys. Kyle—full of innocence, full of mischief, looking at the world with wonder—was really starting to grow up. And Boomer—more complicated, more serious, still finding himself—was a good kid although he was really being a pain in the ass right now, would soon be off to Harvard.

Julie smiled and put a hand on his. "You're a fake, you know that?"

"What do mean?"

"You come across so gruff and unsentimental, but underneath it, you're soft as a marshmallow."

"Only when it comes to my kids," Mario admitted. "And you."

Julie smiled and refilled their wine glasses. "So how was work today?"

Ah, Mario thought, pleased, they were playing house. "Just an ordinary day on Wall Street," he said, "little chicanery, some deceit, plenty of backstabbing, in other words the usual." He certainly wasn't going to tell her about the envelopes, which kept arriving at unpredictable intervals, or about the gun he had bought.

"And how about you?"

"We had a retirement party for Hank Kozloff. It was quite nice."

Mario thought a moment. "He's leaving?"

Julie decided that she might as well tell him about the Washington job and get it over with. She recapped her conversation with Miles, including his offer and the opportunities it could lead to.

"You gonna take it? You going to go to Washington?" Mario asked eating, trying not to look up.

"If I did, it's not as if we would never see each other, Mario. We can always take the shuttle on weekends."

Mario took a deep breath and sighed. "So my brother gotta work out a visitation arrangement with you, too?"

"You could always come with me," she said.

"You know I'm in the thick of it."

"Doesn't have to be right away. It can be after…"

The Washington news came as a surprise. This wasn't the future with Julie that he'd imagined. He'd imagined her at UBS in New York, and himself at Harrison Hart, living together, either at her place or maybe a bigger one in the Village or SoHo. Leaving New York had simply never occurred to him.

"I know that there aren't many investment firms in Washington," she added, "but you'd make an incredible lobbyist or a consultant maybe, Mario."

Mario thought for a moment. "Well, did you think about *this*: I'd never get to see the boys if I relocated."

Julie reached across the table, caressed his hand, and looked into his eyes. "Then we'll fight for custody."

"Be serious, Julie." He got up and walked to the fireplace and lit himself a smoke.

"Why not?" she asked.

"Because I can't put Kyle through that, that's why. The kid has already seen enough fucking shrinks." He feared that looking into Kyle's eyes and breaking his promise might also land *him* in therapy. There was only one way out of this, Mario thought. He had to change Phyllis's mind somehow, or outwit her or something. God, how did things get so fucked up? All he wanted was a little happiness in this shitty life.

About a half hour after dinner—they were still nibbling at dessert—Mario started feeling a cramp in his belly. "I may have eaten too much," he said. "Got any stomach stuff?"

"Let me see." Julie disappeared into the bathroom. By the time she came back, Mario was groaning. "I have Mylanta and Gas-X."

"Jesus," Mario said, squirming. "Give me two of each."

"You're sure?"

Julie brought him some water and put the pills in his hand. He swallowed all four of them in one gulp, and they gave it a few minutes. "Any better?"

Mario wasn't talking now. He doubled over at the stabbing pain in his abdomen.

Julie had him lie down, put a cool, wet washcloth on his head, loosened his clothing, but the pain worsened, until he was actually writhing. "I'm calling the ambulance," she told him. "You're going to the hospital."

A half hour later, an ambulance deposited Mario at NYU Hospital emergency. The harried young ER resident took one look at Mario, poked his belly a couple of times and uttered a single word: "Appendicitis." He summoned a nurse and some orderlies. "Take him to the OR, now," he said. "That thing's ready to pop."

"His appendix?" Julie asked, fearfully.

"Yeah, it's a good thing you got him here."

"You're going to be fine, sweetheart," Julie said, grasping Mario's hand. "It's just your appendix."

Although he was lying on a gurney, Mario still managed a smile. "Good thing it's trivial," he said, trying to be funny, his words blending into another groan.

Julie squeezed his hand one last time and they took him away. She spent the next hour in the waiting room, worrying, until the young doctor reappeared.

"Is he okay?"

"Just a routine open appendectomy," the doctor assured her. "A couple of days and he'll be back on his feet."

"Can I see him?"

He's in recovery now. He won't be awake until mid-morning. No point in you staying. You can see him, tomorrow."

It was the sunlight that woke him up, sunlight from a window whose blinds should have been closed. At first, Mario didn't know where he was—the surroundings were totally unfamiliar. Then he moved, and the pain in his side reminded him of what had happened last night.

Shit! Did anyone besides Julie know where he was? The kids would be worried. He looked at the intravenous feed tunneling into the top of his hand, and at the morphine dispenser to which it led.

Julie walked in a moment later, smiling broadly, and carrying a vase of flowers. "Good morning, sweetheart. How are you feeling?" She said, bending down to kiss him.

"They have this new kind of surgery," Mario said. "It's about as hard to take out your appendix these days as it is to get a good haircut. And speaking about haircuts, they plucked me like a chicken down there. Hey, what's with the flowers?"

"Every hospital room ought to have flowers," Julie said, setting down the vase. "Besides, it's the sentiment that counts. This, my dear, is for you."

She handed him a greeting card, which he took out of the envelope.

"With all my love, now and forever, Julie," he read. "Pretty romantic stuff."

There was a quick knock on the door, and it swung open. A nurse with a meal cart entered the room, set up a lap tray for Mario, and spread out what purported to be breakfast.

Mario looked at the offering with evident distaste. "I'm supposed to eat this crap?" He asked. "Jesus, this is worse than the surgery. Honey, do me a favor. Go across the street and pick me up, a bacon, egg, and cheese on a roll."

Julie looked at the meal nurse, who sternly shook her head. "Sorry, Mario," Julie said. "No can do. Eat what's on your plate. Here, I'll help."

Julie dipped a spoon in the mush and fed it to Mario. "Disgusting," he said with a grimace. But he ate the next bite she offered.

Julie took a deep breath. "I had another conversation this morning with Miles," she said.

"And?"

"He wants me in Washington by the end of the month."

"There goes my appetite," Mario said, refusing the next spoonful.

"Keep eating," Julie smiled. "I turned him down. I told him to find something for me here in New York."

Mario looked into her eyes, trying to gauge what she was feeling. "What about your career?" he asked.

"*You're* my career," Julie said lovingly.

"Are *you* okay with this?"

She took his hand and squeezed it. "You mean, am I happy with just settling for the most important thing in my life?" She smiled, reached for a piece of toast, and held it up to his mouth. After a moment's reluctance, he bowed to the inevitable.

"Look, about dinner—could you bring me something decent tonight?" Mario asked.

"I'm sorry, sweetheart, I can't be here tonight—Miles is hosting a gathering for some of the new affiliate stations, and he wants me there. But I'll call you when I get home, if it's not too late. I promise."

"You're still picking me up tomorrow afternoon, aren't you?" Mario asked.

She smiled. For a moment, Mario seemed vulnerable, and she felt a rush of love. "Of course. I'll be here at 1:30 tomorrow afternoon, on the dot."

Julie stayed a short while longer—until she had to return to work. When she left, Mario asked the nurse to push the phone closer. By now, he realized, the boys would be worried sick about him.

A few hours later, the nurse came in to check up on Mario and found him restlessly flipping through the TV channels. "How are you feeling?" she asked, recalibrating the morphine machine. "Any pain?"

He flipped to *The Young and the Restless,* then grimaced and flipped past it. "You'd think a big hospital like this would have ESPN."

The nurse shrugged, then smiled and left the room, closing the door behind her. A moment later, the door swung open again and Kyle burst into the room, followed by Boomer and Phyllis. Kyle ran toward Mario, crying happily, "Daddy!"

"Easy does it!" Mario said. He held out a hand and Kyle grabbed it. "How's my little soldier doing? Hey, Boomer."

"Hi, Dad."

"Why did you wait so long to call us?" Phyllis asked, snidely. "Your children had no idea where you were, or what might have happened to you."

"I'm sorry about that," Mario said, directing an apology more toward the kids than to Phyllis. "I was pretty much out of it."

"Yes," Phyllis said. "I would imagine someone would have to be. How did you get here?" She smiled when she asked, and it wasn't a friendly smile.

"It's kind of fuzzy," Mario said, trying to invent a plausible lie, or hoping she would show at least a hint compassion and relent, "but I was working late with the Zoo Crew, and they brought me here."

"Not one of those imbeciles gave any thought that your family might have been worried sick?" She was on him like a rabid Johnny Cochran. "If you were at the office, then what are you doing up at NYU Hospital?"

Mario was beginning to get irritated. "Cause I like the food here, Phyllis. You've been here three minutes and you're breaking my freakin' cajones."

The nurse stuck her head in the door. "I'm afraid we have too many people in here," she said."How about we put you into a wheelchair and take you into the sun room, where your guests can be comfortable?"

"I'll help," Kyle offered.

The nurse left the room and brought back an orderly with a wheelchair, and put Boomer in charge of the IV trolley. Everyone cooperated in slowly lifting Mario into the contraption. "Kyle," Mario said, "you're the pilot. Slowly, and no sudden turns."

Kyle took his task very seriously, pushing his father with care and caution, following the orderly's directions, leading the family caravan into the sunroom. Kyle parked Mario, and the rest of family took seats surrounding him, except for Boomer, who stood near a window, looking out at the traffic on First Avenue.

"Here, we brought you some magazines," Phyllis said, handing Mario a *Sports Illustrated* and an issue of *Fortune*. "So how are you feeling?"

"Actually, pretty good," Mario said, "except when I move around too much. And don't make me laugh, please."

Phyllis smiled, sweetly. "I wouldn't think of it," she said.

"When will you be coming home, Daddy?" Kyle asked, wrapping his arms around Mario's neck like a scarf.

"Day after tomorrow, hopefully. I'll ask the doctor." He hoped to have a day alone with Julie before returning back to the world.

"That's too bad," Phyllis said, "Boomer's swimming in the city finals tomorrow against Stuyvesant." Phyllis said. "You'll miss it."

Mario remembered. "That's right, it's tomorrow. You ready to kick some ass?"

Boomer shrugged.

Mario exchanged glances with Phyllis.

"Hey, Boomer, would you mind doing your old man a favor?"

"What?"

"Well the food here is god awful. How about you run across the street and get your father a meatball parm?"

"Should you be having that?" Boomer asked.

"C'mon, don't argue with me. Nurse Ratched is gonna be back soon," Mario said.

Mario instinctively went for his wallet—but the hospital Johnny and bathrobe didn't have pockets. "Shit, I left my wallet in the nightstand next to my bed. Why don't you go get it, Boomer."

"Right," Boomer said, all mopey, and trudged back toward his father's hospital room.

Mario waited till Boomer was out of view and turned to Phyllis.

"What's going on? He's getting worse."

"I'm seriously thinking about having him see someone," she said.

A few blocks from UBS, Julie and two of her Georgetown college friends, Leila, a buyer for Calvin Klein, and Alicia, a writer for *The New Yorker*, were having a relaxing lunch at a trendy French Vietnamese restaurant.

Julie checked her watch.

"You in a rush?" Alicia asked.

"I still have time," said Julie, smiling. "I'm picking up Mario at 1:30."

"How *is* the lion of Wall Street?" Leila asked, teasing. "Feeling better?"

"Will he still be able to *purrr* between the sheets?" said Alicia, joining in the fun.

Despite her best efforts to control it, Julie blushed, and her friends grinned. They relished seeing her happy again.

"Seriously, I can't imagine what that must have been like," Leila said, "I mean, him having an appendix attack in the middle of dinner."

"I was frightened to death," Julie said.

There was some kind of commotion at the *maitre'd*'s station—someone was pushing their way into the restaurant. Julie and her friends turned to look, only to find a teenage boy striding toward them, angry and upset. To their absolute shock and dismay, he stormed right up to their table.

"You, you bitch!" he accused, thrusting his whole arm at Julie. "You think I don't know who you are and what you're doing with my father. Why can't you leave us alone?"

Julie stared at the boy, dumbfounded, and her friends looked on, aghast. Everyone in the restaurant—including the waiters—had turned to see what was going on, and the maitre 'd, having recovered from the shove, was headed toward Julie's table at flank speed.

"How did you even *know* he was in the hospital?" the boy demanded. "How did you know before *we* found out? Were you with him when he got sick?"

"Boomer…" she gasped in shock, for this could be no one else. "Boomer," she pleaded.

"Don't see him anymore! Don't write, don't call! Get out of our lives! Stay the fuck away from my father, you dirty whore!" He was in tears and practically screaming.

Suddenly, his arm flashed across the table like a scythe, sweeping it clean of dishes, glasses, chop stocks, and teacups, flinging chaing mai noodles, stir-fried basil and panang curry over everyone at the table, splattering soy sauce over Julie's cream-colored suit, spraying other nearby diners as well, and bringing chaos to the entire dining area.

Then, with hardly a glance, he turned and loped out of the restaurant, easily evading the maitre'd, who grabbed at him, but missed.

"I'm *so* sorry," Julie apologized to her stunned friends. She rose and hurried after Boomer, but by the time she got to the street, he was nowhere to be seen.

Mario slept through the night and well into the morning. By the time he opened his eyes, it was nearly eleven o'clock. Julie would be there soon to pick him up.

He showered and dressed, then packed his stuff in the little overnight bag she'd brought for him.

Surprisingly, none of the activity caused him much pain. This new kind of surgery was truly amazing—less than forty-eight hours after going under the knife, and all he felt was an occasional twinge.

The door opened and the nurse came in the room, pushing a wheelchair.

"Hey, I can walk now," Mario said.

"The way it works," replied the nurse, "is that we wheel you to the hospital exit. You leave here in one piece. What you do afterwards, well, that's up to you."

Mario laughed, and at that moment, his cell phone rang. It was Julie. "Hey," he said, "I'm ready and waiting for you."

"Mario," she said, voice quivering with emotion.

"Julie? What's wrong? You okay?"

"Boomer knows."

"Knows? Knows what?"

"About us."

"How?"

"I don't know—all I know is he came into the restaurant while I was having lunch with my girlfriends. It was awful. He said the most horrible things."

"What do you mean?" Mario said, angry now. "What things?"

"Doesn't matter—Mario, he's terribly hurt. If only you could have seen the hurt in his eyes."

"Where are you?"

"*Le Colonial,* Fifty-Seventh off Lex. My god, I'm still shaking."

"Just stay put—I'm coming right now."

"Don't come *here,*" she cried. "Go to your son," she pleaded. "He needs you!"

Mario didn't know whether to be furious or devastated. "I'll call you as soon as I can."

He quickly zipped his bag and, as he reached for his coat, noticed something familiar on the floor peeking out from under the nightstand, paper. He bent down, probably faster than he should have, and felt the sharpest pain. He grabbed the paper, and straightened up, carefully.

It was the greeting card Julie had given him, the silly, romantic get well card he'd loved, and it had been ripped into a dozen pieces or more. At first he thought it had gotten caught on a caster, but he slowly realized that it hadn't been torn by accident at all. And then, all he could think about was how he could make his son understand.

Mario grabbed a taxi outside the hospital and told the cabbie to take him uptown, to the Halstead School. He checked his watch. Boomer would be readying himself for his meet against Stuyvesant, he realized. "Let's make it a quick trip," he slammed the door and instructed the cabbie.

The cabbie headed up the FDR Drive, while Mario sat in the back, preoccupied, rehearsing what he might say to his son. He couldn't come down hard on him for confronting Julie. He had to be gentle. Boomer was still on the edge over Danny. And it wouldn't do any good to deny or try to hide anything.

Students were streaming out of school by the time Mario arrived—wealthy white kids trying to look gangsta, girls in tight crop-top sweaters with belly buttons on display, scholarship kids trying to fit in.

Mario moved against the current, wincing, when he had to dodge a kid running down the steps. Inside, he found a stairway door and struggled down the stairwell, toward pool level. He stopped one of the swimmers, a gangly redhead kid wearing a Halstead swim jacket.

"Where can I find Boomer Monelli?"

The boy pointed to the locker room.

Mario squeezed past the boy, flung open the door, and found Boomer sitting at his locker, dressed in a Speedo, a towel horseshoed around his neck. The coach was standing over him.

"Okay, so I can't cut you. But I'm moving you back to third in the 400-meter relay, and taking you off the freestyle. I don't know what the hell's the matter with you, Boomer. I expected a greater effort from you, but you've been dogging it. You're up again in ten minutes. Don't disappoint me."

The coach turned and walked out of the locker room, shooting Mario a curious look as he passed. Boomer spotted his father and turned away.

"Boomer, we gotta talk."

Boomer looked at him coldly. "Talk to yourself. I have a race to swim."

"There's things I need to explain, Boomer—"

Boomer stood, and Mario was taken aback by how frail he was. When had he lost all the weight? "You don't have to explain a thing," Boomer said, shoving some of his things into a gym bag. "I understand, perfectly."

"Please, just listen to me for a minute?" Mario pleaded. He'd forgotten all of his rehearsed lines, and he didn't have any idea where to begin. "Boomer, you know it's been over between me and your Mom...for a long time."

"Why does it have to be over?" Boomer demanded.

"We just don't get along. We haven't in years."

"You got along well enough when you fucked her, and had me," Boomer retaliated.

"We were young and stupid," Mario said. "But that's beside the point. The relationship we have is unhealthy for you, *and* Kyle—*especially* Kyle. I hate to think what all the fighting has done to him."

"And this other woman—you never fight with her?"

"We love each other," Mario admitted.

"You say that to my *face*..." Boomer said, looking at him in disbelief.

"Boomer, I know this might be hard to understand, but sometimes you live with someone, spend half your life with them, until one morning you wake up and see a stranger laying next to you."

"What makes this one so different from the other cum dumpsters you've been with?"

"Don't talk about Julie's as if she's a slut."

"No, she's just a whore. *You're* the slut. Think I didn't know about all the others? Did you, *Dad*? How many of Kyle's Little League games and my swim meets did you miss because you were always out at night, getting hammered and getting laid."

"It was all I could do to keep my sanity," Mario exclaimed, pulling himself into the vortex. "But that was before I met Julie. Before life mattered again."

"I see. So it no longer matters with us?"

"That's not what I meant, Boomer. Stop *twisting* things."

"I just can't handle all this now, Dad, I really can't," he said, choking his words, and holding back tears, his torment obvious.

"What's going on with you, Boomer? It's more than Julie. Ever since Danny..., Dammit, talk to me, please! I'm trying to be a friend."

Boomer's head snapped around. "I *had* a friend, but he's dead. What I need is a *father*!"

The coach stuck his head into the locker room. "We're *waiting*, Monelli," he said tersely.

"Be right there," Boomer said, trying to pull himself together. He gave Mario one last hard look. Mario held out his arms and took a step closer, but, to his surprise and dismay, Boomer backed away, shaking his head.

"If you never loved her," he cried, "then why did you stay?!"

Then he turned and ran out of the locker room, the ribs in his back visible through his sallow skin.

CHAPTER TWENTY-NINE

W hen Mario returned to Harrison Hart the next day after a late lunch, he was surprised by the commotion coming from the hall. "What's going on?" he asked Rose Pheeney.

"Not a clue," she said.

He glanced through the glass partitioning the great stage of the trading floor from the hallway and could hardly believe his eyes. Everyone—every broker, every trader, every research analyst—was on the phone, watching the overhead ticker, talking loudly and rapidly, a few so dumbfounded that all they could do was stare at CNN on the TV monitors that loomed overhead. And each of the offices along the periphery was a chaotic miniature of what was happening outside on the floor.

Mario was thoroughly puzzled. He knew something big was happening—but what? He detoured into Tyler's office, but Tyler was also on the phone, talking quickly to someone, probably one of the partners. He waved to get Tyler's attention, and Tyler momentarily put his hand over the phone. "Microsoft's in play."

"What? Are you fucking serious?" This was a far cry from the nibbling he'd been keeping track of.

"Do I look like I'm joking? Dow's down almost 800 points. It's worse than Black Monday."

Mario looked at Tyler with a mixture of disbelief and concern, then he hurried down to the M&A suite, where every phone was ringing.

"Neil, is it true?"

Neil put a hand over his phone. "I'm afraid it is. Ballmer and Gates have mounted a defense, but after the Gates divorce…well, it's 50-50."

Mario looked out at the trading floor and the overhead ticker looming above it. The market was free falling faster than an elevator with a broken lift cable.

"If Microsoft goes, it's over, paisan," Glen said.

Suddenly, an idea leaped into Mario's consciousness—this was what the Crown Prince had forewarned, orchestrating a sell-off so great it would allow the monarchy to acquire majority ownership of several core companies for a fraction of their true value. And putting Microsoft in play would surely accomplish that.

"Seems every blue chip in the Fortune 500 is trying to mount a defense. The whole fucking world is calling us," Dennis said, panicked. "Fucking

Exxon, Texas Power and Light, Dow chemical. Warren Griffth over at
DuPont called three times."

"Yeah," Kat agreed. "Corporate America just hit a giant iceberg, and
every CEO is scrambling for a lifeboat."

Mario slumped down in his chair in dismay and looked out into the
carnage of the trading floor. "I don't think there's enough room for all of
them," he said, and there was a new and disturbing note in his voice—genuine
fear. Neil and Dennis looked at Mario, then at each other, both struck by the
change in Mario's tone.

Dick Hamilton shook his head, puzzled. "What do these fucking Arab
pirates want from us?"

"They want the country," Mario said.

Then his telephone rang. "This will probably be Jeff at GE again," Barry
said, picking it up.

"Hello...sure, hold on." he said, handing Mario the phone. "It's your
kid."

"Kyle, Daddy's busy now," Mario said into the phone. "Oh, it's *you*,
Boomer."

"Dad, you gotta come to the school," said Boomer.

"I can't leave work now," Mario said. "Are you all right?"

"I'm in trouble. I think I'm going to be arrested."

"Arrested!" Mario repeated, leaping to his feet. "What the fuck have you
done?"

"I'll explain when you get here," Boomer said. "Make it fast, Dad. I'm
scared."

Mario pulled the Maserati into an empty bus stop directly in front of the
Halstead School, his second visit in as many days. This time he vaulted up
the stone steps and hurried down the hallway, barging into the headmaster's
office. The headmaster, a starchy-looking man in a vested brown tweed suit,
with steely gray hair, looked up, unperturbed. Boomer sat on a couch, pale
and frightened, his gym bag on the floor beside him.

"Boomer, are you alright?" Mario said, rushing toward him.

"Your boy's fine, Mr. Monelli," said the headmaster.

"What's going on?" Mario said. "What kind trouble is Boomer in?"

"Please have a seat, Mr. Monelli. I'll fill in the details."

Mario remained standing. He glanced at his son, but Boomer wouldn't
meet his eyes.

"I won't bore you with the preliminaries," said the headmaster. "Our
security staff has found illegal narcotics in your son's locker."

"And what the hell were your *narcs* doing in his locker?"

"Dad..."

Mario silenced Boomer. "Shut up and let me handle this," he warned.

"We found them during a routine search," replied the headmaster.

"That can't be," Mario said. "I know my son. He wouldn't have anything to do with drugs—not even weed."

"What we discovered were packets of crystal meth, according to school security. *Several* packets. That makes this a matter for the police." He tossed a plastic bag on the table. It contained several small envelopes of white powder, a syringe, a pipe, and a length of rubber hose.

Mario stared at the dope in horror. "Maybe someone planted this to make it look that way—someone pissed at him for some reason."

"Such as…?"

"Look, it's no secret he's being held scapegoat for losing the state championship."

"They were in *his* locker. As to his guilt or innocence, that's a police matter, a matter for the courts."

"Boomer, did you have *anything*—anything at all—to do with those drugs?"

"No, Dad, nothing—I tell ya, they're not mine. Someone who didn't like me planted them in my locker, like you said."

But the headmaster wasn't buying Boomer's explanation. "I asked Boomer to have you come in because I wanted to notify you in person that your son has been suspended from school, *indefinitely,* pending a police investigation. If cleared, he will be reinstated with full privileges. If not, well, the suspension will become an expulsion. We have a zero tolerance policy here, Mr. Monelli, for the protection of all of our students. I'm sure you understand that. Remember, we already lost one boy to drugs this year."

"I know. And I completely approve of the policy, but think of the consequences for my son. If he's arrested, he can say goodbye to Harvard. He can say goodbye to his future. He can say goodbye to his life."

"Mr. Monelli, I understand your position as a parent, but I'm not the one who has made the decision. This is the result of your son's choices."

"You've called the police already?"

"Yes. They should be here shortly."

Boomer turned panicky. "Dad, call Uncle Frank."

"Good idea," Mario said, reaching for his cell phone. He started to dial, then he thought better of it and flipped it shut. If he called Frank, he and Boomer would be at a police station before the afternoon was over, making plans for his arraignment.

"Dad, what are you doing? Call him."

"Wait a minute," Mario said to the headmaster. "Let's talk about this."

"I don't see what more there is to talk about," the headmaster said, but he leaned back in his chair, ready to listen.

"Look, if—and I'm just saying *if*—Boomer is using, then he needs first-rate professional help, agreed?"

"Yes, but…"

"Well, he's not going to get it sitting in a jail cell. If he's convicted of possession, he's going to find himself in prison with drug users and murderers and rapists—Christ, look at him. He's eighteen years old. He'll be tried as an adult. How long do you think he could survive in prison?"

The headmaster gazed at Boomer for a moment, then looked away. "People get punished for breaking the law," he said.

"Look, there's something I know about you," Mario said. "I mean we've never talked before, but it's obvious that you care about the students who go to your school, and that you're very protective of them."

"That's true," the headmaster admitted, proudly. "We have a long tradition of looking out for our students' welfare here at Halstead. That's an intrinsic part of our mission."

Mario knew he was in the negotiation of his life, and that he had to conclude it as quickly as possible. His negotiating skills and ability to think on the fly had brought many to their knees, including feared and respected people like Time Warner's Pete Singer. But if he fucked up *this* negotiation, he'd be consigning Boomer to a lifetime of dead ends.

Still, he was pretty sure he'd found the key. "And I know," he continued, "how much you care about the kids who have been victimized through no real fault of their own."

"You have a point," said the headmaster.

Mario looked earnestly into the headmaster's eyes. "That's why I want you to help me," he said. "I need your help to save my son from the dangerous world he's living in, to save him from his own weakness."

"A few weeks in a good facility…"

"Okay," Mario interrupted, in his most persuasive tone, his hands gripping the armrest hard enough to drain the blood from his fingernails. "This is what I have in mind: "I'm going to get Boomer the best help there is—no expense spared. And I'm going to be on his back. And my word counts."

Mario glanced out of the headmaster's window. An unmarked Ford Taurus had pulled up to the school, and two, what appeared to be plainclothes police were getting out of the vehicle.

"Yes," said the headmaster, "I believe you will. But…"

"One more thing," Mario said. "I want to help you make sure other students at Halstead are safer from the same influence. So I'm going to establish a fund to provide the school with a cutting-edge camera-based security system, to make sure no unauthorized people can get inside, and that the administration can keep an eye on the student body. Do you think $25,000 would do it?"

There were loud voices in the outside office, Mario could hear the cops identifying themselves and asking to see the headmaster, immediately. The headmaster's intercom came on. "The police are here, sir."

"Please ask them to wait just a moment," the headmaster said. Then he turned to Mario. "I think that would buy a decent system, Mr. Monelli. Of course, for *$50,000*, we could get something *very* sophisticated." He interlocked his fingers and leaned back in his chair.

Mario raised an eyebrow. He was giving Boomer a lesson in how the world worked. Something he could never learn at Harvard. "Okay then, fifty," Mario said. He reached into his pocket and pulled out his checkbook. "Shall I make it out to Halstead?"

The headmaster paused for a few milliseconds. "You could do that. Or you could simply make it out to *me*."

"Gee, Dad, you oughta get this slime a job on Wall Street."

"I said shut up," Mario warned his son.

Mario wrote the check and handed it to the headmaster, who put it into the top drawer of his desk, along with the contraband.

"Thank the headmaster, Boomer," Mario said, putting away his checkbook, masking his contempt. "He's really looking out for you."

"Thank you," said Boomer, mechanically.

"Why don't you take your son out the back entrance."

Mario grabbed Boomer's gym bag, put his other hand on Boomer's neck, and steered him out of the office, his grip tightening the instant they were out of the headmaster's sight.

He took the hallway at a fast march, occasionally stealing a glance behind him while half-pushing Boomer along, through the doors and out onto the street.

"Wait till I get you in the car, you liar," Mario snarled through clenched teeth.

"I'm not lying. Someone has it out for me."

"The only one has it out for you is *yourself*. If Harvard ever found out…"

"Screw Harvard," Boomer barked. "That's *your* thing—not mine."

Mario realized they were attracting unwelcome attention from some passing students. "Shut the fuck up and get in the car," he commanded. He opened the passenger door and shoved Boomer inside, tossing the open backpack into Boomer's lap.

Boomer poured through his backpack, making sure everything that had been confiscated from his locker was there—books, toiletries, swim gear… and jewelry.

"Is that everything?" Mario asked as the car sped away.

"Yeah," Boomer said. "Everything except the stash."

"The stash you say was planted on you."

"That's right," he taunted. Boomer buckled on his watch and refastened his gold crucifix, adjusting it until it once again hung neatly around his neck. Then he slipped on his Halstead school ring, the one with the red stone.

Mario, his thoughts a turmoil of emotions, had stopped paying close attention, content with watching the process out of the corner of his eye. But the class ring caught his attention. That was strange—hadn't Boomer and Danny traded rings on Halloween night, the last time he'd seen Danny alive?

Yes, that's right, Mario remembered. As a symbol of friendship, Boomer had taken Danny's ring—the one with the black stone—and given his friend the one with the red stone, not to be returned until graduation day. Then how…?

For a while, Mario said nothing and just stared at the road ahead. Then, finally, in a voice devoid of spirit, said, "I had such great plans for you, Boomer. But you broke my heart. You broke my *fucking* heart."

"I guess we let *each other* down," Boomer said.

Suddenly, Mario knew he had to find out the truth, *now*, no matter how painful. Not only the truth about Boomer, but the truth about Danny as well. *Nothing* was more important. But how? What could he do that wouldn't force Boomer into more lies and more denials? What could he do that wouldn't drive his son away, maybe forever?

Mario thought back to that terrible night, to the police telling him about Danny, telling him about the dead body on the roof of a building. And suddenly, he knew what he had to do. Instead of cutting back toward the Queens Midtown Tunnel, he headed north.

"Hey, wait a minute. Where are we going?" Boomer asked, confused. "You missed the tunnel. Where ya going?"

"We're going to find out the truth, Boomer."

"Truth about *what*?"

"The truth what really happened that night with Danny."

"You already *know* what happened?"

"Do I?"

"What does *that* mean?"

"*You'll* find out," Mario stoically replied.

They turned again at Central Park West and roared north, past the park on the right and rows of fancy apartment houses. Then it was east on Cathedral Parkway, at the north end of Central Park, and north again on Seventh Avenue that would plug into Lenox Avenue and into the heart of Harlem.

Seventh Avenue was a four-lane artery, lined on both sides with 19th century brick apartment buildings, several of them housing liquor stores on their first floors, adorned by the occasional graffiti-covered billboard. The cross-streets were narrow corridors of two and three-story brownstones and row houses.

"Come on, turn around. This is stupid."

"Is it? Danny was right, Boomer—everyone has a dark side…and today we'll find out yours."

Boomer slammed his shoulder against the door to let himself out, but Mario used the driver's side override, to lock it.

The Maserati took a screeching left on the 125th Street main thoroughfare, now known as Dr. Martin L. King Boulevard, Harlem's main drag and central business district. He barely recognized the place. In his day, it was all vacant store fronts, big "going out of business" signs plastered on the windows, open stalls selling all kinds of Asian crap and, of course, at least three liquor stores on every block.

But now, in the half-light of dusk, it seemed as if every building on the street had been renovated or at least spruced up, and all kinds of new businesses had moved in—Old Navy, the Disney Store, the Gap, goddammit, there was even a Starbucks on the corner.

Years ago, Mario and the Zoo Crew had often come to Harlem, mainly for the music, to see Ella or James Brown, then cap off the night pigging out on baby backed ribs at Sylvia's. What would *they* have thought of the Harlem Renaissance, of this new place edging toward gentrification. Not much, Mario told himself.

The car whizzed past Malcolm X Blvd., up West 138th Street, past the gothic style structure that was Abyssinian Baptist church.

He glanced at Boomer, who was staring out of the window, scared and confused, looking as though he was in the middle of a nightmare. The old King theater in *Sugar Hill,* Mario remembered, and the phrase kept repeating itself in his mind. And there it was, just short of Eight Avenue, on the north side of 145th St.. Mario pulled up to the curb.

"Why are we stopping?" Boomer asked, voice trembling.

Mario ignored him, got out of the car, and swung opened the passenger door. "Get out." Boomer just stayed in the car and shook his head.

"Not until you tell me what's going on."

"I'm not asking you, Boomer." Mario reached in and yanked Boomer out.

"What about the car?"

"Fuck it."

"You're leaving the Maserati here, are you crazy?"

Mario surveyed the street, mostly commercial buildings with nice retail stores on street level, except for one building on the north corner. It was a four-story structure, painted brick, rusty fire escape on one side, windows that stared down at the streets like dark, lidless eyes, a neon marquis ravaged by time, and a ticket booth covered by a roll-down sheet of corrugated steel defaced with multicolored graffiti, the most prominent of which was a big purple "Crips" in balloon letters.

"There we go," he said, spotting the place. He grasped his arm firmly around Boomer's shoulder, and, after a glance at the traffic, steered him quickly and roughly across the street.

"Why are we here?" Boomer resisted.

"You don't recognize this place? Well, you should. Danny died here, Boomer."

He forced Boomer across the street, to a wooden door on one side of the building, and, with one swift, vicious kick, broke it open. "Inside," he ordered his wide-eyed son.

"What? I'm not going in there," Boomer said, squirming, desperately trying to free himself from his father's grasp.

"You sure as hell are," Mario said. "Now get going."

"Hey, hey, all right, I'm going, I'm *going*."

They walked through the door, and into a dim, dank, rat-infested lobby, whose walls were cracked and crumbling and covered with graffiti. A set of rickety stairs, barely visible in the fading sunlight, lay at the end of the hallway beside an open elevator shaft, near the shattered glass showcase of an old concession stand.

"Get up the stairs," Mario commanded, giving Boomer a shove.

"What for?"

"We're going to where it all happened."

Boomer started up the stairway, which creaked with his every step. Mario followed close behind, the steps groaning with his weight. Aside from a grimy window at each level— all of them were blocked by the brick wall of another structure—there was no light in the building whatever, except the blinking red and green neon signs off 145th Street, barely visible through the haze on a grimy staircase window. Twice, Boomer came to a dead stop and turned, but Mario spun him around and threw him deeper into the abyss.

At both the first and second story landing, Boomer pleaded with his father. "This is crazy—what do you think is up there?" Mario didn't bother to respond.

The higher they went, the worse the odor. It was a disgusting mixture of vomit, urine, shit, and substances that could not be identified. Soiled mattresses littered the floor of a large room that was once an auditorium. Mario could only imagine the things that had occurred here—beatings, rapes, drug deals, murders, thieves dividing the take, addicts shooting up. And his own son...

When they reached the next landing, Boomer stopped again. "Keep going, we're almost there," Mario said, his voice bouncing off the walls with an echo. He was running strictly on instinct now. And his instincts told him that the roof was where the truth awaited him, the truth about Boomer, and why he isolated himself from everyone, the only place the truth could be found.

On the fourth floor, past the projection room, the stairs came to a dead end, blocked by an aluminum door with peeling asbestos. "Up to the balcony," Mario ordered.

Boomer tried the door, which opened to reveal another flight of stairs and another door at the top. "All the way," Mario said grimly. "Up the stairs and through the door."

They came to the last door, the entryway onto the roof.

"Open it," Mario commanded.

Boomer jiggled the door knob.

"Now!"

"It won't open," Boomer cried. "It's stuck."

"But you and Danny got it open that night."

Boomer looked down at his father, at the gleam in his eyes. "Remember?" Mario said.

Boomer wildly tried to thrust past him, but Mario blocked him and took hold, hoisting him up.

Boomer whimpered and clutched the spindles of the banister, then the radiator with both hands, holding on like an animal being dragged to the slaughter house, begging his father to let go. Mario ignored Boomer's resistance, peeled his hands free, then grabbed Boomer's jacket collar, and mercilessly yanked him up the last flight, the boy's toes thumping over each step.

Mario laid a shoulder into the aluminum door, and reached back for Boomer, dragging him up by his arms, his feet thrashing wildly over the door's threshold, until he sent Boomer tumbling onto the roof.

Now, they were outside, in the cool breeze, in the half-light, on top of the building, standing among the ventilation outlets, the ancient air conditioning units, the shack-like entries to mid-building staircases, and the telephone and electric wires, plus assorted trash—cardboard boxes melted by rain, newspapers, crack vials, and the occasional condom. Everything was covered in multiple layers of ancient black roofing felt—tar paper.

Mario looked around. "So *this* is where it happened?"

Boomer glared up at his father, terror stricken and out of breath.

"See, there's nothing here, nothing to see. I think you've really fucking lost it."

"Come with me," Mario said, grabbing the boy hard, Boomer wildly squirming in his father's grasp.

Mario led him around the roof, trying to piece it all together and figure out what happened, and where it all might have gone down. Of course, when they found Danny's body, the cops must have taken any related evidence. There'd be no way to identify the actual spot.

Scanning the roof, Mario saw few obvious places to hide from view except for a shack-like structure, which held the door to the inside staircase. "If you crouched down behind that," he told Boomer, "no one would know you were there, much less notice what you were doing."

He dragged Boomer to the shack, and then behind it, the boy resisting every step. "Is that the place?" he demanded. "Is that where it happened?"

"How should *I* know?" he asked, his father's hand now clutching his jaw.

"Oh, I think you know every well, Boomer. I think you know very well... "

Mario studied the tar paper, looking for he had no idea what, until he noticed something: a tiny fleck of blue. He scraped at it with his fingernail. There were more flecks of blue, a line of them, interrupted in spots, but still a line. He stood back and saw what remained, after the passage of time, after the snows of winter, of a crime scene investigator's chalk outline of where a body once lay.

"That's where Danny died, isn't it?" Mario asked his son. "Go ahead, look at it." He threw Boomer to the ground, then clutching him by the hair, pressed his face to the floor like he was rubbing a dog's nose in its own piss.

"How would *I* know?" Boomer shot back.

Mario turned Boomer's head. "How would you know?" he asked, voice trembling with anger. "You'd know because you were there. You'd know because you saw him die."

"I don't know what you're talking about."

"It all makes sense now, the moodiness, the distance, the weight loss. I thought it was over losing Jenny."

"Dad, I swear I was never here!" he cried.

"I never would have placed you here that night," Mario said. "I never would have known. I would have gone on *not* knowing. Only you made one mistake, Boomer. You needed to go back and claim what was yours. The ring, Boomer, I remembered the ring."

Boomer glanced at the red stone on his hand, broke free, and raced to the front of the roof, toward the fire escape. He got about two rungs down before Mario reached over the ledge, grabbed him, and threw him down to the grated floor.

"So *that's* how you got away with no one seeing you." Mario jumped down from the roof onto the fire escape and lifted Boomer off the grated floor by his shirt collar. Boomer, too petrified to resist, submitted to his enraged father. "You left the party early to baby sit your brother. Danny came back later, but you were both dry, so you left your brother alone in the house, got in Danny's car, and drove out to your dealer, someplace in the city, near Halstead."

"I never left Kyle," Boomer protested.

Mario had a rabid look in his eyes. He swung Boomer around, leaning him over the railing. "Stop lying to me! What you don't know is that Kyle woke up and saw you were gone. He told me so."

"He couldn't have," Boomer cried. "He was still asleep...when I got back." Then Boomer realized his mistake.

"So," Mario said, tightening the snare. "We've proved that you went back out. Where did you go?"

This time, Boomer had no reply.

"When you couldn't find your usual connection at the school, you and Danny drove up to Harlem and bought junk off the street. By then, you were both too sick, and couldn't wait any longer. So you broke into this abandoned shit hole, looking for a place to get well."

"That's not true," Boomer said, but his protests were getting weaker.

Mario tightened his grip around Boomer's collar, just looking at him, in the blinking neon of a nearby store that streaked him in red, green, and blue. "But you couldn't get a room, could you?" Mario continued. "So you came up to the roof."

He violently swung him to another corner the fire escape, arching Boomer's back over the railing, four flights above street level.

"You're hurting me!" Boomer complained, squirming his head away from the suffocating hold of his father, but Mario wasn't about to let him.

"Then what happened, Boomer? You and Danny found that spot behind the stair entry, right?" He was spewing saliva and shaking Boomer violently. "Tell me! Tell me!"

"You know what we did."

"Yeah, you shot up with Danny. Oh that little striptease you played with the cops that night."

Boomer was silent…then, finally, he nodded.

"How long have you been using?" Mario demanded.

"I don't know," cried Boomer. "Six, eight months."

"Six to eight months," Mario repeated to himself. "Only something went wrong this time, Boomer, didn't it? Tell me!"

"He was mainlining in his neck." Boomer cried. "He never did that before."

"He shot up in his neck," Mario repeated and swung him around. "Why didn't you stop him?"

"I tried to, but he said he knew what he was doing. But he started foaming and went into convulsions. Then…"

"Then he died, Boomer. He fucking died!"

"There wasn't anything I could do."

"So you just left him there? How could you leave your friend while he was dying?"

"I got scared."

"If you were scared, why did you came back, Boomer? You were already safe, no one saw you leave. You went back for the ring, didn't you?"

"No."

"Didn't you?!" he shouted, firming his clench.

"Yes!" Boomer finally admitted. Mario released his grip and Boomer dropped to the floor.

Mario stood over him panting, wildly. "Then you snuck down with no one seeing ya, then took the railroad back to the Island," Mario said. He was beyond exhaustion now. He had found the truth, but it had kicked the shit out of him. He slumped down to the fire escape floor, while Boomer cowered in the opposite corner, in a fetal position, sobbing.

"Why didn't you tell me?" Mario asked, his voice etched in sadness.

Boomer lifted his tear-stained face and looked at his father. "Tell you? How could I tell you? You thought I was the perfect son."

Conversation was in short supply on the drive to Long Island. Boomer slept through most of the ride while Mario's mind spun like a revolving door…first Boomer, then there was Rick and Danny, then Julie, then the Saudis move on Microsoft, and finally and surprisingly, Gus. He wasn't going to say this to Boomer, but when he accused the boy of deserting Danny, he knew he'd done pretty much the same thing with Gus. But his thoughts always came back to Boomer.

It was bad enough that Boomer had been a witness to Danny's death, was even involved in a way. Who was *he* to complain, he thought. He was grateful. Rich kids from Alpine, New Jersey were hanging themselves with sash cords in their garages. At least his kid was alive.

But his son, his golden hope for the future, his legacy and prized jewel, was a *bona fide* junkie. That, and his guilt over his best friend, Danny, was destroying him. He needed to find a way to save his son, and if he didn't find it soon, they might both be lost. Rehab, maybe.

But putting his boy in the hands of strangers at some bullshit rehab ranch in Utah was just too much for Mario to seriously consider. Besides, Phyllis might veto any plan he came up with, however sensible. Maybe even use it against him in the divorce. No, this was something he had to do himself. In fact, he was the only one who *could* do it, the only one Boomer would accept.

He'd take time off, that's what he'd do. He'd go away with Boomer, take him somewhere isolated, help him break his addiction, set him on the right path, be a *real* father to him, more than he'd ever been in years past. He knew the perfect place. A place where they could lock the world out and begin salvaging two lives. They'd stay there as long as it took and wouldn't return until it was finished. The rest of his life would have to wait.

"I've got Drummond on the line for you," Elliot Case's secretary told
him on the intercom. Drummond? Case thought. What little goodie does the
FBI-SEC liaison have for him today.

"Got a bunch of stuff for you," Drummond told him. *"Organizational
papers and records. We're not interested in them, but you may be."*

*The bunch of stuff turned out to be a brown Samsonite hard-shell suitcase
filled with Xeroxed documents. More out of curiosity than anything else,
Case looked through the papers himself, instead of passing it down to his
investigative team.*

*This turned out to be a good decision. He'd rarely been more
entertained.*

*It was a truly preposterous thing the FBI had accidentally uncovered—a
secret, posh club involving some of the biggest names on Wall Street. The
Lions' Den, they called it—a phrase that came up during their wiretap
operation. The financing, it was found, had violated a half dozen SEC rules,
and that wasn't the half of it—further scrutiny revealed it also flouted zoning
code and building code laws, and the structure itself had been acquired
illegally.*

*He dropped into the office of Ben Hersh, Acting head of the SEC, to
share his findings and a laugh, and try to wheedle permission to go down
to New York to have a closer look at this thing, himself. He brought a few
documents to make his case.*

*Hersh read through them with the high good humor they merited, until
he came to the papers of incorporation. "Did you read this?" he asked Case,
"I mean, did you look at these names? These are some of the biggest players
on Wall Street." Ben read further.*

"I thought you'd get a kick out of it." Case smiled.

*"Here, take a look at this one," Hersh said, putting a finger to the paper.
"Recognize that name?"*

*"Frank Monelli," Case read. "No. The only Monelli I know of is the guy
who dropped a dime about the Saudis on television. Why?"*

*"I was at Fordham law with a Frank Monelli. Mouthpiece for the
teamsters now."*

"You think they're connected?"

"I don't know," Hersh replied.

"Hey, wait a minute," said Case. "Remember a week ago, that DVD I got in the mail—no return address. The one of the television show Mario Monelli was on?"

"What about it?" asked Ben.

"There was a note that had me go to a particular track where Tom Gallagher is talking about Monelli, saying that he and his team protect American companies like a lion protects her cubs. At first I didn't know what to make of it until just now when I saw the name of Frank Monelli on those Lions' Den incorporation papers."

"That's all that was on the DVD—the television program?"

"That's it," Case said. "Nothing we both haven't seen before."

"Still no idea who sent it?" Ben asked.

"No. But evidently someone's trying to tell us something," Case said.

"And I'll bet I know what it is—that Frank Monelli is related to Mario, and that they're both involved in this..." He paused to find the right phrase.

Case supplied it. "They call it the Lions' Den."

"Interesting—they call Monelli the Lion of Wall Street."

"Are you thinking what I'm thinking?" said Case.

"How soon can you get down to sin city and grab the Lions' tail?"

"I'll be on the next shuttle."

"Just make sure you make an effort to pick a reasonably priced hotel this time?"

Chapter Thirty

Father and son were both quiet on the long drive to the Catskills cabin. Boomer's anger and embarrassment at being outed by Mario was gone, replaced by an attitude of resignation and surrender.

Although Mario still blamed himself for Boomer's derailment, his acute disappointment and outrage had likewise faded away. Instead, he was filled with determination and a sense of purpose: to cast out the demon who'd infected and isolated his son. His own would have to wait.

It was still fairly early in the morning when the Hummer pulled into the cabin driveway, and Mario found himself with a reaction he hadn't anticipated. He remembered the last time he was here. With Julie. He remembered the love, and he remembered his betrayal. Such bittersweet memories. Maybe this time, he told himself, things would turn out better.

They dumped their bags at the cabin and drove into the nearby Hamlet of Swan Lake in search of provisions, loaded up the Hummer, and drove back to the cabin. Mario hopped out of the truck, grabbed a grocery bag, and headed for the front door. Then, realizing Boomer wasn't following, he put the bag down and sprinted back to the truck.

Boomer was sitting in the passenger seat, head against his chest, his breathing ragged. Mario jerked the door open and asked, if he was all right.

Boomer held up a hand. "Dizzy," he said. "It'll pass. I'll be okay."

His face was flushed, but he seemed to be getting his breathing under control. Both knew it was a precursor of what was to come.

They brought the groceries inside, and Boomer started putting things away. "Damn, I forgot to pick up some things at the drug store. Want to come?" Mario asked.

"No, you go ahead. I'll put everything away."

Mario mulled it over for a moment, wondering if whether he could trust him. "Ok. I'll be back in a few."

In town, Mario stopped into the Rexall and bought an armload of ice packs, hot water bottles, pain and headache remedies, as well as a couple of extra blankets—anything he could think of to make Boomer more comfortable once the monkey began to play.

When Mario got back, he found the groceries had all been stowed, but Boomer was nowhere in sight. Mario looked into the bedroom. Boomer was stretched out on the bed, tossing and turning, occasionally twitching, in a sleep that was anything but peaceful.

Mario stood at the doorway, painfully watching. Boomer was exhausted, but his body wouldn't let him rest. His face was a picture of anxiety and discomfort. This was what Mario had been expecting, fearing.

After a few minutes, Boomer noticed Mario at the doorway. "I can't find a comfortable position," he said. "I might as well get up. I'm jumping out of my skin."

Mario walked into the kitchen, Boomer close behind. "Why don't you watch a little TV while I work on dinner."

Boomer sat down on a kitchen chair, crossing and uncrossing his feet, gulping occasionally, as though he was fighting the urge to vomit. Mario watched silently.

"I'm scared, Dad," Boomer said.

"I know, Boomer," Mario replied. "So am I. But we're going to get through this thing. You think you're up for some dinner?"

"That's the strange thing—I didn't expect to be hungry, but I'm starving."

Mario tossed him a box of saltines. "Work on these," he said. "I'm going to fry us up some chicken strips and boil some macaroni."

By the time the chicken was ready, Boomer had eaten half the box of saltines. But that didn't stop him. He buzzed through the chicken like he hadn't eaten for days.

"There's still some left on the stove."

Boomer yawned widely, once, twice, and then a third time, his face contorted. "No, no…" Then he leaped up and ran to the bathroom, retching repeatedly as he reached the toilet. Mario, who'd ran after him, soaked a washcloth in cold water and pressed it against Boomer's forehead.

"No! Get that thing away from me," Boomer snapped. "Lemme alone, can't you?"

Mario backed away as Boomer violently heaved up bile till he was tearing and panting with exhaustion. Afterwards, Boomer reached for the washcloth and wiped his face, catching his breath.

"Sorry about that, Dad," Boomer said. "It's just I feel so rotten."

"It's okay," Mario said.

"I think I'm going to try sleeping again," Boomer said, after awhile. He headed back into the bedroom, and lay down on the bed.

Mario spread a blanket over his son, who was already tossing and turning. "Maybe it'll help if we turn down the lights," Mario said. Then he sat on the wooden chair beside the bed and kept guard.

Boomer lay on one side for a few minutes or so, and then on the other, then shifted back again before dropping off for the night. And for the next few days, the pattern repeated itself. Except to go to the bathroom and, occasionally for a meal, Boomer stayed in his room sleeping, occasionally running to the toilet, doubling over to vomit. Mario was glued to his side and didn't get much sleep.

Then, one morning, Mario decided it was time to get Boomer up and moving. He set the breakfast table, then called his son.

"What?" came the annoyed reply.

"Breakfast," Mario said.

Boomer came out of the bedroom, groggy, wrapped in a blanket.

"Jesus Christ, Dad. Couldn't you let me sleep a little later?"

"Nope. Seven o'clock, time for breakfast, then we have work to do."

"Work? What do you mean?"

"Were you cold last night?"

"It's freezing up here."

"That's because we didn't have the fireplace working. No wood. We gotta chop some."

After breakfast, Mario found a couple of rusty axes in the tool shed behind the cabin, and they went to work, dragging fallen pines and beeches into the driveway, cutting them to length, then chopping them in half.

It was a cool morning, but in a half hour's time, they'd both gotten rid of their jackets and were working in their shirt sleeves, sweating. Before long, it was a competition, Boomer swinging his axe almost effortlessly, splitting his logs with a single blow, Mario out of breath, swinging mightily, missing as often as he hit.

The firewood began to pile up—faster on Boomer's side than on Mario's, despite Mario's best efforts. "Damn, you're strong," he gasped.

"That's because you're outta shape," Boomer responded with a grin.

Then Boomer faltered in mid-swing. He dropped the axe and wrapped his arms around himself, causing Mario to look at him curiously. Then he started shaking, and fell to his knees.

Mario was with him in an instant. "Boomer?"

"It's starting again," Boomer groaned. "Please, Dad, get me to the house."

Mario helped his son back into the cabin and carried him to the bed.

"Get me what I need," he begged, shaking uncontrollably.

"That's exactly what I'm doing, Boomer," Mario said and stuffed a hot water bottle under the covers, fed him some aspirin, and ended up on the bed with the shades drawn, spooned beside him. He was cradling him and gently massaging his temples, occasionally pressing his lips to his hair, trying to stop the violent shivering.

"It hurts bad, Dad," Boomer whimpered. Mario locked his legs around Boomer's ankles to hold him steady and ride it out.

"Shhhh...think of someplace peaceful," he whispered in his son's ear. "Think of last summer in New Hampshire when we walked the falls... remember?" He felt Boomer nod between the shivering.

Finally, Boomer dropped off to sleep. Mario disentangled himself and walked into the living room, shutting the bedroom door behind him as quietly as he could. Then he sat down on the couch, picked up the phone, and dialed Julie.

"Hello?"

"Julie, it's me…"

"Mario! Where have you…"

"Sorry I haven't been able to call you earlier. Everything's gone haywire, with Boomer I mean…and I'm afraid it's just starting."

"What happened?" she asked, voice full of concern. And Mario told her everything.

"So you've brought him to the cabin?" Julie asked.

"I think it's his best chance," Mario said. "And maybe mine as well."

"How long do you think you'll be up there?"

"I don't know. A week, maybe two. As long as it takes."

"Mario, if there's anything I can do, any way I can help."

"Just be patient with me, Julie. I love you. I'll call you whenever I can."

"I love you, too. Boomer has to be your first concern now."

Boomer stumbled out of the bedroom late the next morning, eyes bleary, a sour expression on his face.

"How's it going?" Mario asked hesitantly.

"It's going shitty," Boomer said. "Can't you tell?"

"Is there anything I can do to help?"

"Yeah," Boomer barked. "You can drive me back to the city so I can get what I need."

"That's not going to happen, Boomer."

Boomer sat down heavily on the couch, his body movements awkward and twitchy, grinding his teeth together. Then he yawned, widely and unnaturally, and thrust his head back. "I don't know how much more of this I can stand."

"You're getting into the worst of it."

"Gimme the crackers," Boomer demanded.

Mario reached for the saltines and handed the box to his son, who dug his shaking hands into the box, pulled out a handful and started pushing them into his mouth. Mario pulled a Snapple out of the refrigerator, and Boomer reached for it as though parched beyond belief, and he chugged it down.

The boy remained on the couch, a bundle of twitches and nervous energy, eating and drinking like a madman, crossing and uncrossing his legs, yawning and breathing hard. Finally, after littering the couch with crumbs, he started to regain control of himself. Mario watched it all, helpless, silent, feeling the pain as though it were his own, but remaining strong for his son, trying to support Boomer simply through the strength of eye contact.

But Boomer couldn't meet his father's eyes. He couldn't focus on anything. He stared at the floor, his mouth working involuntarily, his breathing irregular. Finally, he raised his head, revealing a face marred by anger and confusion.

"You knew it wasn't going to be easy," Mario said gently.

Boomer looked at his father, resentment in his eyes. "You son-of-a-bitch," he growled. "*You're* doing this to me. You gotta stop. I can't go cold turkey."

"You can…and you will, Boomer."

To Mario's surprise and dismay, Boomer suddenly broke into manic laughter, then just as suddenly, began sobbing, his episodes of depression now growing worse and more frequent. Mario sat beside him and wrapped his arms around his son again, trying to make him feel safe and loved.

In time, Boomer quieted down. His body stopped quivering. He began breathing normally. Mario leaned back to take a look at him and, aside from the tear-stained face and disheveled hair, he looked pretty much okay.

"You all right? Would you care for some lunch?"

Boomer managed a nod. "Yeah," he said. "But for a while last night, I thought I was going to die."

"You're not going to die, Boomer. You're going to get well. But it's not over yet."

They both knew that.

They were having lunch when the phone rang. Mario picked it up.

"Mario, it's Neil."

"Neil? How did you know I was here?"

"Phyllis."

"She mention *why*?"

"I already know why, but that's not why I called."

"Anything wrong?"

"Plenty—things are getting out of control here, paisan. We're in triage. Half of corporate America is banging on our door, looking for protection. Tyler just got off the phone with the boys over at 390. They need help. And they're not the only one."

"It's no surprise," Mario replied. "The boys over at Greenwich Street have been in bed with that Arab billionaire for years," replied Mario. "I once told the jew, if he ain't careful, he's gonna get that big red umbrella, right up his ass."

"That's why I called. We can't handle it all. You gotta come back."

"Neil, I understand, I really do. But I can't rush it. I have a son to take care of. I'll be back when I can."

"Mario, you don't understand."

"No, Neil, *you* don't."

Mario hung up and looked around for Boomer, who was nowhere to be seen. "Boomer? Boomer?" He walked into the bedroom, thinking his son might be resting. The bed was empty. Mario suddenly felt a draft and saw the cabin's front door was half open. It was raining heavily, and the mat inside the door was getting wet. At that moment, the Humvee's piercing siren cut through the sounds of rain.

Mario sprinted out the door, into the cabin's wooded front yard fifty feet from the lake. Boomer was standing at the truck, desperately punching buttons on the key fob, frantically trying to unlock the front door.

Boomer saw Mario coming, which only increased his fevered anxiety with the key fob, but in seconds, Mario had grabbed the key fob, and had Boomer by the tendons between his neck and his shoulder.

Boomer fell to the ground, collapsing like a marionette whose strings had been cut. Mario managed to ease his fall, but just barely. "Boomer!" he shouted, over the rain. "Boomer!"

For a moment, Boomer's eyes rolled back into his head and he lost consciousness. But Mario slapped him once and that revived him. Boomer looked at his father, slack-mouthed, then shook out the cobwebs. "What happened?"

"You passed out for a moment," Mario told him. He scooped Boomer up in his arms, and carried his rain-drenched body back into the cabin, kicking the door closed behind them, and lying Boomer down on the couch. Then he went outside and hid the car keys in the bushes.

That night, it was more of the same—Boomer in the full throes of withdrawal, the agony gnawing at his gut, him begging for a fix, cursing his father out behind locked doors for not giving it to him. It had gotten so bad, Mario had to forcibly tie Boomer's hands to the bed post to keep him from doing harm to himself. Boomer eventually passed out from exhaustion and slept through the night.

They were up at dawn—Mario had insisted on it. He had something special in mind—a morning fresh water fishing, followed by an afternoon hike up Overlook Mountain, through an inviting maze of woodland hills, strenuous exercise that would be good for him, and even better for Boomer, some good, clean fresh air, and most of all, a chance to talk.

"Okay," Mario told his son, "you get the backpack with the first aid kit, and the sodas. I'll grab the one with the sandwiches."

"Tell me again," Boomer said. "Why are we climbing this friggin' mountain?"

"To see what's on the other side," Mario said. "And because it's there. Choose your own reason."

The mountain—a modest peak—was criss-crossed with trails, surrounded by dense brush and pine trees, as well as exposed rock and the occasional boulder, and there were plenty of nature trails and places to rest.

"Hold on a minute," Mario said, spotting a brown cedar bench. "The old man's dragging."

Half a dozen steps ahead of him, Boomer looked back at his father. "Hey, you know, this was *your* idea, Dad."

"Yeah, just a minute. Let me catch my breath. We don't have much further to go." He looked up ahead at his son. The boy had taken to climbing like a mountain goat. "Okay," he said, taking a deep breath, "let's go."

They reached the summit a short while later. It was mostly flat rock, a perfect sitting place. Spread out before them was a gorgeous panorama of green, forested mountains and shadowed valleys, here and there a small town, a few houses visible on the slopes or at the peaks.

They shook off their backpacks, unpacked the sandwiches, and sat, looking at the world outstretched before them in all its splendor, watching the clouds arriving from the west, disappearing to the east, changing shape, like their own lives, as they traveled across the sky.

"So, Dad...this the first time you've done any climbing?"

"My first time was when I was your age, maybe a little younger. Your uncle and me took the boat up the Hudson to Bear Mountain and climbed it."

"Uncle Frank? Pretty hard to imagine him climbing anything, with that belly of his."

"You should have seen him when he was younger. He was never thin, but he was all muscle."

They ate for a while in silence until Mario mustered the courage.

"Why did you do it, Boomer?" Mario suddenly asked.

Boomer stopped eating and turned away from his father. "I don't really know for sure," he said in a very small voice.

"I know I haven't been the perfect father. . .," Mario began.

"Don't beat yourself up over it. Every kid I know has a father who's practically a stranger. You're better than most of them."

But Mario wasn't ready to let himself off the hook. "Your mother and I, the constant fighting, I guess that's what drew me to Julie..."

Boomer's head snapped up quickly. "Do we have to talk about her?" He briskly got up and walked toward the edge of the mountain, pretending to study the landscape.

"Not if you don't want to," Mario answered quietly.

"What about you?" Boomer asked. "Why did *you* do it?"

"I don't know. I suppose we were both lonely."

"That it?"

"Don't kid yourself, Boomer. Loneliness is a lot for two people to have in common."

Boomer looked down for a moment and shrugged. "You know, the strongest feeling I had, it wasn't unhappiness. I'm not one of those miserable rich kids looking for trouble. I'm spoiled shitless, and I'm bored out of my skull."

"What's to be bored of when you got 'cha whole life ahead of you?"

"Nothing..." He said impulsively, then reconsidered. "Everything. Things were so simple when we were living back in Brooklyn. I remember the great times me and Danny used to have at Coney Island, eating dogs at Nathan's or pizza at Spumoni Gardens, or going out for blues at Sheepshead Bay. Even skateboarding along the promenade under the Verrazano."

"And now?"

"Now it's all gone. Why did everything have to change?"

"Nothing changed, Boomer. You just grew up."

"Life isn't fair, Dad."

"And don't you ever forget it," replied Mario. He studied a passing cloud, trying to think of what to ask next. "Why didn't you tell me how you were feeling or that you were using?"

Boomer laughed bitterly. "You're kidding, right? You're the last person on Earth I'd tell. No, maybe Mom is. Anyway, by the time I realized things got away from me, it was too late. I didn't think you would understand."

"But I'm your father, Boomer. You can always come to me."

"Yeah. And rewrite the life script you wrote for me? No thanks. I never wanted to disappoint you again."

"Again? When did you ever disappoint me?"

"Once. Long ago," Boomer replied. "You had taken me to work with you during the holidays to see Santa. I must've been around Kyle's age. All the big shots brought their little geniuses in, showing 'em off in their nice little bow ties and preppy sweater vests. You were no different. It was all great until the kids started playing the president game in front of all the parents. Each kid rattled off all the presidents of the United States. Then it came my turn, and I didn't know one. Not a single one. I'll never forget the look on your face. You never brought me to work with you again."

Mario looked down. There could be no question that the devastating illustration on what it was like being Mario Monelli's son explained much of Boomer's brokenness.

"Now I understand why you felt you couldn't come to me," he replied, then thought for a moment. "I'm sorry, Boomer. I never should have tried to mold you into a Stepford kid like these other Wall Street clones— brain-wash you into believing you were better than where you came from. I never should have done that to you. I never should have done that to *us*. Can you forgive me?"

"Stop doing that to yourself!" Boomer turned and snapped at him.

"Doing what?" Mario asked, startled.

"Blaming yourself for everything. Danny, Gus, *or* your fucked up marriage. Things happen to people. It's nobody's fault. You did what you thought was best for me."

Mario looked his son in some surprise. "You know," he said thoughtfully, "sometimes you sound older than your years."

"Just because I'm almost eighteen, that doesn't mean I'm a bonehead. At least not *all* the time."

Boomer turned away from his father and scanned the mountain range laid out in front of him. "Pretty spectacular view," he said.

"How far do you think you can see, Boomer?" Mario asked. It wasn't really a question about visibility, and Boomer knew it.

"I don't know, Dad. But things look a helluva a lot clearer than yesterday."

It did for both of them.

After awhile, Mario checked his watch. "Getting late. Maybe we'd better start back."

They started down, but after a few minutes, Boomer stopped and let his head sag. Mario was at his side in an instant.

"Getting the shakes," Boomer grunted, through gritted teeth.

Mario put a hand on Boomer's shoulder. The boy seemed to be shivering, and the shivers got stronger with each passing moment. "Sit," he instructed.

Boomer sat down heavily on a nearby boulder, his breathing ragged, his expression grim. He hugged himself fiercely with both arms and yawned again and again and again.

"Can I do anything for you?" Mario asked, feeling helpless.

Boomer looked up at him. "Do you happen to have a loaded syringe?" he asked sarcastically.

"You've seen the last of those," Mario said.

Boomer grinned and sunk his head in his lap, and tried to shut out the light, the sounds, the smells, the world. He sat still as a statue for a while, then suddenly turned away from his father and vomited into the bushes. Finally, he looked up.

"I think I'm coming out of it," Boomer said, sitting up. "Not used to mountain climbing."

Boomer stood and stretched. The color was returning to his face. Mario handed him a bottle of spring water, and he flushed out his mouth.

The rest of the descent was uneventful. They got back to the cabin before sundown, tired but satisfied. Mario nuked a couple of frozen dinners. Then after dinner, they settled down to a couple of games of chess, Boomer winning both games, and turned in for the night.

During the next few days, Mario spent a lot of time studying the effects of the withdrawal, watching the little boy inside the near-man, seeing his son laugh again with genuine affection and pleasure. It was like a kind of fog was lifting, a fog that had clouded their relationship and prevented them from seeing each other clearly, growing denser over the years.

The next day, Mario made them both grilled cheese sandwiches for lunch, and Boomer's disappeared before his father could even begin eating his. Mario fixed him another, and watched his boy eat. The boy is beginning to put on some weight, he thought.

After lunch, father and son spent the afternoon tossing a baseball around by the lake, looking like the inspiration for a Norman Rockwell painting—until the cravings overtook Boomer again. When they did, they hit like a sledge hammer. One moment, he was punching the pocket of his mitt, the next, he had crumpled to the ground, shivering.

Mario ran to him, but Boomer waved him off and sat up, gasping. "I'm all right," he said. "But I think that's enough playing catch for the day. I'm going to lay down for a while."

Mario walked behind his son, admiring him. The boy had grit and courage. He was going to be all right. He hadn't been sure at first, but he was growing more confident every day.

During dinner Boomer leaned back in his chair, took one last mouthful of meatloaf, and studied his father, who was clearing the dishes. "What would grandpa have done?" he asked.

"About what?"

"You know, if you were me…here, now."

Mario laughed bitterly. "He would have kicked me out on my ass. No wait, he would've opened my skull, *then* kicked me out on my ass."

"I remember him giving me candy, once. He smelled funny."

"Probably beer breath. Vito Monelli was a hard man, my boy, beaten down by life. No give in him." Mario had never really told Boomer about his grandfather, mainly because there wasn't anything good to tell.

"How about grandma, she would have stopped him—wouldn't she?"

"She might have tried," said Mario. "But your grandfather never paid your grandma any mind, unless she annoyed him. At least it was better than him smacking her around."

"Grandpa *hit* grandma?"

Mario smiled, ruefully. "Sometimes."

"You couldn't stop him?"

"I was a kid, Boomer. And he would have gone after me, too, if Frank hadn't gotten me away from him. Your uncle took plenty of beatings for me."

Boomer thought a moment. "Jeez, I just remember a nice old man."

"Yeah, well, things aren't always what they seem."

"So why did grandma stay with him?"

Mario didn't answer right away. This wasn't easy to talk about, especially now, considering what was going on between him and Phyllis. "Italians didn't get divorced in those days," he finally said. "It just wasn't an option."

"But if he was abusing her…"

"Didn't matter, Boomer. You just stuck it out, maybe complained to the priest. To Italians, marriage vows were more sacred than *omerta*."

"What's *omerta*?"

"It was the mafia code of silence? Break *omerta* you *die*, break your marriage vows…your eternal spirit dies. It was never to be broken, regardless if it meant being miserable. And that's what your grandmother was, rest her soul."

"She should have called the cops…"

Mario looked at Boomer, who was regarding him in a new way, as though he'd just learned something important about a man he thought he knew very well. "It was a different era," Mario concluded.

That night, no sooner had Mario stretched out his feet on the ottoman and closed his eyes in front of the fire, than the telephone rang. He was reluctant to answer. No one knew he was at the cabin. No one except Phyllis, Julie, and…"Hello?"

"Mario, it's Neil. We're in deep shit."

"What did our Arab friends do *now*?" Mario asked, alarmed.

"Our trouble has nothing to do with them," Neil replied. "The chief investigator of the Securities and Exchange Commission paid us a little visit today—Enforcement Division, Mario. He was asking questions about the Lions' Den."

Mario sat upright. "What tipped off the boys at the SEC?"

"After that conversation you had with the Crown Prince, is it any wonder?"

"That would be a good guess. Who's the investigator?"

"Are you ready? Elliot Case, himself."

"Muthafucker," Mario shouted, slamming the coffee table. "How much do they know, Neil?"

"They know everything—even about the laundered money to Roger."

"What did you tell him?"

"That's just it, Mario, I didn't tell him *anything*. I told him I didn't know what he was talking about, and he just laughed."

"He laughed?"

"The son of a bitch bastard just laughed at me. He wants to set up a meeting with the board of directors to discuss how we financed the club. He's asked us—all of us—to come to the SEC's New York office tomorrow morning. Voluntarily. And to bring counsel."

"Did he mention my name?"

"You were the one he came looking for. I said you were out of town, couldn't be reached, but I'm sure he didn't buy it," Neil replied.

Mario felt as though the floor had suddenly disappeared, and he was free falling, into a bottomless pit. "Where you calling from?"

"I'm at pay phone outside Grand Central."

"Neil, don't call from the office. I'm sure it's bugged. And use a disposable cell."

"What are we gonna do?"

"First thing we gotta do is get hold of Roger before they do."

"Forget it. I swung by his studio earlier. He's gone."

"Gone? What do you mean, gone?"

"Just what I said, checked out. Corcoran got the place up for sale. No one knows *where* the fuck he is. Do you think Rog dealt us?"

"Forget Roger for now," Mario said. "Neil, you gotta go back to the Den and empty out that safe. Tonight. We can't let them get their hands on the membership list…" Then he heard an awkward silence on the other end. "Neil…Neil, did you hear what I said?"

"They already *have* the membership list," Neil replied in a voice devoid of emotion.

Mario went weak in the knees. He had no more cards to play. "Start getting word to the members," he instructed.

"Dennis and Barry are already taking care of that," Neil said. "Everyone is meeting with their attorneys, and the members are huddled with their spokespeople, working up denials for their companies to issue."

"Where the fuck is Tyler?" asked Mario. "We gotta do the same."

"He's MIA, too, somewhere out in Hong Kong this time."

"Again?" That was very peculiar, Mario thought. Tyler again was in China. "Have you called Frank, Neil?"

"No. I thought *you'd* want to do that. Besides, I don't know what to say to him. I don't really know how exposed he is."

"You gotta call him. Right away. He's gotta get Burt to find Roger before Case does." Frank's going to go ballistic, he thought. His brother didn't deserve any of this. He'd helped only with great reluctance. God, Wall Street is going to get hit with another torpedo. And one with a lot more juice in its tank. The Lions' Den was bound to sink plenty of reputations, and Mario knew his and Frank's were first in line.

"We really need you here, paisan," Neil said." There was just a hint of desperation in Neil's voice, and it cut Mario to the quick.

Mario glanced at the closed bedroom door. "I can't come back yet, Neil. I just can't do it. I'm right on the verge here. If I leave now, I'm going to lose my son, forever."

"If you don't, Case will come looking for you. And he'll find you."

"Once things are settled with Boomer, it doesn't matter. Try to put him off the trail, if you can do that, without taking any risks."

"Mario, I don't want to go to jail…"

"No one's going to jail, Neil," Mario said with a lot more confidence than he felt.

Then he hung up. His first instinct was to get in touch with Tyler, anyway possible, but thought better of it. Tyler couldn't possibly explain the Lions' Den to the partners. Nor could he explain to Judith Clarke, or the women in the firm. And suddenly there were a lot more of them around, in senior positions, who would make sure the scandal, left unaddressed, found its way into the tabloids. He would then be forced to endure day after agonizing day of the slow summer news cycle that produced no war, no terror attack or gruesome murder to drive the The Lions' Den from the headlines, festooned across the front pages in the mainstream media, providing endless fodder for the monologues of late-night comedians. Was there any end to his troubles? Was everything in his life going to turn to shit?

He leaned back and closed his eyes. He was making good progress with Boomer. He felt hopeful things with Julie would turn out okay. But the SEC? How the fuck was he gonna finesse *that*? Was he headed for prison? And Frank for that matter…

He would deal with all that later. He had a son to take care of now. He walked into the bedroom, but Boomer wasn't in the bed as he'd expected. Oh shit, he thought. He ran out the front door calling for Boomer.

There was no sign of him, but the truck was still there. "Boomer?" he called loudly, then listened. No answer. Mario sprinted down the driveway, into the woods, looking and calling.

A few hundred yards into the woods, Mario came to a clearing. There was a rainwater pond there. He and the boys had waded through it a few summers ago before his life became a shit storm.

There he was, at the edge of the pond, dangling his bare feet in the moonlit water, sitting there as though he didn't have a care in the world.

"I've been calling for you," Mario said. "Why didn't you answer?"

"Didn't hear you," Boomer explained. His arm shot out as he tried to capture a tiny frog, but the frog got away.

"I didn't know what to think," Mario said, and sat beside him.

Boomer met his father's eyes. "Yeah. Sorry about that. I should have told you I was going for a little walk."

The tiny frog hopped past Boomer, who caught it with ease.

"What are you going to do with it?" Mario asked, grinning.

Boomer looked directly into his father's eyes. Mario recognized the look. It was the way Gus sometimes looked at him. "I'm going to set it free," Boomer said.

And he did just that.

CHAPTER THIRTY-ONE

If Boomer had been his only worry, Mario would have slept well that night. The boy was really coming around, even faster than he'd hoped. And there was a bonus—he felt closer to his son than he had in years.

But Mario didn't sleep well at all. He had other worries—about the SEC's next move, about what might happen to the Zoo Crew. And Tyler's secrecy kept gnawing at him. What the fuck could he be cooking up in China? And finally there was Julie—he hadn't heard from her more than a week now and he didn't understand why.

Then the telephone rang. Mario picked up the receiver expectantly, pathetically hopeful. "Hello?"

"It's me," Neil said.

"Talk to me."

"It's bad, Mario, *Worse* than bad. They're handing down indictments tomorrow."

"Bullshit."

"Bullshit?" Neil said. "They got our balls in a bear trap. Case knows everything about the Den. Not only member identities, but employees, city officials, even the offshore financing. They're already moving to indict Kat's brothers, along with Bill Bronson and half his team."

"But I told you to burn everything, Neil."

"Except for the membership lists, I *did* burn everything. How they know is anyone's guess."

"Jesus fucking Christ." How could the crown Prince have known about the financing, he thought.

"And that's not all—there were a couple of suits in the room when Case was questioning us. Not Eagle types. My mouthpiece later told me they were...are you ready for this? From Homeland Security."

That stopped Mario cold. Homeland Security? "There's more here than meets the eye, Neil. I'm not sure what, but I think the Eagle must have a reason for swooping down on us that has nothing to do with the Lions' Den."

"What are you talking about?"

"I think we're caught in the crossfire of something."

"Like what?" Neil asked.

"I don't know," said Mario. "But they're leveraging off you to get to me. It's *me* they want, Neil. They came looking for *me*, right?"

Mario knew the drill. The only way he could save Neil and the Zoo Crew was to give Case and the SEC whatever the fuck they wanted. Only he didn't have the slightest idea what they wanted. He wondered if this was the Crown Prince's' back-assward way of keeping his mouth shut while Jaffe's Senate hearings played out on national television. And if the Heir Apparent's tentacles now reached inside the SEC, then the whole country was fucked.

But that didn't make sense. Elliot Case was a straight shooter, the ultimate company man, with higher aspirations. And discrediting Wall Street's King would do it. It was common knowledge people had tried to bribe him—with millions. But they'd just ended up with longer jail terms.

All Mario knew was that by giving Case what he wanted, he might be able to deal everyone else off the hook, maybe even get him to deep-six the membership lists. *Especially* the membership lists.

"Did they offer you immunity, Neil?"

The voice on the other end went mute.

"Neil? I asked if Case offered you immunity if you gave me up?"

"They're talking more than thirty counts of finance fraud and money laundering," Neil said. His voice quivered with raw fear.

"Take the deal," Mario said resolutely.

"No!" Neil objected, "I couldn't live with myself."

"The guilt will go away, Neil." But Mario, an expert in guilt, knew it wouldn't.

"What are you, fucking Jesus Christ? You think I'm gonna give these SEC bastards the nails to hammer you to the cross?"

"Don't worry about me. Friends come and go, but family is forever. Your wife is at a fat farm showing you how much she loves you," Mario reminded him. "Some things in this world you never risk."

"You could go to prison, Mario. Twenty years."

"This is what I need you to do," Mario instructed. "Round up the guys… away from the office. That goes for Frank, too. Tell them to do whatever they need to do to save themselves…NOW." It was Mario giving the Zoo Crew a *get out of jail free* card, and trying to unburden them from their conscience for throwing him under a bus.

"By the way, did Burt find our friend?"

"Roger? Oh, you won't have to worry about *him* anymore."

"He'll keep quiet?"

"He's dead."

Mario was flabbergasted. "Dead? When? How?"

"Out in South Beach. Your brother said it was AIDS."

"I didn't even know he was sick," Mario said.

"I guess the stress did him in." Neil replied.

"And it's gonna do *you* in unless you get the Zoo Crew to cooperate with the SEC."

"Mario, this could all go very bad."

"Lotta bad things happening in my life, Neil. It's time I faced them head on."

"Hey, lady," said the tattooed dolly-wheeling mover in a sleeveless t-shirt, "this go, too?" He pointed at a battered, tan four-door filing cabinet.

Julie thought a moment. It was stuffed, pretty much to the brim, with old scripts, outlines, proposals, program research, all of it spilling out of its drawers. "Yeah," she sighed, "that goes, too."

She looked around the office. There wasn't much, really: a half dozen cardboard file boxes, a computer with a scanner and an external back-up hard disk, the Aeon chair her staff had given her a couple of years ago, and a few potted plants.

"What about *this*?" asked the other mover, a wiry young Latino. He was pointing at a vintage photograph of Mary Tyler Moore and the entire cast of her show on the set of a makeshift news room. It had been autographed by everyone.

Julie laughed. "I think that's part of the office. It was there when I got here. If you take that off the wall, the building might fall down."

The mover shrugged, left the picture as it was, and left the room with his partner.

There was one personal item left, however. The Emmy Julie had won for "*America for Sale*." Taking that down from the shelf was really the end of an era. Now she understood what Hank had been hinting at months earlier when he remarked how he would like to leave something behind when he retired. She hoped she'd given him that.

As she reached for the Emmy, Fred walked into her office.

"Ah," he said, teasing, "I was hoping you'd leave that for *me*."

"Not on your life," Julie said. "Besides, you have plenty of your own."

"It's not possible to have too many of those," Fred told her. They both looked at the gold figurine. "Nobody's ever deserved one of those more than you, Julie."

"Thanks, Fred," Julie said. "That really means a lot coming from you." She gave him a peck on the cheek that was enough to make him blush.

"I'll be expecting more big things from you, Missy," Fred said. It was the first time he called her *Missy*. "Knock 'em dead in Washington."

"I'll do my best."

Fred departed, leaving Julie by herself.

She watched the movers trundle it all away, cleaning out her entire history. It was like her memories were being erased.

Once Julie had told Miles of her decision to accept the Washington job, things started to happen. Fred got cleared by his doctor and was reinstated full time. She was asked to approve renovation plans for the Washington bureau. News releases were prepared to announce the changes.

When they wheeled out the file cabinet, all that remained were two battered aluminum guest chairs, a steel desk sitting on a beige Berber rug, a couple of desk phones, and her plastic nameplate, which she grabbed and stuck into one of the cardboard file boxes.

Of course, she wasn't really leaving UBS, just switching offices. All that was superficial, unimportant. What was important, and what was almost unbearably heartbreaking, was that she was leaving Mario.

It was one of the hardest things she'd ever had to do, almost as hard as standing in the cemetery and watching Jack's coffin disappear into the ground. But that had been involuntary. This time, she was choosing, choosing to leave a man she loved *because* she loved him, because she could not allow herself to cause him more grief, but mostly because she could not bear to come between Mario and his children, especially Boomer.

Now, everyone at UBS, it seemed, dropped by to wish her final farewell— Carol, Tex, Cal, Lisa, and Marty. Then Tom Gallagher along with an army of associate producers, and the tech crews, even the phone operators. One of the last to appear was Hank. He waited till everyone left then stuck his head inside.

"Can an old friend say goodbye?"

"Hey," she said, forcing a smile, "I thought you were off cruising somewhere."

"We sail for Europe on Monday. First stop, Athens, Greece. Margie always wanted to see the Greek islands."

"I envy you," Julie said.

"Nah, I'm the envious one. You're going to love Washington. You'll see some real history in the making, even be part of it."

"I'm looking forward to it," Julie said quietly. Hank had misinterpreted her envy, but now he understood.

"Something may work out anyhow, you know," he said, putting an arm around her shoulder. "Life is like that."

She knew Hank was trying to help her through it all, and she felt a rush of affection for the man who'd stuck his head in a noose for her more than once.

"Maybe you're right," she said.

They stepped outside of what had been her office, giving the movers room to maneuver their dollies, watching everyone riveted to John Ayers on the news room monitors. UBS like all other networks had begun blanket news coverage of the Senate Commerce Committee's Wall Street hearings about foreign investment in the United States. The committee chairman, Senator Milton Jaffe, had introduced a bill to restrict it, but was getting partisan resistance moving the measure out of committee and onto the Senate floor for a vote.

Julie and Hank watched as Jaffe launched his crusade against the embattled industry, addressing his committee, speaking passionately about the Saudi threat to America, proposing an open hearing on the subject. But his voice was alarmingly weak, and the skepticism of the committee was unmistakable.

Hank turned to Julie. "Do you think the old boy got a chance?"

Julie shook her head. "I don't know."

"Yeah, me neither," he sighed. "Well, then…I guess this is it, Julie. Call me when you get settled."

"I will, I promise. And Bon Voyage." They hugged and then he was gone.

Julie walked back into her office—what had been her office—for one last look, and Paige came in behind her.

"Julie…," Paige began.

"Paige I…," Julie started the same moment.

They laughed, having started their goodbyes at the same instant.

"You first," Paige said.

"I was going to say how terribly I'll miss you," Julie said. "I don't know how I could have done anything worthwhile without your help. You've been my rock, Paige." And she found that she meant what she was saying. Paige wasn't that cute Vassar intern she hired out of college a few years ago. She had watched Paige mature personally, as well as professionally.

"I've had an incredible time working with you, Julie. When I think of how little I knew before you got here. I couldn't have asked for a better mentor."

Julie reached out her arms and they hugged, tears in their eyes.

Then Tex stuck his head in the doorway and interrupted the moment. "Julie, your ride is here."

Then they parted, and Paige headed for the office door. Halfway there, she stopped and looked back at Julie, with affection…and sympathy.

"Call him, Julie," she said. "Don't leave without saying goodbye."

Then Paige closed the door behind her, leaving Julie alone in the empty room. She stared at the phone, then picked it up.

Mario was just getting out of the shower when the phone rang.

"It's all right, Dad," Boomer shouted over the kitchen radio, "*I* got it." Boomer picked it up in the living room, before it could ring again. "Hello?" he said cheerfully.

Julie froze, surprised by Boomer's light-hearted greeting.

"…hello…hello," Boomer repeated. She'd been nervous enough about this call, and having Boomer answer unnerved her even more. She resisted the urge to hang up, closed her eyes, swallowed hard, and let the chips fall.

"Hello, Boomer, it's Julie…Julie Chambers. I *do* hope you're feeling well." Boomer said nothing, and Julie knew why. He wasn't happy to hear her voice or to have her calling his father. But she wasn't about to give up.

"Boomer, could I please speak with your father?"

More silence.

"*Please,* Boomer," she implored, pitifully. "Please."

Mario heard Boomer call him to the phone as he was toweling off his hair. He walked into the living room and found Boomer looking at him sourly, holding out the receiver.

"Lower that thing?" Mario said. Without a word, Boomer brushed past his father, handing him the phone. Mario looked at him curiously, lowered the radio, and held the phone to his ear.

"Hello?"

"It's me, Mario."

As he heard the sweet sound of Julie's voice, he watched Boomer disappear into the bedroom.

"Mario, are you there?...Mario?"

"Yes, sweetheart," he sighed. "I'm here."

"How's Boomer doing? He sounds better."

"It was bad there for a while, but I think he's coming along. We're heading back tomorrow. I miss you. Are you home?"

"Actually," she said, "I'm in what used to be my office."

"Boy, *that* was quick. Fisher didn't waste any time bumping you upstairs, did he?"

"That's why I'm calling," she said, and dreading what she was about to say. "I know I shouldn't do it like this, but if we were face-to-face, I couldn't. And I'd have to."

Mario felt his gut go into freefall. "Do what?"

"Mario, I've decided to take the Washington job after all." She said it flatly and directly, as if it was pure fact and not subject to debate.

For a moment, Mario didn't understand. "But, I thought you were...how can you do the Washington job from New York?"

"I can't," Julie said. It was the strangest thing—like someone else was talking, and she were only listening. "I'm going to move."

Mario sat down on the couch. "To Washington?" He was trying to keep the emotion out of his voice.

"Yes, Mario. I'm leaving on the Amtrak tonight." More indisputable fact.

"Tonight? As in...this night?"

"Yes. I'll be on the six o'clock. As a matter of fact, the car is downstairs ready to take me to Penn Station."

Mario was having trouble breathing. "When did you decide all this?"

"Last week."

"And you never said anything, until now?"

"You were going through so much with your son, I just couldn't."

But it was more than that, Mario thought. This was the way she intended it. She wasn't just leaving New York. She was leaving *him.* "Julie, if this about Phyllis giving me a divorce..."

"No, Mario, this has nothing to do with your wife," she said.

"Then what, Julie…please tell me."

"I…I just can't bear knowing what leaving would do to you and your family. The way you love your kids. You'll never survive the collateral damage. And neither will I."

She gallantly fought back the impulse to start crying. When life abruptly snatched away Jack, the love of her life, she was shattered. She went through an almost total shutdown. Fate had done that to her. Now, *she* was doing it, to herself, pushing away the very man who had rescued her from despair.

"I feel like a rudderless ship in a storm," Mario said. "And now I'm losing *everything* that meant *anything*. First Gus, now you…now this mess I find myself in over the Lions' Den with the feds. About the only thing that keeps me from putting a bullet through my head is that my son needs me."

For a moment, all of her determination vanished, as did all of the reasons to break it off with him that she'd so carefully thought out. "Then come with me," she said softly. "It doesn't have to be Washington, Mario. We can run to Europe, maybe Canada, or anywhere they won't extradite you, for that matter."

Mario so desperately wanted to tell her *yes,* that he would be with her on the six o' clock at Penn Station, or some airport, that they would escape and always be together. But what Julie said earlier was right—it would mean leaving something behind. Something he didn't have the will to walk away from. He began to cry softly—and Julie heard him.

"I can't," he said.

"So you're going to stick it out for—the kids," she said. "You're going to suffer through it."

"What else I can do?" Mario replied.

"I understand," Julie cried, reminding herself why she loved him.

"Thank you," he told her.

"For what?"

"For saving me. For letting me know what I've missed." At least he had that, Mario thought. At least he knew what could have been.

"I gotta go, Mario," she managed to say in a voice almost too faint to hear.

Then she quietly hung up the phone.

Mario sat motionless, staring at nothing, the telephone still in his hand.

Mario and Boomer ate leftovers that night, hardly speaking. After they cleaned up, Boomer retreated to the bedroom and tried to get some sleep.

When darkness finally fell, Mario walked out onto the porch and sat on the wooden swing, in the glow of the porch light, trying to figure out how he was going to go on.

The forest sounds intruded into his consciousness—the chirping crickets, the croaking frogs, the hoot of owls. Life in the Catskills as it had been for thousands of years, and as it would be for thousands more. With him or without him.

The cabin door creaked opened and Boomer hesitantly walked out onto the porch, wearing the ratty plaid bathrobe they'd found in the closet.

"Having a little trouble sleeping?" Mario asked.

"Yeah," Boomer sighed.

Boomer walked toward the porch steps and leaned against the roof column, away from his father.

Mario looked up at the glittering night sky. "Every star in the universe must be out tonight. This place is pretty close to Paradise. I'll sure miss it."

Boomer didn't look up. Something was on his mind.

"So, what do you think? Ready to go back to the real world tomorrow?" Mario asked. "I bet you're looking forward to graduation…"

"You really love her, don't 'cha, Dad," Boomer said, out of the blue. It wasn't really a question. Mario was taken aback and didn't know how to respond.

"I listened to the both of you say goodbye," Boomer solemnly reflected. "I never heard you cry before. Not even when Grandma died. It hurts to see someone you love so unhappy. Now I know what you must've felt worrying about *me*." He leaned his back against the roof column, then looked up at the sky and sighed.

"I'll feel better tomorrow," Mario said, his voice laced with sorrow. "But tonight—tonight I'm going to feel bad."

Boomer looked down toward the lake, which perfectly reflected the starry sky, then decided to say what was on his mind. "Dad, I was kinda thinking. Since I'll be away to school in the fall, maybe you'll have time to think more about yourself, what with one less kid to worry about."

"You think just because you're turning eighteen next week I can stop worrying about you?"

"That's not what I meant," Boomer said.

"Then what *do* you mean?"

"Remember when Kyle found the bird with the broken wing that one summer we came up here?"

"Bird?"

"Yeah, a blue sparrow, I think. He brought it into the cabin and we fixed its wing, then kept it in a cage for awhile."

"Vaguely. What about it?" Mario said.

"You made us let it go. You said it wasn't happy living in a cage. It had to be free to live its life, no matter how sad we felt about letting it go or…"

"Or, what?"

"Or how much we loved it," Boomer recalled.

"So what are you telling me—you're like a bird who should be set free to live your life?"

"No, Dad," Boomer said, tears welling up in his eyes. "*You* are."

"Boomer, what are you say…?"

"You belong with her, Dad." He turned his head to his father. "Nothing else matters."

Boomer rushed to his father and fell to his knees, resting his head in Mario's lap. He was crying. Mario held his lips to his son's head, gently petted his hair, and kissed him while rocking him.

That night, while preparing for the long drive back to Long Island, Mario heard a car engine in the distance. He glanced out the window and saw a pair of halogen headlights slicing through the darkness.

As the car approached the cabin, Mario saw it was a big, black Ford Victoria. He stopped what he was doing and walked onto the porch, right into the glare of the high beams. He was totally exposed now. If someone had come to do him harm, there wasn't much he could do about it.

Then the engine cut off, the headlights were switched off, the scene now lit only by dim porch light. A meticulously dressed man got out of the driver's side and stood alongside the car, expressionless, while another man, taller, got out of the back seat. Mario recognized the second man.

"I see you fellas found the place," Mario said.

"We finally meet, Mr. Monelli," Elliot Case replied with gentle sarcasm. "You're not easy to find."

Curious about what was going on, Boomer joined his father on the porch. "Dad?"

"It's alright, Boomer. This is Elliot Case of the Securities and Exchange Commission."

Case shook hands with Boomer, both of them a little flustered, Case because he hadn't expected Boomer, Boomer because he was intimidated.

Then Case looked at his surroundings—at the cabin, at the handsome Hummer in the driveway. "Son, would you mind if I have a few moments alone with your dad?"

"I have no secrets from my son," Mario replied calmly. Boomer is gonna find out everything anyway, he thought.

"Okay—Boomer, is it? You have a driver's license?"

Boomer looked at Case with suspicion. "Yeah," he said.

"Your dad let you drive that vehicle?" Case nodded in the direction of the Hummer.

"Yes, I let him drive it," Mario said, obviously disliking the banter between Case and his son. "Why?"

"Because you're not going to be driving it for a few days," said the other man.

"Are you arresting me?"

"No," Case said in a manner that wasn't reassuring. "Not yet anyway. Let's say I'm detaining you and taking you for a little trip."

"Dad, what's going on?"

"What about my son?" asked Mario. "I can't leave him alone here."

"I just heard the boy say he could drive home," said the other agent.

"It's past midnight, I'm not about to let my son drive…"

"It's okay, Dad, I'll be fine," Boomer said. "Really." Then he turned to Case. "Where are you taking my father?"

"Down to Washington. We have some things to discuss."

"When are you bringing him back?" Boomer asked, trying to sound threatening.

Case smiled at him, indulgently. "Depends on him."

At Case's prompting, Mario went inside the cabin and grabbed his bag.

When he came back out he took a few steps toward the Ford, then stopped and held out his arms to Boomer. Case stood by, not all that patiently, while they slipped into a long and meaningful embrace. Mario fished the car keys out of his pocket and tossed them to Boomer. "Tell your mother I'll be in touch."

Then Mario got into the Ford's back seat, feeling as though he was entering a black hole. Case slipped in beside him and closed the door. "Drive carefully," Mario said to his son. "And don't worry about me. I'll be fine."

Boomer nodded, bravely.

The driver gave Boomer a little wave, then joined his passengers, and the car drove off.

They met along the West Side Highway, a few blocks from Vesey Street and the World Financial Center, in the middle of a ball field that had been used as a Graves Registration in the days following 9/11.

The first to get there was Neil, which wasn't surprising. Barry, who had never been late to anything in his life, was next, then came Dennis, accompanied by Kat, and finally Glen, who was both pissed and confused.

"So what's with the fuckin' cloak-and-dagger stuff, Neil? Handwritten notes instead of just telling us, or e-mailing us. Separate exits. You've been watching the Maltese Falcon?"

"Just taking the necessary precautions. Mario thinks they're watching us."

"Who's 'they,' Neil?" Barry asked, totally baffled.

"Yes," Kat said, "and where is Mario? Wasn't he due back yesterday?"

Neil described the catastrophe that had befallen Mario. And how Case was putting the screws to him in Washington—because of the Lions' Den.

Dennis shot him a worried look. "Washington? Why the fuck do they got him in D.C.? We were grilled right here."

"Washington—New York, who cares?" Glen said. "Just remember, none of this was my idea."

"That so, Glen?" Dennis asked. "Seems to me you spent more time getting your knob polished at that place than all the rest of us put together."

Barry had turned white. "Oy gevalt, when my mother hears about this, she's really going to have a heart attack."

Neil held up a hand. "If we're arrested, Mario wants us all to make deals with the feds. He doesn't want any of us taking the hit."

"He wants us to rat him out?" asked Barry.

"Yes," said Neil. "If it'll save us."

"And you know this, how?" Kat asked, unconvinced.

"I talked to him last night. He was crystal clear—and very stubborn about it."

"No offense, Neil, but I would need to hear that from Mario, himself," Dennis said.

"Me too," said Glen.

"We can't. We're all under surveillance, remember?" Neil replied angrily.

"What kind of deal was he talking about?" Kat asked, worried.

"I'm going for immunity," Barry announced. "I'm telling those fuckers whatever they want to hear. I'm not going to jail or having my licenses revoked."

"Wait a minute," said Glen. "How did that Case prick know where to pinch Mario? None of us knew where he was hiding."

"None of us except you, Neil," said Dennis.

"You Judas Fuck," Glen said, "you shorted him!"

Glen took a step toward Neil, reared back, and slugged him in the face, drawing blood, and shocking everyone. Before he could get off another blow, Dennis and Barry wrestled him away.

"He's the godfather of your daughter, Makarios!" Glen shouted, furious.

"Neil's right, Glen," Dennis said, holding him back. "It's the only card left."

"I love him, too, Glen," Neil said. "You know that. But I can't go down. I can't abandon my family. None of us can, and Mario doesn't want us to."

Kat handed Neil a handkerchief. He held it over his nose, hoping to stop the bleeding.

"If you're smart, you'll all do the same," Neil said, painfully pressing the bloody handkerchief against his nose.

Glen got to his feet. "Denny, you're not going along with this, are you?" Then he saw the expression on Dennis's face, and stopped talking.

"You heard Neil, Glen. In a few days, they'll move against him. And if they do without our help, we lose immunity."

"We swore to always stick by one another, Denny," Glen said, stunned.

"Well the world's changed. You willing to do a dime away from Amanda, Glen? And what about your ole lady, Barry? Or my Marie?"

Glen had tears in his eyes now. They all knew what had to be done, even if it was at Mario's expense.

"So I guess this is it," Kat said, looking at the crestfallen faces around her. "It's time to look out for number one."

They looked at each other again, no smiles, no feelings of camaraderie. Then they broke off in different directions.

CHAPTER THIRTY-TWO

They didn't put him in handcuffs, and no one was showing any artillery, but he still felt like a prisoner. Maybe that was because he'd just spent the night in a two-star hotel room under guard, or because he was sitting here, in his lumberjack clothes, in the office of the acting chairman of the Securities and Exchange Commission, surrounded by five men in suits. Unfriendly men.

Elliot Case introduced them—Ben Hersh, the senior deputy director and acting SEC chairman, grimfaced and grey; Joe Roberts, an FBI special counter-terrorism agent, a good-looking black man with the build of a wide receiver; Oswald Sinclair, deputy director of Homeland Security, tall, thin and angry; and Carl Ryan, from the IRS, short and florid-faced, with eyes gleaming like a timber wolf. No one smiled, no one offered a hand to be shaken.

Hersh was sitting behind his desk in a black leather chair so big it seemed to swallow him. As for Mario, they had him sitting on a small hard wooden stool in the middle of the room.

This didn't make any sense, Mario thought. He and the Zoo Crew may have bent a few minor municipal statutes, and maybe strayed into some grey areas with the SEC, but this turn-out was ridiculous. He could understand the IRS being here, the offshore financing was an issue, kind of. But the FBI? Counter-terrorism? What the hell was *that* all about? And Homeland Security? That was almost comical.

"Mr. Monelli," said Ben Hersh, switching on a tape recorder, "do you know why you're here?"

"I'm here because your enforcement agent brought me," Mario said snidely.

The other men exchanged glances, as if Mario had just confirmed their suspicions—that, among other things, he was an arrogant, over-confident big-mouth whose recent celebrity had swelled his head.

"And did he offer you any reason for bringing you here."

"Yeah. He said I'm in trouble. Except for those indictments you've been handing out like hors d'oeuvre, I have no idea what the hell he was talking about."

"This is an informal meeting. Do you wish to be represented by counsel?"

"Maybe it would've been nice if your guy had made that offer back in New York."

Hersh sighed. "I was hoping we could do this in a cooperative spirit," he said.

"I see," Mario said. "You're about to hang me by the balls and you want me to help."

The black FBI guy looked at him coldly. "Do you think this is a time for jokes, Monelli?"

Why the hell not, Mario said to himself. What did he have to lose anyhow? Julie was gone, the Lions' Den was finished, and probably his career. Marriage, too, although that was good news. And there was Boomer. After the inevitable legal fees and fines, he'd be lucky to put Boomer through trade school. And then there were his friends and all of those indictments.

"I want to let you know you're under investigation."

"You mean you didn't bring me out here for a tour of the White House."

"Let's start with the most serious charges, gentlemen," Hersh said. "They may supersede everything else. Oswald?"

The man from Homeland Security turned toward Mario, looking at him as though he were a child molester. "It is my duty to inform you about certain information that has come into our hands, information concerning you and...your associates. The way I see it, you have two choices, Monelli. You can tell us everything you know—and I mean *everything*—or you can start preparing yourself for a new way of life in the Guantanamo prisons."

Mario laughed, which infuriated Sinclair. This is how these pricks probably scared the shit out of Roger. "You mean to tell me you think I'm a terrorist because I set up a private club?"

"Mr. Monelli," Sinclair went on, ignoring Monelli's protest, "do you know a Roger Duvall?"

Monelli thought a moment. What harm could there be in confessing something they already knew? "Sure I do. So what?"

"Are you aware that his father was an Egyptian who was instrumental in the plot to assassinate Anwar Sadat and a known associate of Osama Bin Laden's bankers."

Mario was flabbergasted. "You can't mean the Roger Duvall *I* know," he said. "The architect?"

"That's exactly who I mean," Sinclair said. He flicked a bit of dirt from under a fingernail. "Do you deny knowing him?"

"No—but it couldn't be the same guy. Roger's just a harmless old queen."

"Then why is he sending tens of thousands of dollars to shady characters in the Middle East, and receiving a secret package destined for your—um—establishment?"

"Before you answer that question," said agent Roberts, "I need to warn you that we have in our possession not only all of the Lions' Club bank records, but also Duvall's records, and certain receipts from the Bank Financiere de la Cite in Geneva."

Sinclair had something to add. "We also have proof of certain cash transfers between the Lions' Den entity and Duvall. Your friend tried to launder the money through a bank in Gibraltar, but he failed."

Mario grinned broadly and glanced at Ben Hersh, behind his desk. "I'm not responsible for what Roger did with the money we paid him. He was our architect and designer. He didn't do it for nothing."

"And what about the package?" Sinclair asked.

"What about it?"

"That had all the earmarks of a terrorist weapons shipment. But we never found it." He stared coldly at Mario, hoping to intimidate him.

"Sure you did," Mario said. "When you broke into the Lions' Den in the middle of the night. It's that stupid lion statue standing at the bottom of the grand stairway."

The FBI agent stared at Mario, astonished. "Who told you we broke..."

"You did," Mario interrupted. "Just now."

Ben Hersh looked at Case, then groaned, reached into his pocket, pulled out a pack of Rolaids, and popped one into his mouth.

Case turned his attention to Roberts. "Don't they teach you anything at the FBI?"

"Don't be too hard on him, Elliot," Mario interrupted. "There's no excess of brains over at the SEC either. You clowns could've had Madoff much sooner if your team didn't have its head up its ass."

"Mr. Monelli, you're not taking this seriously," Hersh admonished.

"I'm glad you noticed, Ben."

The phone on Hersh's desk rang and Hersh picked it up, annoyed. "Hi, sweetheart. I'm in a meeting. No, I *can't* talk now, I'll call you back." He hung up and turned back toward the group a little embarrassed. "My wife," he said, by way of explanation.

"Sounds like a bit of a pain, Benjamin. I may be able to get you a Gold membership at the Den. Seems like a few of the guys won't be renewing their privileges."

"What were we talking about?" Ben said, ignoring Mario's sarcasm.

"Roger Duvall," Sinclair reminded him, then to Mario: "Tell me everything you know."

"I don't know much," Mario said. "except that he died in South Beach a few days ago."

Sinclair pounced. "Did you kill him? Or did you send one of your *associates* to do the job?"

"I got a call from a friend," Mario explained, casually. "I hope they don't let you interrogate any *real* terrorists."

Sinclair's eyes narrowed and he wheeled around to glare at Roberts, the FBI agent. "Weren't you monitoring the calls to the cabin?" he asked.

"Yes, we heard that call, but I didn't think it was relevant."

Steam almost shot out of the top of Sinclair's head. "My God, man, have you people still not learned to share your information with Homeland Security? What if this had been a real..."

Hersh leaned back in his chair and stared at the ceiling.

"I think you're finished here," Mario said. "No sale on the terrorist scenario."

Sinclair looked at Hersh, confused and panicked.

"You go ahead, Oswald," Hersh said. "I think we can handle it from here."

Sinclair picked up his briefcase and left, in a huff, and Roberts got up, too, but Hersh motioned him to stay.

"I see," Mario said. "The FBI isn't finished with me. "Well, bring it on, Mr. FBI. tell me what I'm charged with."

Roberts opened his briefcase and took out a full-sized black-and-white photo of the Lions' Den grand stairway, and the pair of lions at the bottom. He handed it to Mario.

Mario examined the picture with interest. "Hmmm. Taken at night, I see. I guess that's when you broke into the club."

"We had a warrant," Roberts shot back.

"No doubt," Mario agreed. "But I'm sorry you didn't come when we were open. You would have had a good time—well, maybe not. I don't think you're the type."

"Ha, ha," Joe Roberts said without a trace of humor. "These statues are antiquities of almost incalculable value, and try as we might, we haven't been able to locate any custom information to indicate that you legally imported it."

"And the penalty for that would be..." Mario inquired with mild interest.

Case answered. "The penalty for criminal smuggling is a federal offense with up to ten years in prison, and if the object was stolen or illegally removed from its country of origin, there will no doubt be additional criminal charges mandated by an international court. Of course you'll need to be extradited. Agent Roberts, what do you suppose the sentence is in Jordan for theft of a national artifact?"

Agent Roberts grinned fiendishly.

"I had nothing to do with the fuckin' lions," Mario said. "None of us did." This was nothing like Mario had expected. He'd expected to be grilled about the financing of the Lions' Den and perhaps the fraudulent purchase of the building itself—but terrorism? Smuggling? "This is plain bullshit," Mario told the FBI agent. "None of those charges will stick."

"Oh, really?" Roberts said. "Well, we know exactly when, where, and from whom Roger Duvall bought the lions. We can trace the money he used to pay for it. And," he said, waving the photograph, "we know just where it ended up."

Mario just shook his head, sadly. "You know so much, Agent Roberts, and yet you know so little. You know the lions are stolen, but you don't know if *I* knew that. You know Roger bought it, but you don't know if *I* had any idea how he was going to use the money we paid him. You know it was smuggled, but you don't know if *I* knew…"

"When I get you in court…"

"You're not going to be able to convince any jury—without a reasonable doubt—that my friends and I were anything but naïve end users. But if you want to waste the taxpayers' money, and don't mind making a fool out of yourself and the FBI, go right ahead."

Roberts kept quiet, but his eyes were blazing.

"Listen, Ben—you don't mind if I call you Ben, do you?—before you start waterboarding me, mind I get a shot at a urinal? I'd hate to make a mess on your nice Berber carpeting," Mario said.

Hersh nodded to Case, who rose. "Come with me, Monelli."

"Do you want to hold it, Elliot, or can I?"

"You're quite a joker, aren't you, Monelli?" Case said. He pulled himself up out of the deep leather couch.

They walked down the wide marble-floor hallway outside of Hersh's office, into the men's room. Mario looked around, amazed. "I had you boys pegged all wrong," he told Case. "I count fifteen stalls there—"

"Your point?"

"How could anyone at the SEC be full of shit with that many toilets available?"

"Try not to piss yourself," Elliot said.

Mario chose a urinal in the middle of a long line of stainless steel fixtures, and relieved himself at length, while Elliot kept a watchful eye, unable to resist temptation.

"So answer me something, Monelli," he said. "Exactly how many women do you and your degenerate pals need to fuck in that place of yours to prove you can all get laid?"

"Oh, I don't know, Elliott," replied Mario. "How many women would you say live in Manhattan?"

The stinging reply wiped the smug grin off Case.

"You should congratulate me," he told Case, zipping up.

"Yeah? Why is that?"

"I've just made a substantial contribution to government waste."

"You know, Monelli, I think that TV show went to your head. But I have a feeling that by the end of the day, you won't be making jokes anymore."

When they got back to Hersh's office, agent Roberts was gone. But Carl Ryan, the IRS investigative agent, was going through his files and evidently getting his ducks in order.

Mario took his seat and smiled at Hersh. "Okay," he said, "who's the lead-off hitter in this inning?"

"I think that honor is mine, Mr. Monelli," said Ryan, sizing up Mario in the way a tiger regards a gazelle.

Ryan handed Mario a sheaf of papers. "Recognize these?"

Mario leafed through the papers. "My income tax returns," he said. "My God, these go back ten years."

"Twelve," Ryan corrected.

"Well my accountant can support everything in every one of these returns," Mario said.

"I'm sure," the IRS agent said, quietly confident. "But that's not what interests me. It's what *doesn't* show up on your returns."

"Well, you can't mean my casino winnings—and losses. They're all spelled out, to the last penny."

"Be that as it may, there are glaring omissions on your tax return. I'm not sure about previous years, but on this year's return, you have vastly understated your income."

Mario laughed. "That's what you think? Do you know how many tens of thousands of dollars I paid you bastards last year?"

"To the penny, as you would say, but that's not what I'm talking about. You fail to show any income whatever from the entity on Ward's Island. What do you call it…the…"

"Lions' Den," Mario said helpfully. "And you're right. I don't show any income from it."

"And yet you have taken in hundreds of thousands of dollars…"

Mario turned toward Ben Hersh in mock distress. "Please, Ben, tell me what's going on." He checked the gold Cartier on his left wrist. "I've been here for nearly three hours and all I've heard is a litany of bogus charges. I feel like I'm the audience at some kind of ridiculous play. What's the purpose of all this?"

"You're facing criminal tax evasion charges," Ryan pointed out.

Mario put his chin in his hand and thought. "Wasn't it the IRS that finally tripped up Al Capone?" he asked.

"That's right," Ryan said.

"Must have been well before your time, Agent Ryan. If you'd been in charge of that investigation, we'd be calling Chicago Caponeville."

Ryan's already-red face reddened further. "You like to insult government agents, don't you?"

"Only incompetent ones," Mario said. He tossed the returns back to Ryan. "Put these back in the file, Agent Ryan—it will cost you more to audit them than you'll get in back taxes." Mario knew he was taking a risk talking to Ryan this way, but he was damned if he was going to let the IRS see him rattled. Inside, he was trembling almost as much as when Julie told him the show would air live, but he was the only one in the room who knew it.

"Maybe so, but the club income…"

"I had no club income, *Agent* Ryan."

"Well," Ryan said, "according to the papers we've, um, acquired, you're the president of the company."

"True. But it's not a salaried position, and the Lions' Den is not organized to turn a profit. In fact, the facility has construction debts that need to be paid off."

Ryan opened his mouth to say something, then shut it. Then he changed his mind again. "We have no record of any tax return from any corporation known as the Lions' Den."

"Of course you don't. We've only been open a few months…"

"And what about employee withholding?"

"Filed exactly as the law requires. You really didn't do your homework, did you, Agent Ryan?" Frank was some fucking lawyer, Mario thought.

Ryan looked helplessly at Hersh, who shrugged. "Sorry, Carl. I thought it was worth a try."

"This wasn't an awful lot of fun, Ben," Ryan said. He stuffed Mario's returns back into his briefcase and headed for the door. "Next time you throw a party, do me a favor. Don't invite me."

Then there were three.

"Getting warm in here," Hersh said. He stood, slipped off his suit jacket, and hung it over his chair. Case stretched, looking out the window facing the Washington Monument.

Mario checked his watch again. "So, are we all done now?" he asked.

It was Case's turn to laugh, and Hersh just shook his head, ruefully. "That was just act one," he said. "This is a three-act play."

"Well, what about an intermission?" Mario asked, coolly. "I can't be the only one who's getting hungry."

Case and Hersh exchanged glances, and Hersh reached into a desk drawer and pulled out a handful of take-out menus. Hersh flipped through them. "Thai, Chinese, Italian. What's your choice, Elliot?"

"I don't get a vote?" Mario asked.

Hersh looked at him, tolerantly. "What would you like, Mr. Monelli?"

"It's Mario, please, Ben. And I'd like to have lunch at one of the dozens of good restaurants within walking distance of your office."

"Not in the budget, Mario," said Ben.

They ended up ordering deli.

"All right, gentlemen, would you mind telling me what's going on here? This isn't at all what I expected when Elliot here kidnapped me."

Hersh studied Mario for a moment. "Okay, Elliot, you were right. But I'm new at this, you know."

Mario realized Hersh was speaking about himself, but he couldn't figure out what this meant. "Someone mind telling me what's going on?"

"I told him we'd bring some of the fellas in and you'd crack open like a fortune cookie. Elliot here said the intimidation wouldn't work, you'd see right through it. And he was right." Hersh applauded silently a few times in Case's direction.

"But you didn't bring me here to play games either," Mario continued. "You want something, and you're willing to cook up all kinds of false criminal charges against me to force me to...to what?"

"We have some very real charges against you, too," Hersh said, sidestepping Mario's question.

"Yeah, yeah, I know—we bent a few rules financing the club," Mario said. "You got me there, all right. But you didn't get anyone else—it was all my doing, my idea, my plans. You can forget all those indictments you handed out to my friends and associates."

"Very noble," Case offered, sarcastically. "A Wall Street martyr willing to take a bullet for his friends. I'll see if there's an opening for you at the Secret Service."

Mario really didn't care what they thought of him at this point, but he was damned if he were going to let Frank or the Zoo Crew, or even the members take any heat for this. After all, it was *his* idea. It was all on his head.

"That's not all," Hersh said. "You violated a lot of other laws when you put together that little den of iniquity of yours."

"What? Morals laws? So I'm an adulterer? This is the 21st century, Ben. I don't think I have to worry about the Blue Laws."

"You and your friends acquired that building fraudulently," Hersh said. "That's a felony. You've also violated enough building code and zoning code statutes that by the time the courts get finished with you..."

"You'll be screwing your brains out at the Y..." Case interjected.

"...and taking the subway to work," Ben added.

"If you can find anyone who'll employ you," Case added.

"Mario, I think you should know that we questioned your whole crew, and we have enough information to have the justice department bring legitimate money laundering and fraud against you under RICO—and they'd stick. That would mean prison time."

"Please, don't insult me, Benjamin," Mario said. "You and I both know that even if you can prove the charges, they're all penny-ante bullshit. The attorney general has *real* criminals to prosecute. I'll have to pay a fine and do some community service. So I'll spend a month picking up candy wrappers in Central Park, or work on my tan at Club Fed for a little while. So what?"

There was a knock on the door—the deli guy. Elliot paid and he started passing out the food. And they ate for awhile.

"So tell me, gentlemen," Mario said, "what is it you want from me? You might have just asked, you know, instead of trying to trap me. You think I'm going to say no?"

Hersh and Case exchanged glances. "Frankly, yes," Case said. "You already refused Senator Jaffe."

Mario was momentarily confused, then it occurred to him. "I see, you've been talking about me to the senator."

Ben Hersh leaned back in his chair and took a bite from his pickle. "Randy Hollingsworth was a good friend and the finest chairman the SEC ever had. And the Saudis murdered him."

That's what this is all about? Randy Dandy? Mario thought to himself. He didn't have any connection to Randy Dandy.

"Randy and I were working with Milt Jaffe," Hersh said.

"On what?" Mario still didn't have the slightest idea where this was heading.

"Actually, something you were involved in, too," Case put in.

The light finally went on. "You mean the television show I was on—*America for Sale?*"

"Yes," Hersh said. "That was an audacious performance, Mario, especially when you think of what happened to Hollingsworth."

"You still didn't tell me what you want from me?"

"We need you to testify at the hearings," Elliot Case said.

Now Mario knew what was coming. Hersh was using the Lions' Den as leverage into making him testify at Jaffe's hearings. The old man wants to use me, and he's willing to threaten me, even extort me if he has to. Perfect.

"A lot of people are trying to sabotage him, Mario," Ben said. "A lot of people want Jaffe to fail. I think you know some of them."

Mario took a very deep breath. "I've already done my part," he said. "I did a television special and God knows how many interviews. Why does it have to be me again?"

"Jaffe already told you why, Mario," Case said. "You're independent—no lobbyists are knocking on your door—and you have public support."

"And you love this country," Hersh said. "Your testimony will put enormous pressure on the opposition."

"It would also give some cover to others like yourself who are afraid to testify," Case observed.

"Well, before you slap my face on the ten dollar bill, there's something you fellas oughta know," Mario said. "At the risk of sounding unpatriotic, when I did that television show, I did it more out of love for a woman than I did for my country. And it turned my life upside down. If your game plan is for me to walk into the capital, playing my flute in the hopes everyone follows…if you think I'm volunteering for that, you're fucked."

"We *can* subpoena you," Elliot threatened.

"Go ahead. I got nothing to say."

"Even if means you're held in contempt?"

"Do I look like I give a shit? You got me on tax evasion, conspiracy of money laundering, federal immigration laws…"

"We have to put a stop to this while we still *have* a country," Hersh said. "And you're the one with the best chance to do it. Only we don't have much time. The Saudis are getting out of the oil business faster than the Corleones got out of olive oil, and Jaffe is seriously ill."

"Maybe so," Mario said, "but you're asking me to rat on my colleagues, some of whom are Lions' Den members. My loyalty is what I live and survive on. I break that, I'm out of the business."

"Well, someone ratted on *you*," Elliot Case said.

For once, Mario was startled. "What? Who?"

"We don't know," Hersh admitted. "But someone sent us a tape of your little prime time performance in an effort to connect you to the Lions' Den."

Mario thought for a moment. That tape, if it was sent, didn't come from any of his friends, he was sure of that. Maybe it was the Crown Prince, or someone on Wall Street. Well, Jaffe had warned him.

Elliot Case poured himself a drink of water from a pitcher on a side table. "You've got a choice between protecting your country and protecting your friends. Are they really your friends, Mario, those bastards who are selling our country down the river? We're not talking about your little Zoo Crew, you know."

"They're men I've worked with for years, fought with, dealt with, drank with. Not friends, really, but associates. And as associates, we don't rat on each other," Mario told him.

"Don't give us any of that guinea goomba shit," Case barked.

Hersh just shook his head. "You think they're your buddies—Tyler and the rest of them. But they're about to throw you overboard."

That was intriguing. "Tyler? What do you mean?" Mario asked, curious.

The answer came from Elliot Case. "It may interest you to know that Harrison Hart is negotiating a merger with an Asian player. We don't know all the details yet, but I think you can guess that it doesn't include you and the Zoo Crew."

Now that was clever, Mario thought, using Tyler and Harrison Hart as leverage that way. Why would anyone want to protect buddies who are secretly planning to cut you out of the big deal? On the other hand, Mario reasoned, Tyler has been looking to restructure ever since the Intercoastal disaster. This could be good news for the company, including himself and the Zoo Crew. "You seem to know a lot of secrets," he said to Elliot Case. "If they're really secrets, that is."

"It's my *business* to expose secrets," Case said.

"Well, I hope you don't mind if I take your pronouncements with a grain of salt," Mario replied. "I know all about the merger talks." But he didn't.

Hersh had been leaning back in his big desk chair, relaxed and affable, but now he leaned forward, deadly serious now. "We're preparing indictments for just about everyone you're connected with. Let's see now, there's your brother to begin with. And Neil—what's his alias these days?—and..."

"Think of it like a hostage crisis, Mario," Case interjected. "Every day you don't cooperate, we're going to throw another body out."

This was hardball, Mario realized. And it was aimed at his head. "The trouble is, Ben, there's another party involved in this, and they've made me a better deal than you have."

Elliot was startled. "What are you talking about?"

"You haven't even heard the deal we're offering," Hersh said. "But here it is: you testify before the Jaffe committee—you *name names*—and I'll squash all the charges involved in the Lions' Den. And I mean *all* of them—civil suits as well, for you, your brother, and all of your Wall Street fuck buddies. Think of that before you fall on your sword for them."

Mario found a bit of rye bread crust still on his paper plate and he ate it, waiting for the tasty crunch of the caraway seed. "Okay, Ben, I hear your deal. Now do you want to hear what the other side is offering?"

Hersh was confused. "What other side?"

"I think he's talking about the people who want to see Jaffe's bill die a natural death," Case explained.

"Wall Street people?" Ben asked.

"Not exactly," Mario said, surprising them both. "Royal people. The Crown Prince of Saudi Arabia, to be precise. He offered to let me live if I stay away from the Jaffe hearings."

"He said that?" Hersh asked. "He used those words?"

"Of course not," Mario said. "In fact, he said he meant me no harm. He told me he just couldn't be sure of his kissing cousins, even sent me some love letters."

Well, Mario thought, observing the silence that followed, *that* certainly shut them up.

"The government will protect you," Case said.

"Tell that to the people who worked in the World Trade Center," Mario growled.

For a moment, no one said anything. Then Hersh broke the silence. "We'll put you in witness protection..."

"Did you say that to Hollingsworth, too?" Mario asked, and instantly regretted the remark.

Hersh leaned back in his chair, thoughtful. "They let you live because you've already done whatever damage you were capable of doing. It was too late, and it would have caused public outrage."

"So what about Hollingsworth?" Mario asked. "They killed him after he'd passed on the information, and he'd *done* his damage."

"That's true," Case agreed, "but they knew Hollingsworth could hurt them *again*, especially his testimony before the House and Senate. And they knew most Americans had never heard of him."

"That's why we need you, Mario," Hersh said.

"So do my kids," Mario replied, but he knew that was a weak response. They were asking him to stand up for his country. Again. And he was trying to get out of it.

"We'll keep it a secret that you're going to testify," Hersh said. "Then, afterward, they won't go after you—you wouldn't be a continuing threat, and if they hit you, the backlash would finish them."

"And you want me to bet my life and the lives of my children on that? Well fuck you," Mario politely told Ben. Then he turned to Elliott. "And fuck you, too…because I'm not testifying."

Hersh had had enough of this. "I'm not going to argue with you anymore, Monelli. I would have thought what happened to Hollingsworth would convince you that it's your duty to testify, but you're beyond convincing. Just remember, I wasn't kidding about putting you and your friends in jail. I'll do it, I promise you."

Mario's brain was buzzing with conflict, with duty, with consequences, with fear. It was paralyzing.

"Here's the bottom line, Monelli," Hersh said coldly. "I'll give you a week before I turn everything over to the U.S. Attorney General's office. That's when the Jaffe hearings go into their final sessions. After that, your chariot turns into a pumpkin. Meanwhile, I'm freezing all of your personal assets. That goes for your friends' too, as well as all the Lions' Den accounts."

Case pulled his chair up to Mario's and leaned forward until their faces almost touched. "One more thing, Monelli. All of those Lions' Den records— the membership list, for example—someone here at the commission, without authorization of course, might leak them to *The New York Times*, maybe CNN. That would be a shame, wouldn't it, Ben? It might even leak out that you came to us trying to deal your way out. That way, if the Crown Prince doesn't kill you, Wall Street *will*."

Mario turned toward Hersh, hoping for sympathy, but Hersh wouldn't look at him.

CHAPTER THIRTY-THREE

That morning, while driving to work, Mario vacillated between keeping the worst of it from the Zoo Crew and telling them everything. When he walked into Harrison Hart, he still wasn't sure what he was going to do. But now the moment was at hand, and he couldn't hide anything from his friends.

When Mario got off the elevator, he whisked past Rose Pheeney, who was watering the dusty ficus plant outside Tyler's office.

He opened the door to the back offices and walked through the trading floor, then headed down the short hallway toward the heavy glass double doors that led to the M&A suite. The Zoo Crew were all at their desks—even Dick Hamilton. When they saw Mario, their jaws dropped open, like marionettes.

"You're here," Neil observed. "What happened? Are you all right?"

Mario took in the bandage on Neil's nose. "What about *you*? Are you okay?"

Neil glanced at Glen, who wouldn't meet his eyes. "I'll be fine. I hit my nose on the door."

But Mario knew better.

"Well, Mario," Dick Hamilton said sarcastically, "glad to see you could make it in this week."

"Dick, full of good cheer as usual," Mario said. "Listen, could you go to the records room and dig up the Amalgamated Metal Worker's Pension Fund records. I need to look at the period between 1989 and 1994."

Hamilton's eyes narrowed and he failed to move.

"I need them by the open," Mario said, prompting him.

"Why don't you ask Kat to do it?"

"Because I'm asking *you*?"

Hamilton shot Mario a dirty look, then neatened up the papers on his desk, got up and walked out of the door, pissed and not hiding it.

Mario waited until Hamilton was gone. "I think that *cappcazzo* may have sold us out," he said. "Or maybe it was Bart. I don't know. But someone put the SEC wise to us."

"At least you're not in jail," Dennis said wryly.

"Well, not yet, anyhow," Mario allowed. "And I'm glad to see none of you are either."

"Mario," Neil said, "we've all told the attorney general we're willing to testify in exchange for immunity."

Glen couldn't restrain himself. "Come on, Mario—what gives? What's going to happen to us?"

"I don't think you guys are going to jail," Mario said. "In my case, though, I guess you could say the jury is still out."

"Are you going to tell us what happened?" Kat asked. "None of us have slept in two days."

"Well, for starters, they've frozen our accounts," Mario said. "But don't worry about it. It's just intimidation."

"What about the Lions' Den?" Dennis asked.

"Assets frozen there, too," Mario said. "I'm going over there after work, let go of the employees, and lock up."

"We're starting to get a little impatient, Mario," Kat said. "Would you like to tell us what happened to you yesterday, or do you want us to guess?"

"What happened," Mario repeated, hanging up his suit jacket. "It actually started two days ago. I was at the cabin with Boomer..."

He told them how Elliot Case and Ben Hersh had tried to intimidate him, how they, along with the FBI and Homeland Security, bombarded him with phony charges, how Roger unknowingly used a terrorist cell to help smuggle the marble lions out of Jordan, leading U.S. authorities to think it was a weapon of mass destruction, and how, in the end, they'd let Roger go and admitted they didn't have anything—except for the Lions' Den.

Halfway into the story, Neil interrupted him. "I don't understand, Mario? Why do they even care about the Lions' Den? It's gotta be small potatoes for them?"

And now Mario told them what the whole thing was really all about— what the SEC wanted from him—and about the deal Hersh was offering, a deal that would save them all, and probably make him spend what remained of his life living in the shadows in witness protection.

"Now I understand what all the subpoenas are about," Neil said.

Mario was surprised. "What subpoenas?"

"Federal marshals are busy wall papering the Street with Congressional subpoenas," Dennis explained. "They must have something to do with the hearings."

"They didn't give *me* one," Mario said.

"That's what *you* think," said Neil. "They were here this morning. I told them I was you and they were dumb enough to believe it." He handed Mario the subpoena. "With love."

Mario looked at the paper and shrugged. "They have something a lot more powerful than *this*."

"Yeah," Dennis said, "a get out of jail free" card. You testify before the Senate and all the indictments go away, yours and ours."

"Right. We lose the Lions' Den," Mario said, "but we keep our freedom. Too bad the same can't be said for our careers."

"Then let's shoot this pony," said Glen. "The sooner the better."

Mario took a very deep breath. "It's not that simple," he said. Then he reminded them about his encounter with the Crown Prince in Vegas during the Prosperity Ball, as well as the death threats subsequent to that. Afterward, the room fell silent.

"Jeez, Mario," Barry said. "That's like choosing between the electric chair and poison gas."

"Mario, I can't speak for anyone else, but I won't have you risking your life," said Neil. "Let the SEC do what it wants to me, I'll survive."

"We *all* will," Dennis said, and everyone else nodded agreement.

Every last one of them was willing to take a bullet for him, and the bullet wouldn't be a small one—a couple of years of jail time, big fines, a loss of their jobs, and very possibly their livelihoods. How could he possibly throw them under the bus just to save himself?

But did he owe them his life? Was he supposed to get himself murdered just to keep them out of deep water? Or spend the rest of his life hiding out in some Midwest suburban shithole, like he was Henry Hill, always looking over his shoulder. After all, they knew the inherent risks when they got involved with the Lions' Den. Nobody forced them. He just wished they weren't so damn loyal.

"What are you going to do, Mario?" Kat asked.

"I don't know," Mario said, and that was the truth. "Hersh gave me a week to decide."

At that moment, Mario's phone rang. "Monelli," he said.

"Ah, you're here. Good." It was Tyler. "Could you come down to my office? Something I need to discuss with you."

And something *I* need to discuss with *you*, Mario thought. "Sure. I'll be right there." He hung up and looked at the Zoo Crew.

Mario headed for Tyler's corner office. So Tyler wanted to discuss something. Well, for once, he didn't feel as though he were being called on the carpet. Tyler was the least of his problems. And who knows, maybe he was about to hear all about his China shenanigans.

"You wanted to see me," Mario said, entering his office.

Tyler frowned. "Have a seat." His voice exuded hostility.

Mario took the bigger and more comfortable of Tyler's two guest chairs, sat down, and waited for Tyler to continue.

"You get served with a subpoena this morning?"

"Matter of fact, yes. Why?"

Tyler opened his top desk drawer and tossed a folded piece of paper on the desk. "This came for me last night from the Senate Commerce Subcommittee on Foreign Investment—Senator Jaffe's committee. Go ahead, look at it."

Mario opened the paper and read the subpoena.

"They served me in the fucking terminal at JFK. I wasn't even out of customs yet."

"Interesting," Mario said, non-committally. "What does he want with *you*? You still importing those Cuban cigars?"

Tyler scowled. "Of all people, Mario, *you* know what this is all about. You know Jaffe is trying to outlaw foreign purchases of major American companies. So don't play dumb."

"I'm not playing dumb, Tyler," Mario protested. "I have no idea what Jaffe wants with you. As for me, he probably wants me to repeat what I said on television."

"We're not the only ones, you know. I've fielded calls all morning— half a dozen of my friends and associates have been subpoenaed. Big names, Mario. Some of the biggest. Bart, for one. What do you know about this?"

"Me? Nothing."

"Come on, Mario. You were in Washington yesterday, and today the subpoenas are everywhere. You gonna tell me that's a coincidence?"

He got up, walked over to the display cases in his office—the one with the ice axe—and took out a snow white handkerchief and buffed out a smudge on the glass.

"Tyler," Mario said, "I had nothing to do with the subpoenas. Anyhow, how did you know I was in Washington yesterday?"

"For Christ sake, Mario, do you really think anything happens in this office that I don't know about? Why were you in D.C. anyhow?"

"Personal business," Mario said, knowing that probably wouldn't be enough—but it was all he was going to give him until Tyler came clean about China.

Tyler shot him a nasty look. "Personal business. Can't you do a little better than that?"

"All right. It was Lions' Den business."

"In Washington? Don't give me that shit, Monelli."

"The SEC wanted to see me about the way we financed the Lions' Den. It wasn't exactly *traditional*, you know. We did an end run…around some regulations."

"Fuck me! The Lions' Den! There's trouble with the Lions' Den? Mario, you assured me that no one would ever be able to connect me with that place. Wait till the other members hear this."

"The members already know, Tyler."

"Don't say that."

"Relax. We got word to every one of them."

"All except me, Mario."

"Maybe that's because you were in China again and couldn't be reached."

"Don't change the subject."

"Keep your pants on, Tyler. Your secret is safe. We're going to have to pay a fine and close down the Den. No big deal."

"You better be right, Mario. If you're not, it's your ass. You'll never make partner. No joke. I don't care what the ramifications are for the firm."

Mario took a mental inventory of the people who'd threatened him recently. There was the Crown Prince, Barton Mulvaney after the show, Ben Hersh, and now Tyler Gentry. Wait, that wasn't the full list. Oh yes, Phyllis. Can't forget Phyllis. God, he wished Gus were still alive to help him sort things out.

"Interesting thing, Tyler," Mario said, paying close attention to Tyler's expression. "While I was at the SEC, I came across an odd rumor about Harrison Hart."

"Rumor? What kind of rumor?"

Mario acted as though he was trying to remember. "Hmmm…I think it was something about a merger. Was that it? A merger? Yes, I think that's what I heard."

Tyler's face flushed. "They couldn't kn—" he stopped himself. "What did they say?"

"Let's see now…oh yes, something about a big foreign company."

"Foreign?" Tyler actually looked rattled now, a refreshing change, Mario thought, from his usual expression—arrogant, unflappable, supremely confident.

"I didn't know they were talking about Harrison Hart until the conversation was almost over," Mario said.

"Well, you know how rumors are, Mario," Tyler said. "They can't be trusted."

A lot like people Mario thought.

"So Harrison Hart isn't merging with anyone, Tyler?"

"Well, you know we're looking for a cash infusion, Mario. I've been up front with you about that."

"Are you close to a deal, Tyler?"

"The partners are exploring opportunities. I've been talking with several people, but nothing concrete. You know I'll keep you informed. You're my top gun."

Stroke me again, Mario said to himself. I'm gonna cum.

"Well, I'm glad you feel that way, Tyler. And here I thought I'm never going to make partner. That's the way you put it, right?"

Tyler waved a hand, dismissively. "You know me, I was just hot under the collar. This subpoena business has everyone spooked. You know, Mario, you could do me a really big favor," he said.

Mario regarded Tyler skeptically. "Really? And what's that."

"Well, you could sit with me at the hearings. You know, advise me."

"Tyler, you don't need hand holding. Besides, you'll have counsel there."

Tyler sat down again and leaned forward. "True. But you could help me in a way no lawyer could."

"How so?" Mario said.

"Well, you're the big hero, the knight in shining armor. If you're sitting next to me…"

"It will be a kind of endorsement," Mario said, completing the thought.

"Some senior Democrats may see it that way."

Mario leaned back, crossed his legs and marveled at the way fate worked. Tyler was seeking his protection—but who would protect *him*? Who could advise *him*? Mario felt like a sword juggler with at least one too many scimitars in the air. He badly needed his brother's advice.

Frank agreed to meet him at an Italian restaurant on Schermerhorn Street, near his law office.

Mario walked into the place a half-hour later, but no Frank. Just like his brother, Mario thought. He ordered a bottle of Chianti and sat down in a booth with a view of the front door.

Another half hour and Frank still hadn't shown. He called Frank from his cell, but there was no answer. He must be on his way. Fifteen minutes later, Mario decided it was time to see what was going on. It took him only a few minutes to get to 163 Court Street, and he vaulted up the two flights of stairs to Frank's office only to find the door ajar. He stood at the threshold, bewildered now. "Frank?"

Frank's secretary was nowhere to be seen—at lunch, probably. Looking around a file cabinet, he found that the inner office door, the door to Frank's private office, was half open as well. "Frank?" But there was no answer. An eeriness suddenly hit him. He gently pushed the door forward till it creaked open and he looked down.

Frank was lying half on the floor face down. And dead, that was Mario's first thought. He was dead, his brother.

Mario found himself on his knees, tugging at Frank's body, trying to turn it over, shouting, "Frank, Frank, are you okay, Frank?" And not expecting an answer.

Frank groaned. His nose was squished sideways, one eye was swollen shut and his jaw seemed misaligned. Shocked, Mario almost let go of him, then gently tried to rouse him. "Frank, Frank—talk to me, Frank!"

Frank made a half-hearted and unsuccessful effort to lift his head.

"Stay down, Frank. I'll get help." Mario fumbled with the telephone on Frank's desk and called 911.

Paramedics arrived and got a stretcher under him and ran an IV, then peeled off his shirt and checked for other damage. Frank was bruised front and back, but no holes where there shouldn't be holes. He hadn't been shot or stabbed. But his jaw appeared to be broken, and his right knee was busted.

"Is he going to be all right?" Mario asked, anxiously.

"Vital signs are okay and stable. But someone's really pummeled him."

They carried him downstairs, and Mario rode with Frank in the ambulance all the way to Methodist hospital and accompanied him into the emergency trauma unit.

"This is as far as you go, Bud," one of the orderlies said. "Someone will be out in a few minutes to give you the word."

Mario stood in the hallway, impatiently. A half-hour later, the chief resident, a thin, grey-haired man with piercing eyes, came out looking for him, accompanied by a couple of orderlies pushing a wheeled bed. Frank lay on it, heavily bandaged, apparently unconscious. Mario rushed up to him. "Is he gonna be all right?"

"He's busted up pretty bad," said the chief resident. "Jaw wasn't broken, just dislocated. It's back in place now."

"What about his eye?"

"Took five stitches to close a cut below his eyebrow, but his sight wasn't affected."

"His nose..."

"That may require more surgery, I'm afraid," the chief resident said. "It's probably going to take some plastic surgery to make it look right again."

"Maybe they can make it look better," Frank said weakly.

The doctors chuckled. "Sounds like he's on the way to recovery," he said. "We'll check on him again later today."

Mario got out the Benjamins. "Check on him an hour from now. Make sure he's comfortable—no pain, understand?"

The orderlies wheeled Frank down the hall, Mario following, to one of the hospital's best private rooms. A couple of nurses hovered around Frank when he arrived, hooking up monitors and checking the IV morphine drip. Then they left Mario alone with his brother.

"Frank? You awake?"

"Somewhat," he said.

"What the hell happened? Unhappy client?"

Frank shook his head and weakly flipped him the bird.

"Did you get a good look at who did this?"

Frank nodded and slowly wiped his fingers over his face.

"Masks? They wore masks?"

Frank nodded.

"How many were there?"

Frank managed to hold up two fingers.

"They take anything?"

Frank shook his head in the negative.

"Then what did they want?"

Frank pointed to Mario.

"Me? They wanted *me*? Did they say anything?"

Frank tried to talk, but he couldn't move his mouth.

Mario stopped him. He fetched a note pad from the end table drawer and gently placed a pencil in his brother's hand.

Frank scribbled something and Mario read it. The paper read "Warning."

"What kind of warning?"

Frank raised his hand to his lips and made a turn-key gesture with his fingers. Then again he pointed to Mario.

Mario's mouth went dry. "They want me to shut up."

Frank nodded, and managed to rasp out a few words. "Said you'd better keep quiet ...or else. They had foreign accents."

Then the floor fell away. It could only have been a message from the Crown Prince.

Mario knew it was all his fault. He might as well have done this to Frank himself. His brother had always been his protector, but now, when it really mattered, he wasn't there to protect his brother. Like he wasn't there for Danny, like he wasn't there for Boomer, like he wasn't there for Gus.

"If I coulda got to my bat..." Frank said.

Mario remembered the Louisville Slugger Frank always kept in a corner, a finely turned piece of ash that Thurman Munson had once used to hit a home run. If he could have swung the bat, his tormenters would have been in the hospital, not Frank.

"God, I'm so sorry, Frank. It's all my fault. I'm involved in something, and now it's spilled over to you."

Frank groaned and turned his good eye toward Mario. "Involved in what—the Lions' Den? Your friend Neil told me the SEC was leaning on you."

"It's more than that, Frank."

Mario told him everything, from the moment Case hijacked him up at the cabin, until he left Washington, leaving out nothing.

"You got yourself into a hell of a fix, little brother."

Mario put his head in his hands, then looked up. "I know. And I don't see any way out of it. Either I put everyone I know in jail, including you—or I go into self-imposed exile, or worse, get myself killed. What should I do, Frank?"

"I can't make that decision for you, Mario," Frank said. He sounded tired. Mario knew his brother was right. "Why don't you get a little shut-eye," Mario said. "We'll talk more tomorrow."

Frank offered him a feeble grin. "I already got a little shut eye," he joked.

Mario smiled and flipped off the room light to give Frank a better chance to sleep, then walked out into the hallway and called his sister-in-law.

It was getting dark now. Mario didn't know where he wanted to go or what he wanted to do. He didn't want to go home. Neither did he want to go back to the Millennium Hotel where he'd been staying. He needed to sort things out. He had a decision to make, and what happened to Frank made it clear he needed to make it—and soon.

Mario walked along Court Street, half-dazed, and he stopped when he spotted a subway entrance. How long had it been, how many years, how many lifetimes ago? He walked down the dirty concrete stairs and bought himself a Metrocard, feeling nostalgic about the brass tokens that, when he was a kid, cost a quarter, when a quarter was a lot of money for a kid.

He went through the turnstile, he had no idea why. Maybe it was the smell, the unique smell of the subway, that sent him back years. He walked to the platform edge and looked into the tunnel, as he always had. Headlight approaching.

The Q train came rumbling into the station, crowded with commuters going home from work, and it screeched to a stop. Some people got off, some got on. Mario joined those getting on.

Mario didn't know where he was going, at least not consciously, and he let the stops go by without reacting to them, Prospect Park, Kings Highway, Sheepshead Bay...the train emptied out and he sat down. He sat all the way to Brighton Beach, the end of the line.

There were snapshots somewhere in the attic of Mario's mind of what he would find at the bottom of the stairs, old snapshots, not even in color. But when he came down to street level, so much was different that he hardly recognized the place.

He walked along Surf Avenue, which was almost deserted, past the New York Aquarium, and what used to be Astroland, and would soon be a housing development, each new building invalidating one of those old snapshots in his mind.

He could almost hear kids laughing and screaming, the clattering clicks of the metal coaster wheels climbing the wooden track to the peak of the drop of the Cyclone rollercoaster, the hurdy-gurdy of the carousel.

He could almost smell the hot dogs from Nathan's and the cotton candy, his memories superimposed themselves over the present, and he let himself savor them.

He continued past MCU Park, where the old parachute jump now served as a beacon for JFK Airport. He walked along the empty Boardwalk, found a bench, sat down, and looked out at the beach and the dark water beyond it, toward South Jersey, and he remembered being here before, as a boy with Frank and his Dad, looking up open-mouthed at the fireworks.

There were no fireworks anymore except the ones now going off in his life. But he could still see them—flashes of white and green and red and blue, bursting in the sky and raining onto the Brighton waters of Coney Island.

Mario saw a sprinkling of lights in the distance, gliding across the water, outlining the shape of a vessel. He strained to see the ship itself, but that was beyond his visual acuity—was it a freighter? A tanker? A passenger ship? He couldn't tell.

As he peered into the distance, he thought about the Zoo Crew. And Frank. And Boomer. And Gus. And Julie, most of all, Julie.

Was he the man who married Phyllis Nalbani, the man who clawed his way to the pinnacle of his profession despite his upbringing, crushing whomever stood in his way, the man acclaimed as a savior of companies and the thousands of employees who worked for them…so long as a dollar was in it for him. That man might have considered fleeing to Europe or South America with his two boys, *if* his assets weren't frozen.

That man wouldn't hesitate. That man would cut the Zoo Crew loose, and let them fend for themselves. It wouldn't even occur to that man to worry about anyone but himself first, if he had to choose rather than risk being killed by the Crown Prince's thugs?

Was he that man? Mario asked himself. It was certainly the man he had been before all of this started. Not a particularly nice man, not a particularly good man. Selfish, narcissistic, greedy, emotionally MIA, a disloyal husband who suffered from a character flaw that defeated his better angels. Was this the man he was? Was this the man he *wanted* to be? Maybe he wasn't that man at all.

He hadn't been that man in the cabin with Boomer. He'd just done his best. He'd given as much of himself as he could, and thank God it had been enough. He hadn't been that man with Gus, either. Nor was he that man who spent many sleepless nights over Danny, the guilt still tormenting what little remained of his soul. And he certainly hadn't been that way with Julie.

He was a different man when he was with Julie. She was warm, generous, giving, idealistic, and that brought out the same qualities in him. And she loved him despite his complexities and contradictions. He never would have done that television show if it hadn't been for her. Her values, and more than that, her love, had changed him, profoundly. If it hadn't, he wouldn't be having so much difficulty making this decision.

Maybe he'd lost Julie. But in another way, she would always be a part of him. He'd always wanted to be the man she thought he was, the man she wanted him to be. The man *he* wanted to be, if not for her or for himself, then for Boomer and Kyle. He'd always wanted to be that man, in his heart of hearts, but he thought it was beyond him—until he met her. Maybe a way to hold onto the essence of what they shared and fuse the disconnect between his personal life and his public persona was not to let himself slip back to his former self.

So, he had a decision to make. He didn't have to talk to or see Julie to know what she'd advise, or what she'd expect of him. So, in a way, the decision was an opportunity. He could be the man Julie thought him to be, the man he wanted himself to be. Or maybe like that distant ship, it was beyond him.

CHAPTER THIRTY-FOUR

Tyler and Mario took an early shuttle from LaGuardia to Reagan National, found a Yellow Cab, and headed for the Capitol, the driver being an Iraqi immigrant who claimed he'd been a neurosurgeon in his home country.

It was a gorgeous day, a bright blue cloudless sky, Washington's Federal buildings etched in sunlight. In the last decade or two, Mario had been a frequent visitor to Washington.

There was much business to be conducted here, most recently with the boys at the Securities and Exchange Commission. And the sight of the glorious white-domed Capitol building had never failed to move him.

"Beautiful," he said to Tyler as they drove along Pennsylvania Avenue. Tyler nodded absently. His mind was on other matters. "Still worried about testifying?" Mario asked.

"Not really. Jaffe and his bunch aren't going to rattle me. But there are a couple of weak links in the chain. Just remember how we rehearsed it."

"I will, Tyler."

"And don't elaborate on anything."

"Relax, Tyler...I'll be okay."

As the cab approached the Capitol, Mario saw the reception party awaiting them—a battery of reporters and photographers, poised to intercept the parade of investment bankers and financiers scheduled to testify in the widening probe before the Senate that day.

This wasn't exactly surprising, Mario thought. It isn't every day that the princes of Wall Street are summoned by the princes of Washington and asked to explain themselves. And having Wall Street under the spotlight was the grand finale to the hearings, which were being nationally broadcast and which filled the front page of every major newspaper. The crack Carleton Fisher and Randy Hollingsworth had hoped to strike in the critical mass had come to fruition.

As soon as they got out of the cab, they were mobbed by the media—photographers taking pictures, reporters shouting questions, and TV cameramen, some balancing a boom mike overhead, filming it all.

"Are you for Jaffe or against him, Mr. Monelli?" one reporter yelled out, sticking a microphone in Mario's face, while photographers surrounded him with a lightening storm of photographic flashes exploding from their cameras.

"I'm for America," Mario told him. "Aren't *you*?"

"Mr. Gentry, is it true that the White House is working to defeat Senator Jaffe's bill?" Another reporter asked Tyler.

Tyler stopped and smiled for the wall of cameras. "I don't think the White House has taken a stand," he replied, triggering laughter from the reporters and nearby photographers.

They passed through the security barriers just inside the Capitol, and the media frenzy waned a bit, but the torrent of questions continued.

"Hey, Mario, what are you going to say when you testify?" asked a tall female reporter, donning a floppy hat.

"That depends on what the committee asks me."

Suddenly, the coterie of reporters reversed course, heading back toward the security station, hoping to waylay another group of bankers as they arrived. They'd been summoned from everywhere including the heads of the five families, the godfathers of Bank of America, Goldman Sachs, J.P. Morgan Chase, Citigroup, and Morgan Stanley. And all lawyered up.

Across the street, more limos, carrying the czars of Hedge funds, sultans of private equity firms. And bringing up the rear were the high-ranking officers of Blackrock and the Carlyle Group. The attorneys were doing all the talking, and there wasn't much of it.

Tyler and Mario walked through the rotunda where a security team directed them toward the hearing room, a big, high-ceilinged, half-paneled courtroom-like affair, the same room which once held the Watergate hearings. It was stuffed with witnesses, members of the press corps and a gallery of spectators.

At the front of the room was a raised dais. It was topped by a long table and seats for the nine members of the Senate Commerce Subcommittee on Foreign Investment. Half were still vacant.

Mario and Tyler took seats at the end of a long row filled with some of America's wealthiest and most powerful investment bankers, each of them guarded by legal teams all dressed to perfection. Harrison Hart's counsel— two aces from Skadden-Arps, were waiting for them. At the other end of the row sat Barton Mulvaney, suit pressed to a fine edge.

They acknowledged each other, with varying degrees of camaraderie and suspicion. In a way, they were all members of the same brotherhood. They golfed together at Wingfoot, drank each other's single-malt scotch, and smoked each other's Cuban cigars, even exercised their compulsive womanizing together at the Lions' Den. That didn't make them bosom buddies, but it made them allies in this venue, where mere senators, most of them connivers or buffoons, were calling them on the carpet.

No sooner had Mario taken his seat than one of the sergeants-at-arms approached him. "Mr. Monelli?"

"Yes?"

"Could you come with me, sir? Mr. Case wishes to have a word with you. He assures me you'll be back before the hearings get underway."

Mario glanced at Tyler, who inquired, "Case...*Elliot* Case? The SEC sheriff?"

"I guess he wants to kick me around some more over the Den," Mario said.

Tyler smiled sympathetically. "They ought to be going after *real* criminals," he said.

"Yeah, that's what I told them. They weren't interested."

Mario was led out of the hearing room under Tyler's suspicious eye and escorted down a marble hallway to a small office nearby. Elliot Case and Ben Hersh were waiting for him. "I guess I should have expected this," Mario said, annoyed.

"Glad to see you accepted our invite," Ben Hersh said.

"The Committee served me with a subpoena," said Mario. "But I would have come even if it hadn't. I *like* spectator sports. Anyhow, I like the way you made a show of it in front of an audience. Or was that no accident."

"That's just a taste of how rough we can make things," Case warned.

"So, have you changed your mind?" asked Ben Hersh. "Are you going to testify, I mean *really* testify?"

"I'll take the witness chair in the event I'm called."

"And say what?" Case asked.

Mario shrugged. "I guess you'll just have to find out." Now, he thought it was *his* turn to do a little ball-busting, get a little payback.

"Just remember," Case said. "We have you by the short hairs."

"Is that why we're talking now? You haven't threatened me enough?"

Case put his briefcase on the room's heavy, oak conference table, opened it and pulled out a small tape recorder.

"What's this?" Mario said. "You want to record my testimony in advance."

"Yeah," Case said sarcastically, "so we have something if you're assassinated on the way to the hearing room."

"Cute," Mario said, annoyed.

"Actually, we want to play a tape for you," Hersh said, "something that involves Tyler Gentry."

"And might give you some second thoughts about your Wall Street friends," Case added.

Mario laughed. "There's not a lot about Tyler I don't know. But don't let *that* stop you."

"This was recorded in a hotel room outside of East Beijing," Hersh told him. "Play it, Elliot."

Elliot put the cassette into the player and pressed the play button.

After a few seconds of dead air, Mario heard a man's voice on the tape—and he recognized it immediately. It was Tyler Gentry.

GENTRY: *I just wish your guys hadn't gotten physical with him.*

A second voice came on, the unmistakable dulcet tones of Barton Mulvaney, with the affected upper-class accent.

MULVANEY: *He's going to be just fine.*

GENTRY: *I know, Bart—but a simple warning would have been enough.*

MULVANEY: *I'm not so sure. Monelli has more brawn than brains.*

GENTRY: *I don't think he's a threat any more. He has other things to worry about—his marriage is on life support and I got the SEC looking at the Lions' Den financing. Any way you look at it, he's toast.*

Hersh paused the tape. "Recognize the voices, Mario?"

"Of course I do," Mario said. He was trying to control his anger and figure out what this was all about. "When was this recorded?"

"Day before last," Case said, and he held Mario's gaze for a moment.

Tyler was back in the states then, Mario thought. Bart must have called him from China. Case pressed the play button again and the Gentry-Mulvaney conversation continued.

GENTRY: *We're going to Washington together tomorrow.*

MULVANEY: *So he got a subpoena, too? What do they expect him to say?*

GENTRY: *Nothing that can hurt us. I got him on a short leash. My sources tell me they'll just get him to repeat what he said on television. Won't be enough to help Jaffe's bill, you can be sure of that. How are negotiations going?*

MULVANEY: *Should reach a definitive agreement within the week.*

TYLER: *Good, we'll set the closing ceremony in Hong Kong before the Senate vote comes in.*

MULVANEY: *What about Mario?*

TYLER: *Once the deal is official and we lay to rest that bill, then we'll lay the Lion King to rest..."*

Hersh clicked off the cassette player and turned to Mario. "They've been feathering each other's nest for some time, sharing information and dividing the spoils."

"Do you know who they were talking about, there at the start? You know, the remark about getting physical?" Case asked.

"Yeah," Mario said. "They were talking about Frank. My brother. He was banged up bad—Couple of guys dressed like Saudis."

Case glanced at Hersh, surprised.

Mario stood there, grim and furious. Tyler Gentry had knifed him, cutting an artery—and not just him, but the whole Zoo Crew. What's more, he'd been planning this for who knows how long—months, probably, while they'd been living it up in the Lions' Den. He wouldn't have believed it if he hadn't heard it with his own ears. And then there was Mulvaney. That cocksucker would have a blind date with destiny, and she would order the lobster.

Case and Hersh let Mario steam for a few moments, while the implications of the wiretapped conversation washed over him.

"So, those are the guys you want to protect?" Hersh asked.

"That tape has nothing to do with what's going on down the hall." Mario said. "I have *other* ways to settle with those two."

"Meaning?"

"If you sit by the river long enough the bodies of your enemies will float by."

Hersh was simply furious. "I'm gonna give it to you straight, Mario. The senator is dying. He has only a few months, *if* that. He's spending that time in one last attempt to save this country. He's a *real* hero, Mario. Not the kind you find on the cover of a Wheaties box."

Mario shook his head in wonderment. "You're pulling out all the stops, aren't you, Ben? Threats, guilt, now sympathy—next thing I know you'll be offering me a duffle bag full of C-notes. But I doubt that with *your* budget."

Hersh sighed. "I would if it would get you to change your mind."

"Well, it won't."

There was a knock on the office door. "Yes?" Case said.

The sergeant-at-arms stuck a head inside. "All the Committee members are in place," he said. "The senator is about to call the hearing to order."

Mario looked hard at both men for a moment. "It's been fun," he said. "Now if you'll excuse me." Then, leaving his SEC inquisitors completely frustrated, he walked out of the side office, followed the sergeant-at-arms into the hearing room and returned to the empty seat beside Tyler Gentry.

"You mind telling me what that was all about?" Tyler asked, eyes on the Committee members, going through their papers.

"It was Elliot Case," Mario replied controlling his temper.

"Yeah, I know," Tyler said. "I know who it was. What did he want, Mario?"

"Just some unfinished business about the Lions' Den," Mario said.

On the dais, at the center table, Senator Milton Jaffe picked up the gavel, banged it twice, and called the hearing to order. His face was grey, Mario noted, and his breathing seemed a little irregular, but he looked alert and determined. Jaffe banged the gavel twice more, until he was finally rewarded with silence.

"Ladies and gentlemen, Vice Chairman Harland, and members of the Committee," Jaffe said, his voice a tad fainter than Mario remembered it. "We are here today to discuss new legislation that would sharply restrict the ability of foreign investors to acquire controlling interest in American companies.

"In our previous sessions, we have heard testimony from some of America's leading economists and political analysts on the long-term effect of these buyouts."

Jaffe paused for a moment, as though he needed to catch his breath. Then he continued. "Today, we are going to hear from America's leading investment bankers. Our aim is to find out what they know—or what role they may have played or *be* playing—in what we believe is an attempt by the Saudi Royal Family to eviscerate the core of America's economy.

"I wish I could say that they have all come here voluntarily, but that is not the case, as we know. The Committee has had to subpoena most of these people. All I ask from them now is for their complete and honest testimony."

In the audience, Tyler turned to Mario, "Fat chance," he whispered conspiratorially. Fat chance is right, you Judas prick, Mario thought.

"That's a novel thought," Mario whispered back, grinning appropriately.

"I call our first witness of the day, John Pearson, Chairman of Pearson Pryce," said Senator Jaffe. "Could you please take the witness chair, Mr. Pearson?"

In the audience, John Pearson threaded his way through bankers' row, stopping to shake hands or receive encouragement. He was tall, well-dressed and well-built, with grey hair and pleasing, regular features.

He sat down on the witness chair, took the oath, as administered by one of the Committee functionaries, and smiled at Senator Jaffe. "Good morning, Mr. Chairman, members of the Committee."

"Good morning, Mr. Pearson," Jaffe said. "For the record, could you please tell us your name, your position, and the company you work for."

"Certainly. I am John Pearson, chairman and co-founder of the investment banking firm of Pearson Pryce. We are headquartered in New York City, and I reside there as well."

"Thank you, Mr. Pearson," Jaffe said. "Senator Ryan, we'll let you begin today's questioning."

"Thank you, Mr. Chairman," Ryan said. Matthew Ryan was a small, intense man with steely grey eyes and shiny black hair swept back, highlighting his widow's peak.

He was a second-term Republican senator from Wyoming, who cultivated the nickname "Knife," which had been bestowed on him in recognition of his frequent cutting remarks. "Good morning, John, um, Mr. Pearson. I wonder if you could tell us what you know about foreign buyouts of American companies—from your personal knowledge, that is."

"Certainly, Matt—senator. So far as I am aware, everything has been conducted by foreign brokers and financial agents, with very little transparency, so I'm not really able to shed much light as to the value of such transactions."

"I understand, Mr. Pearson, but could you talk for a moment about the mechanics of how these buyouts work?"

"There's nothing mysterious about it, senator. It happens in exactly the same way such buyouts or mergers happen with domestic companies. It's accomplished entirely by the purchase of stock—a controlling interest. Happens every day on Wall Street."

Mario admired the simplicity of the explanation. It was true as far as it went, but it's what Pearson left out that really mattered.

"But these buyouts often come as a shock, at least to the general public," Senator Ryan said. "Could you explain why that happens?"

"Certainly, senator. It's really quite mundane. The stock purchases are not made by public offer, but quietly, on the market, by several individuals, working together. This may sound conspiratorial, but it's really a common practice. It's done to keep the price of the stock from rising too quickly and too far."

The senator smiled, pleased with Pearson's innocuous answers to his questions. "So there's really nothing unusual about these buyouts except for the identity of the buyers?"

Pearson considered the question. "Even that isn't unusual," he said. "Foreign buyers have been purchasing American companies for many decades—Britain, France, Germany, Japan. The Saudis may be new to the game, but it's an old game."

"I see," said Senator Ryan. "I have nothing further. I yield the rest of my time to Senator Cortez."

"Thank you," said Senator Cortez, who was sitting on the left side of the dais, with his fellow Democrats. Cortez was a sharp, hawk-faced, ex-prosecuting attorney from New Jersey, and, at age twenty-eight, a junior member on the Senate Financial Services Committee and the youngest senator in Congress.

"Mr. Pearson," he asked. "Do you think these buyouts are good for America?"

Pearson looked up toward the ceiling, hands clasped on the table in front of him. "My main concern," he said sagely, "would be to see if the investors got a fair price for their shares. In the deals *I've* negotiated, the shareholders have realized an excellent return on their investments."

"But what about for *America*?" Cortez asked, sharply. "Have these takeovers been good for the country?"

Pearson pondered the question. "You have to look at the stockholders. These deals have made many of them very rich. Is that bad for America? You tell me, no disrespect intended, senator."

"I think it depends on how it impacts the rest of us," Cortez said acidly. "You know, the people who make America work. The people who golf at the public courses."

Pearson laughed. "I think they want to get rich, too, don't you?"

Everyone in the room, including the committee members, laughed appreciatively.

After another few minutes sparring, Cortez realized he wasn't going to get anywhere. "I have no more questions, Mr. Chairman," he said.

"Thank you Senator Cortez," Jaffe said. "Senator Butler, I believe the floor is yours."

Senator Butler, a lanky, raw-boned man with an easy grin, thanked the chairman and smiled at Pearson. "Are you having a good time, Mr. Pearson? Enjoying yourself?"

"Well, I'd rather not be in Washington at the moment," Pearson allowed, "but I am encouraged by my pleasant treatment—thus far."

"Good," Butler said. "I trust you'll feel that way after we're finished." He smiled and so did Pearson. Simon Butler was a three-term Democratic senator from Pennsylvania and a moderate Liberal.

"Tell me, Mr. Pearson," he said in his avuncular way, "What happens when foreign investors—perhaps backed by foreign governments—take control of our American defense contractors? Will our military secrets be safe from our enemies? Will we have to rely on the decisions of foreigners in order to arm ourselves?"

Pearson smiled and took a lazy swing at the question. "Well, first of all, we have laws about such things, and I see no reason to assume foreign-owned companies won't obey the law. We already have many foreign-owned companies in the United States and foreign-owned subsidiaries, and from everything I read, they are very law abiding. But I don't know why I should be answering that question. I am in no way involved in these deals, and I am not an expert on their effects."

"All right," said Senator Butler, "I'll stick to areas in which you're an expert. Would you, if you were asked, provide the expertise to help a foreign purchaser engage in a hostile takeover of an American company?"

"They have their own people," Pearson replied politely. "They don't need me."

"I understand," Butler said. "Now tell us this. There have been rumors that you may have been consulted by the Saudis in some of their ambitious endeavors. Could you tell us, under oath, have you ever acted as a liaison for foreign investors or a foreign government in connection with the takeover of a U.S. entity?"

Pearson bent back toward his counsel, who was sitting behind him, and they whispered briefly. Then he turned back to Senator Butler. "Not that I recall," he said.

"So, you've never negotiated on behalf of a foreign entity and obtained *for them* majority ownership of an American enterprise?"

Senator Harland, the ranking Republican from Texas, interrupted. "The witness has already answered that question, Senator Butler."

Butler and Harland exchanged hostile glances. Their distaste for each other was palpable, and clear evidence of the partisan infighting that had preceded the hearing.

"No, no," Pearson said, "I'd like to respond. As you know, our firm is a very large one and we deal with global investors every day, but to answer your question senator, no, not for that specific reason, not that I recall."

"I see," Butler said, uninterested in challenging Pearson. "Well, tell me this: Do you know of any other American investment bankers, individuals or otherwise, who have helped foreign investors in the clandestine acquisition of U.S. companies? I would like to remind the witness that he is under oath."

"No," Pearson said, "I can't say that I have."

Butler smiled, broadly. "So the rumors are nothing more than rumors?"

"That is correct, senator," Pearson replied steadfast. "Nothing you can do about rumors."

"Of course not," Butler said. "Mr. Pearson, I have no more questions. But before I yield my time, I would like to express my admiration for your long and distinguished career and your contributions to the country." The sarcasm in the remark was obvious to everyone.

"Thank you for your kind words," Pearson said, equally sarcastic.

"Senator Guffman," said Jaffe, "I believe you're next."

Guffman was a little man at the end of the committee table. A Republican from Montana, he was known among his colleagues for inattention and lack of preparedness, and he lived up to his reputation this time.

"What's that?" Guffman said, eyes blinking behind thick glasses, "you say it's my turn?"

"That's right," Jaffe said patiently.

"Well, I have a whole list of questions," he waved a paper. But everybody's already asked them. I don't want to repeat anything that's already been said. So I yield my time to the next senator, whoever that is."

The audience laughed, which confused and angered Guffman. "They've already asked all my questions," he said again.

The next senator to take up the questioning was Dennis Wiscowitz, the first-term Ohio Democrat and a known barn-burner, and Wiscowitz was as hostile to the witness as Senator Ryan was appeasing.

"Good morning, Mr. Pearson. I'd like to get into some specifics. According to our investigators, you spent three weeks in Dubai last winter. Am I correct?"

Pearson consulted his counsel again.

"No need to consult counsel, Mr. Pearson. Were you or were you not in Dubai last year from December eighth through the eleventh?" His voice was harsh.

"Yes I was, senator."

"On at least two occasions, you were visited by members of the Saudi Royal Family at the Crown Plaza hotel where you were staying. Can you describe the nature of these meetings?"

Pearson smiled easily, radiating confidence. "They were purely social occasions. I've known some of these men—socially—for several years."

"Did you at any time discuss helping them target Net Global for hostile acquisition? Please remember that you are under oath."

"You needn't remind me, senator," Pearson said, a little testy. "I have every intention of telling the Committee the truth. The answer to your question is no. That subject did not come up in our conversations."

Witkowitz scribbled a note on his pad while Pearson waited patiently for the next question. "Thank you, Mr. Pearson. Next question: did you or any officers at Pearson Pryce set up a shell company in Gibraltar that was intended to mask the purchase of Disney stocks on behalf of the Saudi oil minister."

"I would never do such a thing," Pearson volleyed.

"I didn't ask if you would or wouldn't, Mr. Pearson," Witkowitz said. "I asked if you *did*."

"The answer is still no," Pearson replied.

"One last question," Witkowitz said. "Did you, or any members of your family, or any officers of your firm or any other close associates profit from any foreign mergers rooted to the Middle East, namely the Saudi Royal Family?" He fixed Pearson with a laser-like gaze.

Pearson, however, showed no signs of wilting. "Not a dime," he said.

Butler held Pearson's gaze for a moment, then gave up on it. "No further questions."

From somewhere in the hearing room's balcony, applause burst out among the spectators. Congressional security officers hurried to the noisy offenders and escorted them from the chamber.

In the audience, Tyler touched Mario's sleeve. "No one's going to lay so much as a glove on any of us," he said.

Mario nodded in agreement. "Looks like it's going to be a minute or two before they resume. I'm going to go see a man about a dog."

He got up, squeezed past Tyler, and walked to the back of the hearing room, to one of the sergeants-at-arm. "Bathroom?"

The man pointed to a door not far away. Mario entered the bathroom, did his business, then went to a sink, splashed some water on his face and studied the man looking back at him in the mirror.

When Mario got back to his seat, Carl Doubleday, Republican, senior senator from Kansas, had just started questioning Andrew Reisman, a senior advisor at the Wilkinson Group. He threw the banker half a dozen pitiful softballs, which Reisman knocked out of the park, then apologized for taking the banker's "precious time."

The Committee interrogated Reisman over his ties with the Saudi ambassador, the Republicans lobbing pitches, the Democrats firing fastballs with only an occasional strike. Then Jaffe thanked him for his testimony and reluctantly sent him on his way.

And so it went for the entire morning, until they broke for lunch. A chorus of investment bankers took turns on the witness chair, all singing the same chorus—"I don't know," "I don't remember," "It's not my field," "I don't recollect," even "I would never do anything against my country's interests" or some variation.

It got to the point that Mario and Tyler started predicting to each other what the next witness would say. They were rarely wrong.

One of the witnesses, Philipe de Broca, president of Hayden Loeb Brothers, a private equity firm in Fort Worth, insisted on responding to every question asked of him. "I respectfully refuse to answer on the grounds that my answer might tend to violate my Fifth Amendment privilege."

Senator Jaffe explained to Mr. de Broca that the proposed law was not in effect and that if he admitted to any acts that it might someday penalize, he would not be in danger of incriminating himself. De Broca, however, refused to provide any answers, other than name.

Next to testify was Sanford Connelly of Montgomery Dawes. Connelly, an atheist, was affirmed rather than sworn in, but his testimony was still under the penalty of perjury. He gave them nothing.

By mid-afternoon, it became clear that Jaffe and fellow Democrats on the committee had miscalculated in thinking that the investment bankers' testimony would somehow garner support for anti-takeover measures. The previous weeks' testimony from corporate executives and economics experts had worked in their favor. But the bankers' testimony seemed to erase all the gains.

The next witness called was Tyler Gentry. His performance was the mirror image of John Pearson's—he was friendly, he was superficially cooperative, and he said absolutely nothing of substance. He returned to his seat grinning, but Mario noticed that the armpits of his expensive suit were dark and damp.

Barton Mulvaney followed Tyler. He slid through the row of investment bankers, grinning, shaking hands, and tried, but failed, to step on Mario's shoe. After being sworn in, he cosied up behind a microphone and, with his legal team at his elbow, read a carefully-crafted opening statement, sipping water from a strategically placed glass. On the dais, Committee members listened and took notes.

When Mulvaney finished his opening statement, the Republican members of the Committee lobbed more softball questions at him. Then it was the Democrats' turn, and though they did everything in their power to provoke something revealing, or even significant. Bart batted away their queries with infuriating ease, giving a condensed version of the stock answers his predecessors had given—a litany of denials, engaging occasionally in sharp and contentious exchanges with the ailing committee chairman.

In the audience, Mario turned to Tyler. "His choreography is flawless," he admitted.

"He has good instincts," Tyler agreed. "But so do you, Mario."

"You think they'll come at me as hard?"

"Harder," Tyler said, shooting Mario a sidelong glance. "But if you get in trouble, take a time out," Tyler advised. "Go for the glass. Winston will take it from there. Then we'll pop the cork on the bubbly."

Mario smiled conspiratorially. "Don't worry," he said, "I know what to say."

After Mulvaney finished testifying, Sen. Harland took the microphone. "Well," he said, "we've listened to a great many people, Mr. Chairman, and taken a long time to do it. I think it's time to vote on whether or not we let the bill go to the Senate floor."

Mario focused on Jaffe. It wasn't obvious, but the senator seemed to be having a problem with his left hand—opening and closing his fist. There was also something wrong with his face. It was subtle, but apparent if you looked closely. His lips were sagging slightly on the left side. My God, Mario said to himself, the old man is having a stroke.

"Not quite yet," Jaffe said, his voice fighting to stay strong. "I have one last witness. The committee calls Mario Monelli, of the Harrison Hart Alliance. Mr. Monelli?"

All eyes in the room turned to Mario. Mario took a deep breath and stood up. As he buttoned his jacket, Tyler reached for his arm and locked eyes with him. "Remember what we spoke about."

Mario took one last look around the room, at the row of magnates and took his place at the witness table facing the committee. The sergeant-at-arms administered the oath, and Mario sat down ready to deliver what Tyler and his friends anxiously anticipated would be the death knell to the Jaffe bill.

"Do you have an opening statement, Mr. Monelli?" asked Senator Jaffe.

"As a matter of fact, senator, " Mario said, relishing the moment, "I do. And when I'm finished with it, that's the end of my testimony here—I won't have anything further to say."

Mario looked back over his shoulder at Tyler and the rest. They seemed pleased, which is just what he anticipated. The Committee, however, was shocked and dismayed, and the public gallery was aghast.

"Mr. Monelli," Jaffe said sternly, "we may well have questions for you, and we will expect you to answer them."

"I'm here because you subpoenaed me," Mario reminded him. "But I'm not going to answer any questions."

For once, the reaction from the senators was bipartisan. Everyone was flabbergasted.

"You can't dictate to this committee…" one senator growled.

"Remember, Mr. Monelli, you are under subpoena," Senator Harland coldly commanded.

"This committee is prepared to hold you in contempt right now," Jaffe said, practically standing.

"With all due respect, senator, if you do, you'll get more I-don't-remember and I-don't-knows, and you won't be able to do a damn thing about it. But I think you'll find that my opening statement covers everything. Are you ready to hear it or do I leave?"

Tyler tried to attract the attention of Winston Freehold, who'd taken the counsel's seat behind Mario, but the man just sat there bewildered.

In the gallery, people were buzzing in confusion, and the Wall Street contingent were exchanging concerned whispers. Jaffe took a long pause. His left hand was now quivering almost imperceptibly. He glanced around at the other democrats on the panel, getting nods of approval. "By all means," he said and lowered himself back into his seat.

"Mr. Chairman, Mr. Vice-Chairman, members of the Committee. Many of your previous witnesses—they're sitting in the audience right now—have a pretty good idea of what I'm going to say," Mario began, speaking without notes.

"They know I'm against foreign takeovers of U.S. companies, but they are confident I'm not going to rock the boat. After all, I'm a member of the club. I'm not going to turn on my own—they're pretty sure of that. I have a career to protect and a family to support."

He paused, turned toward the audience and smiled broadly. The audience seemed confused.

"In fact," Mario went on, "my own boss, Tyler Gentry—" He turned toward Tyler. "Hold your hand up, Tyler." Tyler, caught off guard by the cameras, sheepishly raised his hand.

"Yes," Mario said, "Tyler gave me a little advice just before I took the witness chair here. He suggested that I repeat some of the things I said on television during the winter, and that otherwise, I should be vague and generalize. Do I have that right, Tyler?"

Tyler, who was starting to show some discomfort, just sat there.

"Do you know why Tyler said that?" Mario asked rhetorically. "No, of course you don't. Let me explain. Tyler doesn't want me to give any aid and comfort to the supporters of this bill. He wants to see the anti-takeover bill die as I am sure everyone on this side of the room does.

"I know it," Mario glanced back at Tyler, "and *he* knows it. But maybe I'm not being fair by singling him out. He's no different than any of the others whose testimony you've heard from today."

He turned and pointed to the previous witnesses, all of whom were engaged in deep conversations with each other and pretending to ignore him.

"They're not here to provide information or to offer their expert opinions on whether or not foreign take-overs benefit our country. They're here to kill the bill, once and for all. That is the single motive for every word each of them has said today."

The room was totally silent now, and every eye was riveted to Mario. "You may wonder why they are so bitterly opposed to your bill, senator. Well, let me assure you, it's not because they think it's bad for America. They're opposed to limiting foreign acquisition of American assets because such a law would be bad for *them*."

By now, Tyler was staring venomously at Mario, his face blood red, his jaw jutting forward. Mario watched him for awhile, then turned back toward the committee.

"So why are these men, these generals and admirals of capitalism, so set on defeating this bill? Well, they have thousands of reasons, in fact hundreds of thousands of reasons. They are the inheritors of a tradition that began about 2,000 years ago, with thirty pieces of silver.

"Cast your eyes on these titans of the universe, senators. Look at John Pearson, in his $3,000 suit, more secure in his power than any king. Look at Dwight McPhee. Did you know that Dwight has six homes—mansions really. And let's not forget Melvin Taubman. Anytime anyone uses a credit card, *anywhere*, Mel gets a nickel. Look at them all, de Broca, Vashnay, Kahn, Ito, Becker, Smith. Look at them carefully. *They* control the nation's purse strings, not Congress, and they are not willing to surrender even the tiniest fraction of their wealth and power, even if it means selling out their country."

"Now don't drag out that old cliché about Wall Street greed, Mr. Monelli," interjected Senator Harland. "There's nothing wrong with making money."

"Don't interrupt, senator." Mario looked back at the rows of investment bankers and at their lawyers, their advisors and their other servants, and the Congressional Committee did the same. The objects of this rapt attention dealt with it as their personalities dictated—brazenly, nervously, dismissively, angrily.

"I've called your attention to these men," Mario went on, "because they are a new breed of men, first of their kind—at least in the United States. They are *traitors*. Their eagerness to cooperate with the Saudis and profit from betraying their country and their opposition to this bill is nothing less than treason."

There was an audible gasp in the room.

"These people faced a decision—to enlarge their fortunes or to save their country. And I don't think any of them hesitated a moment because nothing is more important to them than the accumulation of wealth, whatever the consequences, and for whom."

Winston Freehold, in an attempt to end the diatribe, reached over and covered the microphone, briefly chastising Mario. Mario gently brushed his hand away.

"And today they sat in this chair, each one of them, and insisted that they *didn't* know, or *didn't* remember, or *couldn't* be sure, or weren't expert in the field. A housewife in Corona, Queens knows more about her income than these people know about theirs, if we are to believe them.

"Senators, these bald-face liars all know, down to the very last dollar, how much they've profited and by whom. And all of them are hiding it, with a network of shell companies and hidden ownerships that dwarf anything the American mafia ever dreamed up. Now ask yourselves this: Why do they need such deception?"

Mario paused and took a deep breath. There was a sense in the room that something truly remarkable was happening. Someone was speaking the truth, and as a result, anything could happen.

"They needed such deception," Mario said, "not because their actions were against the law. They weren't. They needed to conceal what they were doing because they knew it was *immoral*. They knew what kind of judgment they'd face if the public ever learned of their collaboration with our enemies. Well, they can't hide any more. Their treason is public.

"Mr. Chairman, members of the Committee, these are all immensely talented men, *brilliant* men, most of them the sons of other talented and *brilliant* men. They are the products of the finest private prep schools in America, and the most prestigious universities and finance schools. Their academic achievements are exceeded only by their lightning-like rises up the ladder of success. They are the best America has to offer and they've received the best America has to give.

"They'd have to be, actually, to pull off their remarkable feats of financial terrorism—and keep it all hidden. Well, the secrets end today. *Right* now. John Pearson, third from the left over there, engineered the Saudi purchase of General Electric. He did it through a network of shell companies so complex that no one could have connected him with it. Smile for the cameras, John.

"Bernard Kahn, sitting to his right, did the same with Intel. You didn't know that the Saudi Royal Family now owns the controlling interest in Intel? Well, it does, thanks to Mr. Kahn and his web of shell companies in Costa Rica.

"I'm sure you saw the recent headlines about Microsoft, gentlemen. Well, the man who engineered *that* disaster for the Saudis is Philipe de Broca. I understand he cleared over a half billion dollars on the deal. Personally. Paid to him by the Saudi treasury through the Bundesbank."

Philipe de Broca, black-haired, slim, impeccably dressed in a European suit, and a bit younger than his cohorts, stood suddenly, his face a picture of disgust, if not pure hatred, rudely pushed his way past his brethren and marched out of the hearing room, his counsel following him. His departure was greeted by shocked silence.

Mario waited until de Broca had left the room. "Embarrassed, I guess," he said. "Well he should be. And he's not the only one. Here are a few more:

Joshua Becker sold out Alcoa. Melvin Taubman got the Saudis the controlling interest in American Airlines. Dwight McPhee right now is masterminding a play for Time-Warner, fronting the deal through a shell company in the Netherlands. The Saudi Royal Family will be the new owner."

Members of the print media were frantically thumbing their Blackberries and cell phones in a mad rush to get copy to their editors.

"I could go on, but it's all in here, the ones I've mentioned and all the rest." Mario reached into his inside jacket pocket, withdrew a thick envelope, and handed it to the sergeant-at-arms, who gave it to Senator Jaffe.

Bart looked over at Tyler and shook his head.

"In case you're wondering where all that information came from and if it's accurate," Mario said, "let me assure that it is. It is the product of the sharpest research team on Wall Street—Neil Granger, Barry Nussbaum, Glen Novak, Dennis McCurdy, and Kathleen Sweeney, as fine a group of patriots as exists anywhere. America owes a great deal to them."

The ranking Republican on the Committee, Senator Matthew Harland, of Texas, reached for his microphone and interrupted. "Just one second, Mr. Monelli, just one second there. Do you know the gravity of the charges you're making? Are you aware of the impact this could have on the reputations of these fine Americans?"

"I said 'no questions,' senator," Mario replied brusquely. "I'm going to give my statement and school's out."

Mario let that sit a moment, and Senator Harland just stared at him, open-mouthed.

"And you have reminded me about another group of people, senator. I thank you for that. People like you and some of your colleagues on this Committee who, like Wall Street, have dedicated yourselves to killing this bill right here, *in* Committee, preventing it from reaching the Senate floor, where, I am told, it is nearly certain to pass."

Now it was the opposition senators sitting at the Committee table who tried to hide in plain sight, who looked away from the hearing audience, or consulted aides.

"I understand your motives, gentlemen. The Wall Street interest groups are your pals, your buddies. You have dinner with them, you play golf with them, you even vacation with them. You share the same political philosophy. They finance your re-election campaigns. And your re re *re*-election campaigns. You need each other.

"I'm going to be generous now, senators," Mario went on. "I'm going to assume that you were blind to your supporters' treason. Now I'd like to make another assumption. I'm assuming that since you now know about these terrorists—" he waved at the row of bankers—"you will abandon them, as they so richly deserve, and vote for the first and only law that will bring their treason to an end."

Mario's gaze met Jaffe's and he was startled to see that the old man's eyes were filled with tears. But the senator's face was also illuminated by just a hint of a satisfied smile.

"One last thought," Mario said. He turned toward bankers' row, which was glowering at him with a mixture of hatred and shame. "Although you gentlemen are guilty of high moral crimes against your country, it may not be too late for you. I know it will be extremely humiliating, but I urge you to change your testimony and tell the American people the truth. Those among you who can do that will deserve our admiration. That concludes my testimony, Mr. Chairman and members of the Committee, and it is my last comment on this issue, in this forum or anywhere else."

Jaffe slammed the gavel as Mario stood, buttoned his suit jacket, and strode from the hearing room. For a few moments, there was nothing but stunned silence—then, isolated clapping, then by the growing thunder of universal applause and finally, full-throated cheers of approval. The sound reverberated through the Senate's marble hallways—an outburst of pure noise such had seldom been heard in this august building.

No sooner had Mario exited the hearing room than he saw a scrum of reporters and photographers waiting to swallow him. Mario nixed a dramatic exit down the Capitol's alabaster steps and instead headed for a side door. He'd said what he had intended to say, in exactly the way he'd *always* intended to say it. He didn't need anyone else's approval. He had his own, maybe for the first time in his life.

A little more than a mile away, in a beautiful duplex garden apartment overlooking the tree-lined Potomac, Julie Chambers sat in front of her television set, transfixed. She had just witnessed one of the most remarkable moments in broadcast television—the passionate, courageous, stunningly honest, and utterly damning testimony of Mario Monelli—*her* Mario—to the Jaffe Committee.

And now she was watching the tumultuous response—everyone in the hearing room was on his feet, talking excitedly to his neighbor, on his cell phone urging absent colleagues to turn on the hearings, gleefully observing the humiliated and outraged Wall Street elite. The bankers were huddled together, arguing furiously.

The camera came in on Tom Gallagher, who was covering the event for UBS news live from the hearing room. "Ladies and gentlemen," he said, "in all my years as a journalist, I have never witnessed anything like today's testimony from Mario Monelli, who in a courageous quest for truth, reconciliation, and honor singled out over a dozen of America's most powerful investment firms and called them traitors. His charges, if true, are dynamite. And they make it impossible for anyone on this Committee to vote against Senator Jaffe's anti-takeover legislation or face political oblivion."

Suddenly, the well-known voice of anchorman John Ayers cut in from the studio.

"Tom, what will be the backlash to some of the allegations of treason Mario Monelli has made against his colleagues today?"

"John, in ordinary circumstances, publicly calling someone a traitor is slander—grounds for a *major* law suit. But not in this case. Testimony given to Congress is immune from slander or libel suits because it is in the public interest for Congress to hear everything a witness feels should be said. And of course, if the charges are true—well, that's an absolute defense against libel."

Gallagher cupped an ear, evidently listening to his producer, then UBS switched to a camera focused on Senator Jaffe, who was still in his seat. Someone was leaning over the table talking to him.

"Wait," Gallagher, said in a voice-over, "Samuel Sicorra, one of Dwight McPhee's legal advisors is conferring with Senator Jaffe. Something is happening here, John. Tony, can we pick up any sound? No? They've muted the mikes at the Committee tables? Well, we'll just have to see…"

Sicorra broke off his conversation with Jaffe and headed back to his seat, and Jaffe banged the gavel on the table. The noisy hearing room slowly grew quiet. "I am informed," said the senator, switching on his mike again, "that one of this morning's witnesses, Mr. Dwight McPhee, wishes to revise his testimony. Mr. McPhee, you may take the chair."

As the audience went wild with excited speculation, the television camera panned across the room, coming in on a man who was slipping out of his seat and heading toward the witness chair, a fat, florid-faced fellow with tiny eyes and a head full of carefully cut salt-and-pepper hair. He looked as though his dog had just died.

"Here he comes," Gallagher said. "We have no indication of what he intends to say."

Julie leaned forward, unsure of what was about to happen, her heart pounding nonetheless.

"Mr. McPhee," Jaffe said, "this Committee reminds you that you are still under oath."

McPhee, who seemed unable to meet Jaffe's eyes, mumbled something, and despite the silence in the room, his words were inaudible.

"Could you repeat that please?" Jaffe asked.

"Yes, senator," he said, in a voice that was at least two octaves higher than it had been earlier that day. "I wish to recant my previous testimony."

A sudden buzz of surprise broke out in the room. Gallagher took the opportunity to have a hushed conversation with anchorman Ayers, on air, for the viewers' benefit. "John, this is a most remarkable development…"

McPhee testified for almost an hour, corroborating Mario's testimony, adding details Mario had left out. He was followed by three more of the nation's key acquisition advisors, all admitting their direct complicity in the vast scheme to transfer ownership of America's top-tier corporations to the Saudi Royal Family. They revealed the network of shell companies, revealed the names of those involved, and described in detail the tactics they had employed.

Each one of them also tried to explain why he had lied. McPhee said that Monelli had shamed him. Kahn told the Committee that Monelli had given him the courage to break with his co-conspirators. "I never wanted to be a part of it," he insisted. De Broca tearfully begged his adopted country to forgive him and proclaimed his undying love for the United States.

After awhile, Julie turned off the television. It didn't matter what anyone else said now. What mattered was what *Mario* had said and done. In a few minutes of electrifying testimony, he had changed the course of a nation.

CHAPTER THIRTY-FIVE

Mario briefly considered not going in to work on Monday morning. He considered not going back...ever. After all, he wasn't likely to be warmly welcomed, not after his whistle-blowing performance on national television.

He stepped off the elevator and into the sacrosanct domain of Harrison Hart just after the opening bell. The pretty, blonde receptionist glanced up at him, then, nervously, back at some papers on her desk. He continued on through the trading floor, and as the traders spotted him, they stopped talking to each other on the phone and simply stared.

"Good morning," Mario said with a smile, but he got no response, except for timid nods and winks from the few who'd come with him from Hart. Well, Mario thought, so that's how it's going to be. Then he passed Rose Pheeney, sitting at her desk outside Tyler's office, sorting through a stack of papers. She didn't look up as Mario approached her desk.

"Morning, beautiful. How's my sweet Irish rose?"

She still didn't look up. No, Mario thought, he wasn't going to be getting a warm welcome. In fact, it looked like he'd be a pariah to most everyone except those who'd been very close to him at Hart.

He made the journey to M&A like he was walking through a trappist monastery—more stares—and when he came through the glass doors, everything changed. The entire Zoo Crew greeted him with applause and praise.

"Damn, boss, you were *beautiful* up there," Glen gushed.

"Made me proud, paisan," Dennis said. "No bullshit."

"Yeah, Mario," said Barry. "My mother was watching with all her mah jong friends. She told me to ask you over for dinner sometime. You like gefilte fish?"

Neil stepped forward and embraced Mario. "That was totally amazing. Just the way we planned it. Did you hear what all the Monday morning quarterbacks had to say about your testimony?"

"I stayed away from the tube this weekend," Mario said.

Neil couldn't contain himself. "Well, I *didn't*. They said you were a goddamn folk hero, Mario. Even those Fascist assholes over at Fox. Can I touch you?"

Everyone laughed.

"Have you seen today's *Wall Street Journal*?" Dennis asked.

Mario shook his head.

Dennis held it up, and Mario read the bold headline at the top of page one: *Jaffe Committee unanimously passes anti-takeover bill, Senate passage almost certain, president won't veto.*

"He had no choice," Barry said.

"That's a grand slam homerun, Mario," Kat said.

"I couldn't have pulled it off without you guys. That was the most amazing research work I've ever seen."

"Yeah," Barry said. "Maybe the SEC will employ us. I have a feeling we're not going to be with the firm much longer."

Mario didn't like that at all. "Why?" he asked. "What have they said to you?"

"They didn't say *anything*," Kat told him. "They didn't say hello, they didn't say goodbye. They didn't say, 'coffee wagon is here,' they just didn't say anything."

"If I didn't know any better, I'd think they didn't like us anymore," Neil laughed.

The Zoo Crew took their seats, but Mario remained standing. "I do have a couple of pieces of news for you, *bad* news…"

"Let us guess, the Lions' Den," Dennis said.

"Yeah," sighed Mario. "Frank's associate arranged for the closing at two o'clock this afternoon. We're giving it back to the city…*as is*. He suggested we all drop by after lunch to pick up some of our things and to have Duncan wrap things up."

"That's gonna be hard…about Duncan wrapping things up."

"Why?" asked Mario.

The Zoo Crew looked at each other.

"They deported the chap," said Glen..

"Shit," Mario muttered. "Fucking feds wasted no time." He took a deep breath. "I got one more piece of news left. I don't know exactly how it's going to affect us."

"Might as well tell us," Neil said.

Whatever it was, it clearly wasn't going to throw them.

"Our good friend Tyler has managed to find us an overseas bride. Looks like we're getting hitched again."

"Which outfit?" asked Dennis.

"Don't know, but I'm sure we'll all find out soon enough," Mario replied.

"Ain't no surprise," said Glen. "After the Intercoastal deal it was to be expected."

"That's not the surprise," replied Mario. "The surprise is the partners hired Barton Mulvaney to perform the ceremony."

"They hired Bart as justice of the peace?" said Dennis.

"You heard this from Tyler himself, Mario?" Barry asked.

"...and Bart," replied Mario. "Although not directly."

Kat put a finger to her mouth and neatly bit off a sliver of unruly cuticle. She didn't say anything. Neither did anyone else. Everyone knew what this meant.

Mario held up a hand. "One more wrinkle—the bride—she's Chinese."

Glen was dumbfounded. "He went to the gooks for the money? Are you fucking sure?"

"I have it on *very* good authority."

"So that's why that scumbag was in Beijing," Dennis said.

"I'll bet he parachutes outta here with at least $200 million," said Barry.

Mario's phone chirped. "Monelli here. Yeah, Rose." He looked at the Zoo Crew. "Right now? Sure thing." He hung up the phone slowly and turned to his friends. "Well as they say in La Cosa Nostra, I been sent for."

"You're finally getting your button?"

"I seriously doubt that, Denny."

"Did I hear that right?" Neil asked. "E. Peter Patterson II has summoned you?"

"The very same," Mario said. "After years of total invisibility, Harrison Hart's senior partner has unexpectedly materialized and has invited me in the woodshed."

Dennis was wearing a droll smile. "You remember that's how Pesci got it."

"You want a little protection?" Glen asked, playfully. He pulled a pink and black striped condom from his wallet, and drew laughter from everyone in the room.

"I don't think that's going to help," Mario told him.

Mario grabbed his jacket and headed down the hallway. The last time he'd seen E. Peter Patterson was days after 9/11 when it was learned Austin Keyes was among the missing. The old man had reminded him that Harrison was an old and very well-respected firm, and said he expected Monelli, as Keyes' de facto regent, to uphold its tradition, and not to do anything that would reflect badly on the name. Mario had felt like a little boy in the principal's office being told that he'd better straighten up and fly right.

He didn't know exactly what Patterson wanted to say to him this time, but he knew in the wake of his testimony before the Senate, his position with Harrison Hart was no longer tenable.

Mario walked upstairs. The front desk was manned by a stunning blonde with a pneumatic figure who, sad to say, only showed up at Harrison Hart on those rare occasions when Patterson made an appearance.

"I'm Mario Monelli," he told her.

She looked at him as though his face was dirty. "Yes," she acknowledged, her eyes drifting down to the newspaper in her lap. "He'll be right with you."

While waiting, the door from the executive dining room opened and out walked four impeccably dressed Asian men. They were engaged in conversation with some of Harrison's high-ranking officers. Mario watched as they disappeared into the elevator banks.

"You may go in now, Mr. Monelli," she said.

Mario opened the door to Patterson's office, a heavy bleached-oak affair, and walked in. The room was a duplicate of Louis XIV's master bedchamber at the Palace of Versailles, complete with preposterous crystal chandeliers, heavy damask drapes, and enough gold leaf to cover the dome of a state capitol.

Five men were waiting for him: E. Peter Patterson, a tall, pious-looking gent with pink cheeks, a fringe of white hair and the look of money; J. G. Caldwell, a Texas oil billionaire who wore cowboy boots with his Dolce and Gabbana suit; Col. Brentwood Bargus, of the Philadelphia Barguses, and not too proud to tell anyone, whether or not they asked; and Sidney Cohn, a small, shrunken, gnome-like person, son of the man who invented aspartame. And last but not least, Tyler Gentry. The partners. There were also two unfamiliar faces in the room—attorneys, Mario assumed.

Patterson was the only one to meet Mario's eyes. "Good to see you again, Mr. Monelli," he said smoothly, his on-off smile switch was on. "I hope all is well with you and yours."

He extended a hand and Mario took it. "As well as can be expected, sir. Please convey my best to Mrs. Patterson and Deborah. How is she doing?"

Patterson frowned. "Still in the hospital, sadly, but her new team of psychologists think there may be a light at the end of the tunnel."

Mario glanced at the other faces in the room and exchanged pleasantries. Everyone except Tyler was looking at him now. "Greetings, Tyler."

Tyler muttered a hello without looking up. The others were slightly more cordial.

"Please have a seat, Mr. Monelli," Patterson said, indicating the sole empty chair in the room, a fragile-legged Louis XIV reproduction in the center of the circle of partners.

"I see you like the Cubans," Mario said, noticing the box of cigars on Patterson's desk.

"Very much so," Patterson replied. "These were given to me personally by Premier Castro when I was down there—grown on his own plantation. The tobacco is quite rare I was told. Enough to make only a few every year. I would offer you one, but they're just, ah, decorative."

"Of course," said Mario.

"Mr. Monelli—Mario, if I may—we are all adults here…"

"A fact not in evidence, but go ahead," Mario said, smiling graciously.

"Yes, well, be that as it may. I think everyone would appreciate it if I didn't engage in meaningless chit-chat, so let me get right to the point. The other partners and I have thoroughly discussed the direction of Harrison Hart, and we have voted not to renew your contract.

"Mergers and Acquisitions will be undergoing a reorganization, and we have come to the general agreement that you no longer fit with our future plans."

"I see," Mario said wryly. He was having a very good time. Not giving a shit did that for you. "And what might those plans be if I may ask, Peter?"

"The climate is shifting, Mario. In wake of this new law the president signed over the weekend, we now find it necessary to turn to our one guaranteed source of income. Takeovers. The kind that come with, shall we say…collateral damage."

"The kind you refrain from doing," J.G. interjected.

Mario nodded. He understood everything that wasn't being said openly, and so did they. The exit strategy was like a little play, each person speaking his lines.

Patterson continued. "We feel that you simply do not share our philosophy of hostile acquisition. Because of that, the synergies between our two firms have never really quite meshed…and never will."

"What about my team?" Mario asked. "You'll still need a support structure."

"We're bringing in another team…from overseas, one with greater expertise in the area."

"I assume there was a vote."

"Yes," Patterson said, "all in accord with the corporate by laws."

Mario nodded. "And it was unanimous, I gather?"

"The vote was…" Patterson began, but Mario interrupted.

"No, Peter, I'd rather hear it from Tyler."

Tyler looked up from his pipe and engaged Mario. "It was unanimous, Mario," he said without expression.

"We have a generous severance package for you, Mario," said Sidney Cohn with a disarming smile.

"You'll never need to work again," grinned Brentwood Bargus.

Mario craned his neck and glanced at the figure. "My, that's quite a goin' away kiss," he said, leaning back. The sarcasm sailed over their heads.

"Our spokesman will issue a statement saying that you've resigned in order to pursue other endeavors."

"Endeavors," Mario laughed. "Hard to argue with that," he said, sowing confusion. He patted his breast pocket. "But I seem to have left my resignation at home."

"Not a problem," J.G. Caldwell harrumphed. "We've taken the liberty of drafting one for you."

Of course, Mario thought. You don't stage a play without having all the necessary props on hand.

"We've also prepared a statement for your signature, agreeing to the details of the severance agreement with the caveat you refrain from any public comment," Peter added.

One of the attorneys fished a folded piece of paper from his suit jacket and handed it to Mario, who opened it and read it carefully.

"I'm sure you'll find everything is in order," Peter said.

Patterson unclipped his Mont Blanc pen and handed it over. "From me to you," he said pompously, "with thanks for your service."

Mario looked curiously at the pen, then at Tyler. "I don't have any problem with the resignation," he said. "But I can't sign the severance agreement as it is."

"Beg pardon?" Patterson said, blinking.

"You gonna try to squeeze us for more?" Sidney said, instantly perturbed.

"I don't want any of your *damn* money," Mario said. "*You* keep it."

"What *do* you want?" said Peter Patterson, dropping his pretense at politeness.

Good. Mario thought. Now we're communicating. "What I *want...* is for you to keep the Zoo Crew, every one of them. Give them all three-year contracts. You do that and I'll go...*quietly.*"

"Listen, Monelli, getting rid of that crude bunch of yours is half..."

"Now, Sidney," Patterson said, raising his voice almost imperceptibly. "I think Mr. Monelli has made a very reasonable request, and I admire his loyalty. I'm inclined to grant him what he wishes."

The partners looked at each other.

"...Colonel...Sidney..."

The two men came aboard with a feeble nod.

"Good, then it's settled," said Peter.

Patterson called his beautiful secretary, and five uncomfortable minutes later, she appeared with a new document. Mario glanced at it, signed it, then signed the resignation.

"From me to you," he said, returning the pen to Peter Patterson with the same pompous demeanor in which it was offered.

"Are you sure you want to walk out empty handed?" asked Peter.

"Who said I'm walking out empty handed?" Mario scooped up the box of Cubans and walked out of Louis XIV's bedroom for what he knew was the very last time. He walked back to the M&A suite, and the Zoo Crew pounced. "Well?" Neil asked.

Mario explained what had happened down to the unanimous vote that sealed his fate. "Nothing surprising—considering my Senate testimony and what's going on with the firm. I'm out...as of right now," he said.

"They whacked you?" Kat said, aghast.

Mario smiled. "I resigned. At least that's what sweet Maria will say on MSNBC in about an hour from now."

"They gave you some excellent parting gifts, I hope," Neil said.

"A very good one, actually," Mario said. "Anyone care for a cigar?" He handed them out like it was a celebration.

Just then a scratchy sound alerted the Zoo Crew to an imminent announcement over the company public address system. Mario sensed what was about to come.

Someone at a distant microphone cleared his throat, then said, "Good morning, ladies and gentlemen. This is Michelle Conyers with an announcement for all of the employees of the Hart division. Please put your present business on hold and report immediately to the auditorium on the twenty-sixth floor. Everyone's presence is mandatory. I repeat…"

The loudspeaker system crackled off, leaving the members of the Zoo Crew gazing at each other in surprise and confusion. Mario looked at them with a reassuring smile. "You already know what Patterson is going to say. The bottom line is that most Hart people are getting pink slips today. But not you guys. Your jobs are guaranteed, at least for the next three years. I made sure of that."

Barry relaxed visibly. "Thank God. I don't know what I would have told my mother. She hates having me around the house."

"That's not fair," Glen said angrily. "Those bastards have no business cutting our people loose."

That drew a shrug from Mario. "Well, *they* think they do. Anyhow, you know we'll all hit the ground running."

"Sure, *we'll* be standing," said Neil, "but what about everyone else, all our friends?"

Mario sighed. "You can't save the world, Neil."

The Zoo Crew watched as hundreds of befuddled Hart employees emptied the cube farms and perimeter offices surrounding the trading floor, heading toward the stairwells like it was an impromptu fire drill.

"Is everyone going to just sit there and take it like sheep?" Kat said.

"I'm going up there," Barry said. "Glen, Kat…?"

"Right behind you," Kat piped up.

"I beg you guys not to go up there," Mario implored. He wanted to protect his friends from what was about to unfold.

"You coming, Denny?" Neil asked, ignoring him.

"No, you go. I'll be at Harry's, getting loaded," Dennis said, disgusted.

"Mario?" Kat asked.

"Not me. I'm not an employee anymore. Besides, I got to pack my stuff. I'll catch up with you guys later this afternoon."

Mario found some cartons in a closet, entered his private office, and began cleaning out his desk.

He picked up the etched nameplate. "Mario Monelli," it said on the top line, "Managing Director Mergers and Acquisitions." Mario tossed it at the wastebasket, but missed. He was reaching for it when Tyler appeared at his doorway, smoking his pipe. He was accompanied by an armed security guard.

"Ah, Tyler. And you've brought a friend. How nice. Is he here to protect you or me?"

"It's standard procedure, Mario," Tyler said placidly.

"I understand. You don't want me walking out with the stapler."

"We have to protect our client files. We wouldn't be responsible if we didn't."

"Oh, now you're telling me you're responsible?" Mario was poking pins at Tyler's balloon.

"I need your corporate card," Tyler said. "And your card key."

Mario surrendered both items to the guard. "Sorry, Mario."

"It's ok, Stevie, it wasn't a good picture anyway."

"I also came by to return *this,*" Tyler said, tossing Mario his key to the Lions' Den. "By the way, leaving with the old man's cigars…a sweet touch."

Tyler surveyed the contents of the boxes. "Hard to believe how much garbage you accumulate through the years," he said.

"I'm leaving most of the crap here," Mario sighed, dropping a wooden plaque into a box. He looked past Tyler, through the plate glass window that had an unobstructed view of the practically deserted trading floor and gazed at the gaggle of well-dressed Asian men surveying the field. Tyler followed Mario's gaze.

"It was nothing personal, Mario."

"Except to the people in my division," Mario said, not kindly.

Tyler changed the subject. "So what are your future plans?"

"I resigned less than an hour ago, Tyler. I'm still *working* on my plans."

"Rumors have it the attorney general found themselves a gravedigger," Tyler said, hinting at something. "Someone with a big shovel."

"Must be someone who knows just where to dig."

"Do you think *you* know, Mario? Wall Street is an awfully big boneyard."

"Well, I've attended plenty of burials," Mario said with a gleam in his eyes. "But don't you worry, Tyler. When they exhume the bodies they won't find the ones *you* buried. When our two firms married, I vowed you my loyalty."

He clicked shut the locks on his briefcase, then gave Tyler a menacing grin. "But then again, I gave it to my wife."

Tyler noticed the photo of Boomer on Mario's desk and reached for it. "The boy has a promising future I hear. It would be a shame to have that evaporate." His eyes were cold and threatening.

"You know, Tyler," Mario said, taking the photo and measuring his words carefully, "I misjudged you. I always thought somewhere deep inside, there was a decent and loyal guy. But you just cleared up all of that. And you answered a couple of questions for me." Mario was now standing almost toe to toe with him.

"Like?"

"I never knew until today it was you who tipped off the SEC about the Lions' Den. You wanted to keep me so preoccupied with saving my ass that I wouldn't see this little shotgun wedding you've been planning."

He glanced over Tyler's shoulder at the Chinese suits now taking possession of the Hart employees' offices along the trading floor perimeter. "Well, here comes the bride."

"I always looked out for you, Mario."

"Is that what you said when you had my brother busted up?"

"I had nothing to do with that. Patterson wanted to wash his hands of you long ago, and I stopped him..."

"Screw Patterson? That *strunzo* barely knows my name. It was you, Tyler. I don't know how I could have been so fucking blind. That's what Intercoastal was all about. You and Bart had been planning this little reception of yours even before then."

"I was just trying to strengthen the company, Mario. I wasn't trying to hurt anyone."

"Tell that to my people up on twenty-six whose lives are being butchered. No Tyler...we lost Intercoastal because you *wanted* us to lose it. It was set up to fail from the start. You knew I'd never agree to a marriage—not with the Chinese or any other foreign entity. And that's where you wanted to take the business. But first you had to be rid of the one person who was in your way, and that required approval from the partners. Only you couldn't get it.

"So you altered the proxies," Mario continued. "You're the only one who could have done it. You're the only one who knew my plan. You altered the Intercoastal proxies and handed them over to Bart."

"You can't prove that," Tyler insisted. "And even if I had, what would I have gained? What would be my motive?"

"To weaken my position," said Mario, "even if it weakened Harrison Hart. And you knew losing Intercoastal would be my Achilles' heel and it would discredit me, not just with the partners, but throughout the Street."

Tyler just looked at him, saying nothing.

"Well, don't keep me in suspense, Tyler. Who's giving away the bride?"

"Actually, the deal was arranged offshore through intermediaries who choose to remain anonymous—even to us."

"You don't say. And how much are these *silent partners* paying for you, Tyler? Ten billion...a hundred?"

Once more, Tyler had nothing to say. But Mario *did*. "I always knew one day you'd knife me—after Keyes it was to be expected. But I never imagined you'd betray your own outfit to do it."

"If you go public with that, my lawyers will strip you down to your underwear," Tyler warned. "Maybe you'll be able to find work again in some executive cafeteria."

"Spoken like a man born to power, status, and money, Tyler."

He picked up his briefcase, reached for the carton with his belongings, and brushed past Tyler. "Forgive me if I don't hang around for the exit interview."

Tyler followed Mario out into the aisle.

"Go ahead, Mario. Go to Washington. Bite the head off the monster. She'll only grow another one."

"Maybe," Mario turned and said. "Maybe not. You Ivy League assholes, you sit in boardrooms and sell out everything that matters…jobs, pensions, families…*people*, Tyler. In the end we *all* lose. Because when you lose ownership, you lose control. You should know that, Tyler. It's our business. It's happening to *you*."

"I'll be here when the sun goes down," Tyler said confidently.

"That's what Julius Caesar said."

Mario turned, then snapped his fingers as if remembering something. "Oh, before I forget, Tyler, that tape you sent the SEC, that was a violation of the Lions' Den discretion code…" Mario said slyly. "As president, I am hereby revoking your charter. You forfeit all of your privileges, and all penalties apply…*you cocksucker.*"

As Mario approached the corridor, a noise filtered into his ears from somewhere else on the floor—the sound of shouting. He edged toward the trading floor—more shouting, this time louder. Around a corner, he found a woman loudly arguing with her boss.

"John, who is that Asian woman sitting at my desk?"

"It's hers now, Claudia, we're moving you to a cubicle."

Mario continued down the hall, moving through the elevator banks and saw an angry mob coming down from the twenty-sixth floor, teaming out of the stairwell and elevators, spilling into the hallways and cursing-loudly.

Mario spotted Barry in the hallway amidst the anarchy. "Barry, how many?"

"In total…over fifteen hundred, including Midtown and Jersey City."

"All of them! Jesus Christ, they'll tear the place apart."

"What did you *think* would happen after the announcement?"

Mario never pictured anything like this. He hadn't known the Chinese would be arriving *today*, and right after the merger announcement was made. One of the spokespeople had fucked up the time of the official news release. News of the merger had sailed across the ticker just as Hart employees were being dismissed, compounded by the stunning news of Mario's resignation on MSNBC. There was no partnership, no representation for Hart.

Two young men—fairly recent hires, Mario recalled—came racing down the hallway, in hot pursuit of their Asian counterparts. Two desks away, a wiry Asian banker was keeping a trio of Hart people at bay by holding up his briefcase to ward off the blows of his attackers.

Nearby, a panicked Hart secretary was stuffing papers into her desktop shredder as though they were secret codes and had to be kept from the enemy.

Mario knew this was more than a mass termination. He recalled the horror during E.F. Hutton's merger with Shearson-Lehman American Express back in '87—the brutal way it was handed out to Hutton's rank and file—and how in the end it resulted in the demise of the firm itself. But this was far worse than anything he'd ever seen. It was a bloodletting, an execution done with extreme prejudice, done without warning, without even the polite precursor of a rumor. An ambush. And now it was happening to Hart, to the very people who were loyal to him.

He couldn't help feeling responsible somehow. He'd thought about how the Hart people would react to his resignation, and how the merger announcement would affect them—although he never dreamed the firings would be on such a scale. He'd expected shock, anger, bitterness, grumbling even, then an orderly departure. But he hadn't foreseen this…this brawl, this bedlam.

Ken Bushwald, Harts CFO, sliced through the pandemonium and jumped on top of a desk. He was waving a piece of paper and holding a fire warden's bullhorn. "Listen to how Tyler and his band of rogues feathered their nests while selling us out," his voice bellowed. He began to read aloud. "Peter Patterson, $110 million; Tyler Gentry, $90 million; J.G. Caldwell, Brentwood Bargus and Sidney Cohn, $50 million each…" Holy shit, the golden parachutes Mario thought. Someone must have leaked the numbers. The genie was out of the bottle. There wasn't any stopping it now.

Some senior directors from the Harrison side had barricaded themselves in perimeter offices, locking their doors and pushing the desks against them. But some Hart employees managed to wrench the fire extinguisher off the wall and were slamming it against the locked door of one of the senior manager's offices. The civil war Tyler and Mario so desperately wanted to avert was turning into South Central.

Something about the all-out brawl Mario was witnessing seemed familiar to him. He had seen this before, a long time ago, but for a moment, he couldn't remember just when. Then it came back to him all at once. It was a varsity football game, when he was a junior at New Utrecht High. He was playing its big rival Lafayette and his guys lost. Afterward, everyone got drunk on both sides and the two teams met under the stadium bleachers at New Utrecht field with bricks and baseball bats.

The fight lasted for better than two hours and it took more than half the 61th precinct to squelch it, and five kids had to spend a night at Victory Memorial hospital.

He got a split lip that took two weeks to heal, but he gave better than he got and was among scores of students arrested and suspended that day.

The Daily News gave it two columns on page three, under the headline "Mayhem Beneath the Bleachers."

And here it was again, only this time it was adults, educated ones from nationally ranked schools, polished and articulate professionals. And it was Caucasians against Asians, with the usual ugliness of a race war, and no one was drunk. But the anger was the same, as was the very real intent to injure. There wasn't any visible blood yet, but bloody noses and broken bones were inevitable.

It was time, Mario decided, for an exit. He'd had his fifteen minutes, and it was more than enough for him.

Mario hurried back to his private office. He quickly sealed the file boxes that contained his personal belongings, scribbled a D.C. mailing address on them, and stacked them with the rest of the mail. Then he took the back route to the freight elevator.

When the freight elevator door opened, police in riot gear poured out, batons at the ready. Mario squeezed past them and rode the elevator downstairs.

Mario had intended to take the lobby elevator to the garage level, and get his car, but the police had sealed off that exit. With the garage elevator blocked, Mario was forced to take the outdoor route to the basement level. He walked around the Winter Garden, through the Merrill Lynch building's west wing and came out on Chambers Street. Looking backward to the WFC's front entrance, he saw half a dozen police cars, a paddy wagon, and an ambulance haphazardly parked at the front of the building and a TV news van pulling in behind them. The old regime was certainly going out with a bang, he observed.

No sooner had he started down the street, toward the garage entrance, when he heard a voice calling out to him. It was Dennis, trotting across the pavement to join him.

"It's like fucking Tiananmen Square in there," Dennis said, panting.

"I thought you were going to Harry's," Mario said.

"I just *left* Harry's. Where ya headed?"

"Anywhere but here," Mario said, as police led a string of handcuffed Hart employees out of the building and into the paddy wagon.

"PD ain't the only ones busy today," said Dennis. "The feds are busting everyone all over the place. Two guys just got pinched over at Harry's. You happen to know anything about that?"

Mario didn't say anything.

"Thought so. You'll need help."

"Thanks Denny, but you got a lot of good years left."

"You're damn right I do," said Dennis. "But I don't want to talk about my sex life."

Mario laughed.

"*You'll* never change…thank *God.*"

"I quit, Mario. Wasn't going to be the same without you."

"I hope you didn't do it for *me*."

"I did it for myself," said Dennis.

They stood on Chambers Street, talking and watching the action.

"So what's your next move?" Mario asked.

"Who knows." Dennis gazed at the WFC building and shook his head at the growing group of police cars.

"They invited me to announce the roll call at the 9/11 memorial next month. You know it's been almost ten years, Mario, and me and Marie still can't walk inside the pit. But I'm hoping she'll go *this* year. We miss our boy, Mario," he said with the hint of a smile. "I think it's time we miss him *together*.

Dennis spotted an asian man pulling a rickshaw.

"Here's my turn. Well, paisan, it's been a good run."

"All the best, Denny." They shook hands for what they both knew would be the last time.

Dennis hopped in the back, opened up an issue of Playboy and offered Mario a mock farewell salute as the driver trotted away.

Mario headed down the outside ramp and into the quiet of the World Financial Center's maw, and walked toward his car. He turned a corner, and standing in front of his Maserati was a face he hadn't seen in more than a year, Vinny Maldonado, older, sharply dressed and carrying an expensive leather briefcase.

"Vinny?" Mario said, totally astonished. "Is that *you?*"

"It's good to see you again, Mario," Vinny said, attempting a smile.

Same here kid, look at you." He threw his arms around Vinny and hugged him for a moment. "You look like a million," Mario said, holding Vinny at arm's length, "but what are you doing *here*?"

"I'm back now, Mario," Vinny said. He looked and sounded a bit embarrassed.

Mario looked at him with a puzzled expression. "You, you work here…"

"That's right, Mario, I…"

"Wait a minute," Mario said, taking a step back. "Oh, *now* I get it. This isn't a social call. You're part of the merger. The other party…its Minsheng. You muthafucker, you knew all along." The suspicion had turned into anger.

Mario slammed Vinny against his car and raised a fist.

"If you just give me a minute, Mario," Vinny pleaded.

"Like the minute you gave me to let me know what was going on?"

Vinny faced him, hands at his sides, ready to take whatever Mario was going to hand out. But Mario couldn't deliver the blow. He backed away, glowering at his one-time protégé, eyes blazing with contempt.

"I wanted to tell you. I begged Rick, but he said if I did, I'd be out of a job. I have a family now to think about."

Then it occurred to Mario. Vinny was just a pawn—a delivery boy sent by grocery clerks to collect on a bill. He hadn't meant any harm. This act of treachery had only one creator—Rick Bernard. Tyler's deceit was politically driven, but Rick's…Rick was a whole other story, Mario realized.

The cloak-and-dagger negotiations with nameless intermediaries had little or nothing to do with merger synergies or escaping a political backlash. It was about Rick exacting revenge over Danny. And for Tyler and the partners…vengeance for their dismantling of Austin Keyes. A vendetta Rick delivered with a single blow. It was vicious and unforgiving, but it was also brilliant, and meant to be very personal.

"So you're part of the transition team," Mario said, still smoldering.

"Actually, I'm *heading* the transition," Vinny said. "Rick and I were lead advisors on the deal. No one was meant to know. I'm the new head of Harrison Hart mergers and acquisitions, soon to be Harrison Minsheng."

Mario was simmering down now. He just shook his head, amazed. "You popped your cherry kid," he said. "You cut your first throat."

"My only regret is that it had to be yours."

"You're gonna fit into this town just fine," Mario said, still coming to terms with what he'd just learned. "So, you back for good?"

Vinny straightened his tie and put himself back together again. "A year or two, maybe, then back to China. Of course, I'm not alone. Inez came with me."

"Yeah? How is she?"

"She just a had the baby, Mario. I mean *we* did. A boy."

"Really? Well, I guess congratulations are in order." He tucked one of Patterson's Cubans in Vinny's suit jacket pocket, but he still wasn't smiling.

"Anyhow, Inez and I talked about it and, well, we'd both like if you would stand up as godfather. That's what I came to ask you."

"Give me one reason why I should," Mario said.

"I can give you a *million* reasons why, Mario."

For a moment, Mario didn't get it. Then, it slowly came to him. And then he understood.

"Well, I better get going," Vinny said. "I'm on my way upstairs to tell Tyler I'm in charge. Rick wanted to save the best for last."

Vinny walked to the elevator bank and pushed the button and waited for the doors to open.

"So when is it?" Mario called out to him.

Vinny looked up.

"The christening," Mario said. "When is it?"

"Oh… it's next month. I'll send you an invite."

"I can't promise anything," Mario said, but his voice was softer now.

The elevator doors opened, and Vinny stepped inside. He turned and looked at Mario standing by his car, and smiled.

"*You'll* be there, Mario."

Then he reached for the button and the doors closed.

Mario waited till the elevator left, then parked his briefcase on the car hood, snapped it open and took out his wallet. And deep in a compartment he rarely used, he found what he was looking for.

For a moment, he imagined the expression on Bart's face when he learned he'd lost the bet and would have to fork over a million dollars or be so deeply humiliated he'd never be able to make his presence known on Wall Street again.

Then something else occurred to him. If he didn't collect on this bet promptly, he might never get it. He had a feeling that Bart wasn't going to be liquid very much longer.

Mario collected his car, and revved up to the mechanical gate. His buddy Widell came out from the attendant booth, his longshoreman's cap in his hand. He had a sad look in his eyes.

"I hear 'bout what happen. I'm real sorry, boss."

"You take care, Widell."

"Ya know, you was the only one say hello every mornin'…ask about my kids. Even throw me a little sumthin' come holiday time. I'll sure miss that respect." He smiled and patted the Maserati. "An' I'll sure miss greetin' this little lady ever' mornin'," he said. "Well, I'll go open the gate."

Widell walked back inside the booth and the gate lifted. But the car didn't move. Mario shut the engine off and thought for a moment. He leaned over and opened the glove box and took out a pink slip. "It's Widell with two L's, right?" he asked.

Widell looked at him. "Two L's, yes."

Mario filled out the paper, shoved it back in the glove box, and closed it. He popped open the trunk from the inside and got out of the car.

"Who's got the best car in the place, Widell?"

"Why, you do, boss?" Widell answered. "*You* know that." It was a playful ritual they shared each morning.

Mario found a pair of gloves and an old umbrella in the trunk and decided to leave them where they were. He slammed the lid shut. "No, Widell," he said, tossing the car keys to him. "*You* do."

Widell looked at the keys open-mouthed.

Mario rested his hand on Widell's shoulder. "The title is in glove box… along with a few stogies."

Mario walked up the garage ramp and outside into the blinding sunlight. He looked back toward the front entrance. Now the cops were stuffing handcuffed, black-suited Chinese into a second paddy wagon. The confused expression on their faces was priceless.

In the midst of the chaos, he saw Kat on West Street struggling to open the door of a taxi, and juggling a box in her hand. He hurried over and opened the door for her. "Here, let me get that," he said, and helped her in.

"Fucking driver sits on his ass..." she grumbled, loud enough for the driver to hear. She climbed into the back seat, and Mario closed the door after her.

Kat rolled down the window. "Well, I'll be seeing you, Mario. It was a blast."

"I take it you've also resigned," Mario said, noticing the box beside her.

"That's right."

"Well, if ever you need a reference..."

"Thanks, but I think I had enough of Wall Street."

"Don't let *this* kill you?"

"Kill *me*? Don't be silly," she said with her wonderfully sarcastic laugh. "This 'Kat' has plenty of lives left."

"So what are you gonna do with the next one?"

"Don't really know," she said. "Maybe go back to teaching. Instead of trading futures, I'll do more *shaping* them. After all, everyone remembers their third-grade teacher."

"Lady, I know *I* certainly would have, if you'd been mine."

Kat smiled. She reached out the window and tenderly touched Mario's cheek. Then, to his absolute amazement, she kissed him. Then, before he had a chance to say anything, the window went up, and the taxi pulled away from the curb and drove up the West Side Highway.

Barton Mulvaney was only a few blocks away from the WFC building. Mario hoofed it, and a few minutes later, he entered the belly of the beast—the corporate headquarters of the Blackwell Group.

In the past, he might have been uncomfortable here—a Pentagon general paying a visit to his opposite number in the Kremlin. But that feeling had disappeared, as a result of his separation from Harrison Hart, and the wonderfully unpleasant news he had for Bart.

Mario took the elevator to the seventeenth floor and walked past the receptionist unannounced and onto Blackwell's small trading floor. The Blackwell traders were doing business as usual, their eyes boring into their computers, fingers dancing over the keys, both ears festooned with telephone receivers. Mario tapped one on the shoulder and asked for the whereabouts of the Investment Banking Division.

The trader pointed to a group of Blackwell people—Mulvaney included—crowded around a big, flat-screen television, laughing uproariously. CNN was displaying a live feed from the Harrison Hart executive bathroom, where half-a-dozen uniformed cops were about to attack the heavy oak door with a battering ram. In the background, Mario could hear the shouts and screams of a continuing riot.

The cops swung the battering ram into the door with an enormous crash, and the crash was followed by a tortured scream from inside the bathroom. "If you hit that door one more time, I'll *kill* myself!" Mario recognized the annoying and pompous voice of Dick Hamilton.

One more swing of the battering ram, and the oak door splintered its final splinter and flew open. Hamilton was sitting on a toilet, the stall visible from the door. His pants were down and Tyler's shotgun was in his mouth. "Give me that thing," said an annoyed cop, who snatched the weapon from the sniveling investment banker. Hamilton began sobbing as police wrestled him to the floor.

At Blackwell, the entire trading floor stopped what it was doing and burst into guffaws and shouts of derision.

Mulvaney finally looked up and saw Mario approaching. "Well, well, if it isn't the dethroned King," he announced for all to hear. "And look, fellas, he's packed up and leaving the jungle."

"Very amusing," Mario said mildly.

"Sorry about what happened to you at Harrison Hart. We're all watching it." Mulvaney surveyed the smiling audience around him. "But I hear they gave you a generous package."

"Turned it down, Bart," Mario said. "I'm going to get my package from *you*."

Bart laughed. "I only give to recognized charities," he said.

"Oh, I'm not asking for a charitable donation," Mario said. "I'm just asking you to pay a debt of honor...or have you forgotten."

"Talk sense, Mario."

"Let me refresh your memory, Bart. Two kids with potential, working their way to the top, first one there wins a million for one of us. Remember?"

"Sure I do," Bart laughed. "But who said *you* won?"

"Minsheng Bank...that was Vinny's deal," Mario said with a wicked grin.

Bart laughed. "You expect me to believe that bullshit?"

"Call Tyler Gentry and ask him." Mario was enjoying this even more than he had imagined.

Bart laughed uncertainly. He turned to his Phi Beta Kappa groupies. "Someone get Gentry on the phone. Find out what this loser is talking about."

Vaughn picked up the phone and punched some numbers.

"The one time I ever lost to you, Bart, the deal was rigged," Mario said. "But you couldn't rig *this* one."

"Losers never win, Mario," Bart said. "They just learn to lose more graciously."

"What do you mean he's not available?" Vaughn could be heard saying on the phone. "He's been what?"

"Well," Bart said. "Do you have him?"

Vaughn looked nervously at Mario. "Tyler Gentry's not in charge anymore."

"What do you mean, *not* in charge?"

"He…He's been arrested."

Bart swung his legs off the desk and leaped to his feet.

"Gimme that thing," Bart said, grabbing for the phone. "Who is this? Well, Miss Rose Pheeney, this is Barton Mulvaney, and I need to talk to Tyler Gentry. Now." Bart listened for a moment. "Then, goddammit, who *is* in charge?"

Bart listened for a moment, then looked up at Mario.

Mario took out his wallet and gingerly pulled out a wrinkled, tattered napkin that was now worth a cool million dollars.

"My contract, Bart," he said loudly for all to hear. "I believe this is your name. And next to it is a one with five…no Bart, I believe *six* zeroes."

Bart hung up the phone and just stared at Mario. Everyone on the floor was watching Mulvaney to see what he was going to do. Meanwhile, news of Tyler's arrest scrolled across the bottom of CNN's news coverage.

"Oh, yes," Bart said, realizing how his own people were looking at him, "*that* bet. What was the amount again?"

Mario spread out the napkin, and Bart peered at it for a moment. "I see," he said with a weak grin, trying to imply that he'd just been kidding. "One million dollars. Okay. Come with me."

Bart nervously headed down the hallway, Mario right behind him. An entourage of onlookers managed to ditch what they were doing and hurriedly followed along, knowing what they were about to witness would become Wall Street lore.

Bart entered his office, took a seat and opened his desk drawer. He pulled his checkbook out and Mario handed him a pen. Then, hands shaking, he scribbled a check while everyone struggled for a glimpse. He stuffed it into Mario's front shirt pocket, playing for the crowd like it didn't bother him. Mario retrieved it and examined it. "Thank you, Mr. Mulvaney. It was a pleasure betting with you," he said.

Mario licked the napkin and slapped it on Bart's forehead.

"Here's your receipt."

He pushed his way past the mob outside the office, Bart following after him. "Go fuck yourself, Mario. You know I'll make that back in a month, because—unlike *you*—I *have* a career."

"A month?" Mario said as though he were calculating. "I think it will take a lot longer than that, folding underwear at ten cents an hour."

Bart was about to respond when three men in trench coats split the crowd and marched toward him. "Barton Mulvaney?" asked the first, a squat, red-haired man.

"Yes," Bart said. "And you are…?"

"George McNutt, U.S. Attorney General's Office," the redhead said, flashing his badge. "And this is Philip Da Silva, Inspector General of the Securities and Exchange Commission, and James Brody, U.S. Postal Inspector. You're under arrest for conspiracy to commit stock fraud and for violating the insider trading sanction act in relation to the sale of Intercoastal, Inc. Put your arms behind your back."

They swung Bart around making no pretense at gentleness and cuffed him. The Blackwell traders stared in horror as the wrist locks clicked home.

"Take care, Bart," Mario said, sounding friendly. "Don't bend over for any soap. Oh, and if you need a character reference, have them call on me. I can testify that you don't welsh on your bets."

CHAPTER THIRTY-SIX

Mario had the taxi drop him off at the downtown Manhattan Heliport along Pier 6, where a waiting chopper ferried him up to Wards Island for the last time. He started toward the building, heading along the log-bordered flagstone path. And sure enough, he heard the jungle drums. Well, he thought, at least the electricity is still on.

A few steps more, then the Den hove into view. He smiled, once again and for the last time, admiring Roger's work. It had been wonderful for all of them, an escape from the rules and conventions, a place to be who they wanted to be, who they were *meant* to be, and do what they wanted to do. And now the dream was over.

The rough-hewn log doorway was unguarded—no Massai warriors in loincloths, carrying spears—and the door was ajar. Mario stepped inside tentatively.

"Honey, I'm home," he called playfully. No answer, but the lights and the music were on, and images danced over the giant plasma screens. "Hey," he said, this time a little louder, "anyone here?"

Neil's voice came back. "We're at the bar, Mario. Come on back."

Mario walked through the grand hallway, and stopped for a moment at the great stairway, with its gorgeous elephant tusk railings, and he patted the head of one of the giant stone lions that flanked the bottom steps.

For a moment, he let the sounds and scents carry him away—the exotic birds, the buzzing insects, the perfume of the jungle foliage, the dank smell of the rivers. He and Roger had sure done it right, all of it, every detail. There'd never be anything like it again.

"You coming, boss?" It was Glen's voice.

"Yeah," Mario sighed.

He walked into the cocktail lounge and aboard the replica of the *African Queen*. Glen, who was wearing an incongruous Hawaiian shirt, was playing bartender. The rest of the Zoo Crew—everyone but Dennis and, of course, Kat, was sitting bunched together at the long hunk of highly lacquered mahogany that served as the Lions' Den's main bar.

"Where ya been?" Barry asked. "You missed the closing. The lawyers just left."

"What'll you have, Mario?" Glen asked.

"Pour me some Glengoyne 1967 single malt, if we have any left," Mario said, taking a seat at the bar.

Glen bent down, under the bar, and emerged with a black-labeled bottle of golden liquid. He filled a crystal shot glass and slid it over to Mario. "Only the best," he said. Then he poured shots for everyone else.

"To the Lions' Den," Mario said, raising his glass. "I'm sure gonna miss this place."

"To the Lions' Den," said the others, in chorus.

They clinked glasses, then drank up, slamming the empties down on the bar with a resounding clunk.

"Again?" Glen asked. He refilled their glasses without waiting for an answer.

"To the Zoo Crew," Neil said, lifting his glass again.

"The best of the best," Glen said.

They clinked and drank again.

"To quitting Harrison Hart," Barry said.

Another round of glass-clinking.

Glen offered refills, but no one was interested. "Mario! Mario, you don't know yet, do you?"

"About what?"

"About Tyler. He's been…"

"Arrested," Mario said, finishing Glen's sentence. "Yes I know. I heard it on CNN."

"I was there when they slapped the cuffs on," Glen went on excitedly. "I thought Tyler was going to shit himself."

"Well," Neil said, "here's something you *don't* know, Mario—Vinny…"

"I know all about that, too," Mario interrupted, with a wry smile. "I ran into the kid as I was leaving the building. He told me everything."

"Then you know it was Rick's outfit," Neil said.

"And after all you did for that fucking kid," said Glen. "Bringing him up like that. What a fucking waste."

"Oh I wouldn't say it was *all* a waste," Mario said. He pulled Bart's million dollar check out of his pocket and put it on the bar.

"Boys, the drinks are on *me*."

Neil was the first to take a look. "Is this for real?" he asked, before handing it to Barry to see.

Barry looked at it without comprehending. "How in the world…"

By now, Neil had figured it out. "The bet," he said, grinning. "You son of a bitch. You won the damned bet!"

"Let me see that!" Glen said, grabbing the piece of paper and staring at it, astonished.

"Vinny won it," Mario said, taking it back. "I just collected it."

"I wish I'd been there to see the expression that fuckstick's face," Barry said.

"It was priceless," Mario told him, "but it was nothing compared to the way he looked when he was arrested."

Glen was confused. "Bart got pinched, too?"

"Who do you think helped Tyler alter the Intercoastal proxies," Mario said.

"Twenty years from now," Glen predicted, "they'll still be talking about all this."

"They'll be talking about *you,* Mario," Barry said.

"They'll be talking about *all* of us," Mario observed.

"Yeah," Glen agreed, "and I know what they'll be saying. They'll be asking how the fuck a ragtag bunch of maniacs managed to take down the biggest conspiracy against America in history."

"So, Mario," Neil said, changing the subject, "what are you going to do with the million?"

"Try to keep it out of Phyllis's hands," Mario replied.

They laughed.

"Pour me another," Neil told Glen, who dutifully did the honors. Neil took a sip, shaking his head in wonder. "Damn," he said, "it's been a strange and wild ride."

Glen started chuckling to himself.

"What's so funny?" Neil asked.

"I was just thinking back, you know, back to our very first deal."

"You're talking about Allied-Bendix," Barry remembered.

Mario thought back. "God, that was in—what—1985?"

"We didn't have the first fuckin' clue what we were doing," Neil said.

"Damn—we were just kids then, but we were fast learners," said Mario.

"*Damn* fast," Glen agreed. He turned and looked through the rows of bottles, passing most of them by, finally settling on Laphroaig, another pricey single-malt Scotch and filled everyone's glass.

"How many jobs were at stake?" Neil asked, trying to remember.

"Hmmm—eight or nine thousand, maybe ten," Glen guessed.

"More like twelve," Barry estimated.

"12,631," Mario said.

The Zoo Crew looked at him in surprise, then at one another. Then it was back to their drinks.

"Remember the blood in the water over Unical?" Glen asked, still reminiscing."And how we kept it out of the jaws of Kravis and the sharks."

"I'll never forget it—even if I get Alzheimer's," Mario said. "More than 26,000 people kept their jobs because of that poison pill we dropped."

"And over 15,000 families kept their houses *and* their pensions and were able to keep providing for their kids," Neil added, proudly.

They clinked glasses and drank again.

"But my favorite," Neil said, "my all time favorite was Kraymerica."

Barry excused himself and headed for the bathroom.

"That was also in '89, wasn't it?" Mario asked.

Glen shook his head. "No, couldn't have been. Reagan was still president. Hadda be in '87. Remember, Bush practically had a fuckin' heart attack when Jerry Rogers tried to leverage that plant in his home state."

"You're right," Mario said, "1987."

"I remember now," Neil said. "Keyes said we weren't ready for it."

"And that was the last time he said that," Glen said, grinning.

They drank a toast to their old boss, Austin Keyes.

Mario sighed. "We did good work out there, gentlemen," he said proudly.

"We did good work in here, too," Neil joked, pumping his fist in a gesture filled with testosterone. Everyone laughed.

Glen raised his glass and offered a toast. "They can kill the Lions' Den, but they can never kill the lion."

Just as they raised their glasses, Barry came barreling out of the bathroom.

"Quick, turn on the news…"

"We're in the middle of…"

" Do it!"

Glen reached for the remote and switched to CNN where a reporter was broadcasting outside 1 New York Plaza.

"Turn it up," Barry said.

"…had planned to put a radioactive RDD inside the New Year's Eve ball over Times Square set to go off at midnight…," the reporter said. "The NYPD estimates, such a plan, if carried out, could have resulted in thousands, maybe *hundreds* of thousands of casualities. Homeland Security puts the figure at almost a million…"

"My God," Glen said in a voice, barley audible, "that's what they must've been looking for?"

"Shh…"said Mario.

"…the FBI took four men into custody today at a mosque in Flatbush Brooklyn, including Mohammed Zamarri Quanfi, a Syrian with known ties to Al Qaeda and Osama Bin Laden…"

Neil pointed at the TV. "You mean, they thought *that*… " he looked over at the granite statues in the adjacent room, *"was that*?"

"Thank God they got it in time," said Mario.

Neil nodded then checked his watch. "Oh, jeez, speaking of the time," he said, "Elaine flies in at three. I gotta pick her up at Newark. You believe she lost twenty more pounds? We're going out to celebrate."

"Yeah, I gotta get moving too," said Glen, gulping down what was left of his drink. "Amanda has a doctor's appointment."

"What about you, Barry?" Mario said. "Have time for another drink?"

"Sorry, Mario," Barry said, slipping on his trench coat. "Gotta get home to Ma. It's our Bingo night…double jackpot."

They exchanged looks. And then, a little awkwardly, they exchanged hugs as well.

Mario watched them go, then after a long final look at the Lions' Den, he walked through the door one last time and closed it behind him. He'd almost reached the helicopter when he realized he'd forgotten something. He turned around and walked back to the Den, and opened the door.

Sam was looking up at him, meowing, apparently annoyed at being forgotten. Mario scooped him up, tucked him under his arm and walked back to the helipad.

It was late afternoon when the taxi pulled up at the Monelli home in Sands Point, and Mario was in no mood to get out to face Phyllis. It had been a life-altering day, filled with both tragedy and triumph, but it wasn't over yet. The hardest part was yet to come.

"Wait for me," Mario told the driver, a slim dark-haired Rastafarian with a lilting Jamaican accent.

"Okay, mon."

He walked toward the house and slipped his key in the lock. Well, he thought, here goes. The door swung open and, a moment later, he heard Phyllis's inimitable accent. "Who the fuck's there?" she yelled.

"It's me," he replied, loud enough for her to hear.

There was a return screech. "Me who?"

"Cut it out, Phyllis, it's me, Mario."

Phyllis appeared at the top of the stairway, wearing sweat pants and a blouse tied in a knot, baring her trim waist. "Well, whadda you know," she said sarcastically, "If it isn't Sammy the rat. My lawyer never said you were coming over."

Mario came upstairs and she followed him into the master bedroom.

"Get out or I'm calling the cops."

"I'm not going to be here long, Phyllis," Mario told her. "I've just come to pack a few things."

"Pack?" she said, furious. "Then *what*? Back to Washington to spill your guts to the feds and kill any chance of getting a partnership."

"I'm not working for Harrison Hart anymore, Phyllis. Oh I forgot, you don't watch the news. I resigned this morning."

Phyllis blanched. "What? You better be kidding, Mario. If you screw up my appointment to the Wellborn Foundation, I'm going to make your life miserable. You better have a new job before the week is over."

Mario got a suitcase out of the storage closet and began tossing clothes on the bed.

"If you leave me now," she said, "so help me, we'll go to trial. I'll clean you out."

Mario spotted the brandy decanter on the dresser and he handed it to Phyllis. "Here," he said, "suck on this."

She grabbed the bottle and threw it at him, but missed. The bottle flew into the closet, hit a grey, pinstriped Armani suit, and rolled to the floor, intact.

"Do you think you can just grab some clothes, then ride off into the sunset?"

Mario dropped a stack of shirts into the suitcase. "Let's face it, Phyllis, the sun set on us long ago."

Phyllis paced across the room and back, trying to think of something to say, something that might at least give him pause, when a horn honked from outside. She moved to the window. "What's that gypsy cab doing out front," she finally said. "Where's the car?"

"Gave it to Widell," Mario said with an up-your-ass grin.

"Widell? Who the fuck is Widell?"

"The garage attendant where I used to work. He was very appreciative."

Phyllis was apoplectic. "You gave away our $200,000 Maserati to a fucking garage attendant?"

Mario scooped up some cufflinks and dropped them into one of the suitcase's many little pockets. "Not *our* Maserati, Phyllis. *My* Maserati."

"It's under both names, like everything else," Phyllis said. She was looking around the room wildly, and she found a framed wedding picture. She grabbed it and held it up to Mario, two inches from his nose. "Till death do us part, remember?"

Mario pushed the picture out of his way and continued packing. "Death may last forever, Phyllis, but marriage doesn't come with guarantees."

He reached into the back of his sock drawer and pulled out a stack of bills. He stashed them in his jacket pocket and reached over to an electric outlet, plucked off his cell phone charger, and dropped it into his suitcase, then he sat down on the bed, flipped open his cell phone and dialed.

"Who's that?" Phyllis barked. "Who ya calling?"

"Monelli, room 246," he said into the phone, ignoring her.

"Your prick brother? You're calling your brother? He should only die in that fucking hospital."

"Yeah, Frank, it's me."

"Are you okay, Mario? It's all over the TV…," Frank said.

"Never mind that. Look, Frank, I can't make it down there. Don't ask me to explain."

"But they're discharging me today."

"Now that's a coincidence," Mario laughed. "I'm getting discharged today, too."

"I know," said Frank. "You quit your job…"

"No, Frank, I *resigned* my job. I quit my marriage. Effective immediately."

There was a pause on the other end of the line while Frank absorbed what his brother was telling him. "You're shitting me, Mario."

"Think so? I'm sitting on my bed right next to my suitcase. And my darling of a wife is standing five feet away from me. Wanna ask her?"

"Jesus, Mario, that's abandonment. You'll lose everything."

Mario hesitated a moment, then spoke. "I told you what Hef said to me that night—didn't I?"

"Remind me."

"He said, 'Don't live your life as though you'll do better next time.'"

"Oh, yeah," Frank said. "That. Seems to me that's what Gus was trying to tell you as well."

"He was, only I was too wrapped up over Danny to see it," Mario said, thinking of the old boxer. "I've finally decided they were right."

"Damn," Frank said. "Quite a step, little brother. You sure you're ready to take it?"

"If I waited to be sure, I might not know until they lowered me into the ground."

"That's not the step I mean Mario and you know it." Frank said.

Mario moved toward the window and saw Kyle happily riding his bicycle with his friends. "Yeah Frank," he said a bit softly. "I know what you meant."

"Well, little brother, if you got the courage to look into his face and do *that,* then you deserve to be happy. Call me when you get settled."

"You can bet on it." Mario hung up and took one long look at Phyllis, who was staring at him as though he'd lost his mind. Then he walked into his closet and stuffed a few of his best suits into a garment bag, zipped it closed, and slung it over his shoulder.

"I'll let you know where to send the rest of my things," he said, pushing past her.

"*Your* things?" Phyllis said, venomously pursuing him into the hallway. "You'll tell me where to send *your* things? You know where I'm going to send your things? I'm going to send them into the fucking garbage."

Mario put his hand up to his chin, reflectively. "You know, this is turning out exactly the way I imagined it."

Phyllis ignored him. "You leave now, I'll nail your ass. I'll get you for abandonment. My lawyer won't leave you a pot to piss in."

"Works for *me*, Phyllis," Mario said wearily. "That's all this marriage is worth—a piss pot."

"You're bluffing, asshole." She stopped at the top of the stairs. "You ain't got the balls to walk away empty-handed."

"Really? Watch closely." He started down the stairway, struggling a little with the bags.

"You'd never give up your home," Phyllis insisted.

"This was never my home. My house, maybe, but not my home."

"Oh, so the house in the Hamptons was your home?"

"Take it all, Phyllis. It's yours." He turned and looked up at her. "I don't need the big houses and fancy cars anymore. They never did much for me anyhow—just took my mind off how miserable I was. Only not anymore," he said, before continuing down the stairs.

Phyllis folded her arms across her chest and shifted her weight to one leg. "You're willing to give up your sons?" she said, throwing her ace with a heinous grin.

Mario was about halfway down the stairs. He stopped, but only momentarily. "They'll always be my sons," he said stoically, without turning to look at her. Then he started walking again. She dropped her arms in a moment of panic.

"You aren't kidding. You *do* mean it." She ran past him down the stairs and blocked his path at the foot of the staircase, almost tripping over the dog. "I know where you're going, you son-of-a-bitch. You're throwing it away to live in sin with that television whore." She turned the last word into a growl.

Mario considered Phyllis's remark for a moment. "I'd rather live with her in sin than be married to you in hell. Goodbye, Phyllis." He squeezed around her, opened the front door, and walked out of the house.

"Hell is just where you're going, you bastard," she yelled, slamming the door behind him.

The cab driver saw Mario exit the house, popped open the trunk, and came around to help his fare stow the luggage.

"Any more, mon?"

"This should be everything," Mario said. As the driver made room, the upstairs window flew open, and Phyllis leaned out, spewing a tirade of profanity. The cab driver glanced back at the house, eyebrow raised, and Mario followed his gaze. Pants and jackets and shirts and ties were raining out of the master bedroom window, littering the front lawn.

At that moment, a BMW stuffed with rowdy high school kids pulled up behind the cab. Boomer emerged wearing a Halstead sweatshirt cut off at the sleeves and holding a basketball. He waited till the car pulled off. "Hi, Dad," he said, walking over to his father. He looked up at the open window, at the clothes floating onto the lawn. "Mom seems pissed."

"Does she?" Mario said ruefully. "I hadn't noticed."

Boomer nodded, then spotted the suitcase. "Business trip?"

"The personal kind," Mario said, looking into his son's eyes.

"You mean the *permanent* kind," Boomer said, misplacing his smile.

Mario nodded and Boomer understood. Then Boomer made note of the livery. You're taking a cab to the airport? What happened to the car?"

"Let's just say it's one less thing for your mother to get in the settlement."

"Wait a minute, Dad, is that *Gus's* cat in the back?"

Mario turned and looked at Sam through the rear glass. He was lying atop the speaker shelf behind the seat.

"Yeah. I'm gonna take him with me."

"I think Gus would've liked that," Boomer said and smiled. "By the way, I'm real proud of what you did."

"Are you?"

"Yeah."

They were both trying to avoid saying the words they knew had to be said.

"Listen, Boomer, about your graduation…"

Boomer half smiled, "That's okay, Dad," he said, letting his father off the hook. "You'll come to my next one."

"You bet I will," Mario said.

As they stood on the sidewalk, talking, Boomer looked over his father's shoulder and spotted Kyle fast approaching on his bike. "Dad," he warned, "Kyle's coming. You'd better go before he sees you. I'll explain everything…"

"No, Boomer," Mario said. "That's *my* job." He turned toward his youngest son and forced a smile.

Kyle's eyes flew open wide when he saw Mario. He hopped off his bike, letting it fall where it was, and ran to his father, throwing his arms around his neck and wrapping his legs around his waist. "Daddy, Daddy, where have you been? I've missed you!"

"I know, Kyle," Mario said, closing his eyes and clinging to him. "I'm sorry, I really am."

Kyle pulled back to look at his father. "All the kids at school are talking about you, Daddy, especially that mean Robert Conner. He said you were a stool pigeon. What's a stool pigeon mean, Daddy?"

This is *already* impossible, Mario thought. What could he possibly say that would make everything all right?

"I'll put my bike away, Daddy, and we'll go for some Italian ice."

Kyle climbed down from his father and as he bent to pick up his bicycle, he saw the driver putting Mario's bags into the taxi's trunk. A wave of anxiety washed over his face as he slowly walked the bicycle up the driveway.

Mario looked at Boomer, then followed Kyle into the garage. The boy lowered the bike's kickstand, but conspicuously avoided turning back toward his father. Mario realized the boy sensed something.

"Hey, buddy…"

Kyle pretended to have trouble leaning his bicycle.

"Kyle...forget the bike."

Kyle finally turned. His face was a rain cloud waiting to burst. His eyes were on the cab driver, who was stashing Mario's garment bag in the trunk, on top of his luggage.

Mario laid down his shoulder bag. He knew what his son was thinking. "Oh, the bags, don't worry, Daddy's taking a little trip," he explained. "But I'll be back."

Kyle looked at him, unsure, and Mario realized he couldn't lie, not now...not ever. "No," he continued, "that's not true. The truth is, Kyle, that Daddy's *never* coming back, at least not to live here with Mommy, you, and your brother, the way it was."

Kyle's expression was a mixture of fear and confusion. "But you promised...."

Mario nodded sadly and kneeled to meet him. "I know I did, Kyle. But sometimes things happen, and daddies can't keep every promise they make, even though they want to."

Kyle looked at Mario without understanding. "But a good soldier doesn't leave his buddy behind. Remember?"

God, Mario thought, this is awful. But he could see that no matter how hard it was, he'd have to try to explain, hoping that the words would come. "Do you remember the last time you saw Mommy and me hug each other? Or tell each other 'I love you'?"

The little boy shook his head, still confused.

"No," Mario said. "You probably don't. Well, neither do we. Mommy and I haven't felt that way toward each other in a very long time. Guess you can say we just...don't *like* each other very much anymore."

"You both fight a lot," Kyle said.

"Yes, and that's why. We just don't want to be together anymore."

Kyle was still holding back the tears, but just barely. "But don't you want to be with me and Boomer?"

Mario hugged his son again, and he was having trouble holding back the tears too. "Of course I do, Kyle. I love you very much, and I love your brother, too. I wish I could stay. But it wouldn't be good for any of us if I did—especially you. I don't want you to grow up in a home without love. You can never think that is normal. So I can't stay."

Kyle's eyes began overflowing. "I'll never see you again?"

"Oh, no! No! You'll see me a lot. You'll come and stay with me sometimes when I have a new house, and we'll do everything we always did. More. We'll go to ball games. They got a team in Washington. And we'll talk to the players, and we'll have lots of fun. Like we always did. And that's a promise nothing can stop me from keeping."

"Maybe you and Mommy will stop being mad at each other," Kyle said hopefully.

"That's not going to happen, Kyle. But you and I will see each other a lot."

"Billy Parker's daddy told him the same thing," Kyle said, sniffling, "and he doesn't even call Billy anymore."

"That's because Billy Parker's father is a piece of shit," Mario barked. "It's going to be different with us. I guarantee it."

"Is it because I don't do good in school," Kyle said. "I'll do better, I promise."

The school reference was like a kill shot for Mario. "Kyle, I know you're trying your hardest. I'm not leaving because of *you*."

"When will I see you?" Kyle managed to ask. He was gasping for air, as if he were having an asthma attack.

"As soon as Uncle Frank can work it out," Mario said. "I swear, Buddy."

"Would you tell me something, Daddy?"

"Anything Buddy. What do you want to know?"

"The other lady—is she prettier than Mom?" he cried.

Mario felt a flash of fury and did his best to repress it. He hadn't even left the house and that bitch was already poisoning Kyle against him. "Kyle, I'm not leaving your mother for someone else," he said, even though he knew this wasn't the whole truth.

He held out his arms and Kyle slipped into his embrace, wrapping his arms tightly around his father's neck, sobbing into his ear. "The Dow closed at 12,000," he cried, hoping that would change his father's mind.

Mario closed his eyes, overcome for the love he felt for his little boy. He had to leave, he knew, and he had to do it now, while he still could.

Kyle's grip tightened.

"Please, Kyle, Daddy needs to go."

He reached behind his neck and tugged Kyle's hands till they broke apart. Then he stood.

Kyle glared up at his father, scowling, then reared back and walloped Mario in the thigh, hitting him for what Mario knew to be the promises he broke, and for the ones Kyle believed would be broken eventually. Mario looked at his son with dismay, trying to deal not with the blows, but with the unexpected anger and desolation. Kyle swung again and again, wildly, eyes full of pain and resentment.

Finally, Kyle turned away and marched angrily into the house, leaving his father standing in the garage, helpless and bereft. Mario stood there a moment, a crippling look on his face, then picked up his shoulder bag and walked slowly up the driveway, toward the cab—and Boomer.

Until then, Boomer had managed to cage his emotions. But now, his face began to twist into the beginnings of a cry.

"Don't you do this," Mario implored, caressing his son's face and pressing his forehead against Boomer's, their noses touching. "I won't make it, I just won't."

Even though he tried, Boomer couldn't keep his feelings within him. He tried, in spite of his best efforts. Mario gently brought his son's head onto his shoulder and held him, and he felt his boy break.

"You're going to be fine, Boomer," he said in his ear. "You'll be away at school most of the time, and you can come up to D.C. and visit me whenever you want."

Mario thought desperately as they held onto each other, ignoring the torrent of clothing falling on the lawn. He couldn't bear to go through life with two estranged sons.

He couldn't give Julie half a man.

He turned to the driver.

"Take the bags out of the car."

The driver looked at him.

"I said take 'em out," he said harshly.

"No. Leave them," Boomer said, wiping his eyes with his palm. Then he looked at his father. "You better get going. You got a plane to catch," he sniffled, braving it. "I'll call you from Harvard."

For a moment, Mario stood paralyzed, unsure what to do.

"Please go…just go, Dad," Boomer begged, gently pushing his father away. "Don't worry about Kyle. He'll be fine."

The driver loaded the last bag into the trunk and closed it. Mario picked up his shoulder bag and walked over to the car. And as he reached for the door handle, he looked back at his son.

"Boomer," he said, "if it means anything, I never loved your mother more… than the day you were born. That reminds me…"

He unzipped his shoulder bag, reached inside, and pulled out the leather jacket.

"Happy birthday, kid." He winked, tossing it to his son. "The *King* never forgets."

He blew his son a kiss, then opened the door of the cab and got in.

"LaGuardia."

Epilogue

E xcept for a few puffs of cotton fleece floating by, the sky had never been
bluer, and the grass never greener. A broad swath of it was spread out
in front of them, dotted by many long rows of small stone crosses and the
occasional Star of David.

The two of them had taken up positions just behind the row of dignitaries—
the President and Vice President, the Chief Justice, the Secretary of State,
the Secretary of Defense, both the majority and the minority leaders of the
House and Senate, and a few dozen other VIPs, and their spouses, everyone
dressed somberly.

From where they were standing, they could see an American flag taut
over an elaborate mahogany coffin, resting on the straps of the casket-
lowering device above the freshly-dug grave itself. Mrs. Jaffe, frail, but
erect, was standing next to her young son, who had recently announced
his candidacy for Congress. They were talking quietly with Rabbi Pincus,
a calm, composed white-haired gentleman who, despite the nature of the
event, could not suppress an occasional mischievous smile.

Behind them were all the rest, two or three hundred of them—senators
and former senators, agency heads, union leaders, ministers both black
and white, Harry Belafonte and Shirley Maclaine, and a few other older
Hollywood legends, plus a large contingent of Jaffe family and friends.
A sprinkling of Secret Service agents and military personnel dressed in
ceremonial uniforms completed the picture.

It was a solemn time, and the crowd was quiet and subdued, but the
atmosphere was not one of paralyzing grief. Those attending had come to
say goodbye to a man who had left the world a far better place than when he
had entered it.

Milton Jaffe had been a friend to most of the people assembled here
at Arlington National Cemetery for the final farewell. But he had been a
respected and feared enemy of some of the others, an opponent of unwavering
strength and commitment. Nothing attested to this more than his final
legislative triumph, the unexpectedly successful uphill struggle to pass the
Foreign Investment Limitation Act.

The Rabbi moved away from Mrs. Jaffe and stepped up to the head of
the coffin, and all conversation among those attending quickly ceased. The
eulogies—more than two hours of them—had been delivered at the funeral

itself, at the historic reformed synagogue at Sixth and I. But the Rabbi had a few last words.

He cleared his throat, and all the men in the audience donned the white silk yarmulkes they'd received when entering the synagogue. Then he intoned the brief Hebrew prayers familiar even to many of the gentiles in the gathering. After he finished, he said, "Goodbye, my friend."

A few yards behind the coffin, a lone trumpeter played taps, then a six-man military honor guard smartly raised its rifles skyward and fired in unison nineteen times.

Finally, as the echoes of the last shots faded away, a soldier tripped the casket-lowering device, and Milton Jaffe's coffin sank slowly into the opening prepared for it, disappearing from view. A young marine presented Mrs. Jaffe with the flag that had been draped over the senator's coffin and rendered the final salute.

Mrs. Jaffe bent at the fresh mound of dirt next to the grave, scooped up a handful, and tossed it on top of the coffin. Then her knees buckled. The Rabbi caught her before she fell, and others came out of the crowd to help, Julie Chambers among them. She comforted Mrs. Jaffe, who quickly regained her composure. Meanwhile, a procession of dignitaries filed past the grave, each of them tossing in a handful of earth.

Mario was observing all this when a tall young man appeared in front of him, almost out of nowhere—a man with dark glasses, a non-descript little pin on his lapel, wearing a tiny earphone in one ear, and the kind of face on which you rarely saw a smile. "Mr. Monelli?"

Mario nodded.

"POTUS—the president—would like to have a private word with you."

Mario looked over the Secret Service agent's shoulder and spotted the president a few feet away, looking directly at him and brandishing a rehearsed and hollow smile.

Mario smiled back, with more irony than humor. "I'll pass," he said.

"Sir, I can't tell the president that."

"You tell him that," Mario said. "You tell him *exactly* that."

"As you wish," said the Secret Service agent, hiding any surprise he may have felt. He turned away, toward the president and spoke a few words. Anger—vicious, brutal, unforgiving anger—briefly flashed across the president's face, then transformed itself into a ugly twisted smile, which he directed toward Mario. Then POTUS turned away, the Secret Service man at his side, and headed for his limousine.

A moment later, Mario was approached by Ben Hersh, the newly confirmed head of the SEC, who was smiling wryly and shaking his head in appreciation. "Damn it, Monelli," he said, "you *do* have a set of brass ones, don't you?"

"I didn't want to be seen having a polite conversation with him," Mario said. "Anyhow, all he was going to do is shake my hand, grin like the buffoon he is, and tell me he'd been on my side from the beginning. Then he'd put his arm around my shoulder, and make sure the press got a shot of it."

"Yep," Hersh said, looking back at the president, "that's our commander in chief all right."

They both watched as the president got into the armored limo and his convoy drove away.

"So tell me, Ben, how are the investigations going? Is it true that some of your targets have skipped to South America?"

"Just a few. We pulled the passports from the rest, and we're bringing them in at our leisure."

"How high up in the government is it reaching?" Mario asked.

"We're inside 1600," Ben said. "But that's off the record. I think we're going to bring down at least one cabinet member on obstruction of justice, and a couple of the president's close advisors who directed aides to defy congressional subpoenas, claiming executive privilege."

"Too bad," Mario said.

"Too bad? You wanted us to leave the higher-ups alone?"

Mario smiled. "No, I just hoped you'd get all the way up to the crown."

"Well, speaking of the crown," Hersh said, eyes twinkling, "there's something else you should know, Mario. It's not public yet, but I'm told that the Heir Apparent has been demoted."

Mario broke out into a grin. "I'll be damned."

"Not many people can say they brought down a prince," Hersh observed.

"What will happen to the rest of the Royal Family?"

"It's anyone's guess" Ben said. "But whatever *does* happens, it won't happen on *our* soil. Thanks to you…and the senator."

"We're not out of the woods yet," replied Mario. "The Saudis can still make good on their threat to liquidate their trillions here without warning."

"Not a chance of that happening," said Ben.

"You know something I don't?"

"This isn't for public consumption, Mario, but we've frozen all Saudi assets in U.S. banks—more than a trillion dollars worth. And we have quietly purchased eighty-nine percent of the world's oil tanker fleet. If the Saudis continue to annoy us, we can make it impossible for them to sell oil to anyone. Either they get friendly again, and fast, or they'll end up eating camel meat."

"That should teach them not to threaten us," Mario said, grinning.

Hersh chuckled. "And what about *you*? What's next for *Time* magazine's Person of the Year?"

"I think that's a question on a great many minds," Mario replied. "But I haven't really decided."

"You're not planning to go back to Wall Street, are you?"

Mario shook his head. "I don't think that's an option. Besides, I think I'm going to be here in Washington for the foreseeable future." He looked over to Julie, who was still consoling Mrs. Jaffe.

"Ah," Hersh said, grinning. "I see. Well that job offer still stands with me and Elliot over at the commission. Always will."

"Let me think about it."

"Sure, don't give me an answer yet. Think it over. Discuss it with a friend."

"I already am," said Mario.

Ben smiled and walked away.

Mario took the milk out of the refrigerator and warmed up a glassful. Then he felt Sam rubbing against his pajama leg. He poured half the milk into a saucer and set it on the floor, then filled a small glass for himself.

While Sam began lapping up the treat, Mario slid open the terrace door as quietly as he could, and stepped outside into the night, glass in hand. The terrace drapes waved in the autumn chill until he closed the door behind him. He leaned on the railing and looked out over the Potomac, at the beautiful lights of D.C.—at the Capitol, the White House, the Lincoln and Washington Monuments, the steady flow of traffic across the bridges, and the airplanes arriving and departing from Reagan National. And he thought about the year that had just passed.

If someone had sat him down a year ago and laid out the events he was about to experience, he thought, he would have laughed out loud. So many things had happened that no one could have anticipated, and they had lifted him out of one life and set him down in an entirely different one, a new one, a better one. And it wasn't just a new life. He was a different man as well, a better one.

Mario hardly knew how it had happened, or even how it had started. But after a moment, it began to come back to him. It all started the night he nearly lost his life in Cortlandt alley, maybe the luckiest thing that ever happened to him, because it brought him Gus—and started the whole amazing chain of events.

He thought about Gus and he couldn't help smiling. What was it about the old fighter that had affected him so deeply. It was the wisdom…and the humor…and the love. No, that wasn't it, or not *all* of it. There was something else, something deeper, maybe something unintentional, or maybe *quite* intentional.

Gus had forced him to tear open his soul and find the hidden part of himself. And make peace with a past that would forever remain with him. Gus helped him understand that only *he* was responsible—to himself—for not only changing the trajectory of his life, but for living it the best way he could, without regret and being the man he wanted to be. In a way, Mario thought, he *had* died that night in Cortlandt alley. But that night he was also reborn.

Still, nothing would have happened if it hadn't been for Julie. More dumb luck. It was almost as if someone had planned out the whole thing, almost as if the choices had been made for him. Perfect choices.

He gazed at Washington's twinkling lights, and raised his glass to the stars.

"Thanks, Gus," he said to no one but himself. Then he drank down the milk and opened the sliding door and walked back into the apartment. Sam was now asleep atop the bookshelves. Everything was calm.

Mario tiptoed into the bedroom, slid off his robe, carefully pulled back the covers, and climbed into bed beside her while she slept. For most of the night he lay there in the half-light watching her eyes, her lips, and her face. And in the stillness he felt peace. Then as he closed his eyes, Julie stirred in her sleep…and reached out for him.

ABOUT THE AUTHOR

Scott Noto is a Magna Cum Laude graduate of SUNY and holds degrees in Finance and English with a Masters in American Literature. A 25-year veteran of Wall Street combat, he served over a decade in the trenches at Lehman Brothers, then on the front lines as Vice President of Salomon Smith Barney.

During his career, he's written many news articles for its financial publications and served as guest speaker and periodic host on radio FCN, broadcast nationally. Recognized for his hard hitting and gritty literary style, he has been the recipient of numerous collegiate writing awards. His critically acclaimed novel The Lions' Den is his national debut.

Don't forget to read Scott Noto's upcoming novel "Sam I Am" due for release in summer 2013. "Sam I Am" is the gripping saga of Sam Mckenna, a baseball teen phenom who—despite his controlling father—climbs from the rubble of the depression-ravaged west and is launched into the limelight of the major leagues and Connie Mack's Philadelphia A's, only to have it unravel when he falls under the thumb of the Chicago underworld on the dawn of WWII.